MARVEL

SPIDER-MAN
MAXIMUM VENOM

MARVEL

SPIDER-MAN
MAXIMUM VENOM

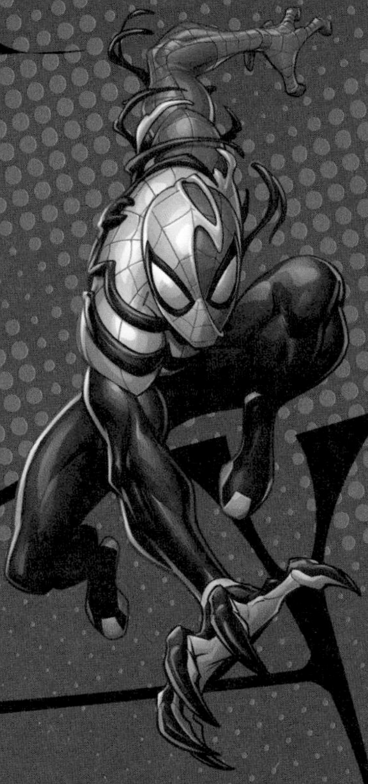

A Random House SCREEN COMIX™ Book

Random House • New York

All rights reserved. Published in the United States
by Random House Children's Books, an imprint of Penguin Random House LLC,
1745 Broadway, New York, NY 10019, and in Canada by Penguin Random House
Canada Limited, Toronto, in conjunction with Disney Enterprises, Inc. Screen Comix
is a trademark of Penguin Random House LLC. Random House and the Random House
colophon are registered trademarks of Penguin Random House LLC.

ISBN 978-0-7364-4143-8 (paperback)
ISBN 978-0-7364-4144-5 (ebook)
rhcbooks.com

Printed in the United States of America
10 9 8 7 6 5 4 3 2 1

WEB OF VENOM

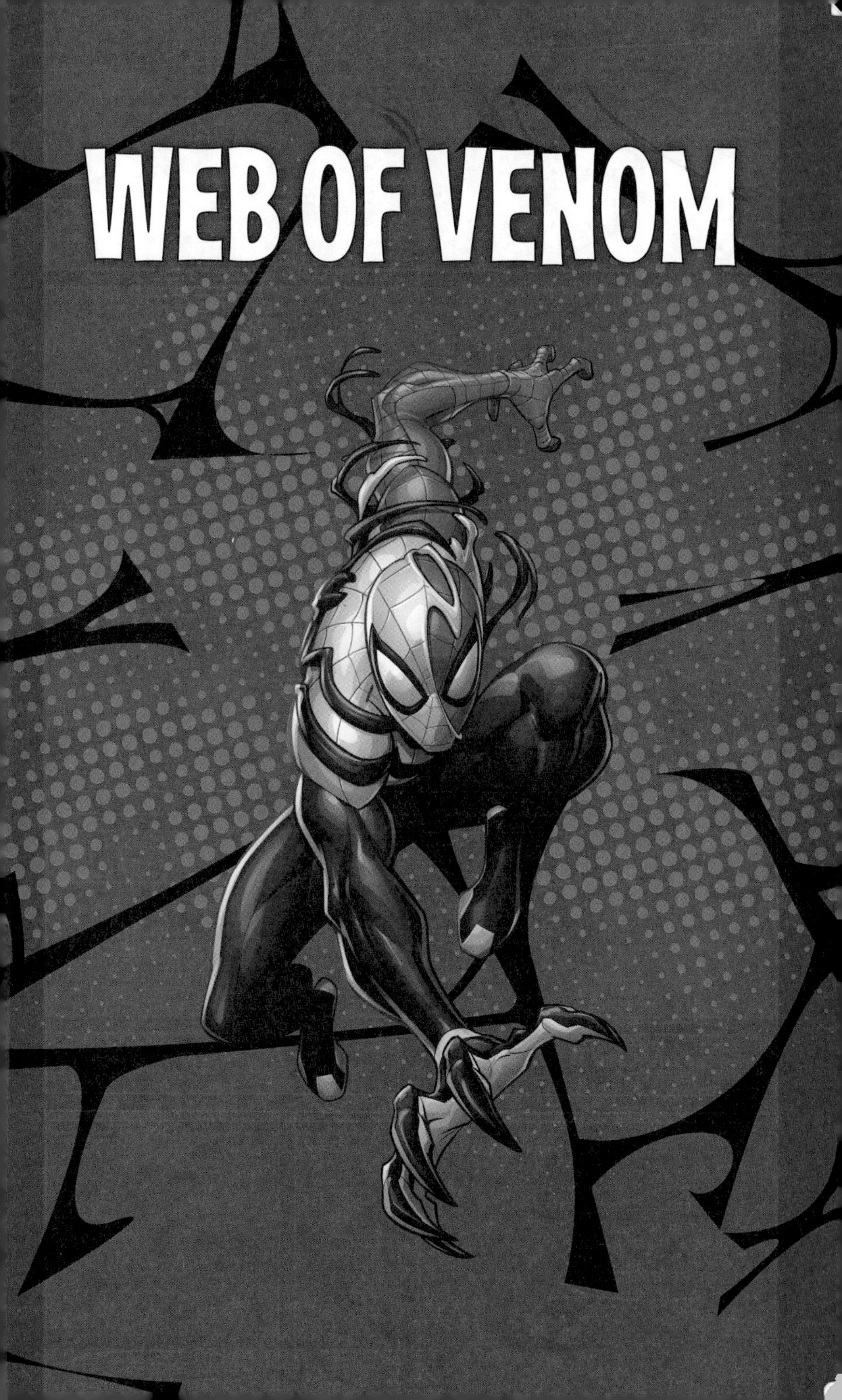

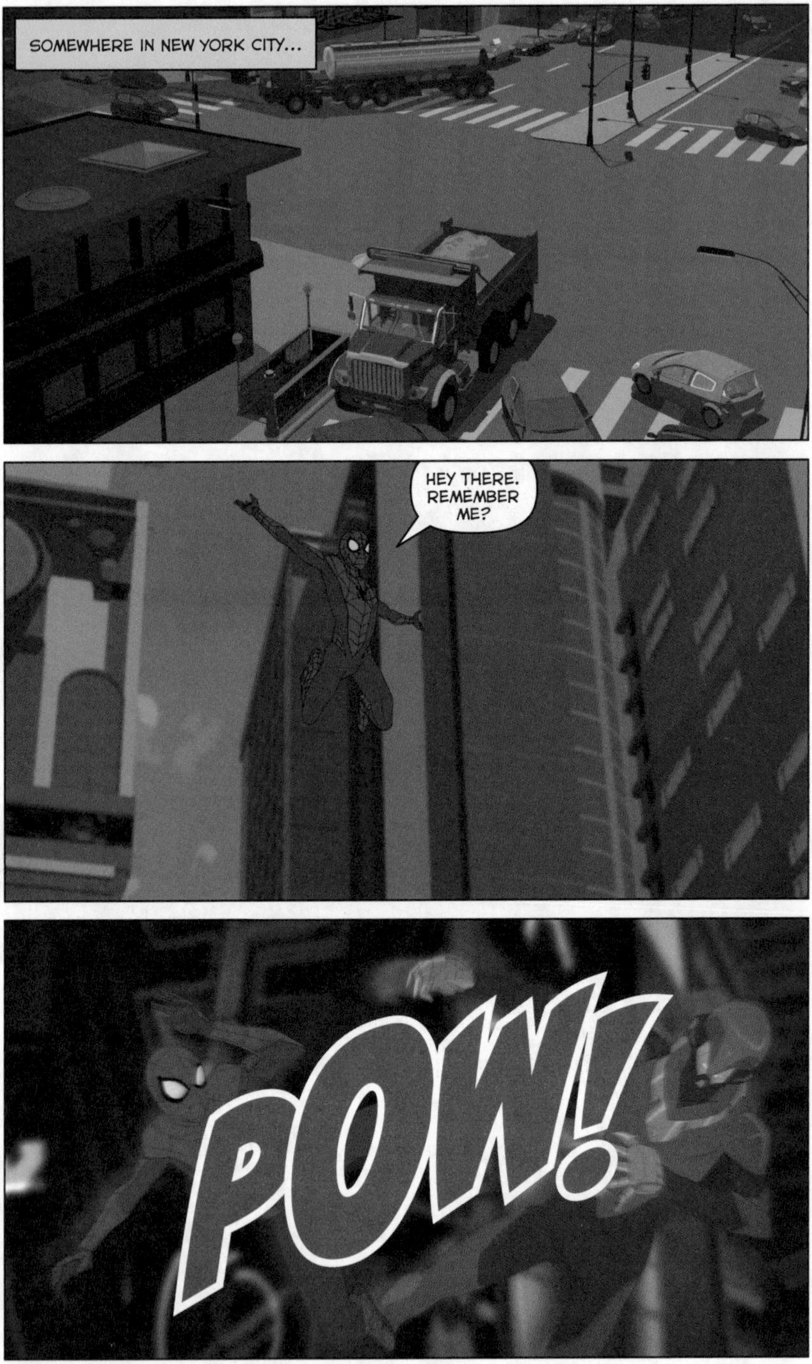
SOMEWHERE IN NEW YORK CITY...
HEY THERE. REMEMBER ME?
POW!

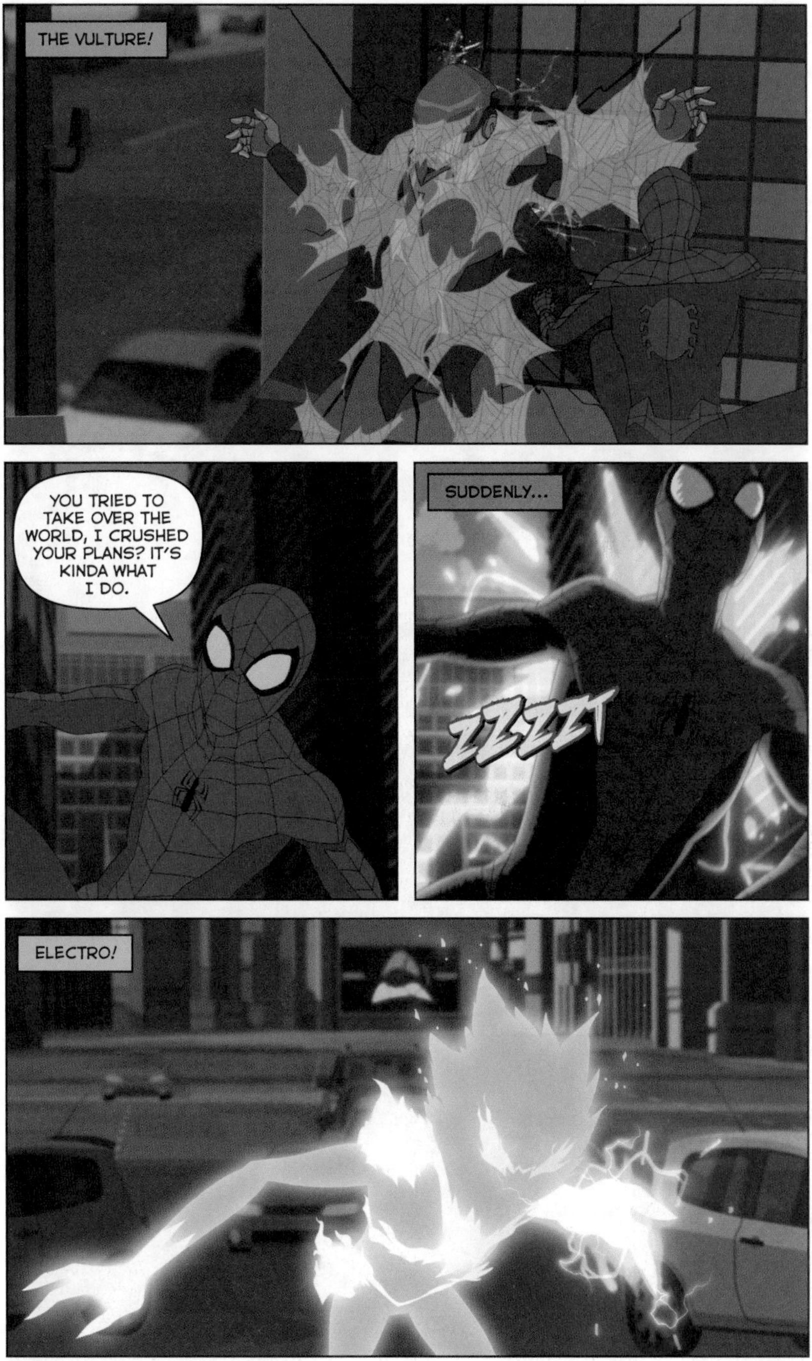
THE VULTURE!
YOU TRIED TO TAKE OVER THE WORLD, I CRUSHED YOUR PLANS? IT'S KINDA WHAT I DO.
SUDDENLY...
ZZZZT
ELECTRO!

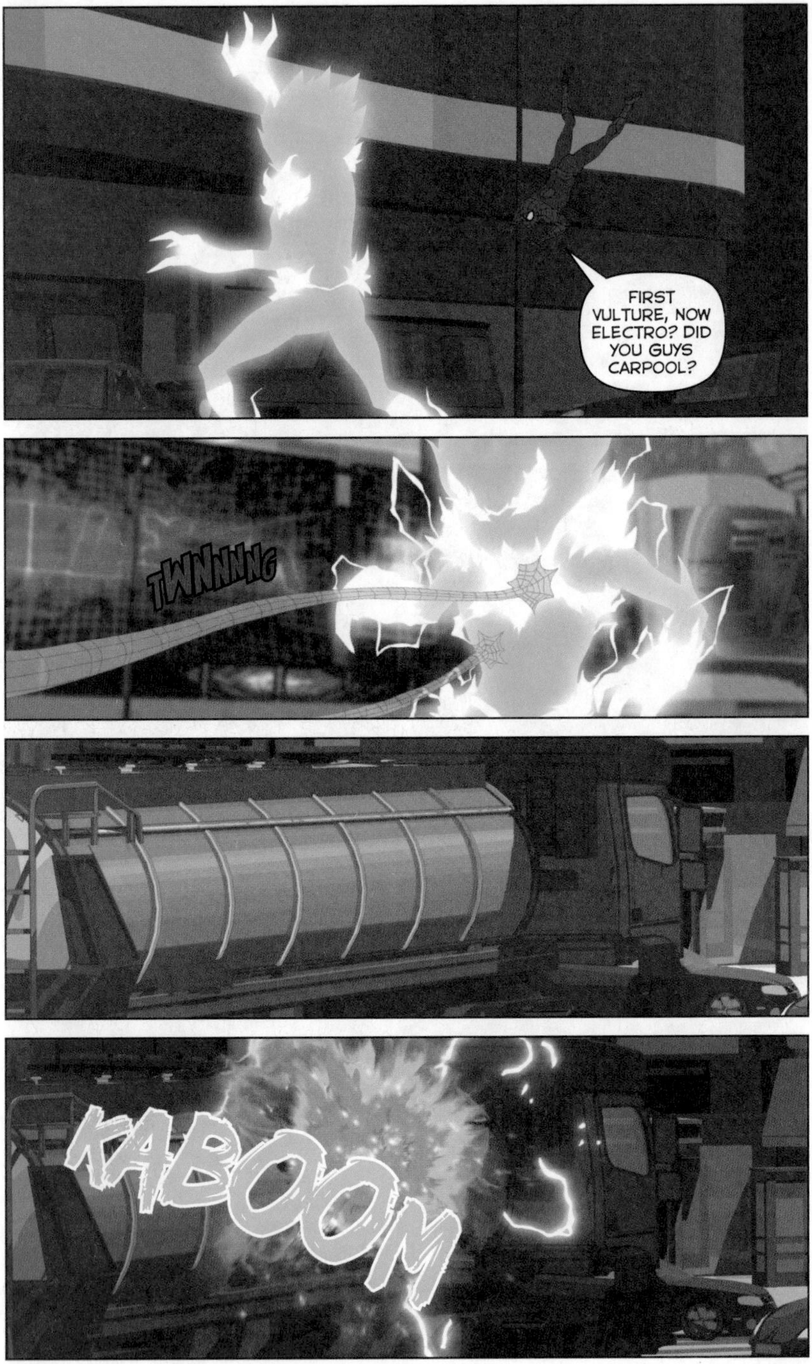
FIRST VULTURE, NOW ELECTRO? DID YOU GUYS CARPOOL?
TWNNNNG
KABOOM

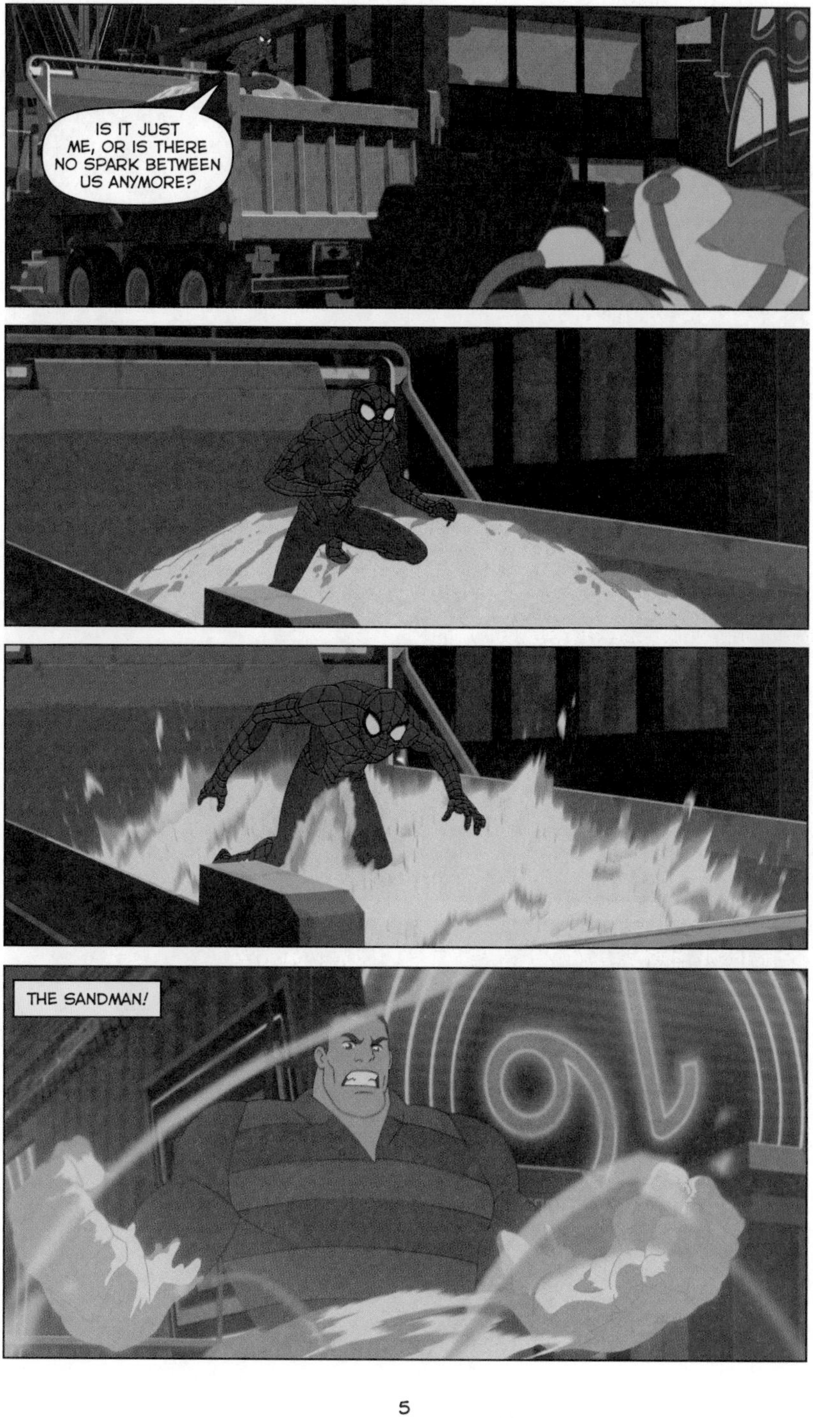
IS IT JUST ME, OR IS THERE NO SPARK BETWEEN US ANYMORE?
THE SANDMAN!

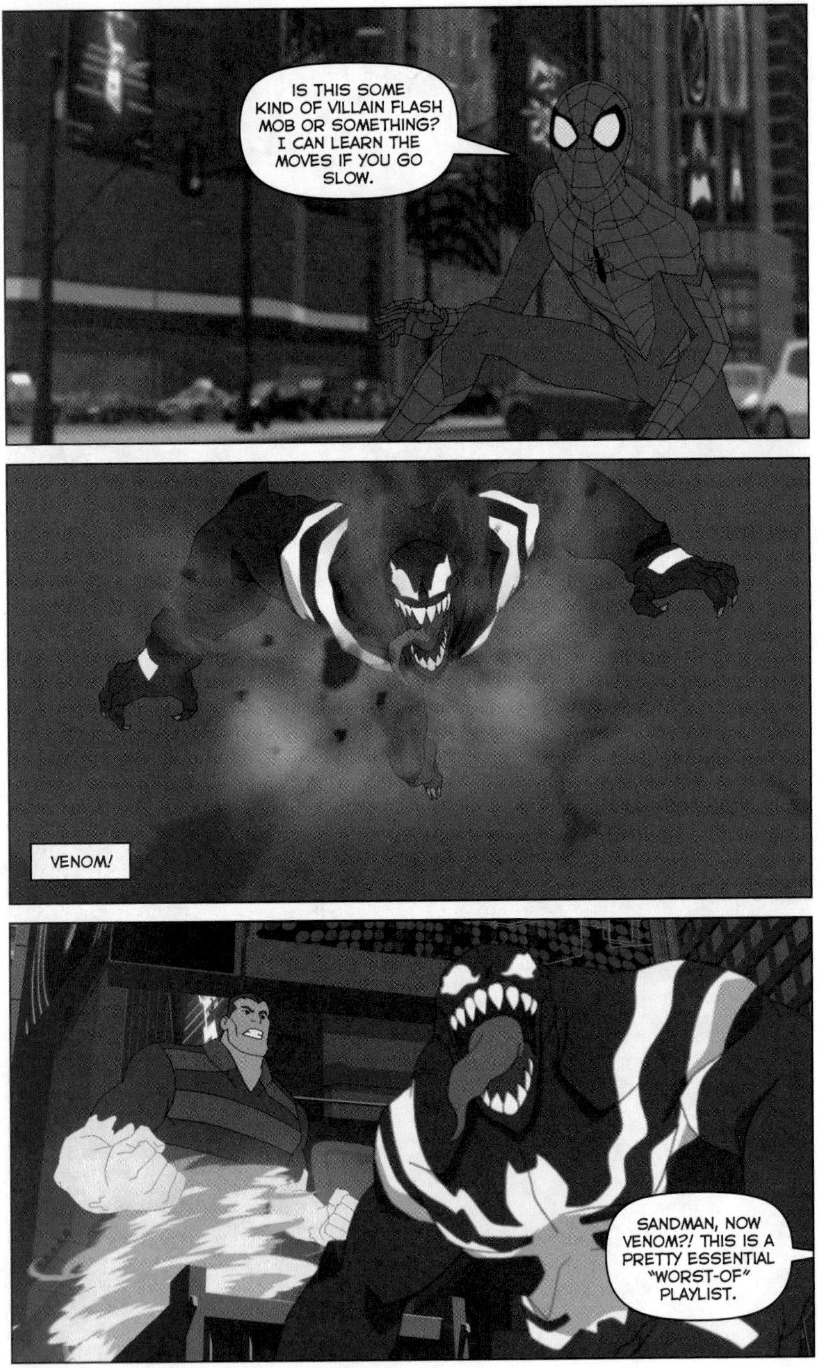
IS THIS SOME KIND OF VILLAIN FLASH MOB OR SOMETHING? I CAN LEARN THE MOVES IF YOU GO SLOW.
VENOM!
SANDMAN, NOW VENOM?! THIS IS A PRETTY ESSENTIAL "WORST-OF" PLAYLIST.

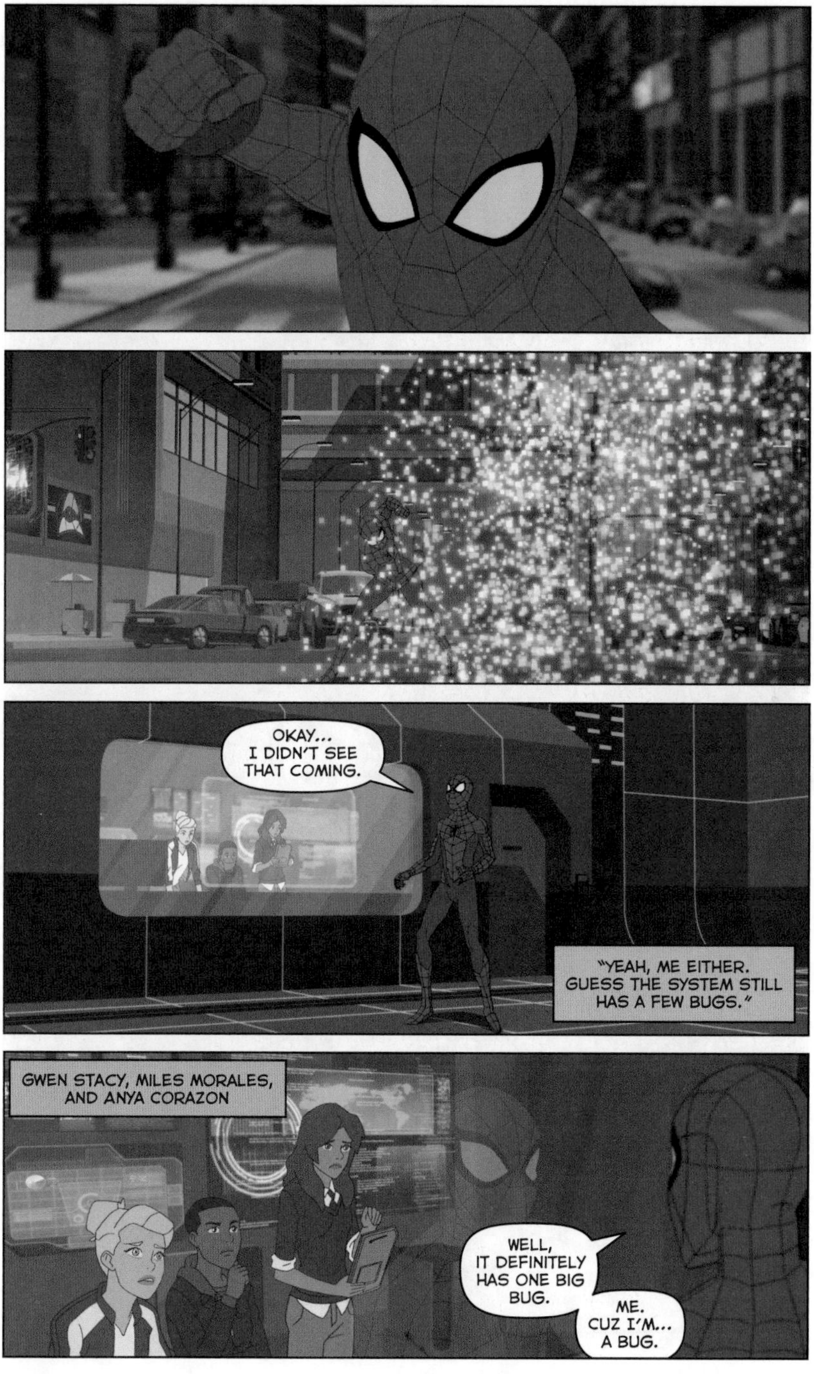
OKAY... I DIDN'T SEE THAT COMING.
"YEAH, ME EITHER. GUESS THE SYSTEM STILL HAS A FEW BUGS."
GWEN STACY, MILES MORALES, AND ANYA CORAZON
WELL, IT DEFINITELY HAS ONE BIG BUG.
ME. CUZ I'M... A BUG.

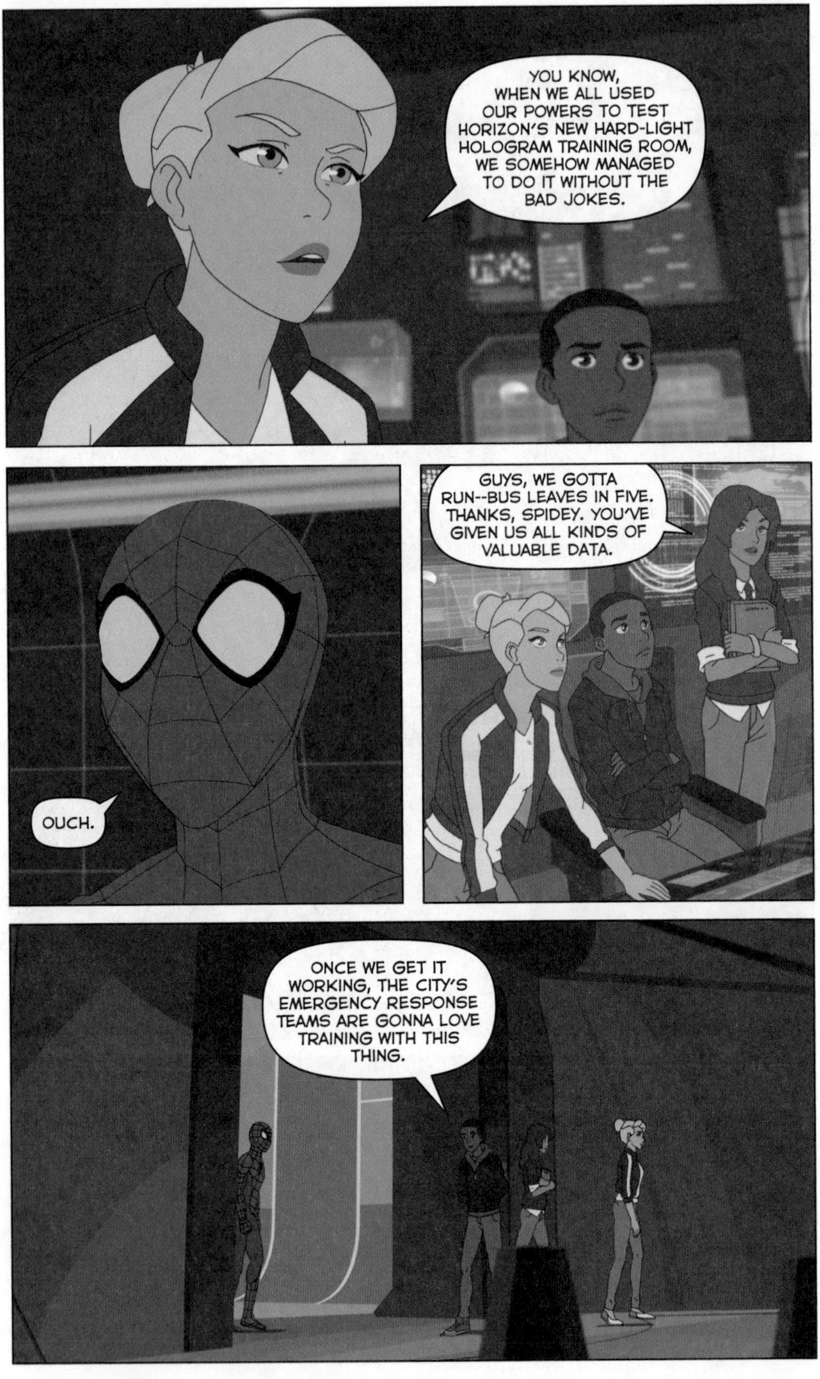
YOU KNOW, WHEN WE ALL USED OUR POWERS TO TEST HORIZON'S NEW HARD-LIGHT HOLOGRAM TRAINING ROOM, WE SOMEHOW MANAGED TO DO IT WITHOUT THE BAD JOKES.
OUCH.
GUYS, WE GOTTA RUN--BUS LEAVES IN FIVE. THANKS, SPIDEY. YOU'VE GIVEN US ALL KINDS OF VALUABLE DATA.
ONCE WE GET IT WORKING, THE CITY'S EMERGENCY RESPONSE TEAMS ARE GONNA LOVE TRAINING WITH THIS THING.

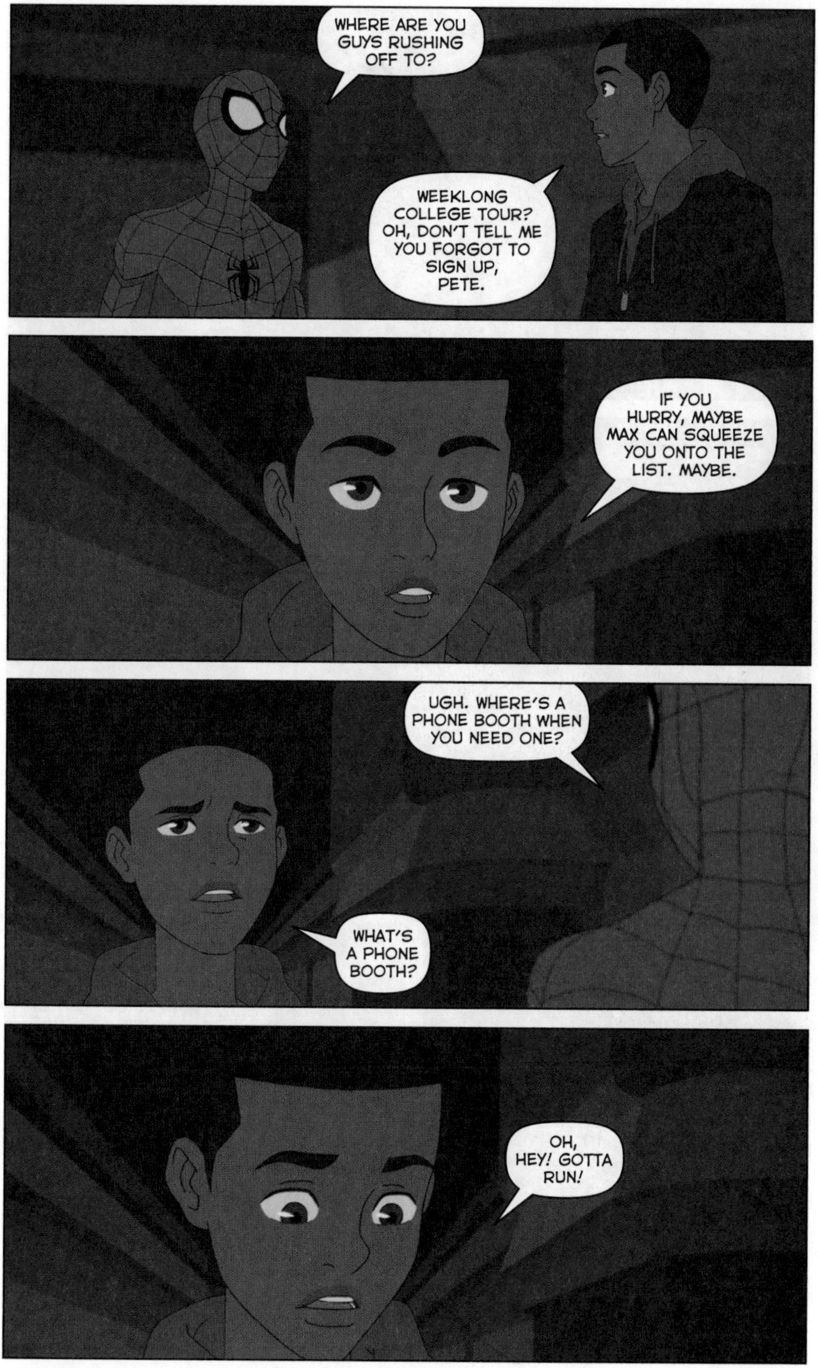
WHERE ARE YOU GUYS RUSHING OFF TO?
WEEKLONG COLLEGE TOUR? OH, DON'T TELL ME YOU FORGOT TO SIGN UP, PETE.
IF YOU HURRY, MAYBE MAX CAN SQUEEZE YOU ONTO THE LIST. MAYBE.
UGH. WHERE'S A PHONE BOOTH WHEN YOU NEED ONE?
WHAT'S A PHONE BOOTH?
OH, HEY! GOTTA RUN!

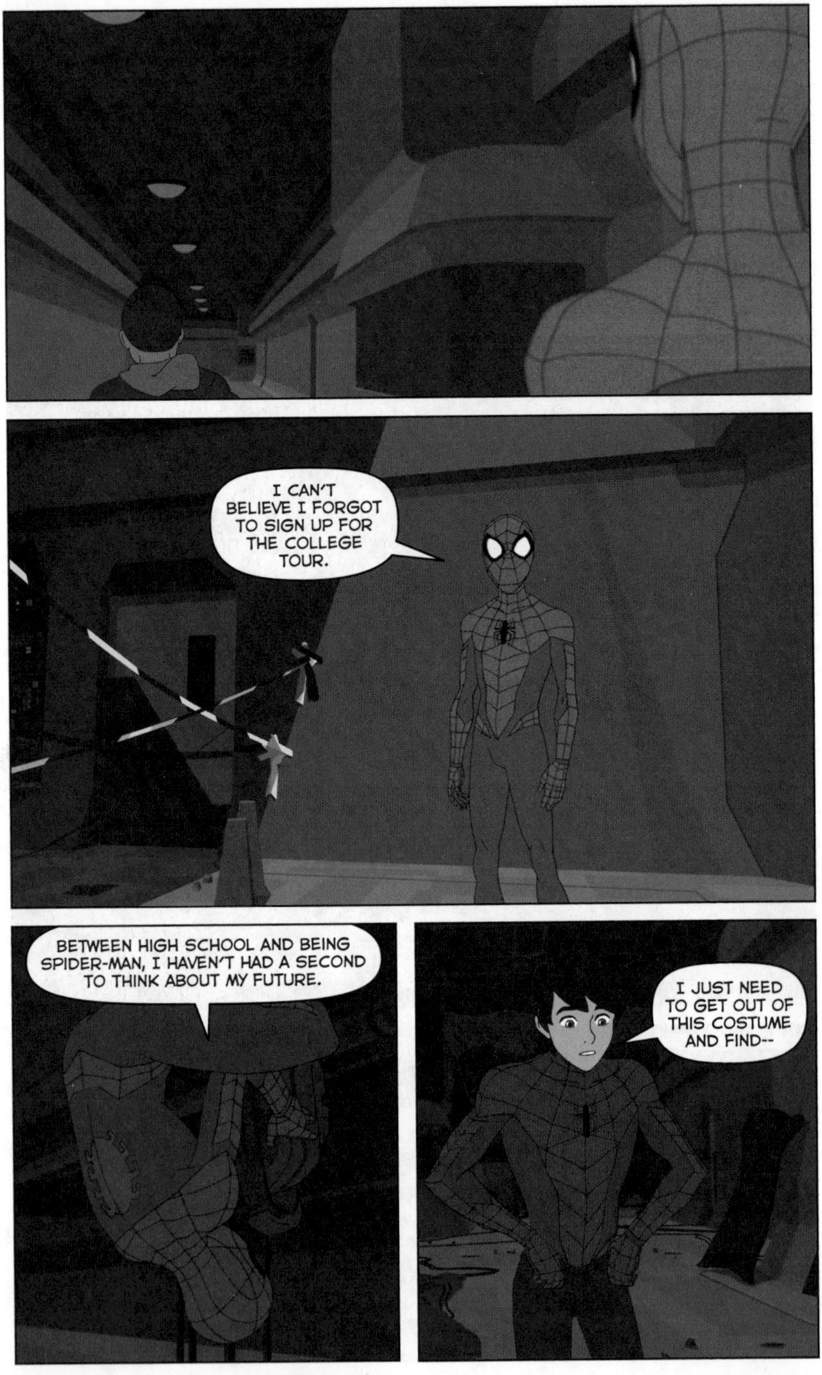
I CAN'T BELIEVE I FORGOT TO SIGN UP FOR THE COLLEGE TOUR.
BETWEEN HIGH SCHOOL AND BEING SPIDER-MAN, I HAVEN'T HAD A SECOND TO THINK ABOUT MY FUTURE.
I JUST NEED TO GET OUT OF THIS COSTUME AND FIND--

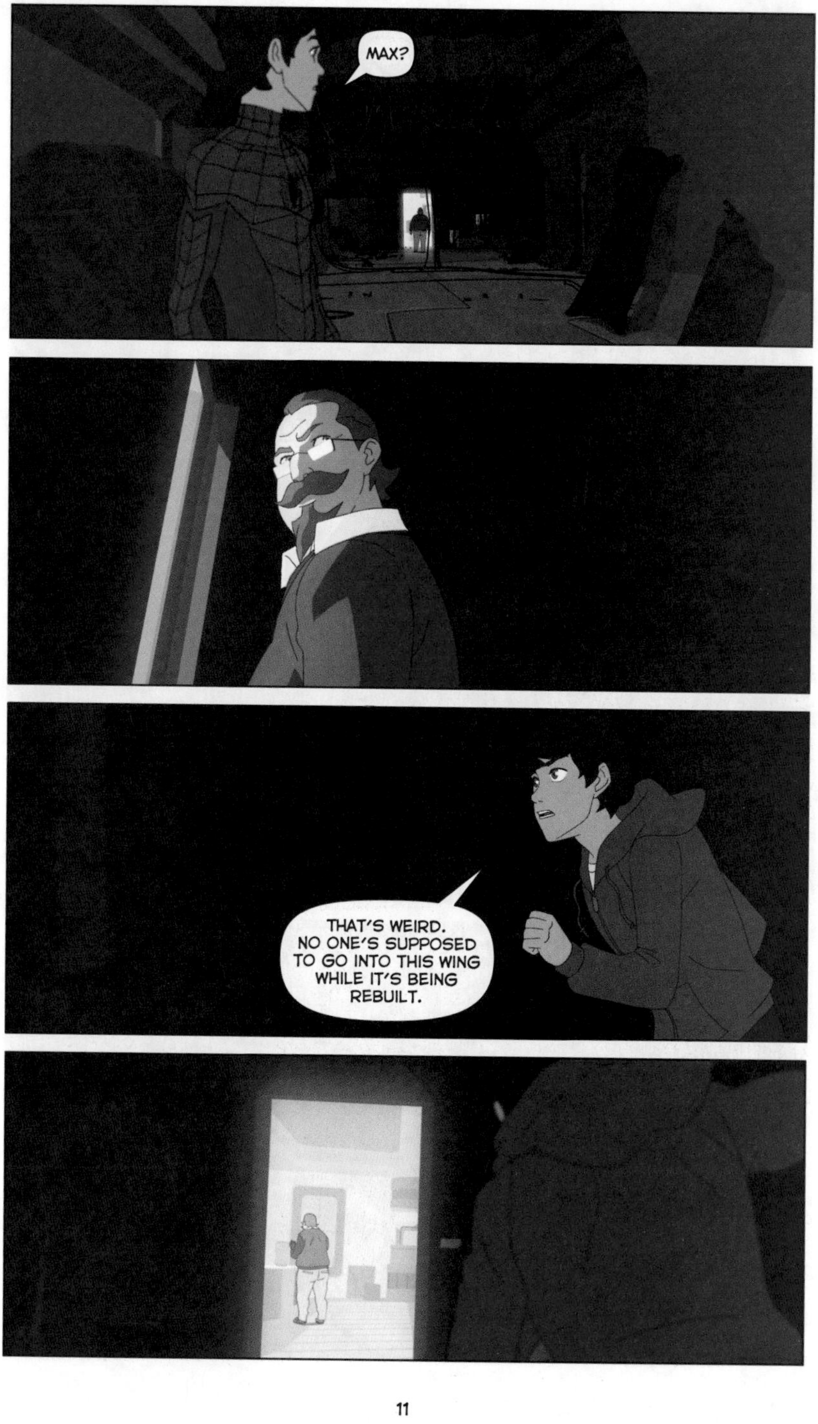
MAX?
THAT'S WEIRD. NO ONE'S SUPPOSED TO GO INTO THIS WING WHILE IT'S BEING REBUILT.

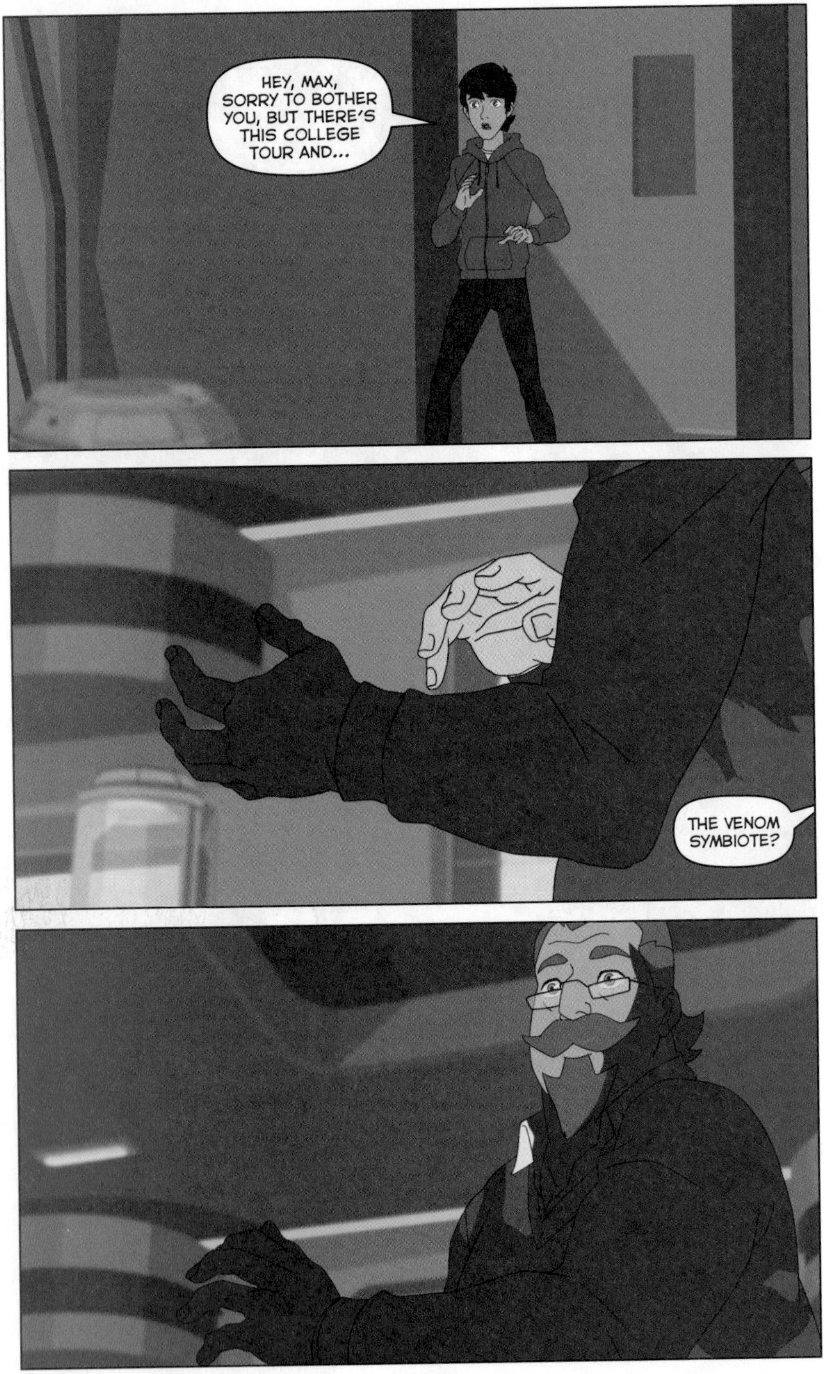
HEY, MAX, SORRY TO BOTHER YOU, BUT THERE'S THIS COLLEGE TOUR AND...
THE VENOM SYMBIOTE?

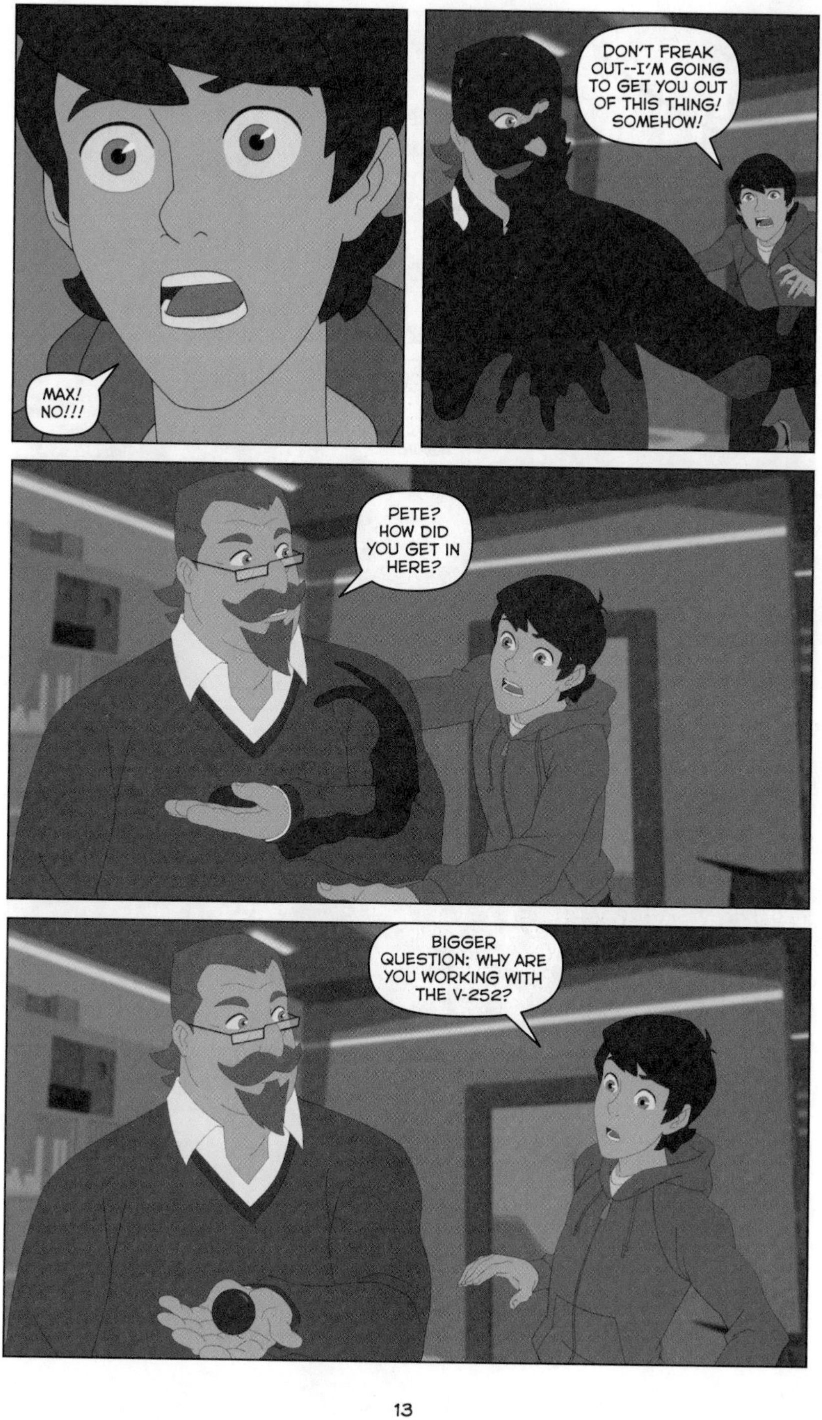
MAX! NO!!!
DON'T FREAK OUT--I'M GOING TO GET YOU OUT OF THIS THING! SOMEHOW!
PETE? HOW DID YOU GET IN HERE?
BIGGER QUESTION: WHY ARE YOU WORKING WITH THE V-252?

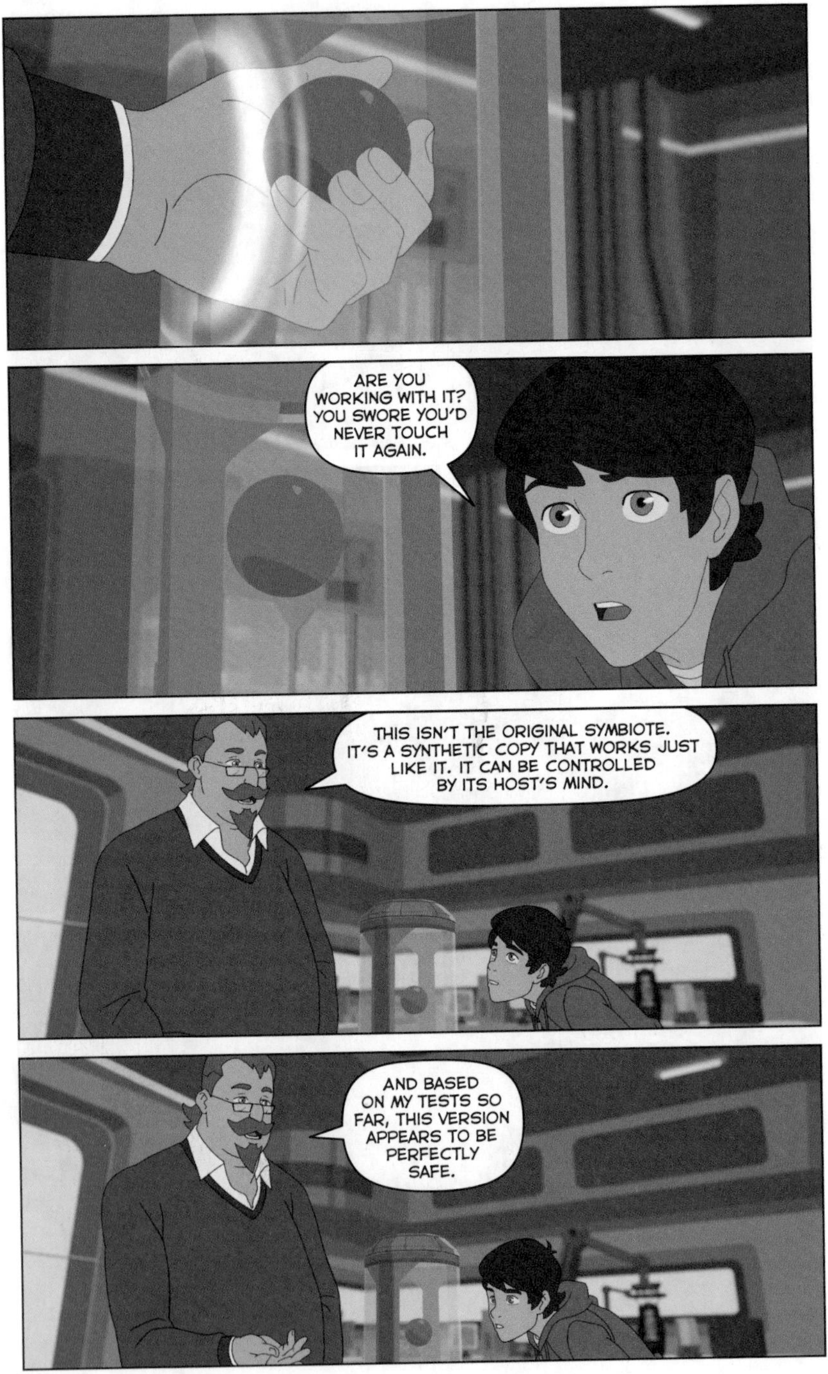
ARE YOU WORKING WITH IT? YOU SWORE YOU'D NEVER TOUCH IT AGAIN.
THIS ISN'T THE ORIGINAL SYMBIOTE. IT'S A SYNTHETIC COPY THAT WORKS JUST LIKE IT. IT CAN BE CONTROLLED BY ITS HOST'S MIND.
AND BASED ON MY TESTS SO FAR, THIS VERSION APPEARS TO BE PERFECTLY SAFE.

A SAFE VENOM SYMBIOTE? I'M SKEPTICAL.

AFTER VENOM WAS DEFEATED, I WAS ABLE TO GATHER A TINY SAMPLE OF THE ORIGINAL ALIEN SYMBIOTE, KEEPING IT UNDER HEAVY SECURITY.

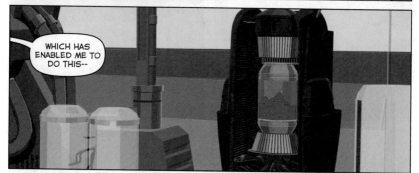

WHICH HAS ENABLED ME TO DO THIS--

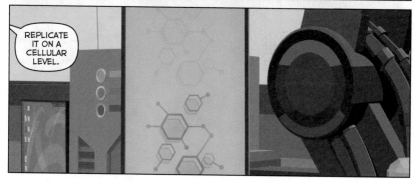

REPLICATE IT ON A CELLULAR LEVEL.

BUT UNLIKE THE ORIGINAL V-252, THIS NEW SUBSTANCE ISN'T ALIVE.

REMEMBER MY DREAM OF USING IT TO REVOLUTIONIZE THE WORLD?

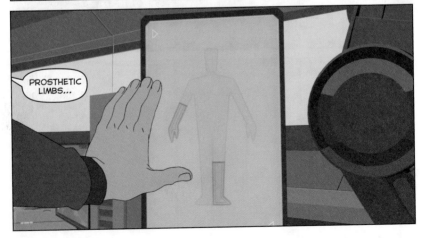

PROSTHETIC LIMBS...

16

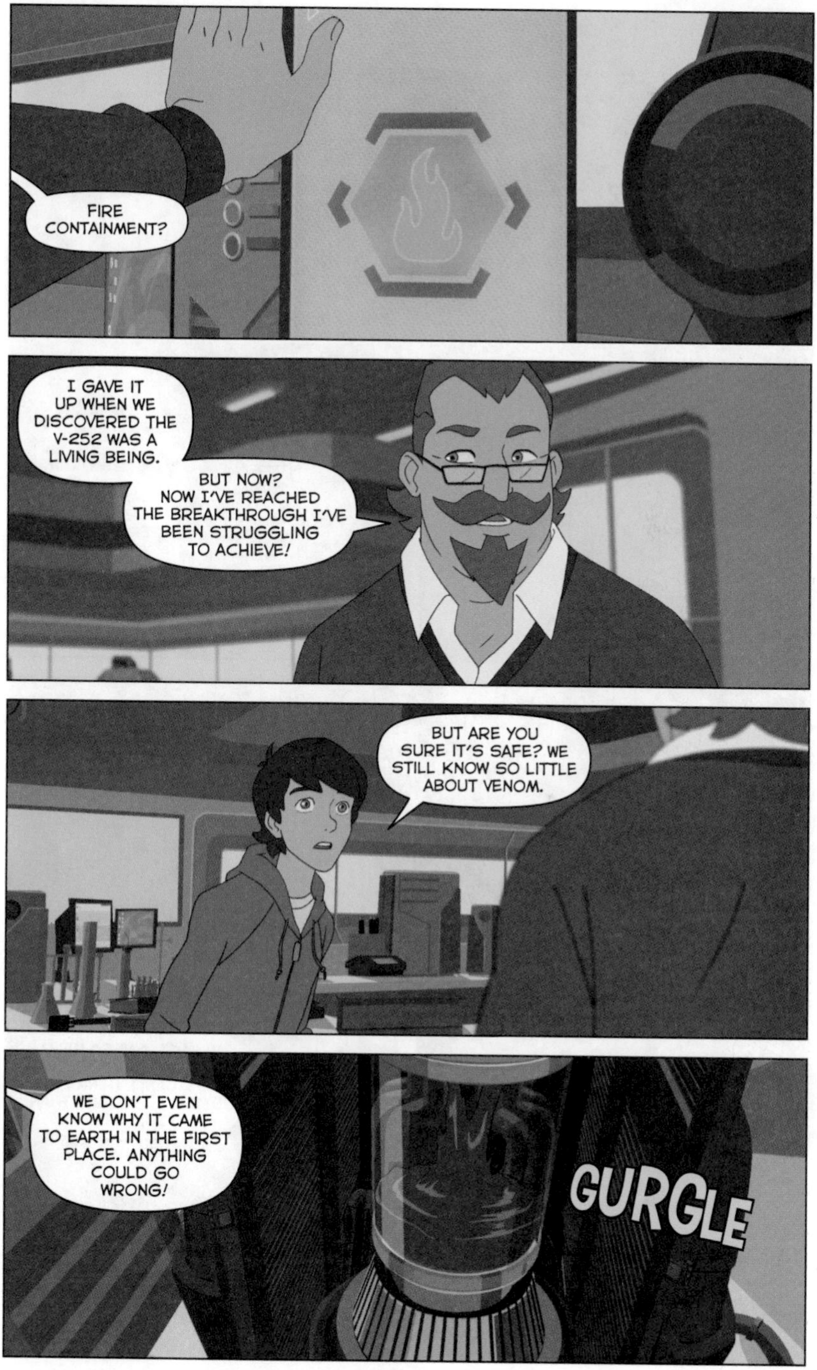

FIRE CONTAINMENT?
I GAVE IT UP WHEN WE DISCOVERED THE V-252 WAS A LIVING BEING.
BUT NOW? NOW I'VE REACHED THE BREAKTHROUGH I'VE BEEN STRUGGLING TO ACHIEVE!
BUT ARE YOU SURE IT'S SAFE? WE STILL KNOW SO LITTLE ABOUT VENOM.
WE DON'T EVEN KNOW WHY IT CAME TO EARTH IN THE FIRST PLACE. ANYTHING COULD GO WRONG!
GURGLE

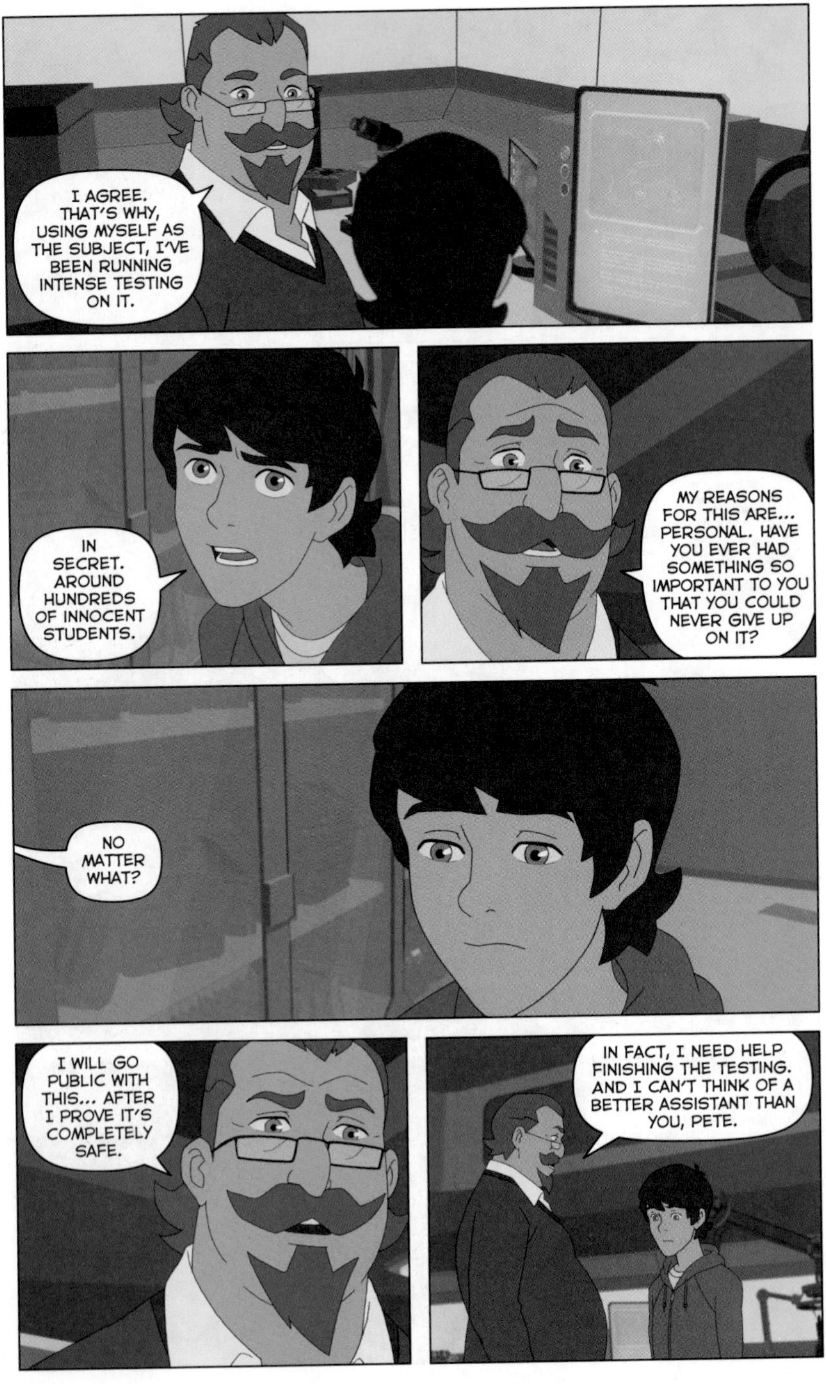
I AGREE. THAT'S WHY, USING MYSELF AS THE SUBJECT, I'VE BEEN RUNNING INTENSE TESTING ON IT.
IN SECRET. AROUND HUNDREDS OF INNOCENT STUDENTS.
MY REASONS FOR THIS ARE... PERSONAL. HAVE YOU EVER HAD SOMETHING SO IMPORTANT TO YOU THAT YOU COULD NEVER GIVE UP ON IT?
NO MATTER WHAT?
I WILL GO PUBLIC WITH THIS... AFTER I PROVE IT'S COMPLETELY SAFE.
IN FACT, I NEED HELP FINISHING THE TESTING. AND I CAN'T THINK OF A BETTER ASSISTANT THAN YOU, PETE.

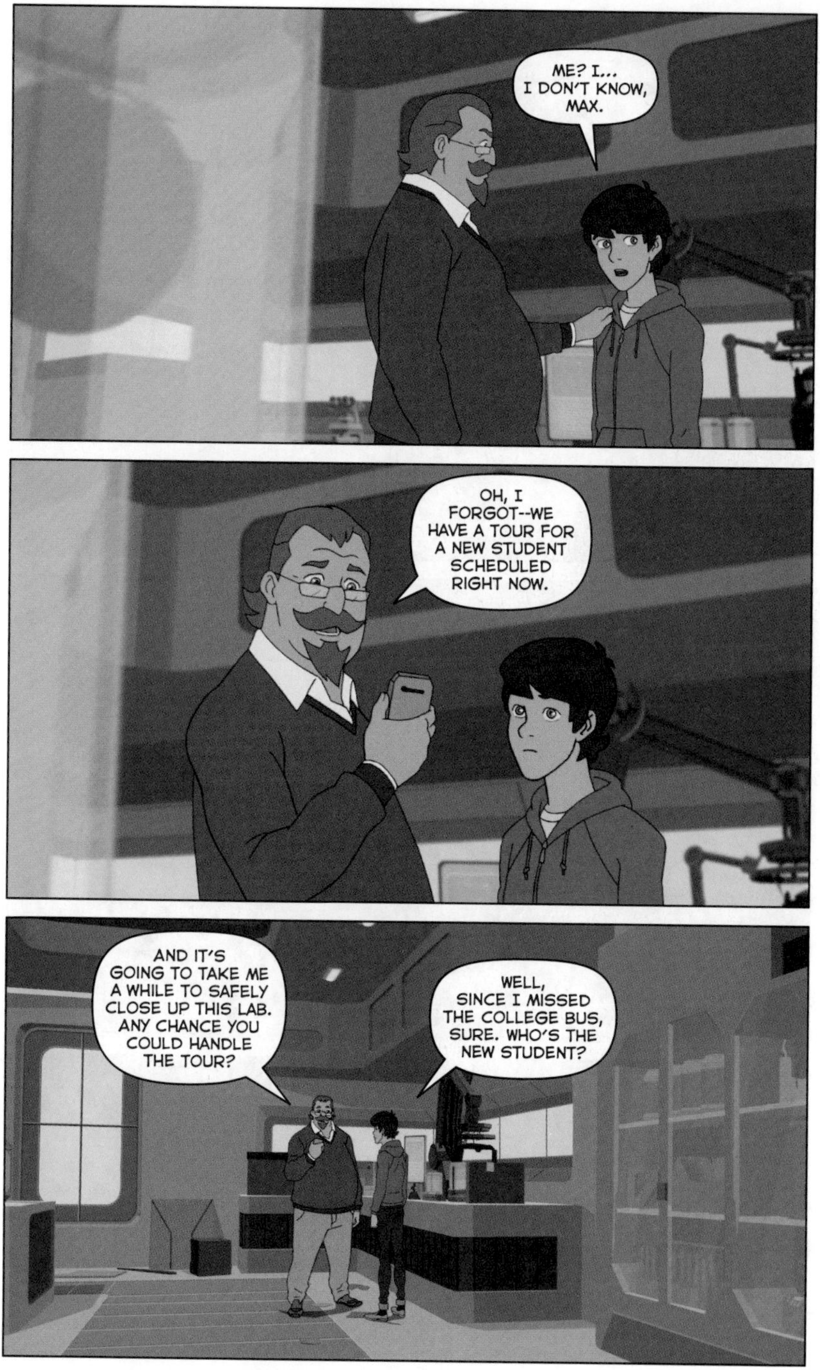

ME? I... I DON'T KNOW, MAX.
OH, I FORGOT--WE HAVE A TOUR FOR A NEW STUDENT SCHEDULED RIGHT NOW.
AND IT'S GOING TO TAKE ME A WHILE TO SAFELY CLOSE UP THIS LAB. ANY CHANCE YOU COULD HANDLE THE TOUR?
WELL, SINCE I MISSED THE COLLEGE BUS, SURE. WHO'S THE NEW STUDENT?

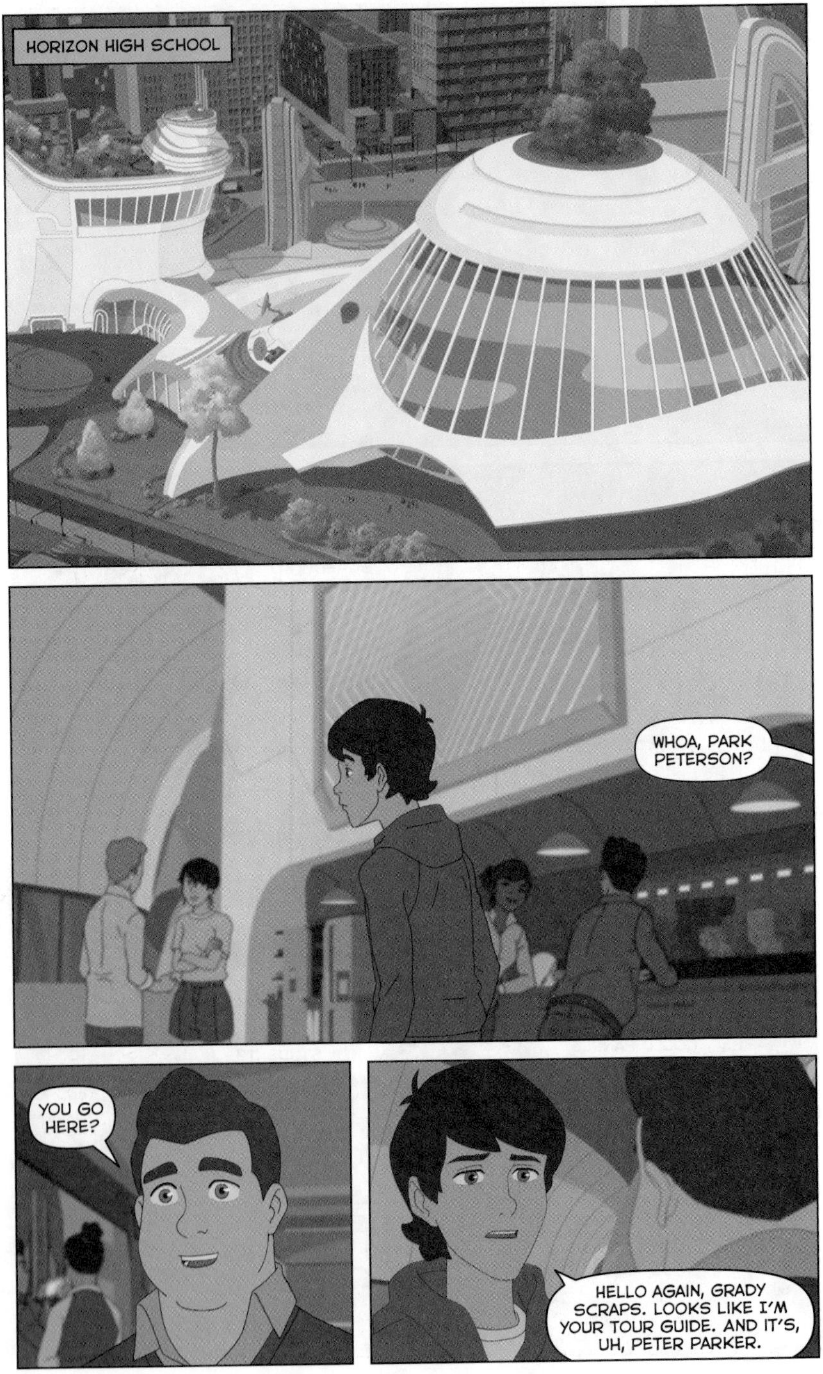
HORIZON HIGH SCHOOL
WHOA, PARK PETERSON?
YOU GO HERE?
HELLO AGAIN, GRADY SCRAPS. LOOKS LIKE I'M YOUR TOUR GUIDE. AND IT'S, UH, PETER PARKER.

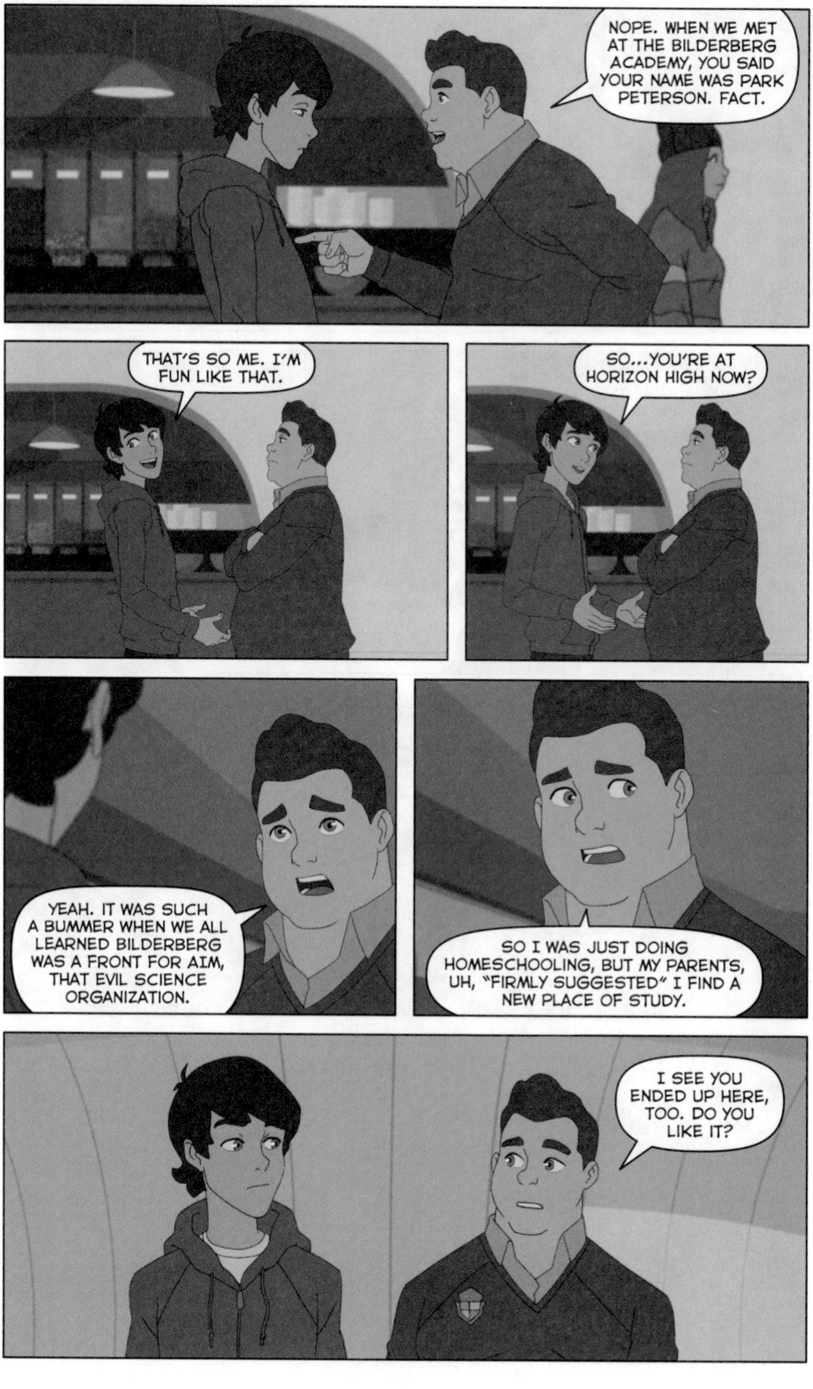
NOPE. WHEN WE MET AT THE BILDERBERG ACADEMY, YOU SAID YOUR NAME WAS PARK PETERSON. FACT.
THAT'S SO ME. I'M FUN LIKE THAT.
SO...YOU'RE AT HORIZON HIGH NOW?
YEAH. IT WAS SUCH A BUMMER WHEN WE ALL LEARNED BILDERBERG WAS A FRONT FOR AIM, THAT EVIL SCIENCE ORGANIZATION.
SO I WAS JUST DOING HOMESCHOOLING, BUT MY PARENTS, UH, "FIRMLY SUGGESTED" I FIND A NEW PLACE OF STUDY.
I SEE YOU ENDED UP HERE, TOO. DO YOU LIKE IT?

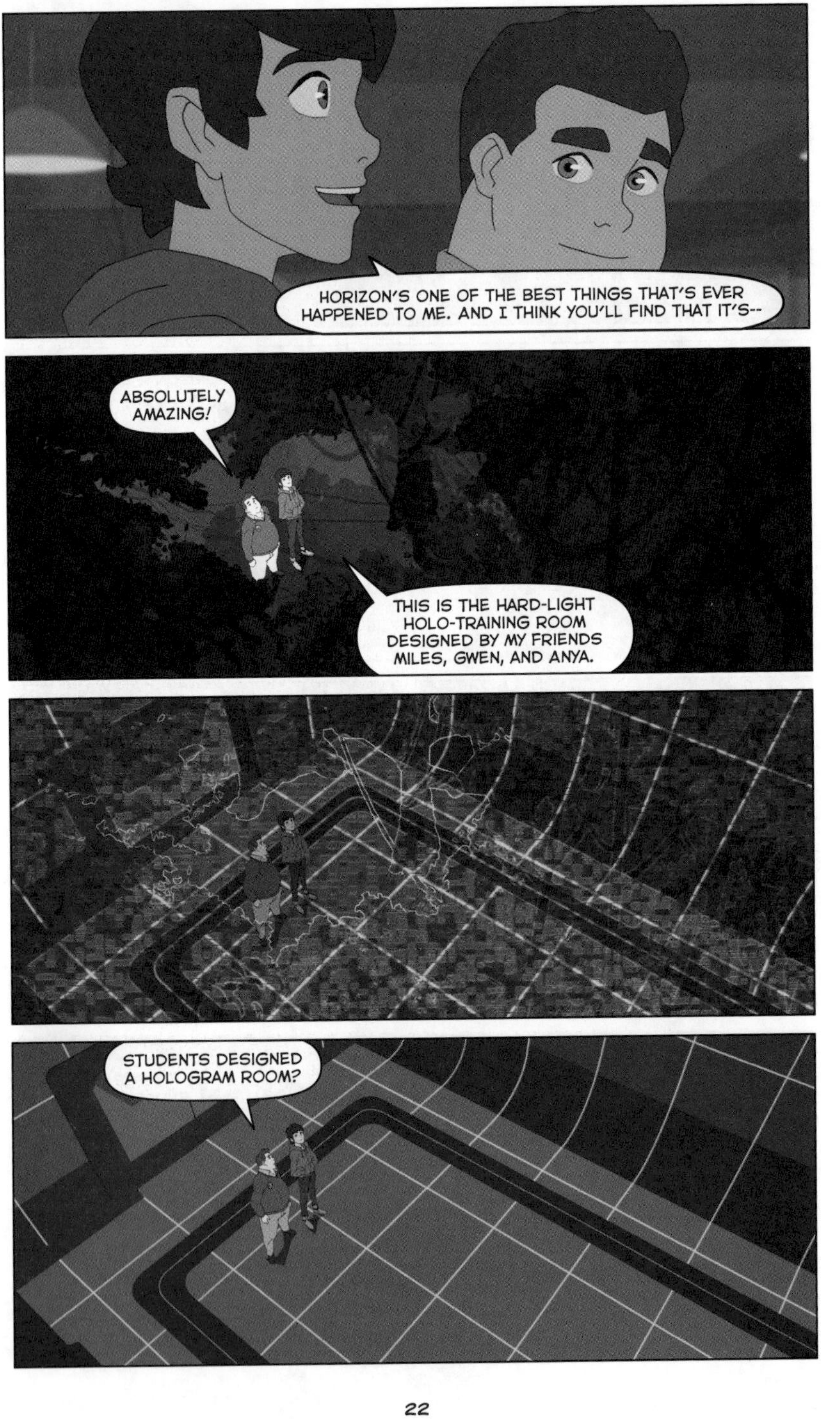
HORIZON'S ONE OF THE BEST THINGS THAT'S EVER HAPPENED TO ME. AND I THINK YOU'LL FIND THAT IT'S--
ABSOLUTELY AMAZING!
THIS IS THE HARD-LIGHT HOLO-TRAINING ROOM DESIGNED BY MY FRIENDS MILES, GWEN, AND ANYA.
STUDENTS DESIGNED A HOLOGRAM ROOM?

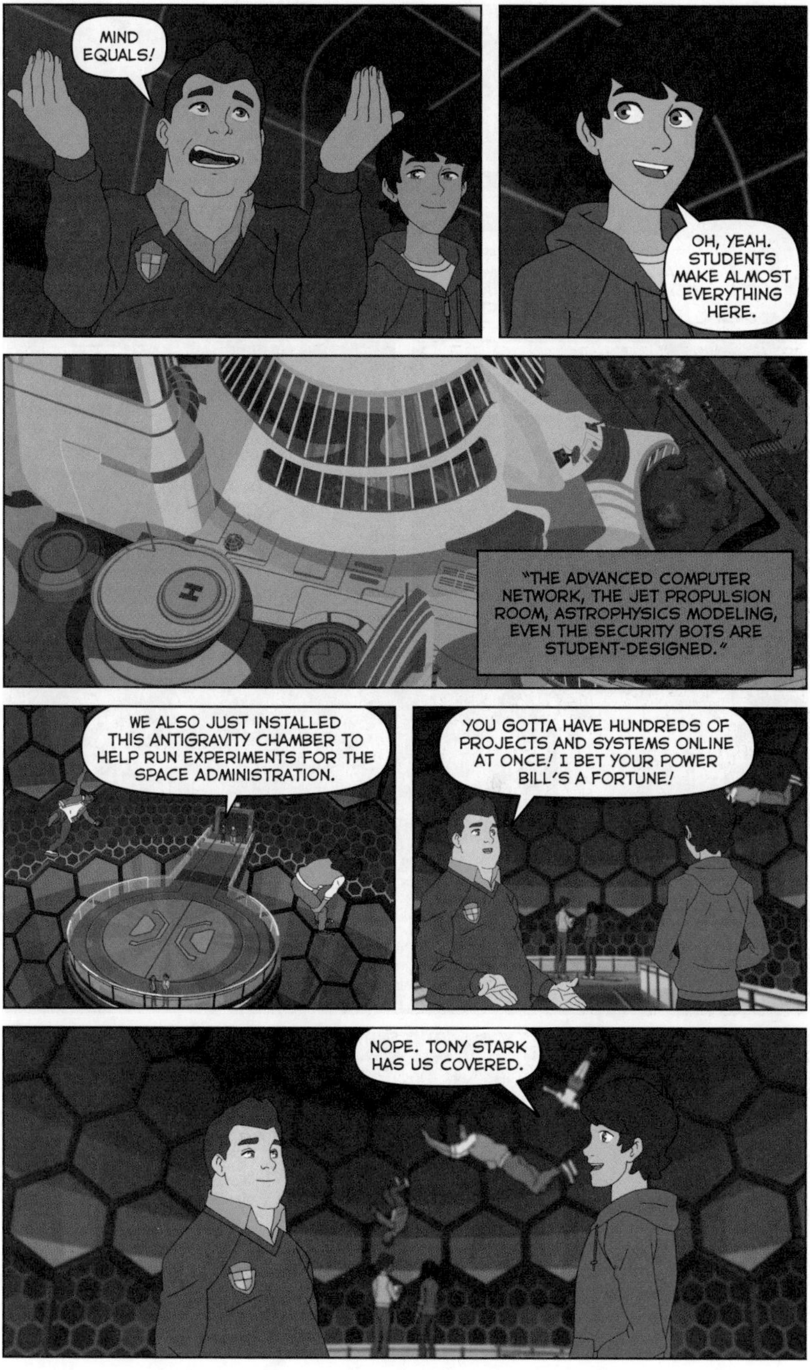
MIND EQUALS!
OH, YEAH. STUDENTS MAKE ALMOST EVERYTHING HERE.
"THE ADVANCED COMPUTER NETWORK, THE JET PROPULSION ROOM, ASTROPHYSICS MODELING, EVEN THE SECURITY BOTS ARE STUDENT-DESIGNED."
WE ALSO JUST INSTALLED THIS ANTIGRAVITY CHAMBER TO HELP RUN EXPERIMENTS FOR THE SPACE ADMINISTRATION.
YOU GOTTA HAVE HUNDREDS OF PROJECTS AND SYSTEMS ONLINE AT ONCE! I BET YOUR POWER BILL'S A FORTUNE!
NOPE. TONY STARK HAS US COVERED.

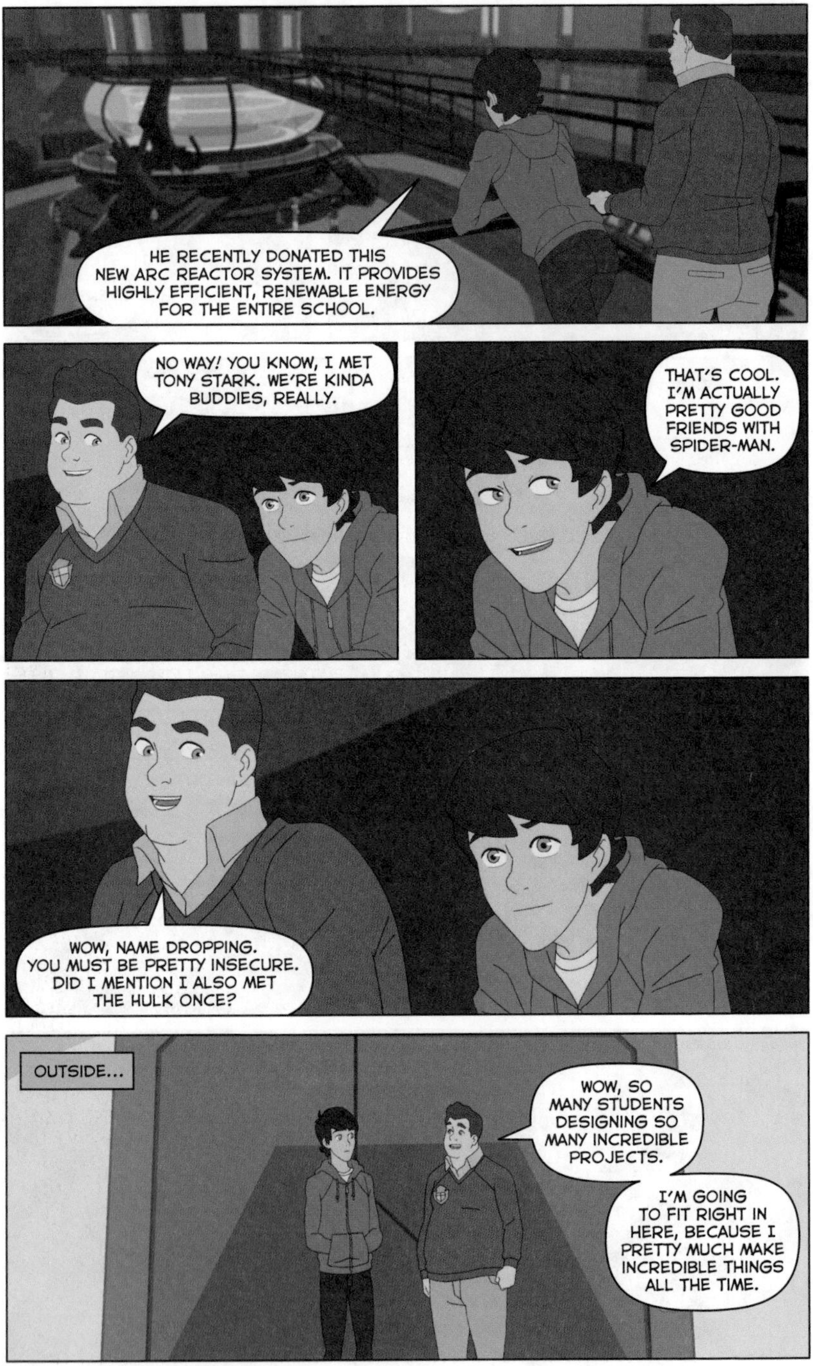
HE RECENTLY DONATED THIS NEW ARC REACTOR SYSTEM. IT PROVIDES HIGHLY EFFICIENT, RENEWABLE ENERGY FOR THE ENTIRE SCHOOL.
NO WAY! YOU KNOW, I MET TONY STARK. WE'RE KINDA BUDDIES, REALLY.
THAT'S COOL. I'M ACTUALLY PRETTY GOOD FRIENDS WITH SPIDER-MAN.
WOW, NAME DROPPING. YOU MUST BE PRETTY INSECURE. DID I MENTION I ALSO MET THE HULK ONCE?
OUTSIDE...
WOW, SO MANY STUDENTS DESIGNING SO MANY INCREDIBLE PROJECTS.
I'M GOING TO FIT RIGHT IN HERE, BECAUSE I PRETTY MUCH MAKE INCREDIBLE THINGS ALL THE TIME.

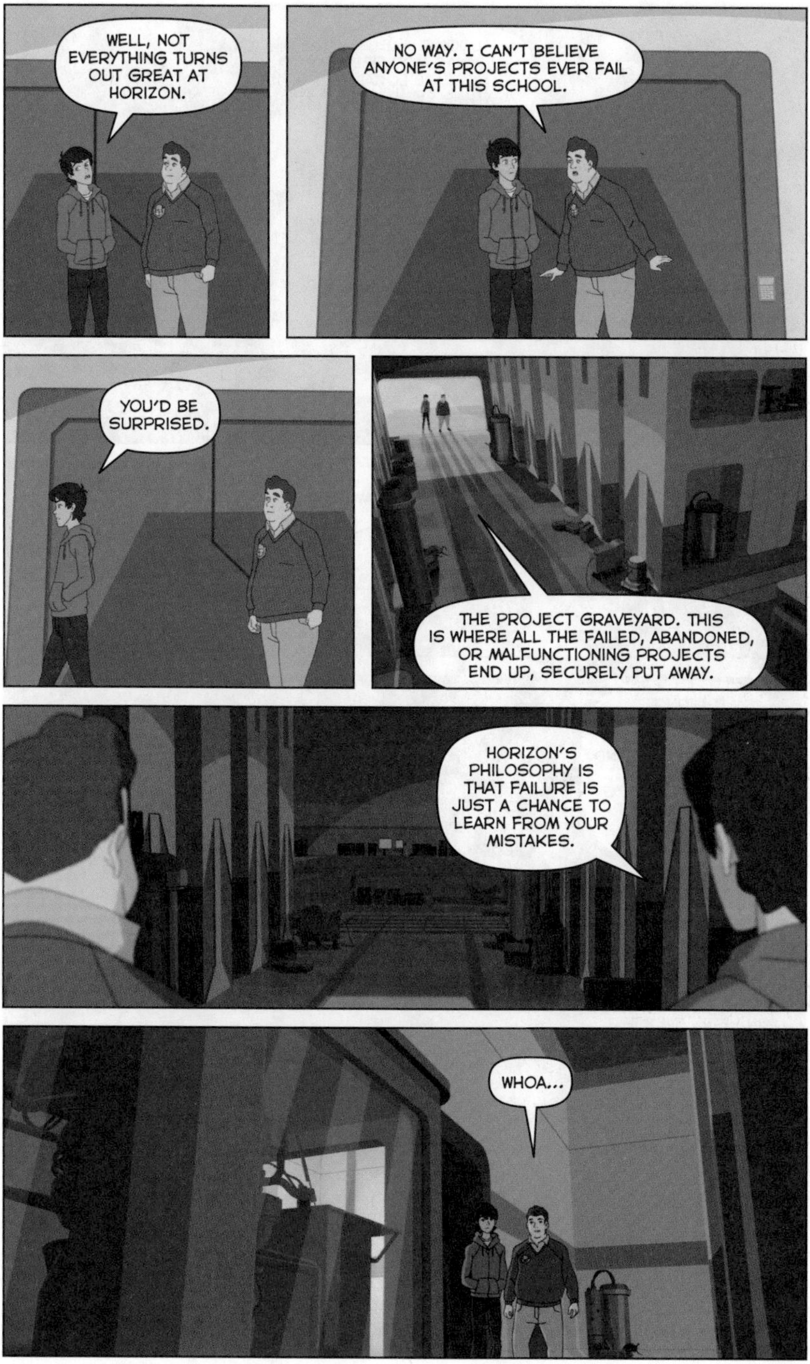
WELL, NOT EVERYTHING TURNS OUT GREAT AT HORIZON.
NO WAY. I CAN'T BELIEVE ANYONE'S PROJECTS EVER FAIL AT THIS SCHOOL.
YOU'D BE SURPRISED.
THE PROJECT GRAVEYARD. THIS IS WHERE ALL THE FAILED, ABANDONED, OR MALFUNCTIONING PROJECTS END UP, SECURELY PUT AWAY.
HORIZON'S PHILOSOPHY IS THAT FAILURE IS JUST A CHANCE TO LEARN FROM YOUR MISTAKES.
WHOA...

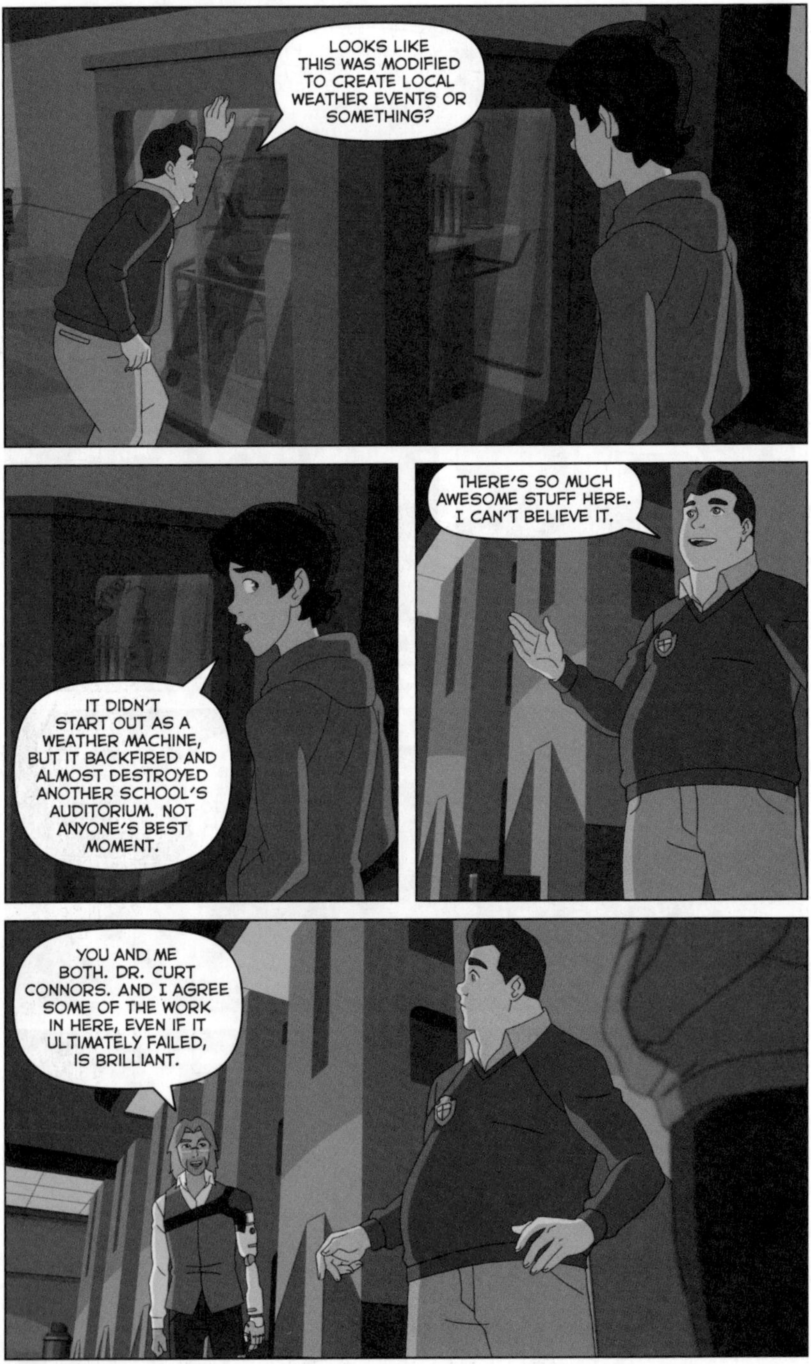
LOOKS LIKE THIS WAS MODIFIED TO CREATE LOCAL WEATHER EVENTS OR SOMETHING?
IT DIDN'T START OUT AS A WEATHER MACHINE, BUT IT BACKFIRED AND ALMOST DESTROYED ANOTHER SCHOOL'S AUDITORIUM. NOT ANYONE'S BEST MOMENT.
THERE'S SO MUCH AWESOME STUFF HERE. I CAN'T BELIEVE IT.
YOU AND ME BOTH. DR. CURT CONNORS. AND I AGREE SOME OF THE WORK IN HERE, EVEN IF IT ULTIMATELY FAILED, IS BRILLIANT.

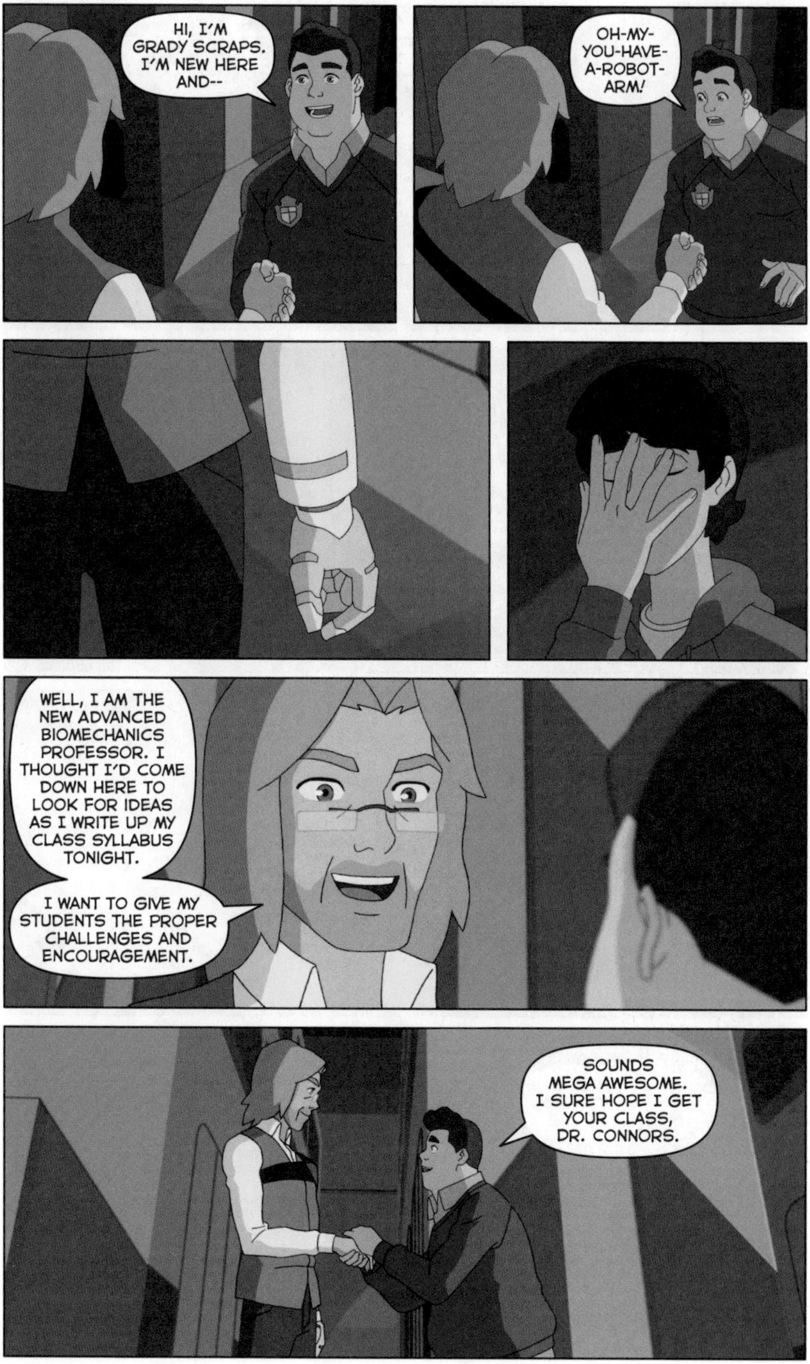
HI, I'M GRADY SCRAPS. I'M NEW HERE AND--
OH-MY-YOU-HAVE-A-ROBOT-ARM!
WELL, I AM THE NEW ADVANCED BIOMECHANICS PROFESSOR. I THOUGHT I'D COME DOWN HERE TO LOOK FOR IDEAS AS I WRITE UP MY CLASS SYLLABUS TONIGHT.
I WANT TO GIVE MY STUDENTS THE PROPER CHALLENGES AND ENCOURAGEMENT.
SOUNDS MEGA AWESOME. I SURE HOPE I GET YOUR CLASS, DR. CONNORS.

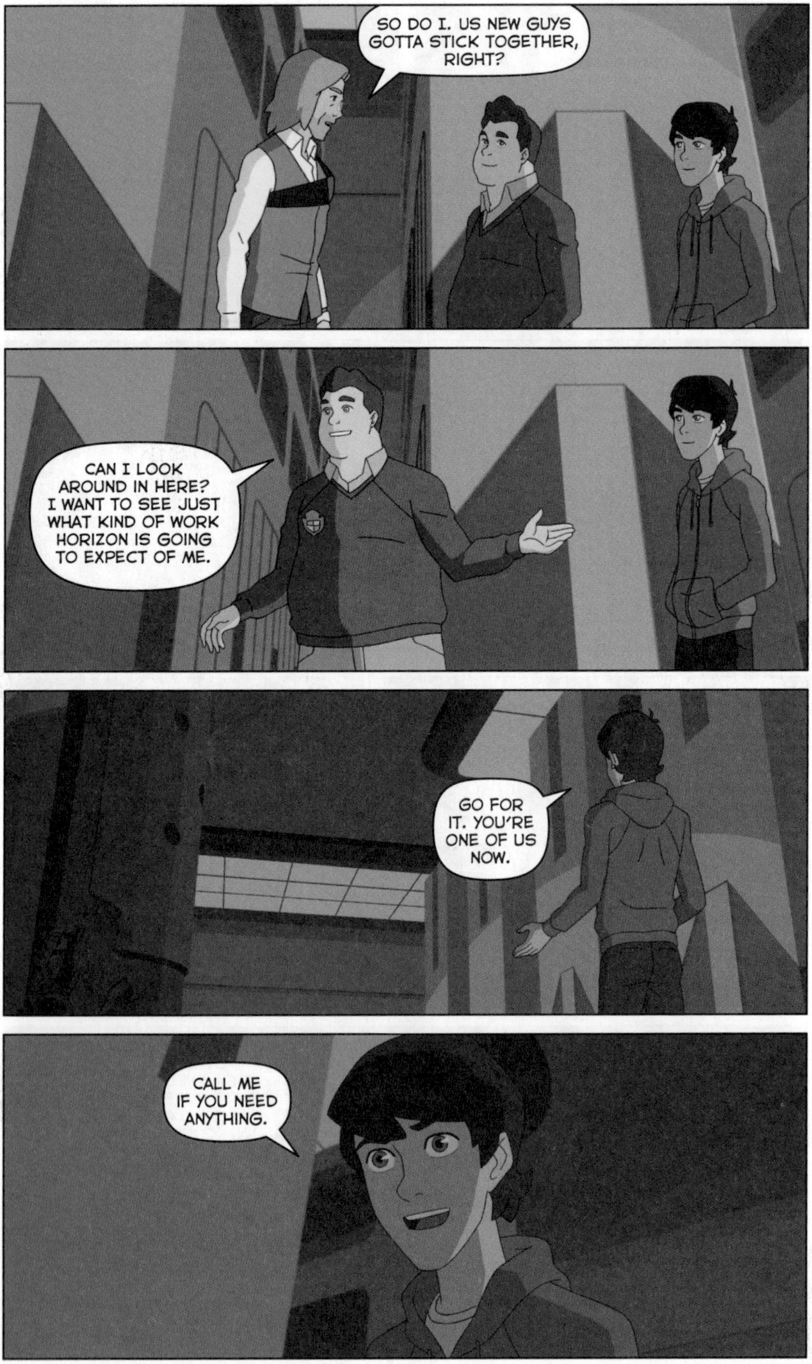
SO DO I. US NEW GUYS GOTTA STICK TOGETHER, RIGHT?
CAN I LOOK AROUND IN HERE? I WANT TO SEE JUST WHAT KIND OF WORK HORIZON IS GOING TO EXPECT OF ME.
GO FOR IT. YOU'RE ONE OF US NOW.
CALL ME IF YOU NEED ANYTHING.

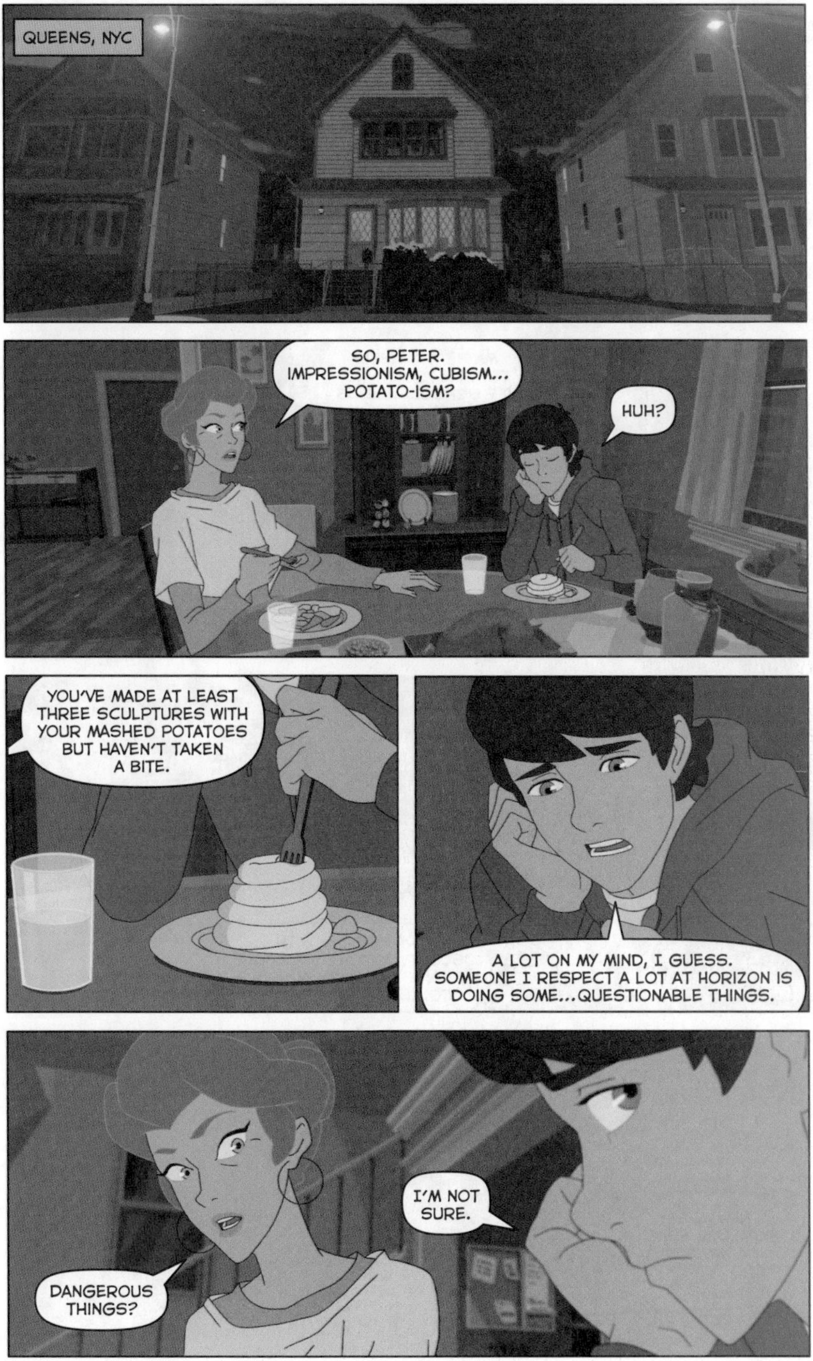
QUEENS, NYC
SO, PETER. IMPRESSIONISM, CUBISM... POTATO-ISM?
HUH?
YOU'VE MADE AT LEAST THREE SCULPTURES WITH YOUR MASHED POTATOES BUT HAVEN'T TAKEN A BITE.
A LOT ON MY MIND, I GUESS. SOMEONE I RESPECT A LOT AT HORIZON IS DOING SOME...QUESTIONABLE THINGS.
DANGEROUS THINGS?
I'M NOT SURE.

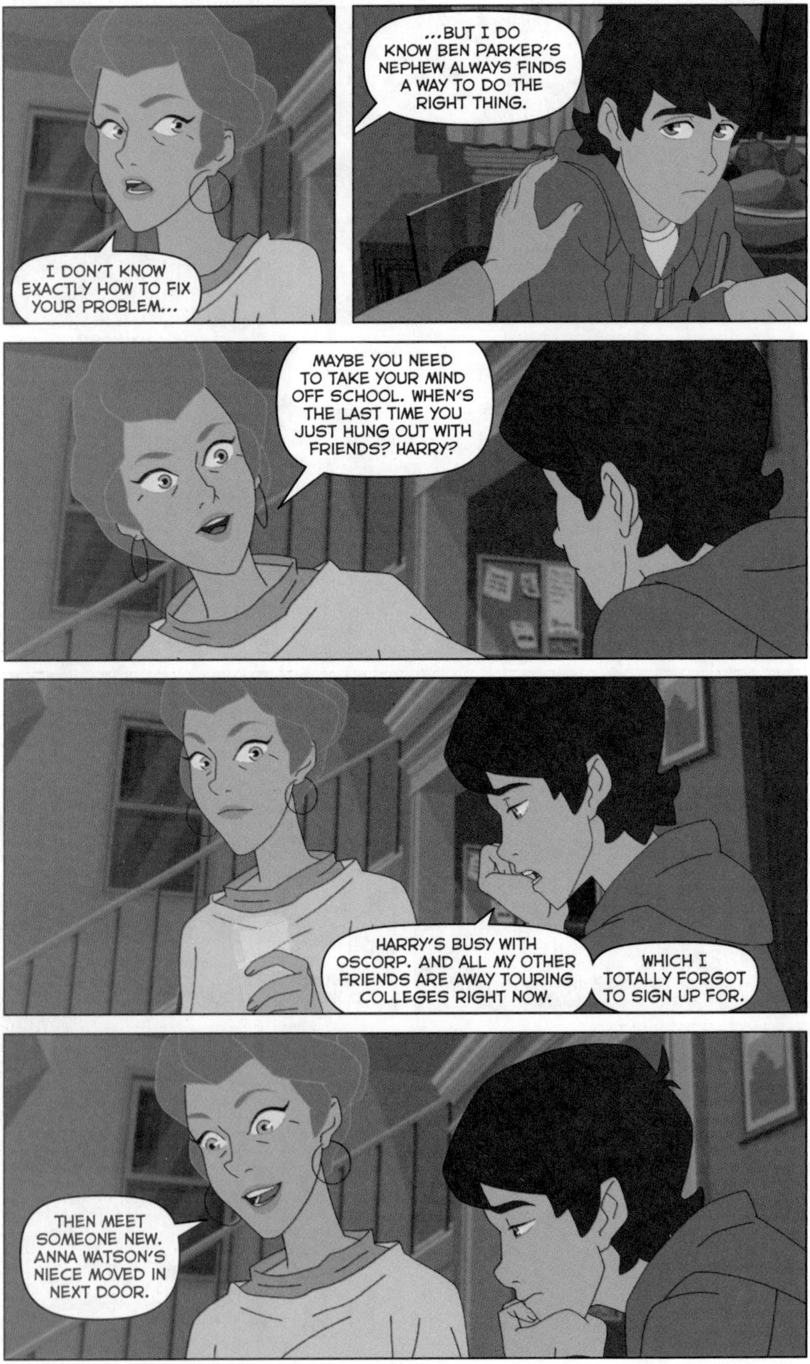
I DON'T KNOW EXACTLY HOW TO FIX YOUR PROBLEM...
...BUT I DO KNOW BEN PARKER'S NEPHEW ALWAYS FINDS A WAY TO DO THE RIGHT THING.
MAYBE YOU NEED TO TAKE YOUR MIND OFF SCHOOL. WHEN'S THE LAST TIME YOU JUST HUNG OUT WITH FRIENDS? HARRY?
HARRY'S BUSY WITH OSCORP. AND ALL MY OTHER FRIENDS ARE AWAY TOURING COLLEGES RIGHT NOW.
WHICH I TOTALLY FORGOT TO SIGN UP FOR.
THEN MEET SOMEONE NEW. ANNA WATSON'S NIECE MOVED IN NEXT DOOR.

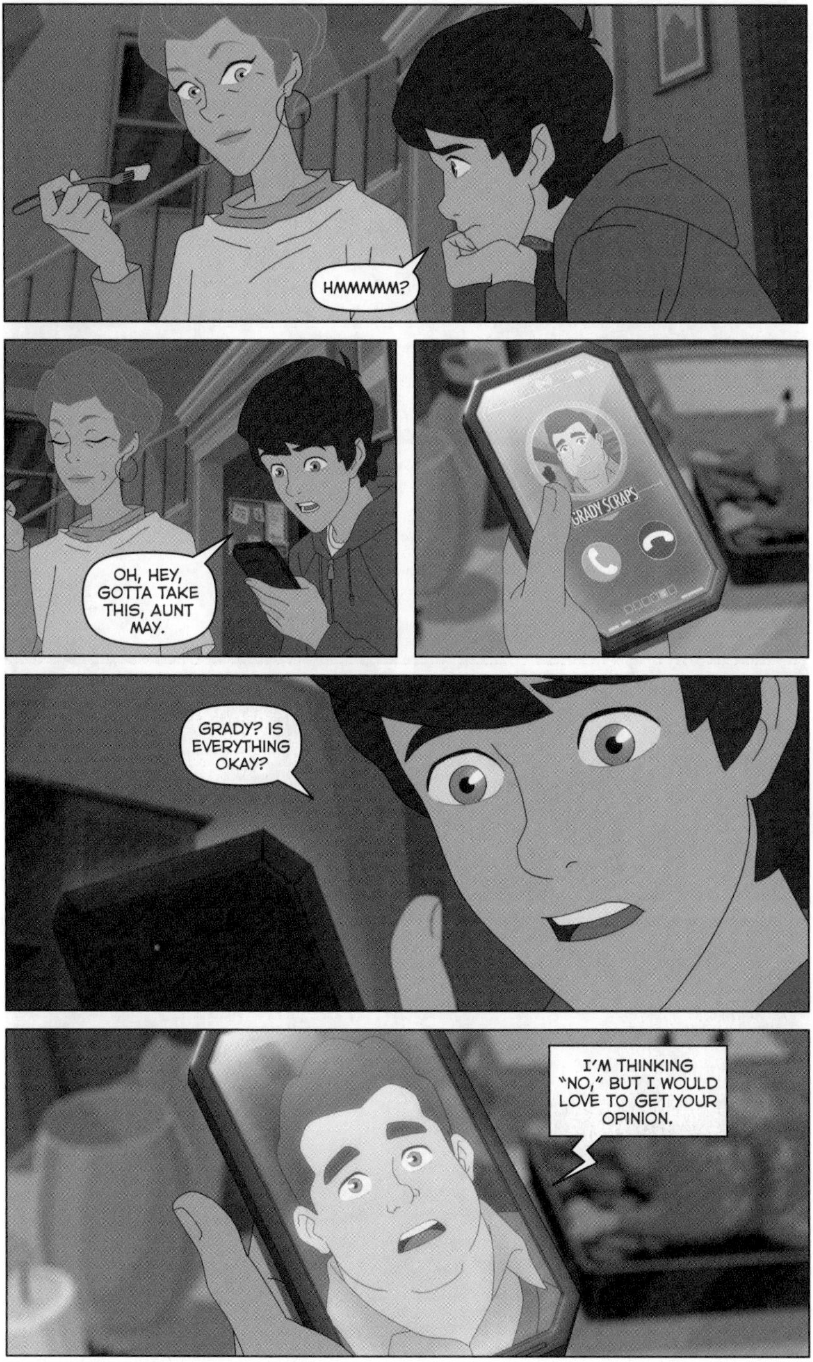
HMMMMM?
OH, HEY, GOTTA TAKE THIS, AUNT MAY.
GRADY SCRAPS
GRADY? IS EVERYTHING OKAY?
I'M THINKING "NO," BUT I WOULD LOVE TO GET YOUR OPINION.

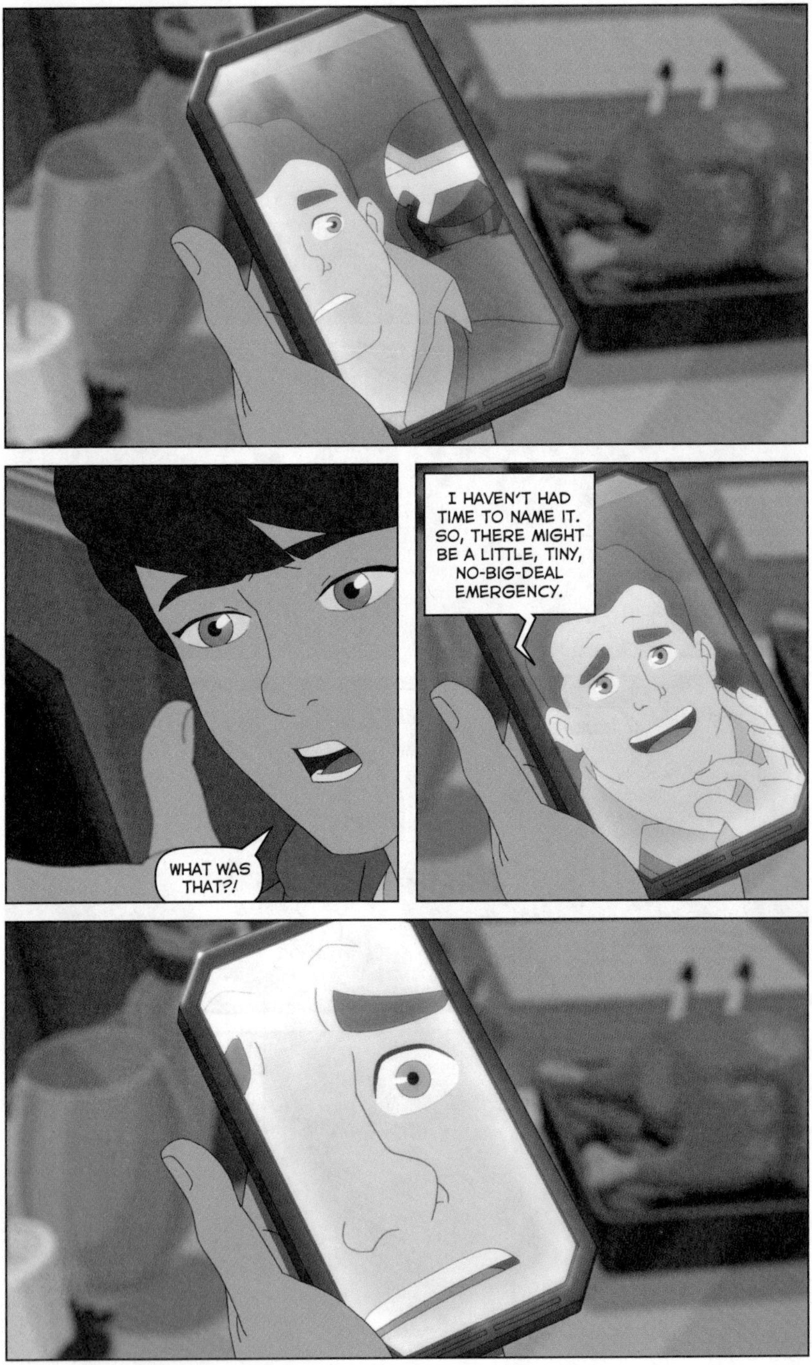
WHAT WAS THAT?!
I HAVEN'T HAD TIME TO NAME IT. SO, THERE MIGHT BE A LITTLE, TINY, NO-BIG-DEAL EMERGENCY.

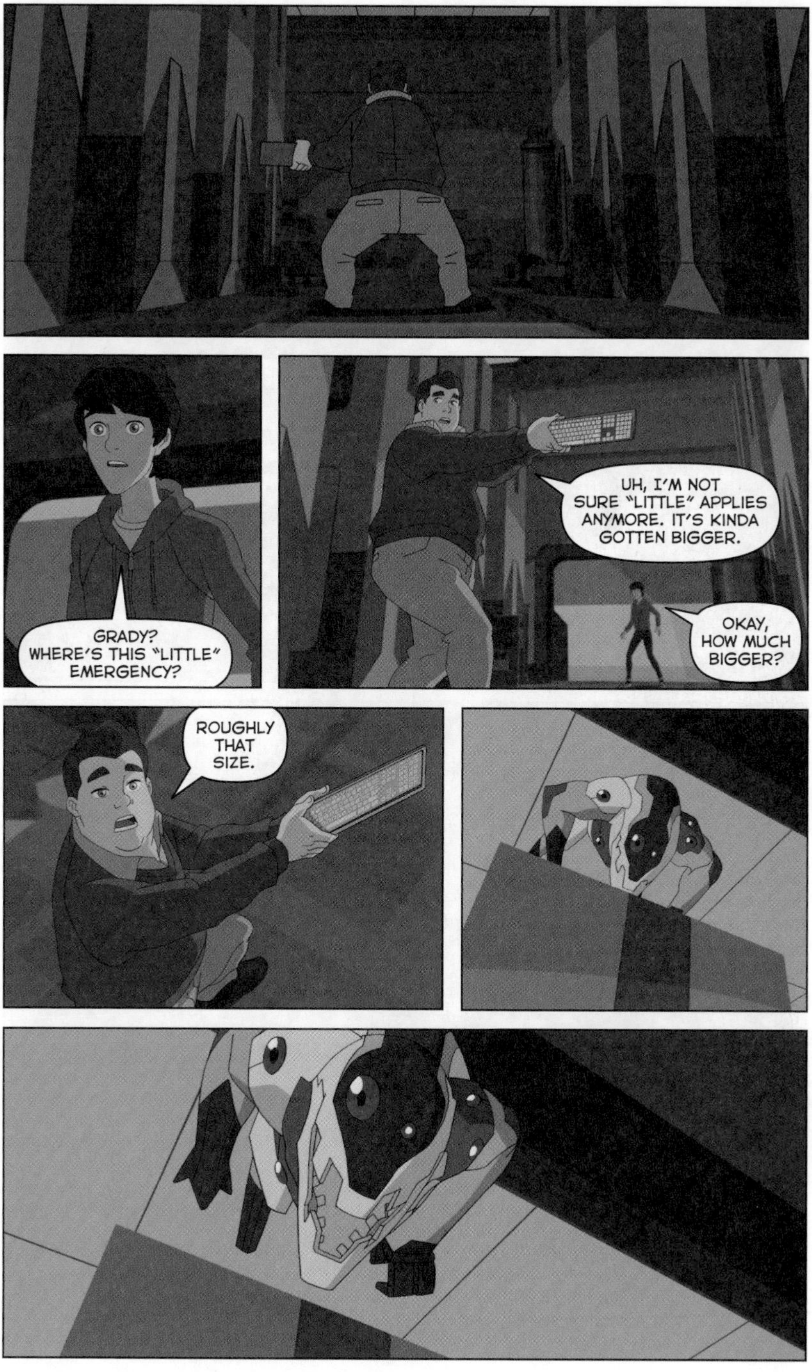
GRADY?
WHERE'S THIS "LITTLE" EMERGENCY?
UH, I'M NOT SURE "LITTLE" APPLIES ANYMORE. IT'S KINDA GOTTEN BIGGER.
OKAY, HOW MUCH BIGGER?
ROUGHLY THAT SIZE.

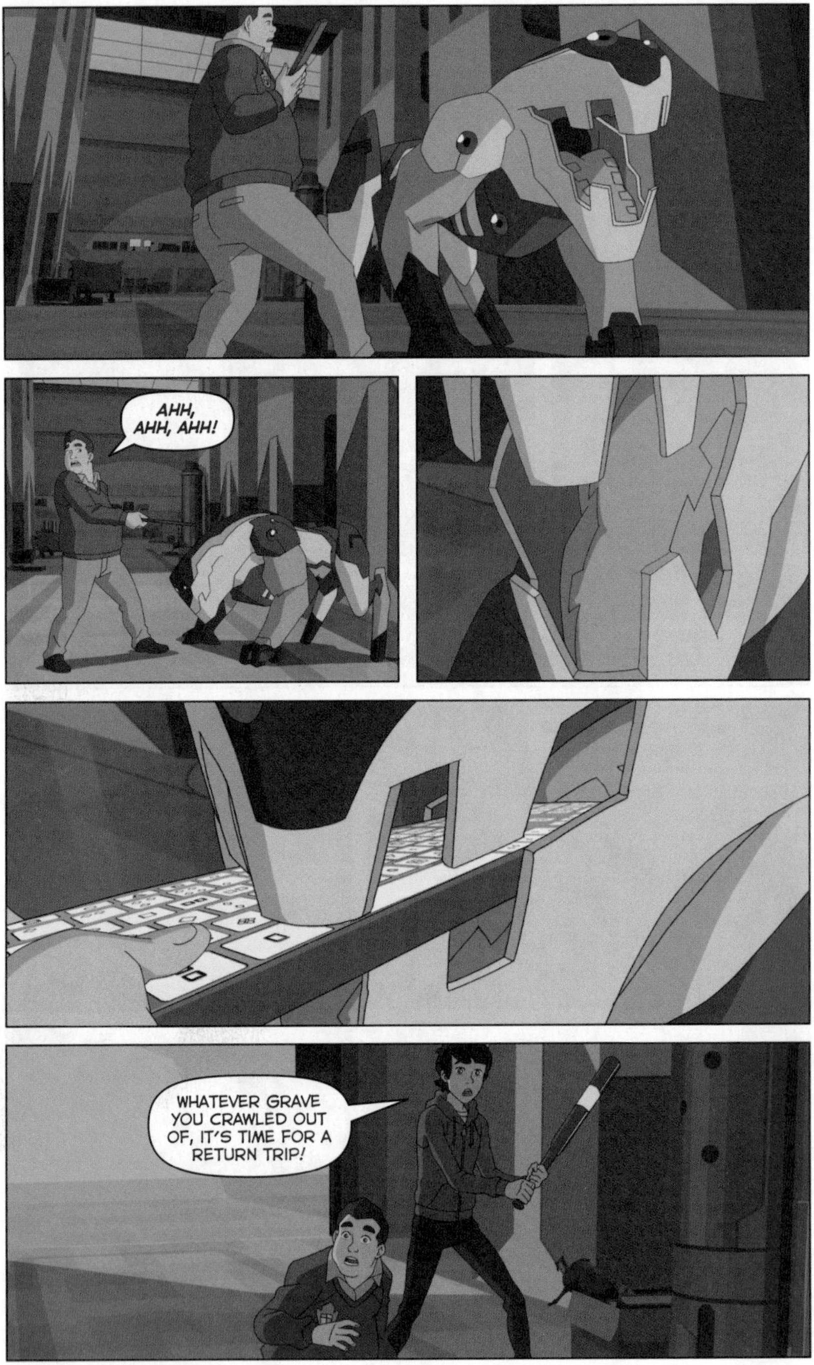
AHH, AHH, AHH!
WHATEVER GRAVE YOU CRAWLED OUT OF, IT'S TIME FOR A RETURN TRIP!

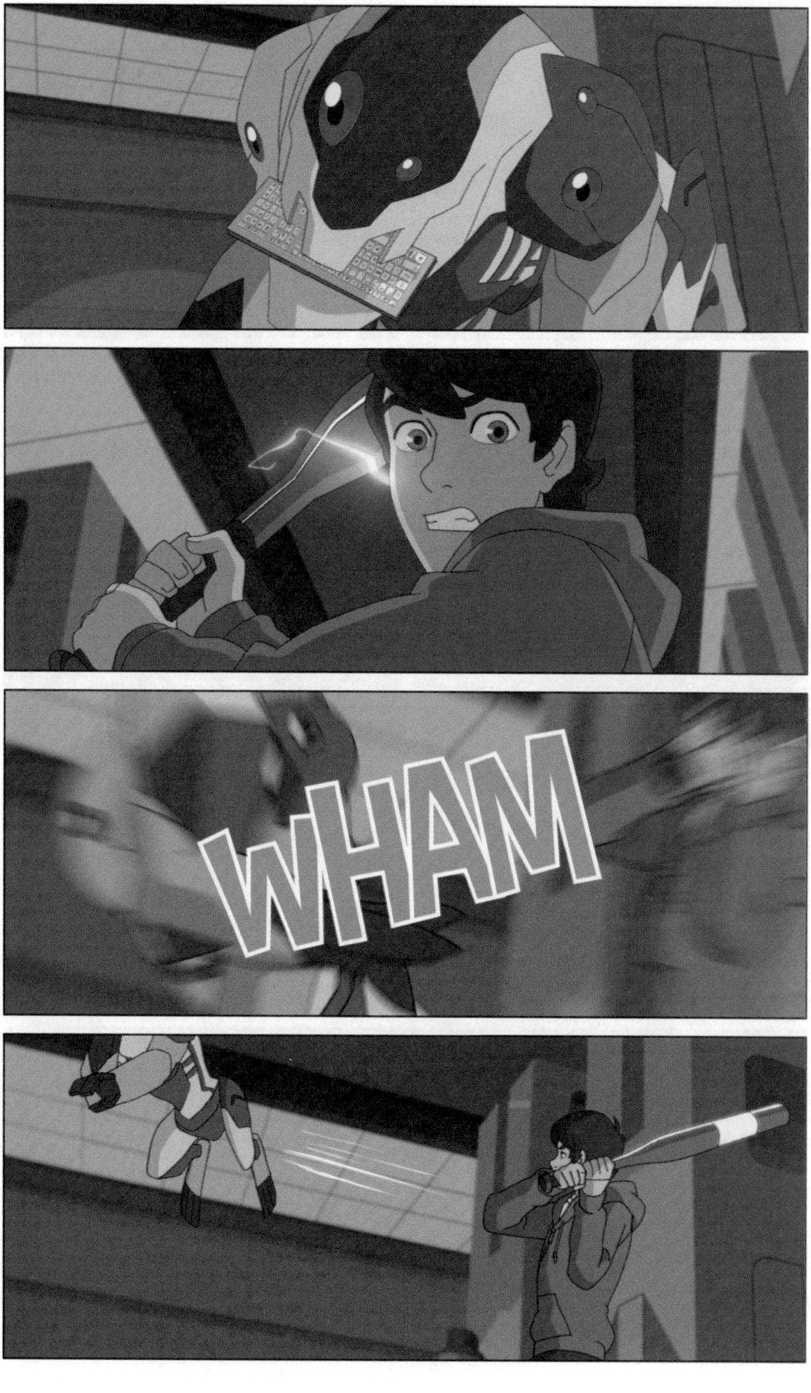
WHAM

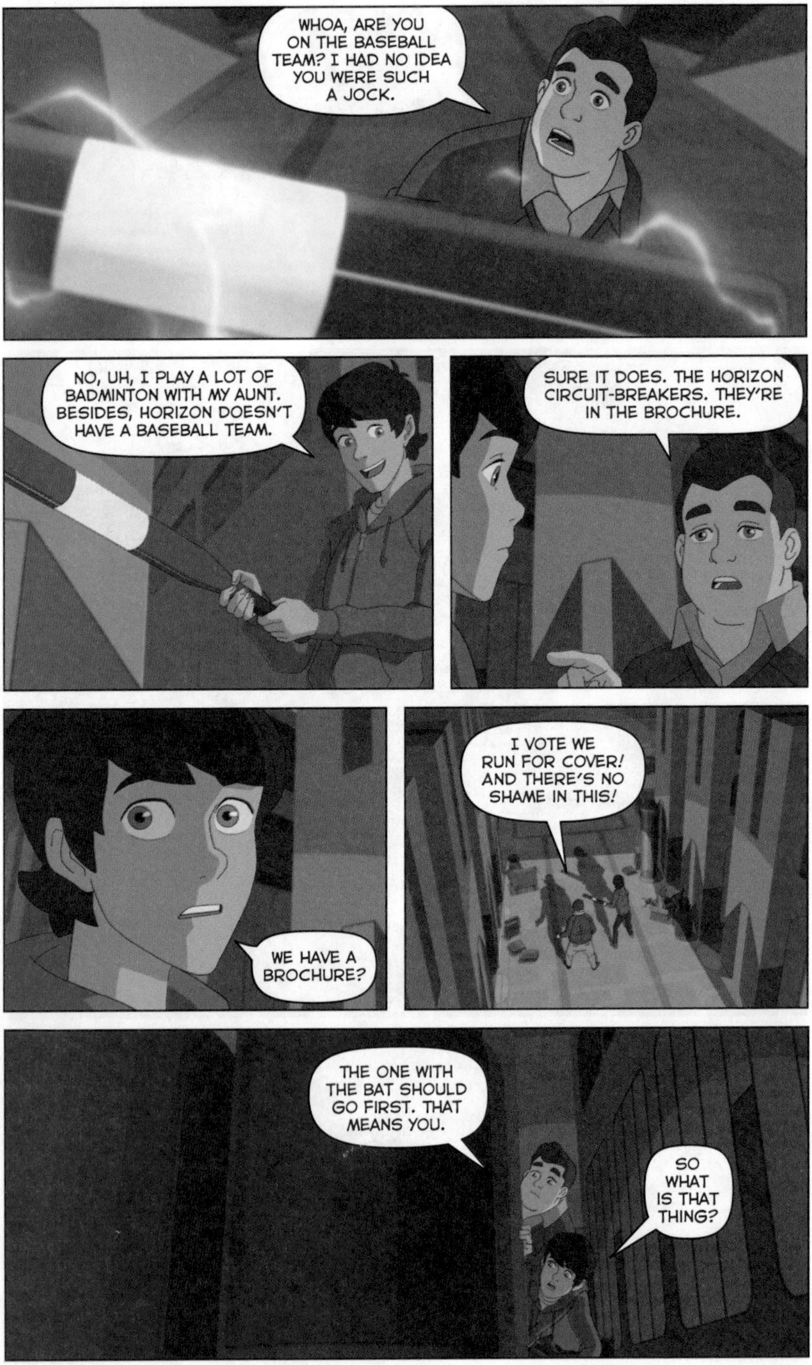
WHOA, ARE YOU ON THE BASEBALL TEAM? I HAD NO IDEA YOU WERE SUCH A JOCK.
NO, UH, I PLAY A LOT OF BADMINTON WITH MY AUNT. BESIDES, HORIZON DOESN'T HAVE A BASEBALL TEAM.
SURE IT DOES. THE HORIZON CIRCUIT-BREAKERS. THEY'RE IN THE BROCHURE.
WE HAVE A BROCHURE?
I VOTE WE RUN FOR COVER! AND THERE'S NO SHAME IN THIS!
THE ONE WITH THE BAT SHOULD GO FIRST. THAT MEANS YOU.
SO WHAT IS THAT THING?

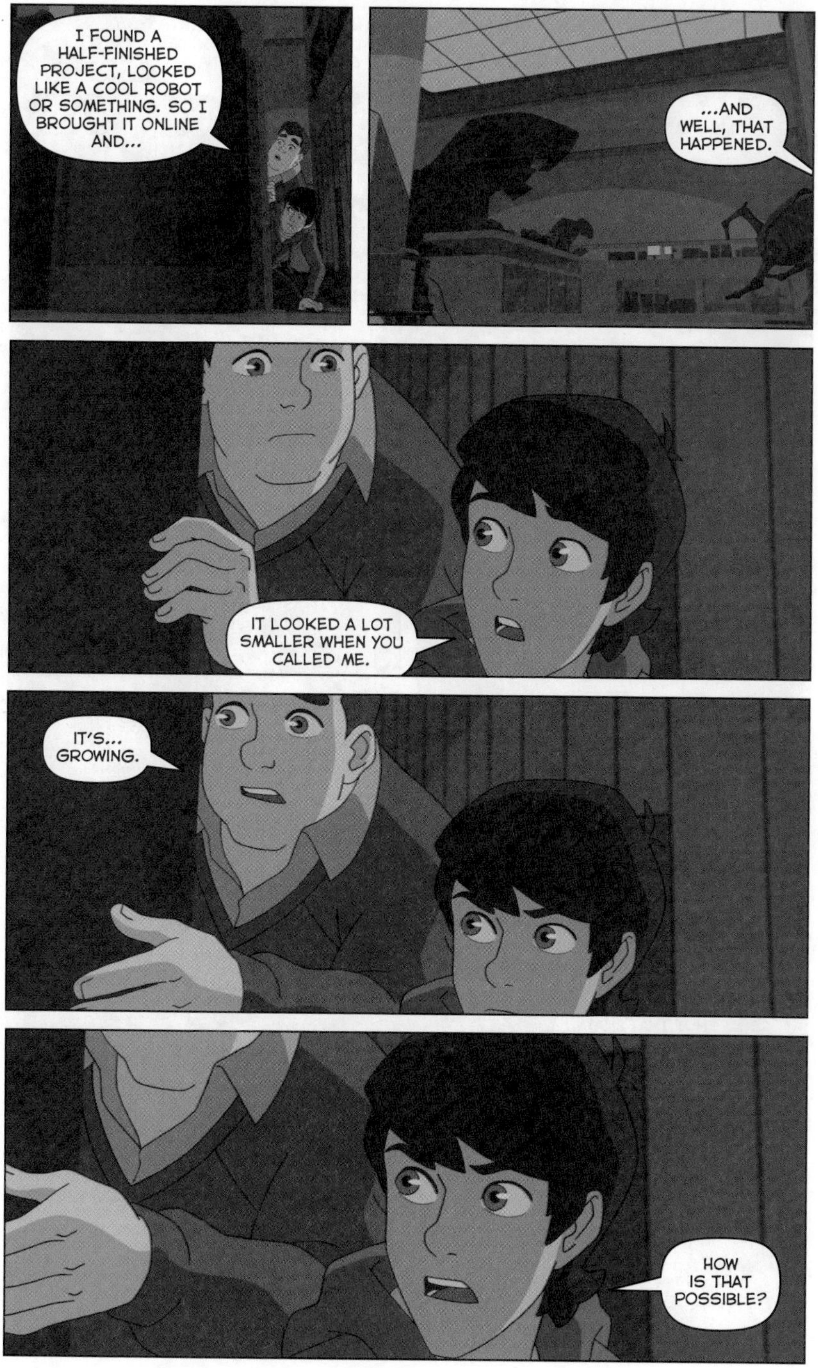
I FOUND A HALF-FINISHED PROJECT, LOOKED LIKE A COOL ROBOT OR SOMETHING. SO I BROUGHT IT ONLINE AND...
...AND WELL, THAT HAPPENED.
IT LOOKED A LOT SMALLER WHEN YOU CALLED ME.
IT'S... GROWING.
HOW IS THAT POSSIBLE?

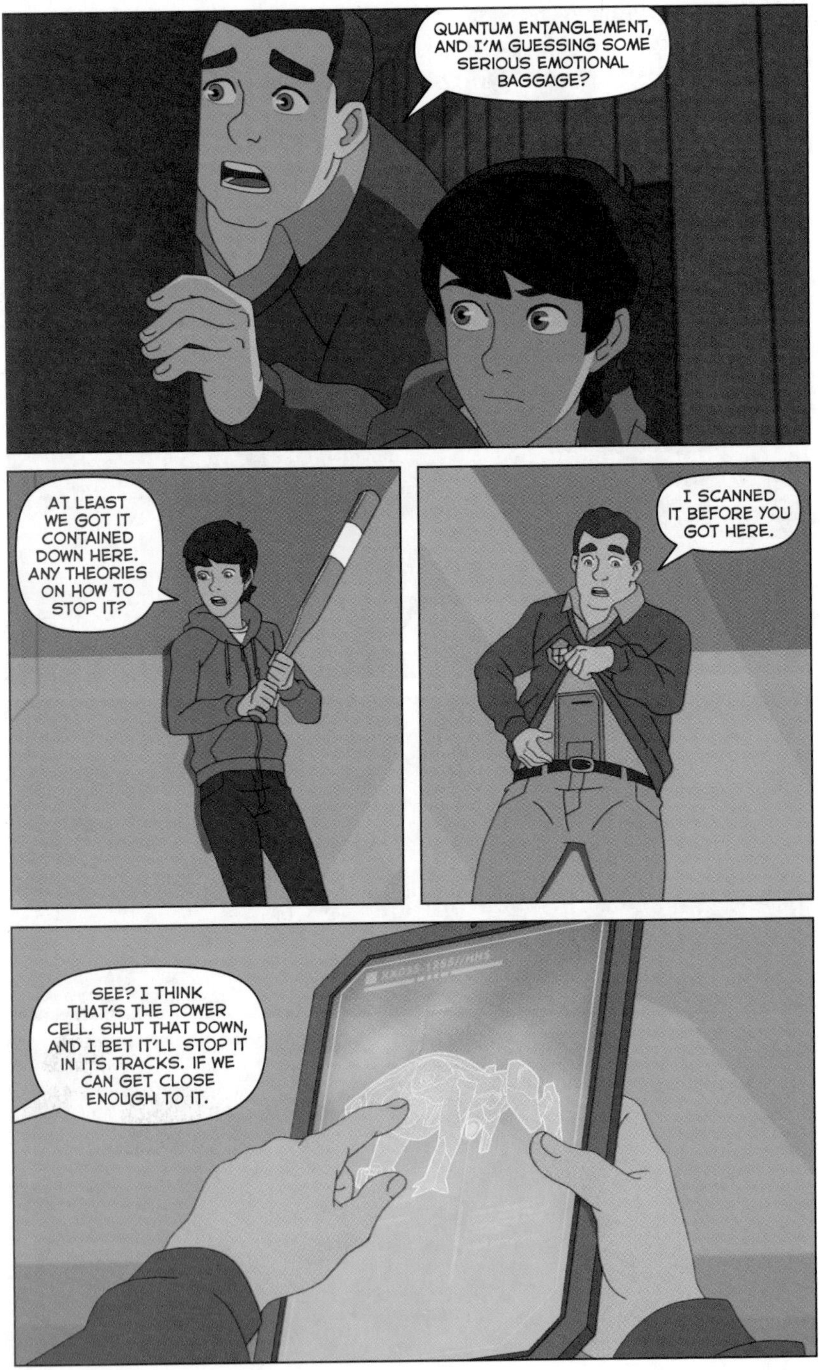
QUANTUM ENTANGLEMENT, AND I'M GUESSING SOME SERIOUS EMOTIONAL BAGGAGE?
AT LEAST WE GOT IT CONTAINED DOWN HERE. ANY THEORIES ON HOW TO STOP IT?
I SCANNED IT BEFORE YOU GOT HERE.
SEE? I THINK THAT'S THE POWER CELL. SHUT THAT DOWN, AND I BET IT'LL STOP IT IN ITS TRACKS. IF WE CAN GET CLOSE ENOUGH TO IT.

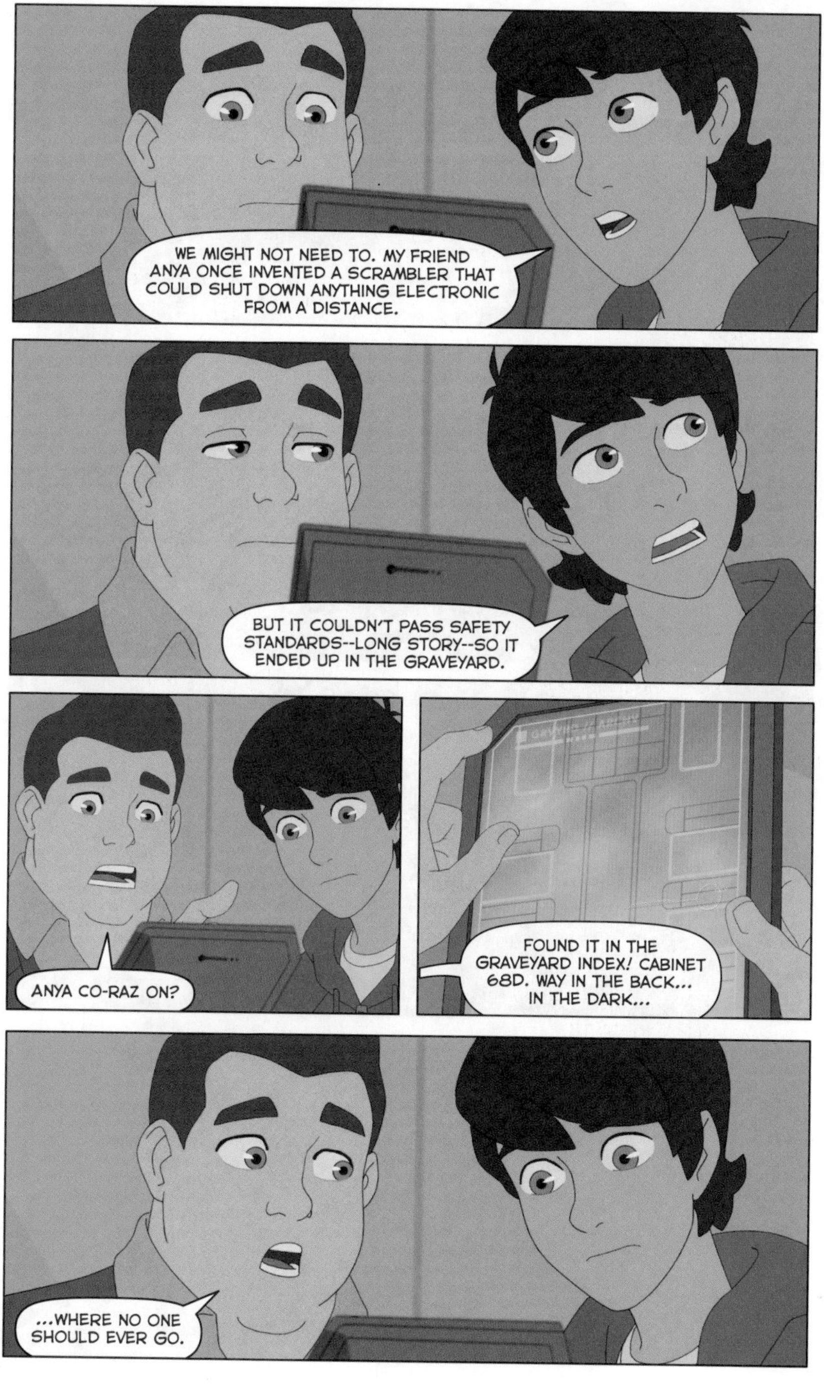
WE MIGHT NOT NEED TO. MY FRIEND ANYA ONCE INVENTED A SCRAMBLER THAT COULD SHUT DOWN ANYTHING ELECTRONIC FROM A DISTANCE.
BUT IT COULDN'T PASS SAFETY STANDARDS--LONG STORY--SO IT ENDED UP IN THE GRAVEYARD.
ANYA CO-RAZ ON?
FOUND IT IN THE GRAVEYARD INDEX! CABINET 68D. WAY IN THE BACK... IN THE DARK...
...WHERE NO ONE SHOULD EVER GO.

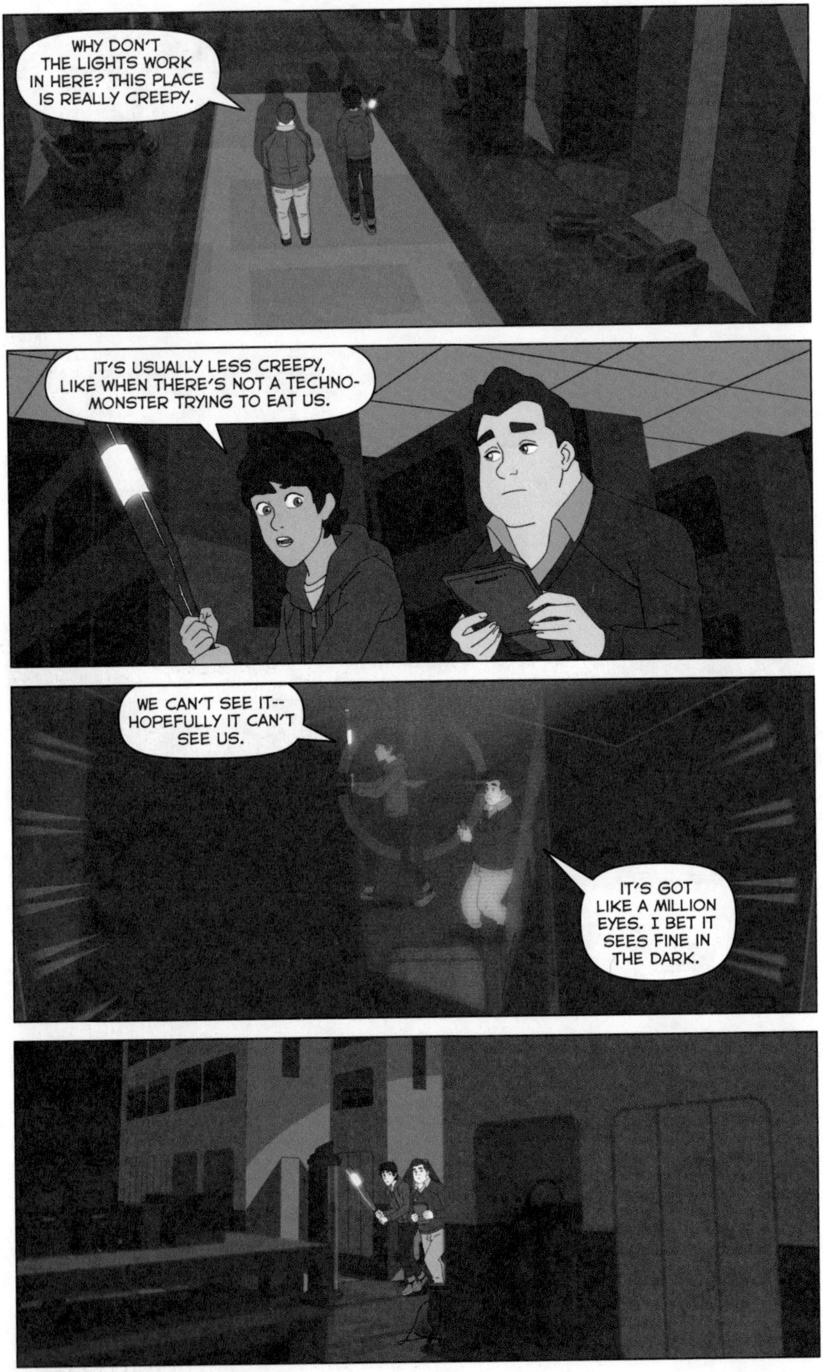
WHY DON'T THE LIGHTS WORK IN HERE? THIS PLACE IS REALLY CREEPY.
IT'S USUALLY LESS CREEPY, LIKE WHEN THERE'S NOT A TECHNO-MONSTER TRYING TO EAT US.
WE CAN'T SEE IT-- HOPEFULLY IT CAN'T SEE US.
IT'S GOT LIKE A MILLION EYES. I BET IT SEES FINE IN THE DARK.

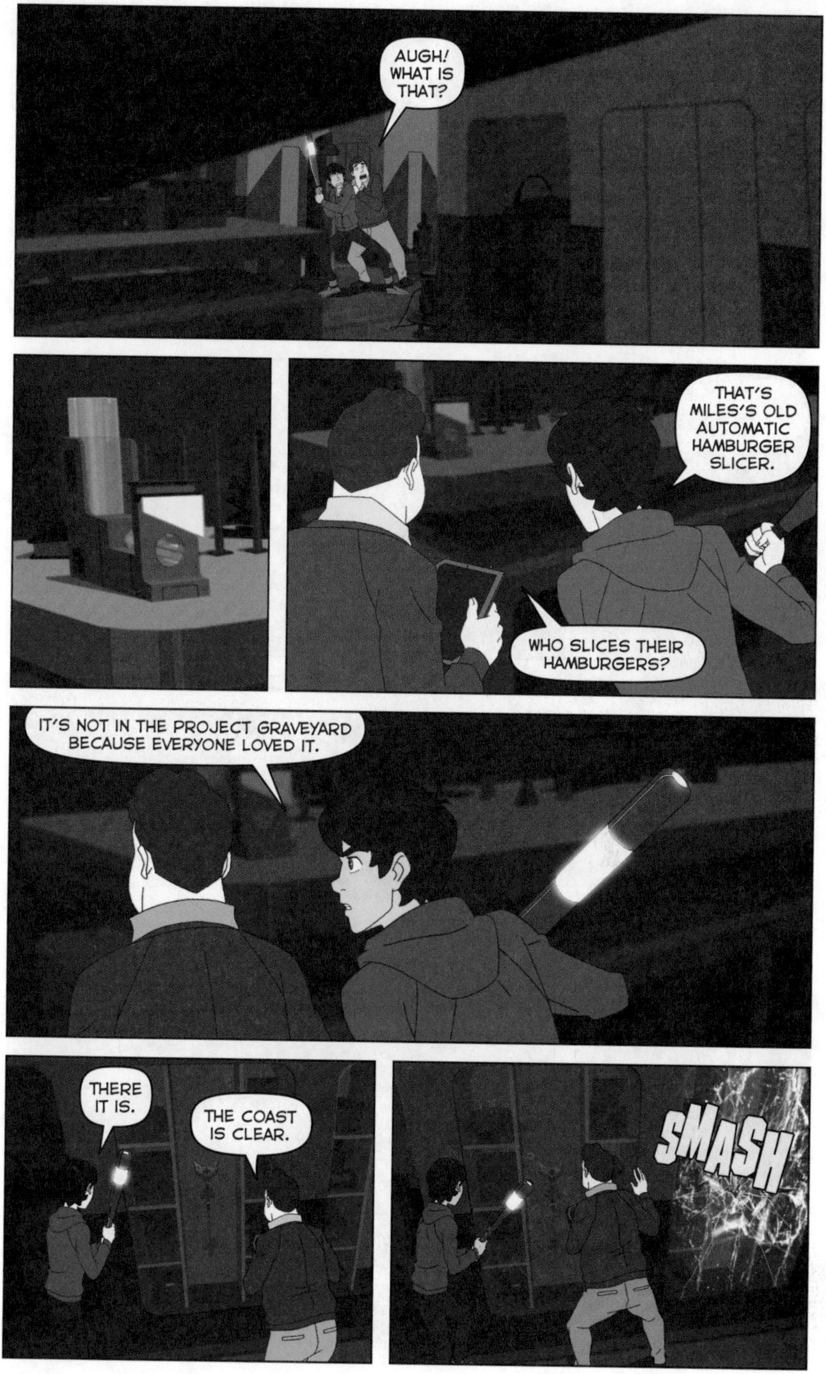
AUGH! WHAT IS THAT?
THAT'S MILES'S OLD AUTOMATIC HAMBURGER SLICER.
WHO SLICES THEIR HAMBURGERS?
IT'S NOT IN THE PROJECT GRAVEYARD BECAUSE EVERYONE LOVED IT.
THERE IT IS.
THE COAST IS CLEAR.
SMASH

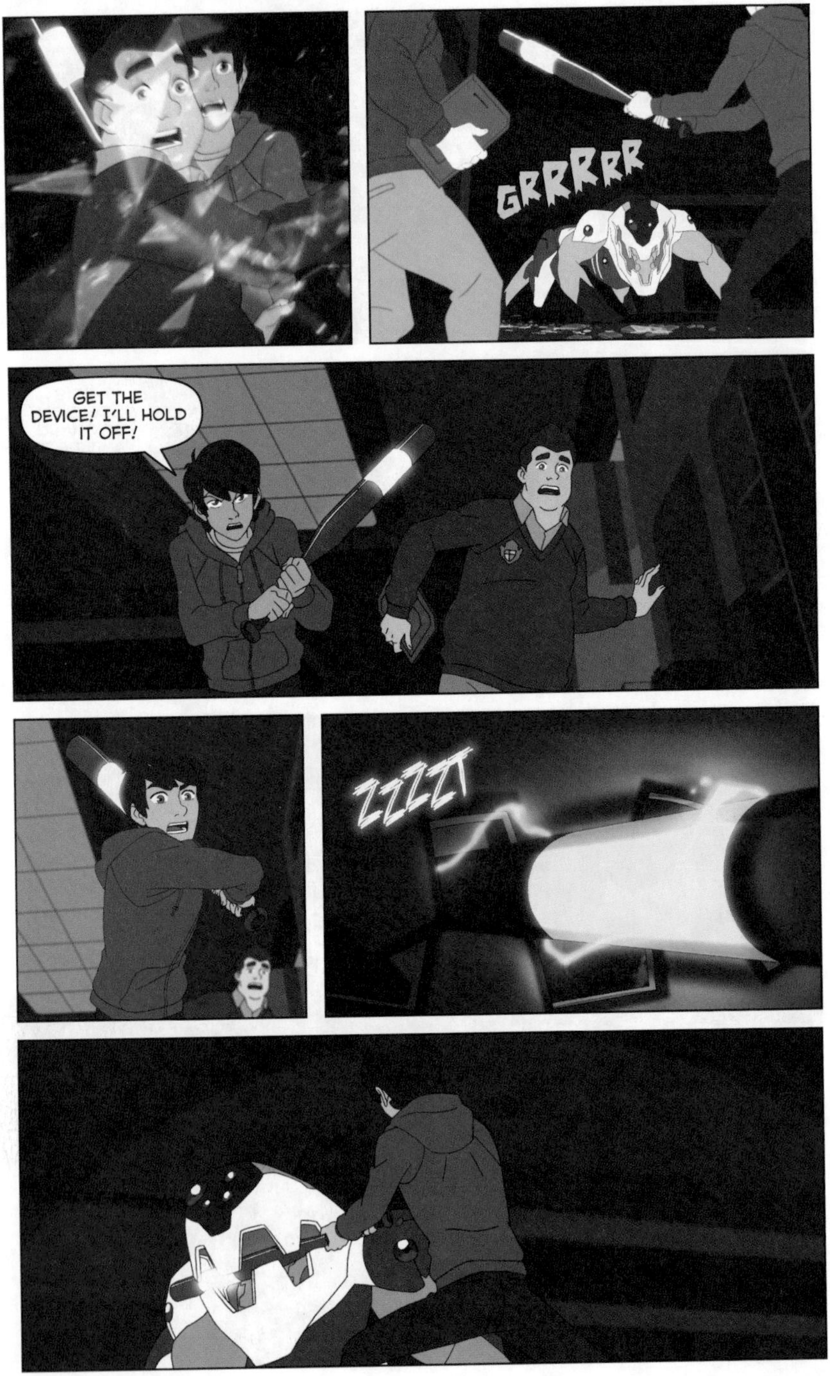
GRRRRR
GET THE DEVICE! I'LL HOLD IT OFF!
ZZZZT

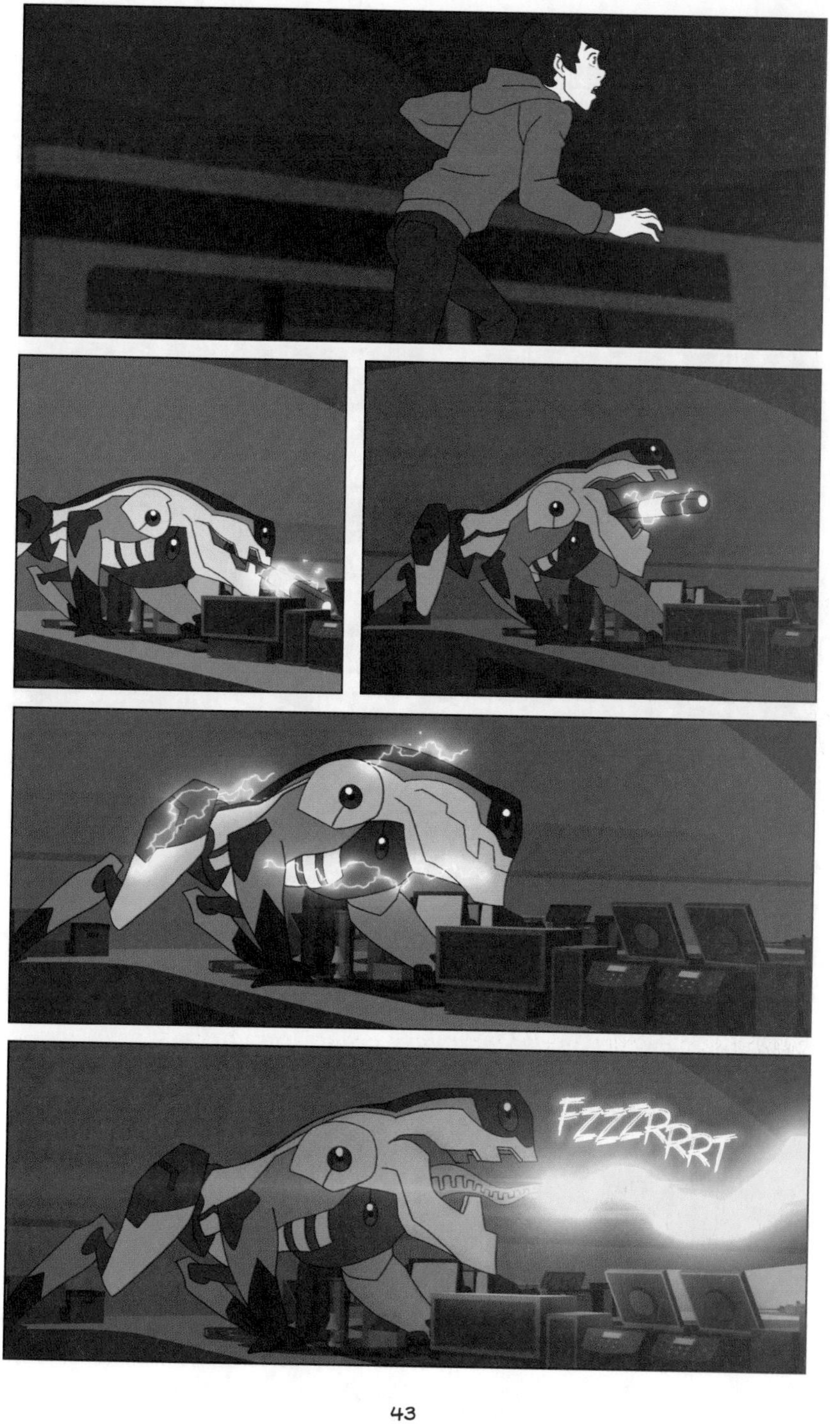
FZZZRRRT

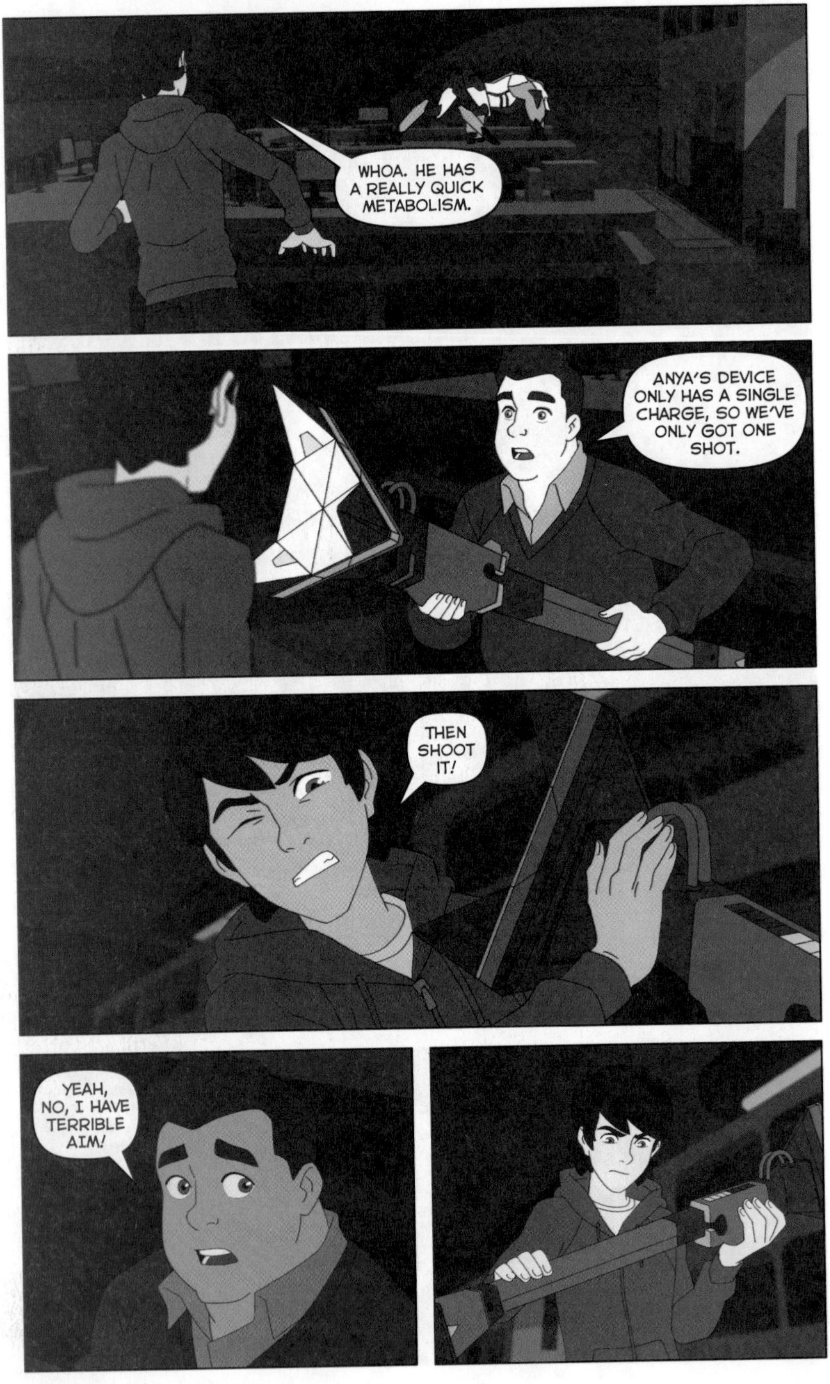
WHOA. HE HAS A REALLY QUICK METABOLISM.
ANYA'S DEVICE ONLY HAS A SINGLE CHARGE, SO WE'VE ONLY GOT ONE SHOT.
THEN SHOOT IT!
YEAH, NO, I HAVE TERRIBLE AIM!

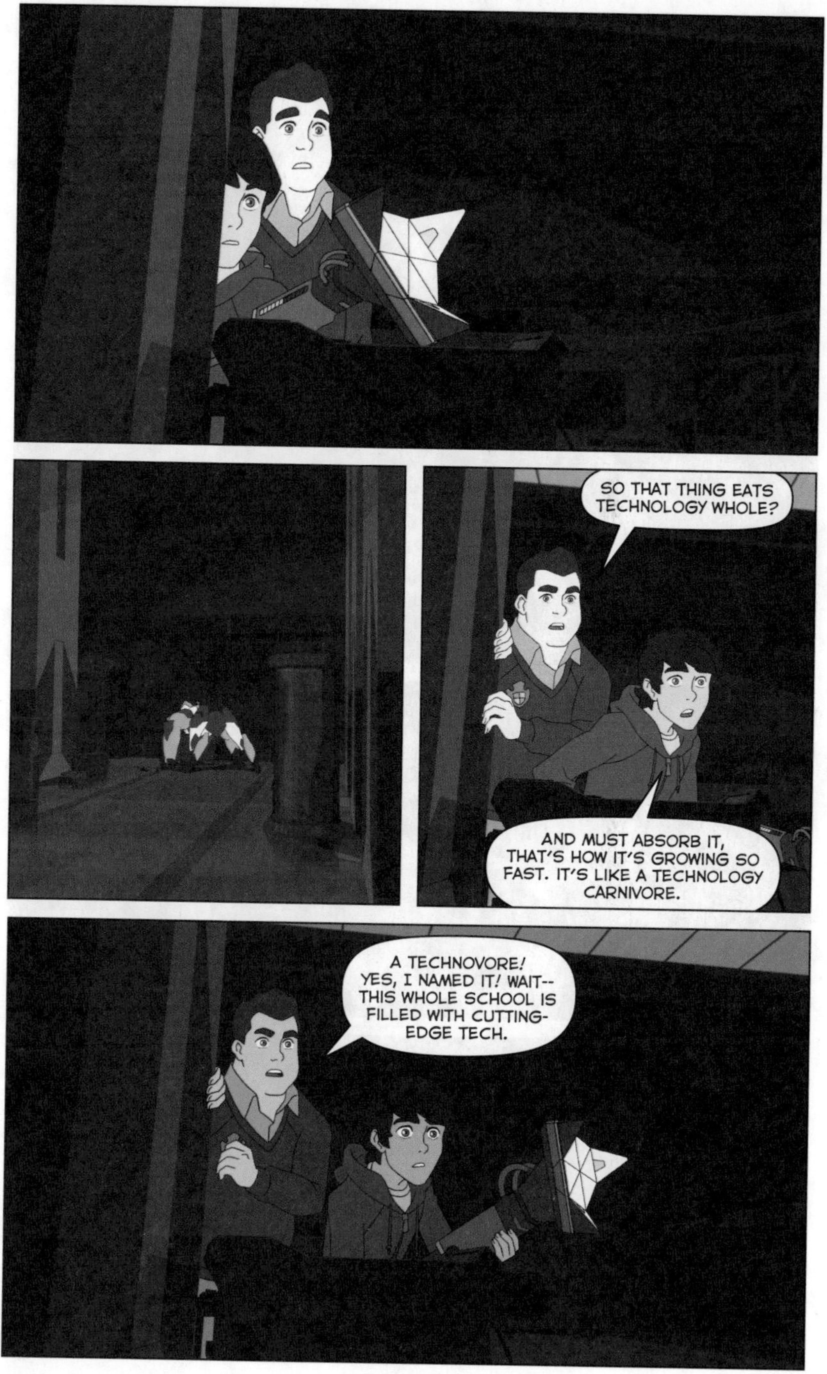
SO THAT THING EATS TECHNOLOGY WHOLE?
AND MUST ABSORB IT, THAT'S HOW IT'S GROWING SO FAST. IT'S LIKE A TECHNOLOGY CARNIVORE.
A TECHNOVORE! YES, I NAMED IT! WAIT-- THIS WHOLE SCHOOL IS FILLED WITH CUTTING-EDGE TECH.

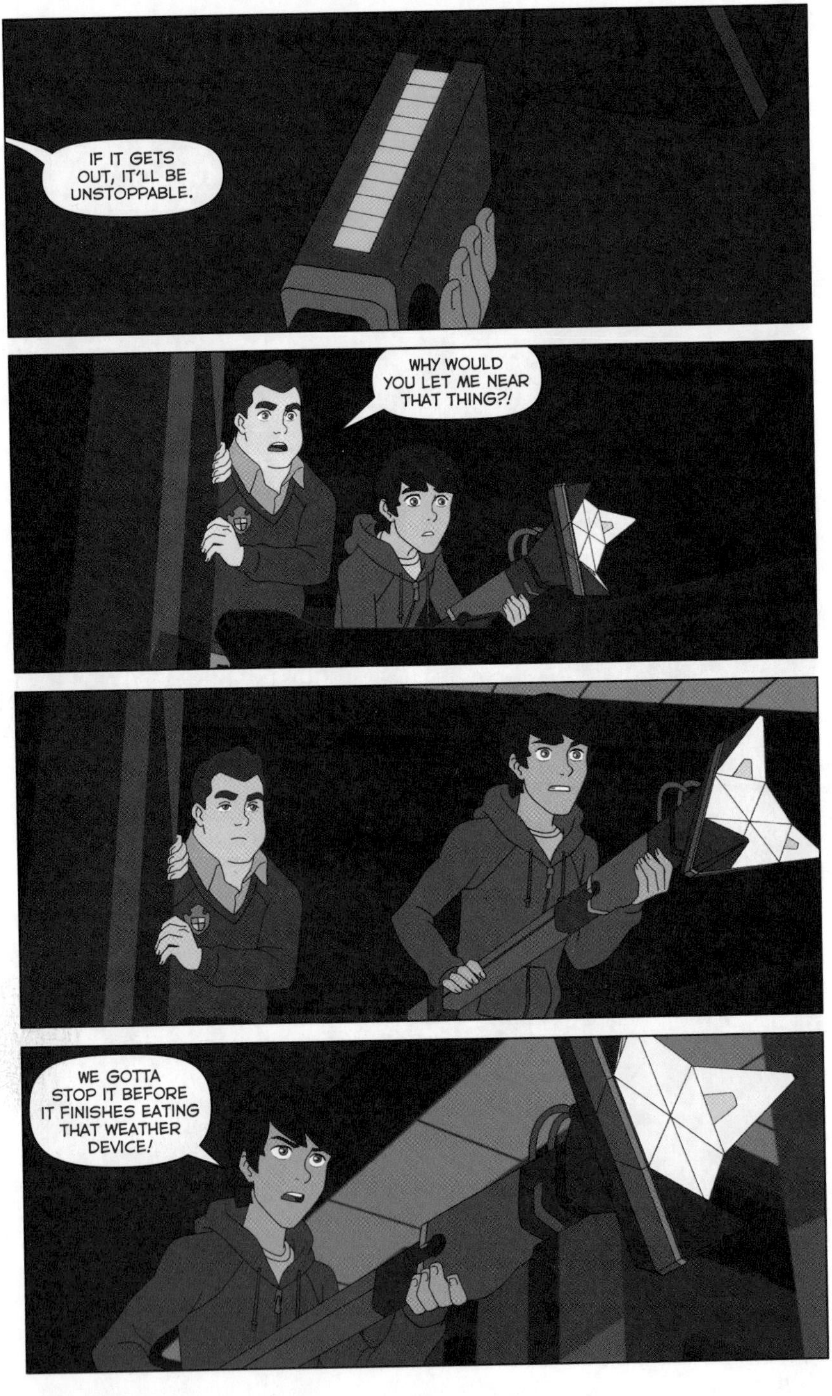
IF IT GETS OUT, IT'LL BE UNSTOPPABLE.
WHY WOULD YOU LET ME NEAR THAT THING?!
WE GOTTA STOP IT BEFORE IT FINISHES EATING THAT WEATHER DEVICE!

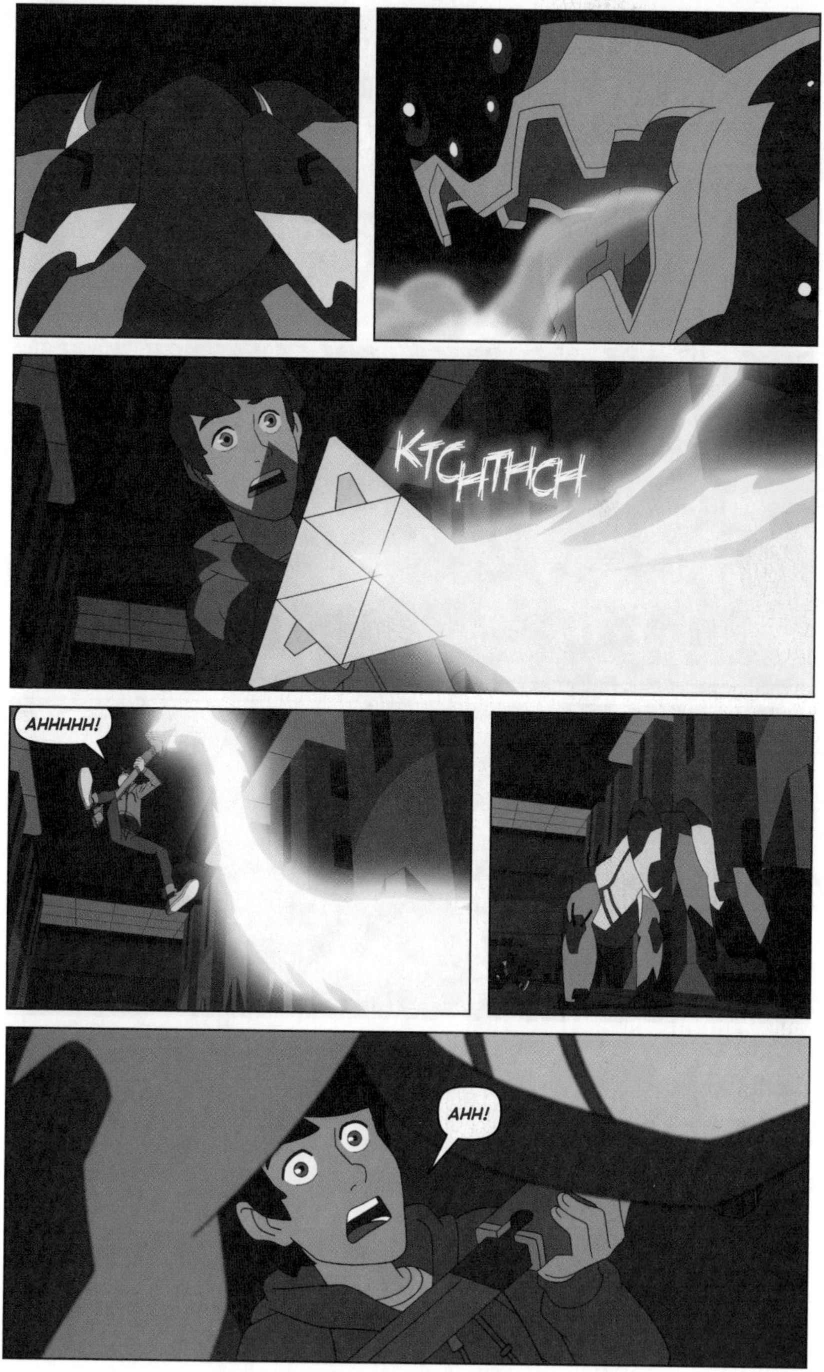
KTCHHTHCH
AHHHHH!
AHH!

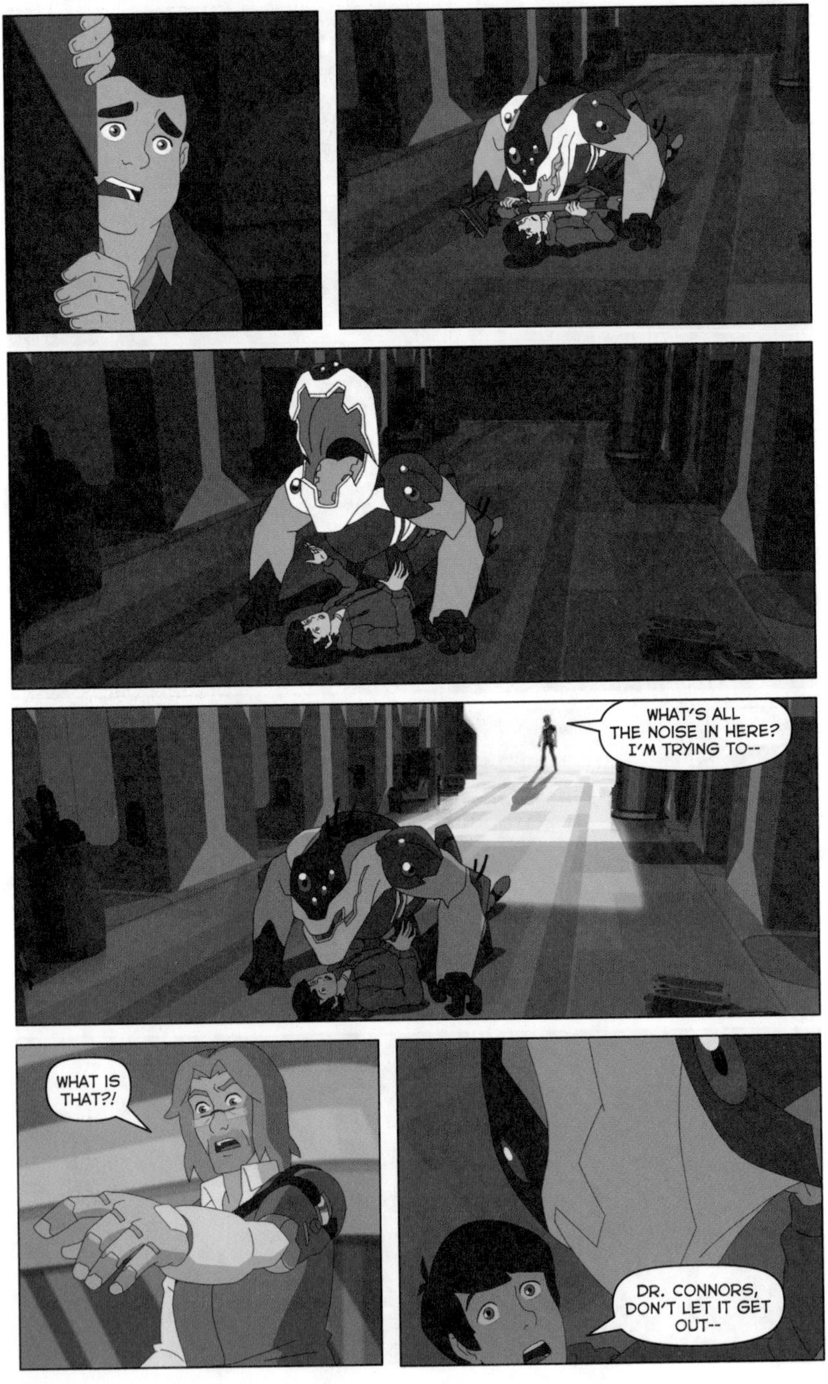
WHAT'S ALL THE NOISE IN HERE? I'M TRYING TO--
WHAT IS THAT?!
DR. CONNORS, DON'T LET IT GET OUT--

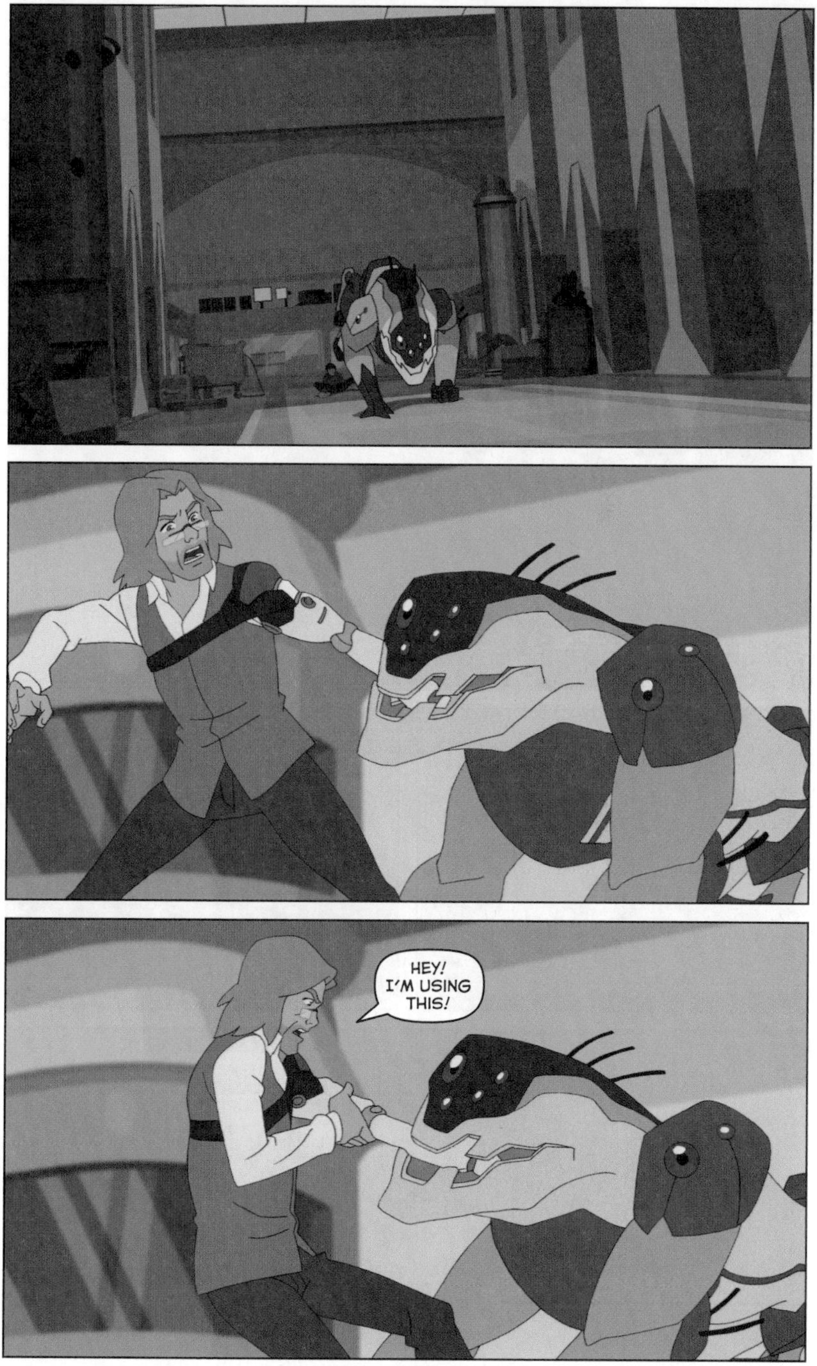
HEY! I'M USING THIS!

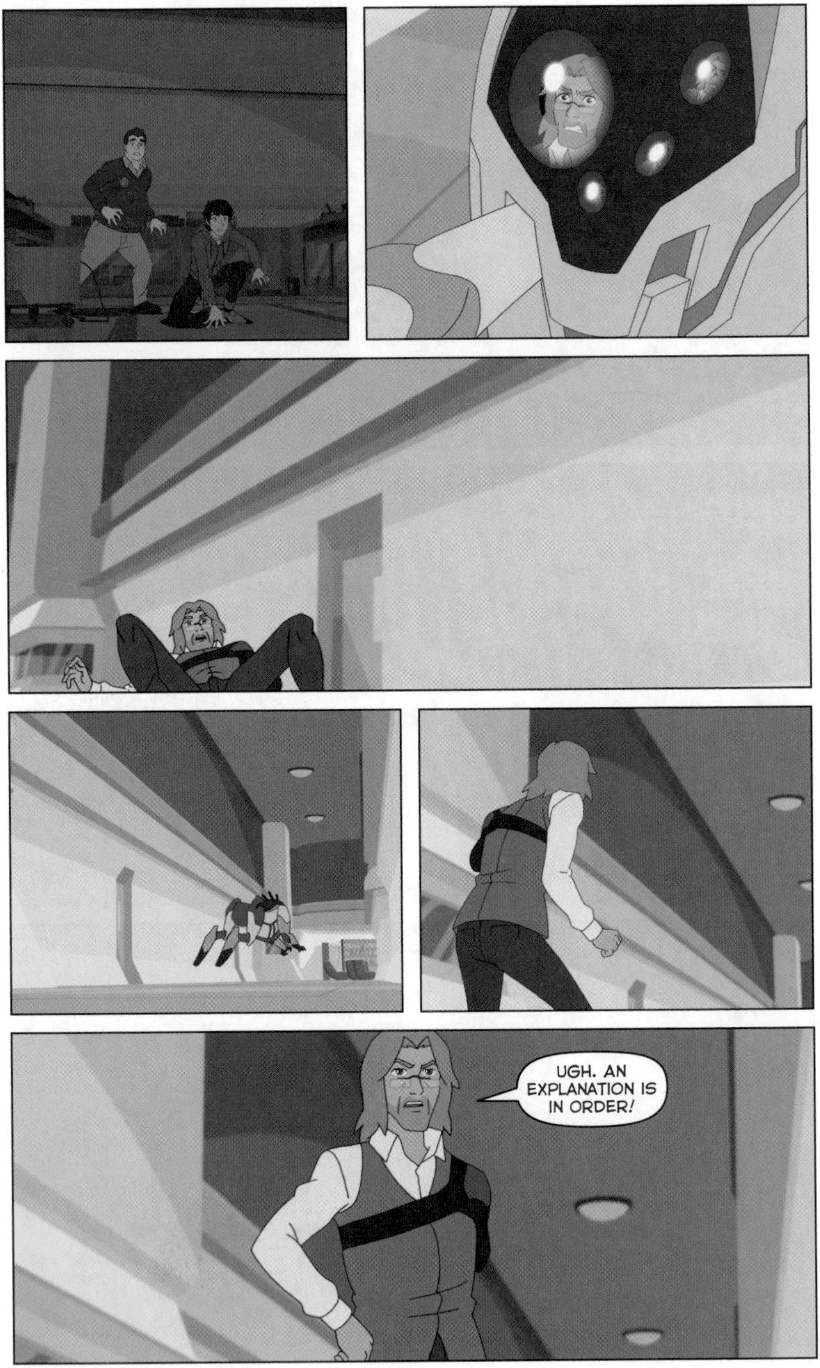
UGH. AN EXPLANATION IS IN ORDER!

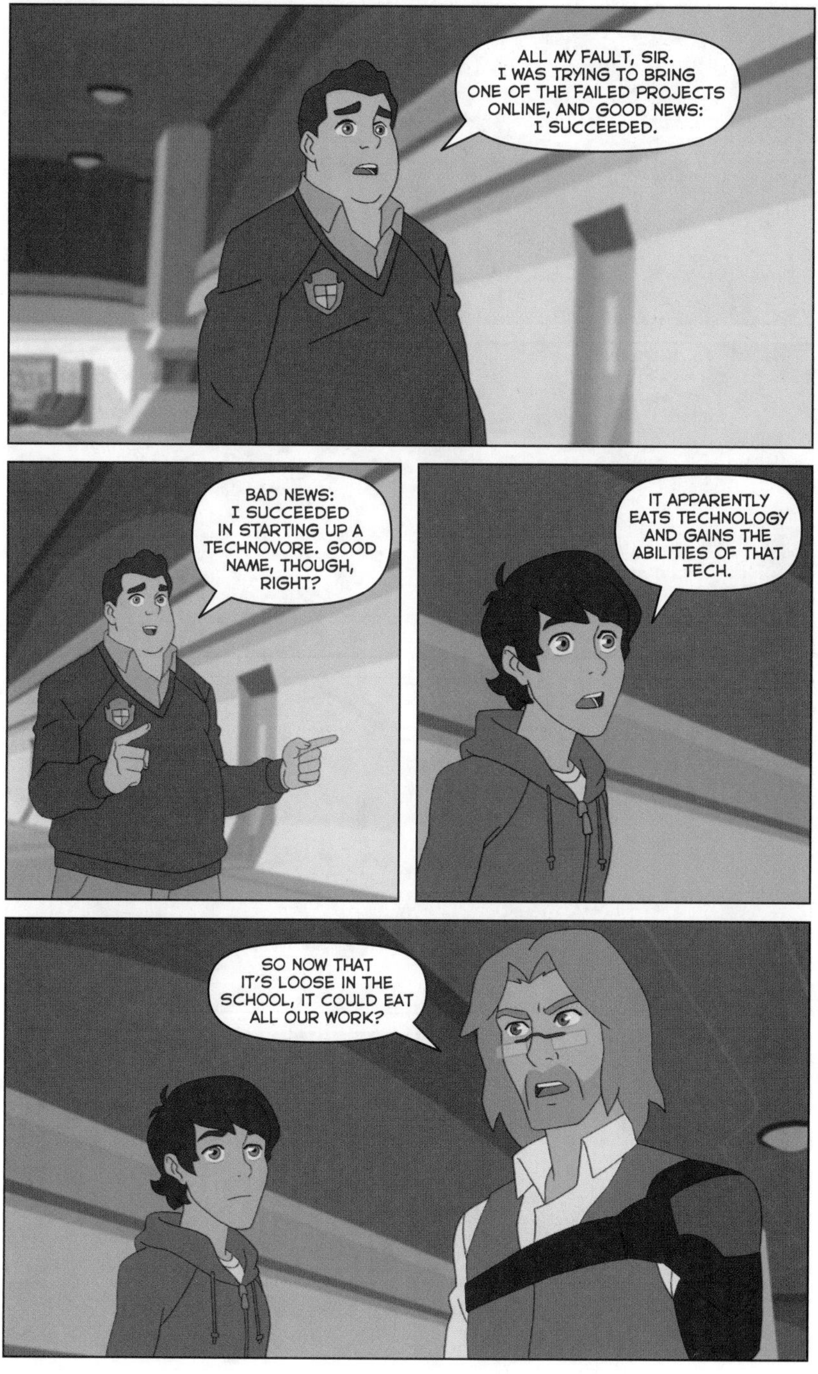
ALL MY FAULT, SIR. I WAS TRYING TO BRING ONE OF THE FAILED PROJECTS ONLINE, AND GOOD NEWS: I SUCCEEDED.
BAD NEWS: I SUCCEEDED IN STARTING UP A TECHNOVORE. GOOD NAME, THOUGH, RIGHT?
IT APPARENTLY EATS TECHNOLOGY AND GAINS THE ABILITIES OF THAT TECH.
SO NOW THAT IT'S LOOSE IN THE SCHOOL, IT COULD EAT ALL OUR WORK?

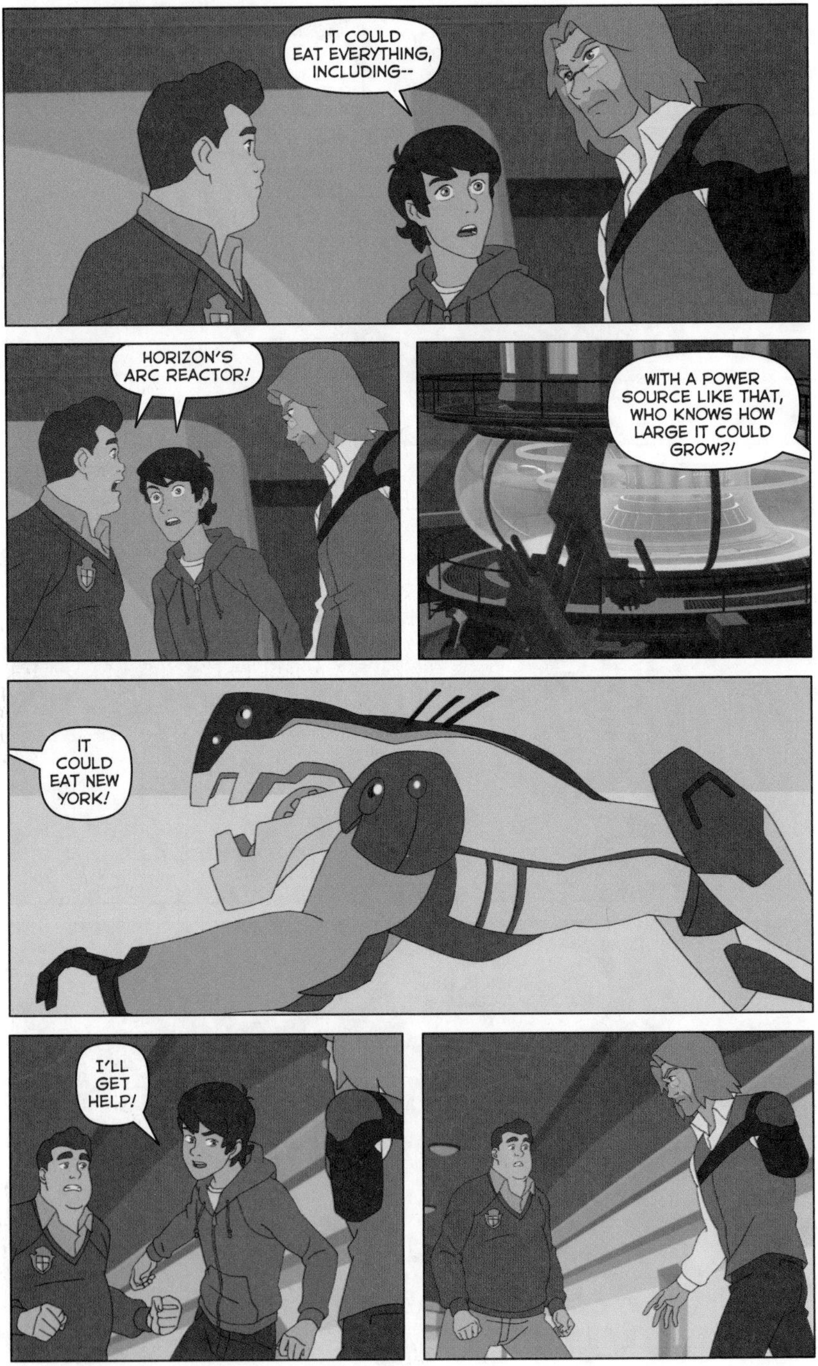
IT COULD EAT EVERYTHING, INCLUDING--
HORIZON'S ARC REACTOR!
WITH A POWER SOURCE LIKE THAT, WHO KNOWS HOW LARGE IT COULD GROW?!
IT COULD EAT NEW YORK!
I'LL GET HELP!

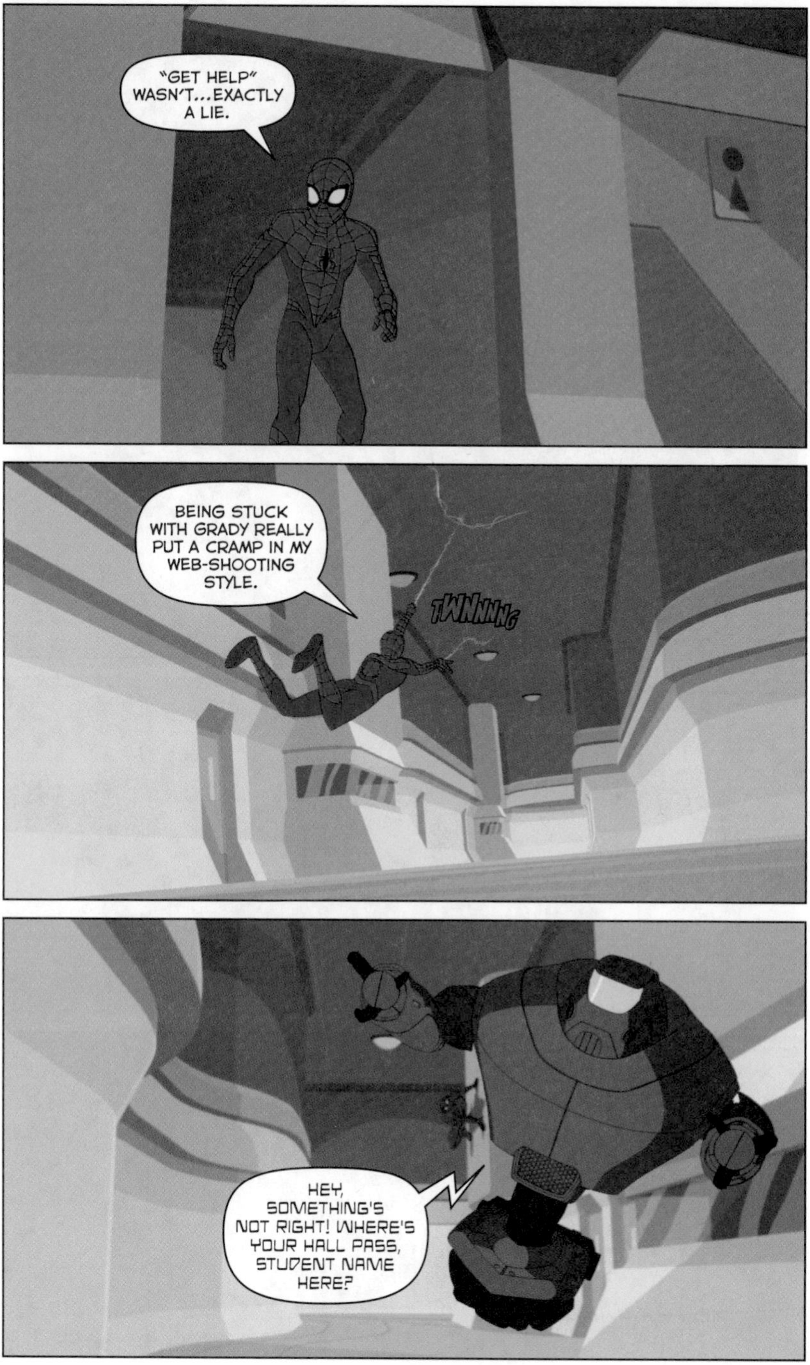
"GET HELP" WASN'T...EXACTLY A LIE.
BEING STUCK WITH GRADY REALLY PUT A CRAMP IN MY WEB-SHOOTING STYLE.
TWNNNNG
HEY, SOMETHING'S NOT RIGHT! WHERE'S YOUR HALL PASS, STUDENT NAME HERE?

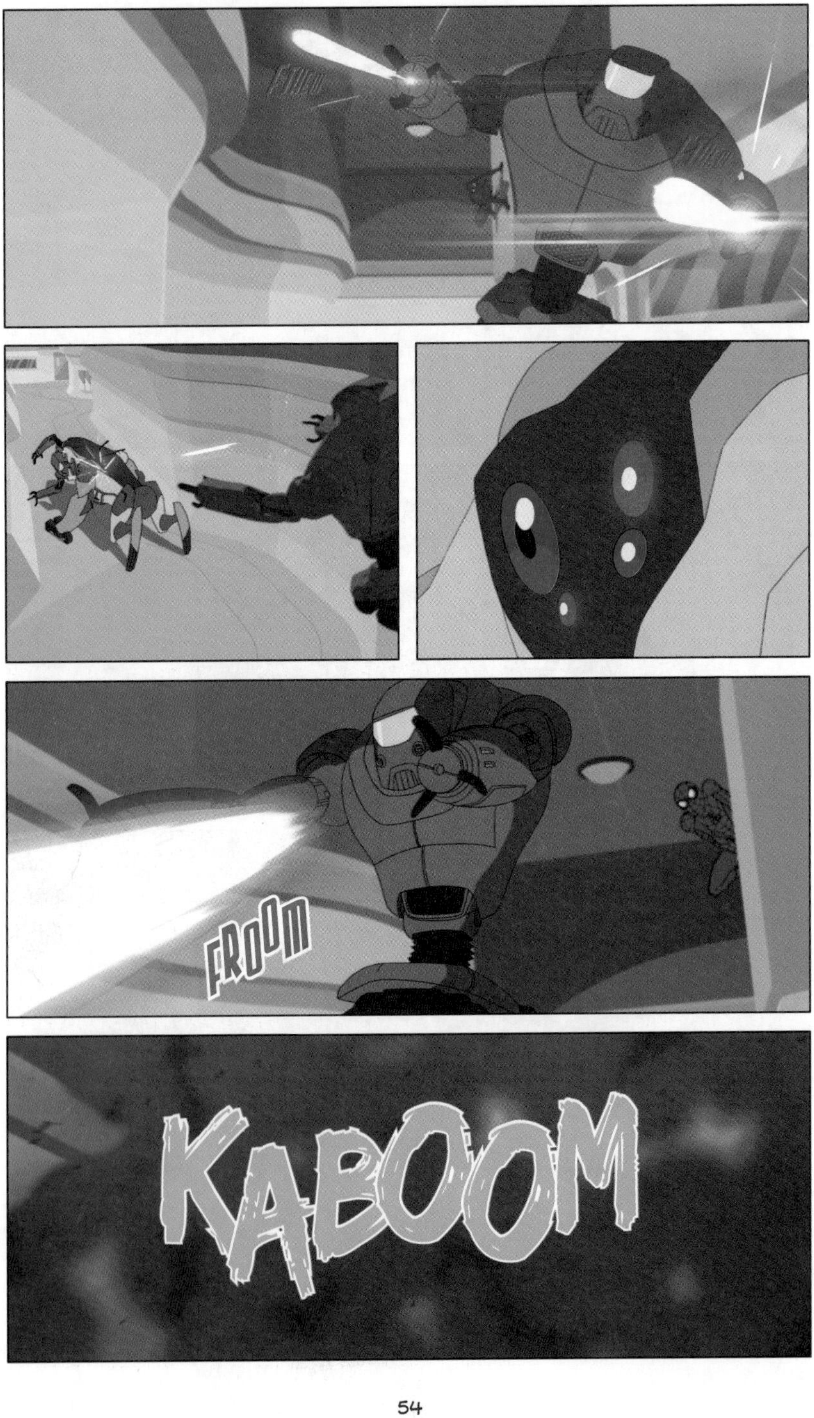

FROOM
KABOOM

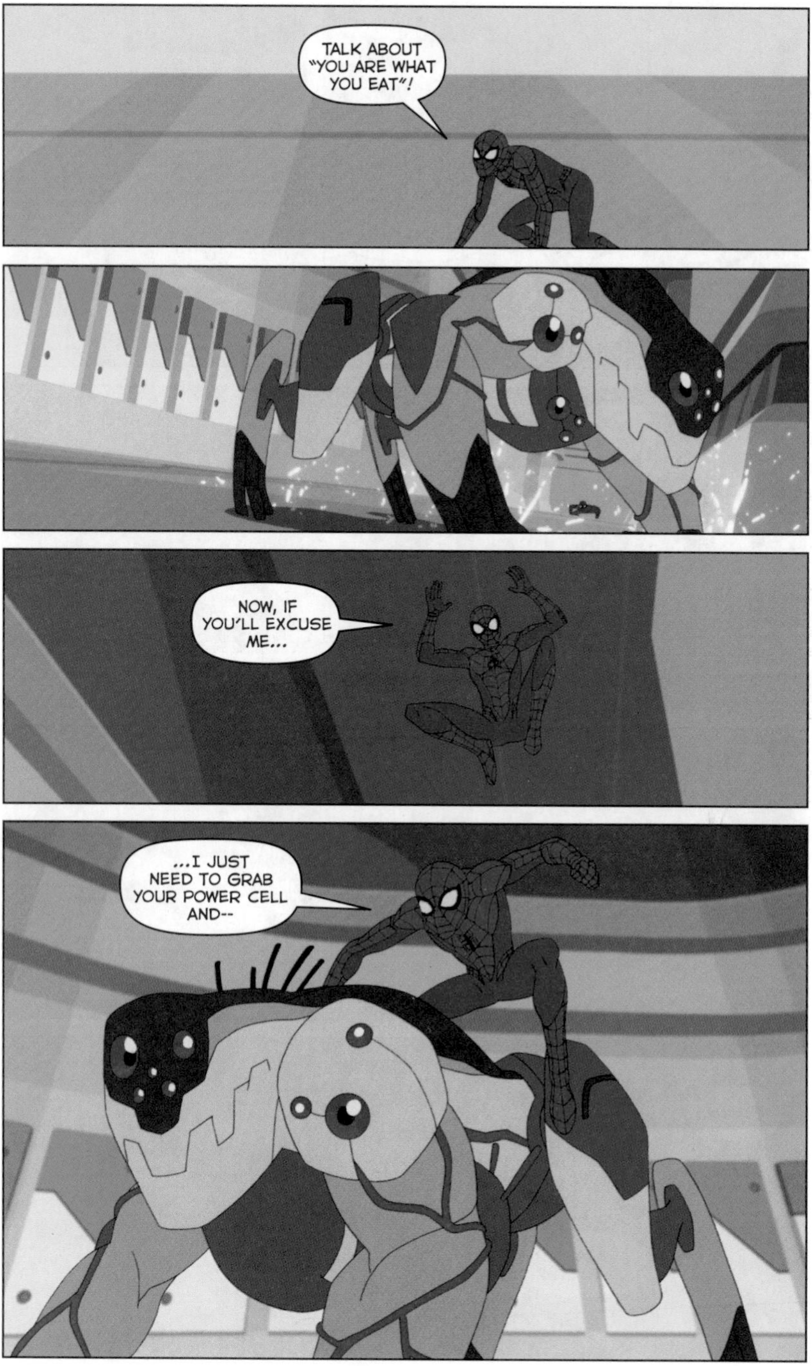
TALK ABOUT "YOU ARE WHAT YOU EAT"!
NOW, IF YOU'LL EXCUSE ME...
...I JUST NEED TO GRAB YOUR POWER CELL AND--

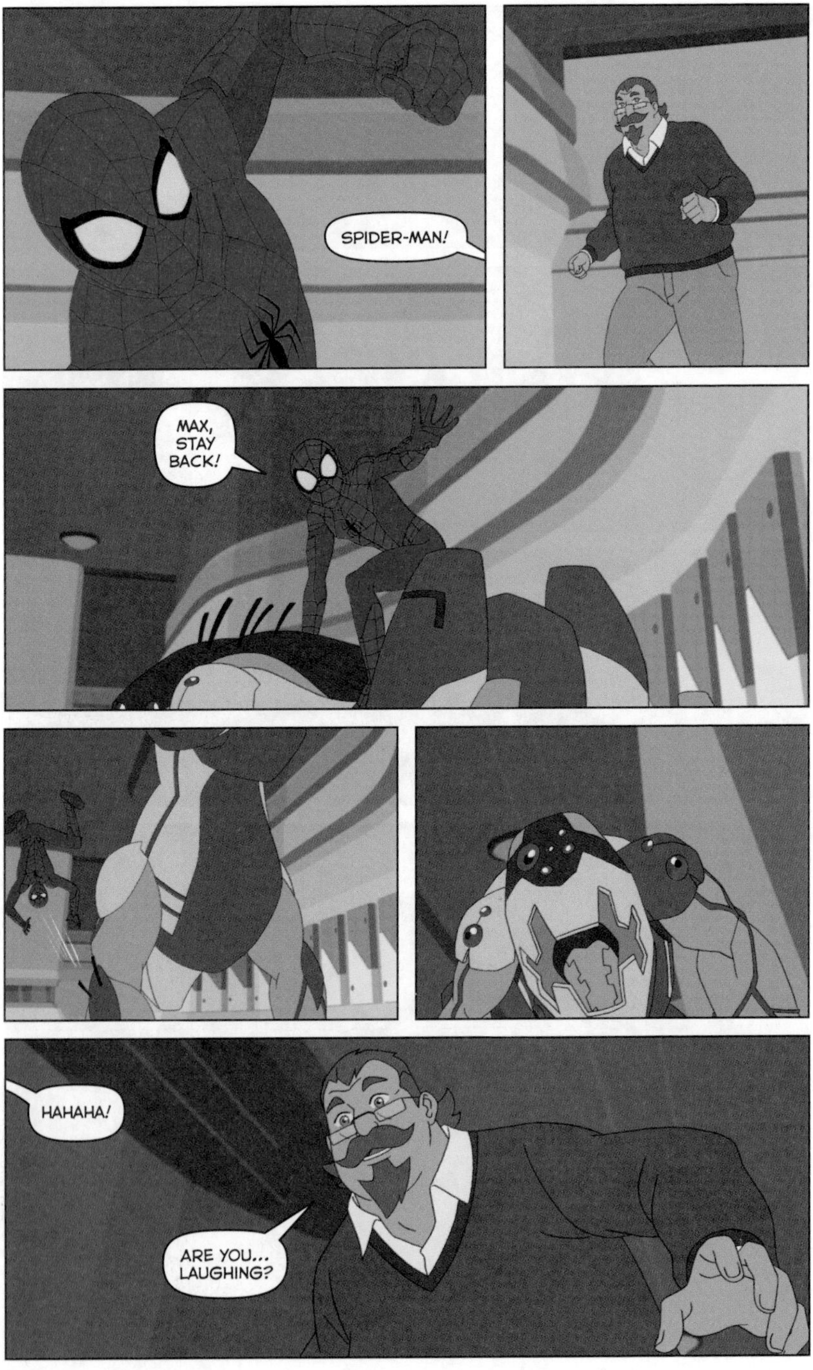
SPIDER-MAN!
MAX, STAY BACK!
HAHAHA!
ARE YOU... LAUGHING?

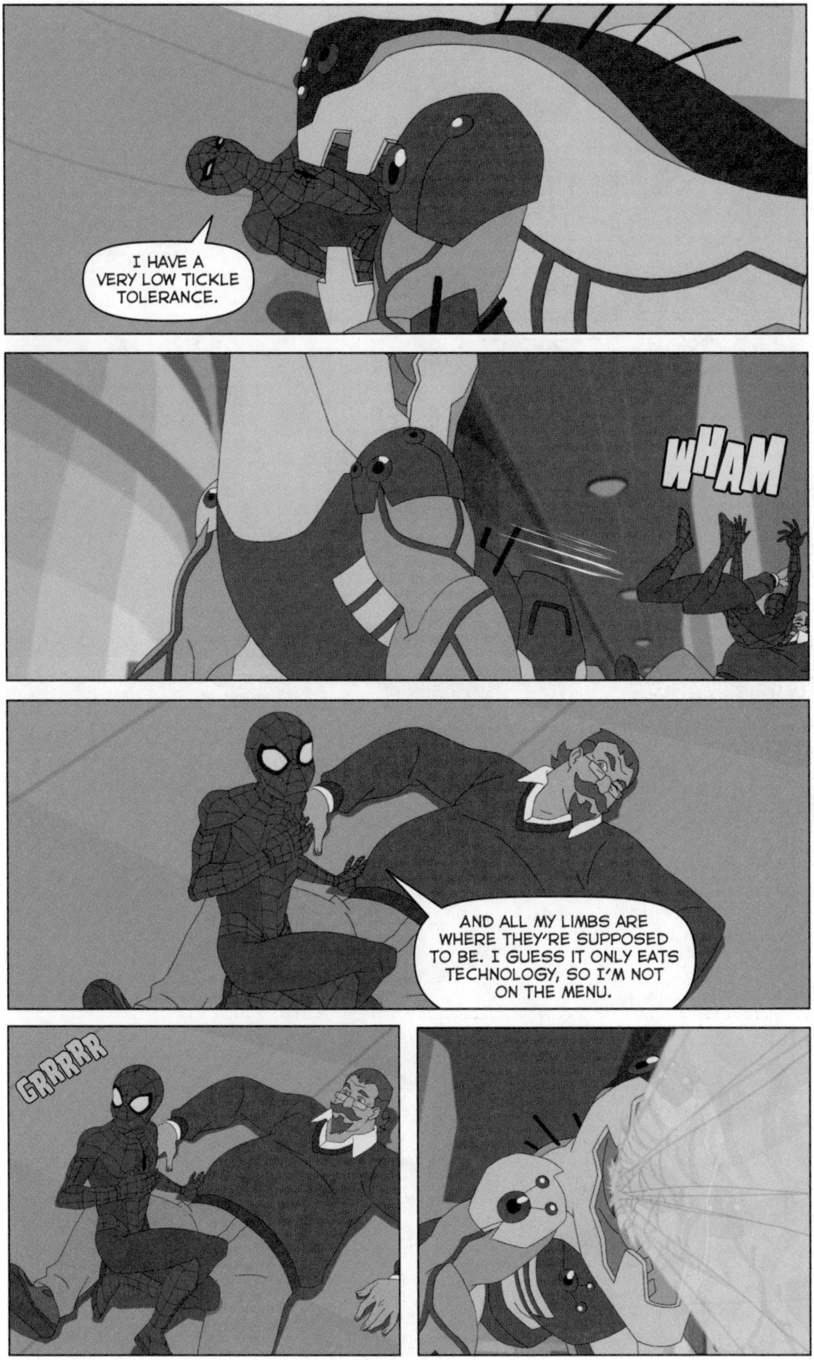
I HAVE A VERY LOW TICKLE TOLERANCE.
WHAM
AND ALL MY LIMBS ARE WHERE THEY'RE SUPPOSED TO BE. I GUESS IT ONLY EATS TECHNOLOGY, SO I'M NOT ON THE MENU.
GRRRRR

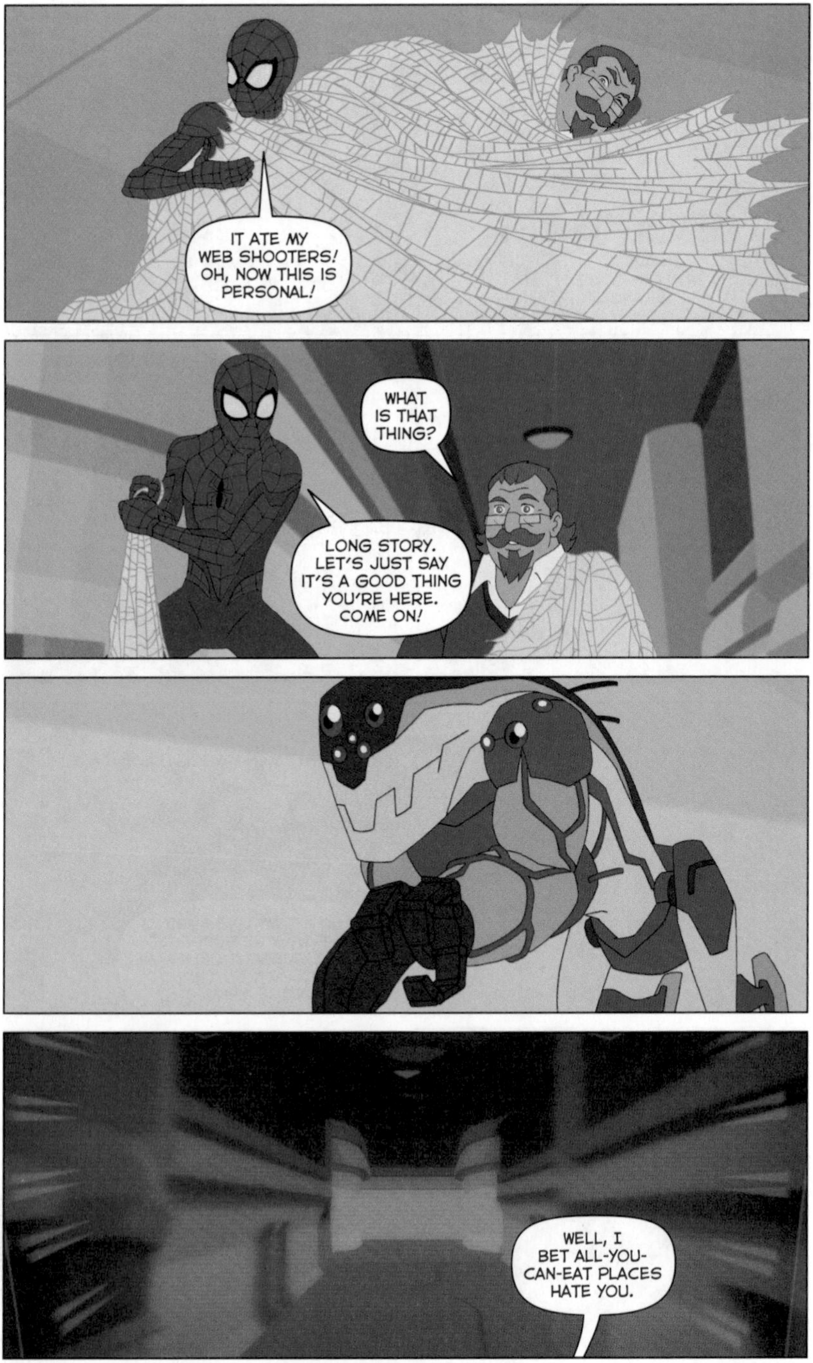
IT ATE MY WEB SHOOTERS! OH, NOW THIS IS PERSONAL!
WHAT IS THAT THING?
LONG STORY. LET'S JUST SAY IT'S A GOOD THING YOU'RE HERE. COME ON!
WELL, I BET ALL-YOU-CAN-EAT PLACES HATE YOU.

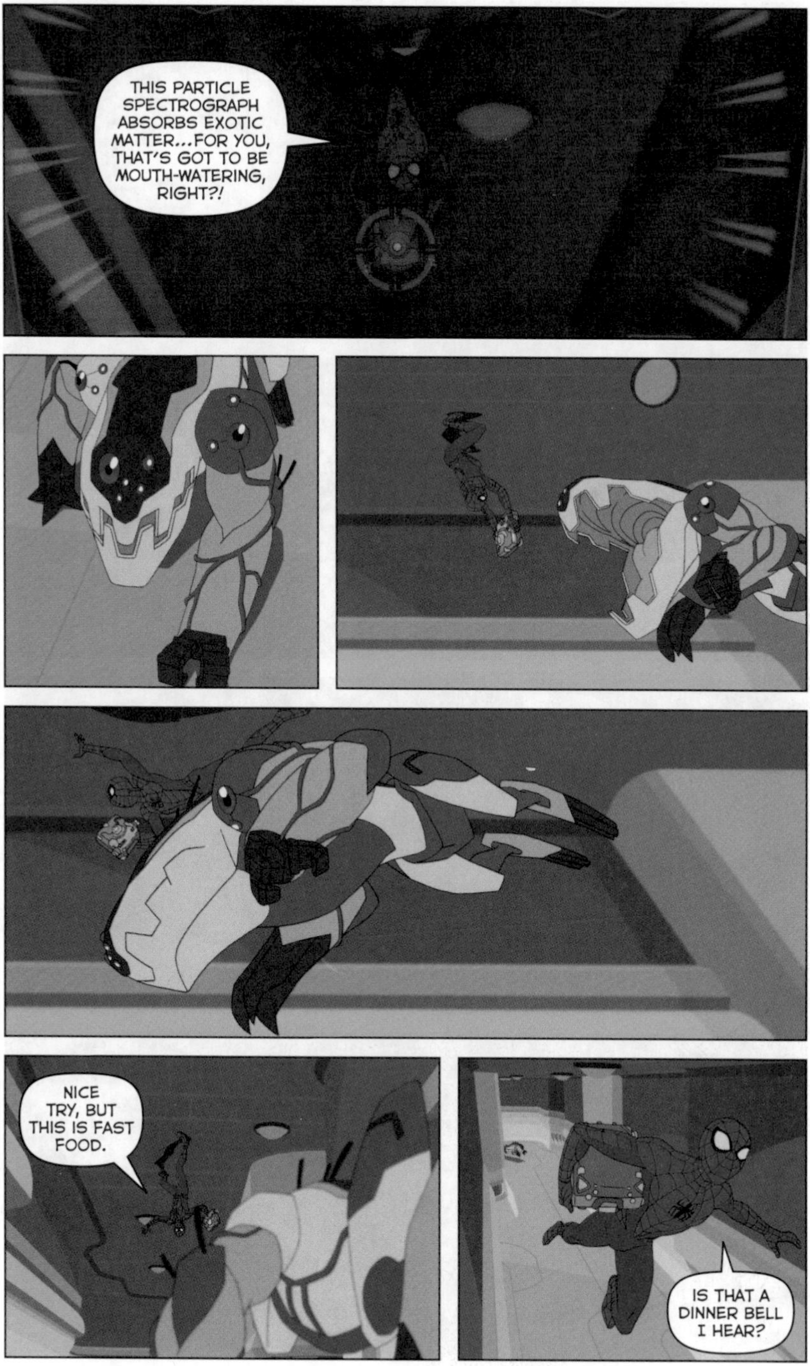
THIS PARTICLE SPECTROGRAPH ABSORBS EXOTIC MATTER...FOR YOU, THAT'S GOT TO BE MOUTH-WATERING, RIGHT?!
NICE TRY, BUT THIS IS FAST FOOD.
IS THAT A DINNER BELL I HEAR?

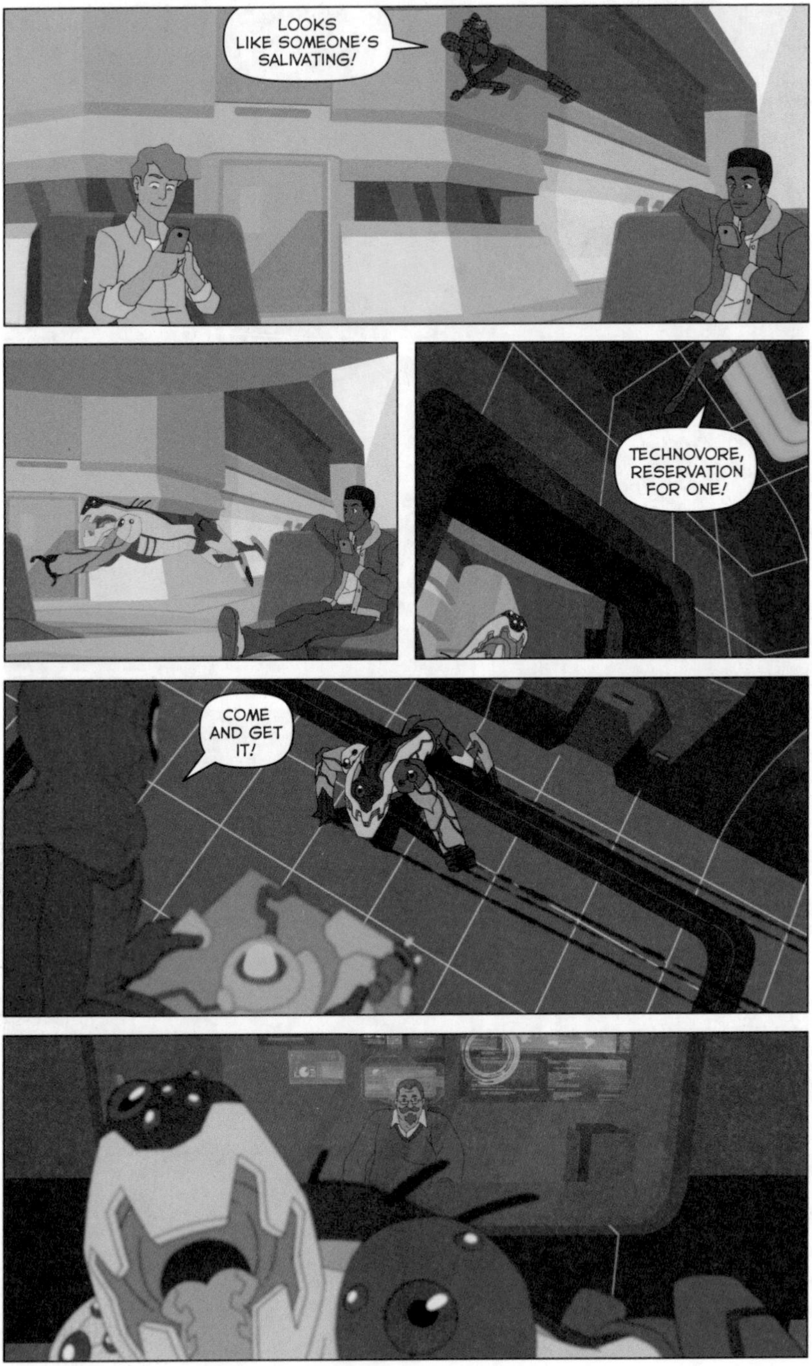
LOOKS LIKE SOMEONE'S SALIVATING!
TECHNOVORE, RESERVATION FOR ONE!
COME AND GET IT!

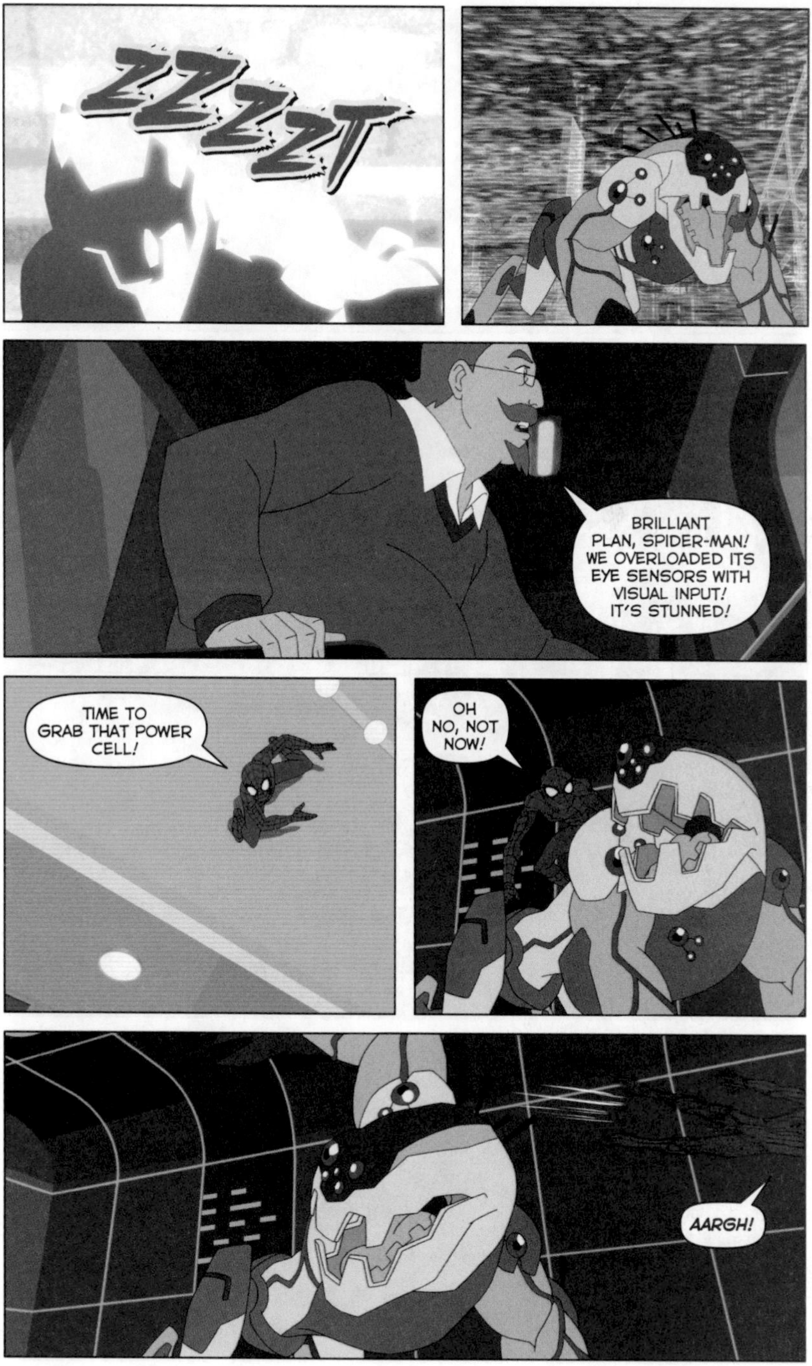
ZZZZZT
BRILLIANT PLAN, SPIDER-MAN! WE OVERLOADED ITS EYE SENSORS WITH VISUAL INPUT! IT'S STUNNED!
TIME TO GRAB THAT POWER CELL!
OH NO, NOT NOW!
AARGH!

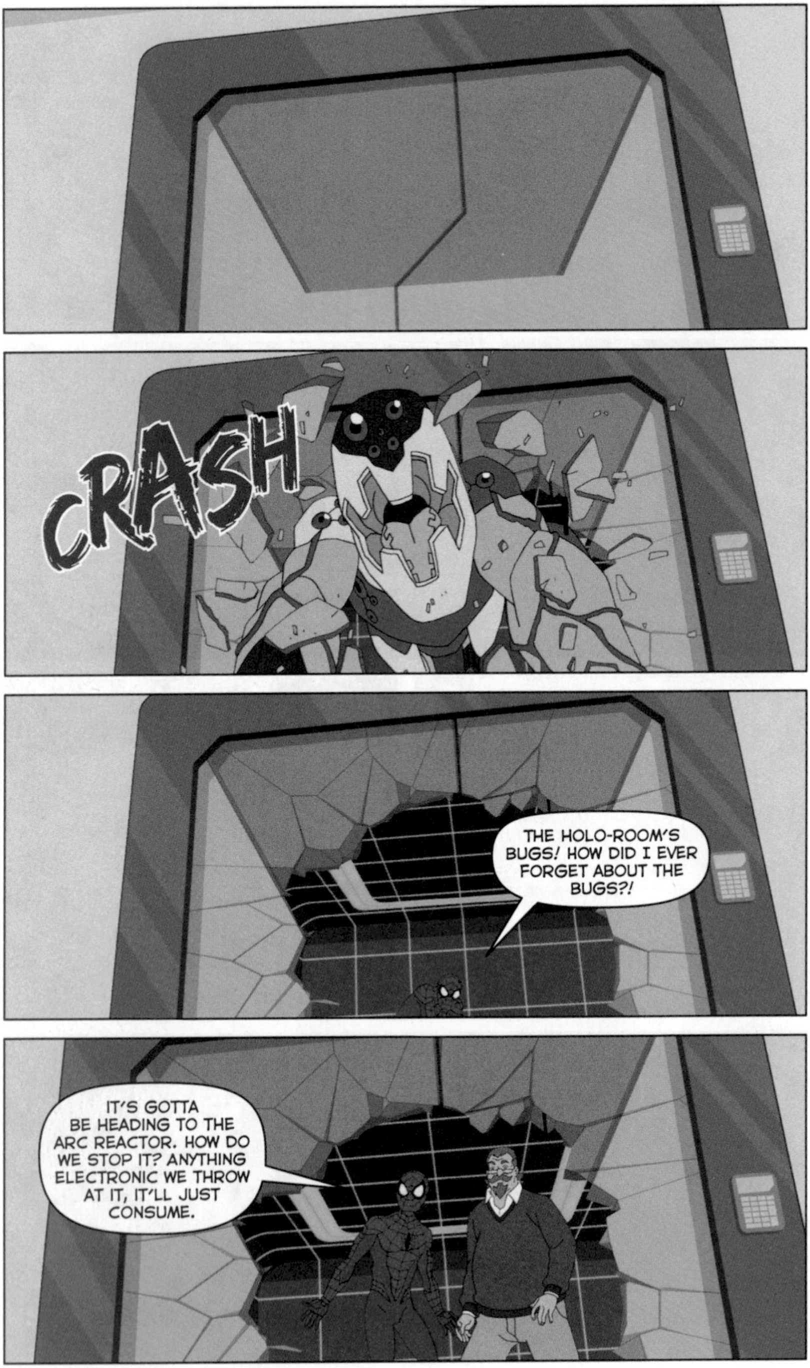
CRASH
THE HOLO-ROOM'S BUGS! HOW DID I EVER FORGET ABOUT THE BUGS?!
IT'S GOTTA BE HEADING TO THE ARC REACTOR. HOW DO WE STOP IT? ANYTHING ELECTRONIC WE THROW AT IT, IT'LL JUST CONSUME.

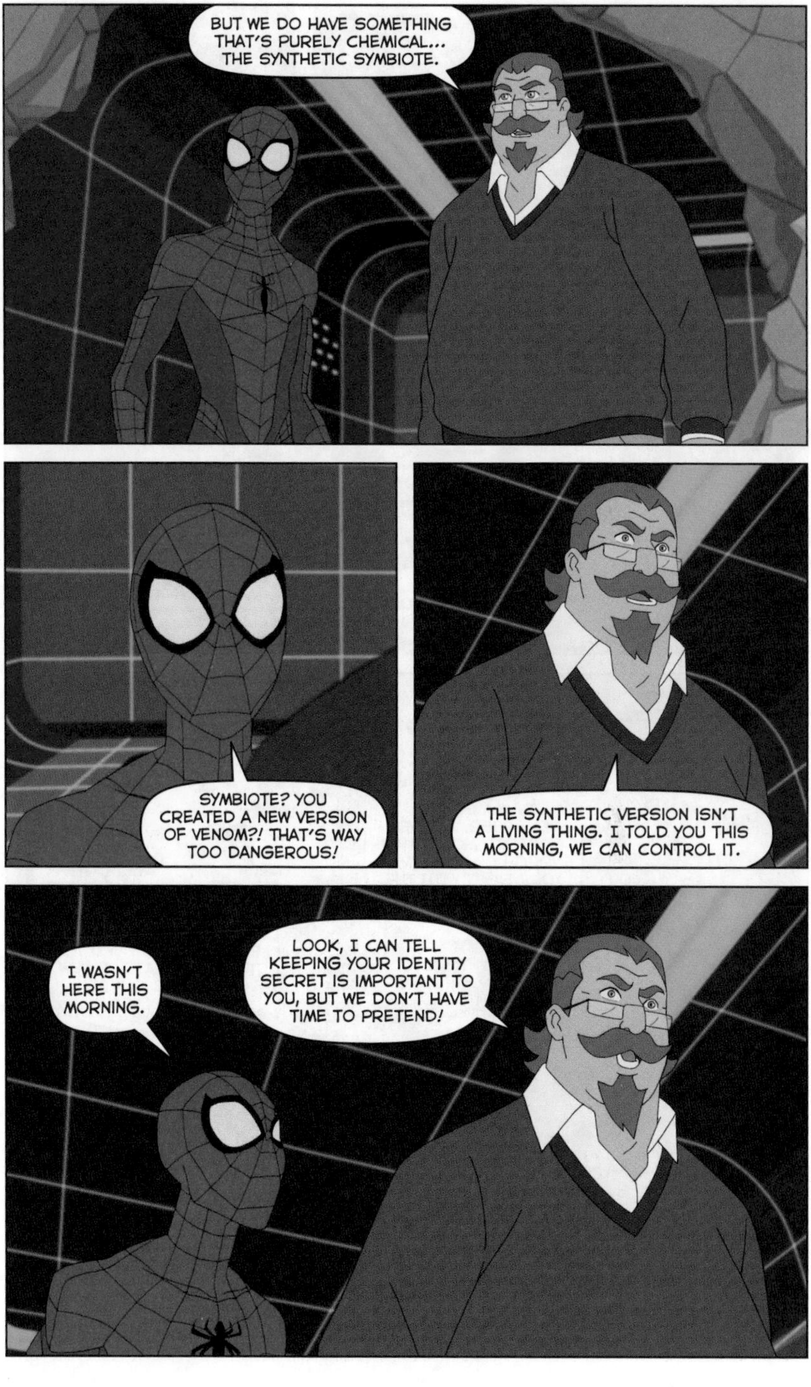
BUT WE DO HAVE SOMETHING THAT'S PURELY CHEMICAL... THE SYNTHETIC SYMBIOTE.
SYMBIOTE? YOU CREATED A NEW VERSION OF VENOM?! THAT'S WAY TOO DANGEROUS!
THE SYNTHETIC VERSION ISN'T A LIVING THING. I TOLD YOU THIS MORNING, WE CAN CONTROL IT.
I WASN'T HERE THIS MORNING.
LOOK, I CAN TELL KEEPING YOUR IDENTITY SECRET IS IMPORTANT TO YOU, BUT WE DON'T HAVE TIME TO PRETEND!

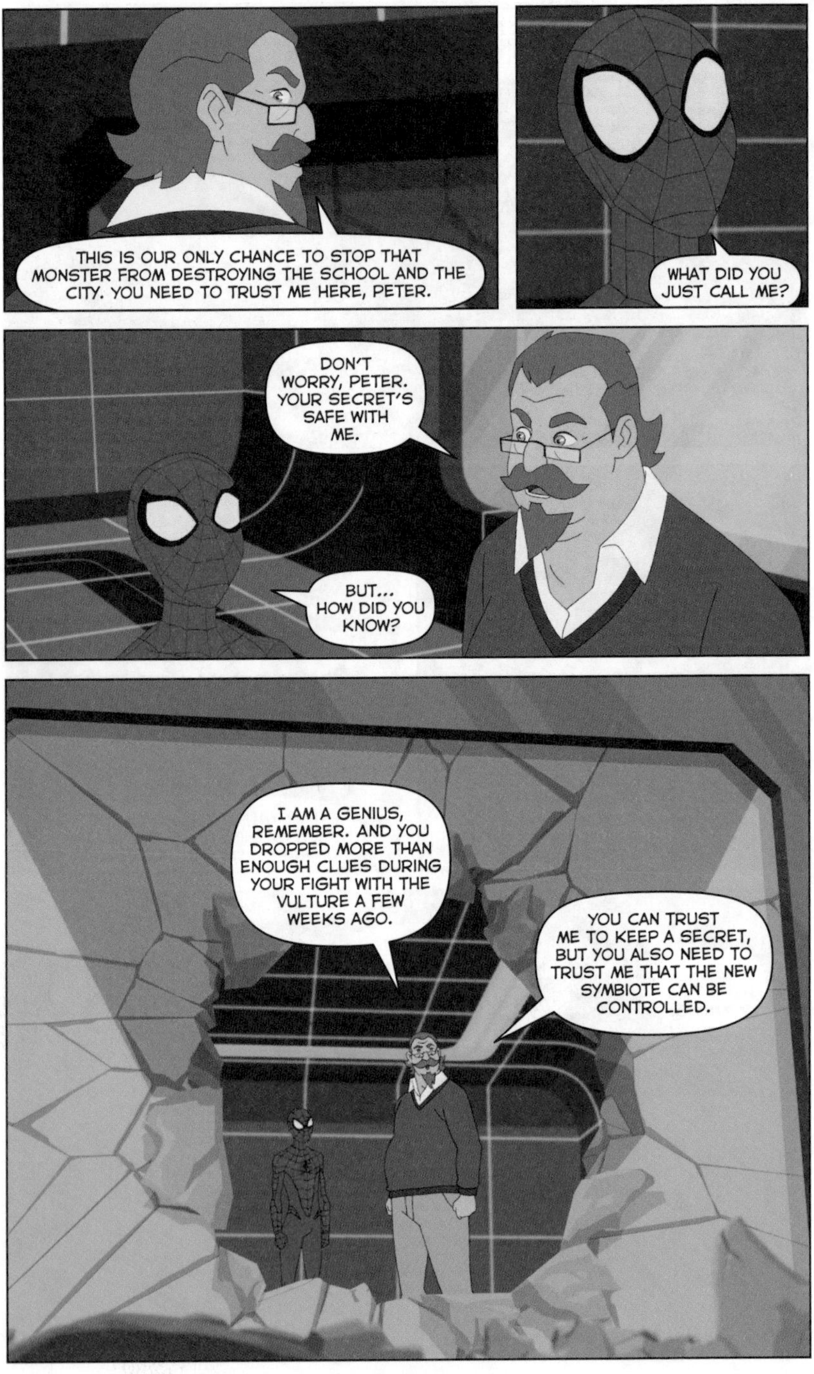
THIS IS OUR ONLY CHANCE TO STOP THAT MONSTER FROM DESTROYING THE SCHOOL AND THE CITY. YOU NEED TO TRUST ME HERE, PETER.
WHAT DID YOU JUST CALL ME?
DON'T WORRY, PETER. YOUR SECRET'S SAFE WITH ME.
BUT... HOW DID YOU KNOW?
I AM A GENIUS, REMEMBER. AND YOU DROPPED MORE THAN ENOUGH CLUES DURING YOUR FIGHT WITH THE VULTURE A FEW WEEKS AGO.
YOU CAN TRUST ME TO KEEP A SECRET, BUT YOU ALSO NEED TO TRUST ME THAT THE NEW SYMBIOTE CAN BE CONTROLLED.

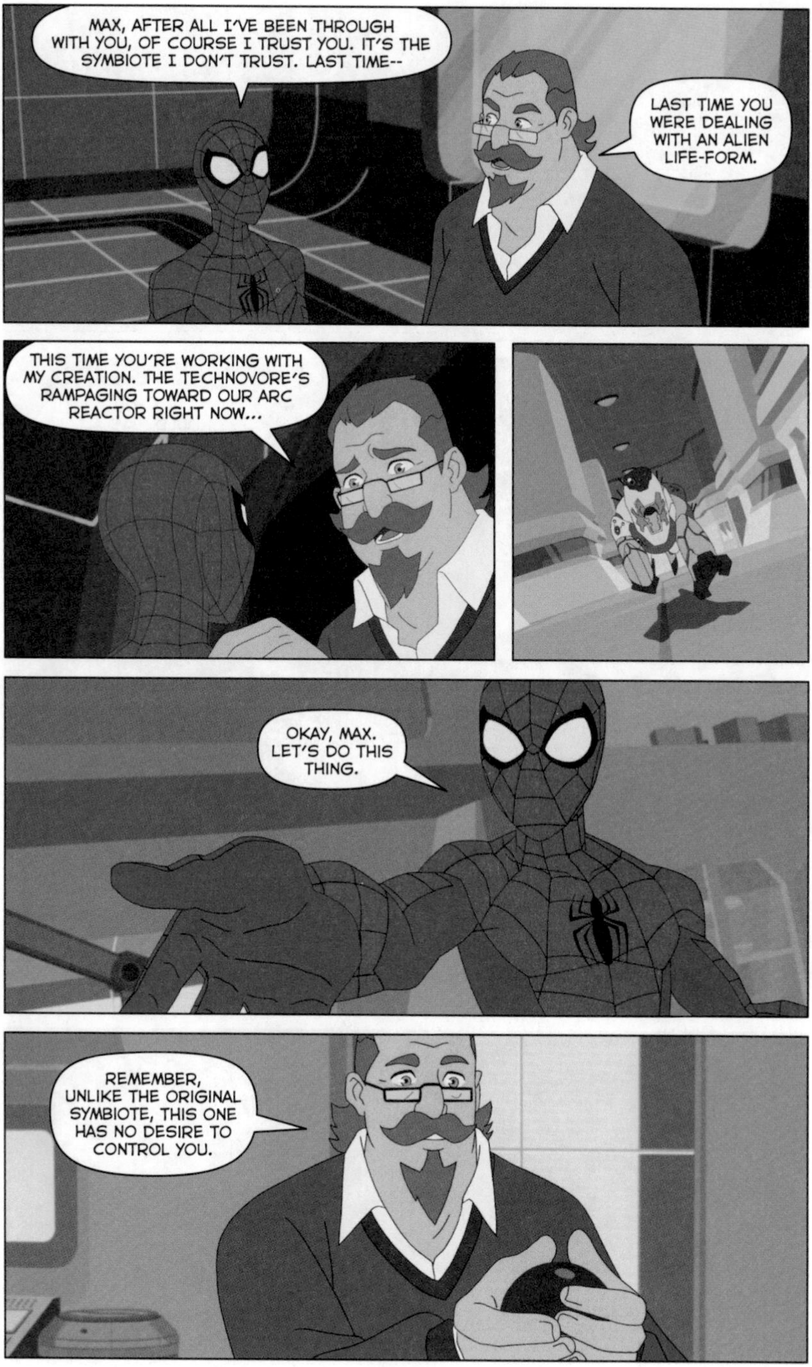
MAX, AFTER ALL I'VE BEEN THROUGH WITH YOU, OF COURSE I TRUST YOU. IT'S THE SYMBIOTE I DON'T TRUST. LAST TIME--
LAST TIME YOU WERE DEALING WITH AN ALIEN LIFE-FORM.
THIS TIME YOU'RE WORKING WITH MY CREATION. THE TECHNOVORE'S RAMPAGING TOWARD OUR ARC REACTOR RIGHT NOW...
OKAY, MAX. LET'S DO THIS THING.
REMEMBER, UNLIKE THE ORIGINAL SYMBIOTE, THIS ONE HAS NO DESIRE TO CONTROL YOU.

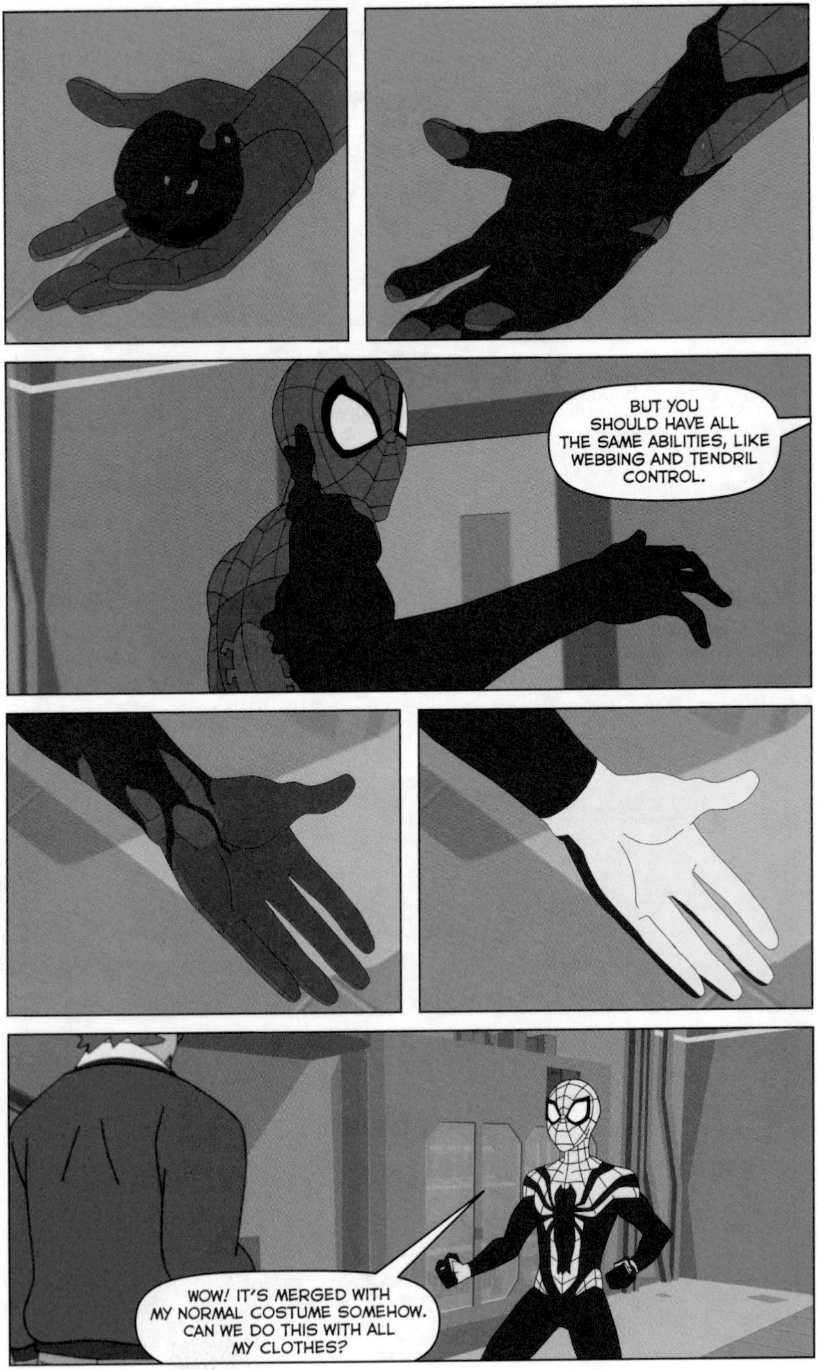

BUT YOU SHOULD HAVE ALL THE SAME ABILITIES, LIKE WEBBING AND TENDRIL CONTROL.
WOW! IT'S MERGED WITH MY NORMAL COSTUME SOMEHOW. CAN WE DO THIS WITH ALL MY CLOTHES?

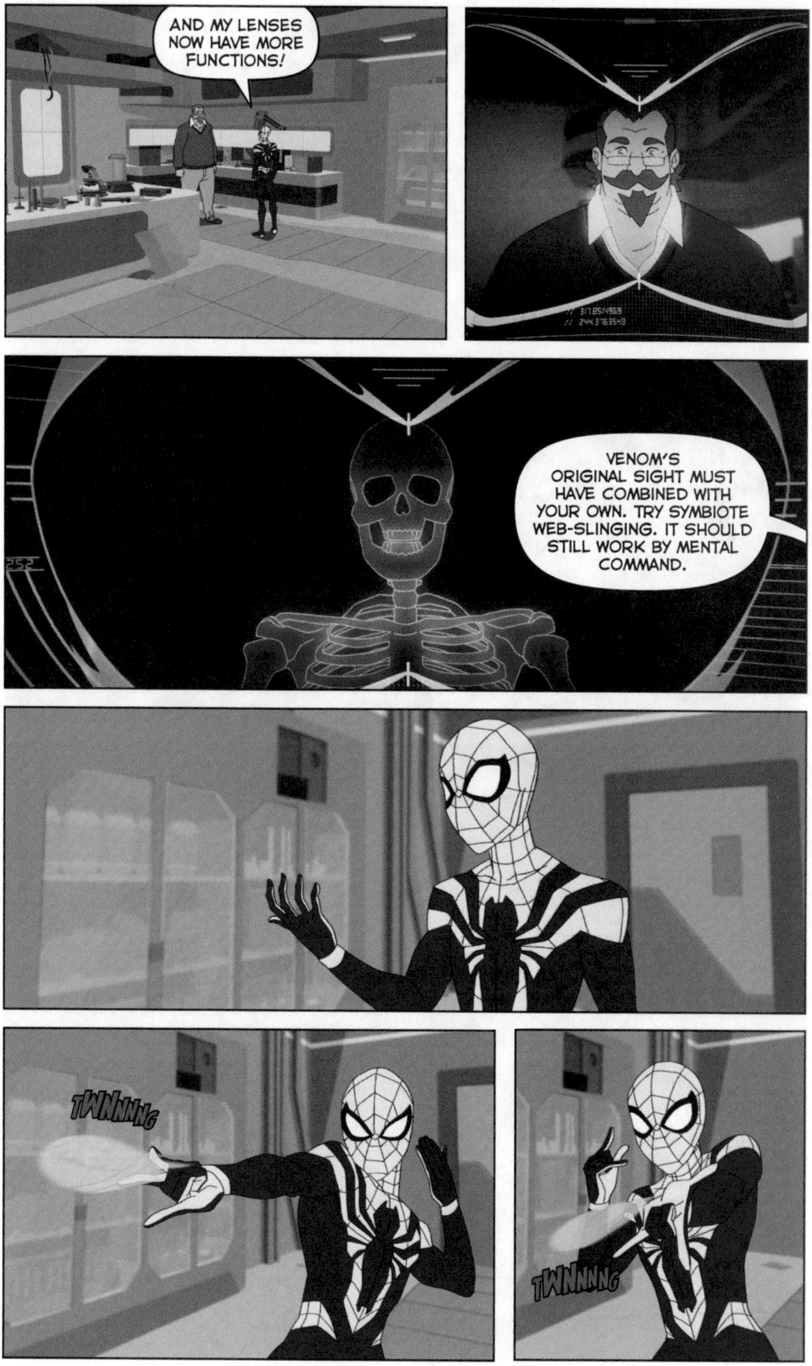
AND MY LENSES NOW HAVE MORE FUNCTIONS!
VENOM'S ORIGINAL SIGHT MUST HAVE COMBINED WITH YOUR OWN. TRY SYMBIOTE WEB-SLINGING. IT SHOULD STILL WORK BY MENTAL COMMAND.
TWNNNNG
TWNNNNG

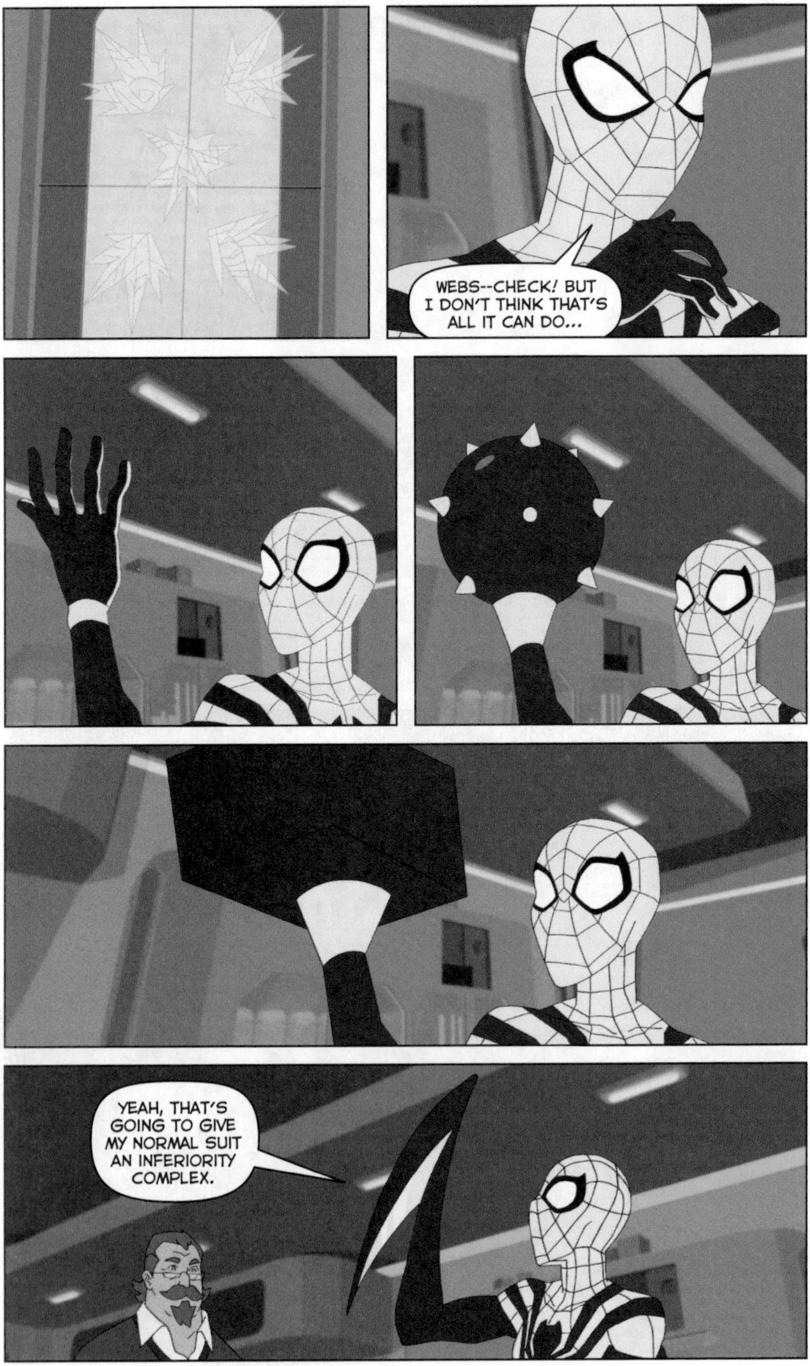
WEBS--CHECK! BUT I DON'T THINK THAT'S ALL IT CAN DO...
YEAH, THAT'S GOING TO GIVE MY NORMAL SUIT AN INFERIORITY COMPLEX.

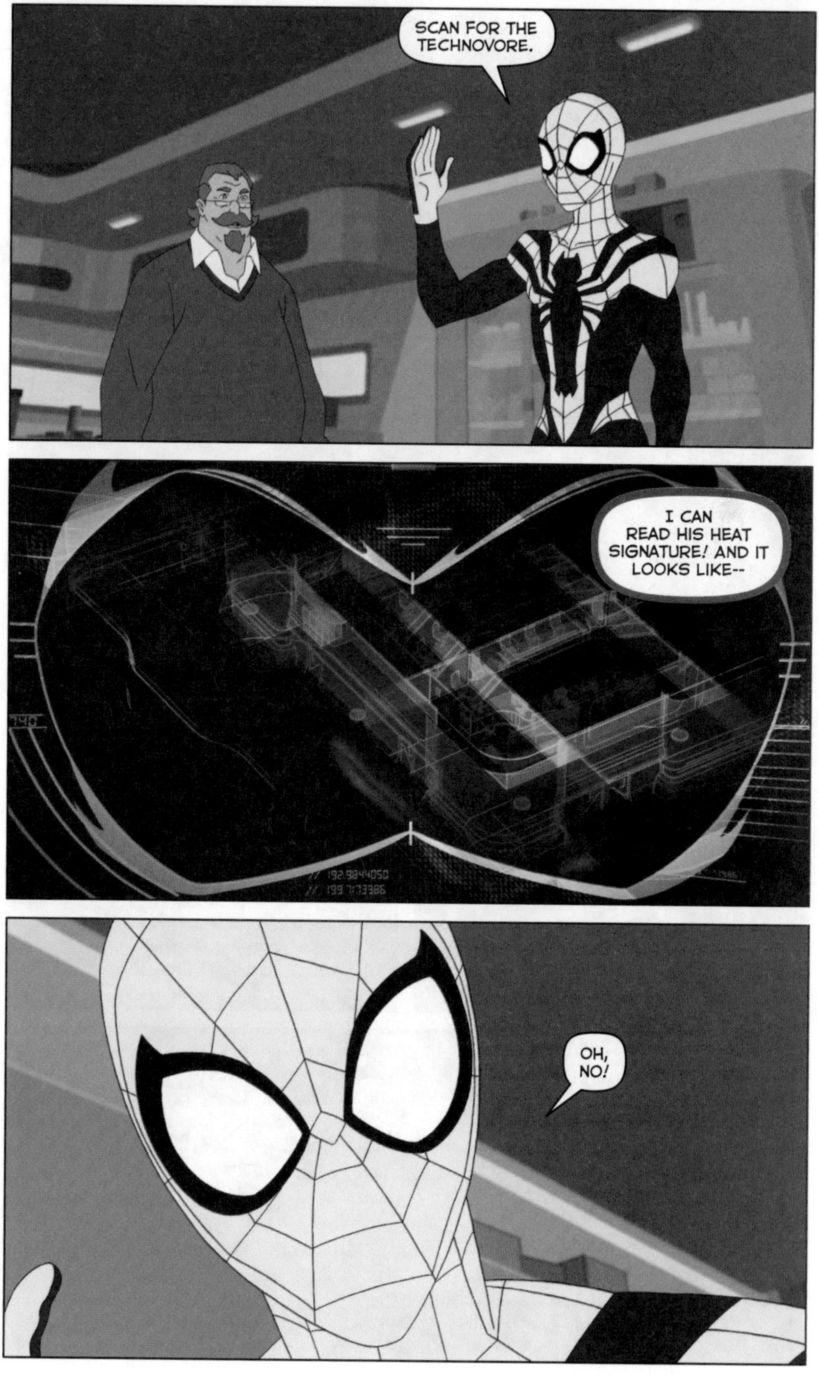
SCAN FOR THE TECHNOVORE.
I CAN READ HIS HEAT SIGNATURE! AND IT LOOKS LIKE--
OH, NO!

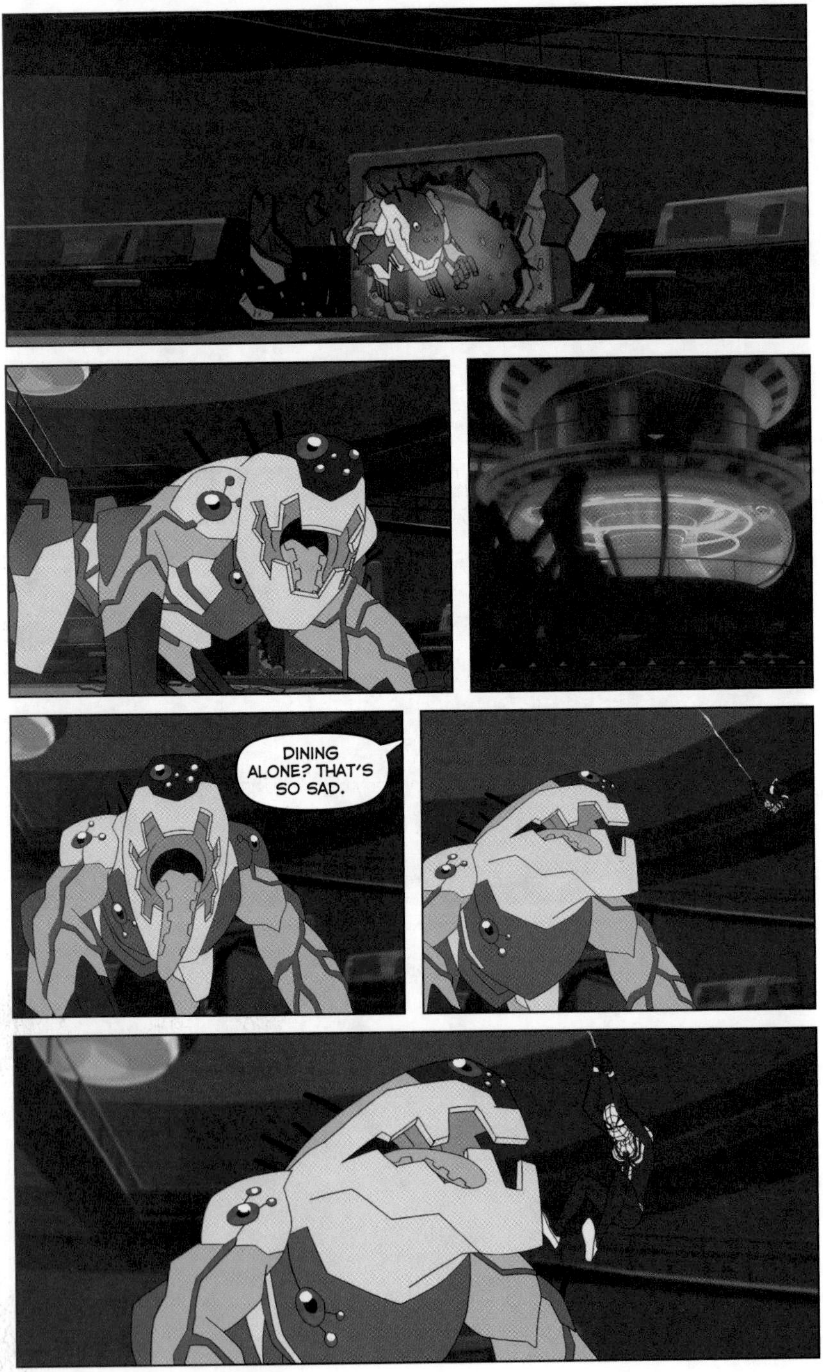
DINING ALONE? THAT'S SO SAD.

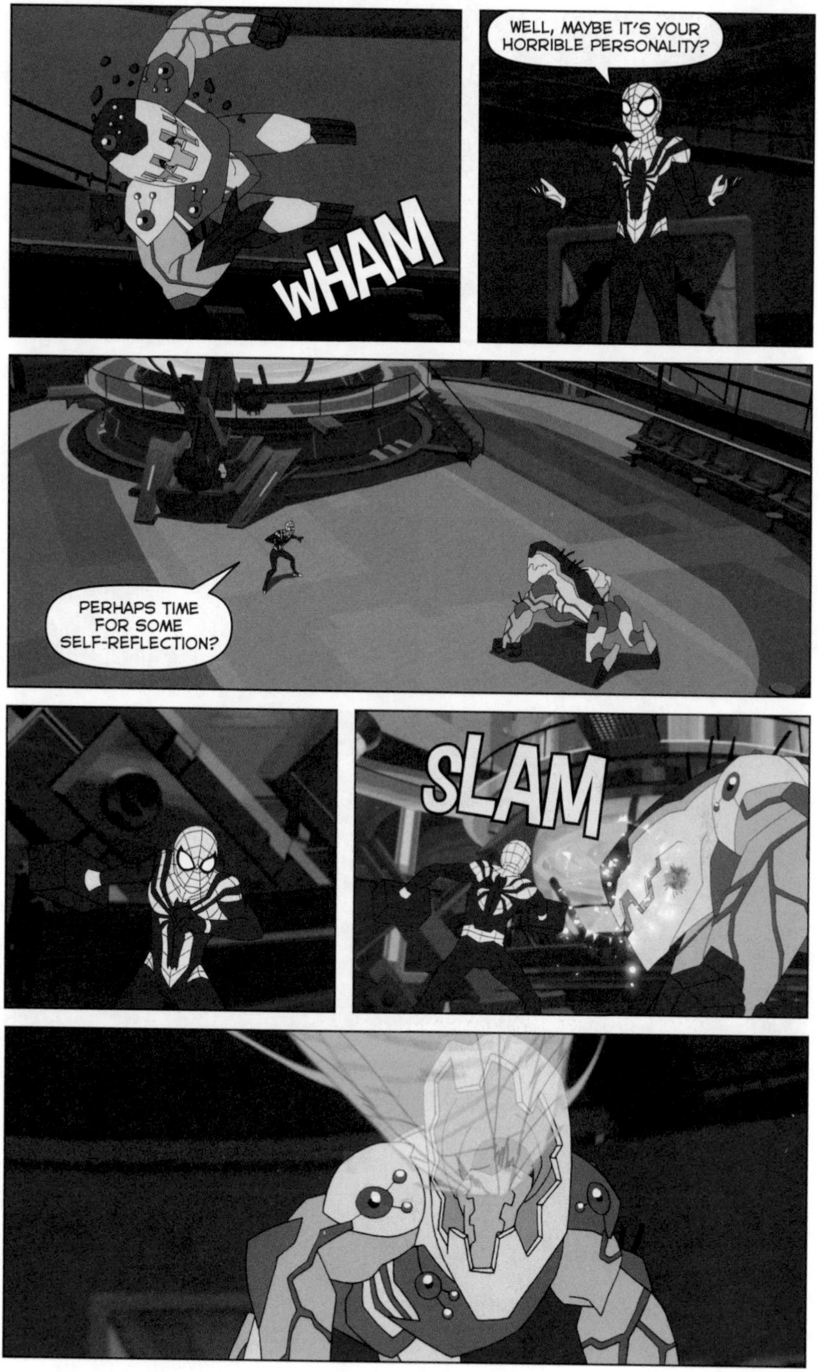
wHAM
WELL, MAYBE IT'S YOUR HORRIBLE PERSONALITY?
PERHAPS TIME FOR SOME SELF-REFLECTION?
SLAM

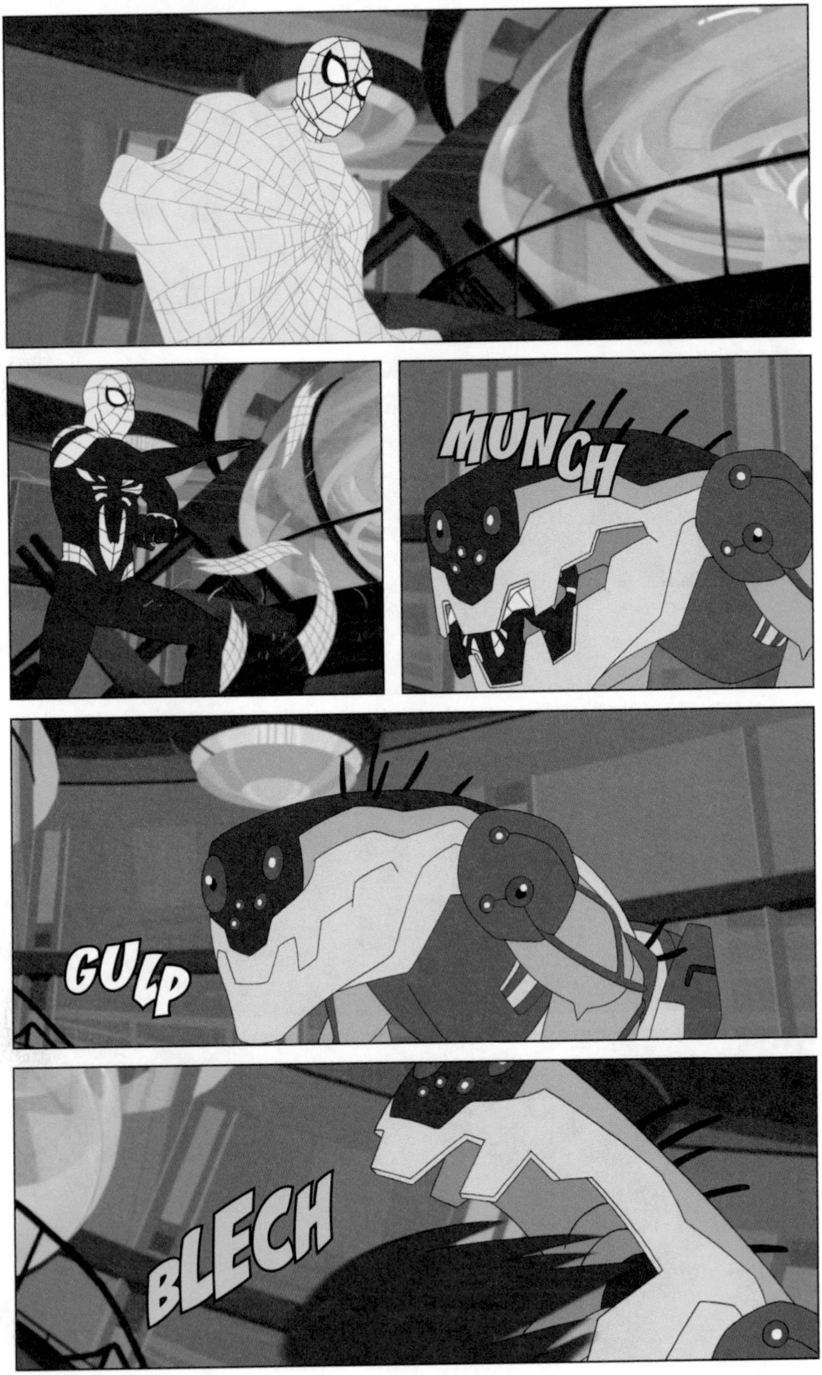
MUNCH
GULP
BLECH

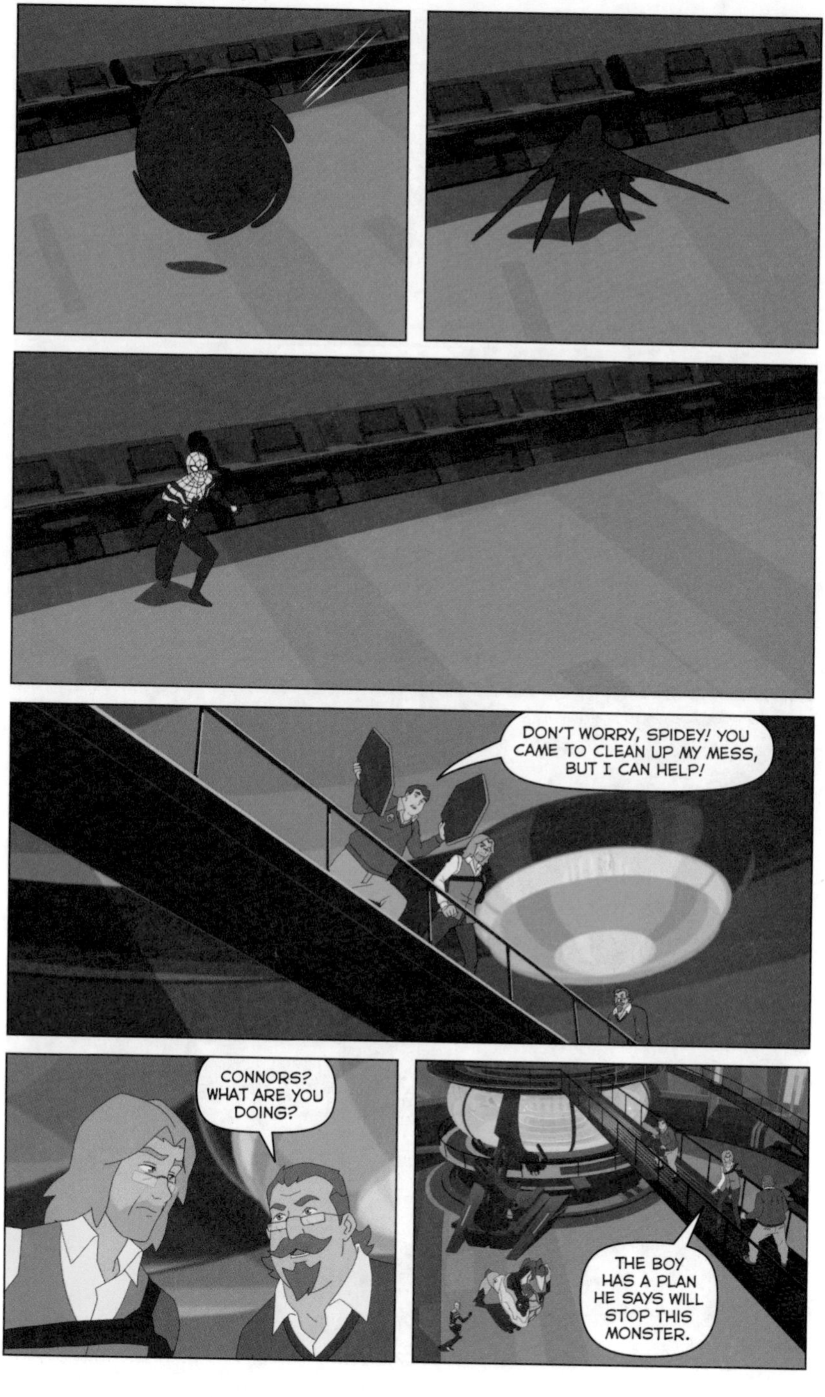
DON'T WORRY, SPIDEY! YOU CAME TO CLEAN UP MY MESS, BUT I CAN HELP!
CONNORS? WHAT ARE YOU DOING?
THE BOY HAS A PLAN HE SAYS WILL STOP THIS MONSTER.

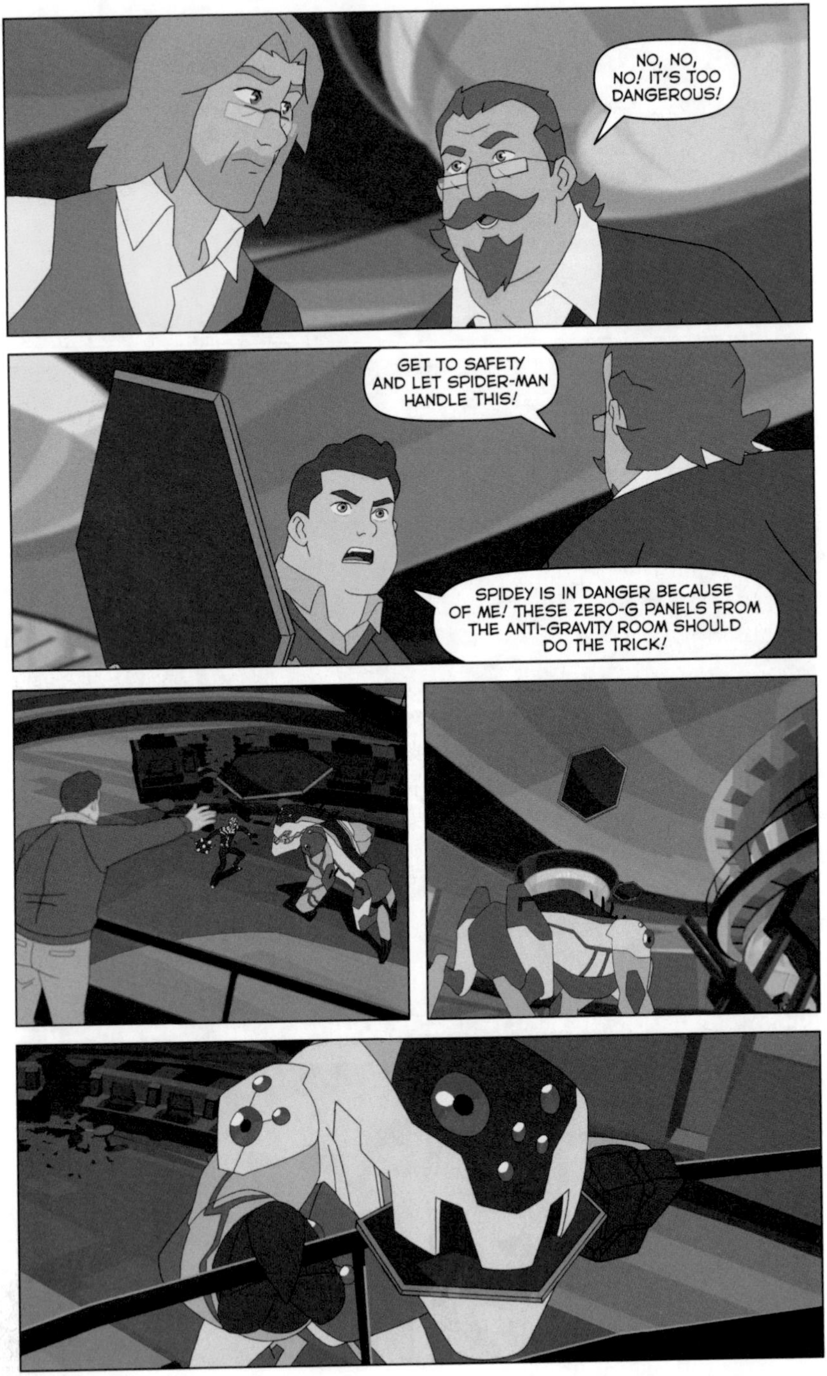
NO, NO, NO! IT'S TOO DANGEROUS!
GET TO SAFETY AND LET SPIDER-MAN HANDLE THIS!
SPIDEY IS IN DANGER BECAUSE OF ME! THESE ZERO-G PANELS FROM THE ANTI-GRAVITY ROOM SHOULD DO THE TRICK!

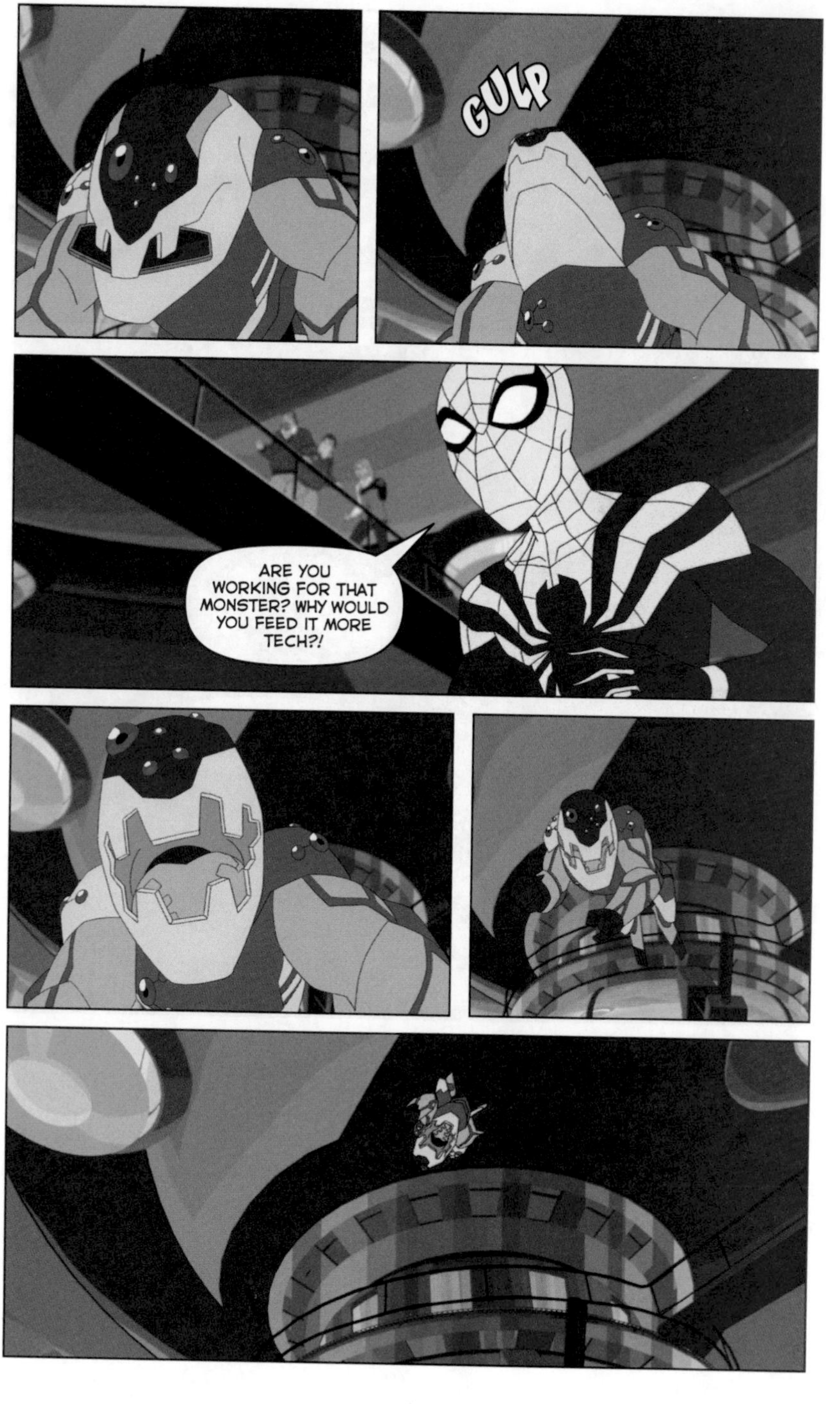
GULP
ARE YOU WORKING FOR THAT MONSTER? WHY WOULD YOU FEED IT MORE TECH?!

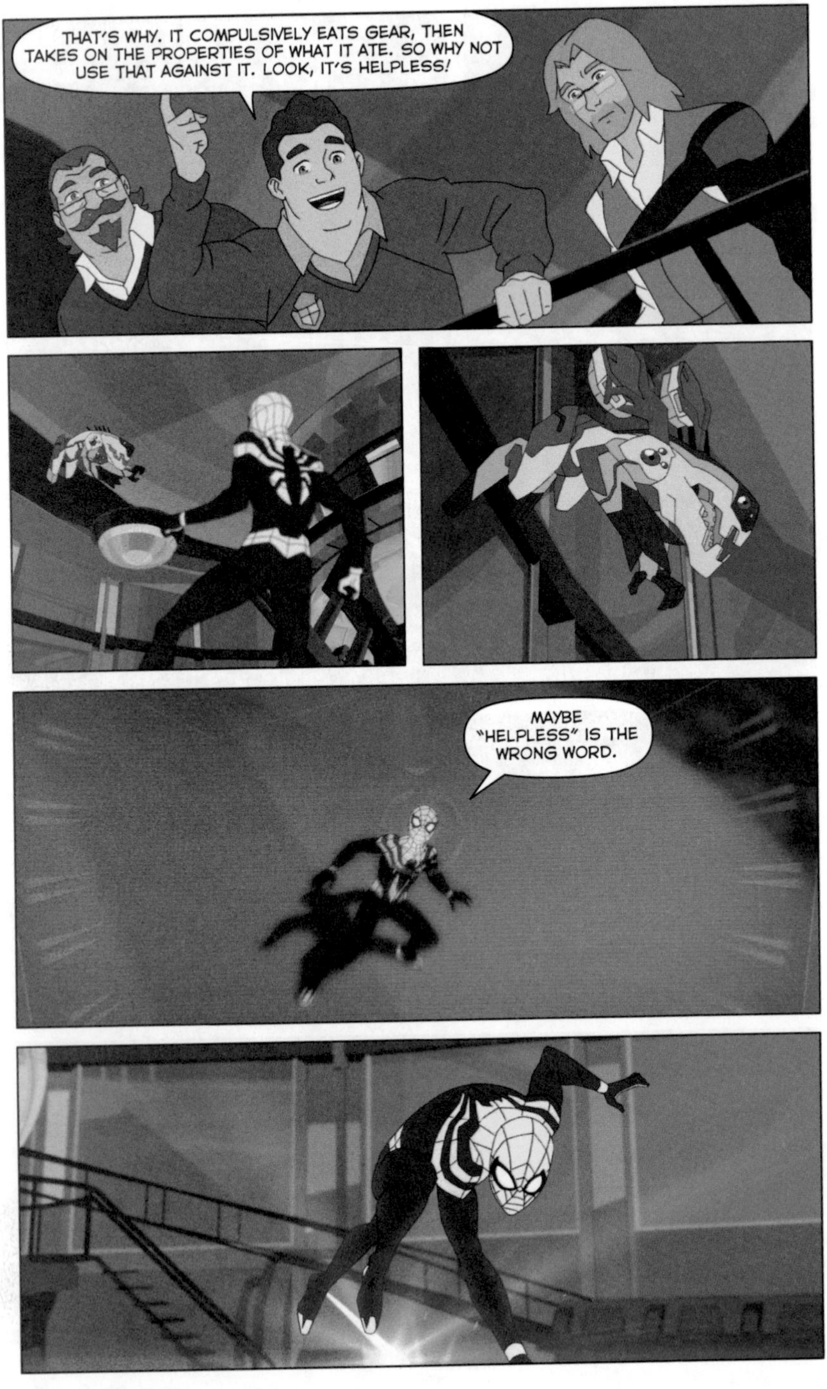
THAT'S WHY. IT COMPULSIVELY EATS GEAR, THEN TAKES ON THE PROPERTIES OF WHAT IT ATE. SO WHY NOT USE THAT AGAINST IT. LOOK, IT'S HELPLESS!
MAYBE "HELPLESS" IS THE WRONG WORD.

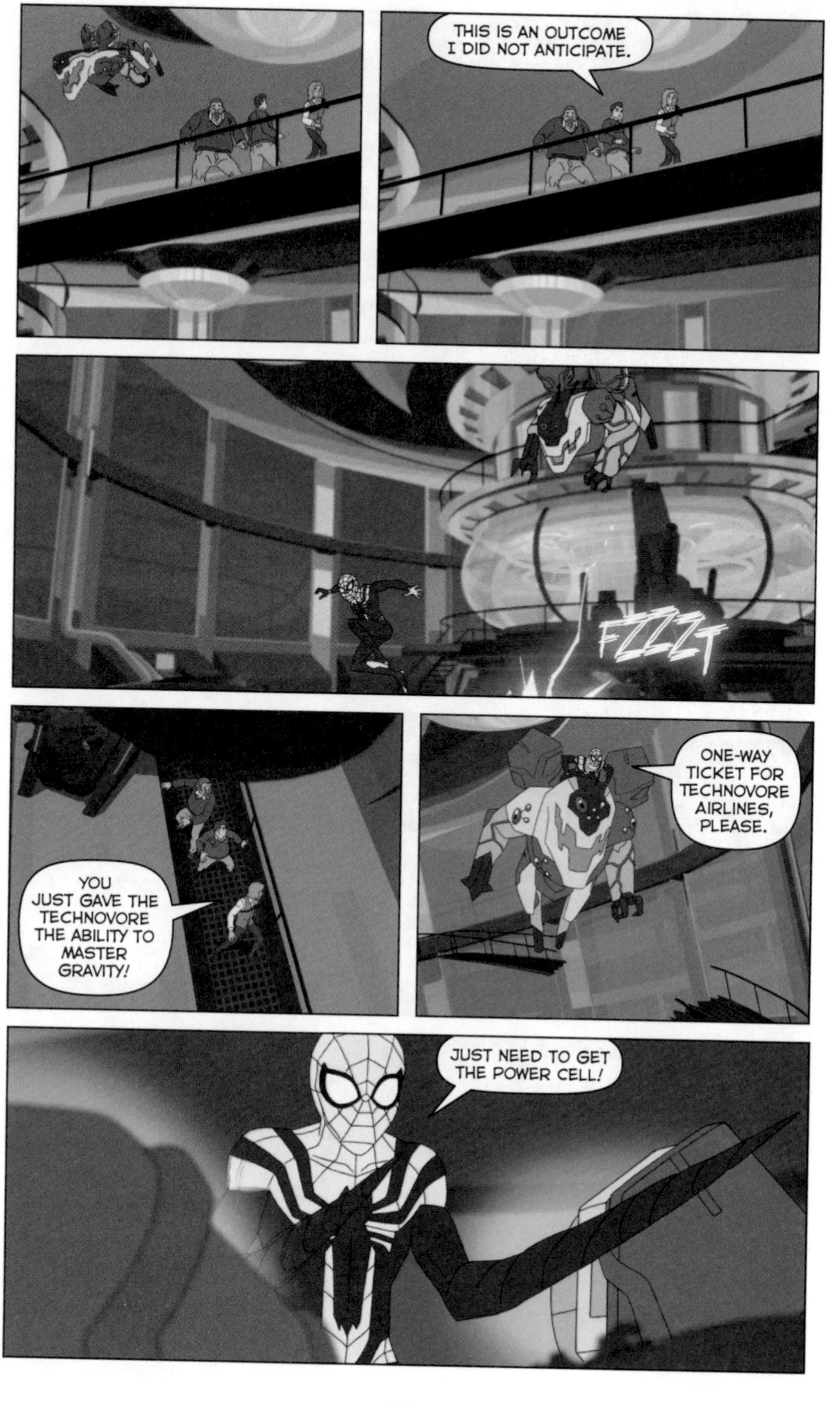
THIS IS AN OUTCOME I DID NOT ANTICIPATE.
FZZZZT
YOU JUST GAVE THE TECHNOVORE THE ABILITY TO MASTER GRAVITY!
ONE-WAY TICKET FOR TECHNOVORE AIRLINES, PLEASE.
JUST NEED TO GET THE POWER CELL!

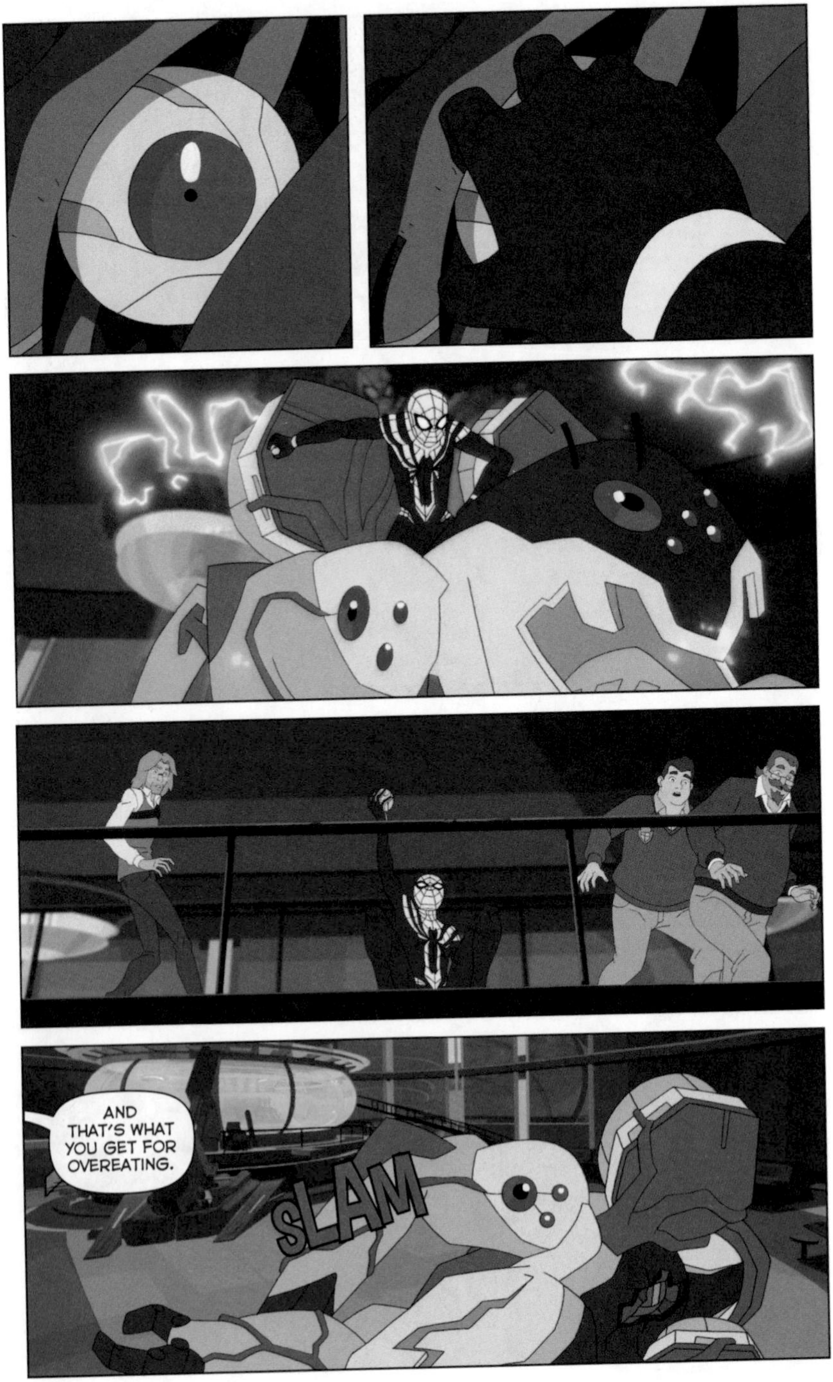
AND THAT'S WHAT YOU GET FOR OVEREATING.
SLAM

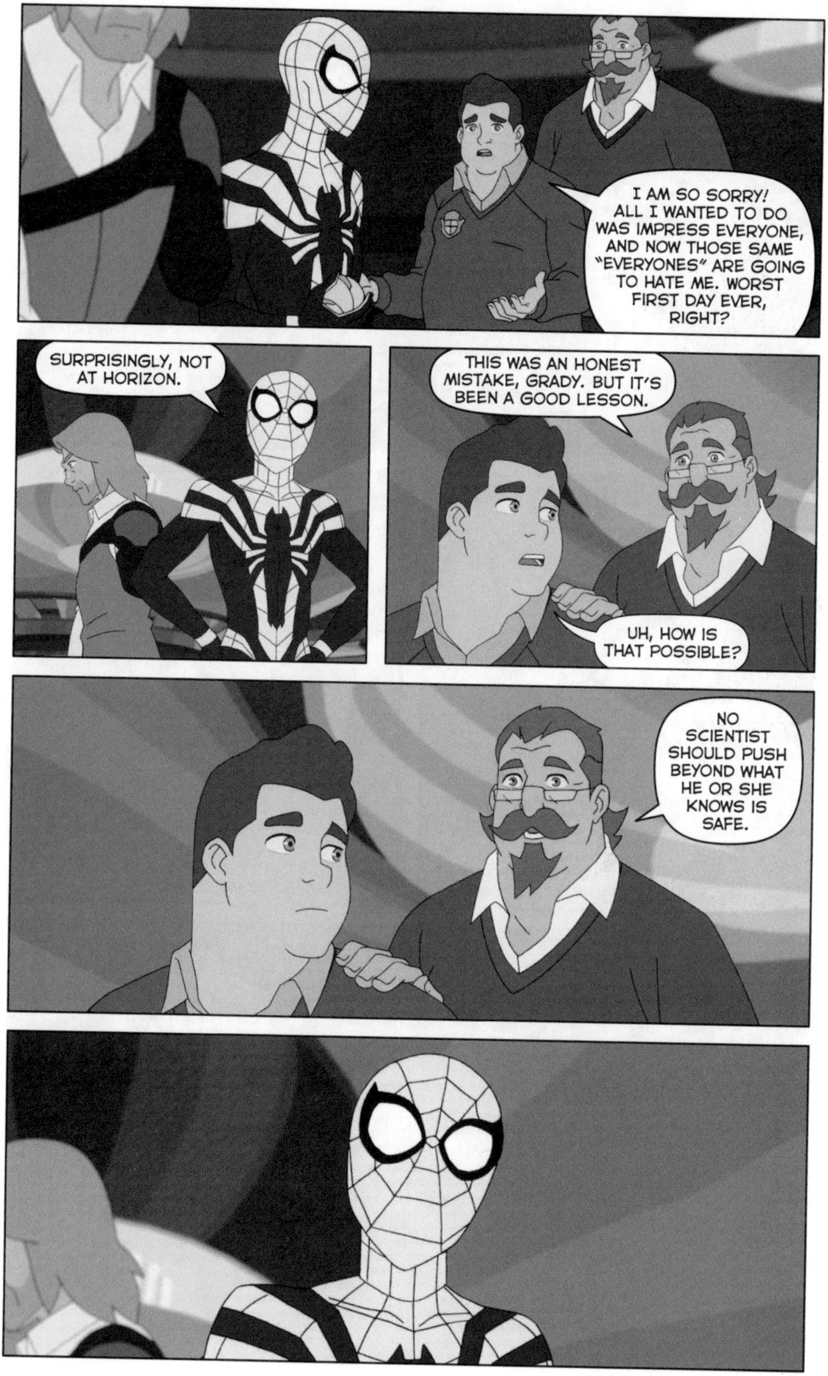
I AM SO SORRY! ALL I WANTED TO DO WAS IMPRESS EVERYONE, AND NOW THOSE SAME "EVERYONES" ARE GOING TO HATE ME. WORST FIRST DAY EVER, RIGHT?
SURPRISINGLY, NOT AT HORIZON.
THIS WAS AN HONEST MISTAKE, GRADY. BUT IT'S BEEN A GOOD LESSON.
UH, HOW IS THAT POSSIBLE?
NO SCIENTIST SHOULD PUSH BEYOND WHAT HE OR SHE KNOWS IS SAFE.

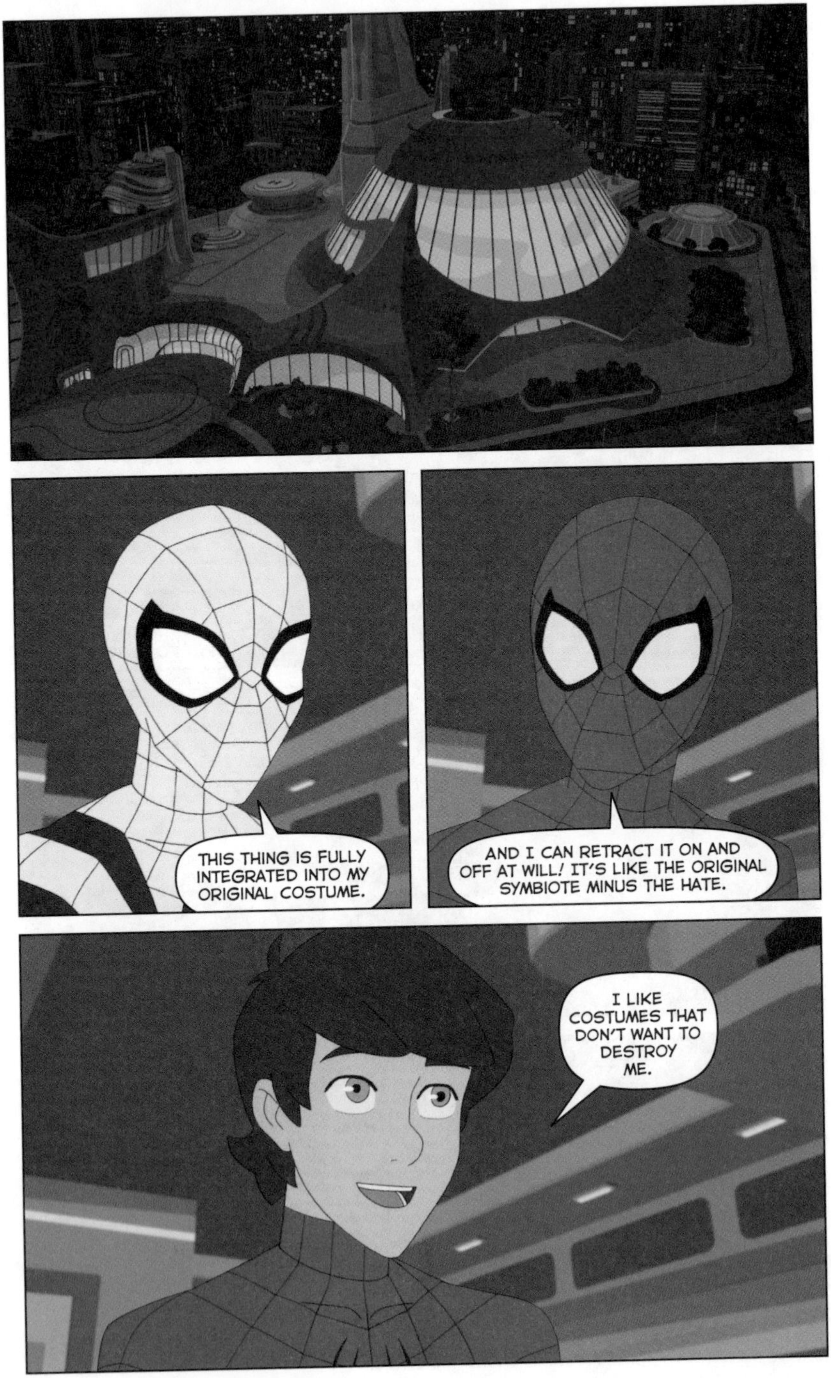
THIS THING IS FULLY INTEGRATED INTO MY ORIGINAL COSTUME.
AND I CAN RETRACT IT ON AND OFF AT WILL! IT'S LIKE THE ORIGINAL SYMBIOTE MINUS THE HATE.
I LIKE COSTUMES THAT DON'T WANT TO DESTROY ME.

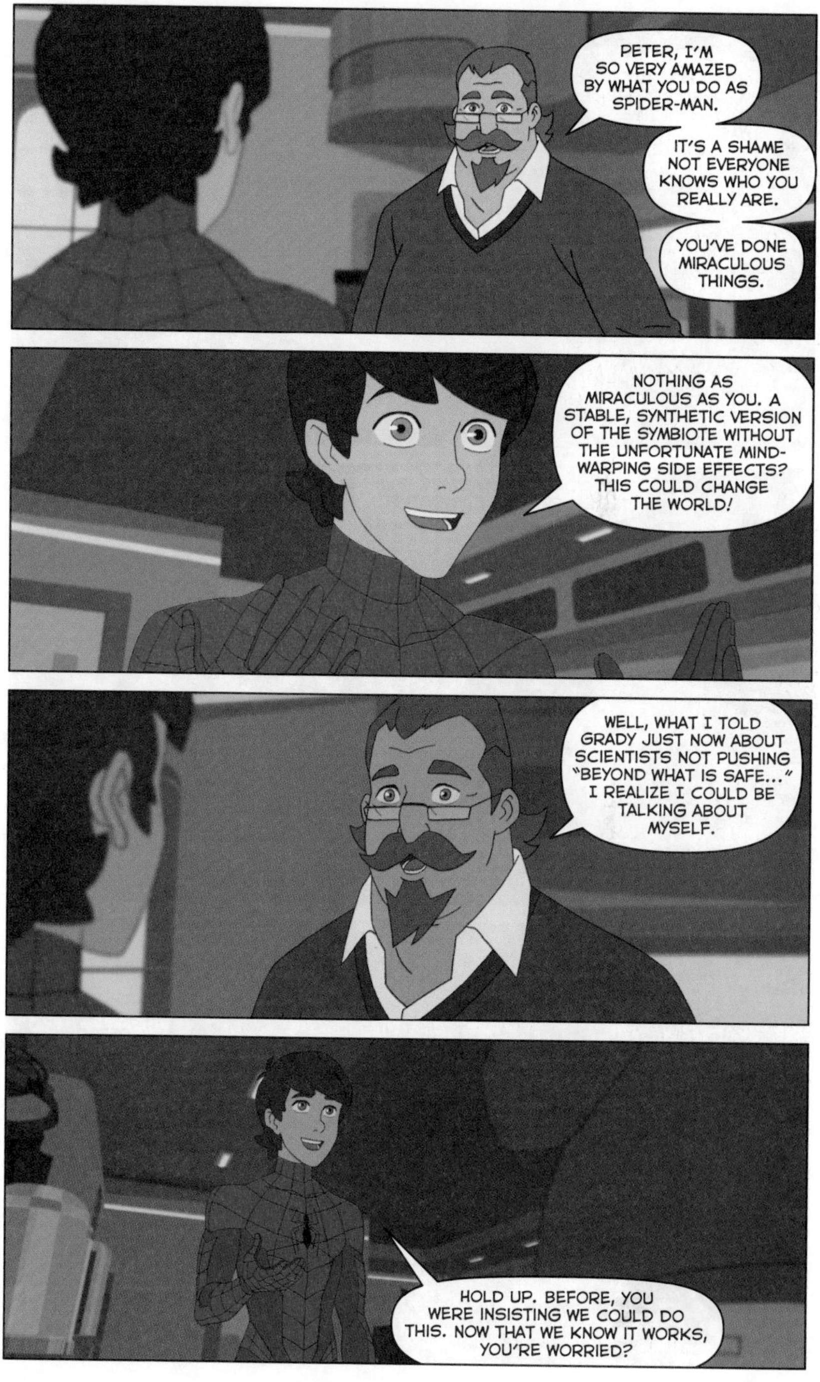
PETER, I'M SO VERY AMAZED BY WHAT YOU DO AS SPIDER-MAN.
IT'S A SHAME NOT EVERYONE KNOWS WHO YOU REALLY ARE.
YOU'VE DONE MIRACULOUS THINGS.
NOTHING AS MIRACULOUS AS YOU. A STABLE, SYNTHETIC VERSION OF THE SYMBIOTE WITHOUT THE UNFORTUNATE MIND-WARPING SIDE EFFECTS? THIS COULD CHANGE THE WORLD!
WELL, WHAT I TOLD GRADY JUST NOW ABOUT SCIENTISTS NOT PUSHING "BEYOND WHAT IS SAFE..." I REALIZE I COULD BE TALKING ABOUT MYSELF.
HOLD UP. BEFORE, YOU WERE INSISTING WE COULD DO THIS. NOW THAT WE KNOW IT WORKS, YOU'RE WORRIED?

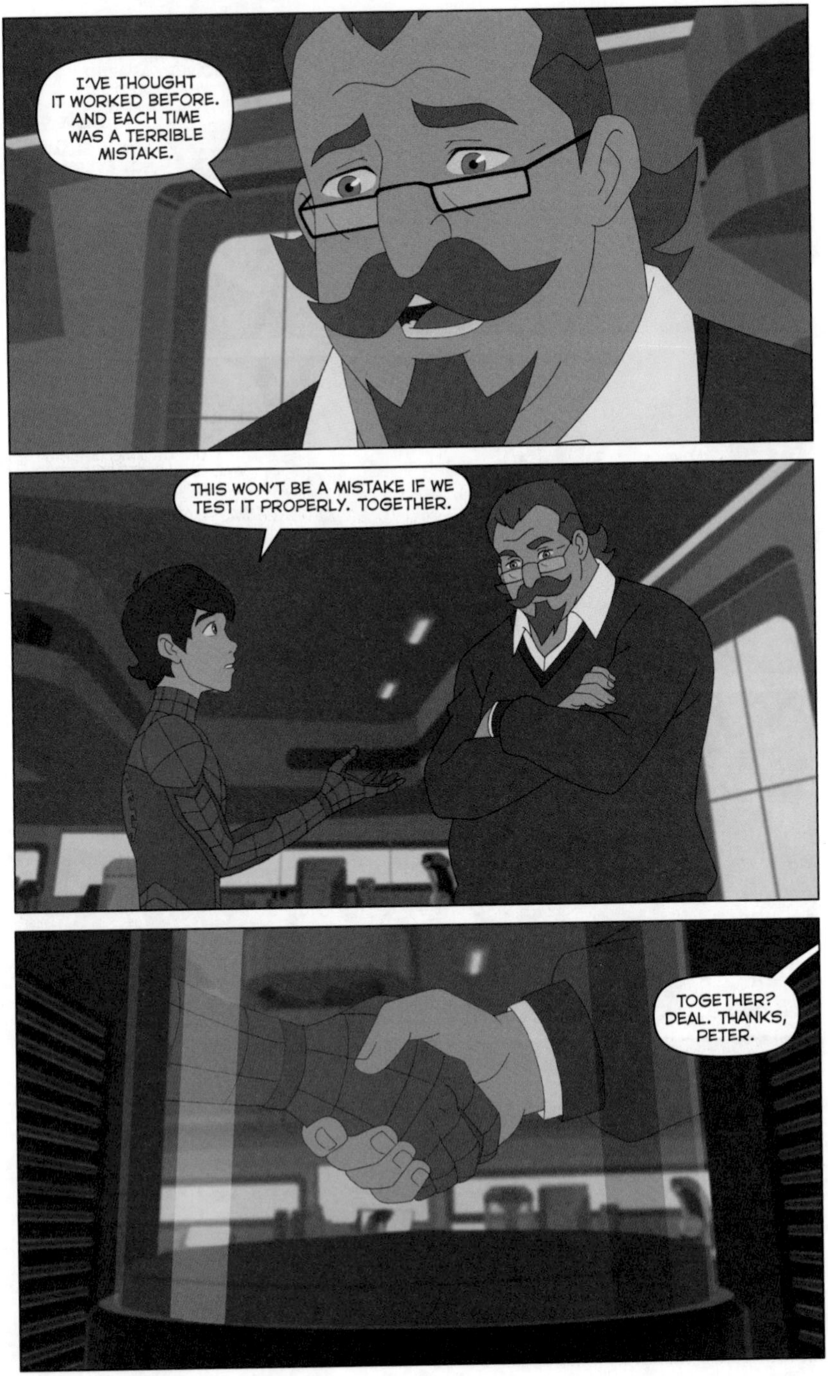
I'VE THOUGHT IT WORKED BEFORE. AND EACH TIME WAS A TERRIBLE MISTAKE.
THIS WON'T BE A MISTAKE IF WE TEST IT PROPERLY. TOGETHER.
TOGETHER? DEAL. THANKS, PETER.

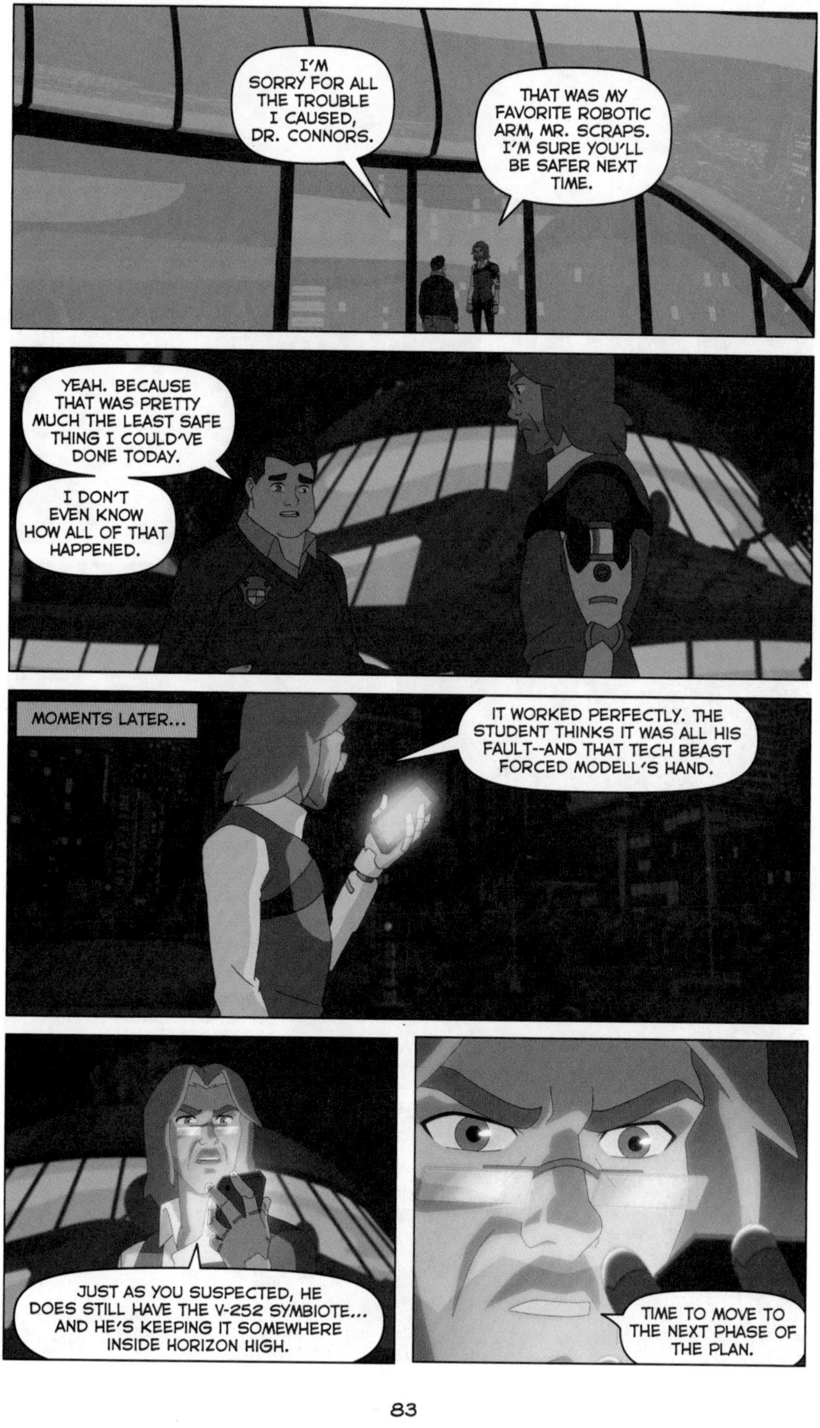
I'M SORRY FOR ALL THE TROUBLE I CAUSED, DR. CONNORS.
THAT WAS MY FAVORITE ROBOTIC ARM, MR. SCRAPS. I'M SURE YOU'LL BE SAFER NEXT TIME.
YEAH. BECAUSE THAT WAS PRETTY MUCH THE LEAST SAFE THING I COULD'VE DONE TODAY.
I DON'T EVEN KNOW HOW ALL OF THAT HAPPENED.
MOMENTS LATER...
IT WORKED PERFECTLY. THE STUDENT THINKS IT WAS ALL HIS FAULT--AND THAT TECH BEAST FORCED MODELL'S HAND.
JUST AS YOU SUSPECTED, HE DOES STILL HAVE THE V-252 SYMBIOTE... AND HE'S KEEPING IT SOMEWHERE INSIDE HORIZON HIGH.
TIME TO MOVE TO THE NEXT PHASE OF THE PLAN.

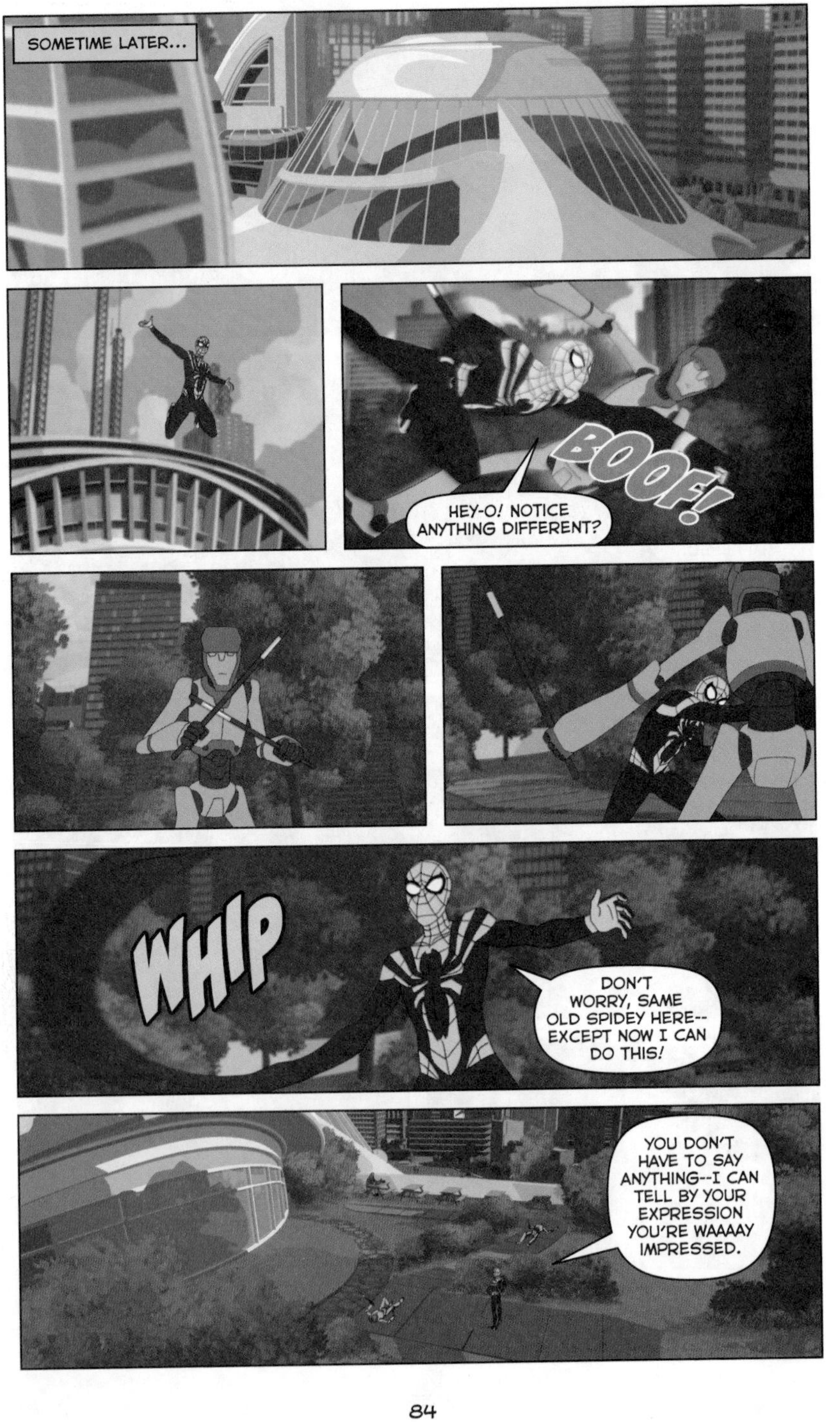
SOMETIME LATER...
HEY-O! NOTICE ANYTHING DIFFERENT?
BOOF!
WHIP
DON'T WORRY, SAME OLD SPIDEY HERE--EXCEPT NOW I CAN DO THIS!
YOU DON'T HAVE TO SAY ANYTHING--I CAN TELL BY YOUR EXPRESSION YOU'RE WAAAAY IMPRESSED.

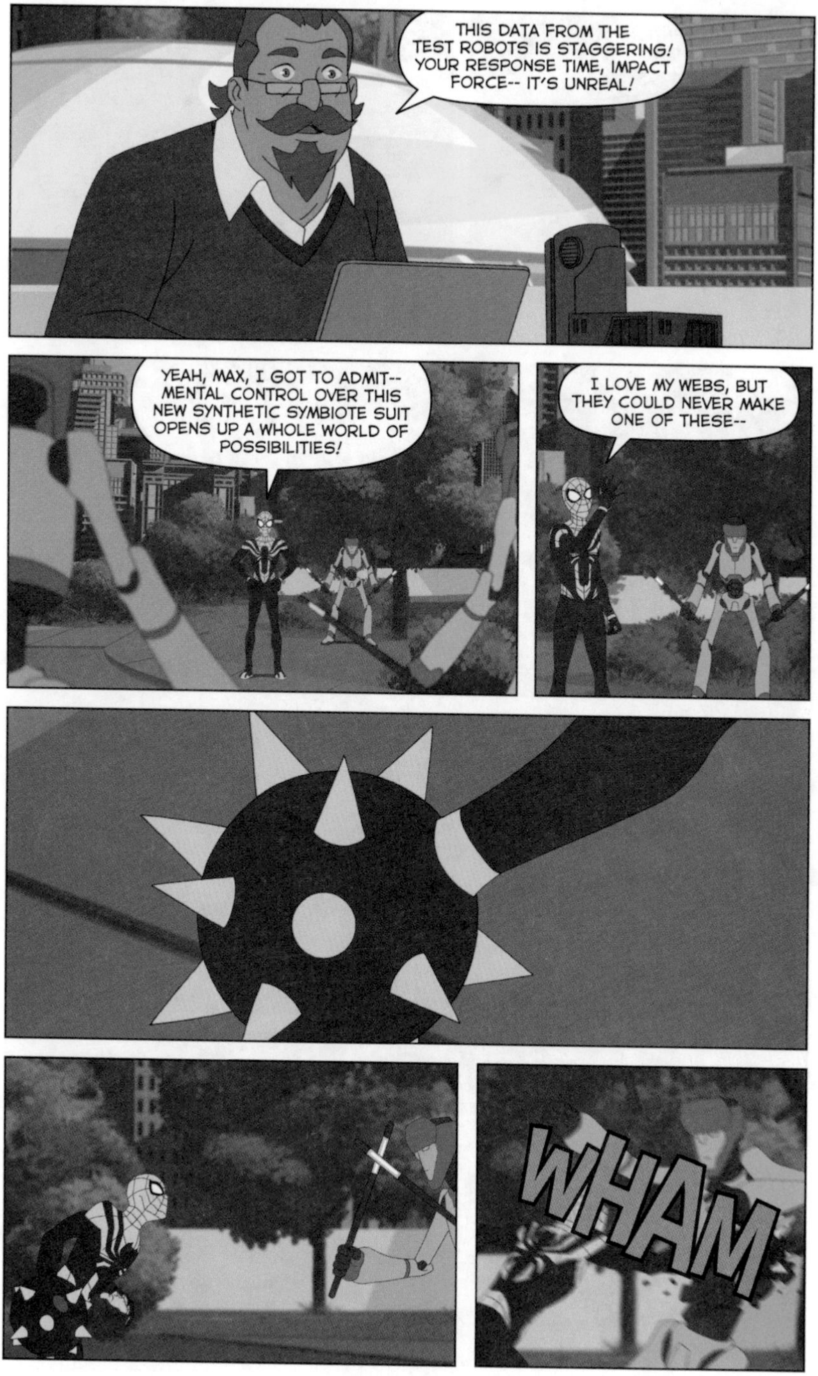
THIS DATA FROM THE TEST ROBOTS IS STAGGERING! YOUR RESPONSE TIME, IMPACT FORCE-- IT'S UNREAL!
YEAH, MAX, I GOT TO ADMIT-- MENTAL CONTROL OVER THIS NEW SYNTHETIC SYMBIOTE SUIT OPENS UP A WHOLE WORLD OF POSSIBILITIES!
I LOVE MY WEBS, BUT THEY COULD NEVER MAKE ONE OF THESE--
WHAM

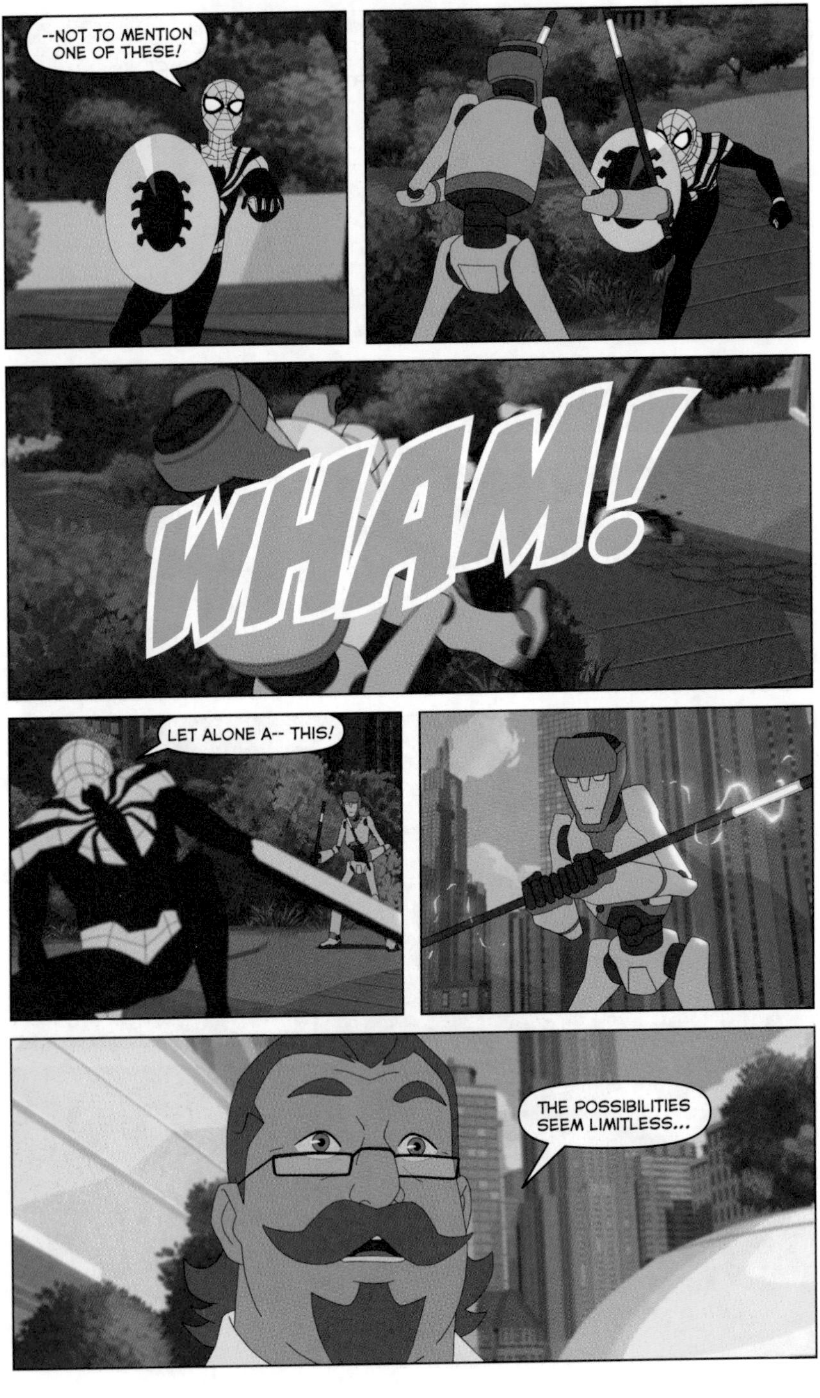
--NOT TO MENTION ONE OF THESE!
WHAM!
LET ALONE A-- THIS!
THE POSSIBILITIES SEEM LIMITLESS...

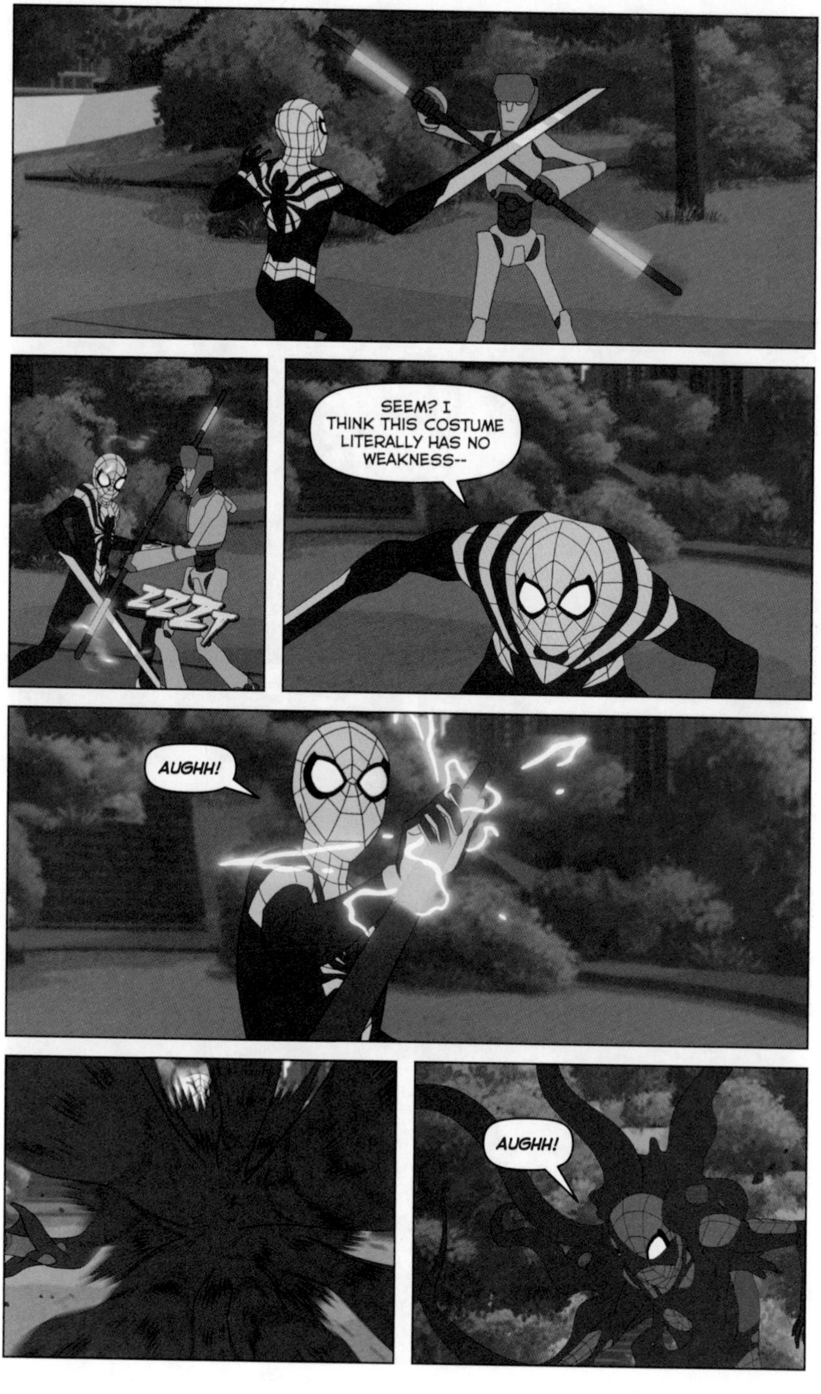
ZZZT
SEEM? I THINK THIS COSTUME LITERALLY HAS NO WEAKNESS--
AUGHH!
AUGHH!

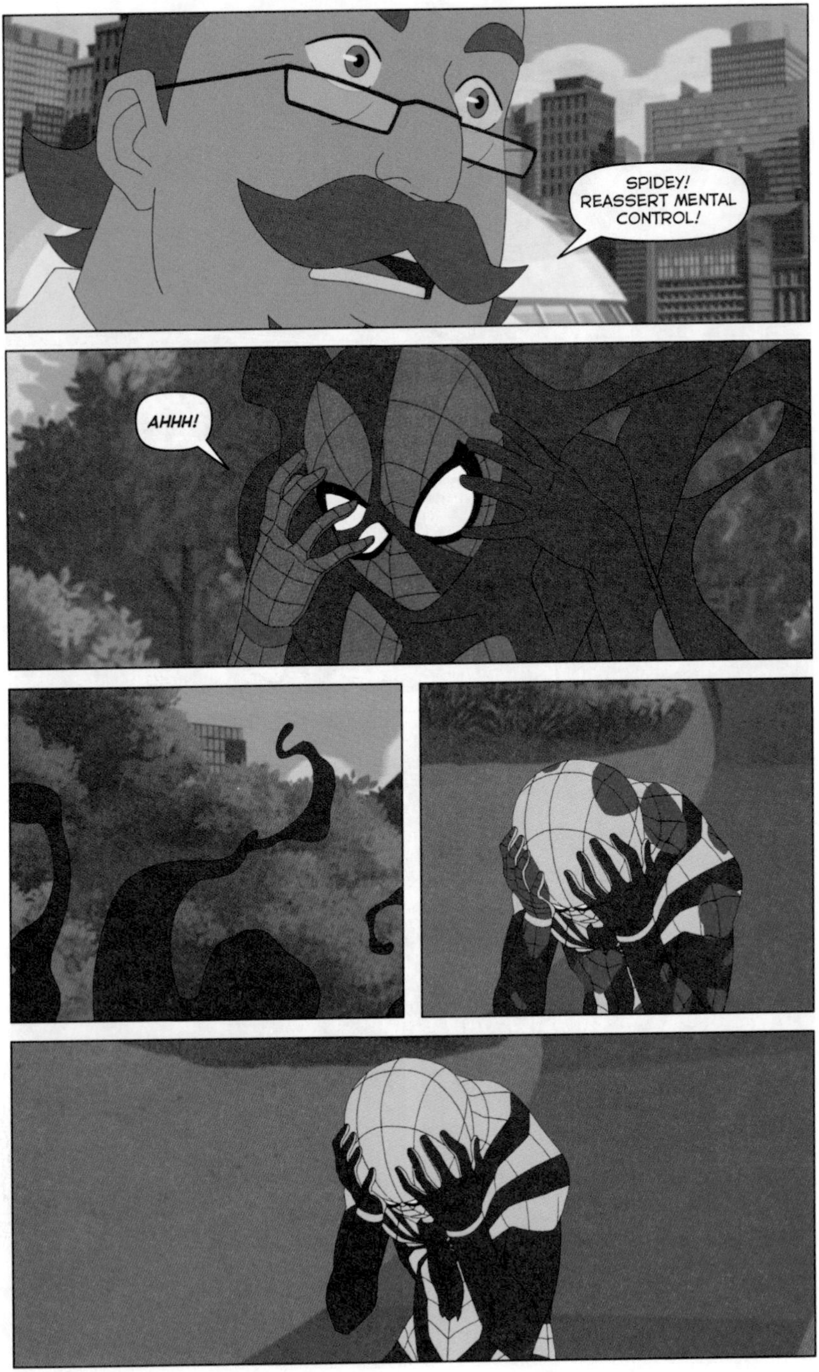
SPIDEY! REASSERT MENTAL CONTROL!
AHHH!

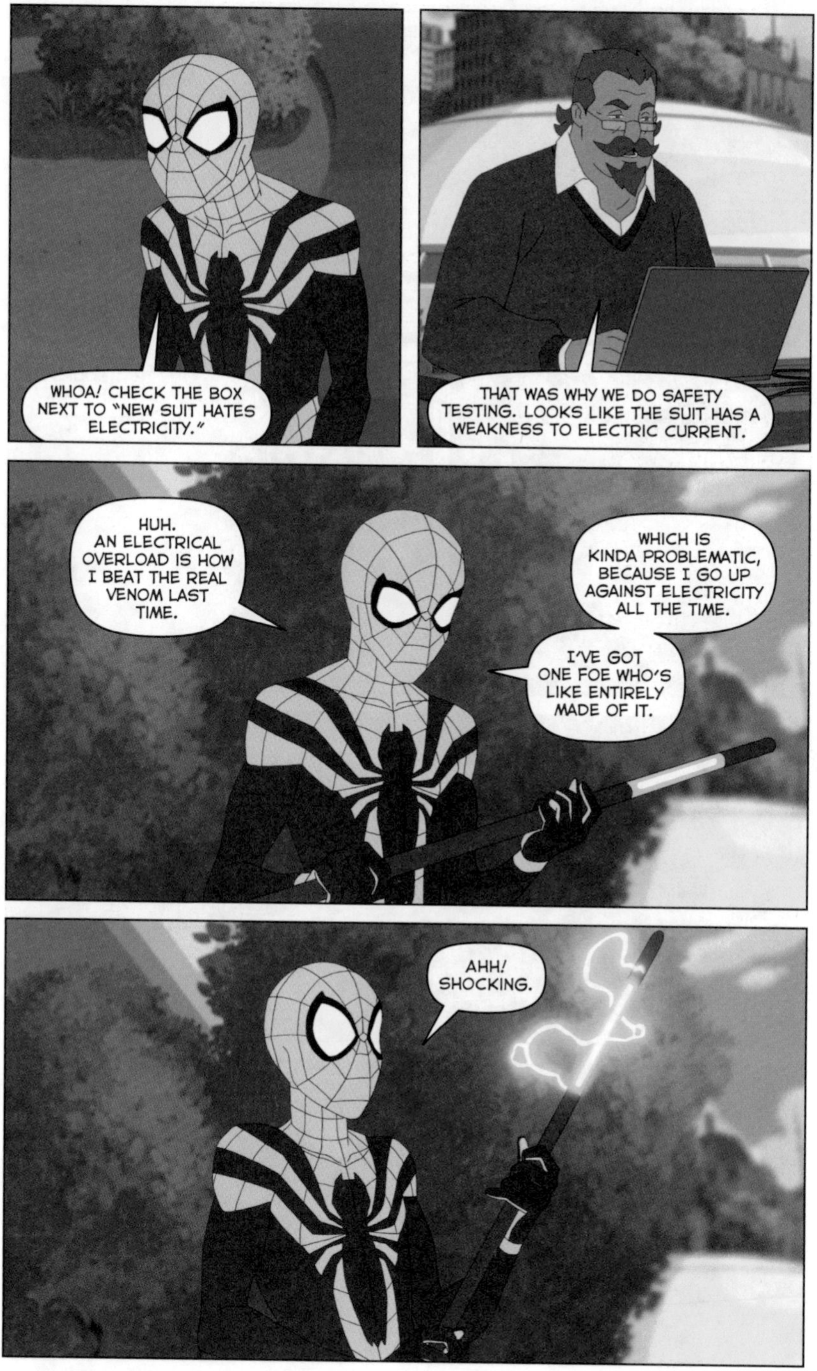
WHOA! CHECK THE BOX NEXT TO "NEW SUIT HATES ELECTRICITY."
THAT WAS WHY WE DO SAFETY TESTING. LOOKS LIKE THE SUIT HAS A WEAKNESS TO ELECTRIC CURRENT.
HUH. AN ELECTRICAL OVERLOAD IS HOW I BEAT THE REAL VENOM LAST TIME.
WHICH IS KINDA PROBLEMATIC, BECAUSE I GO UP AGAINST ELECTRICITY ALL THE TIME.
I'VE GOT ONE FOE WHO'S LIKE ENTIRELY MADE OF IT.
AHH! SHOCKING.

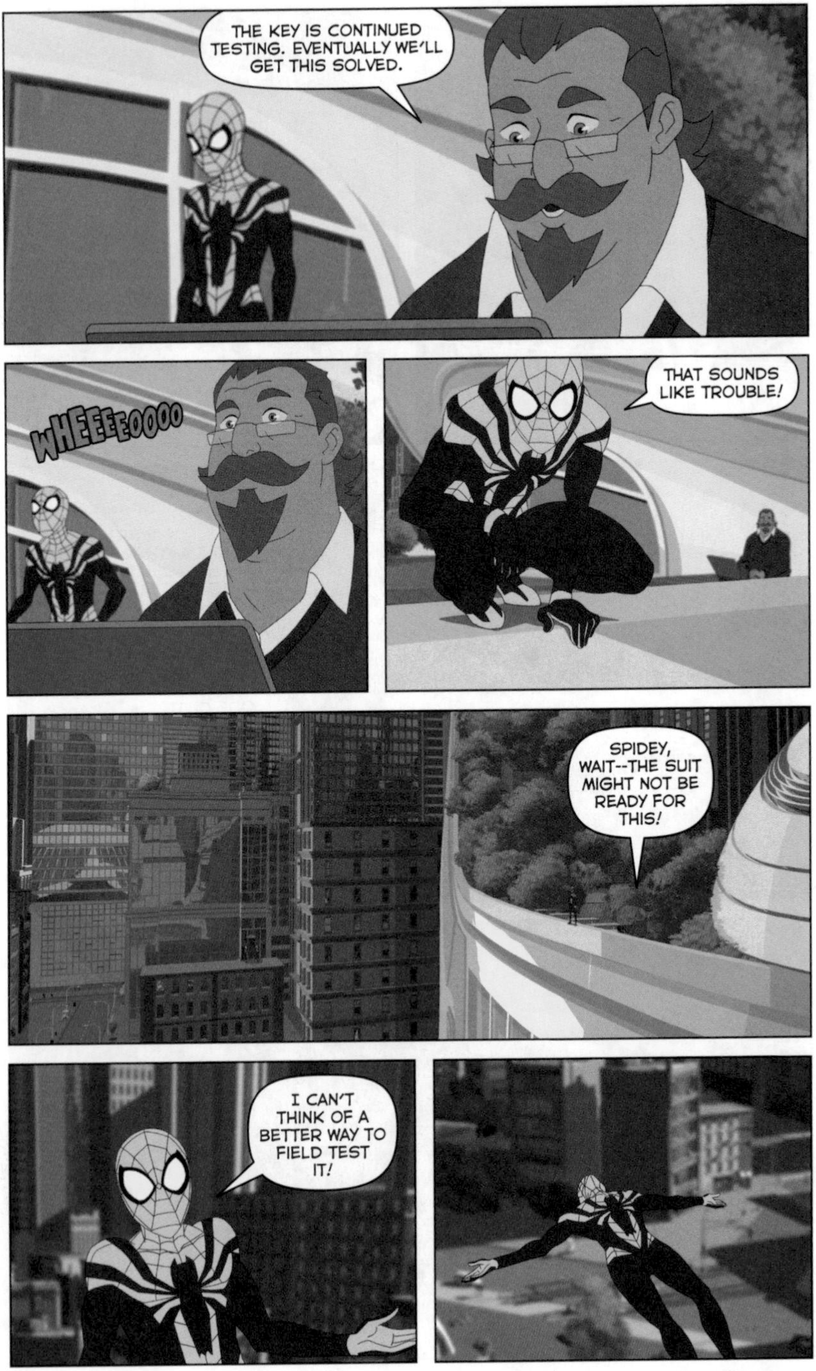
THE KEY IS CONTINUED TESTING. EVENTUALLY WE'LL GET THIS SOLVED.
WHEEEEOOOO
THAT SOUNDS LIKE TROUBLE!
SPIDEY, WAIT--THE SUIT MIGHT NOT BE READY FOR THIS!
I CAN'T THINK OF A BETTER WAY TO FIELD TEST IT!

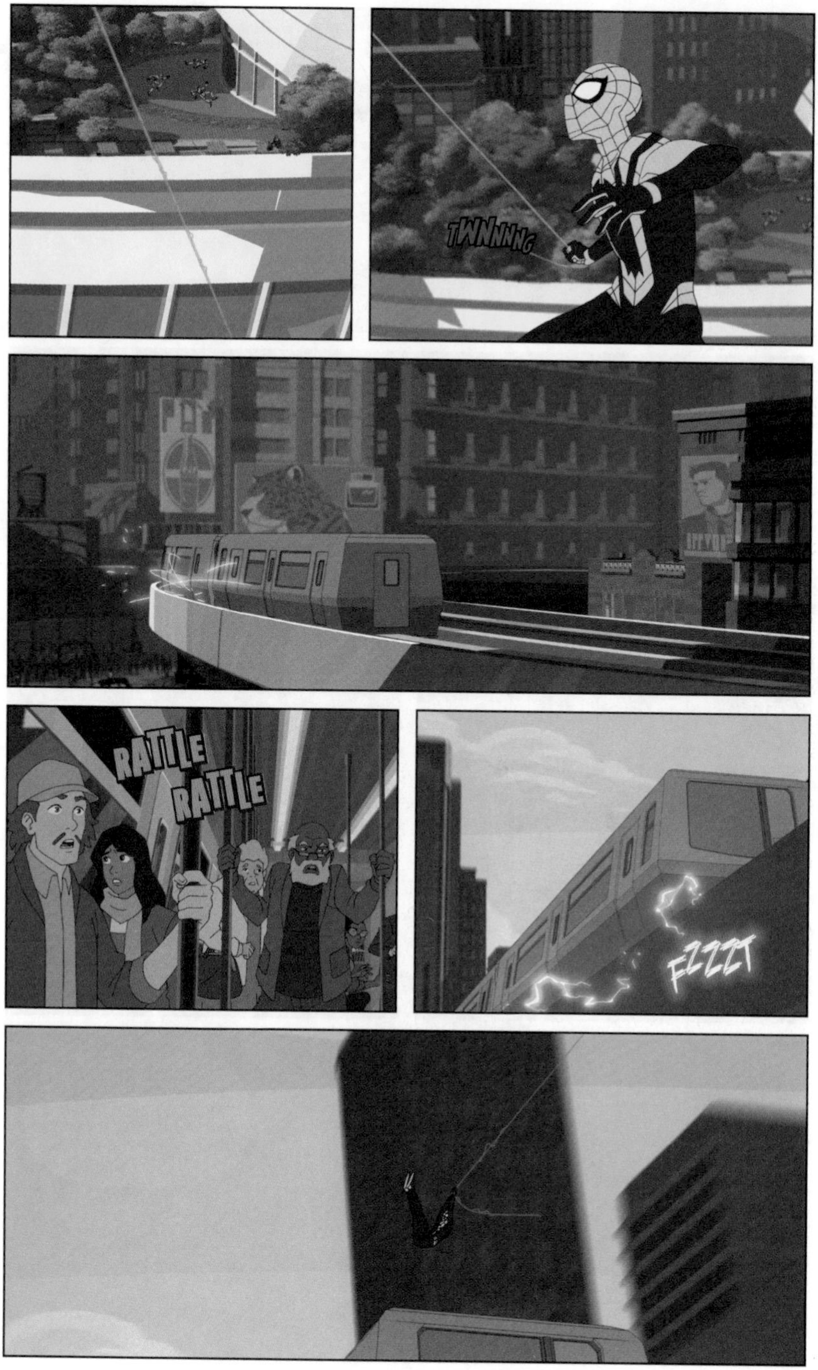
TWNNNNG
RATTLE
RATTLE
FZZZT

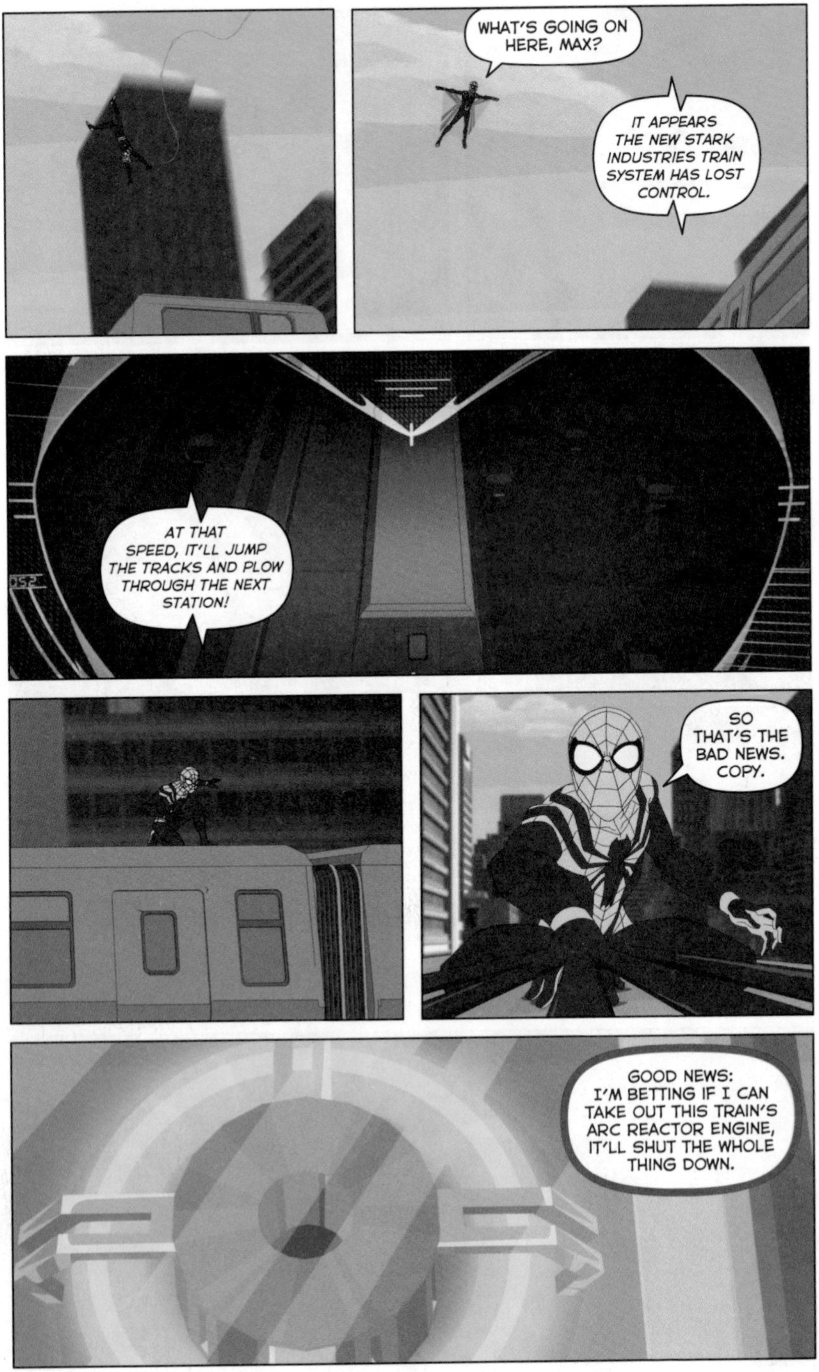
WHAT'S GOING ON HERE, MAX?
IT APPEARS THE NEW STARK INDUSTRIES TRAIN SYSTEM HAS LOST CONTROL.
AT THAT SPEED, IT'LL JUMP THE TRACKS AND PLOW THROUGH THE NEXT STATION!
SO THAT'S THE BAD NEWS. COPY.
GOOD NEWS: I'M BETTING IF I CAN TAKE OUT THIS TRAIN'S ARC REACTOR ENGINE, IT'LL SHUT THE WHOLE THING DOWN.

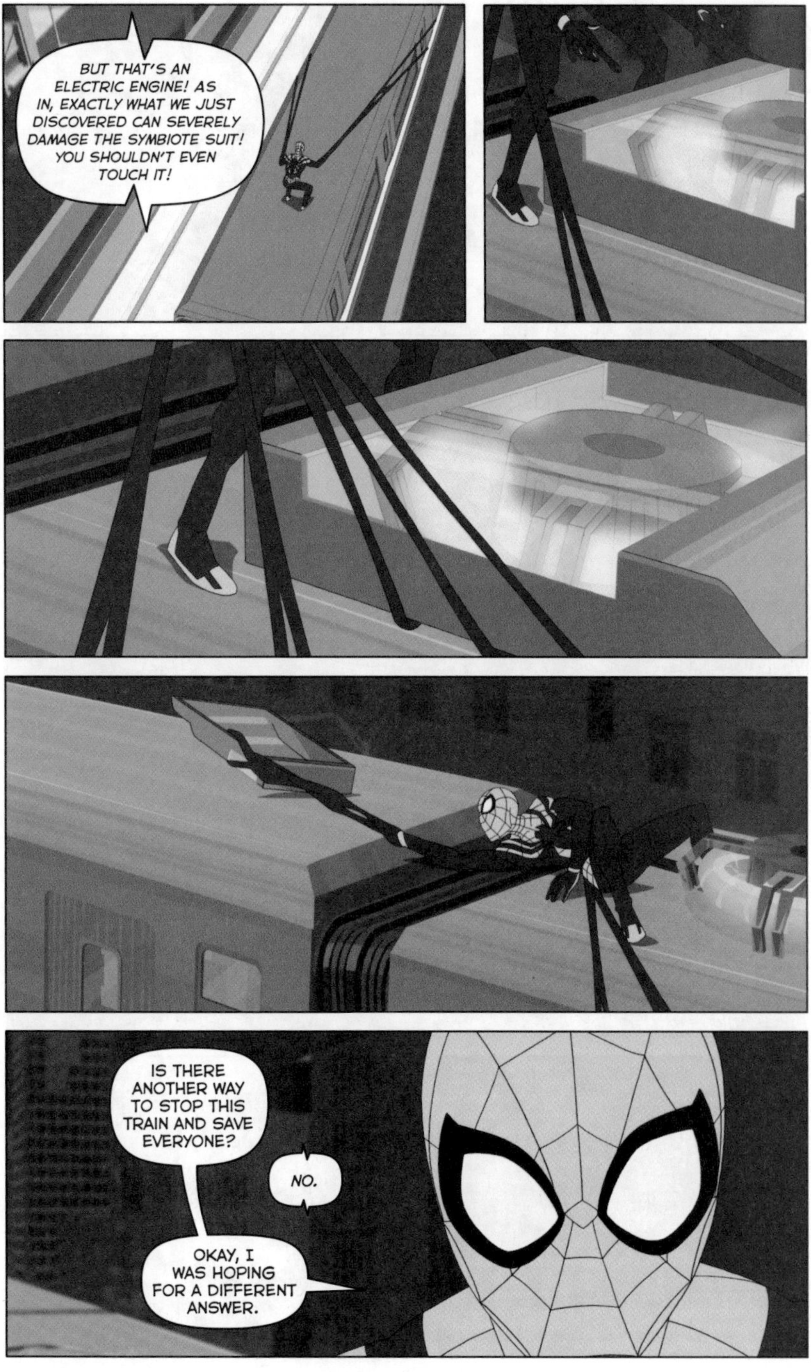

BUT THAT'S AN ELECTRIC ENGINE! AS IN, EXACTLY WHAT WE JUST DISCOVERED CAN SEVERELY DAMAGE THE SYMBIOTE SUIT! YOU SHOULDN'T EVEN TOUCH IT!
IS THERE ANOTHER WAY TO STOP THIS TRAIN AND SAVE EVERYONE?
NO.
OKAY, I WAS HOPING FOR A DIFFERENT ANSWER.

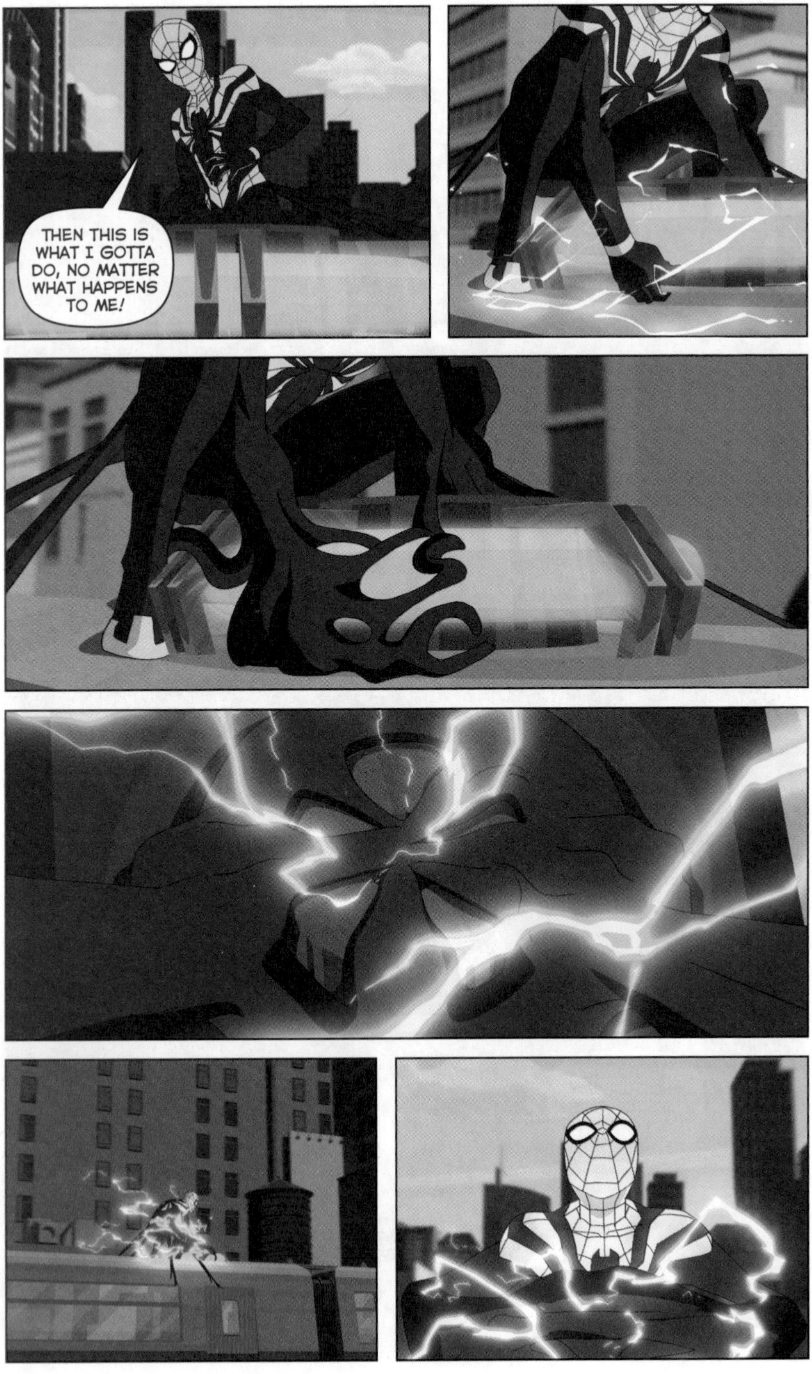
THEN THIS IS WHAT I GOTTA DO, NO MATTER WHAT HAPPENS TO ME!

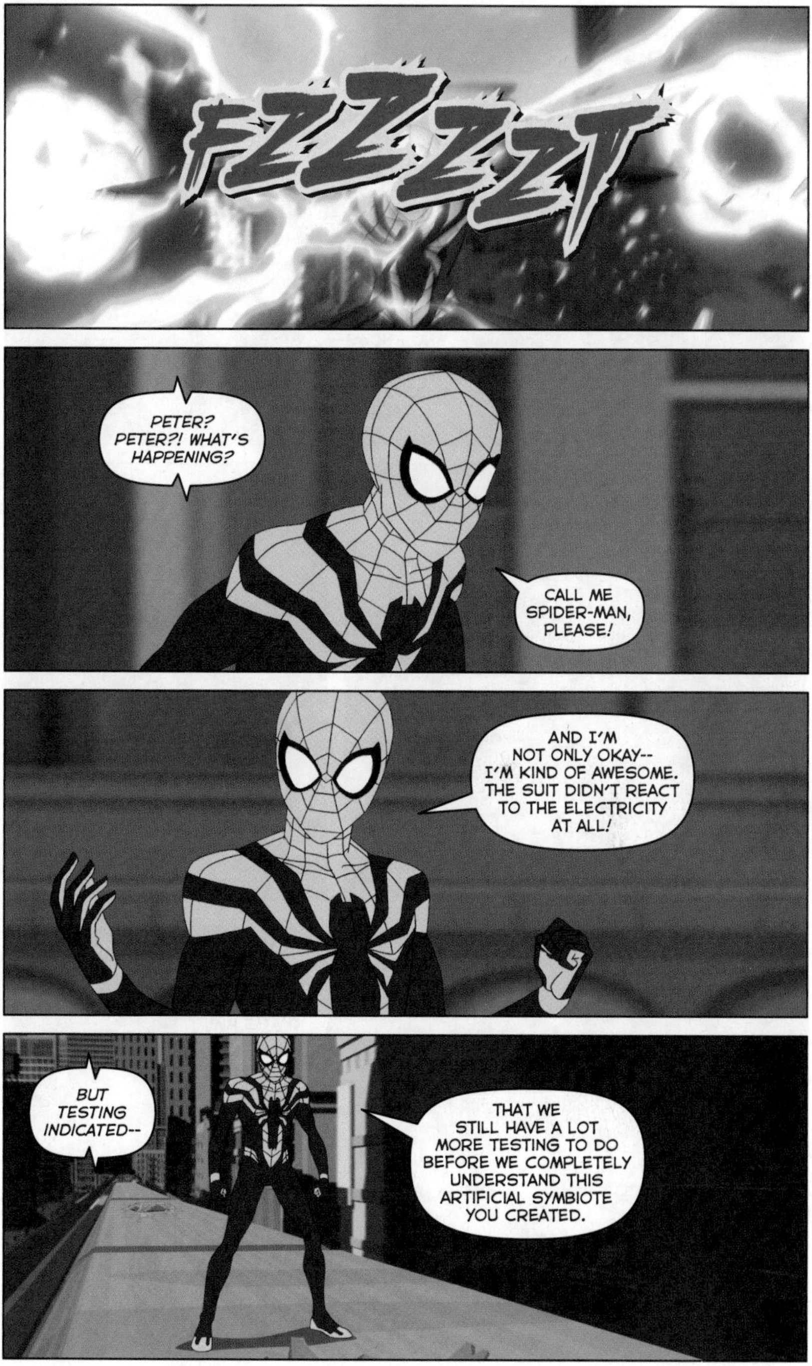
FZZZZZT
PETER? PETER?! WHAT'S HAPPENING?
CALL ME SPIDER-MAN, PLEASE!
AND I'M NOT ONLY OKAY-- I'M KIND OF AWESOME. THE SUIT DIDN'T REACT TO THE ELECTRICITY AT ALL!
BUT TESTING INDICATED--
THAT WE STILL HAVE A LOT MORE TESTING TO DO BEFORE WE COMPLETELY UNDERSTAND THIS ARTIFICIAL SYMBIOTE YOU CREATED.

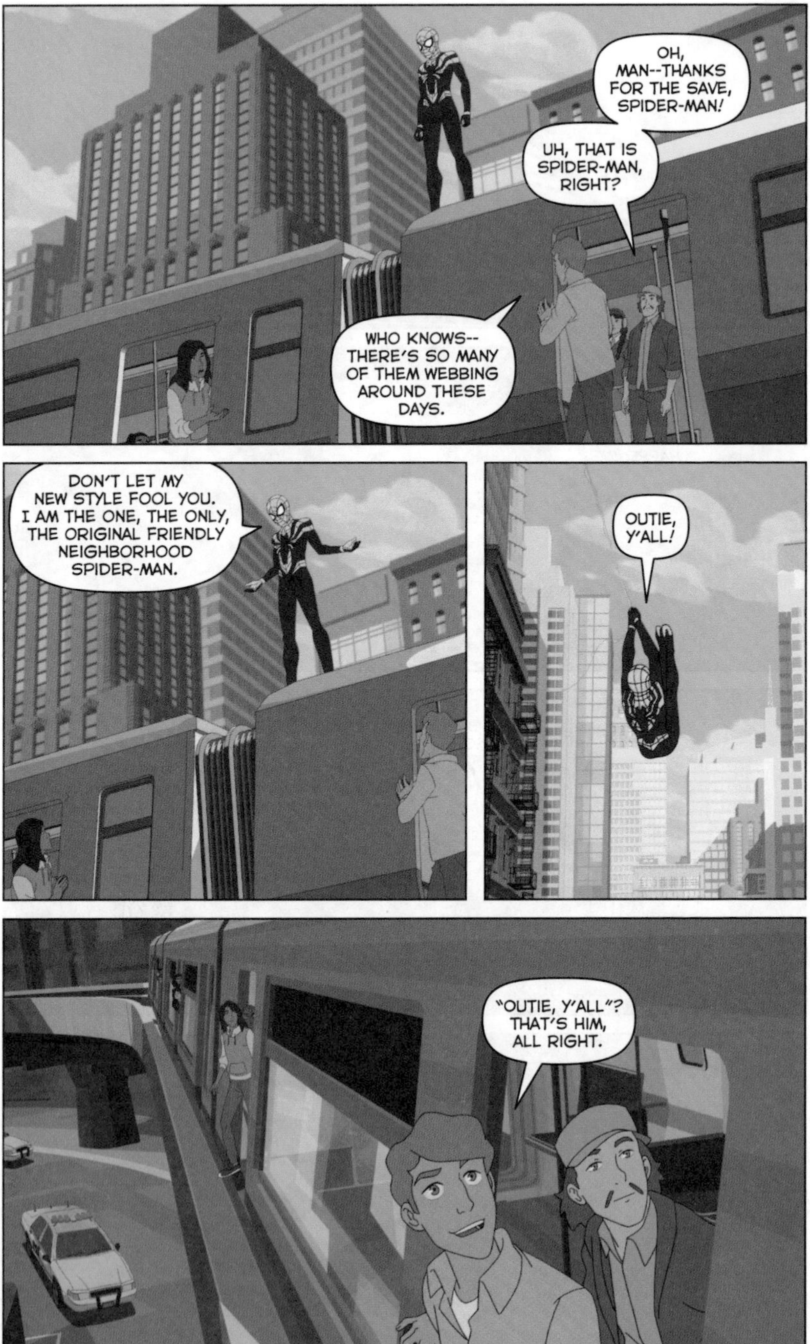
OH, MAN--THANKS FOR THE SAVE, SPIDER-MAN!
UH, THAT IS SPIDER-MAN, RIGHT?
WHO KNOWS-- THERE'S SO MANY OF THEM WEBBING AROUND THESE DAYS.
DON'T LET MY NEW STYLE FOOL YOU. I AM THE ONE, THE ONLY, THE ORIGINAL FRIENDLY NEIGHBORHOOD SPIDER-MAN.
OUTIE, Y'ALL!
"OUTIE, Y'ALL"? THAT'S HIM, ALL RIGHT.

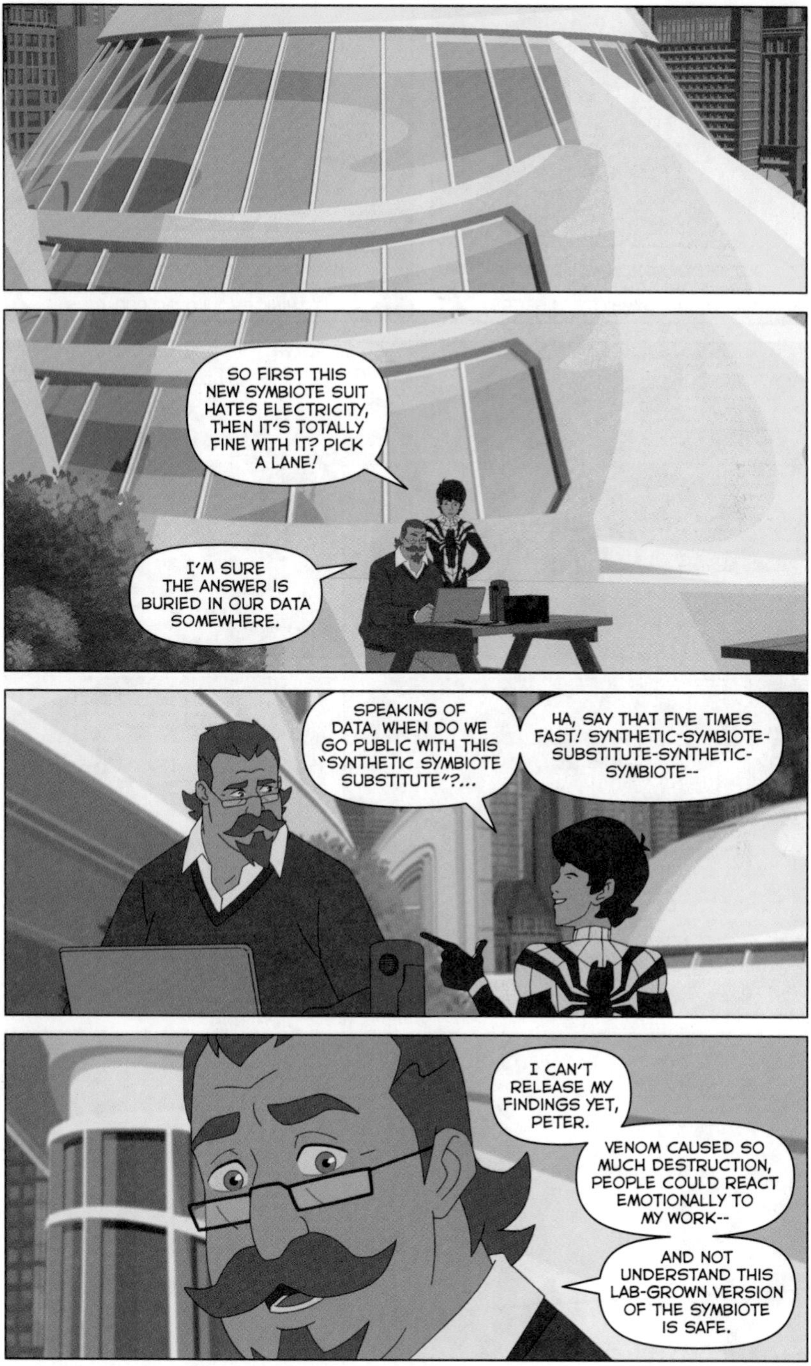
SO FIRST THIS NEW SYMBIOTE SUIT HATES ELECTRICITY, THEN IT'S TOTALLY FINE WITH IT? PICK A LANE!
I'M SURE THE ANSWER IS BURIED IN OUR DATA SOMEWHERE.
SPEAKING OF DATA, WHEN DO WE GO PUBLIC WITH THIS "SYNTHETIC SYMBIOTE SUBSTITUTE"?...
HA, SAY THAT FIVE TIMES FAST! SYNTHETIC-SYMBIOTE-SUBSTITUTE-SYNTHETIC-SYMBIOTE--
I CAN'T RELEASE MY FINDINGS YET, PETER.
VENOM CAUSED SO MUCH DESTRUCTION, PEOPLE COULD REACT EMOTIONALLY TO MY WORK--
AND NOT UNDERSTAND THIS LAB-GROWN VERSION OF THE SYMBIOTE IS SAFE.

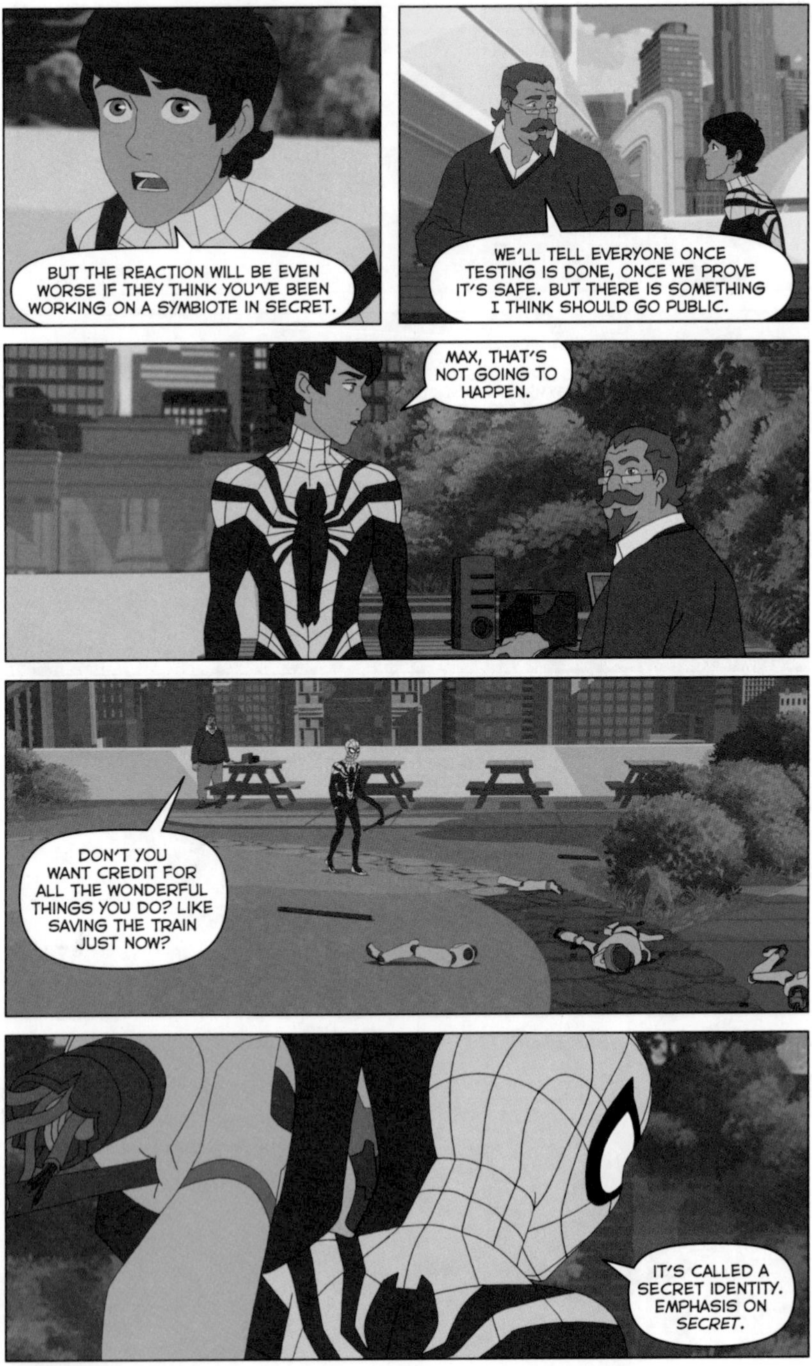
BUT THE REACTION WILL BE EVEN WORSE IF THEY THINK YOU'VE BEEN WORKING ON A SYMBIOTE IN SECRET.
WE'LL TELL EVERYONE ONCE TESTING IS DONE, ONCE WE PROVE IT'S SAFE. BUT THERE IS SOMETHING I THINK SHOULD GO PUBLIC.
MAX, THAT'S NOT GOING TO HAPPEN.
DON'T YOU WANT CREDIT FOR ALL THE WONDERFUL THINGS YOU DO? LIKE SAVING THE TRAIN JUST NOW?
IT'S CALLED A SECRET IDENTITY. EMPHASIS ON *SECRET*.

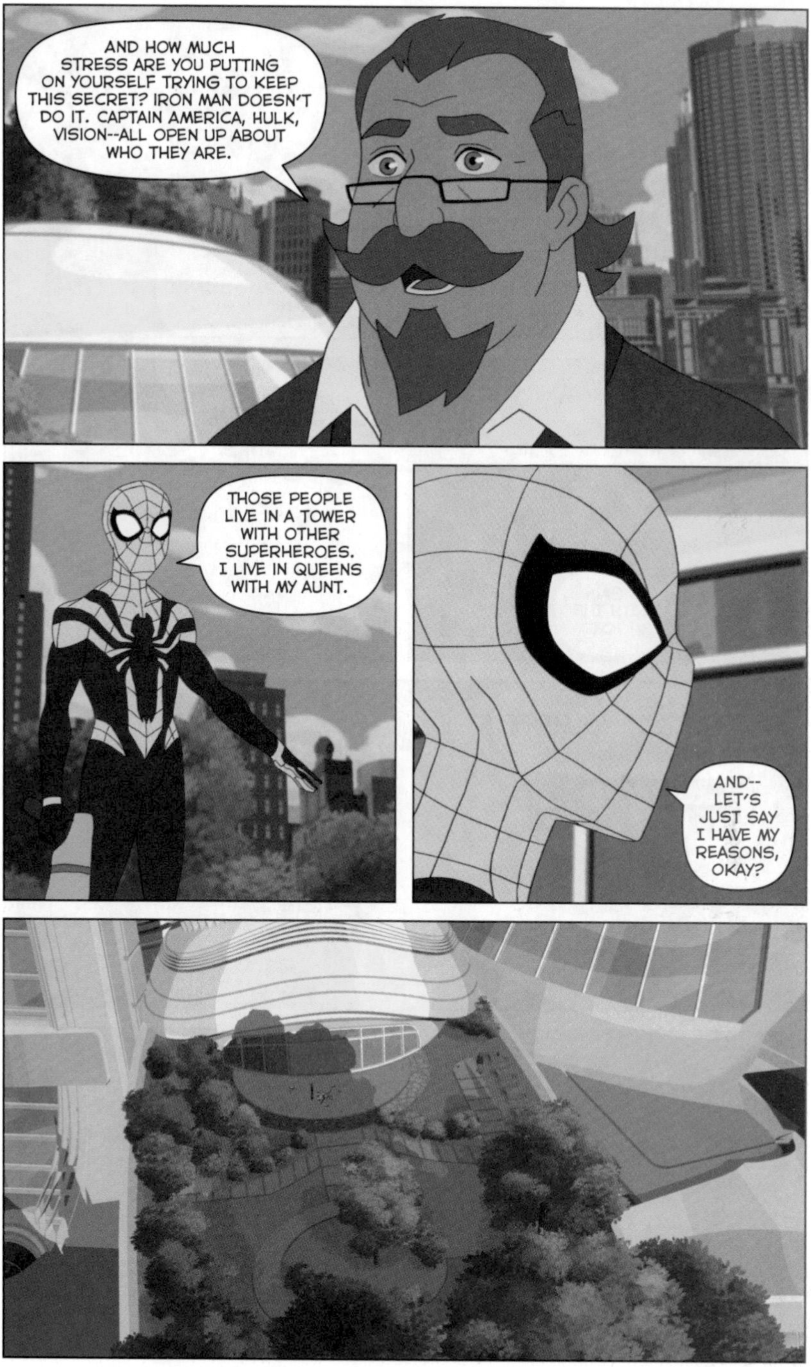
AND HOW MUCH STRESS ARE YOU PUTTING ON YOURSELF TRYING TO KEEP THIS SECRET? IRON MAN DOESN'T DO IT. CAPTAIN AMERICA, HULK, VISION--ALL OPEN UP ABOUT WHO THEY ARE.
THOSE PEOPLE LIVE IN A TOWER WITH OTHER SUPERHEROES. I LIVE IN QUEENS WITH MY AUNT.
AND--LET'S JUST SAY I HAVE MY REASONS, OKAY?

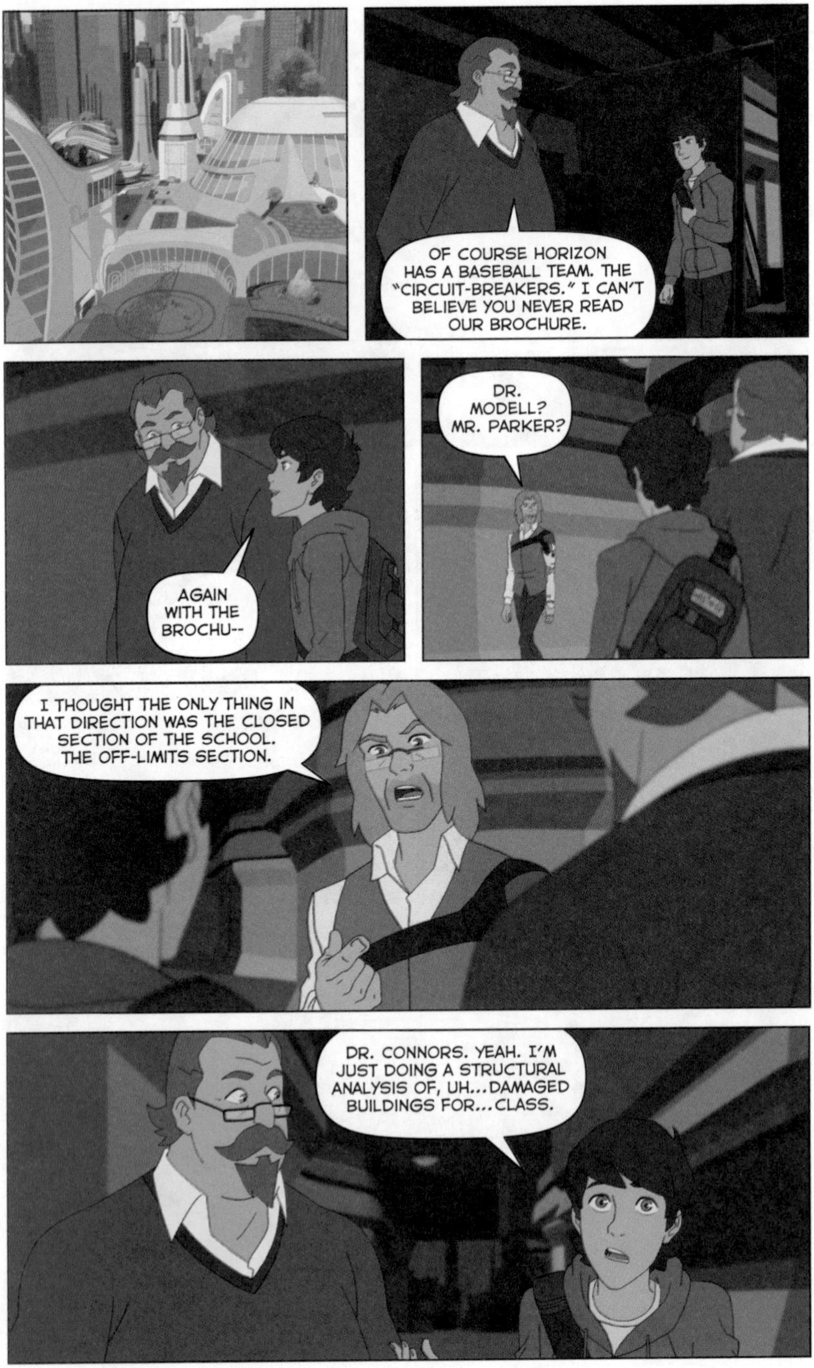
OF COURSE HORIZON HAS A BASEBALL TEAM. THE "CIRCUIT-BREAKERS." I CAN'T BELIEVE YOU NEVER READ OUR BROCHURE.
AGAIN WITH THE BROCHU--
DR. MODELL? MR. PARKER?
I THOUGHT THE ONLY THING IN THAT DIRECTION WAS THE CLOSED SECTION OF THE SCHOOL. THE OFF-LIMITS SECTION.
DR. CONNORS. YEAH. I'M JUST DOING A STRUCTURAL ANALYSIS OF, UH...DAMAGED BUILDINGS FOR...CLASS.

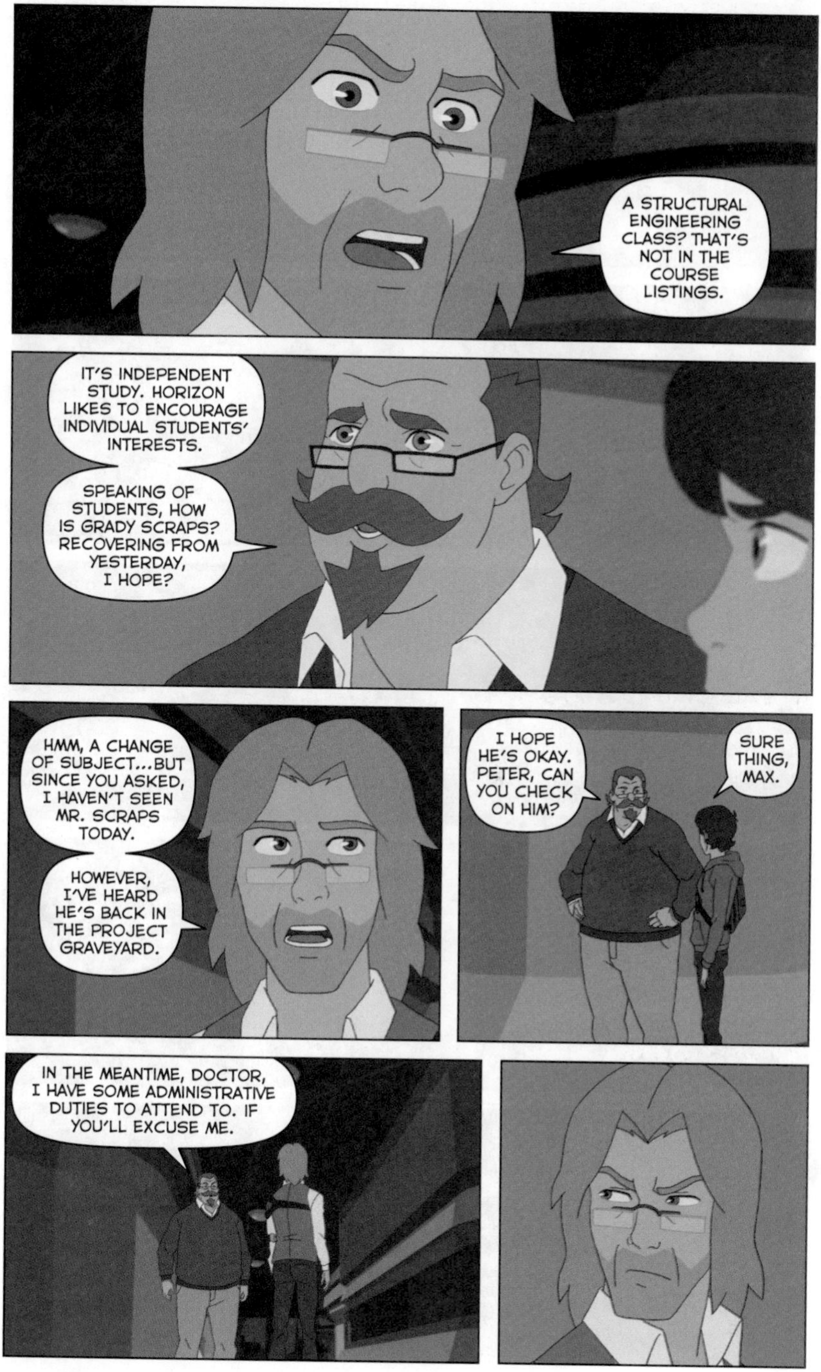
A STRUCTURAL ENGINEERING CLASS? THAT'S NOT IN THE COURSE LISTINGS.
IT'S INDEPENDENT STUDY. HORIZON LIKES TO ENCOURAGE INDIVIDUAL STUDENTS' INTERESTS.
SPEAKING OF STUDENTS, HOW IS GRADY SCRAPS? RECOVERING FROM YESTERDAY, I HOPE?
HMM, A CHANGE OF SUBJECT...BUT SINCE YOU ASKED, I HAVEN'T SEEN MR. SCRAPS TODAY.
HOWEVER, I'VE HEARD HE'S BACK IN THE PROJECT GRAVEYARD.
I HOPE HE'S OKAY. PETER, CAN YOU CHECK ON HIM?
SURE THING, MAX.
IN THE MEANTIME, DOCTOR, I HAVE SOME ADMINISTRATIVE DUTIES TO ATTEND TO. IF YOU'LL EXCUSE ME.

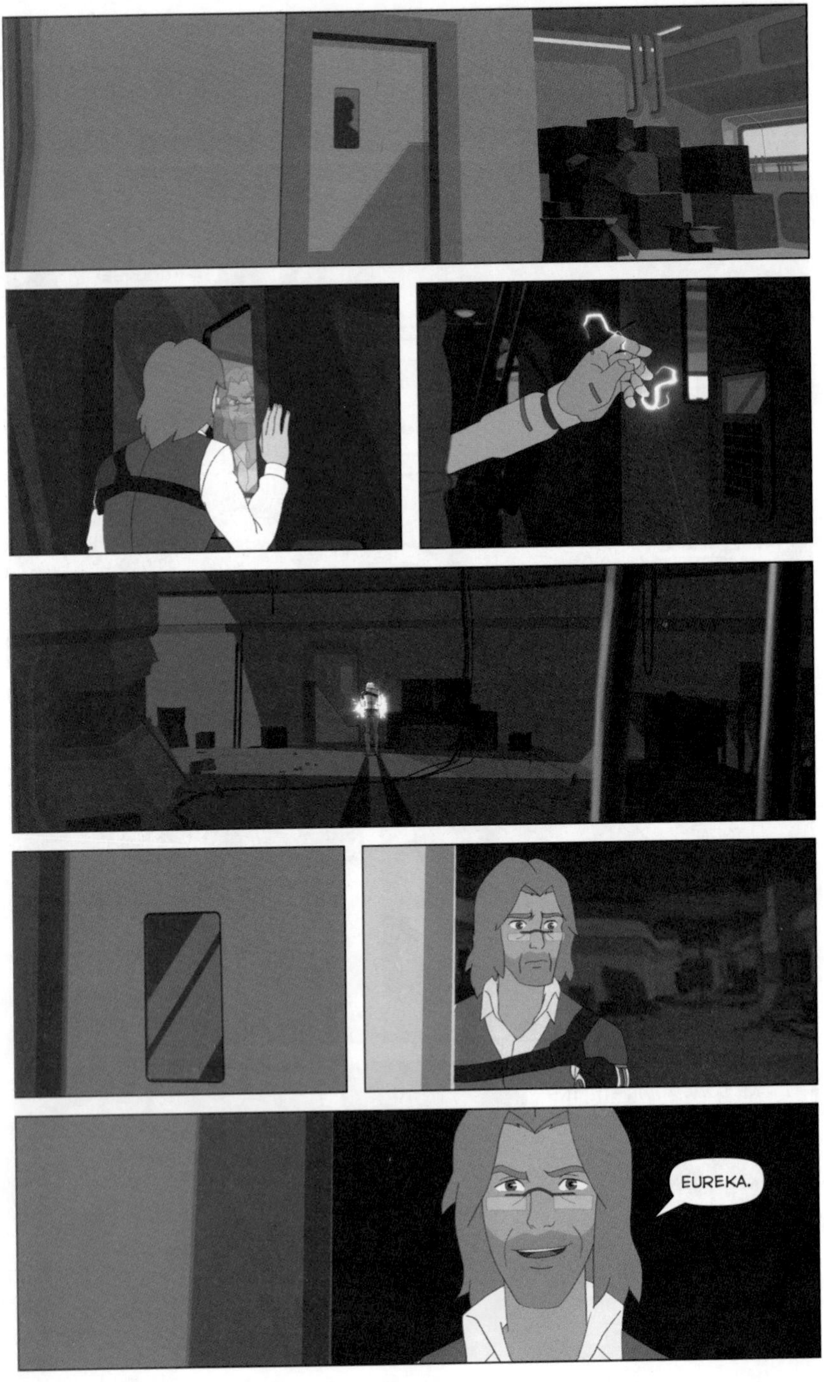
EUREKA.

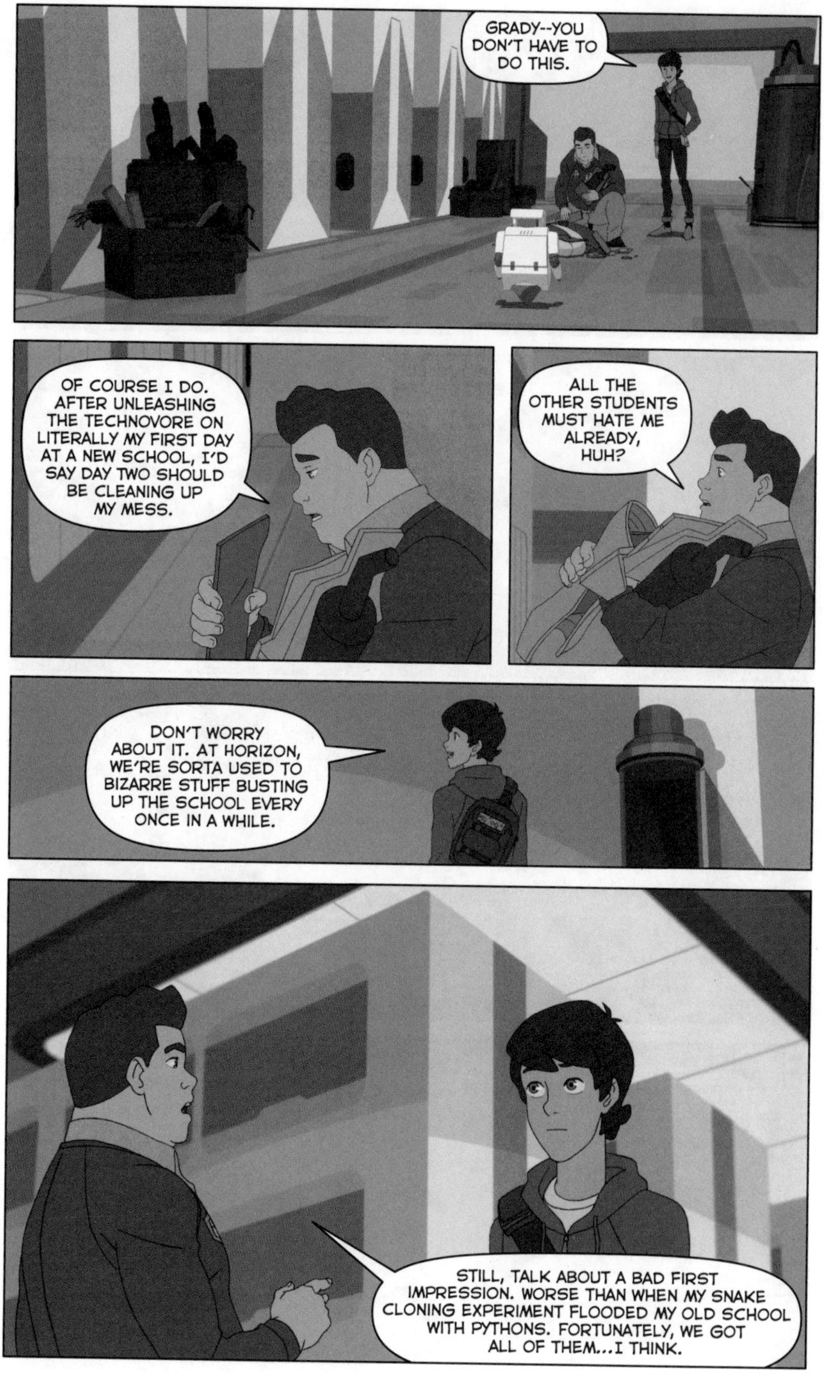
GRADY--YOU DON'T HAVE TO DO THIS.
OF COURSE I DO. AFTER UNLEASHING THE TECHNOVORE ON LITERALLY MY FIRST DAY AT A NEW SCHOOL, I'D SAY DAY TWO SHOULD BE CLEANING UP MY MESS.
ALL THE OTHER STUDENTS MUST HATE ME ALREADY, HUH?
DON'T WORRY ABOUT IT. AT HORIZON, WE'RE SORTA USED TO BIZARRE STUFF BUSTING UP THE SCHOOL EVERY ONCE IN A WHILE.
STILL, TALK ABOUT A BAD FIRST IMPRESSION. WORSE THAN WHEN MY SNAKE CLONING EXPERIMENT FLOODED MY OLD SCHOOL WITH PYTHONS. FORTUNATELY, WE GOT ALL OF THEM...I THINK.

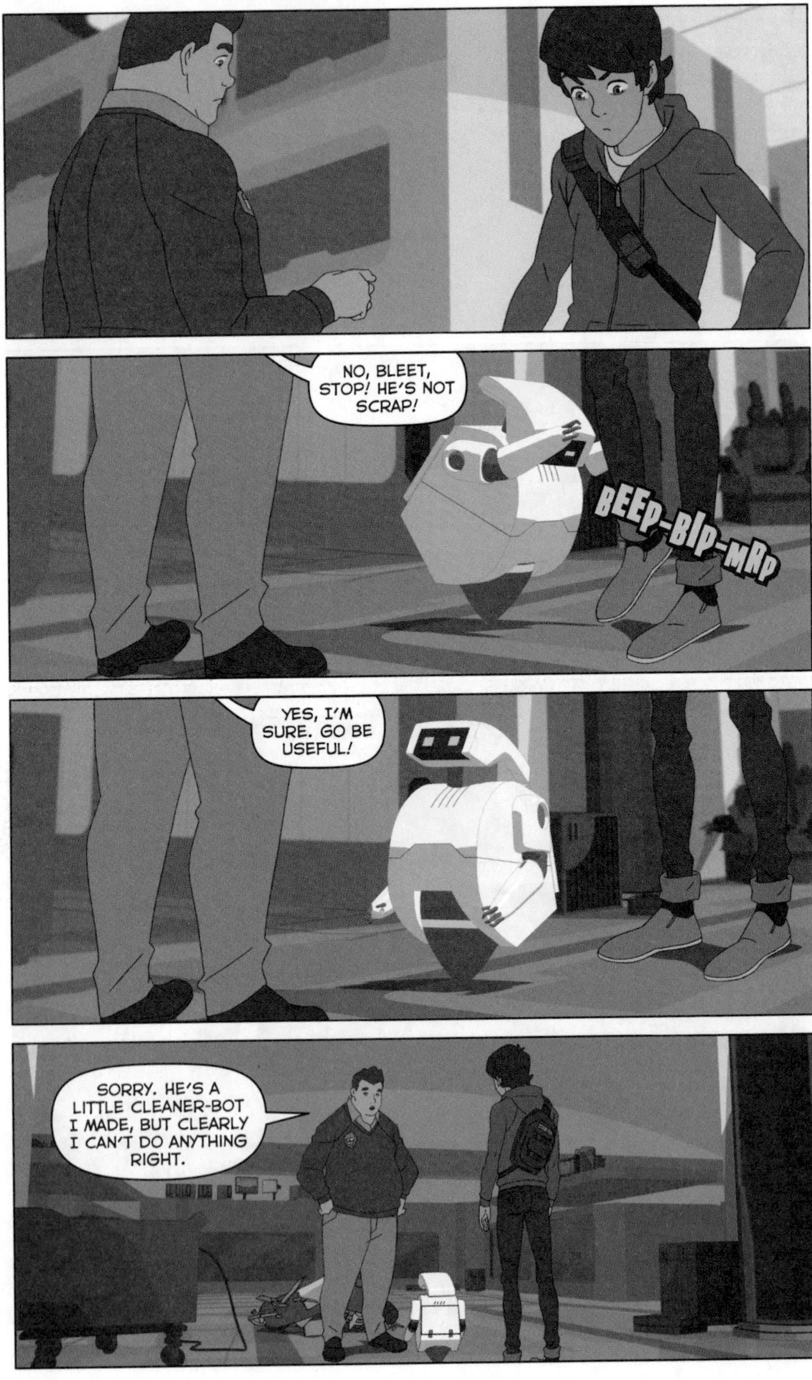
NO, BLEET, STOP! HE'S NOT SCRAP!
BEEP-BLP-MRP
YES, I'M SURE. GO BE USEFUL!
SORRY. HE'S A LITTLE CLEANER-BOT I MADE, BUT CLEARLY I CAN'T DO ANYTHING RIGHT.

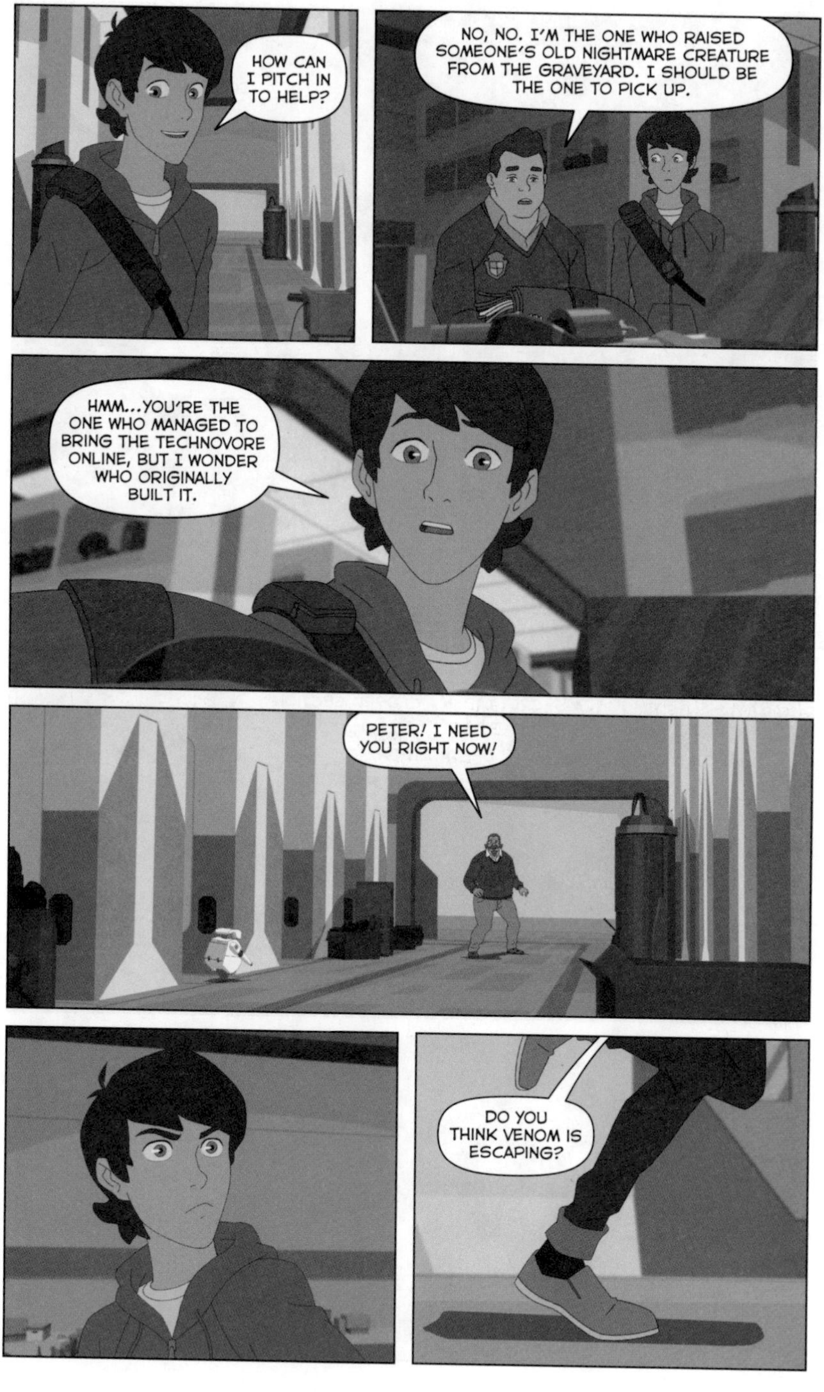
HOW CAN I PITCH IN TO HELP?
NO, NO. I'M THE ONE WHO RAISED SOMEONE'S OLD NIGHTMARE CREATURE FROM THE GRAVEYARD. I SHOULD BE THE ONE TO PICK UP.
HMM...YOU'RE THE ONE WHO MANAGED TO BRING THE TECHNOVORE ONLINE, BUT I WONDER WHO ORIGINALLY BUILT IT.
PETER! I NEED YOU RIGHT NOW!
DO YOU THINK VENOM IS ESCAPING?

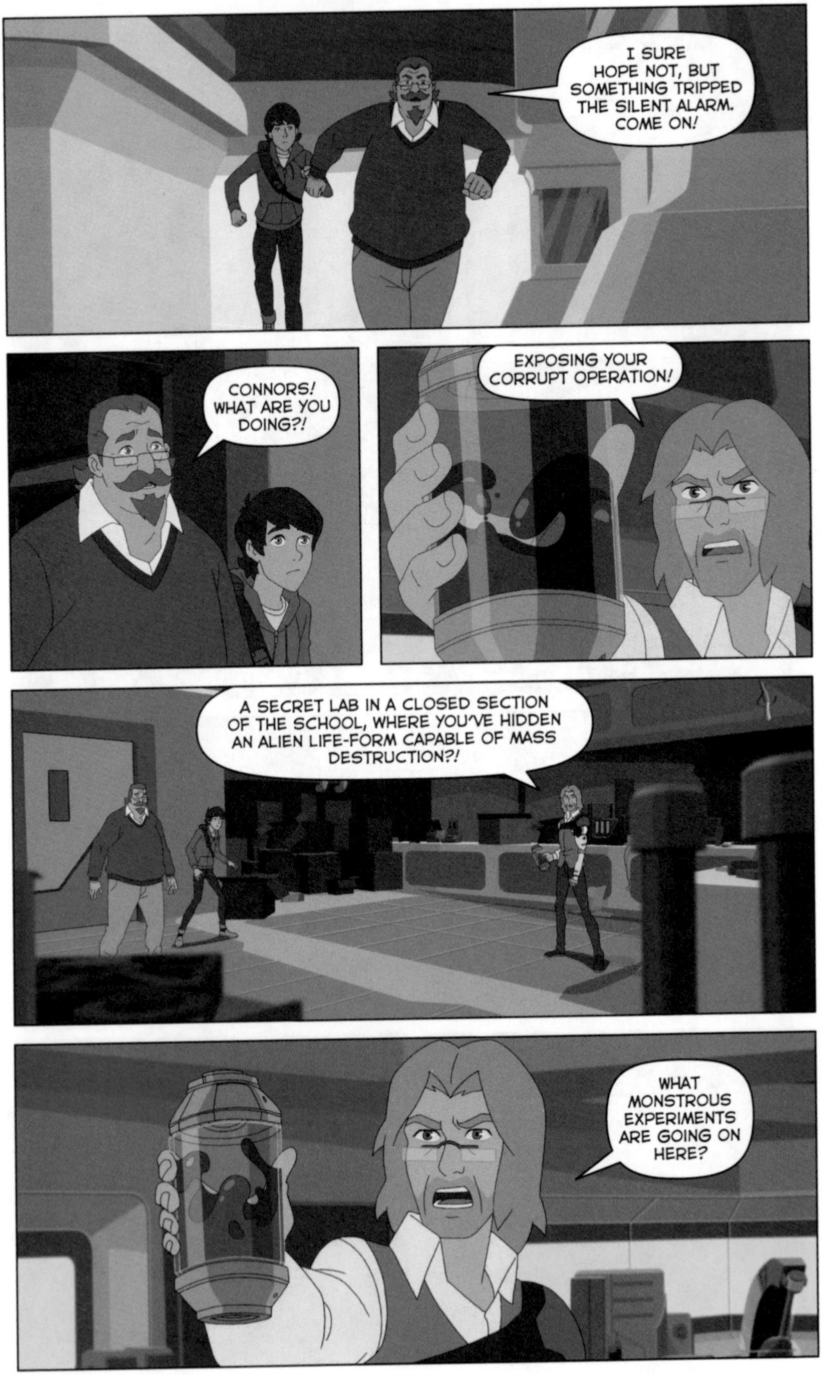
I SURE HOPE NOT, BUT SOMETHING TRIPPED THE SILENT ALARM. COME ON!
CONNORS! WHAT ARE YOU DOING?!
EXPOSING YOUR CORRUPT OPERATION!
A SECRET LAB IN A CLOSED SECTION OF THE SCHOOL, WHERE YOU'VE HIDDEN AN ALIEN LIFE-FORM CAPABLE OF MASS DESTRUCTION?!
WHAT MONSTROUS EXPERIMENTS ARE GOING ON HERE?

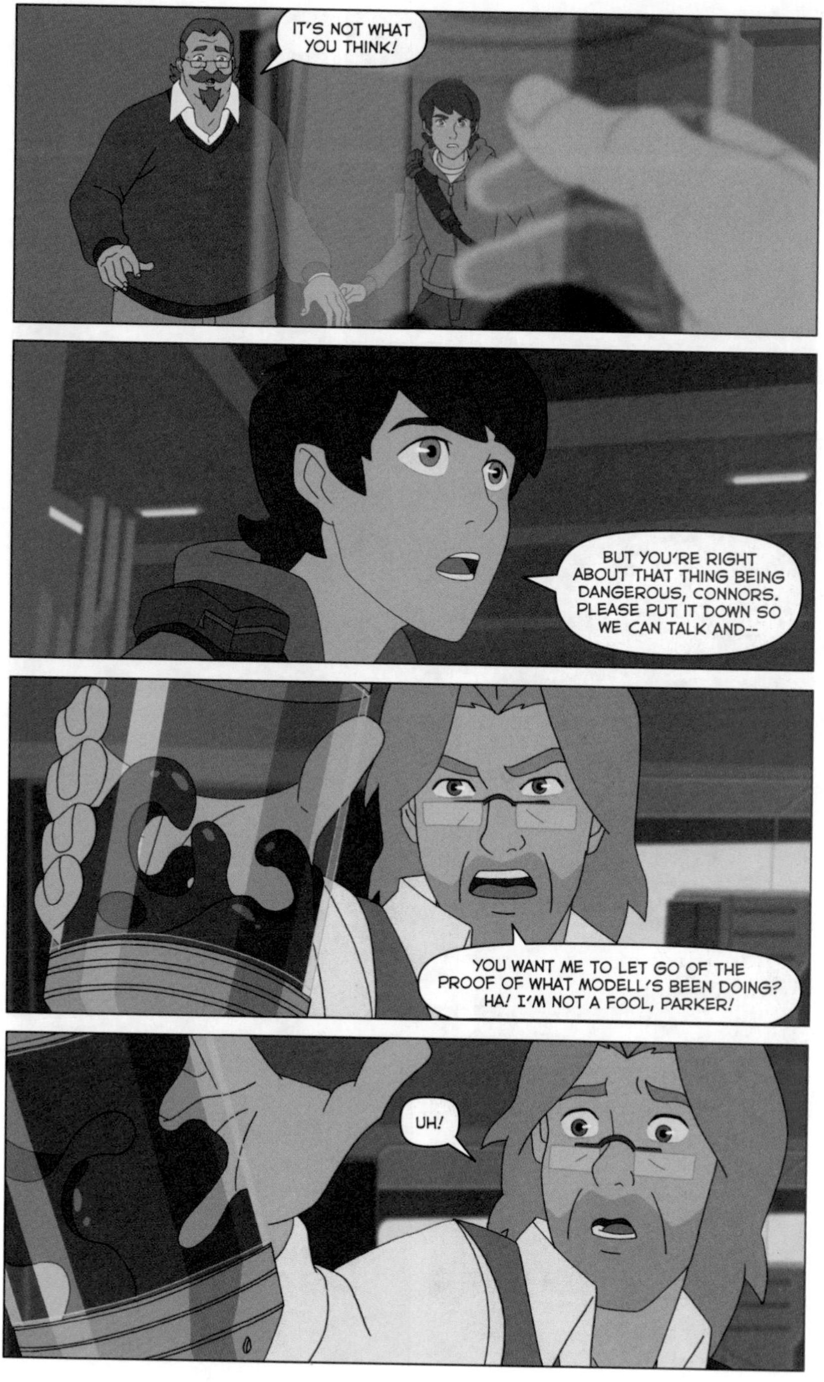
IT'S NOT WHAT YOU THINK!
BUT YOU'RE RIGHT ABOUT THAT THING BEING DANGEROUS, CONNORS. PLEASE PUT IT DOWN SO WE CAN TALK AND--
YOU WANT ME TO LET GO OF THE PROOF OF WHAT MODELL'S BEEN DOING? HA! I'M NOT A FOOL, PARKER!
UH!

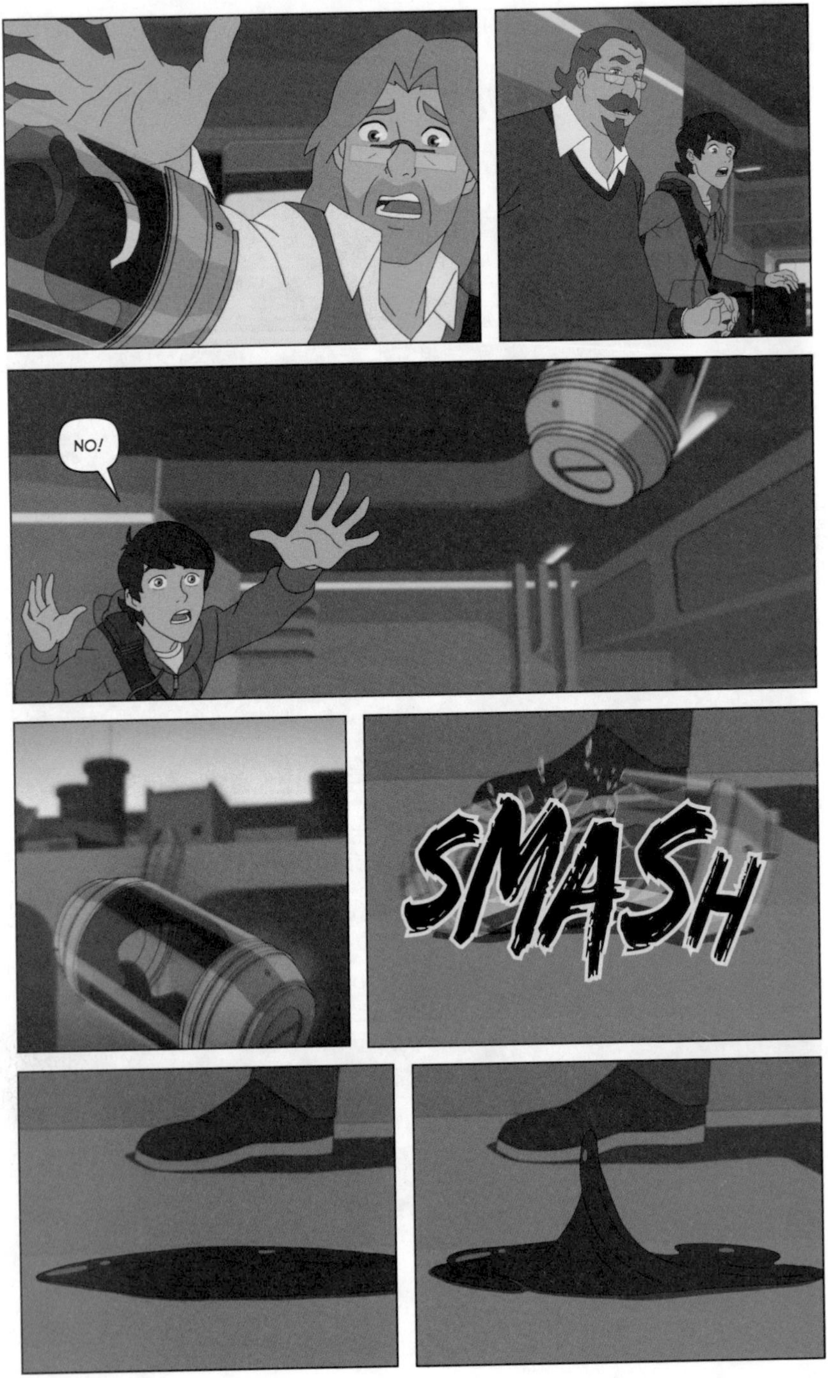
NO!
SMASH

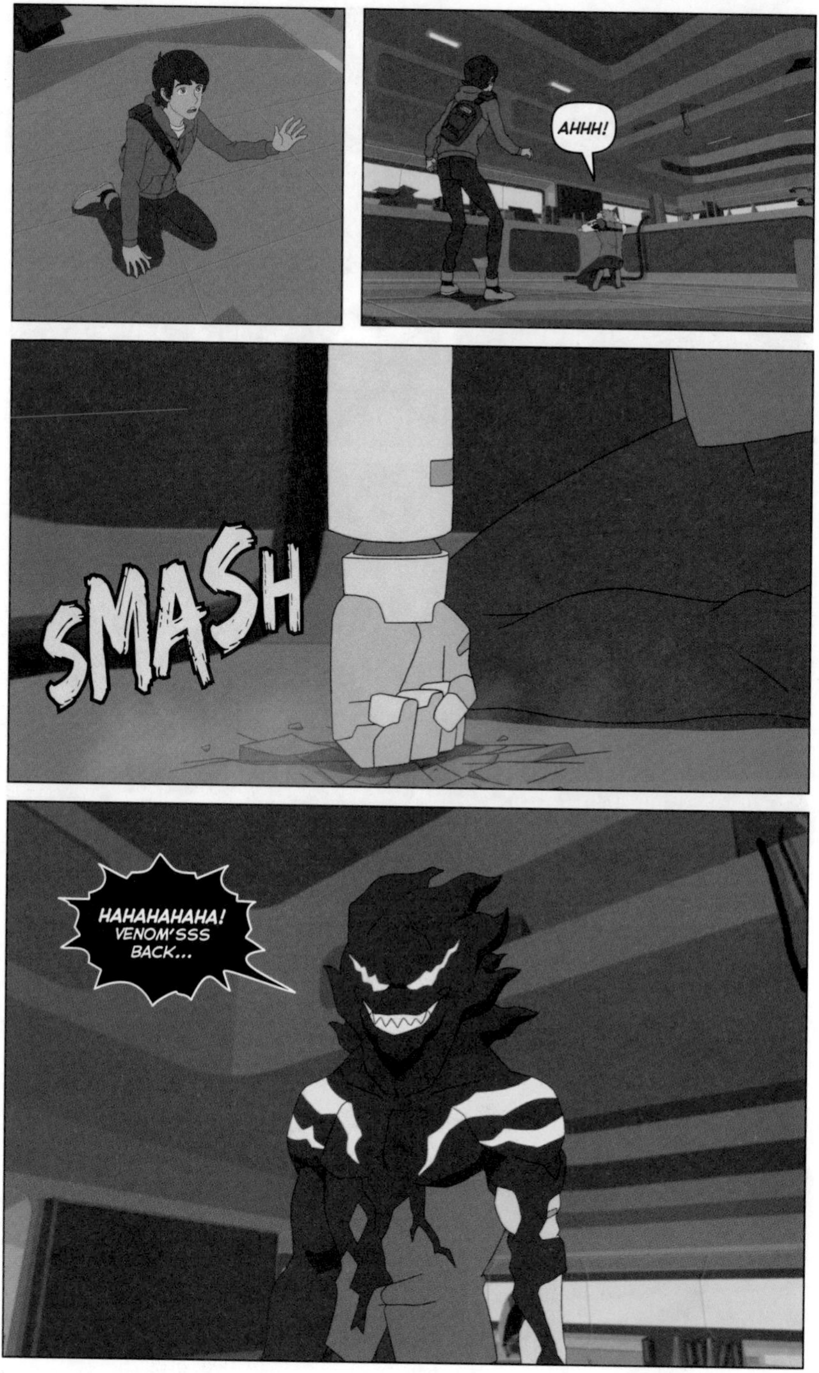
AHHH!
SMASH
HAHAHAHAHA! VENOM'SSS BACK...

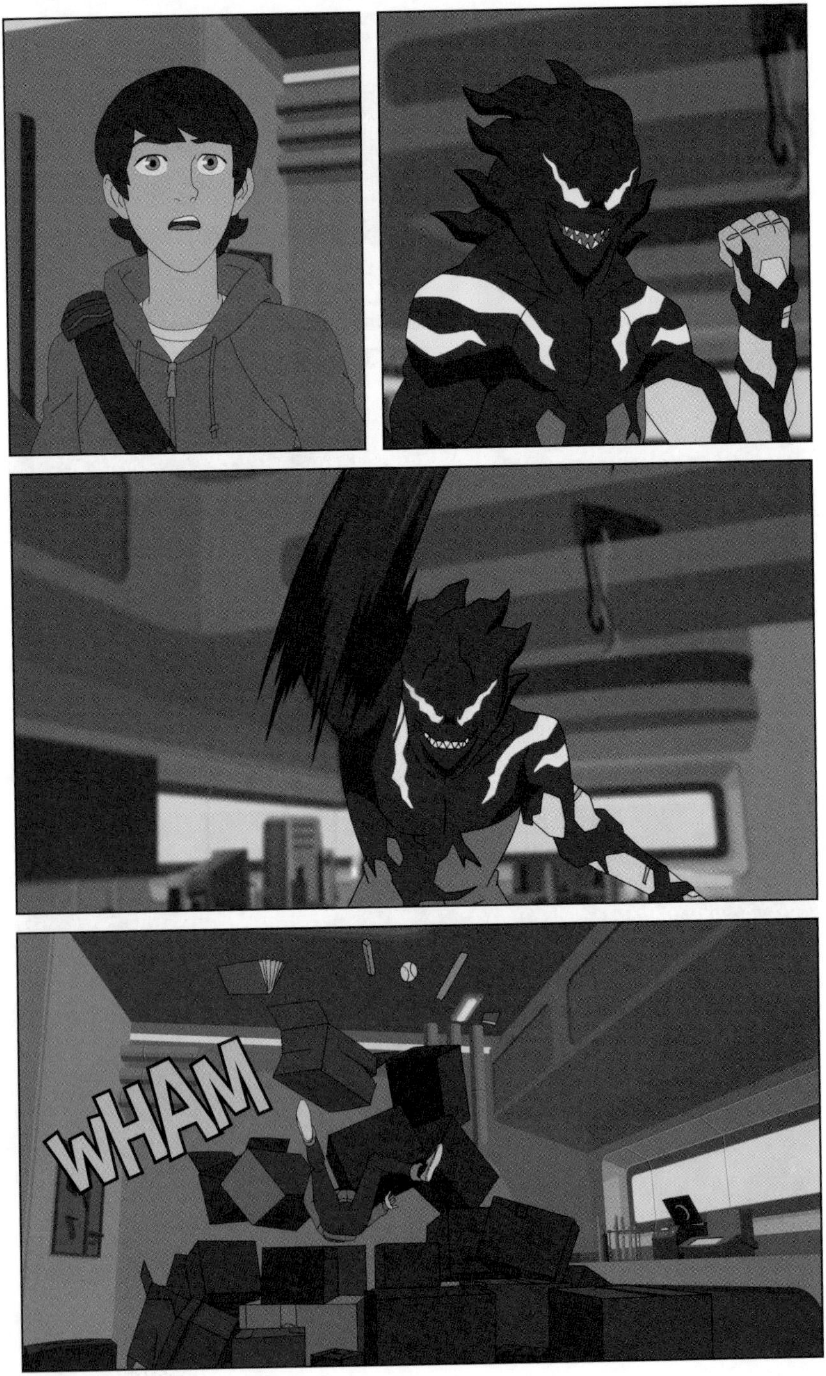
wHAM

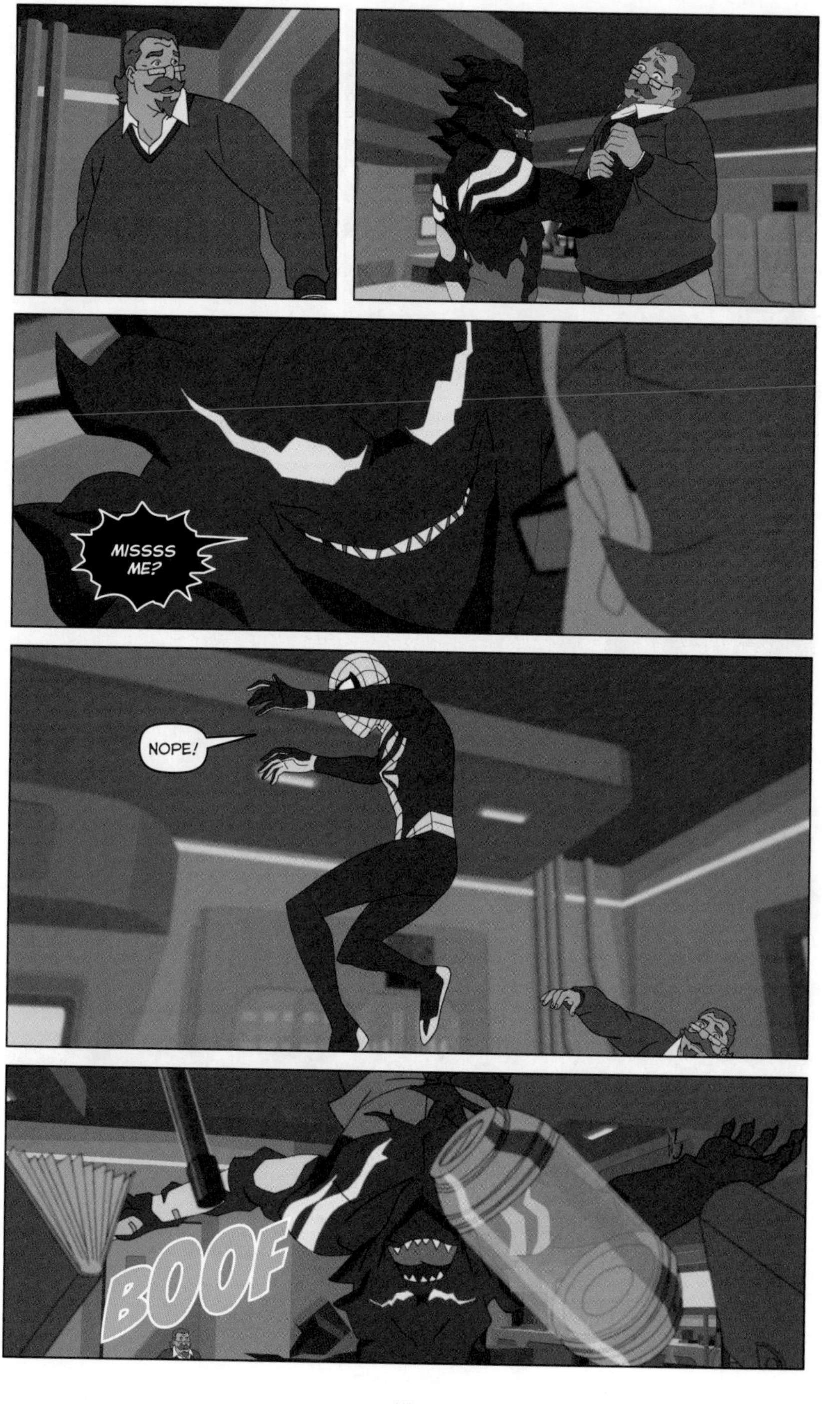
MISSSS
ME?
NOPE!
BOOF

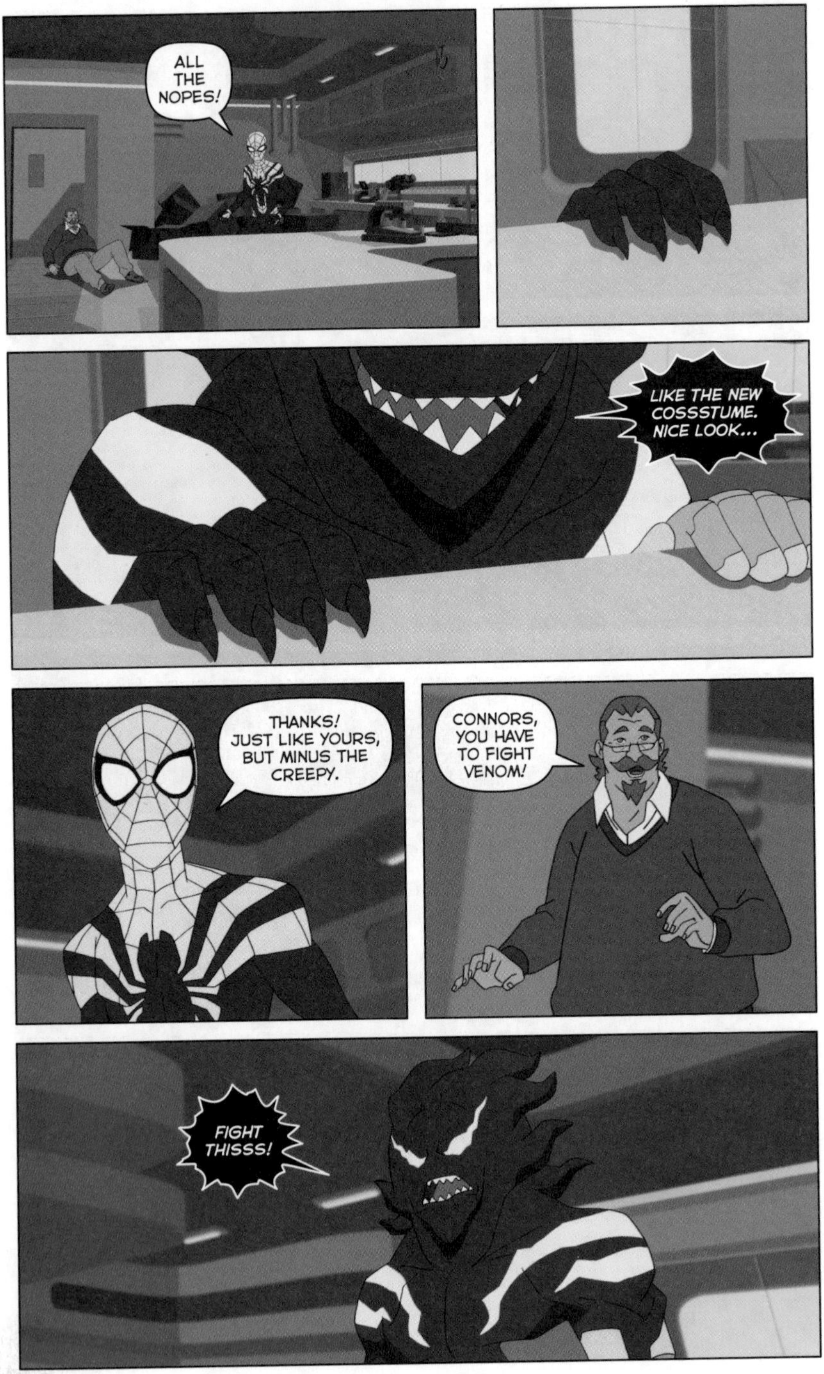
ALL THE NOPES!
LIKE THE NEW COSSSTUME. NICE LOOK...
THANKS! JUST LIKE YOURS, BUT MINUS THE CREEPY.
CONNORS, YOU HAVE TO FIGHT VENOM!
FIGHT THISSS!

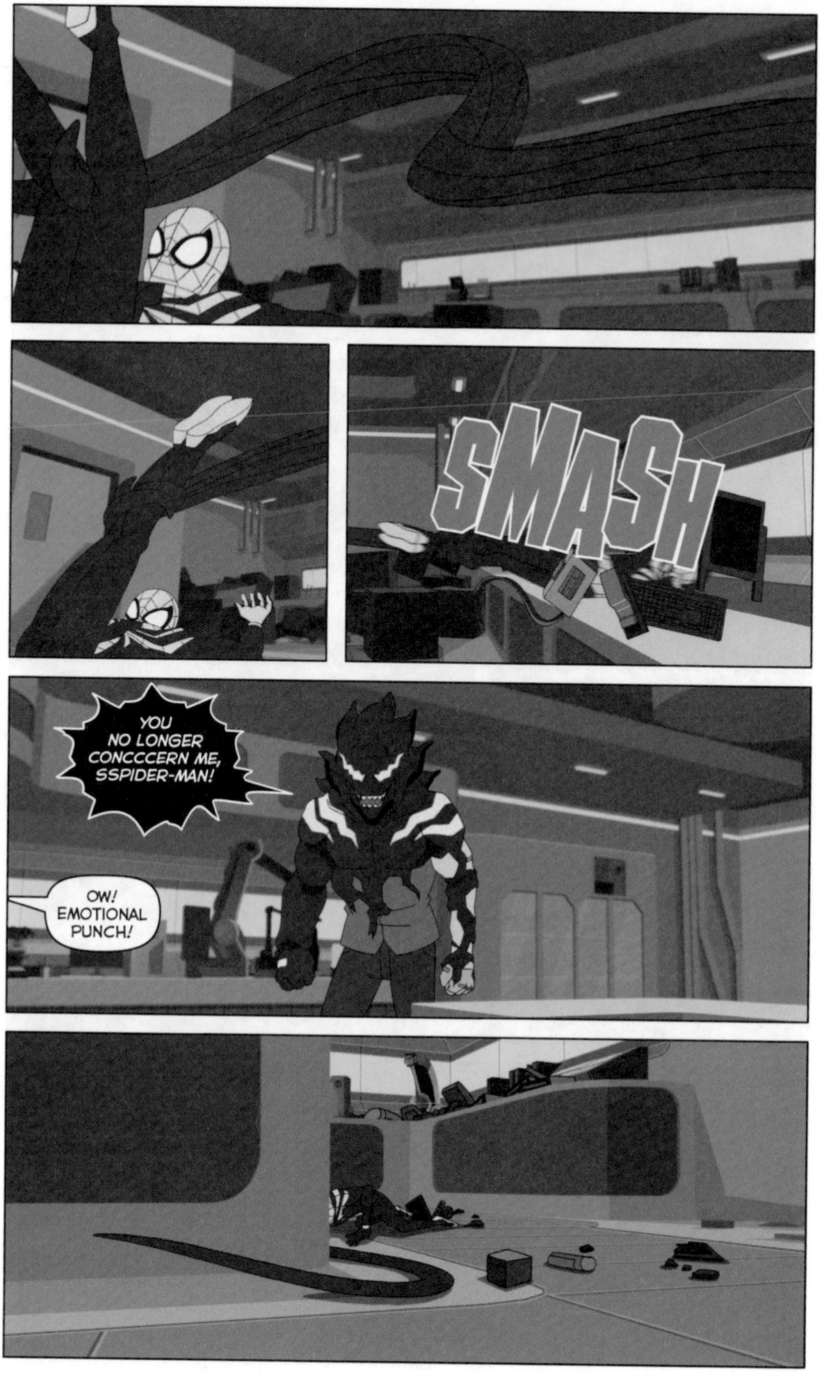

SMASH
YOU NO LONGER CONCCCERN ME, SSPIDER-MAN!
OW! EMOTIONAL PUNCH!

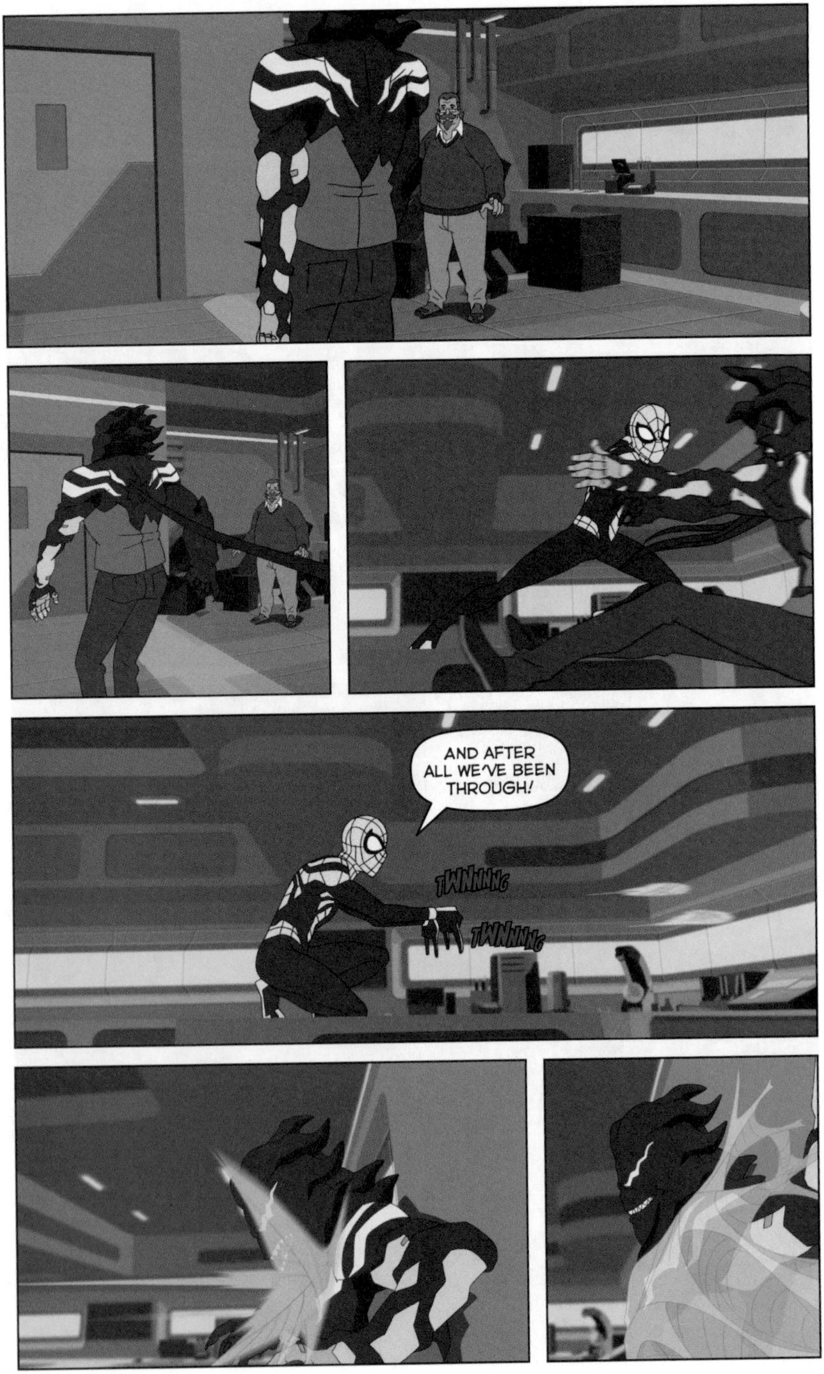
AND AFTER ALL WE'VE BEEN THROUGH!
TWNNNNG
TWNNNNG

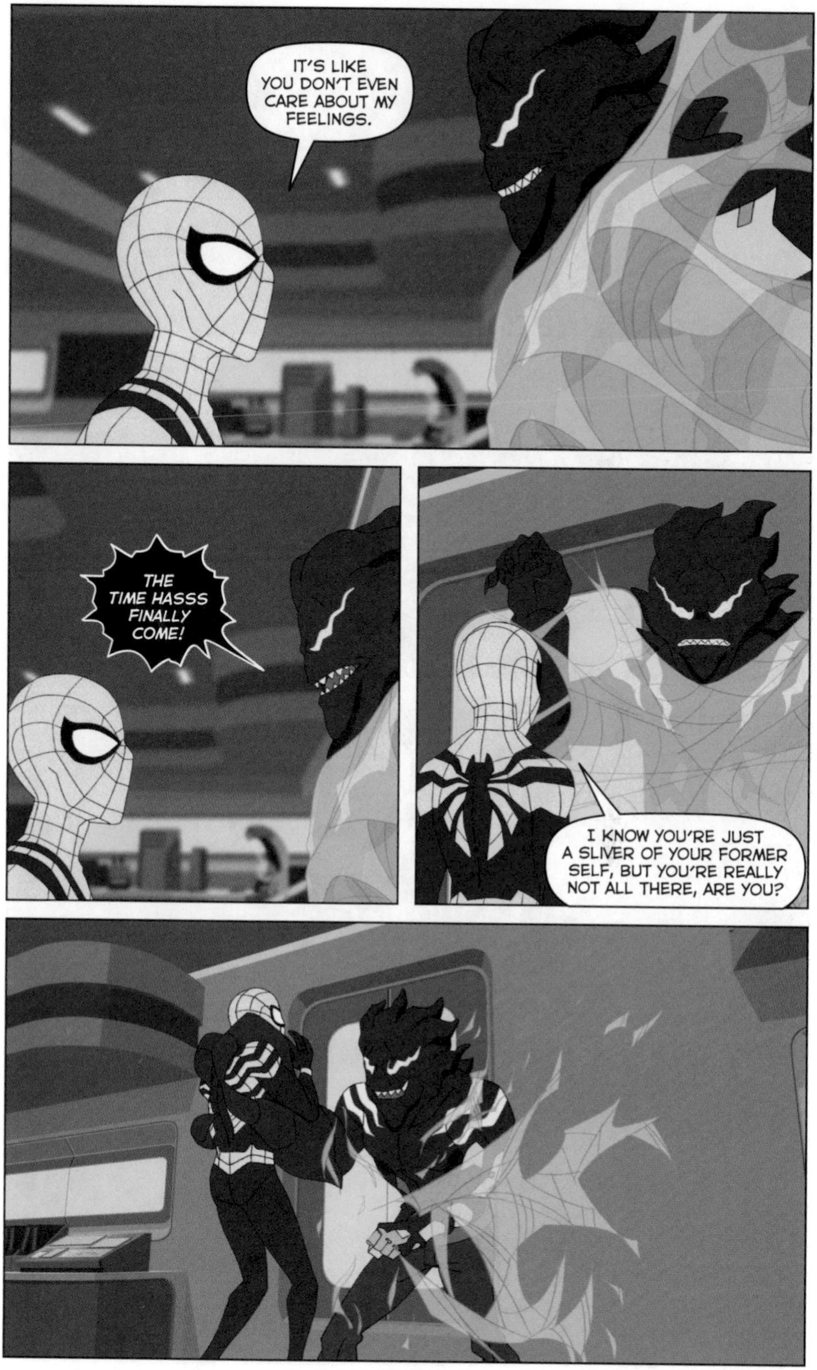
IT'S LIKE YOU DON'T EVEN CARE ABOUT MY FEELINGS.
THE TIME HASSS FINALLY COME!
I KNOW YOU'RE JUST A SLIVER OF YOUR FORMER SELF, BUT YOU'RE REALLY NOT ALL THERE, ARE YOU?

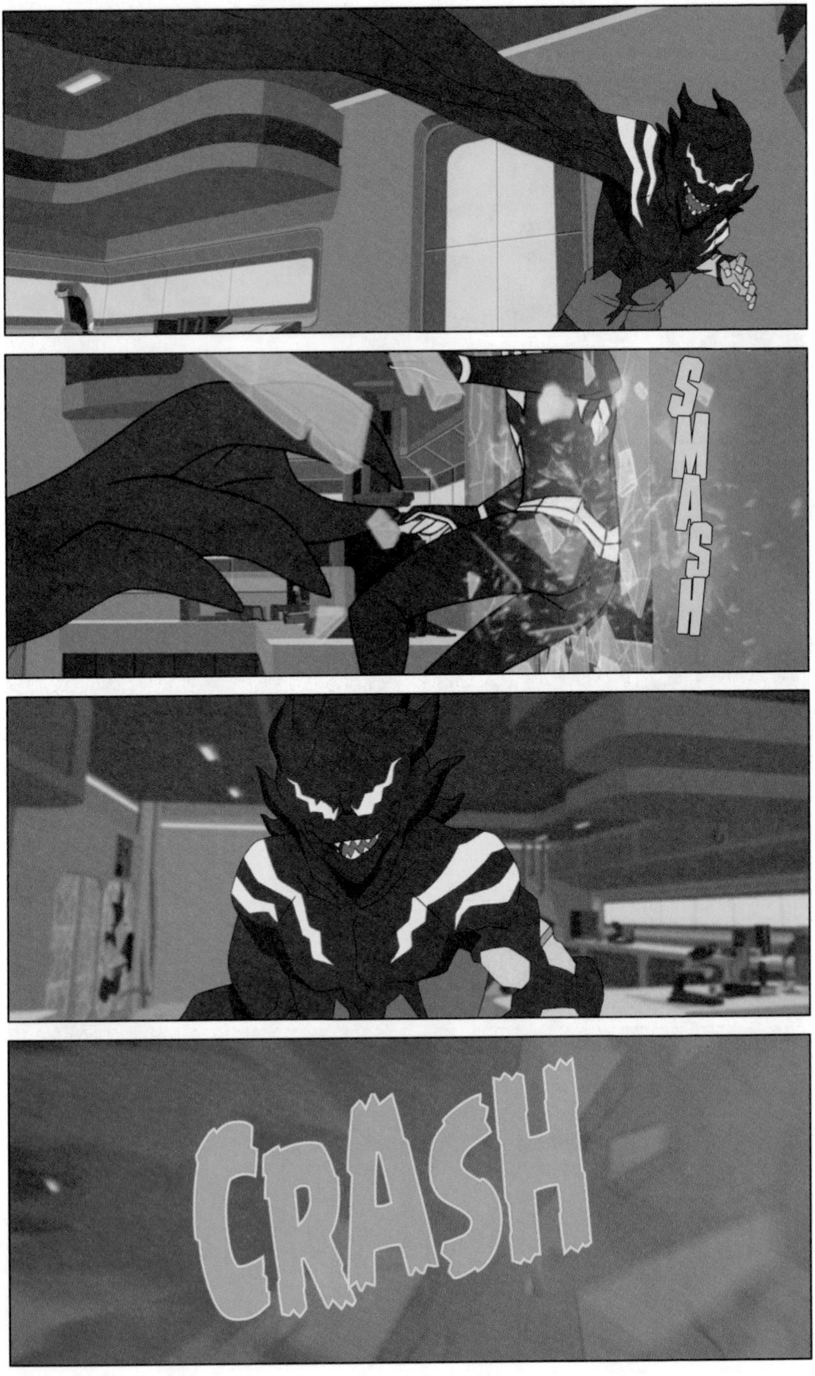
SMASH
CRASH

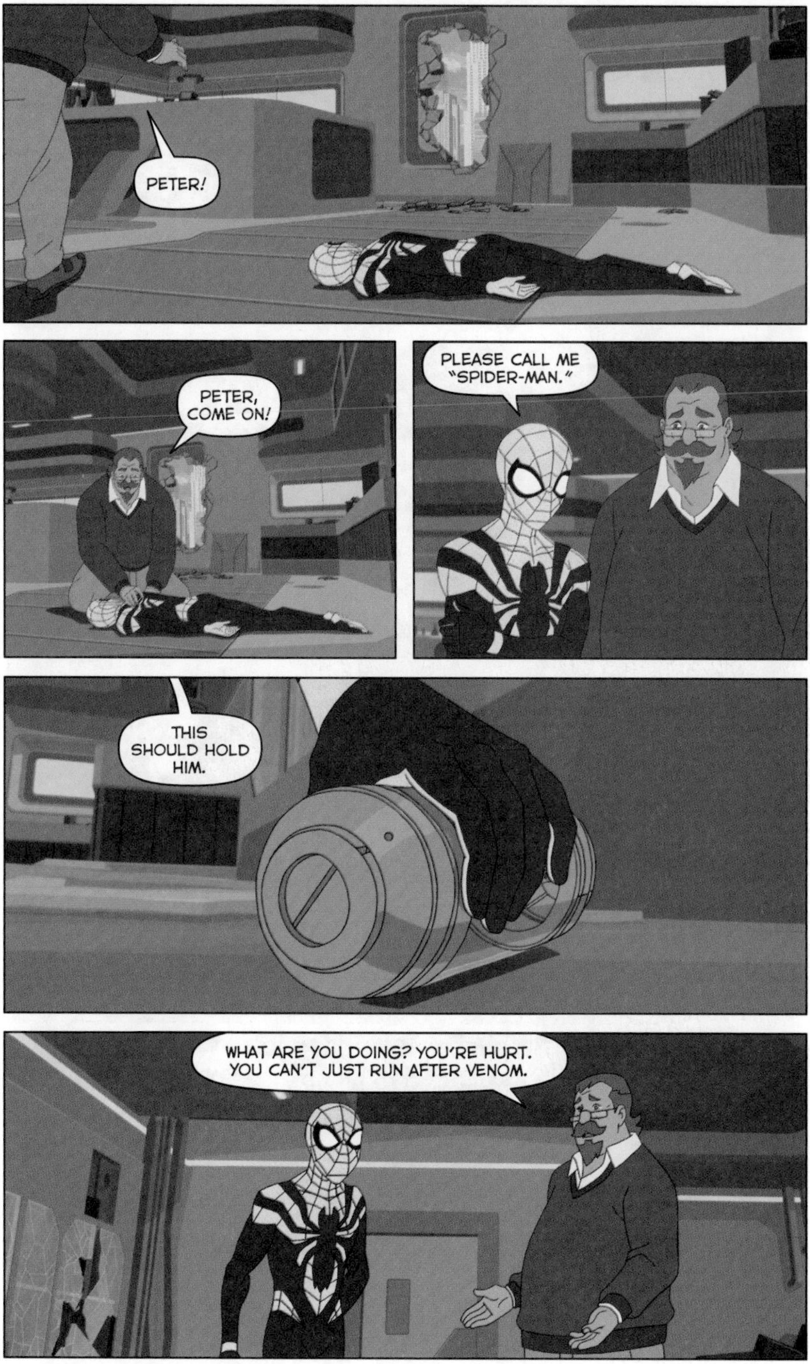

PETER!
PETER, COME ON!
PLEASE CALL ME "SPIDER-MAN."
THIS SHOULD HOLD HIM.
WHAT ARE YOU DOING? YOU'RE HURT. YOU CAN'T JUST RUN AFTER VENOM.

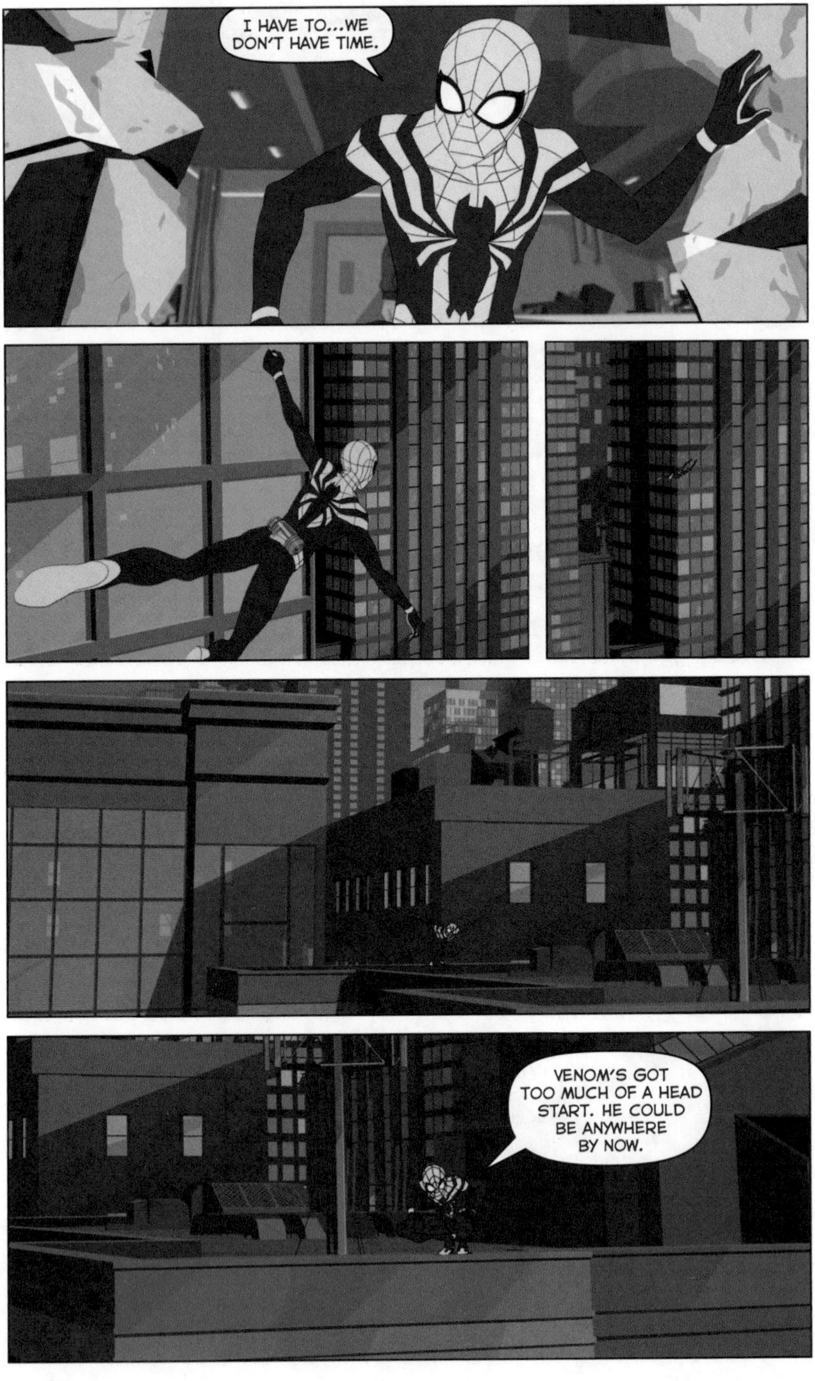
I HAVE TO...WE DON'T HAVE TIME.
VENOM'S GOT TOO MUCH OF A HEAD START. HE COULD BE ANYWHERE BY NOW.

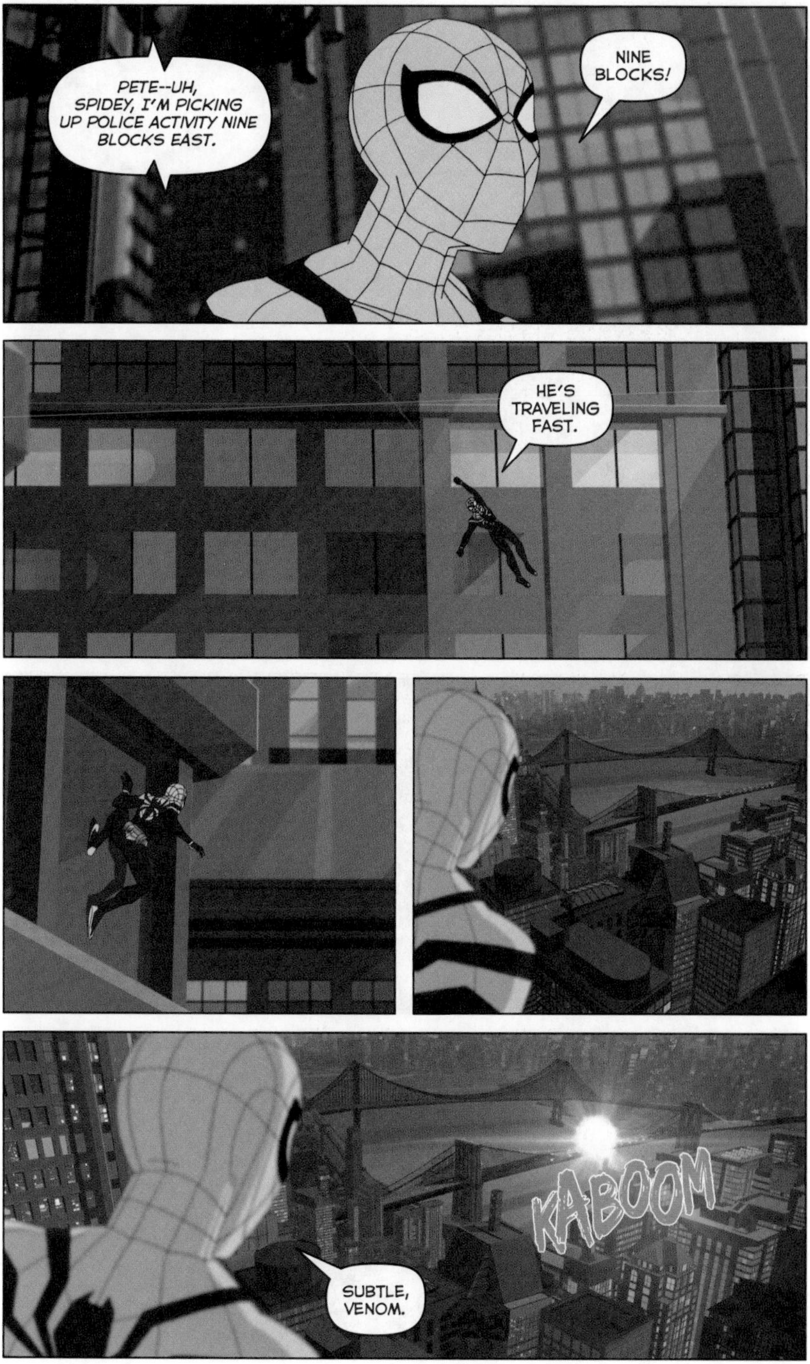
PETE--UH, SPIDEY, I'M PICKING UP POLICE ACTIVITY NINE BLOCKS EAST.
NINE BLOCKS!
HE'S TRAVELING FAST.
KABOOM
SUBTLE, VENOM.

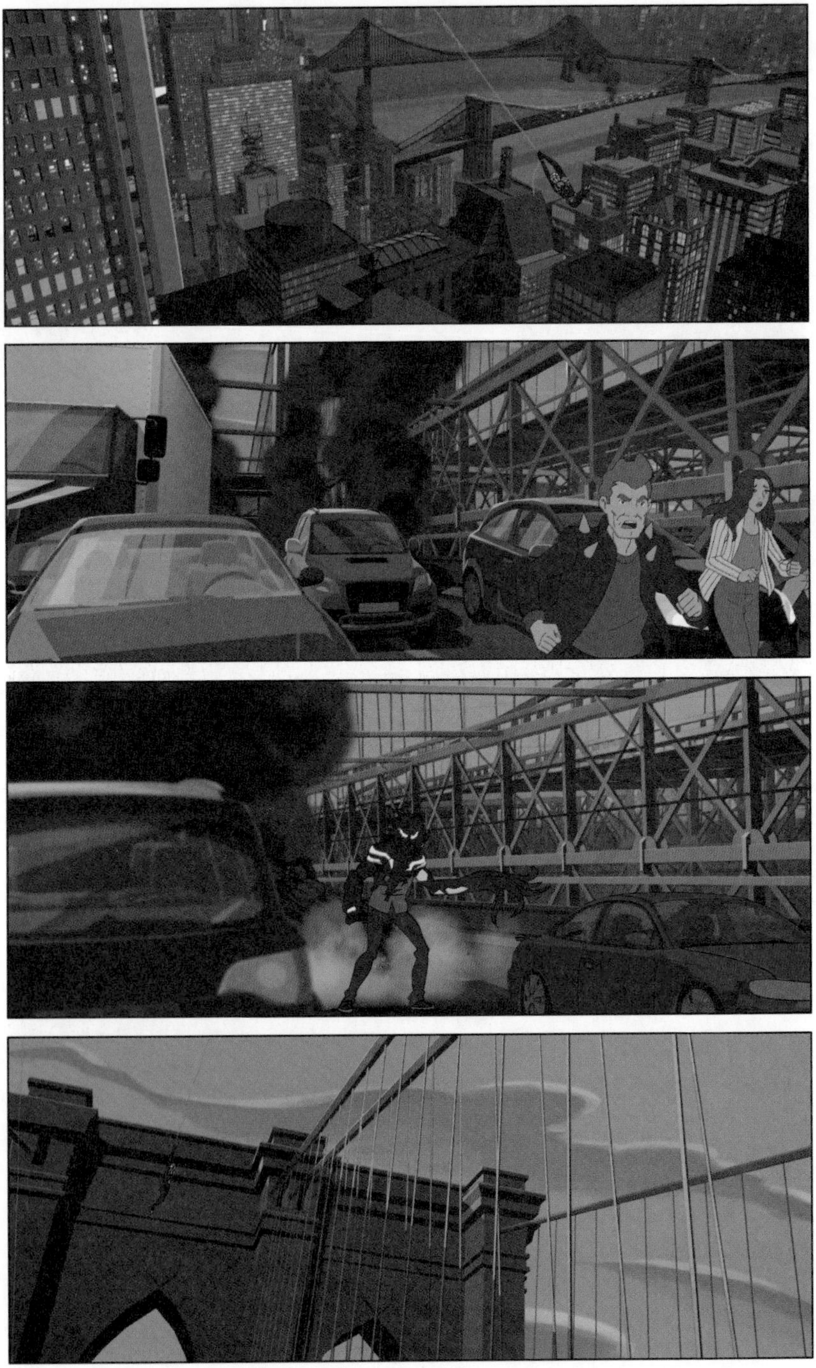

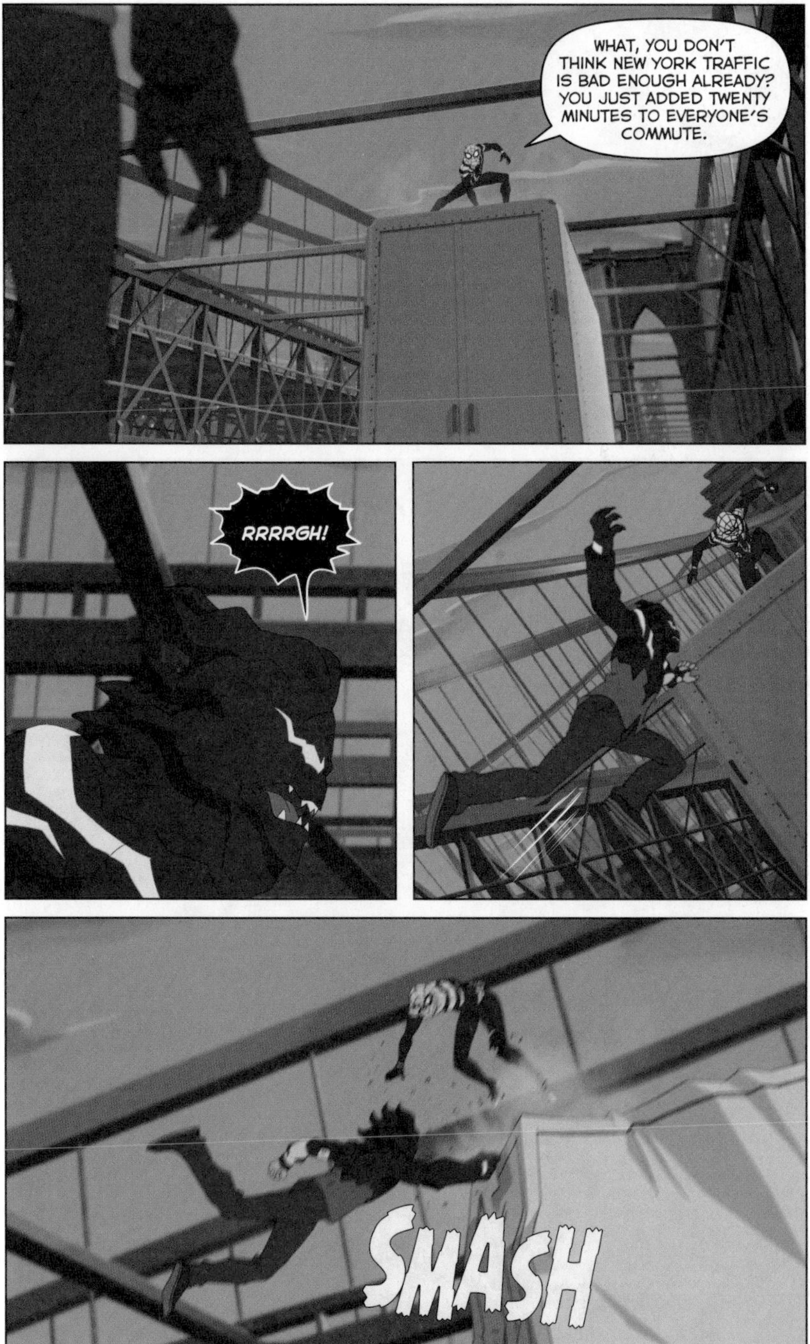

WHAT, YOU DON'T THINK NEW YORK TRAFFIC IS BAD ENOUGH ALREADY? YOU JUST ADDED TWENTY MINUTES TO EVERYONE'S COMMUTE.
RRRRGH!
SMASH

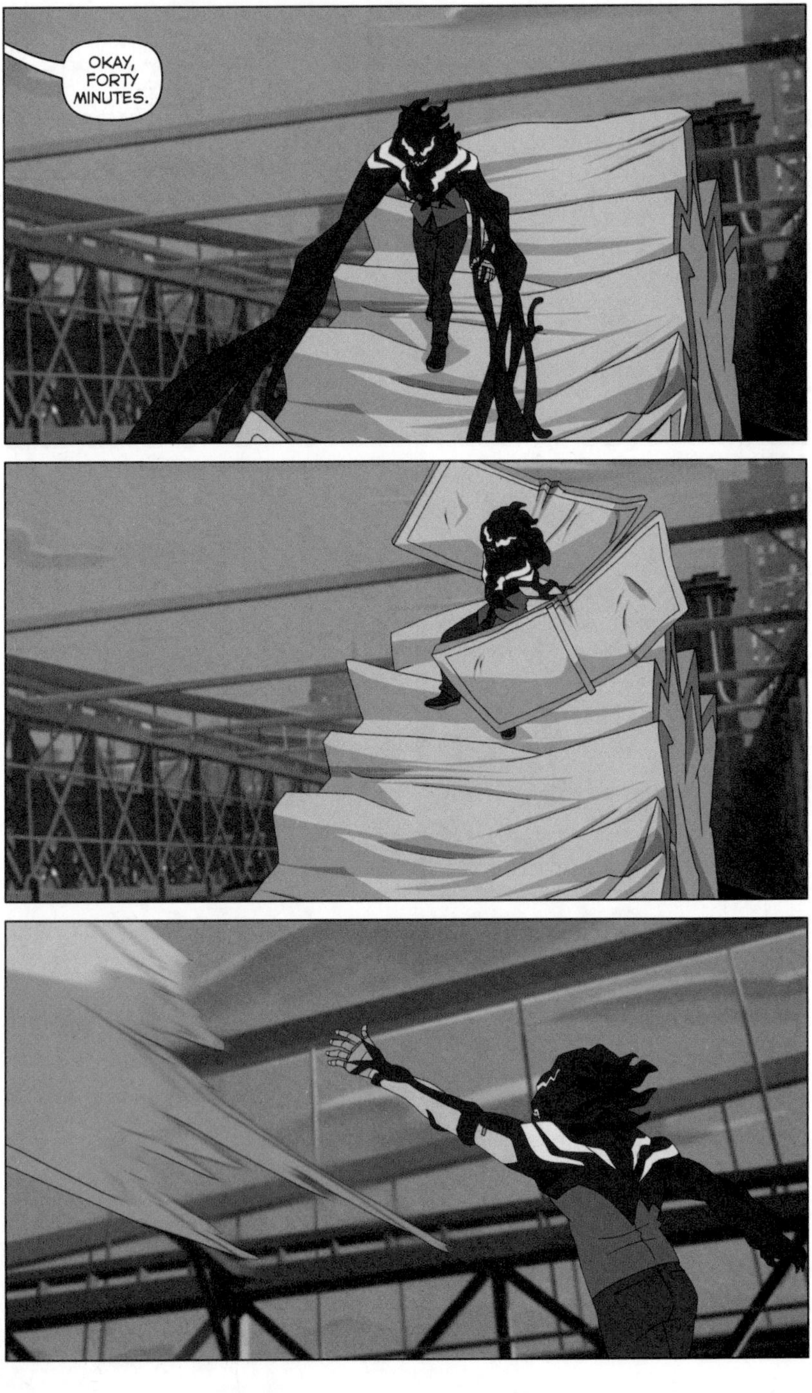
OKAY, FORTY MINUTES.

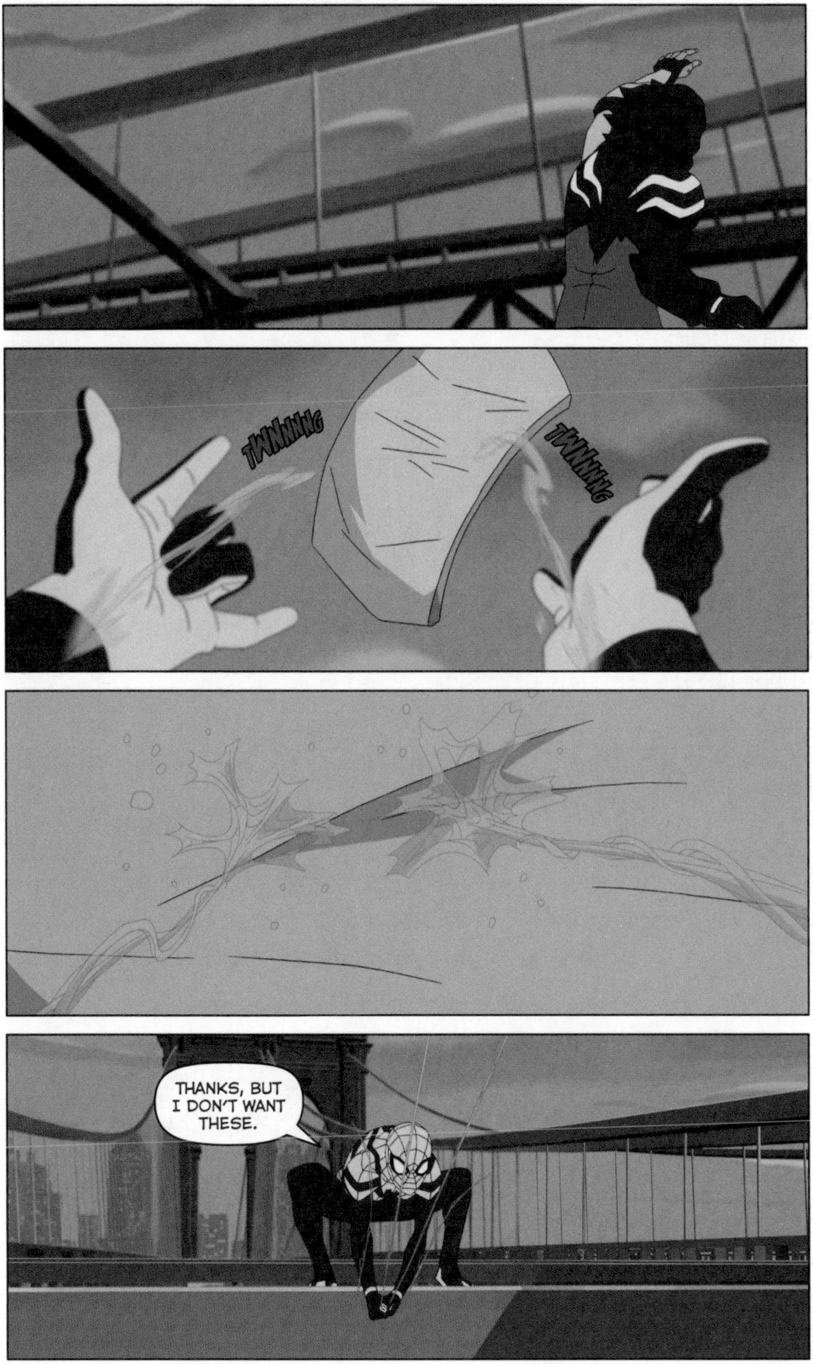
TWNNNNG
TWNNNNG
THANKS, BUT I DON'T WANT THESE.

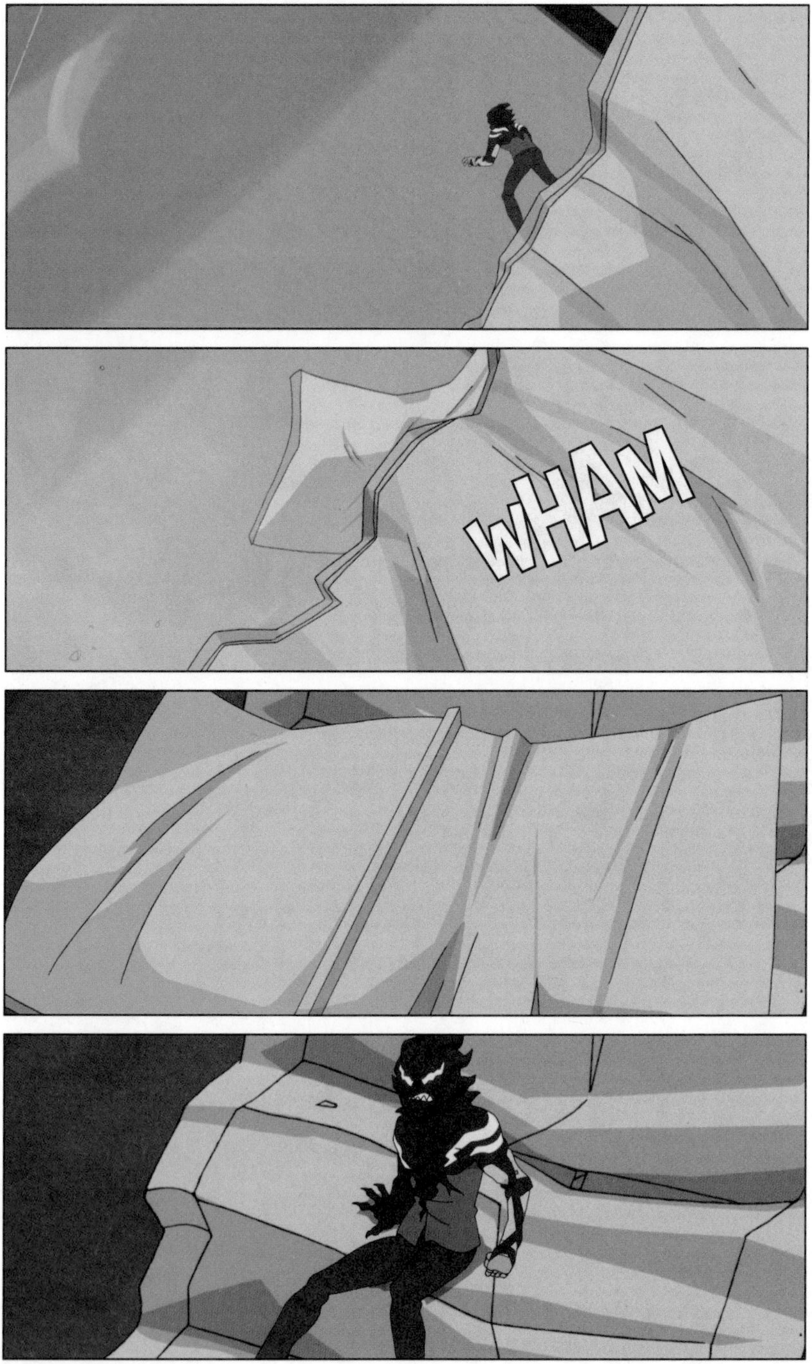
wHAM

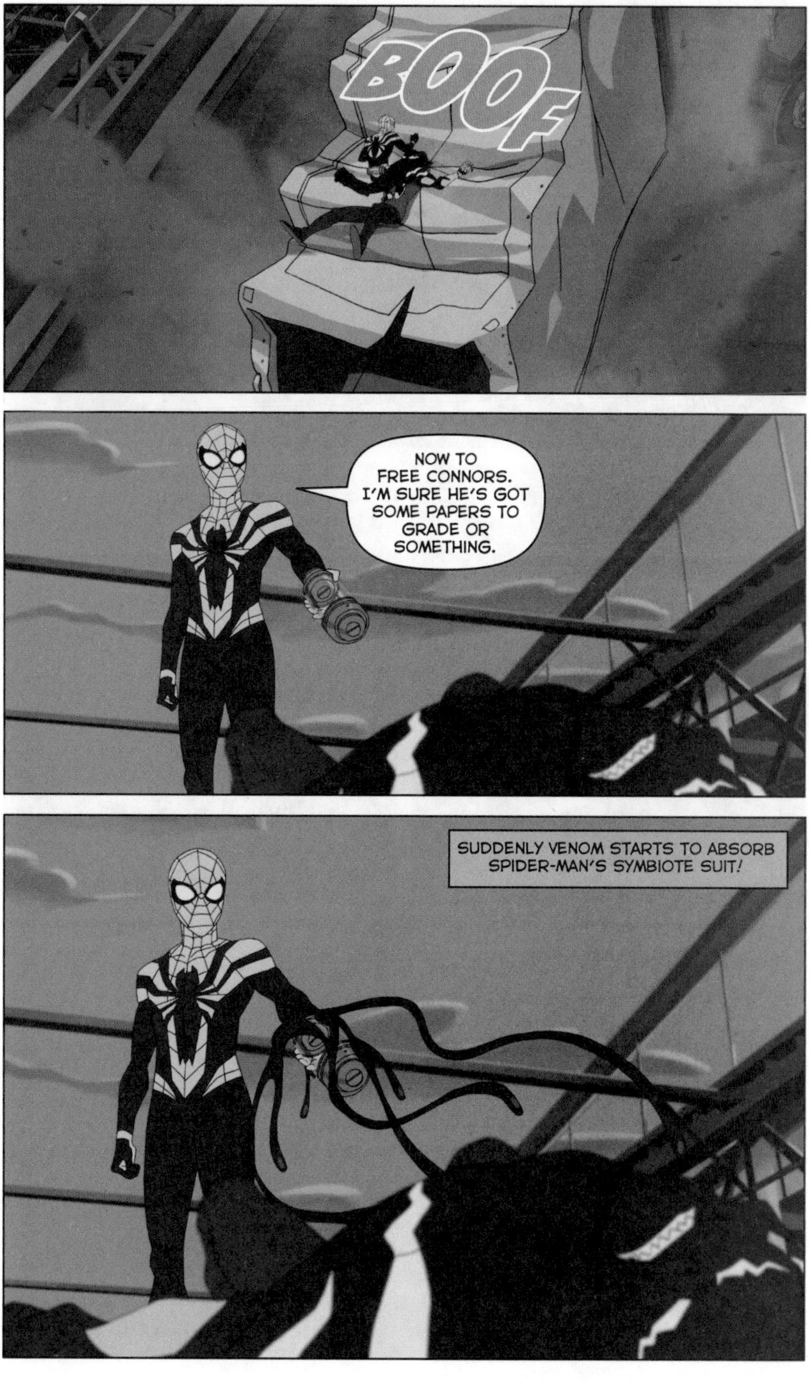
BOOF
NOW TO FREE CONNORS. I'M SURE HE'S GOT SOME PAPERS TO GRADE OR SOMETHING.
SUDDENLY VENOM STARTS TO ABSORB SPIDER-MAN'S SYMBIOTE SUIT!

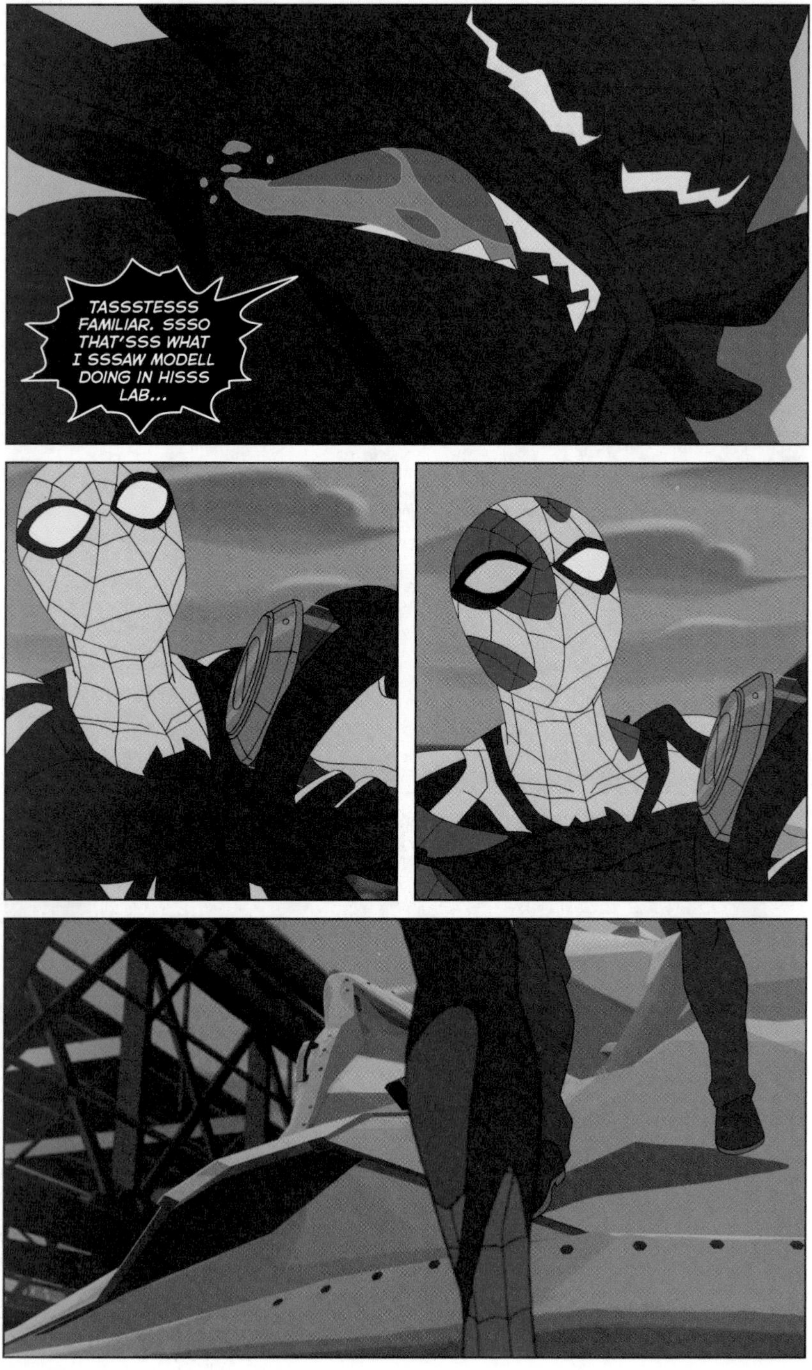
TASSSTESSS FAMILIAR. SSSO THAT'SSS WHAT I SSSAW MODELL DOING IN HISSS LAB...

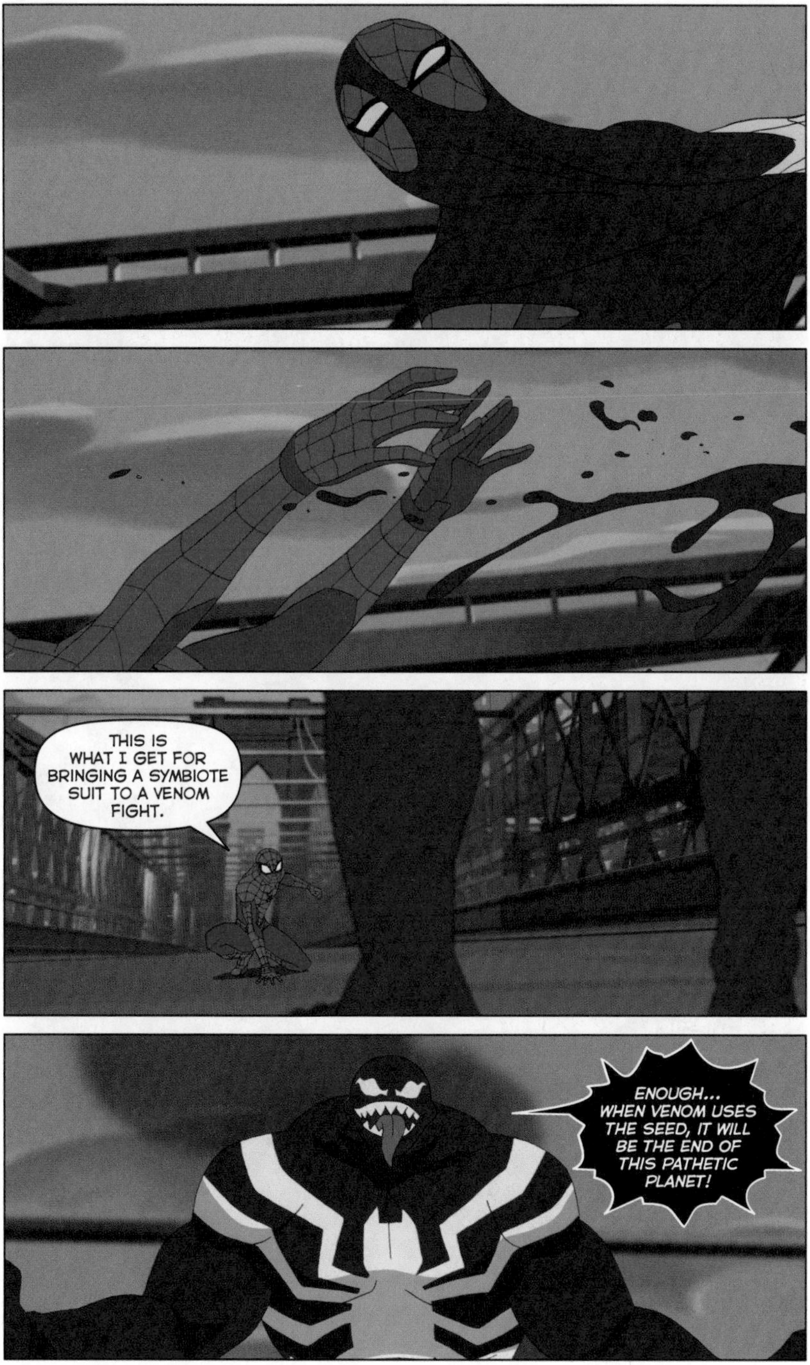
THIS IS WHAT I GET FOR BRINGING A SYMBIOTE SUIT TO A VENOM FIGHT.
ENOUGH... WHEN VENOM USES THE SEED, IT WILL BE THE END OF THIS PATHETIC PLANET!

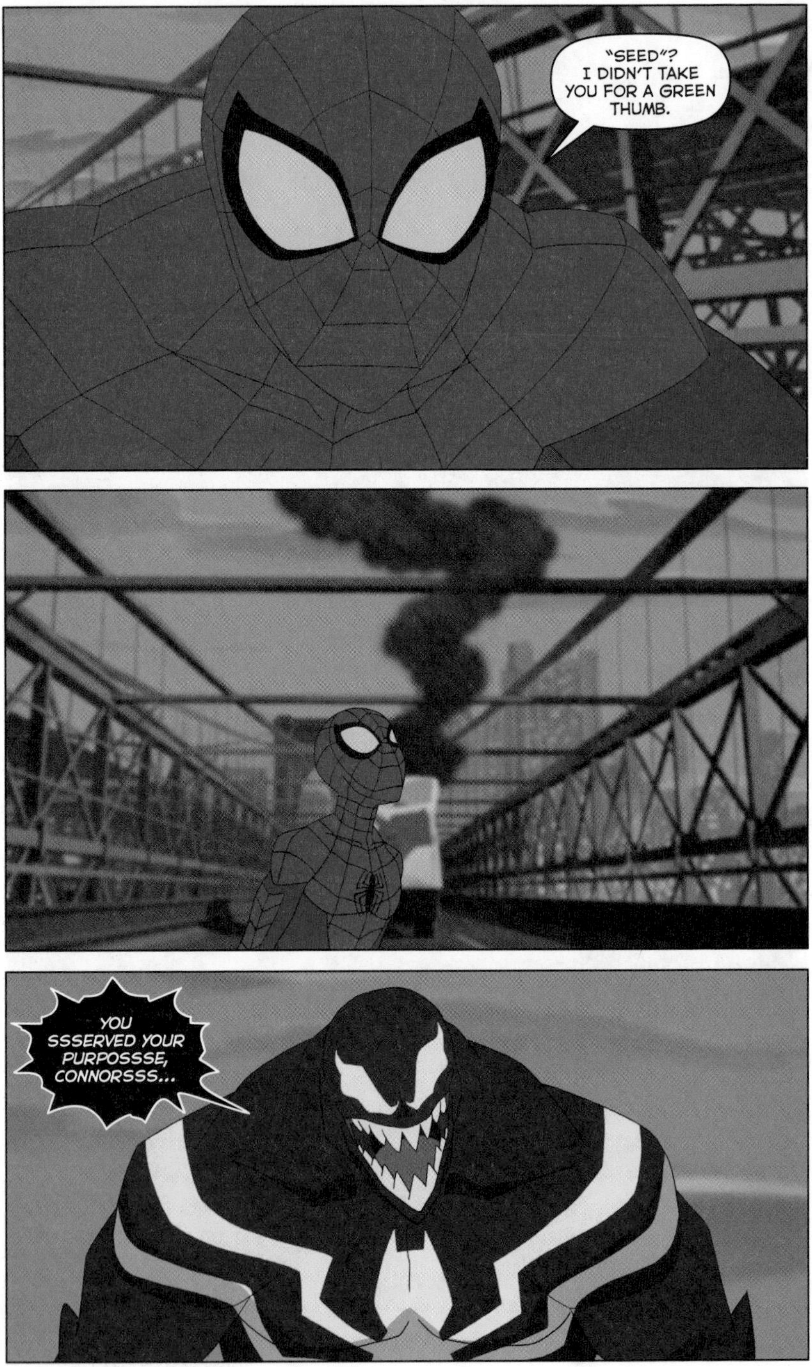
"SEED"? I DIDN'T TAKE YOU FOR A GREEN THUMB.
YOU SSSERVED YOUR PURPOSSSE, CONNORSSS...

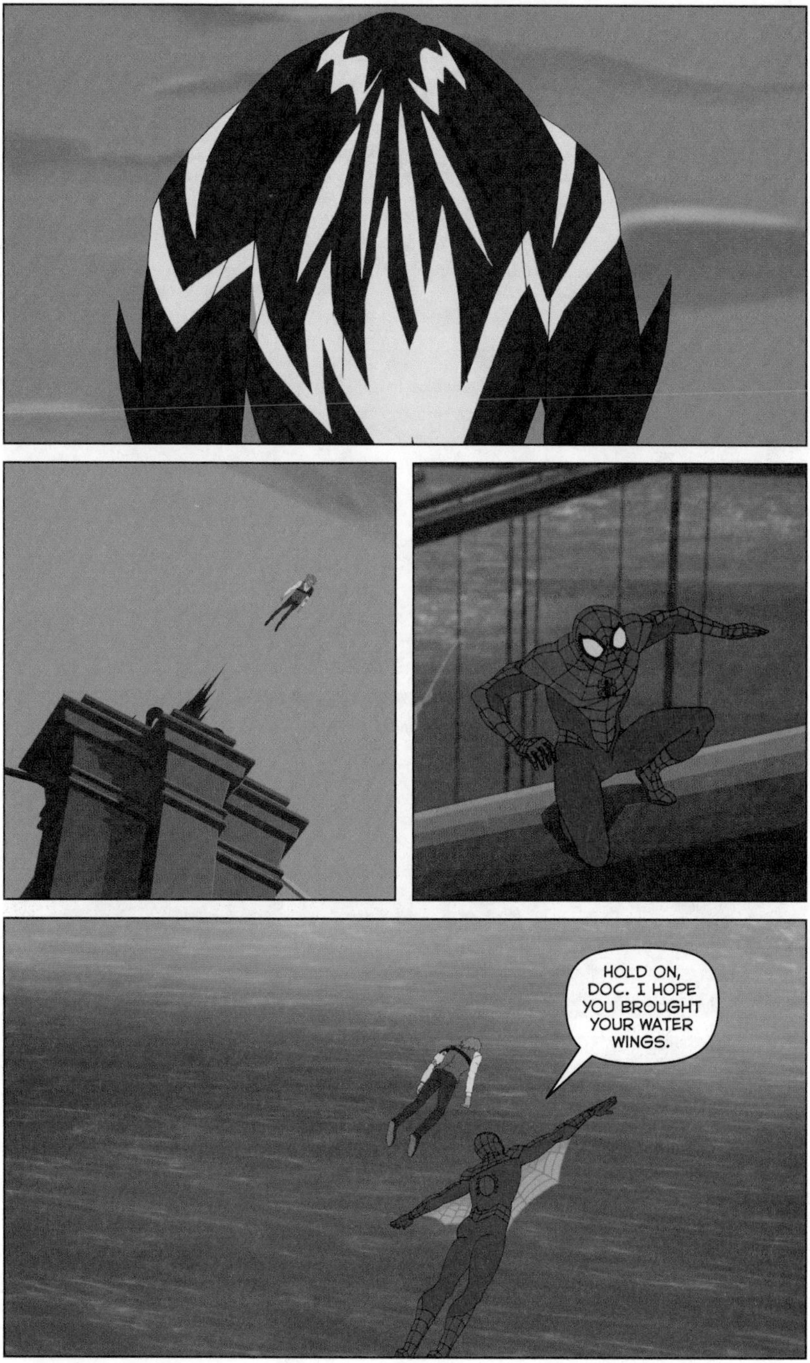
HOLD ON, DOC. I HOPE YOU BROUGHT YOUR WATER WINGS.

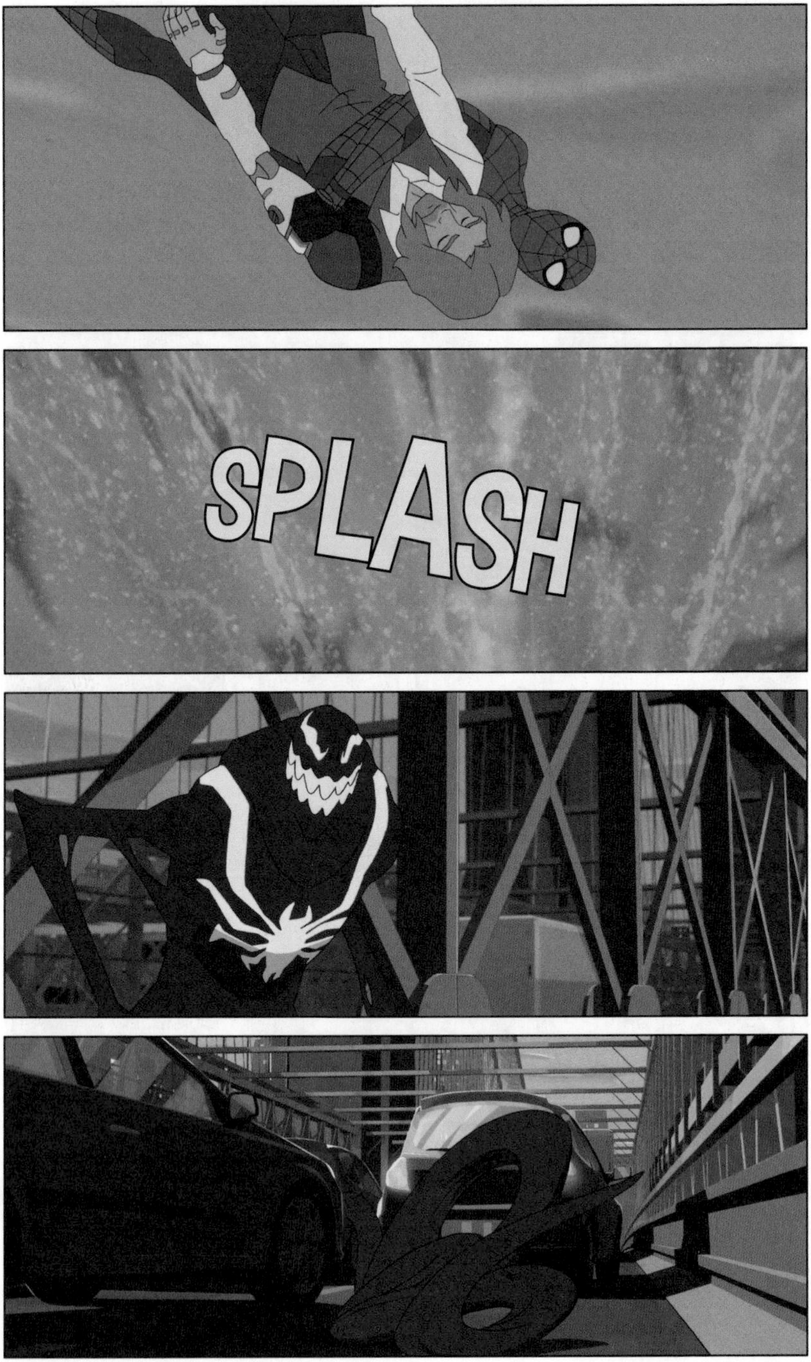
SPLASH

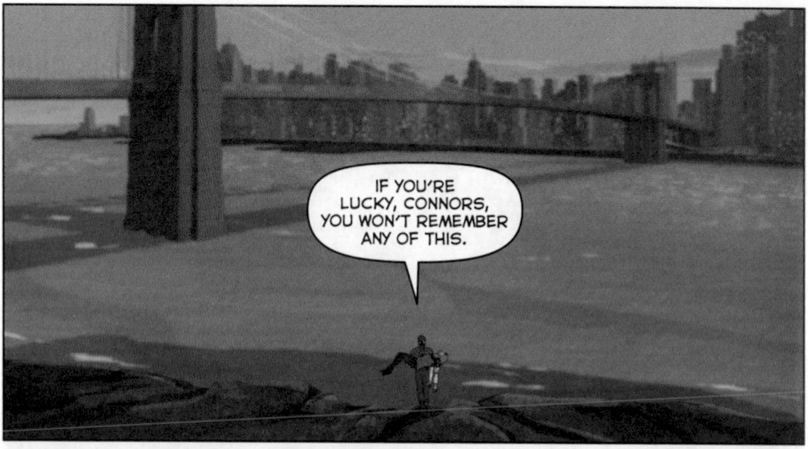
IF YOU'RE LUCKY, CONNORS, YOU WON'T REMEMBER ANY OF THIS.

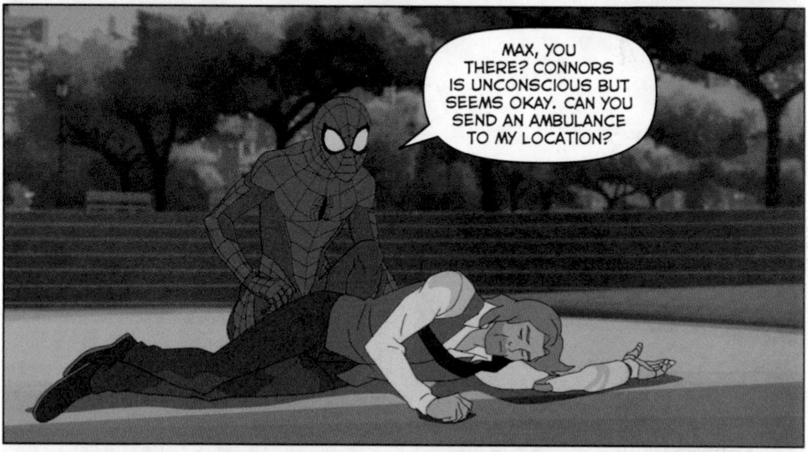
MAX, YOU THERE? CONNORS IS UNCONSCIOUS BUT SEEMS OKAY. CAN YOU SEND AN AMBULANCE TO MY LOCATION?

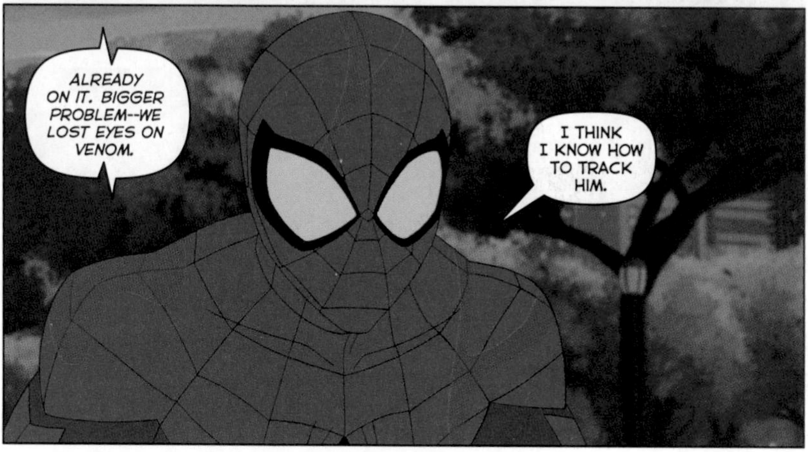
ALREADY ON IT. BIGGER PROBLEM--WE LOST EYES ON VENOM.
I THINK I KNOW HOW TO TRACK HIM.

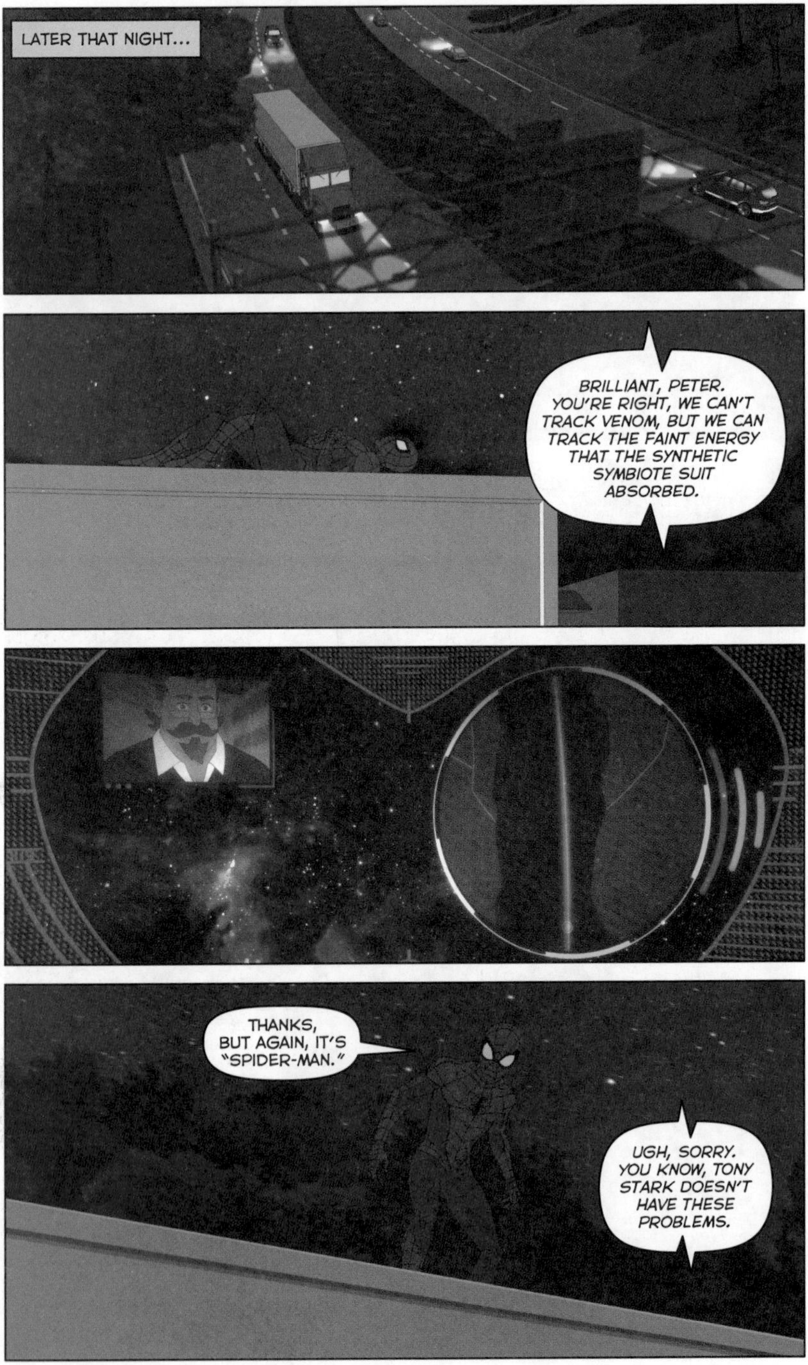
LATER THAT NIGHT...
BRILLIANT, PETER. YOU'RE RIGHT, WE CAN'T TRACK VENOM, BUT WE CAN TRACK THE FAINT ENERGY THAT THE SYNTHETIC SYMBIOTE SUIT ABSORBED.
THANKS, BUT AGAIN, IT'S "SPIDER-MAN."
UGH, SORRY. YOU KNOW, TONY STARK DOESN'T HAVE THESE PROBLEMS.

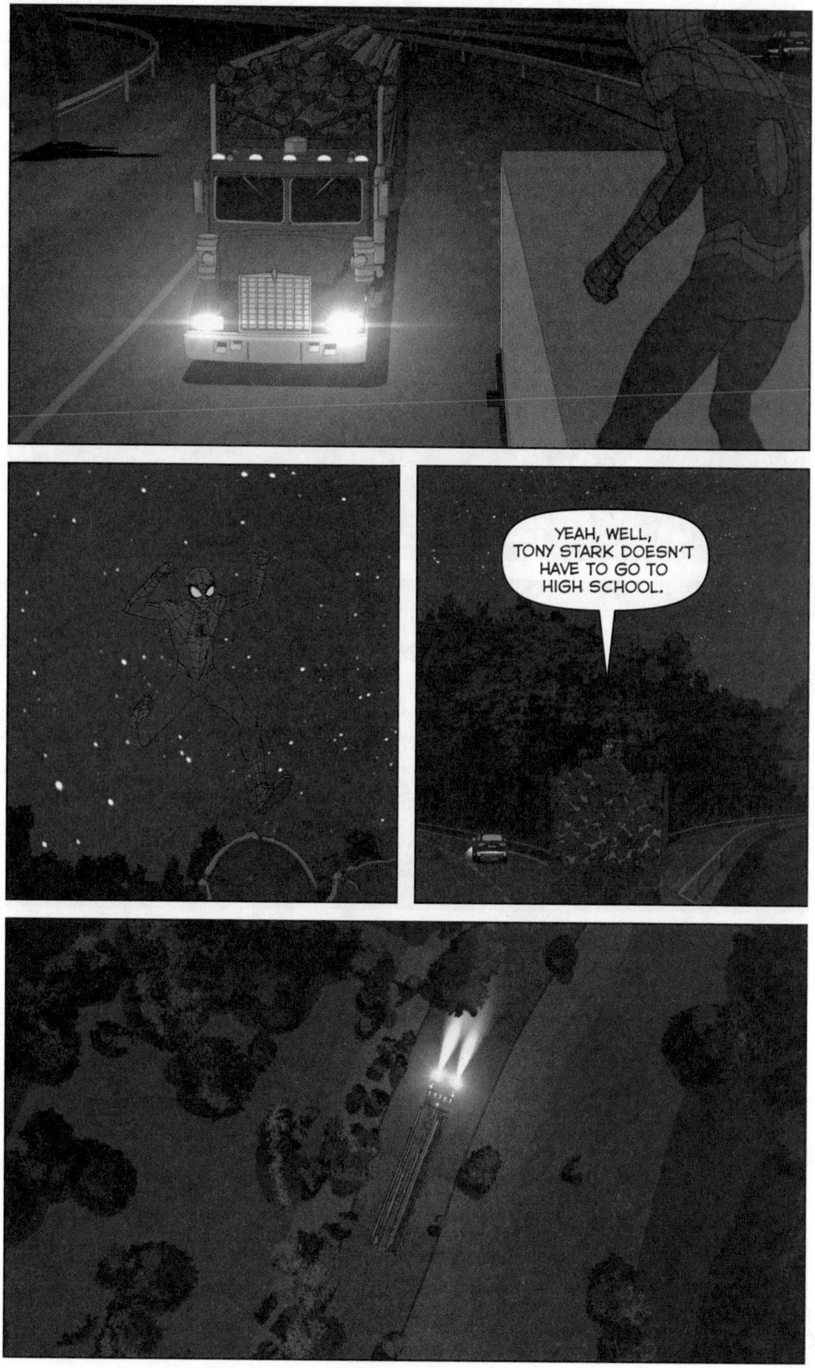
YEAH, WELL, TONY STARK DOESN'T HAVE TO GO TO HIGH SCHOOL.

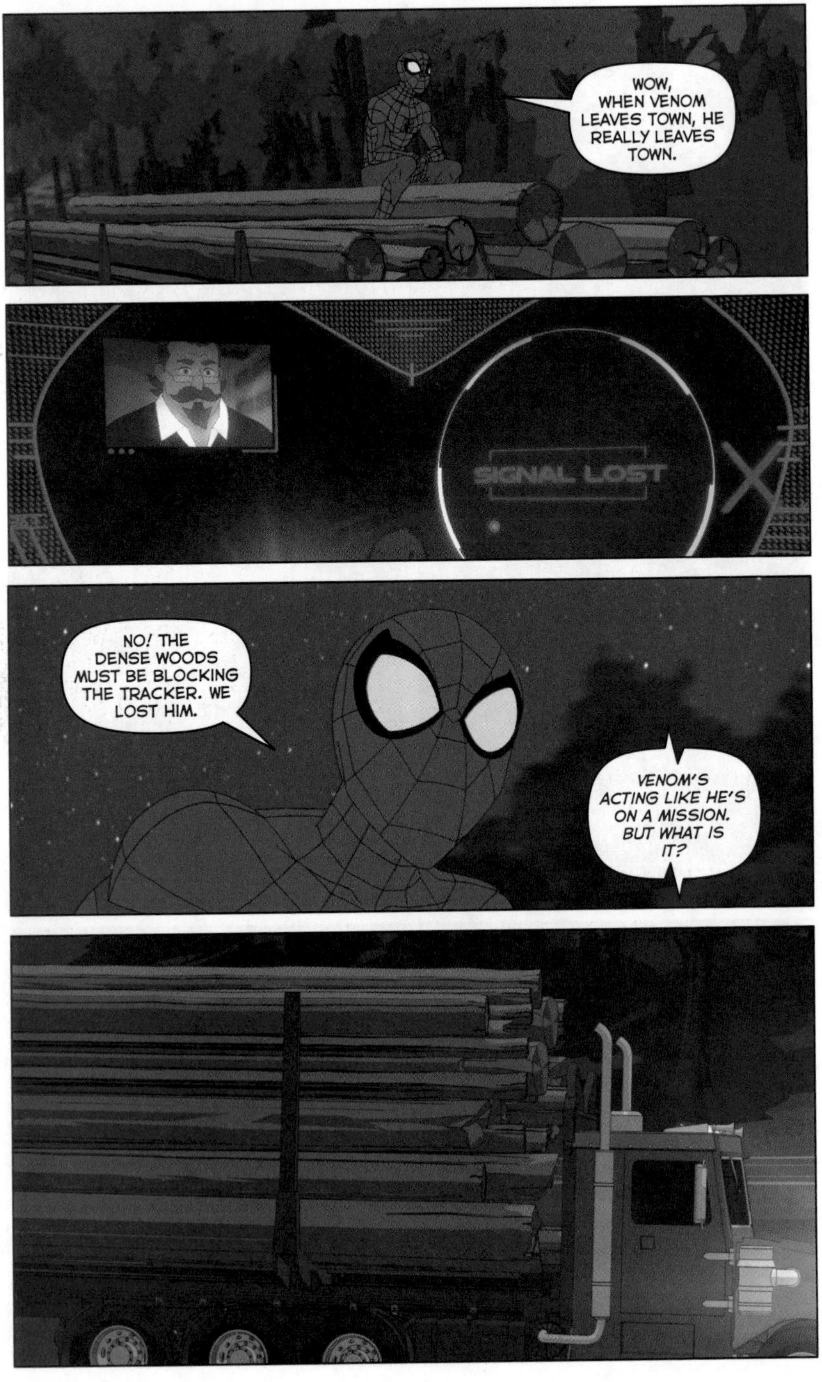
WOW, WHEN VENOM LEAVES TOWN, HE REALLY LEAVES TOWN.
SIGNAL LOST
NO! THE DENSE WOODS MUST BE BLOCKING THE TRACKER. WE LOST HIM.
VENOM'S ACTING LIKE HE'S ON A MISSION. BUT WHAT IS IT?

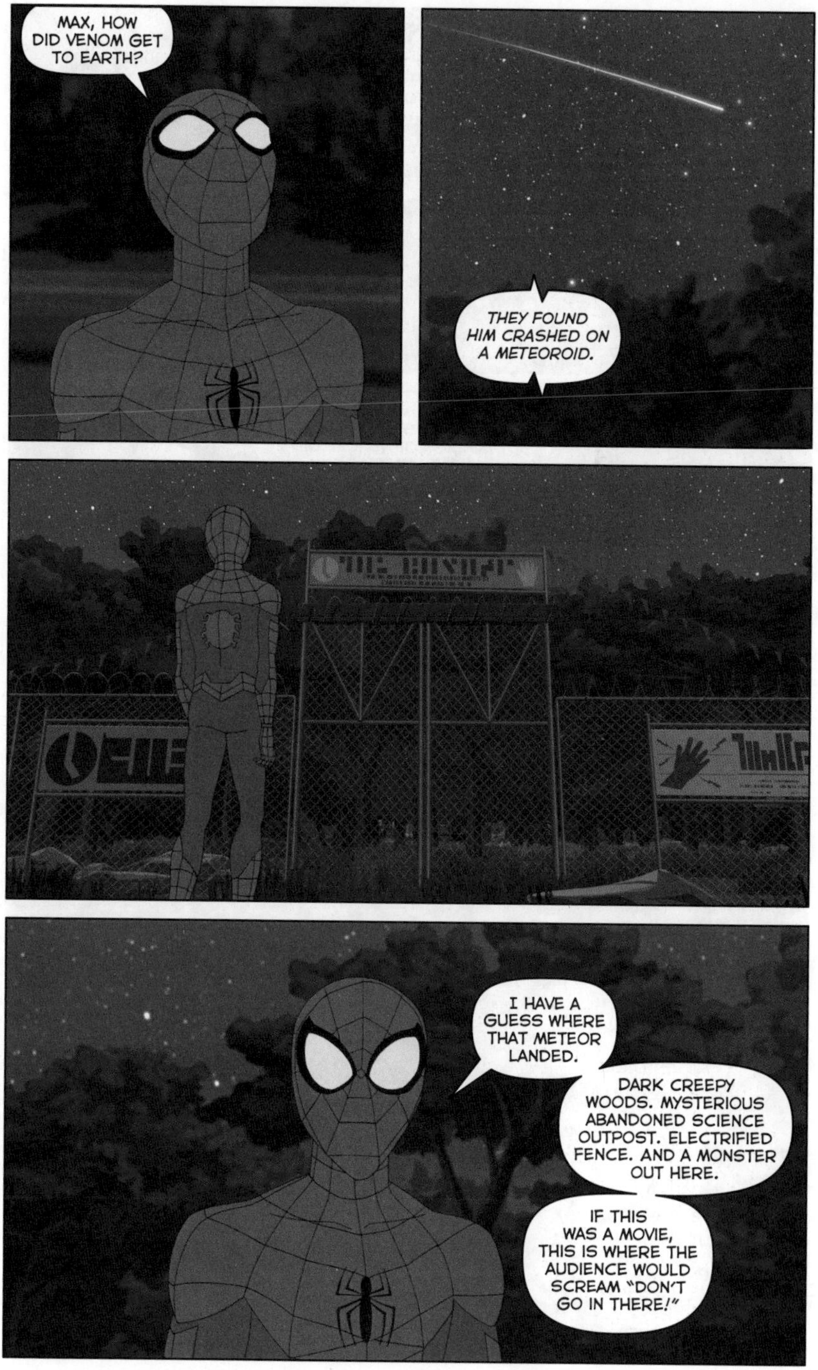

MAX, HOW DID VENOM GET TO EARTH?
THEY FOUND HIM CRASHED ON A METEOROID.
I HAVE A GUESS WHERE THAT METEOR LANDED.
DARK CREEPY WOODS. MYSTERIOUS ABANDONED SCIENCE OUTPOST. ELECTRIFIED FENCE. AND A MONSTER OUT HERE.
IF THIS WAS A MOVIE, THIS IS WHERE THE AUDIENCE WOULD SCREAM "DON'T GO IN THERE!"

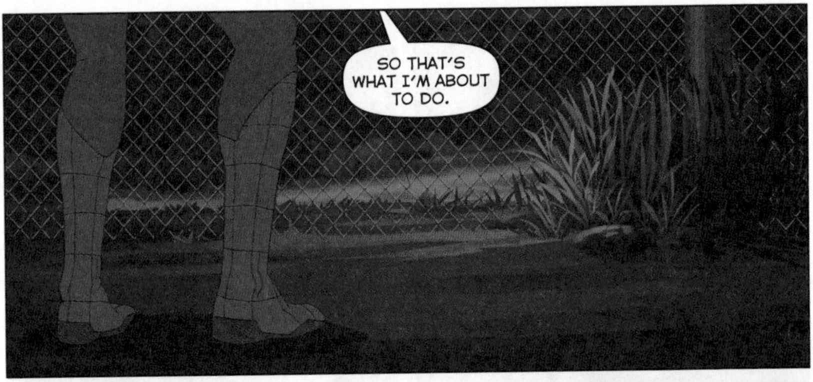
SO THAT'S WHAT I'M ABOUT TO DO.

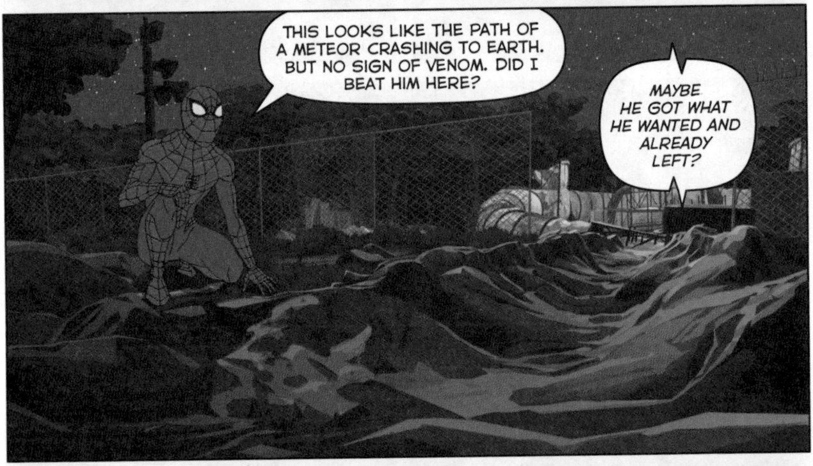
THIS LOOKS LIKE THE PATH OF A METEOR CRASHING TO EARTH. BUT NO SIGN OF VENOM. DID I BEAT HIM HERE?
MAYBE HE GOT WHAT HE WANTED AND ALREADY LEFT?

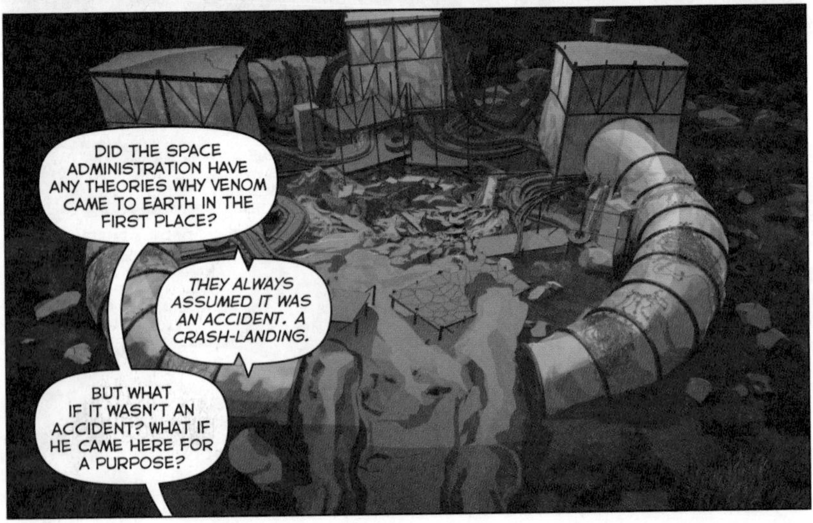
DID THE SPACE ADMINISTRATION HAVE ANY THEORIES WHY VENOM CAME TO EARTH IN THE FIRST PLACE?
THEY ALWAYS ASSUMED IT WAS AN ACCIDENT. A CRASH-LANDING.
BUT WHAT IF IT WASN'T AN ACCIDENT? WHAT IF HE CAME HERE FOR A PURPOSE?

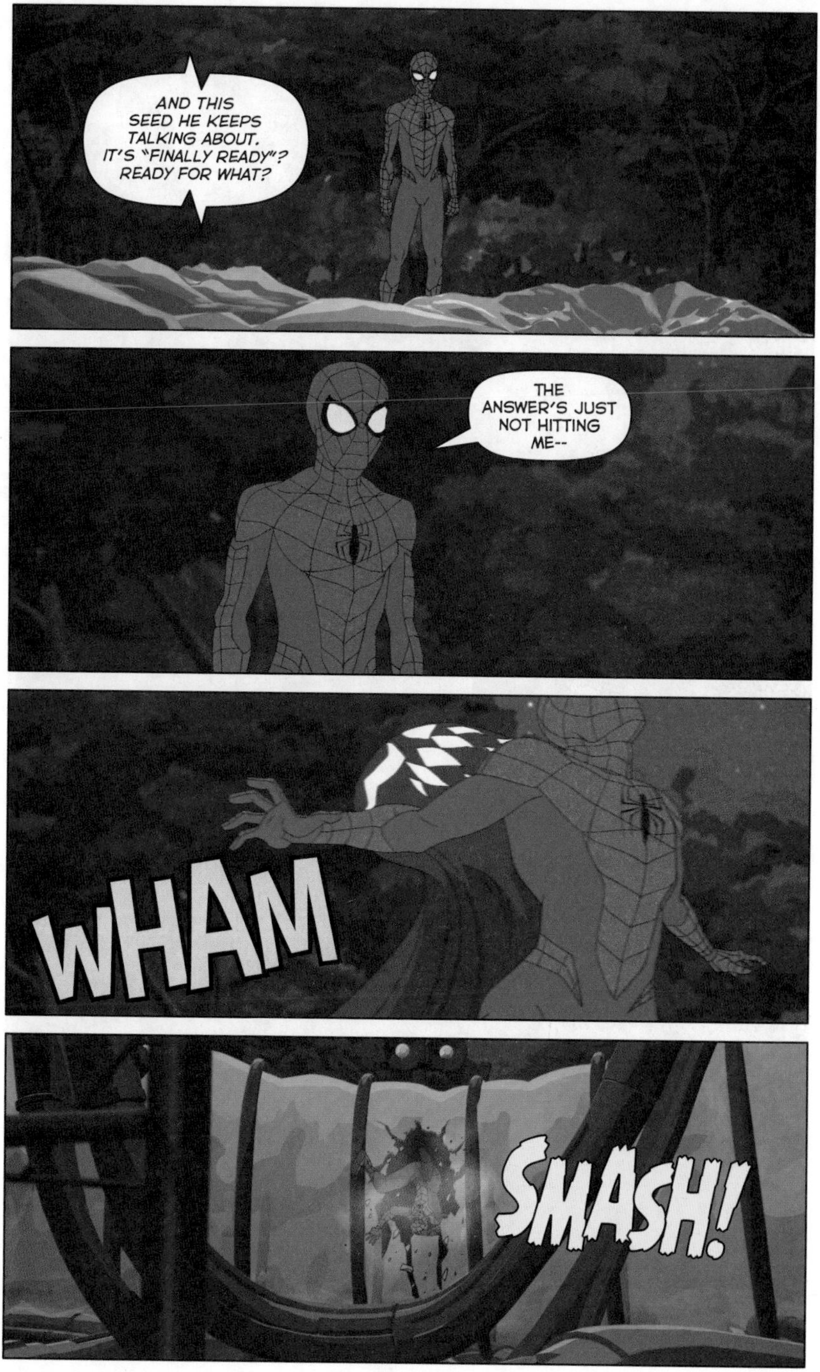
AND THIS SEED HE KEEPS TALKING ABOUT. IT'S "FINALLY READY"? READY FOR WHAT?
THE ANSWER'S JUST NOT HITTING ME--
WHAM
SMASH!

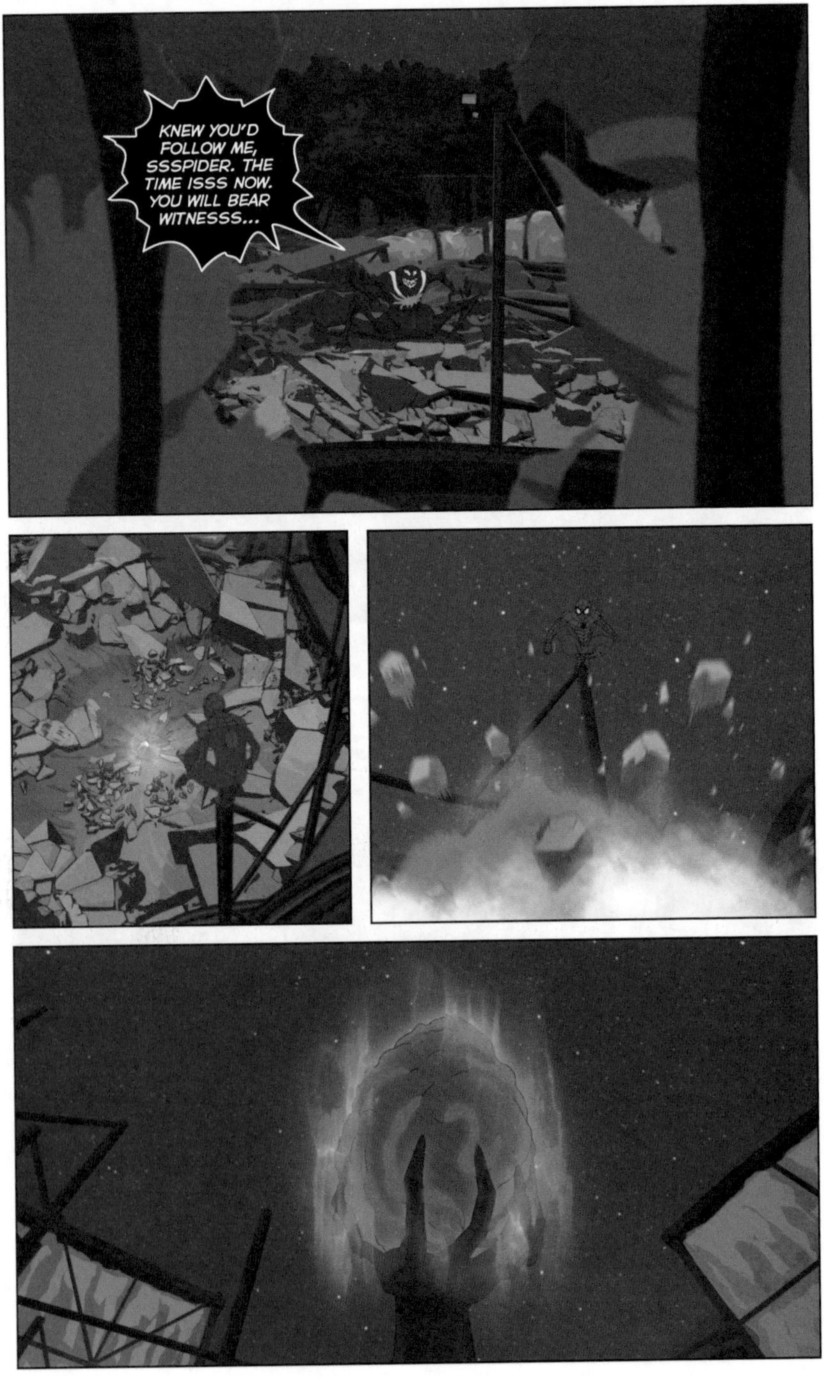
KNEW YOU'D FOLLOW ME, SSSPIDER. THE TIME ISSS NOW. YOU WILL BEAR WITNESSS...

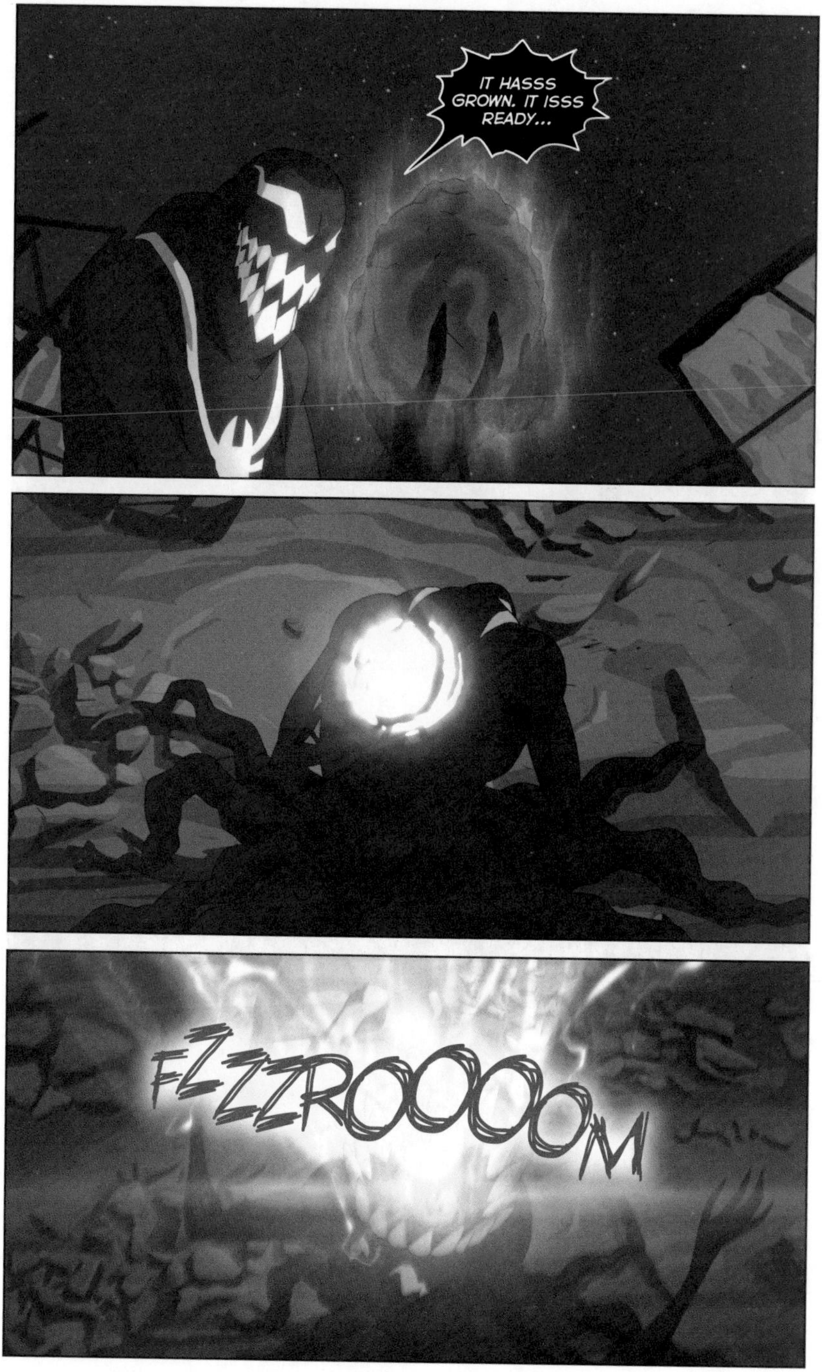
IT HASSS GROWN. IT ISSS READY...
FZZZROOOOOM

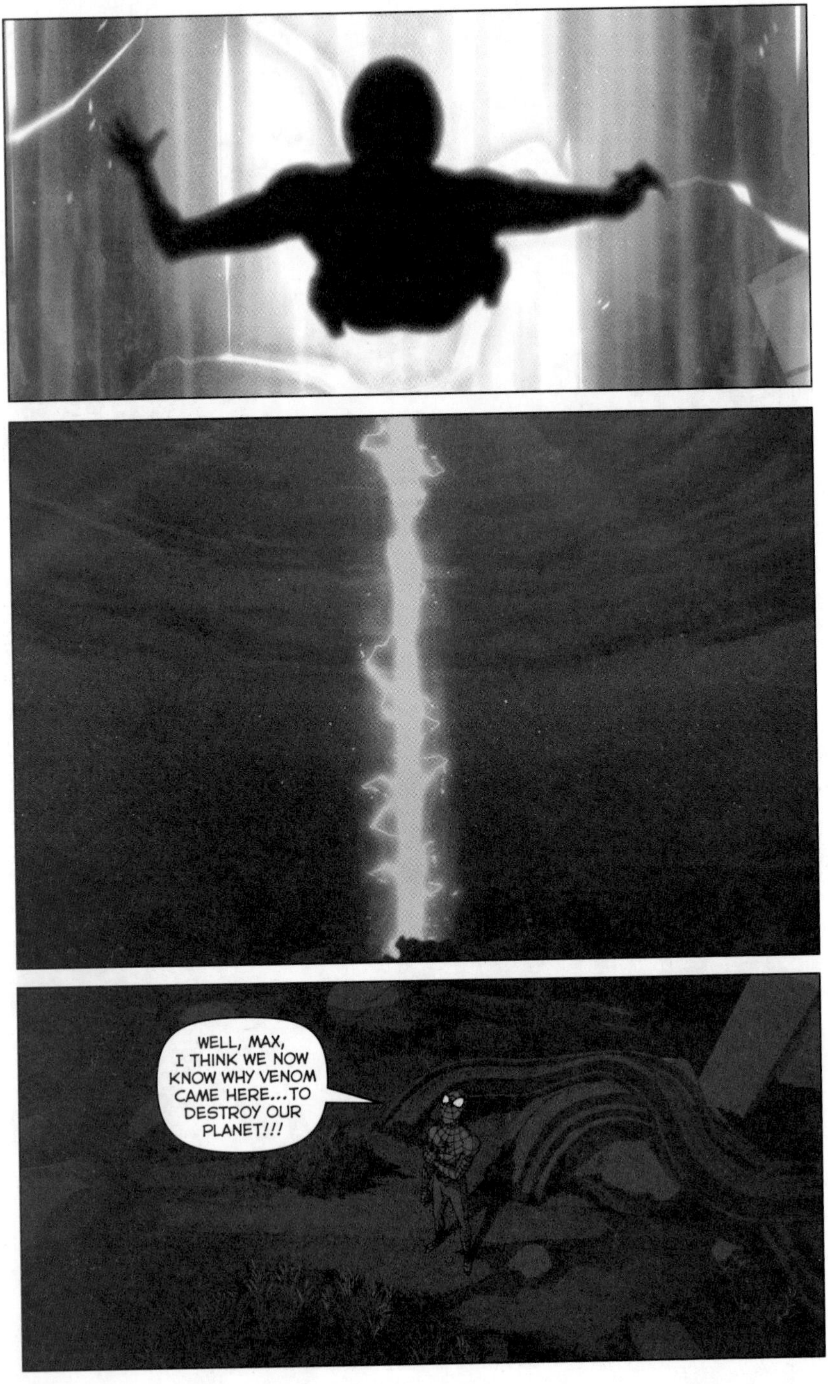
WELL, MAX, I THINK WE NOW KNOW WHY VENOM CAME HERE...TO DESTROY OUR PLANET!!!

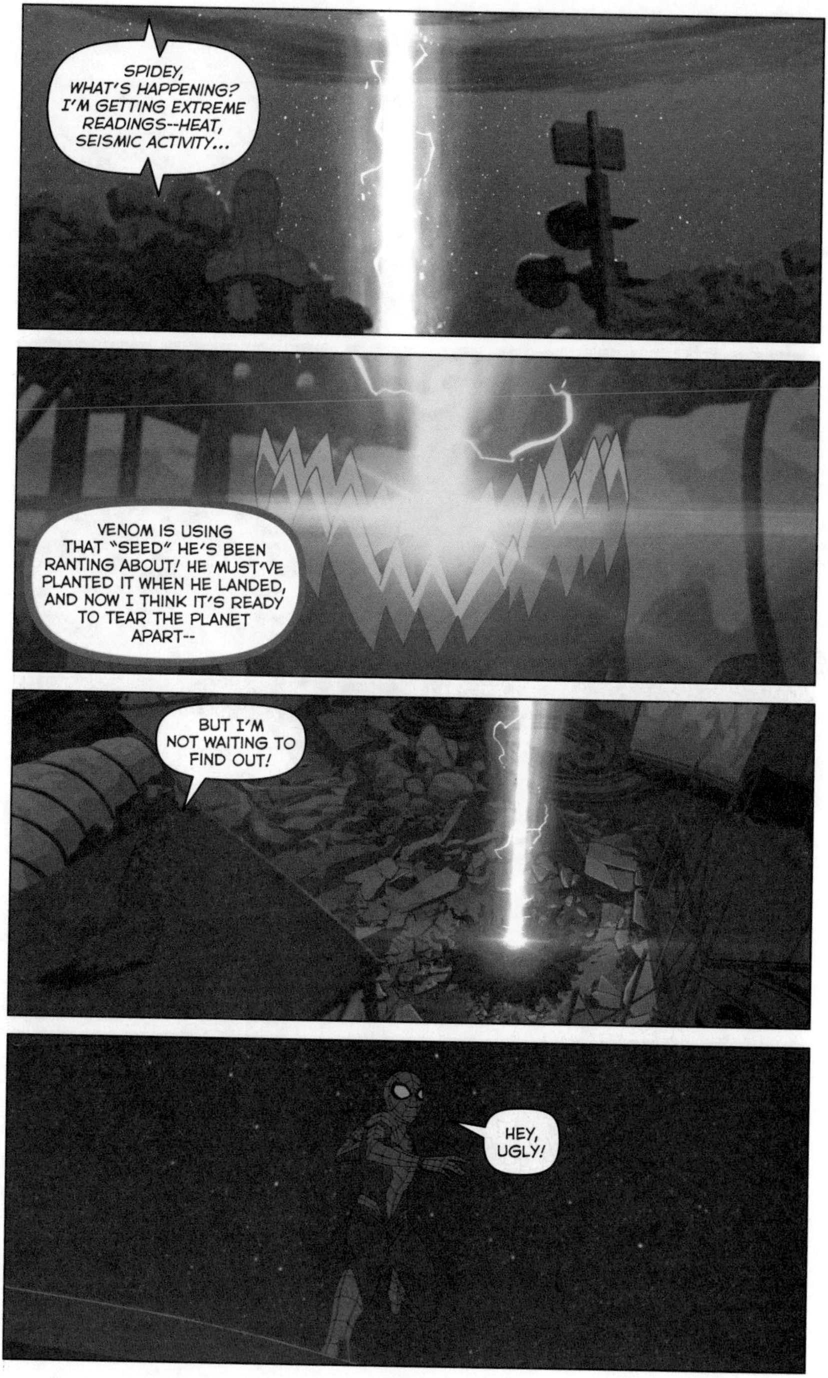
SPIDEY, WHAT'S HAPPENING? I'M GETTING EXTREME READINGS--HEAT, SEISMIC ACTIVITY...
VENOM IS USING THAT "SEED" HE'S BEEN RANTING ABOUT! HE MUST'VE PLANTED IT WHEN HE LANDED, AND NOW I THINK IT'S READY TO TEAR THE PLANET APART--
BUT I'M NOT WAITING TO FIND OUT!
HEY, UGLY!

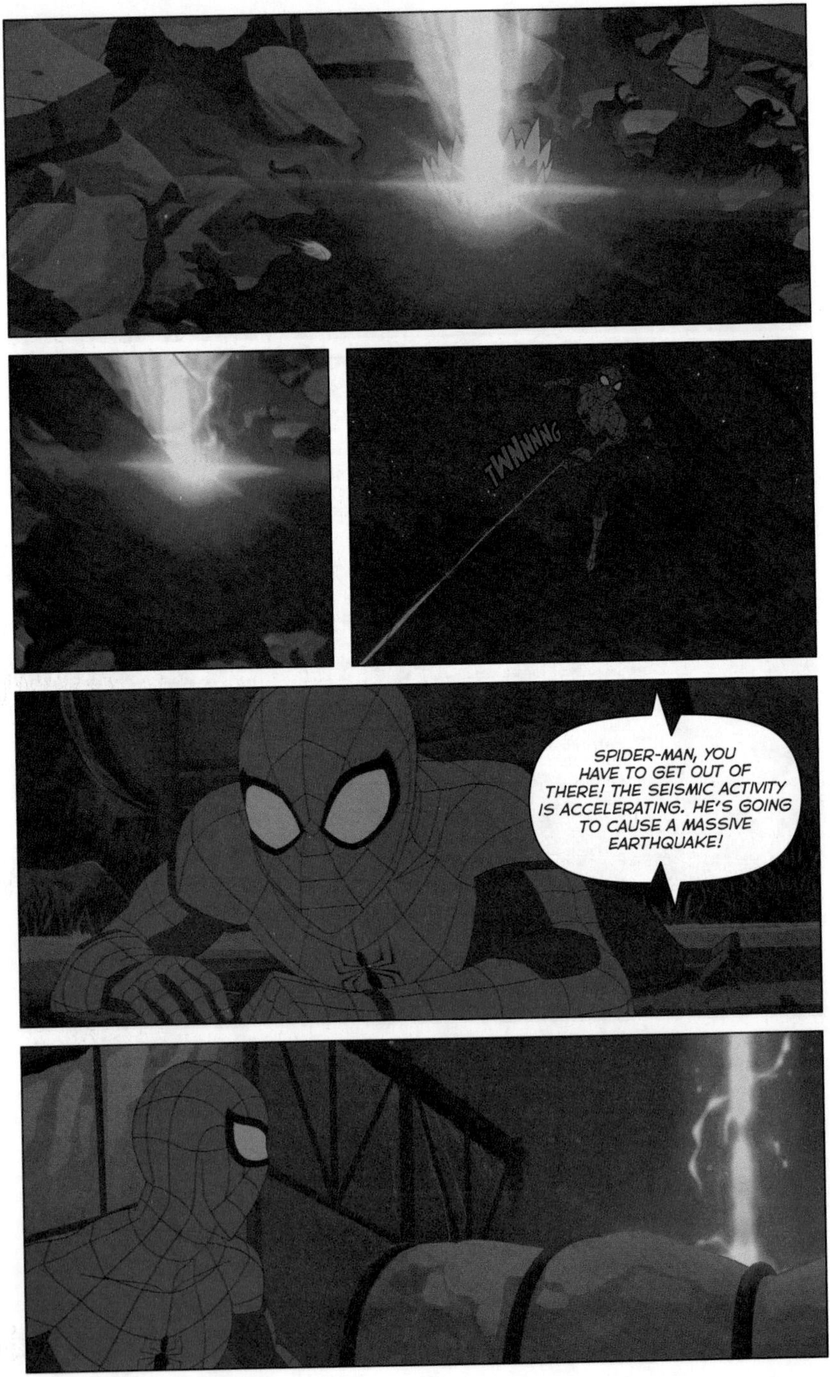
TWNNNNG
SPIDER-MAN, YOU HAVE TO GET OUT OF THERE! THE SEISMIC ACTIVITY IS ACCELERATING. HE'S GOING TO CAUSE A MASSIVE EARTHQUAKE!

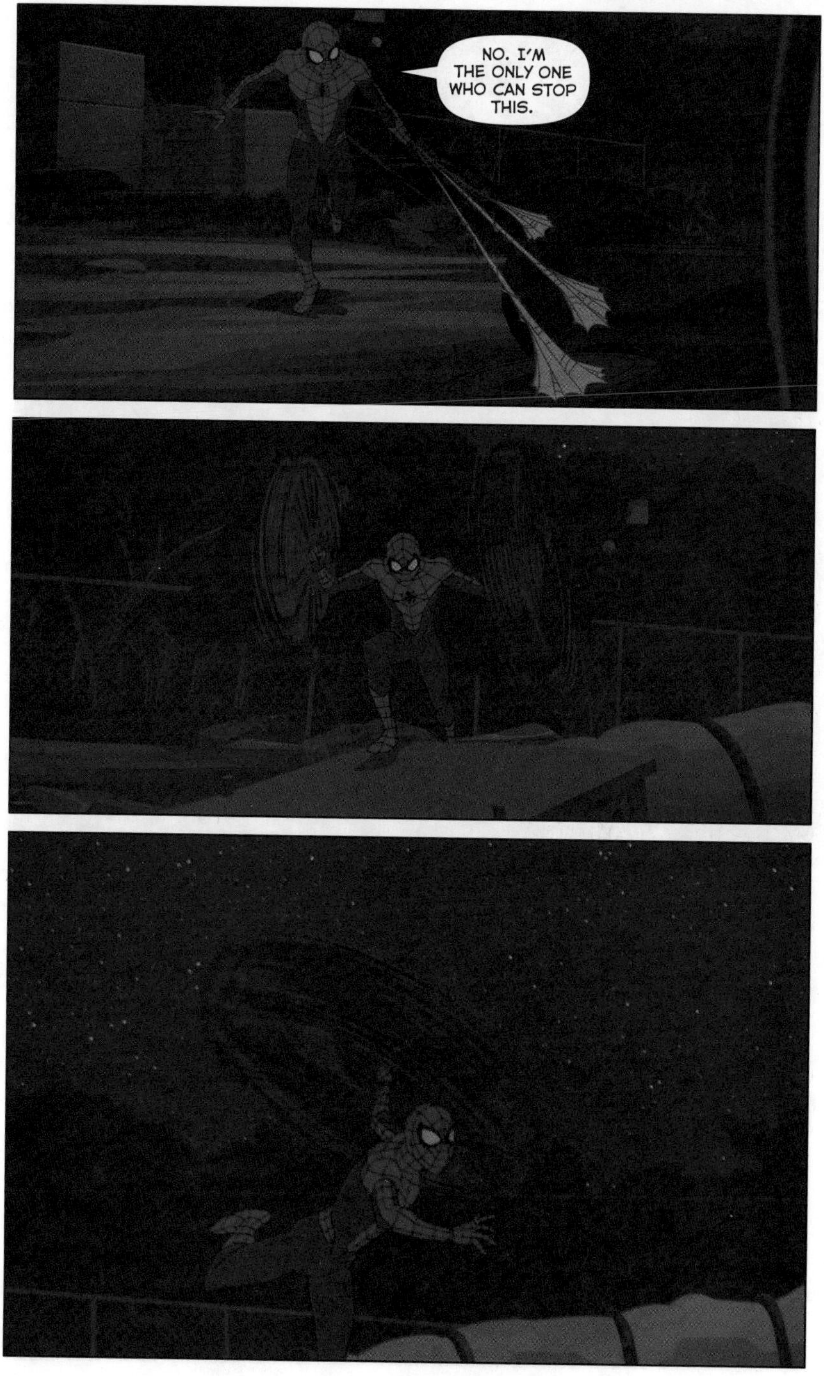
NO. I'M THE ONLY ONE WHO CAN STOP THIS.

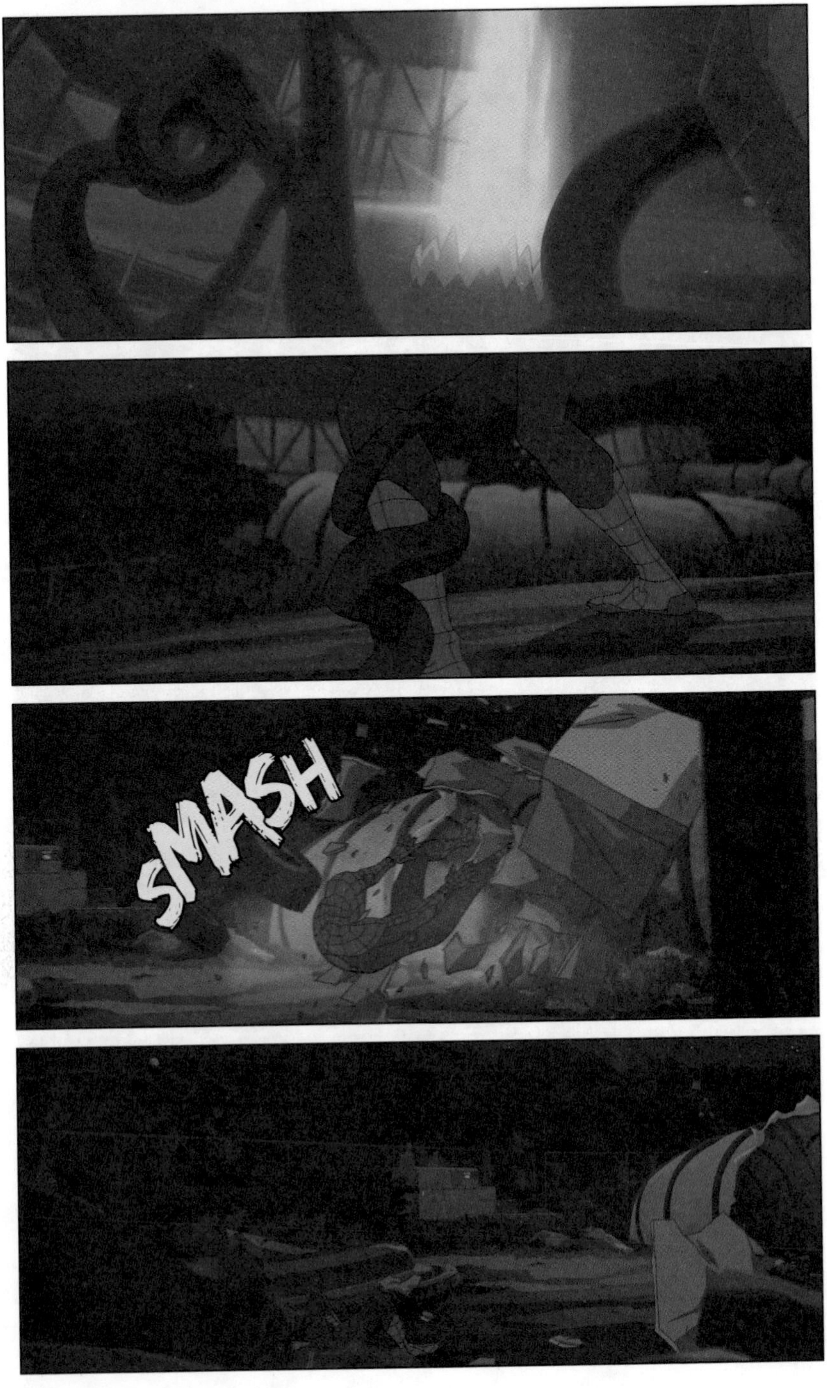
SMASH

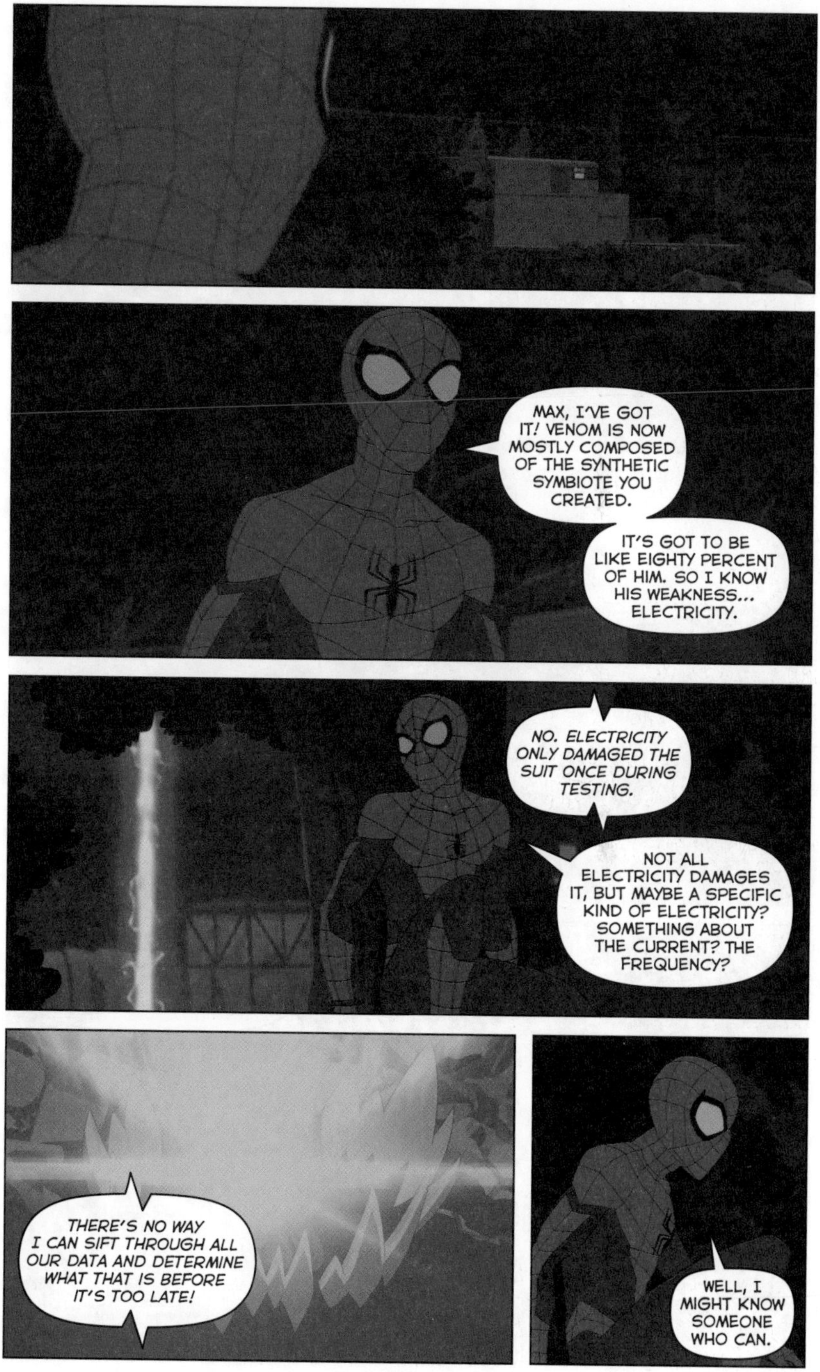
MAX, I'VE GOT IT! VENOM IS NOW MOSTLY COMPOSED OF THE SYNTHETIC SYMBIOTE YOU CREATED.
IT'S GOT TO BE LIKE EIGHTY PERCENT OF HIM. SO I KNOW HIS WEAKNESS... ELECTRICITY.
NO. ELECTRICITY ONLY DAMAGED THE SUIT ONCE DURING TESTING.
NOT ALL ELECTRICITY DAMAGES IT, BUT MAYBE A SPECIFIC KIND OF ELECTRICITY? SOMETHING ABOUT THE CURRENT? THE FREQUENCY?
THERE'S NO WAY I CAN SIFT THROUGH ALL OUR DATA AND DETERMINE WHAT THAT IS BEFORE IT'S TOO LATE!
WELL, I MIGHT KNOW SOMEONE WHO CAN.

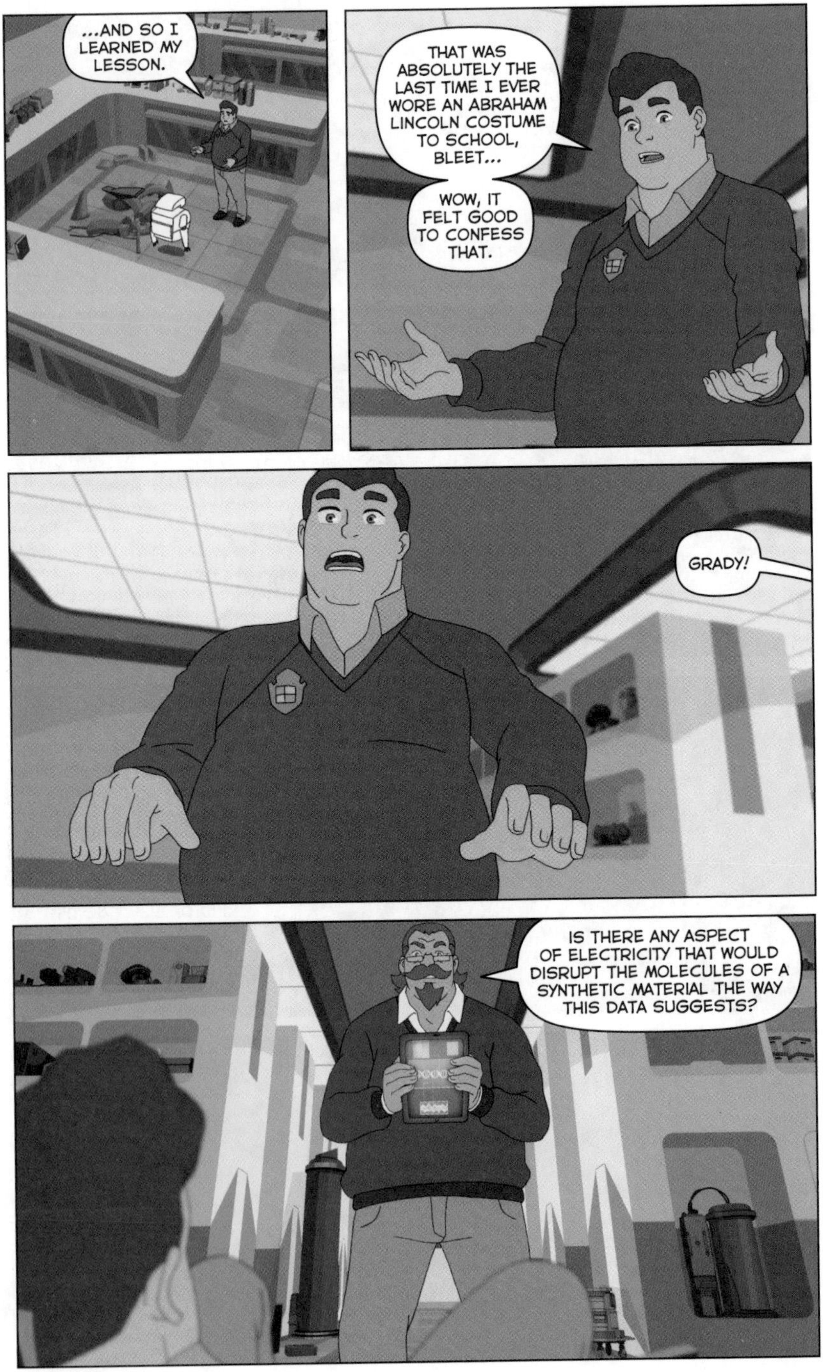
...AND SO I LEARNED MY LESSON.
THAT WAS ABSOLUTELY THE LAST TIME I EVER WORE AN ABRAHAM LINCOLN COSTUME TO SCHOOL, BLEET...
WOW, IT FELT GOOD TO CONFESS THAT.
GRADY!
IS THERE ANY ASPECT OF ELECTRICITY THAT WOULD DISRUPT THE MOLECULES OF A SYNTHETIC MATERIAL THE WAY THIS DATA SUGGESTS?

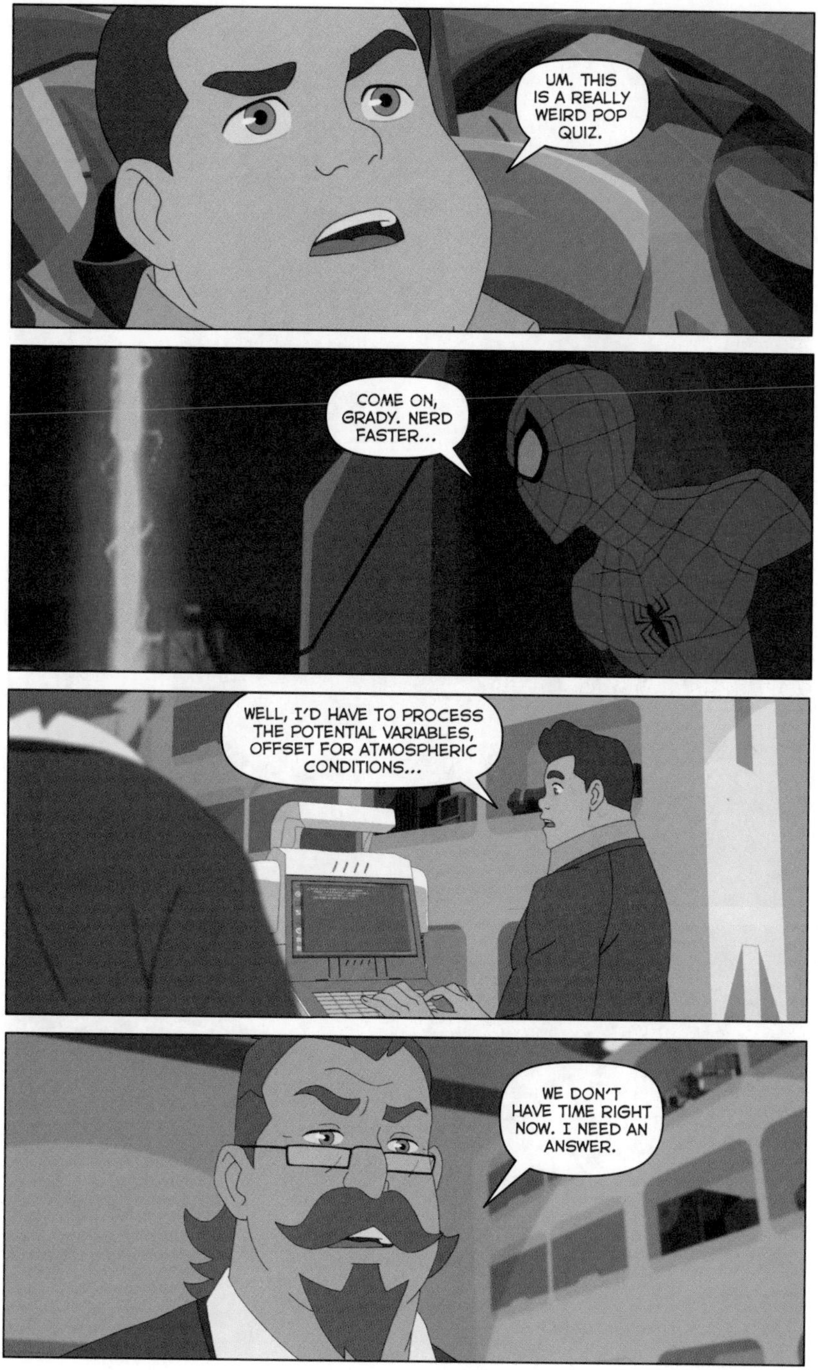
UM. THIS IS A REALLY WEIRD POP QUIZ.
COME ON, GRADY. NERD FASTER...
WELL, I'D HAVE TO PROCESS THE POTENTIAL VARIABLES, OFFSET FOR ATMOSPHERIC CONDITIONS...
WE DON'T HAVE TIME RIGHT NOW. I NEED AN ANSWER.

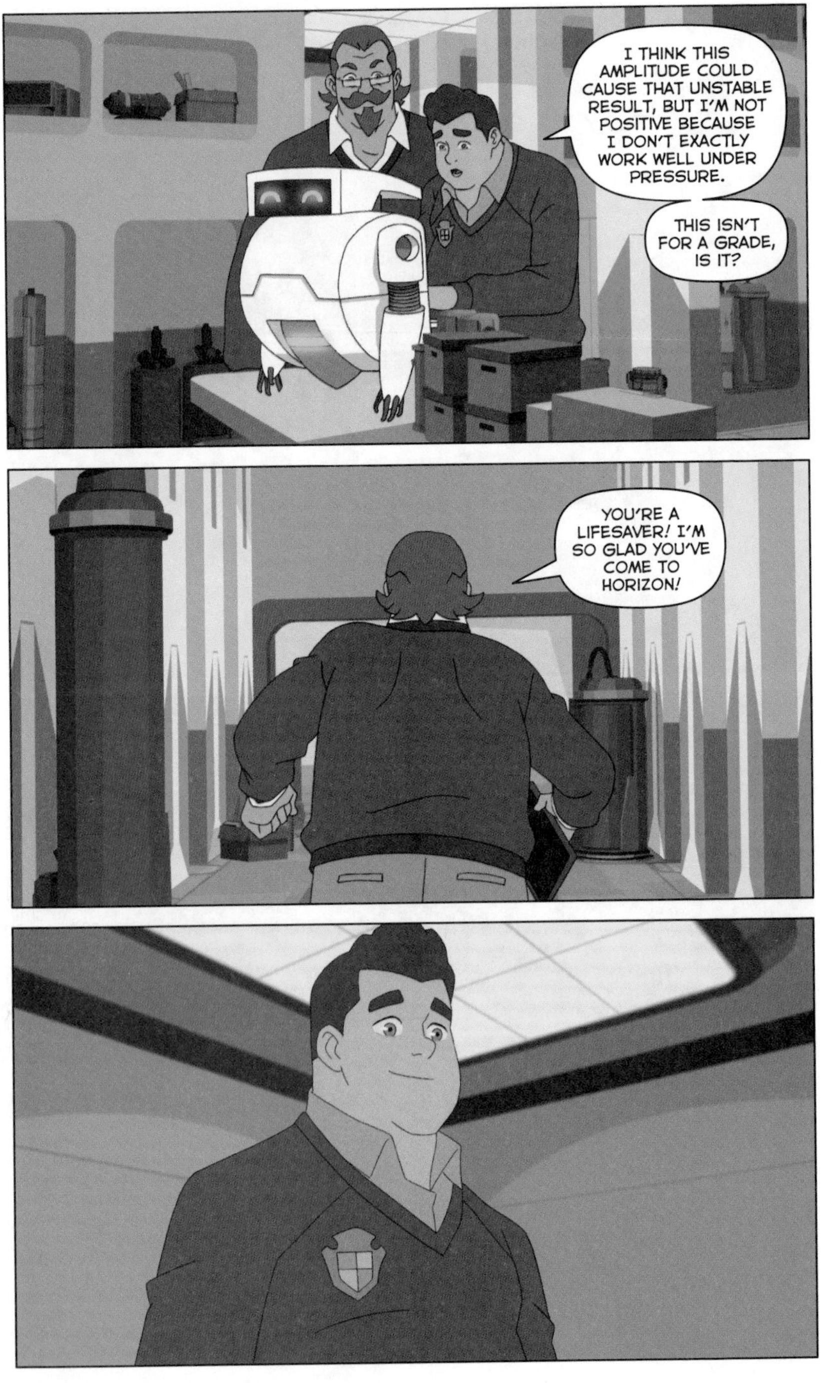
I THINK THIS AMPLITUDE COULD CAUSE THAT UNSTABLE RESULT, BUT I'M NOT POSITIVE BECAUSE I DON'T EXACTLY WORK WELL UNDER PRESSURE.
THIS ISN'T FOR A GRADE, IS IT?
YOU'RE A LIFESAVER! I'M SO GLAD YOU'VE COME TO HORIZON!

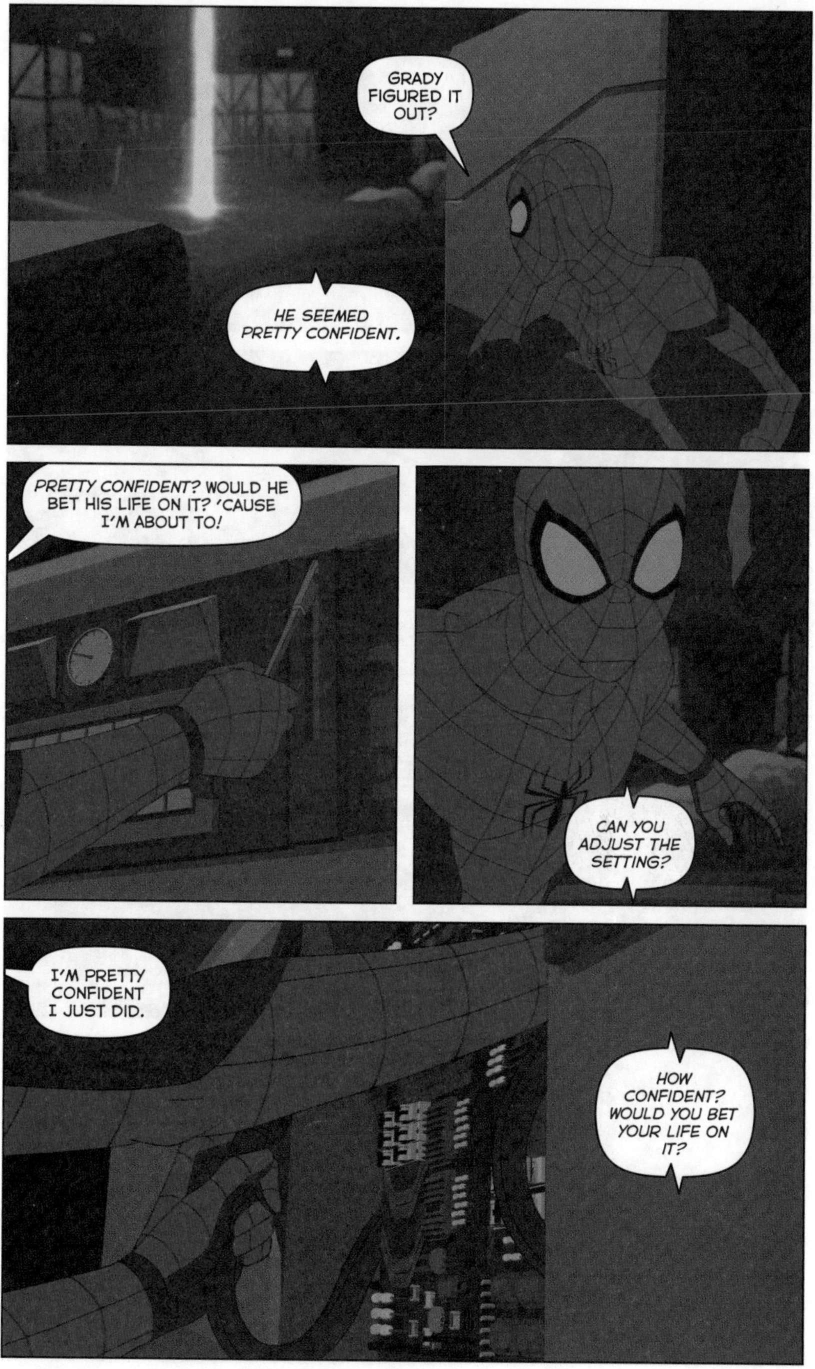
GRADY FIGURED IT OUT?
HE SEEMED PRETTY CONFIDENT.
PRETTY CONFIDENT? WOULD HE BET HIS LIFE ON IT? 'CAUSE I'M ABOUT TO!
CAN YOU ADJUST THE SETTING?
I'M PRETTY CONFIDENT I JUST DID.
HOW CONFIDENT? WOULD YOU BET YOUR LIFE ON IT?

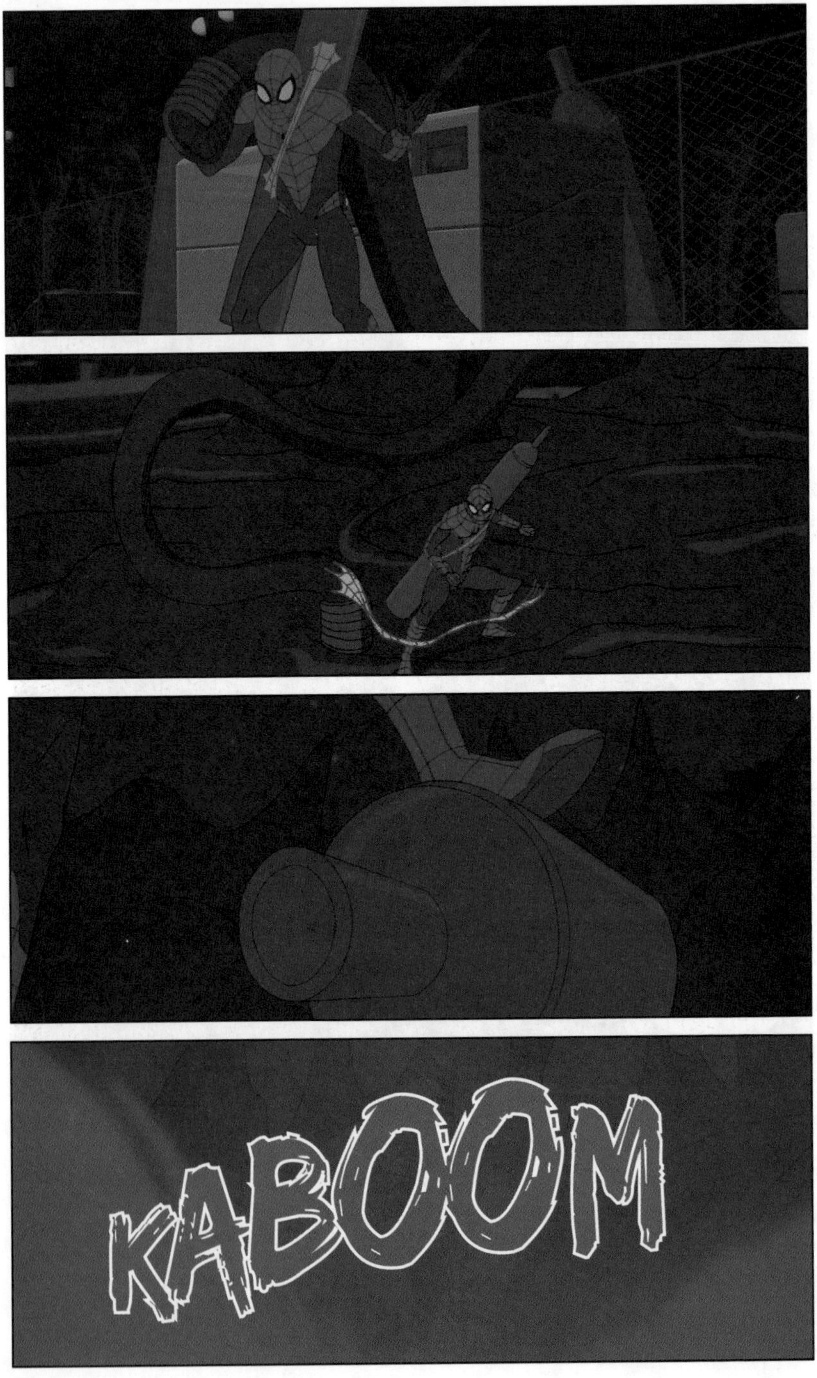
KABOOM

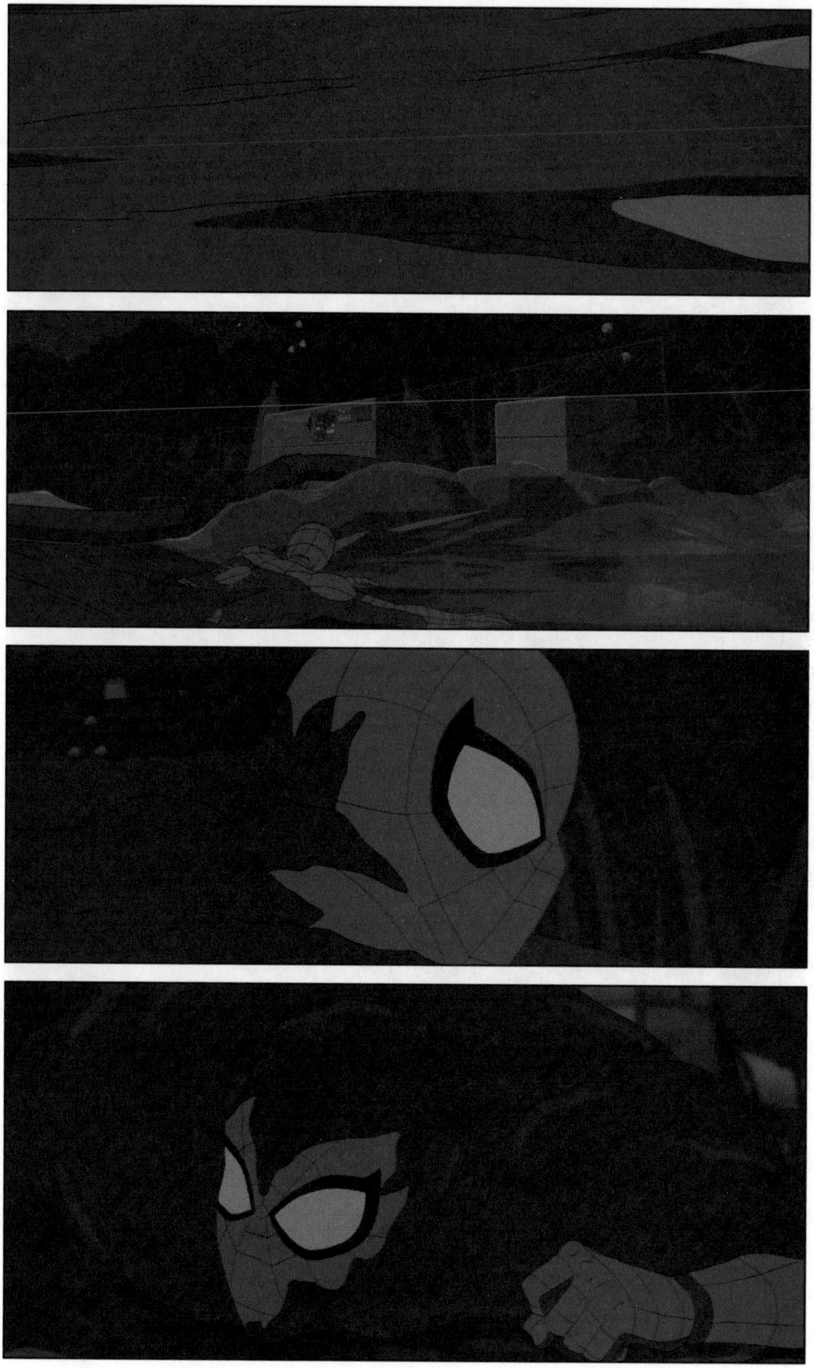

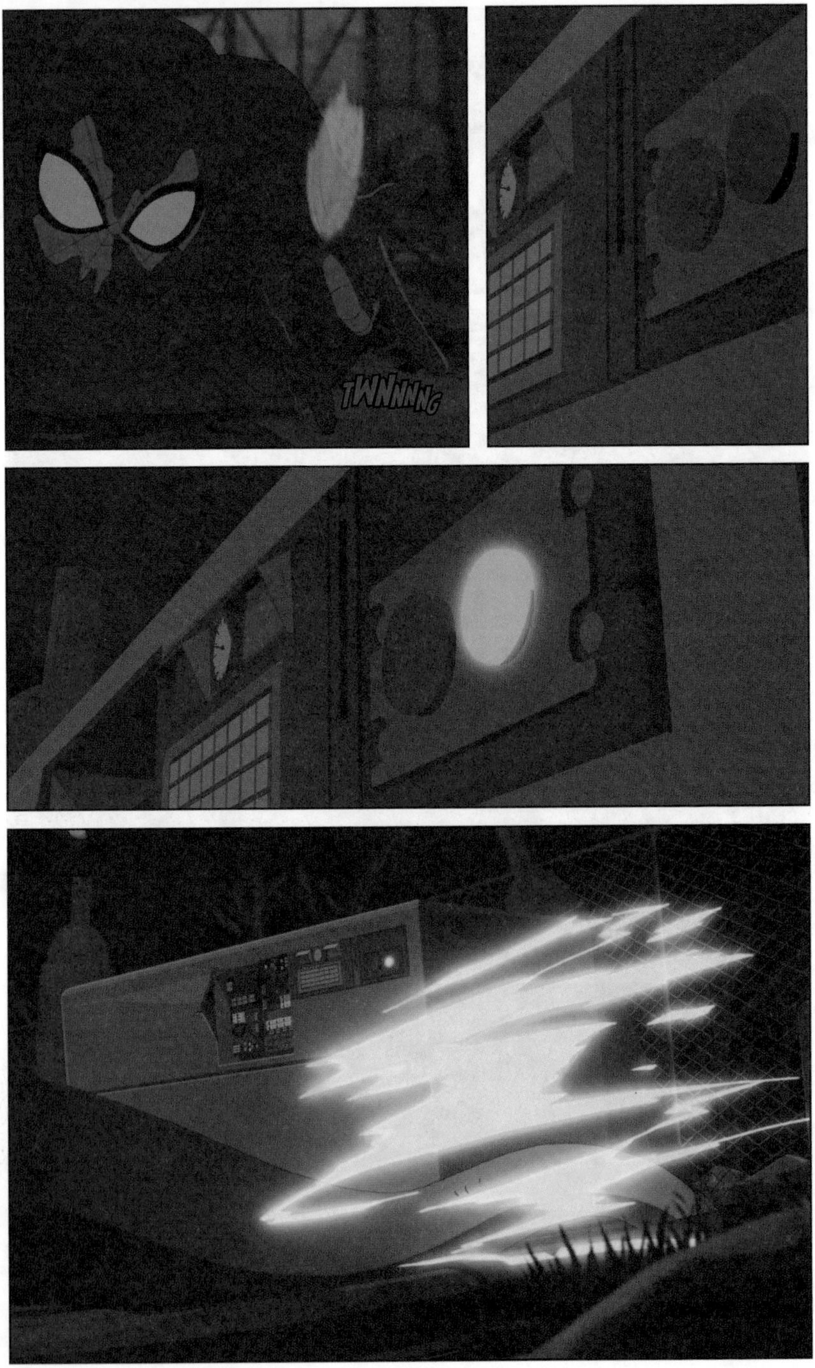
TWNNNNG

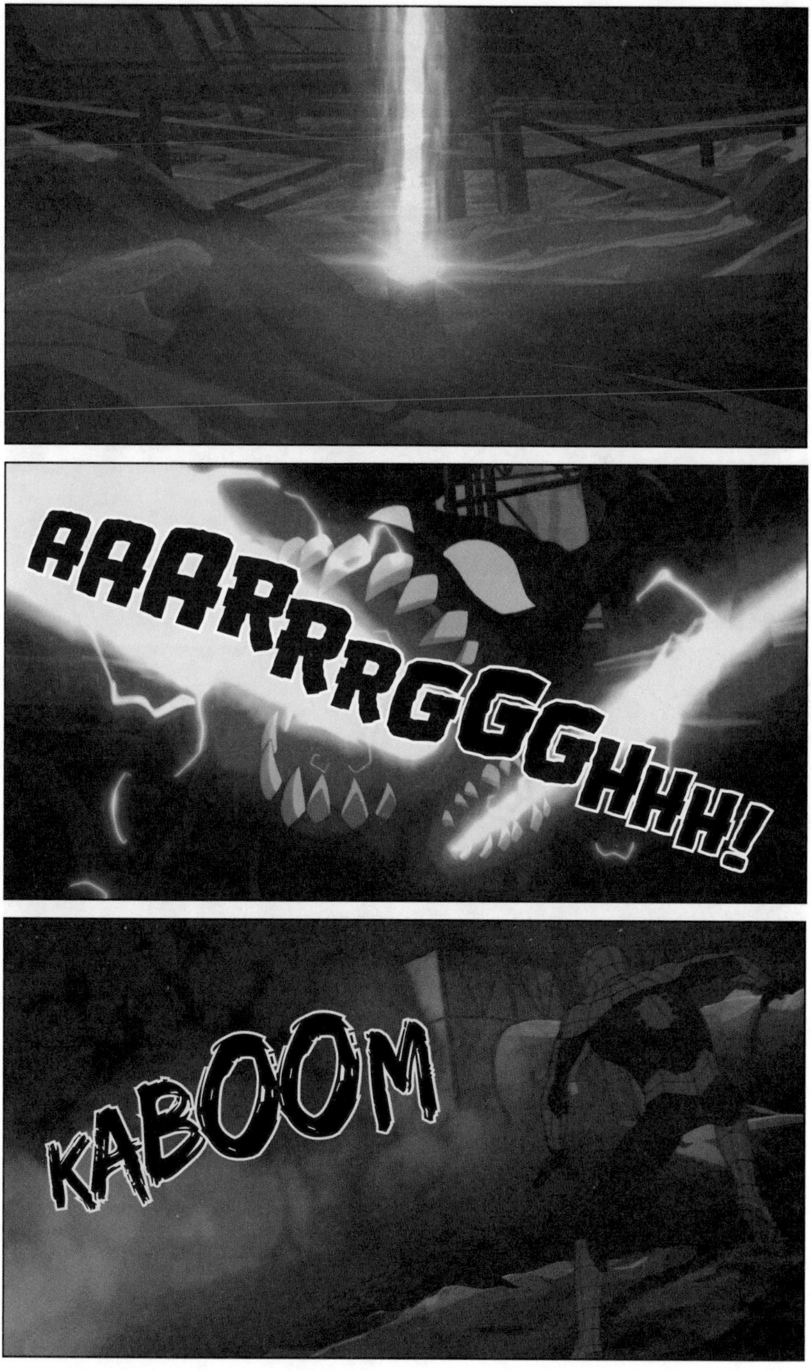
AAAARRRRGGGHHH!
KABOOM

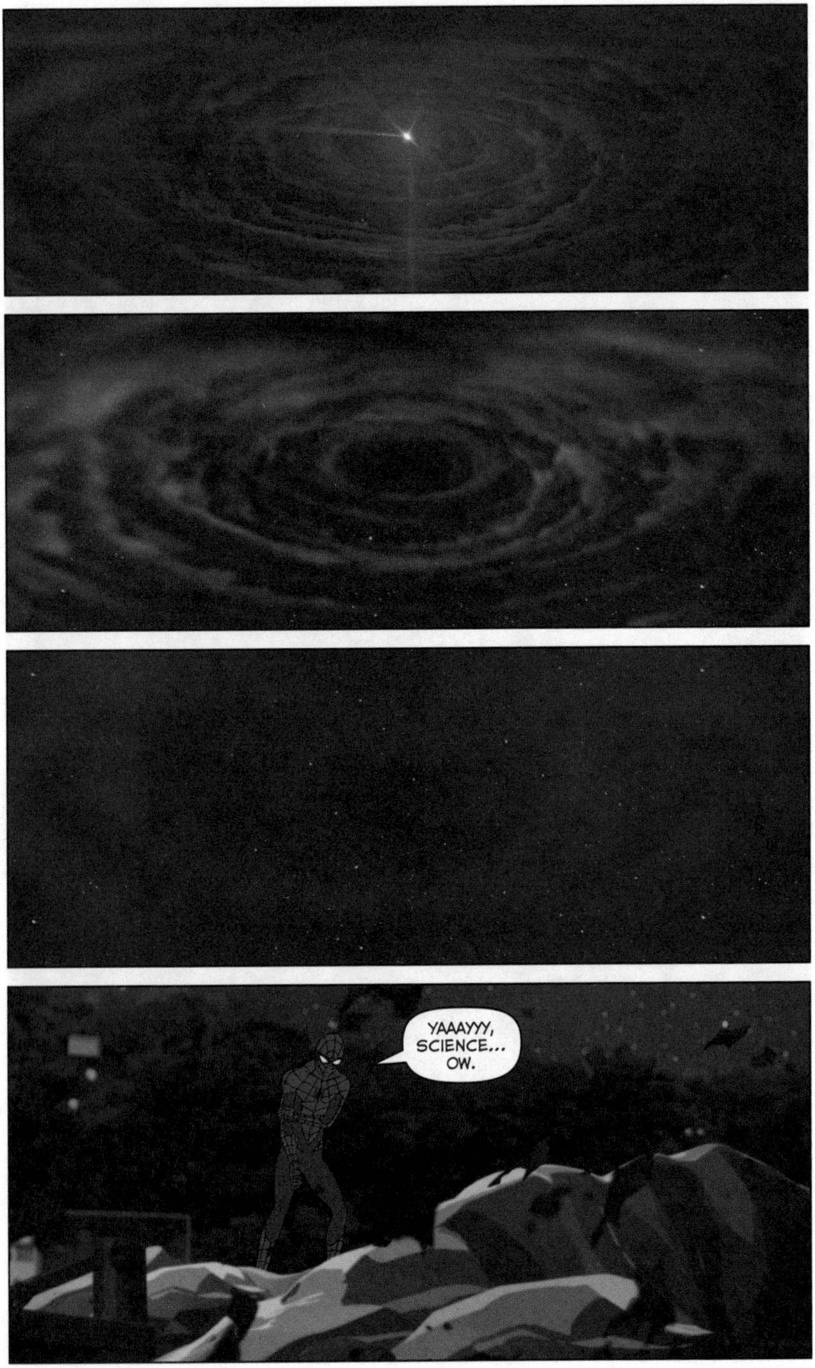
YAAAYYY, SCIENCE... OW.

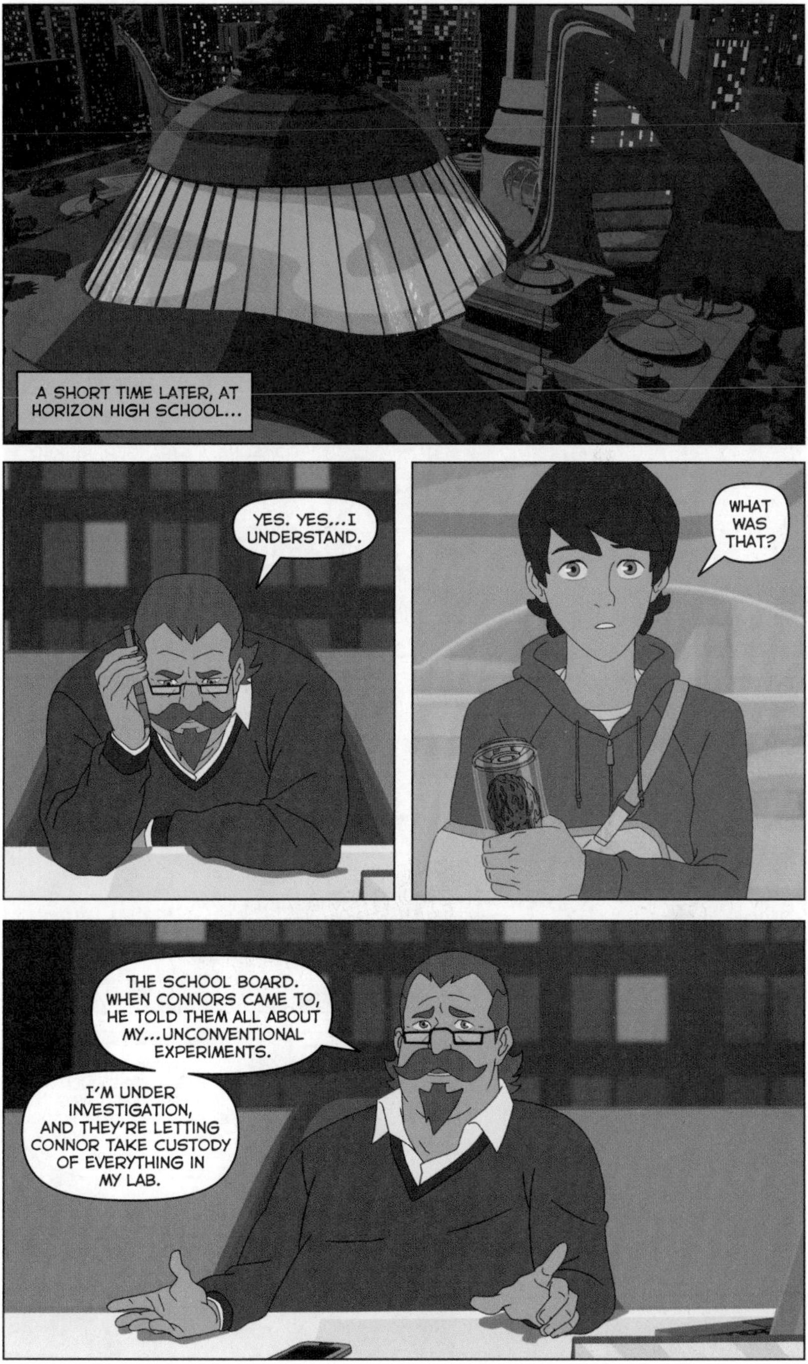
A SHORT TIME LATER, AT HORIZON HIGH SCHOOL...
YES. YES...I UNDERSTAND.
WHAT WAS THAT?
THE SCHOOL BOARD. WHEN CONNORS CAME TO, HE TOLD THEM ALL ABOUT MY...UNCONVENTIONAL EXPERIMENTS.
I'M UNDER INVESTIGATION, AND THEY'RE LETTING CONNOR TAKE CUSTODY OF EVERYTHING IN MY LAB.

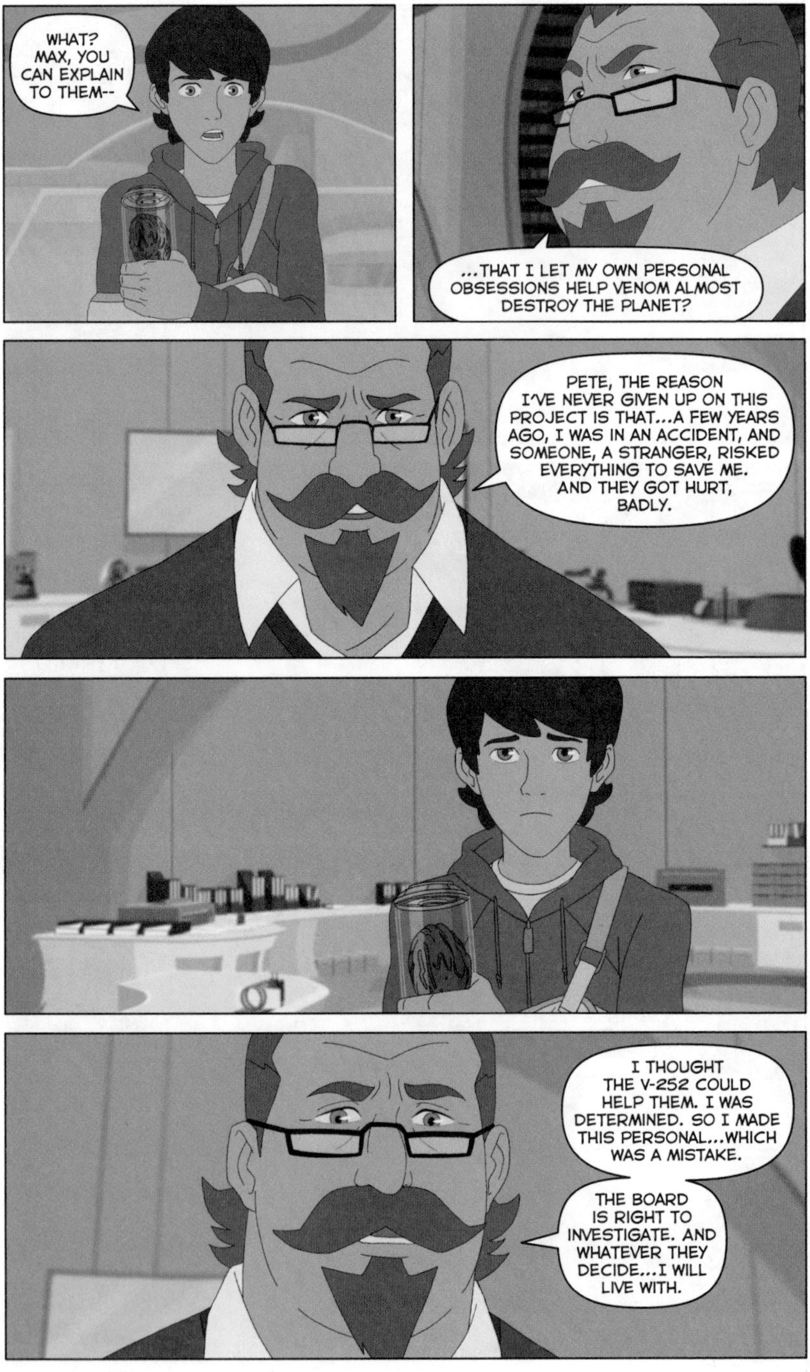
WHAT? MAX, YOU CAN EXPLAIN TO THEM--
...THAT I LET MY OWN PERSONAL OBSESSIONS HELP VENOM ALMOST DESTROY THE PLANET?
PETE, THE REASON I'VE NEVER GIVEN UP ON THIS PROJECT IS THAT...A FEW YEARS AGO, I WAS IN AN ACCIDENT, AND SOMEONE, A STRANGER, RISKED EVERYTHING TO SAVE ME. AND THEY GOT HURT, BADLY.
I THOUGHT THE V-252 COULD HELP THEM. I WAS DETERMINED. SO I MADE THIS PERSONAL...WHICH WAS A MISTAKE.
THE BOARD IS RIGHT TO INVESTIGATE. AND WHATEVER THEY DECIDE...I WILL LIVE WITH.

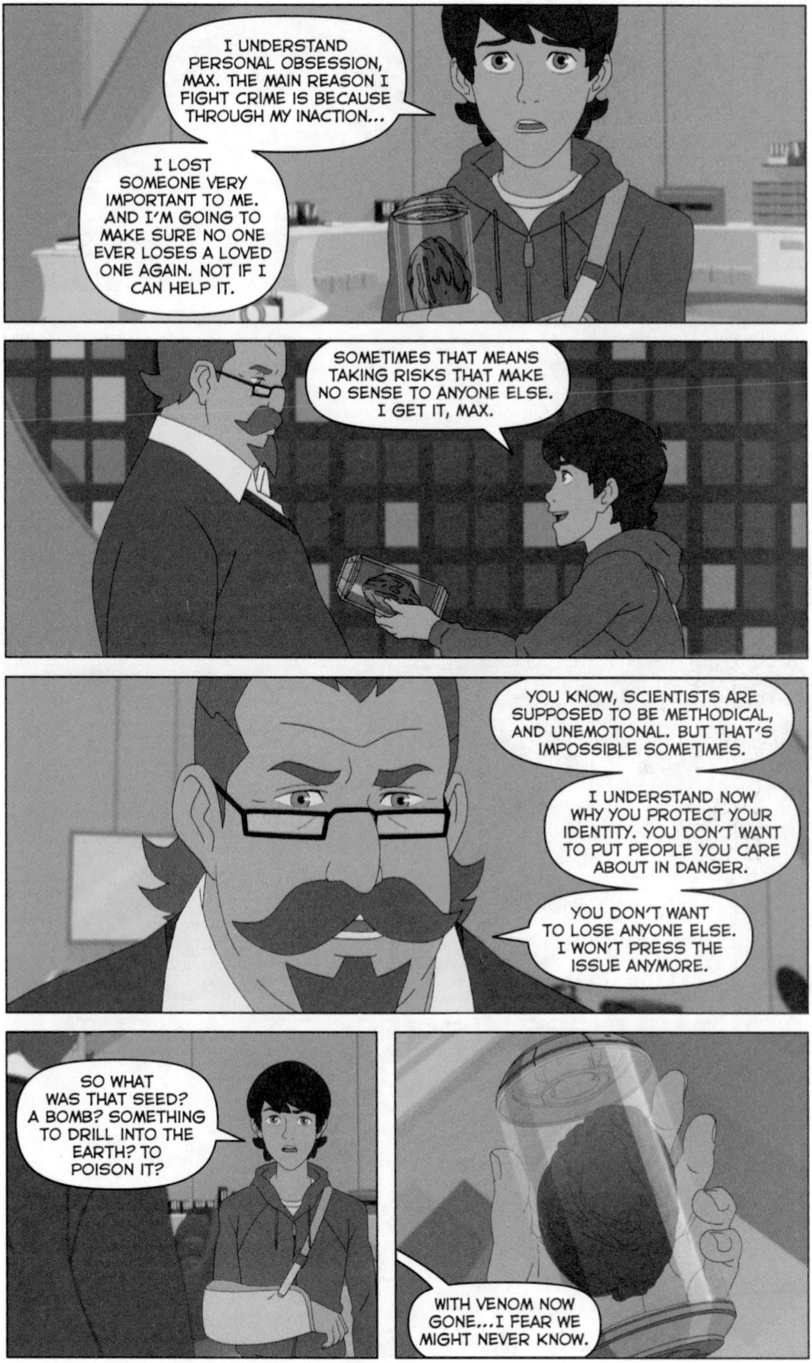
I UNDERSTAND PERSONAL OBSESSION, MAX. THE MAIN REASON I FIGHT CRIME IS BECAUSE THROUGH MY INACTION...
I LOST SOMEONE VERY IMPORTANT TO ME. AND I'M GOING TO MAKE SURE NO ONE EVER LOSES A LOVED ONE AGAIN. NOT IF I CAN HELP IT.
SOMETIMES THAT MEANS TAKING RISKS THAT MAKE NO SENSE TO ANYONE ELSE. I GET IT, MAX.
YOU KNOW, SCIENTISTS ARE SUPPOSED TO BE METHODICAL, AND UNEMOTIONAL. BUT THAT'S IMPOSSIBLE SOMETIMES.
I UNDERSTAND NOW WHY YOU PROTECT YOUR IDENTITY. YOU DON'T WANT TO PUT PEOPLE YOU CARE ABOUT IN DANGER.
YOU DON'T WANT TO LOSE ANYONE ELSE. I WON'T PRESS THE ISSUE ANYMORE.
SO WHAT WAS THAT SEED? A BOMB? SOMETHING TO DRILL INTO THE EARTH? TO POISON IT?
WITH VENOM NOW GONE...I FEAR WE MIGHT NEVER KNOW.

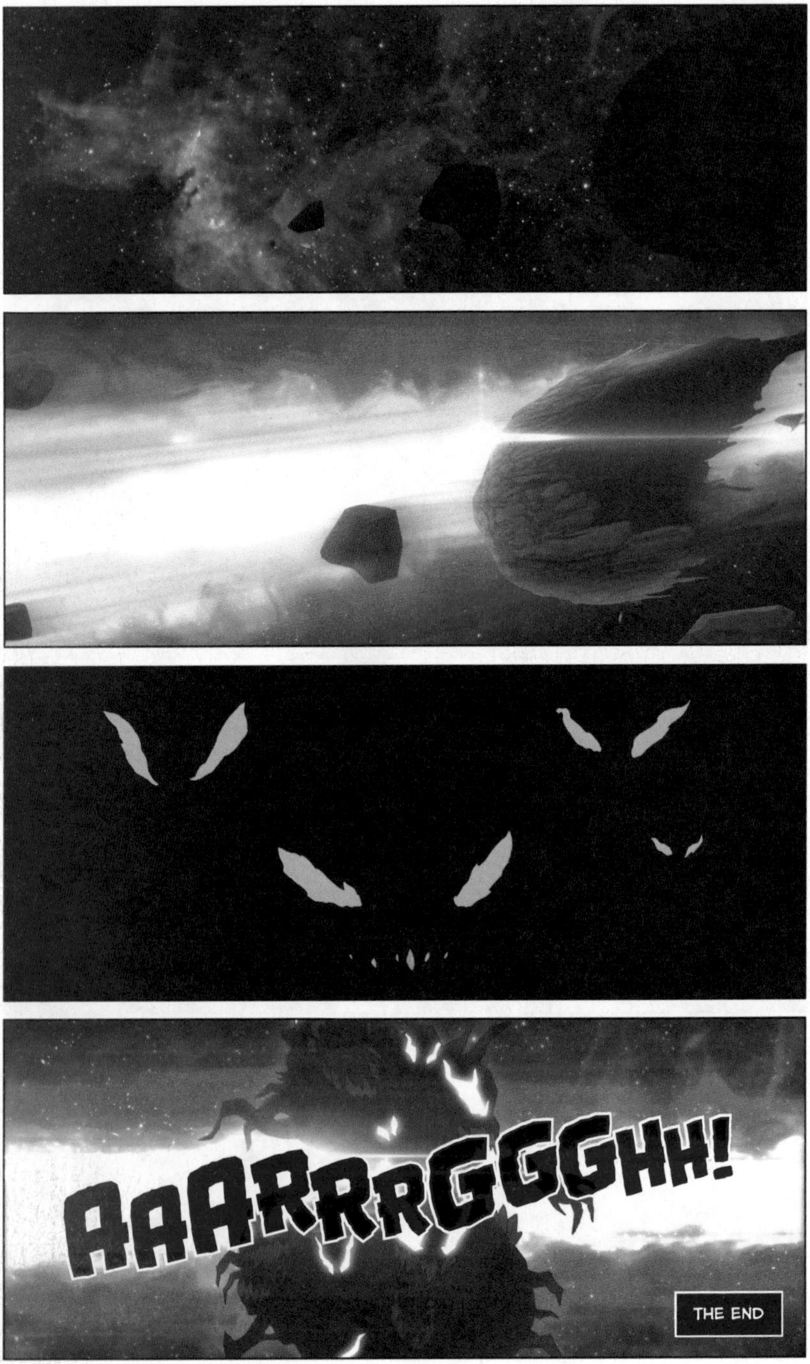
AAARRRGGGHH!
THE END

AMAZING FRIENDS

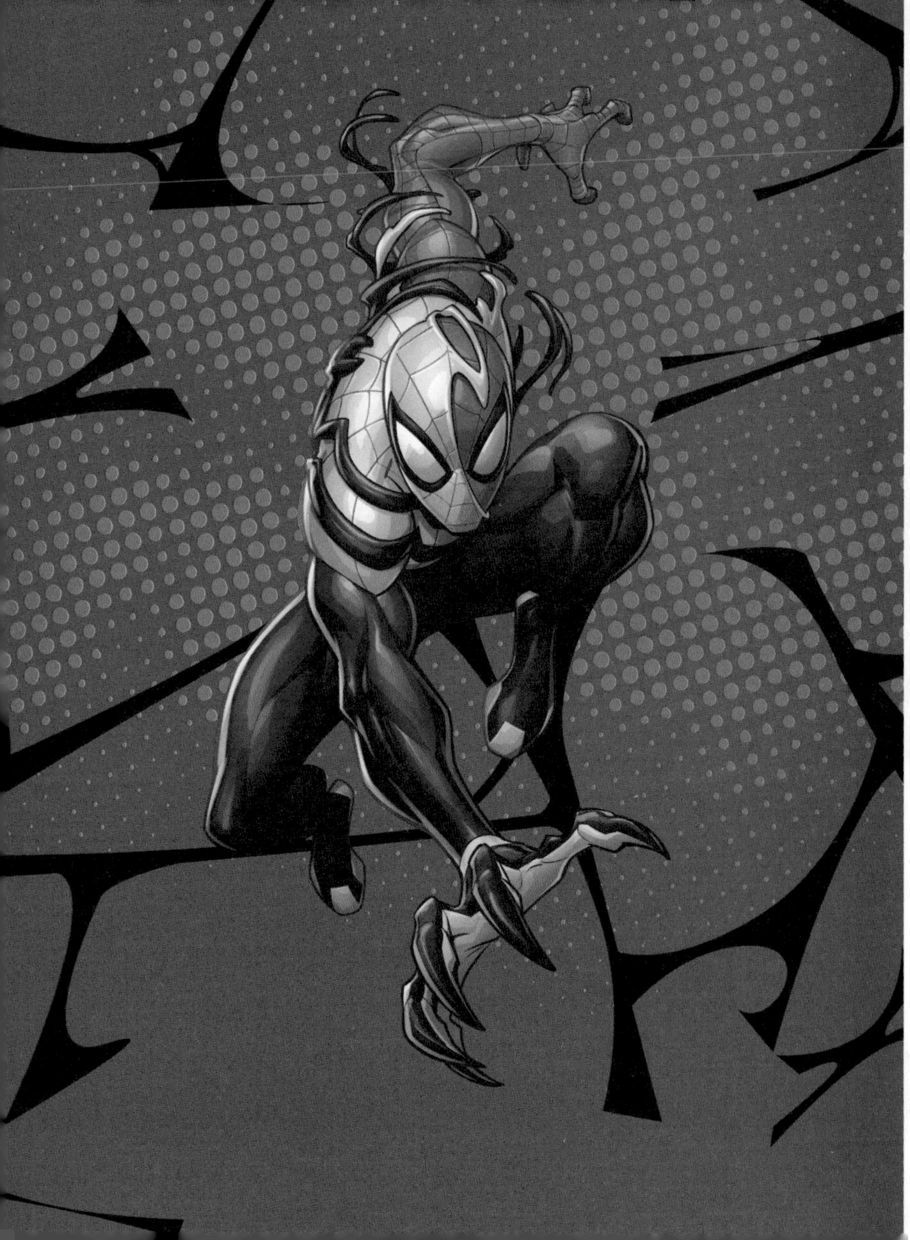

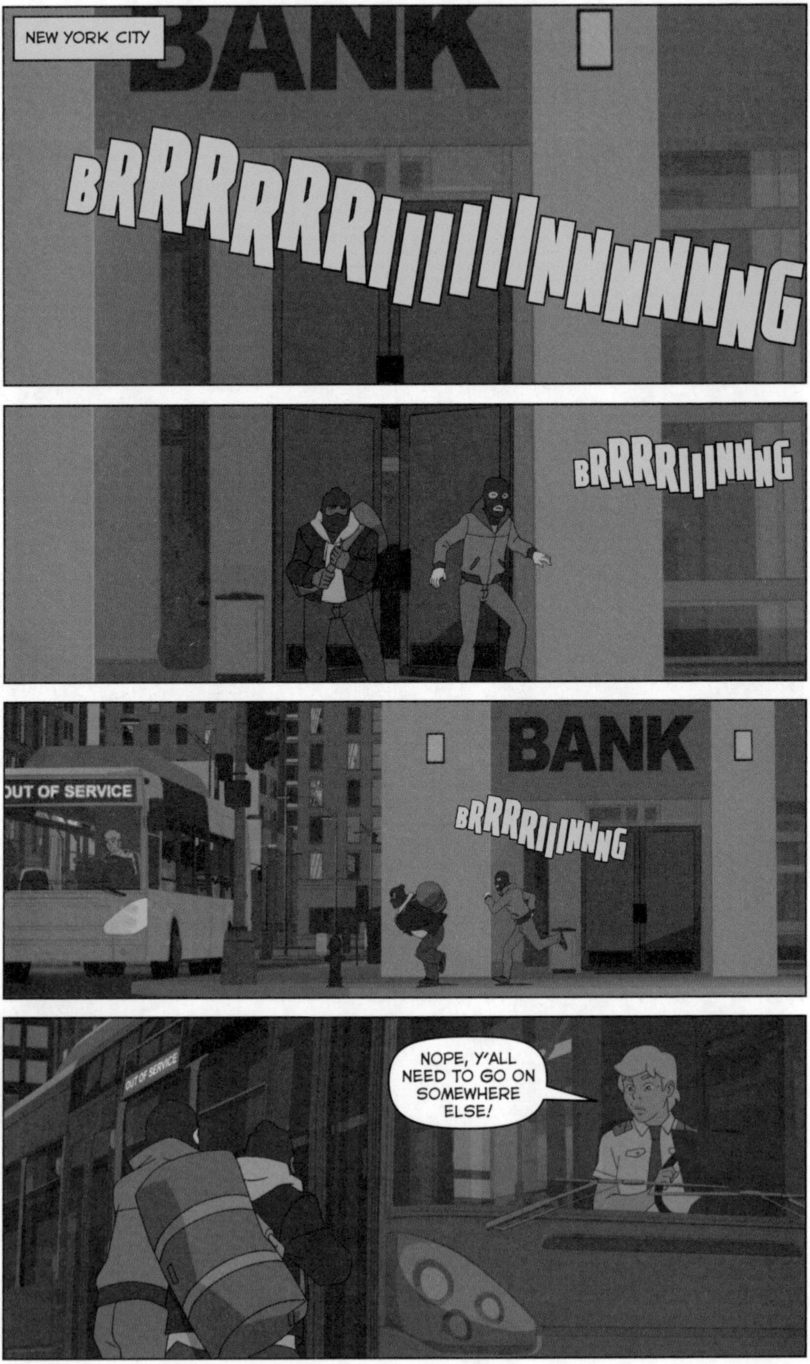
NEW YORK CITY
BANK
BRRRRRRIIIIIIINNNNNNG
BRRRRIIINNNG
OUT OF SERVICE
BANK
BRRRRIIINNNG
OUT OF SERVICE
NOPE, Y'ALL NEED TO GO ON SOMEWHERE ELSE!

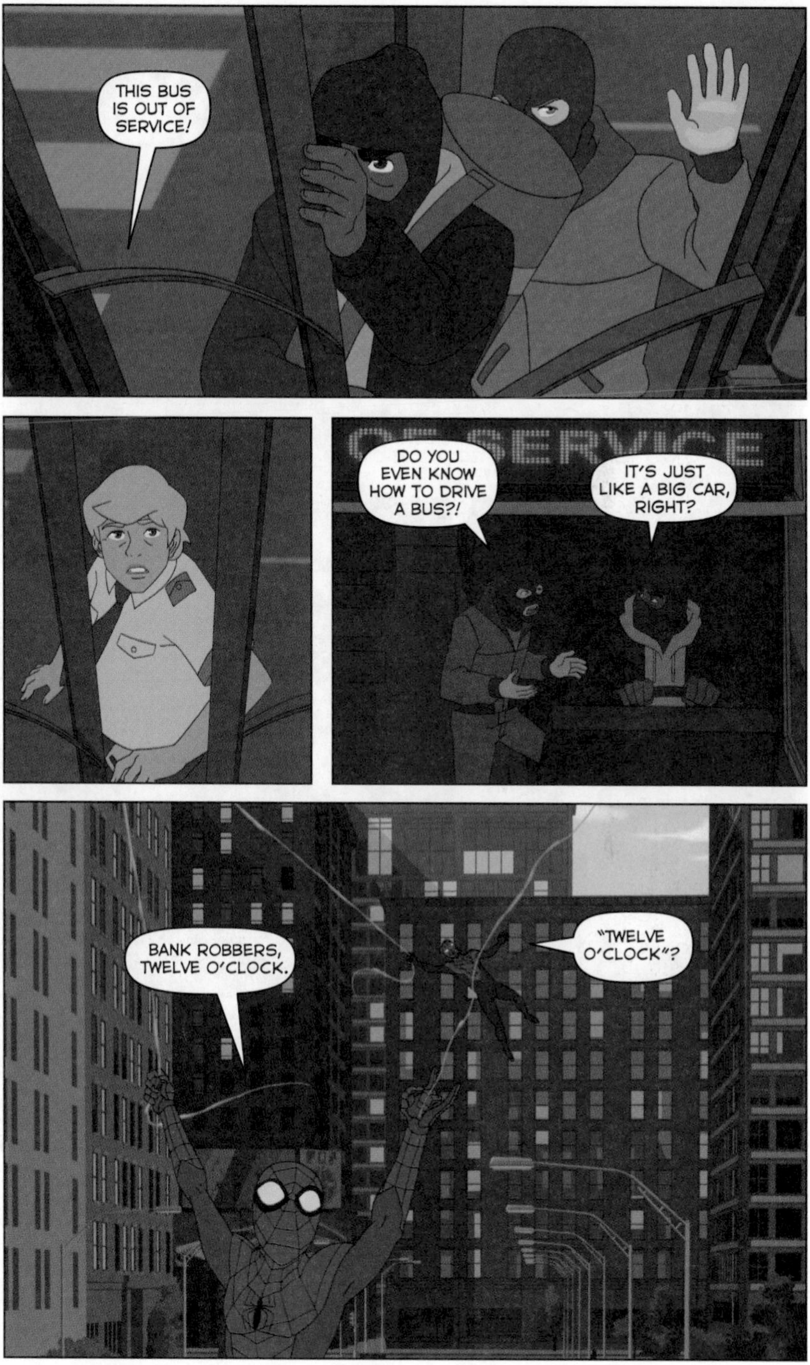
THIS BUS IS OUT OF SERVICE!
OF SERVICE
DO YOU EVEN KNOW HOW TO DRIVE A BUS?!
IT'S JUST LIKE A BIG CAR, RIGHT?
BANK ROBBERS, TWELVE O'CLOCK.
"TWELVE O'CLOCK"?

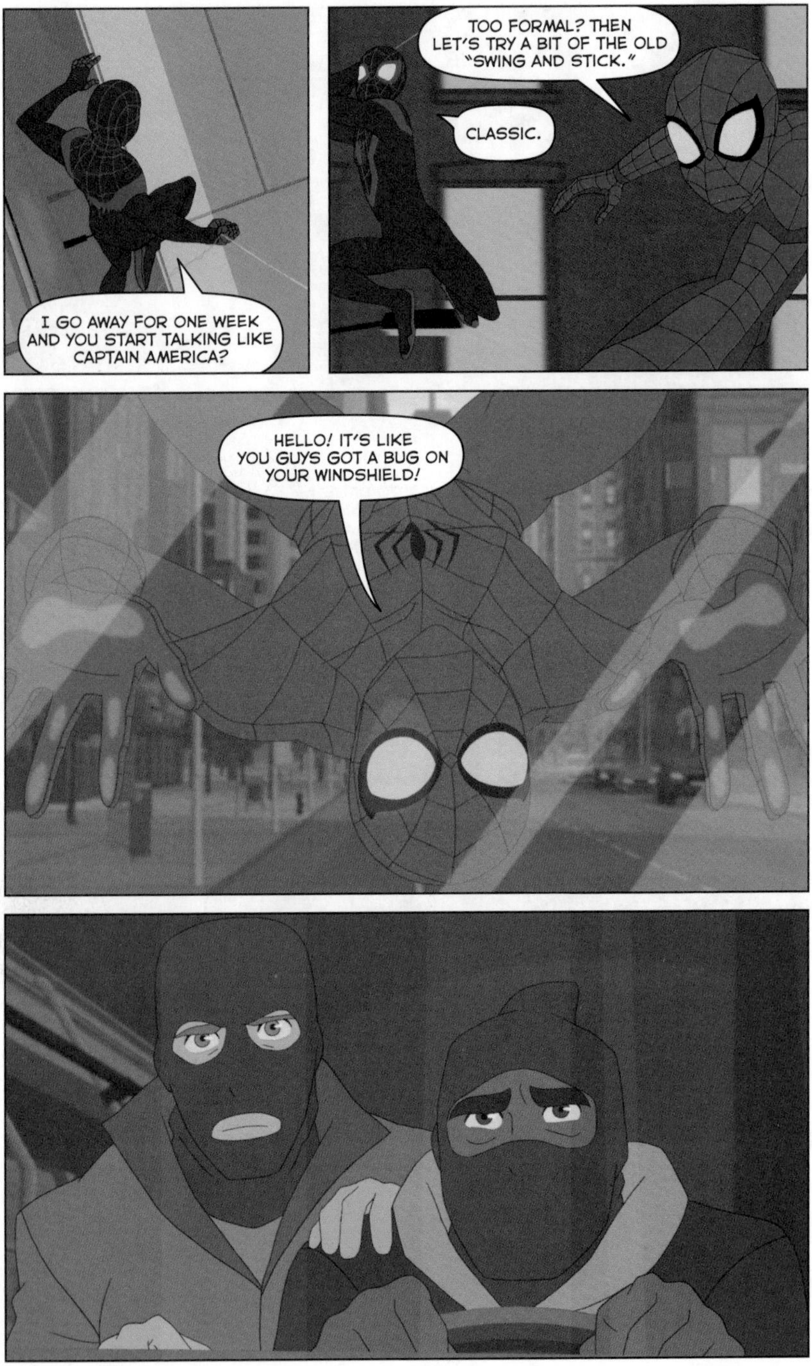
I GO AWAY FOR ONE WEEK AND YOU START TALKING LIKE CAPTAIN AMERICA?
TOO FORMAL? THEN LET'S TRY A BIT OF THE OLD "SWING AND STICK."
CLASSIC.
HELLO! IT'S LIKE YOU GUYS GOT A BUG ON YOUR WINDSHIELD!

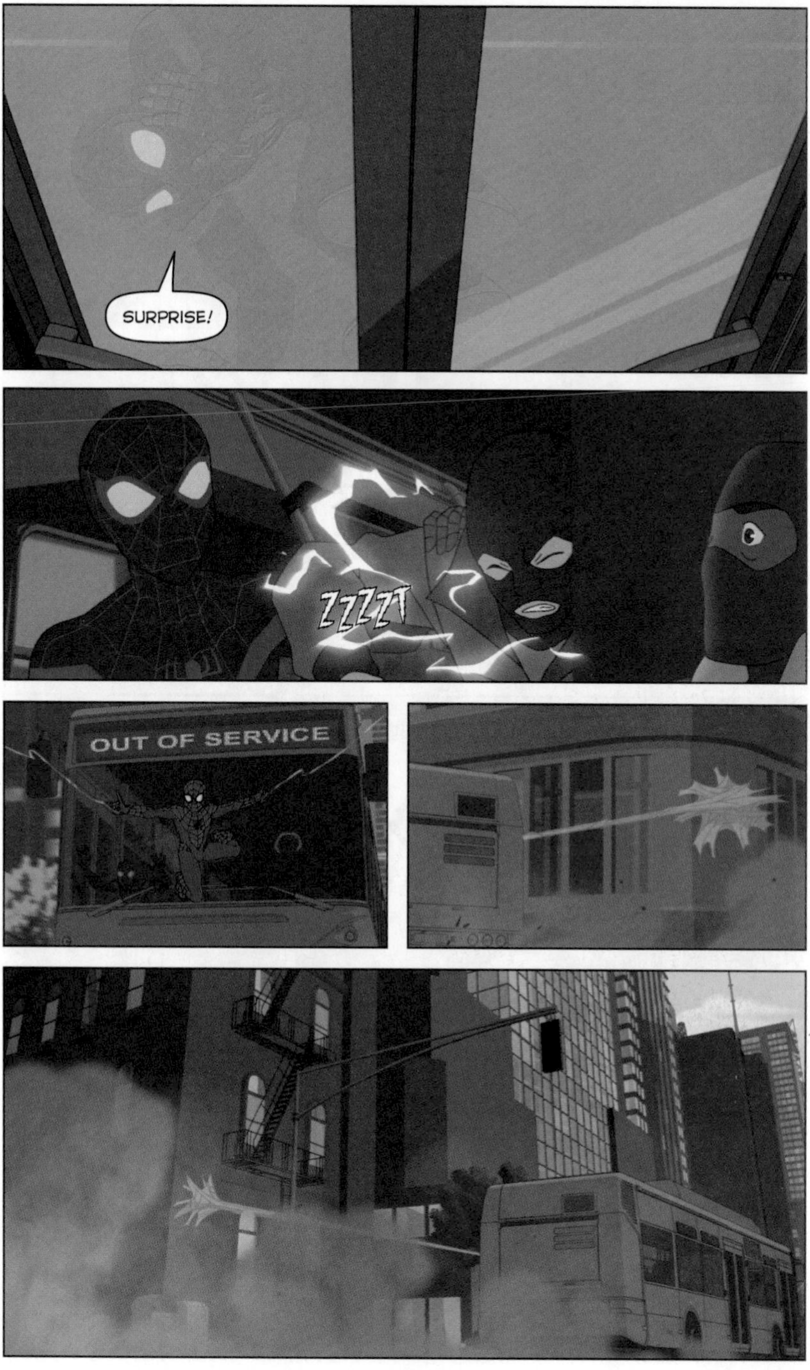
SURPRISE!
ZZZZT
OUT OF SERVICE

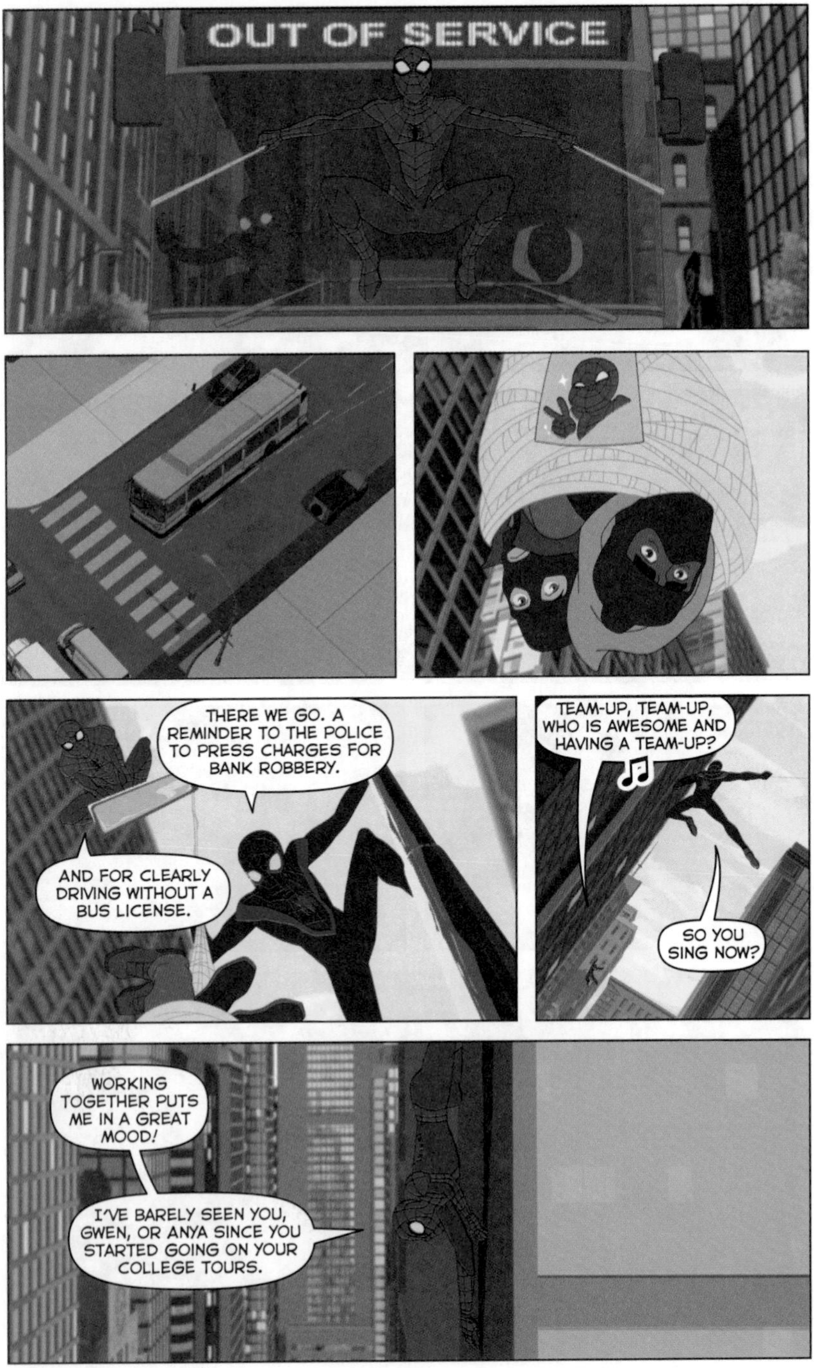
OUT OF SERVICE
THERE WE GO. A REMINDER TO THE POLICE TO PRESS CHARGES FOR BANK ROBBERY.
AND FOR CLEARLY DRIVING WITHOUT A BUS LICENSE.
TEAM-UP, TEAM-UP, WHO IS AWESOME AND HAVING A TEAM-UP?
SO YOU SING NOW?
WORKING TOGETHER PUTS ME IN A GREAT MOOD!
I'VE BARELY SEEN YOU, GWEN, OR ANYA SINCE YOU STARTED GOING ON YOUR COLLEGE TOURS.

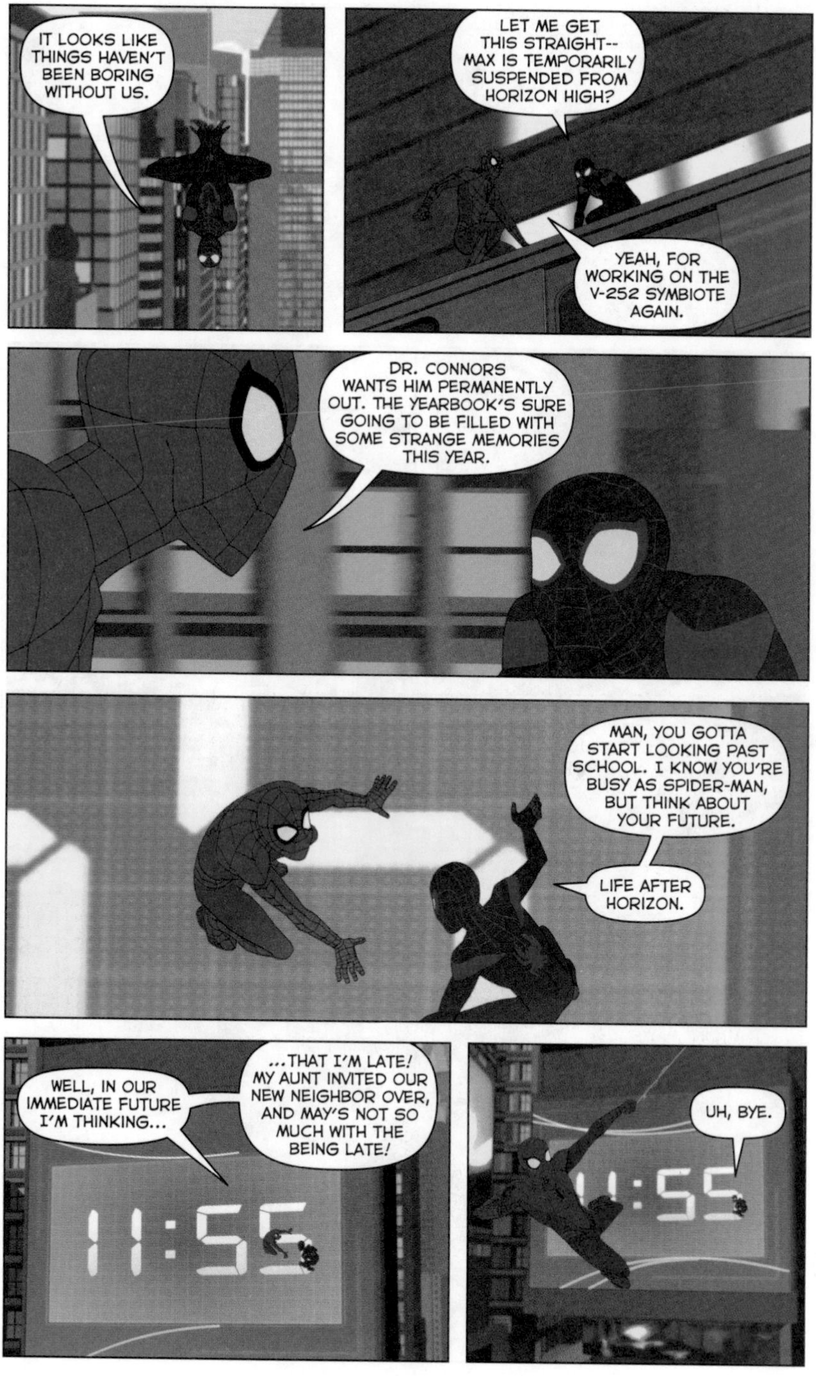
IT LOOKS LIKE THINGS HAVEN'T BEEN BORING WITHOUT US.
LET ME GET THIS STRAIGHT-- MAX IS TEMPORARILY SUSPENDED FROM HORIZON HIGH?
YEAH, FOR WORKING ON THE V-252 SYMBIOTE AGAIN.
DR. CONNORS WANTS HIM PERMANENTLY OUT. THE YEARBOOK'S SURE GOING TO BE FILLED WITH SOME STRANGE MEMORIES THIS YEAR.
MAN, YOU GOTTA START LOOKING PAST SCHOOL. I KNOW YOU'RE BUSY AS SPIDER-MAN, BUT THINK ABOUT YOUR FUTURE.
LIFE AFTER HORIZON.
WELL, IN OUR IMMEDIATE FUTURE I'M THINKING...
...THAT I'M LATE! MY AUNT INVITED OUR NEW NEIGHBOR OVER, AND MAY'S NOT SO MUCH WITH THE BEING LATE!
11:55
UH, BYE.
11:55

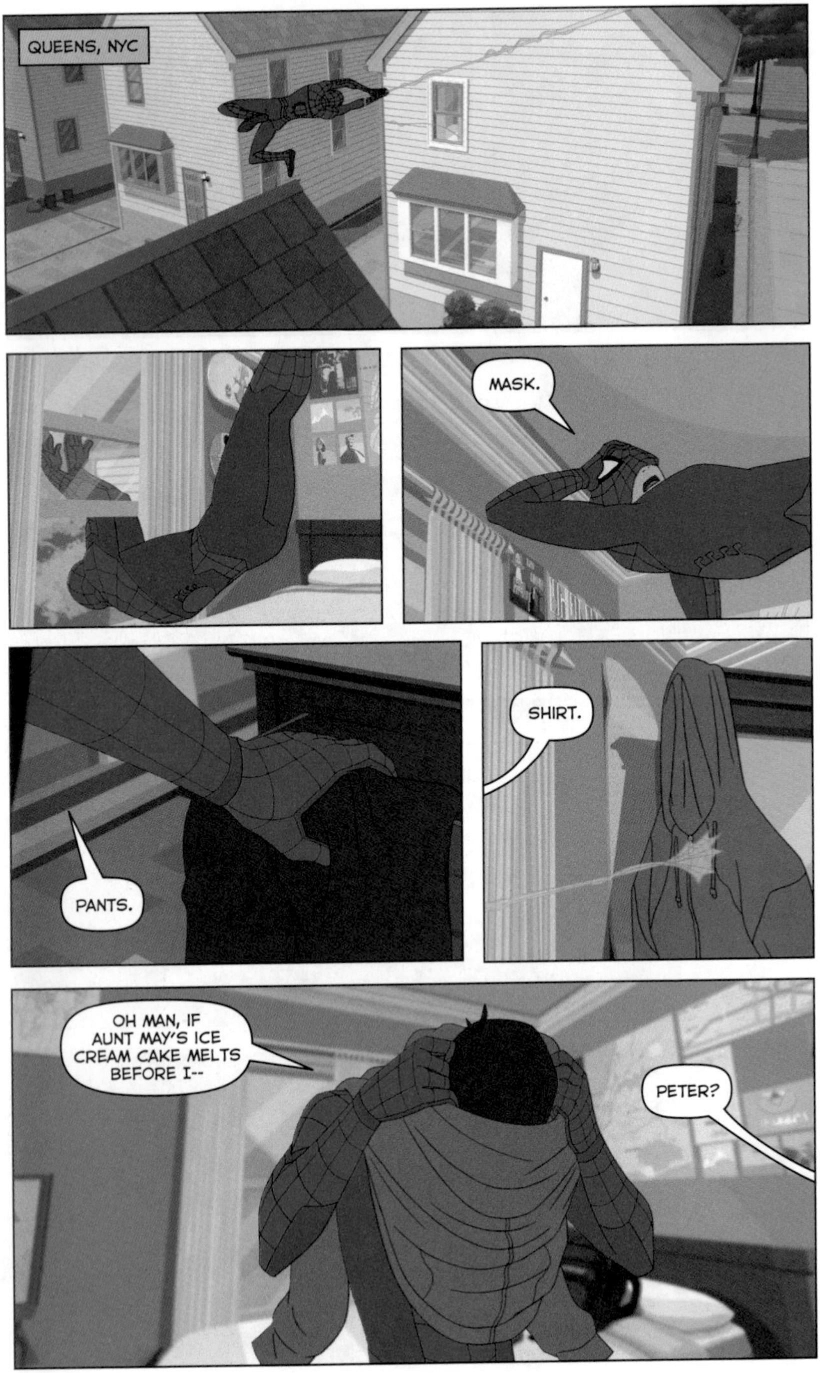
QUEENS, NYC
MASK.
PANTS.
SHIRT.
OH MAN, IF AUNT MAY'S ICE CREAM CAKE MELTS BEFORE I--
PETER?

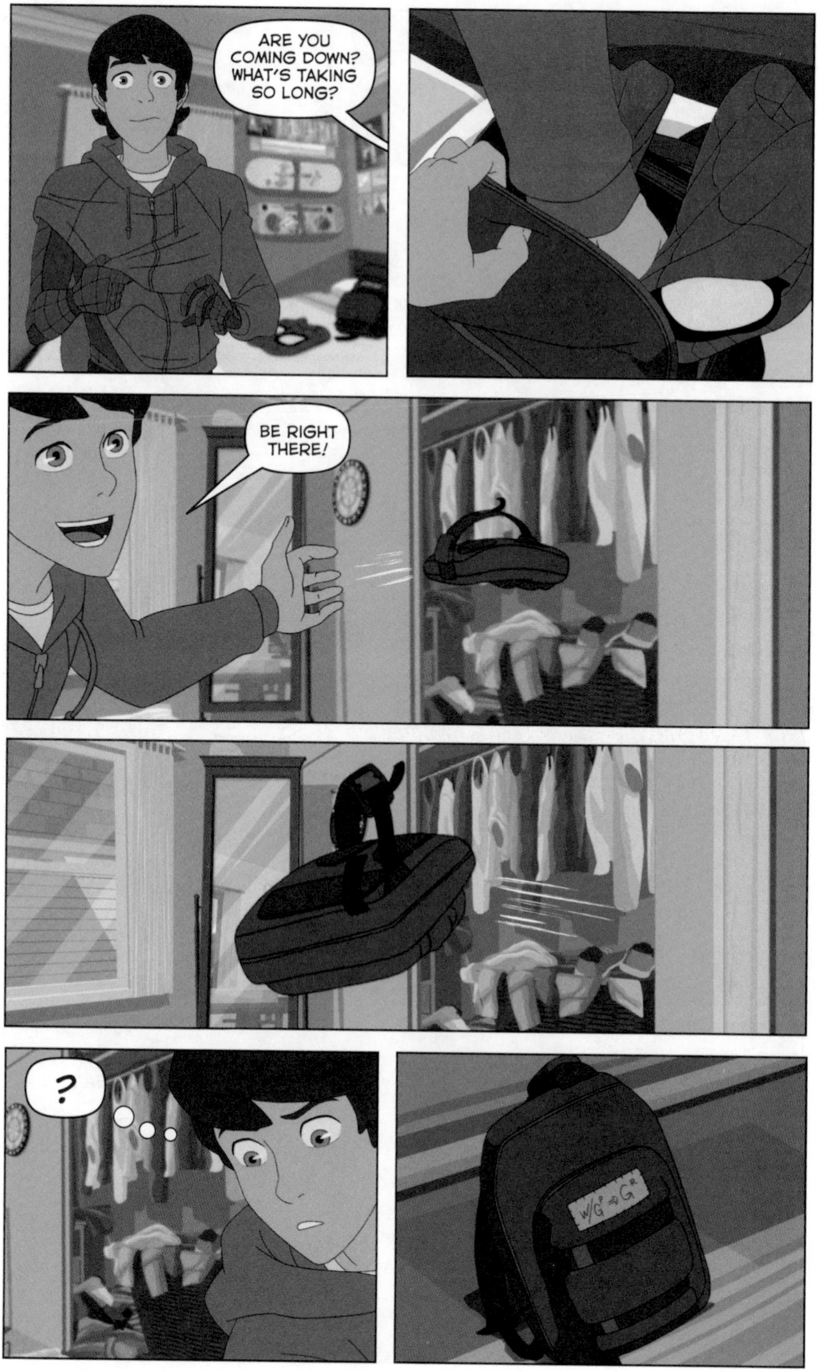
ARE YOU COMING DOWN? WHAT'S TAKING SO LONG?
BE RIGHT THERE!
?

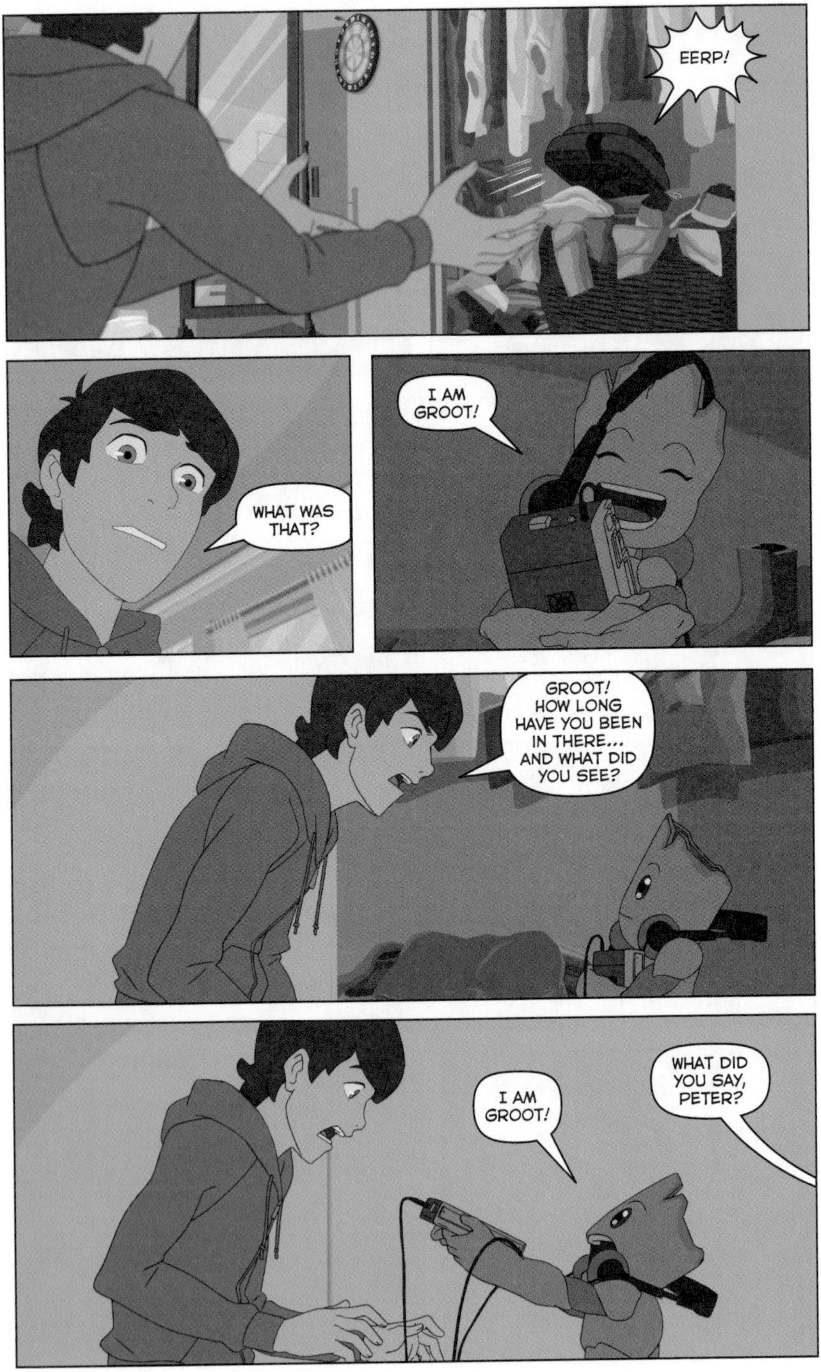
EERP!
WHAT WAS THAT?
I AM GROOT!
GROOT! HOW LONG HAVE YOU BEEN IN THERE... AND WHAT DID YOU SEE?
I AM GROOT!
WHAT DID YOU SAY, PETER?

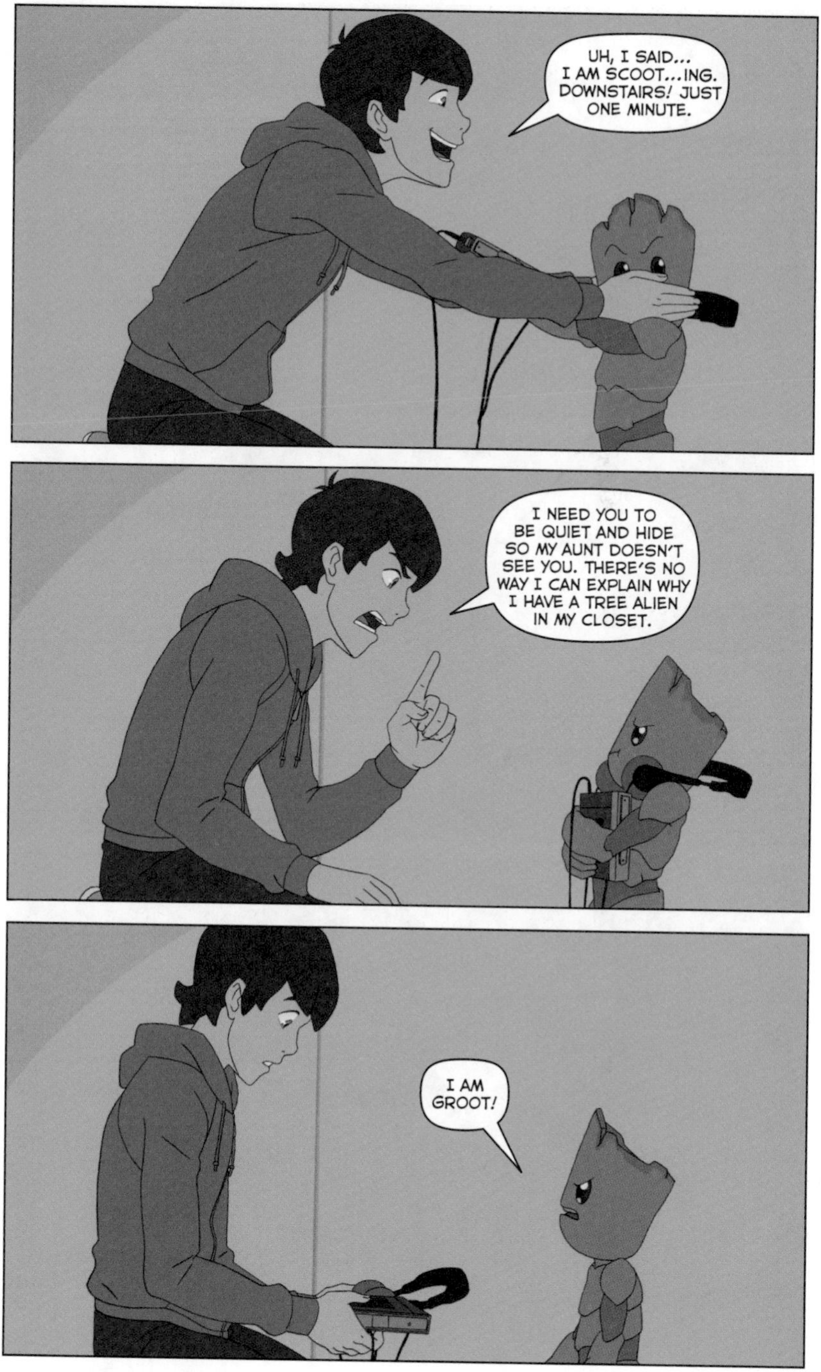
UH, I SAID... I AM SCOOT...ING. DOWNSTAIRS! JUST ONE MINUTE.
I NEED YOU TO BE QUIET AND HIDE SO MY AUNT DOESN'T SEE YOU. THERE'S NO WAY I CAN EXPLAIN WHY I HAVE A TREE ALIEN IN MY CLOSET.
I AM GROOT!

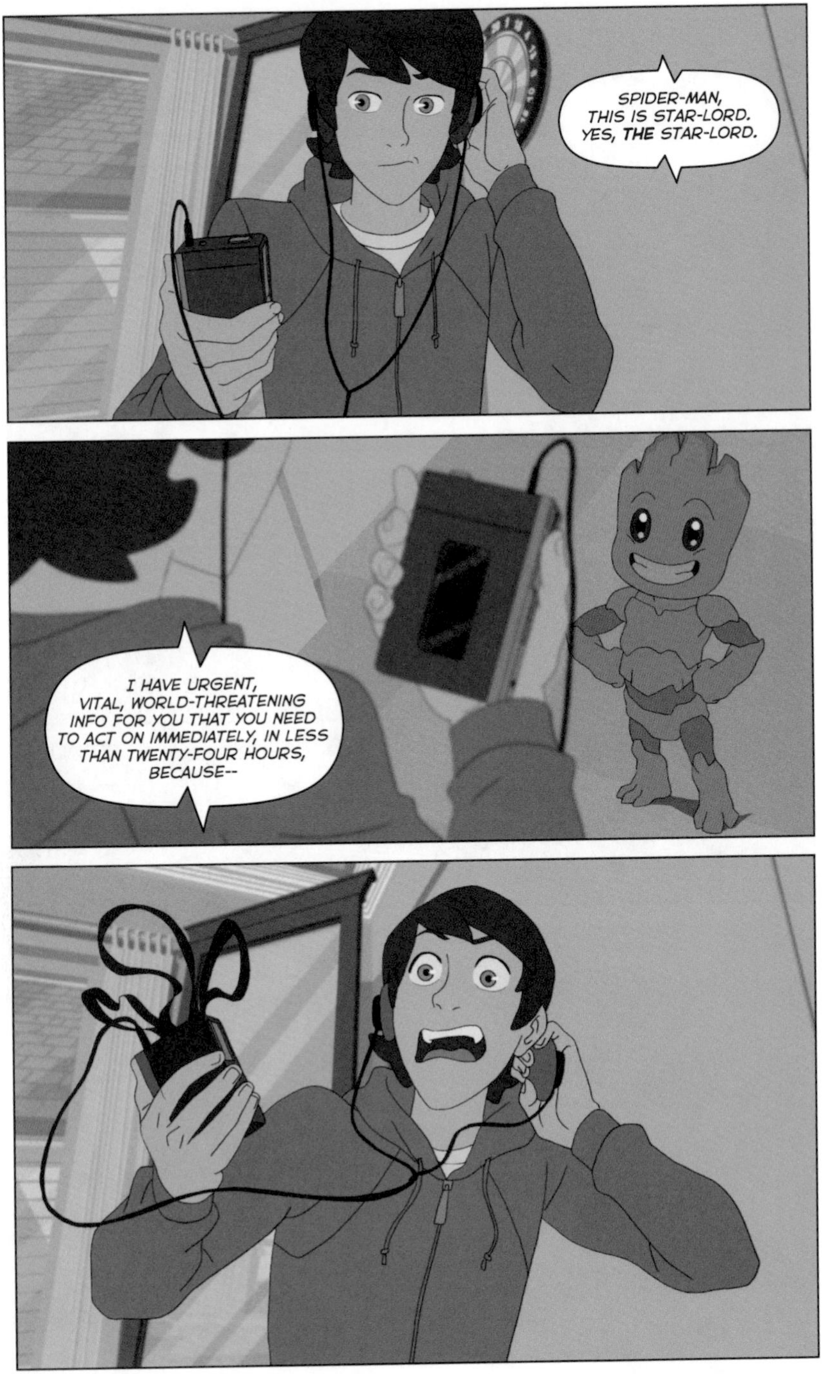
SPIDER-MAN, THIS IS STAR-LORD. YES, THE STAR-LORD.
I HAVE URGENT, VITAL, WORLD-THREATENING INFO FOR YOU THAT YOU NEED TO ACT ON IMMEDIATELY, IN LESS THAN TWENTY-FOUR HOURS, BECAUSE--

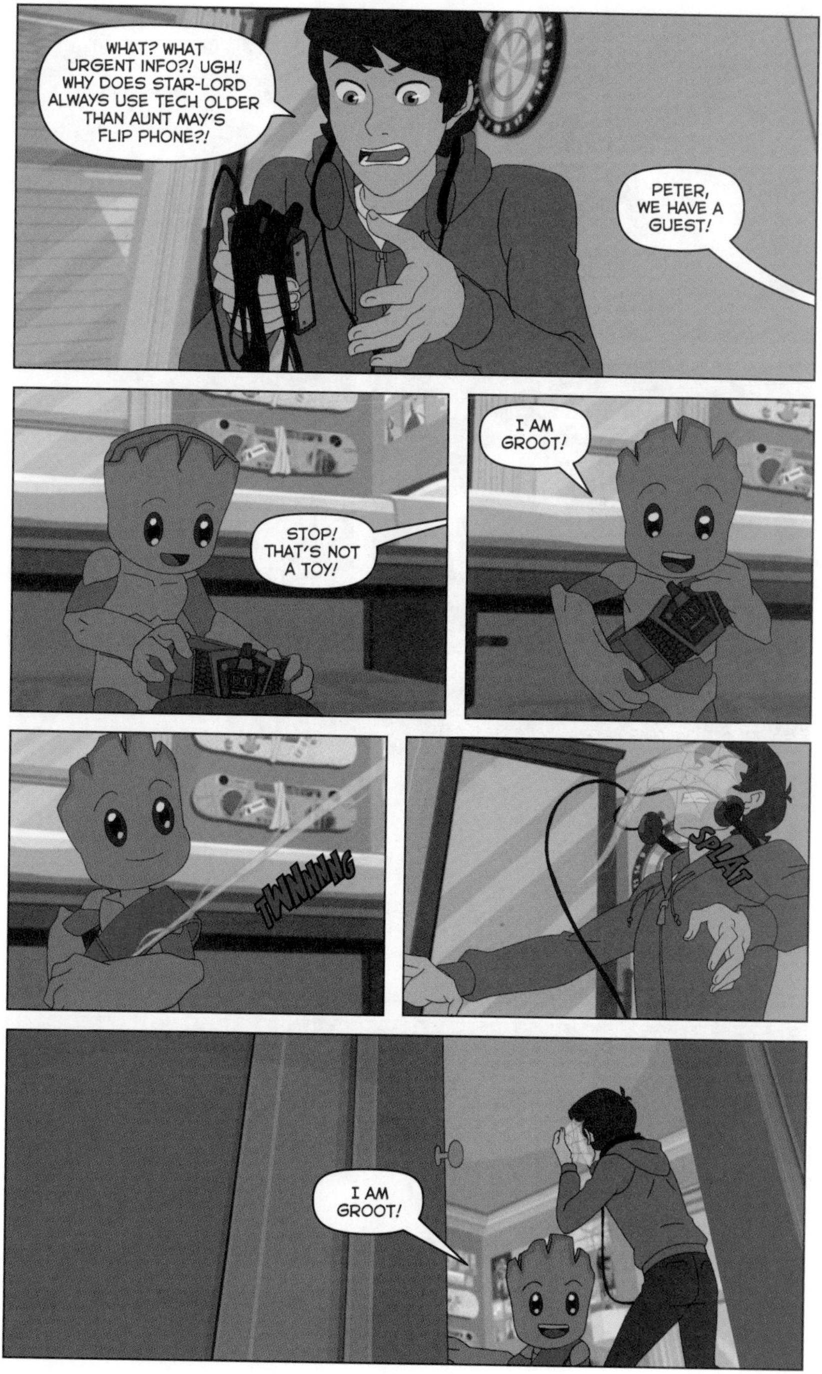
WHAT? WHAT URGENT INFO?! UGH! WHY DOES STAR-LORD ALWAYS USE TECH OLDER THAN AUNT MAY'S FLIP PHONE?!
PETER, WE HAVE A GUEST!
STOP! THAT'S NOT A TOY!
I AM GROOT!
TWNNNNG
SPLAT
I AM GROOT!

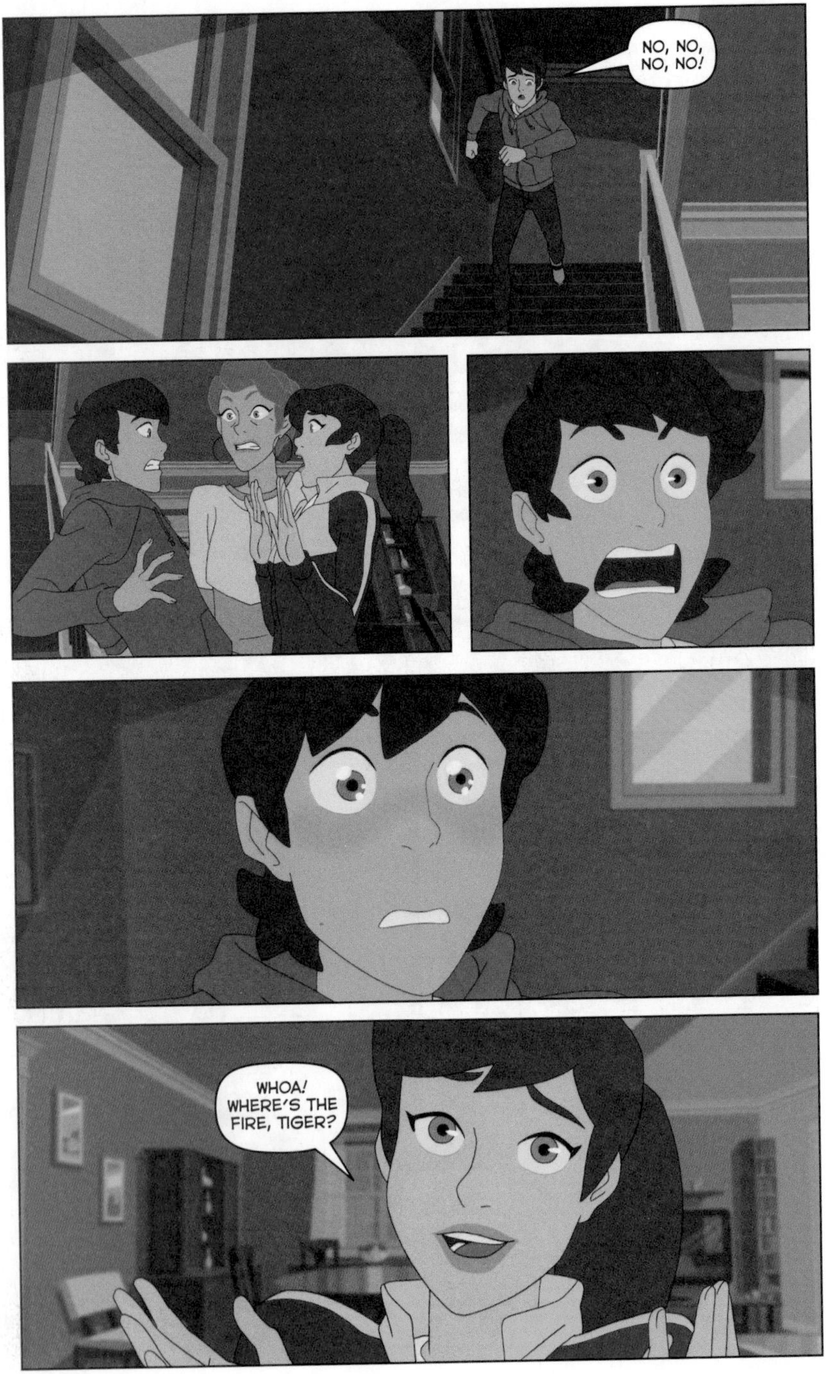
NO, NO,
NO, NO!
WHOA!
WHERE'S THE
FIRE, TIGER?

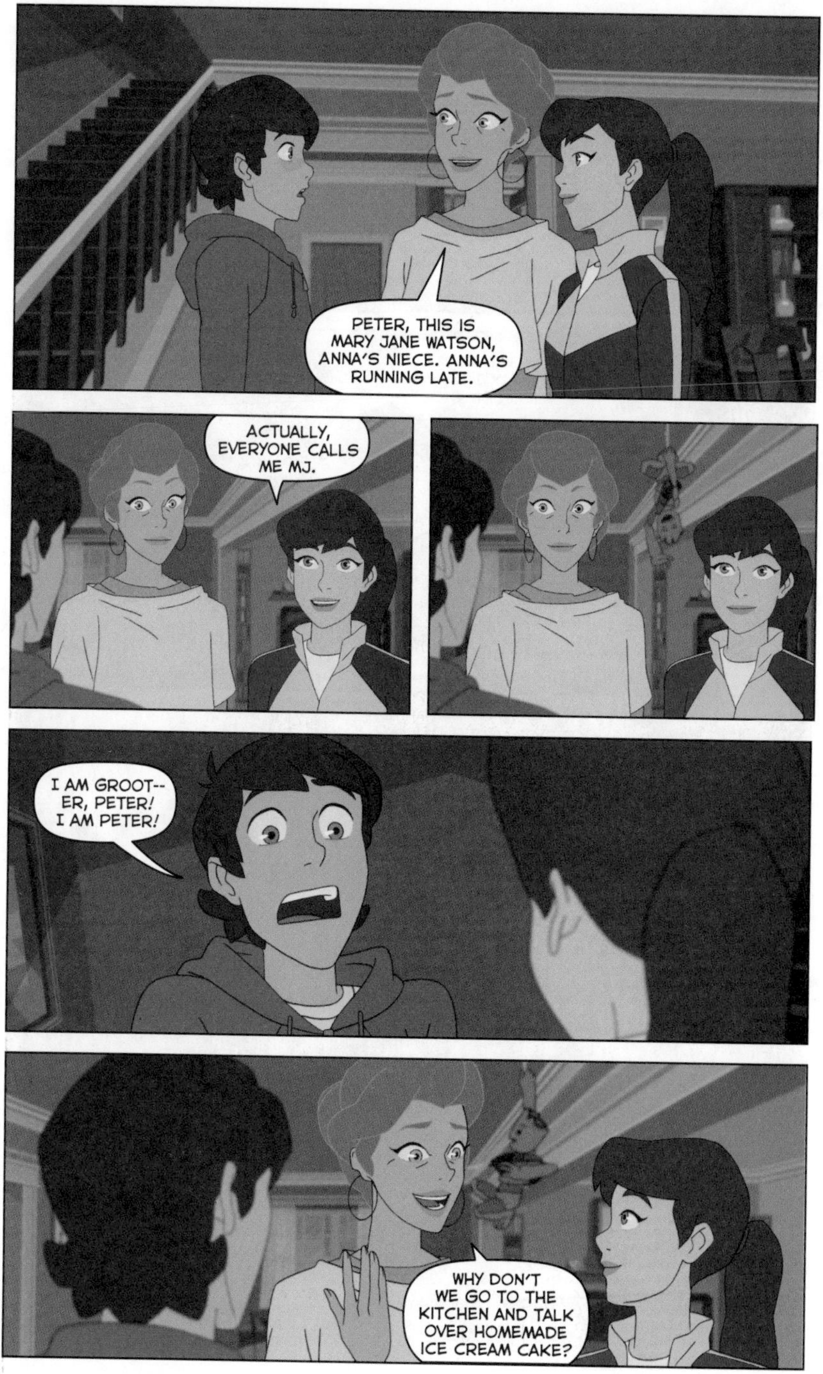
PETER, THIS IS MARY JANE WATSON, ANNA'S NIECE. ANNA'S RUNNING LATE.
ACTUALLY, EVERYONE CALLS ME MJ.
I AM GROOT-- ER, PETER! I AM PETER!
WHY DON'T WE GO TO THE KITCHEN AND TALK OVER HOMEMADE ICE CREAM CAKE?

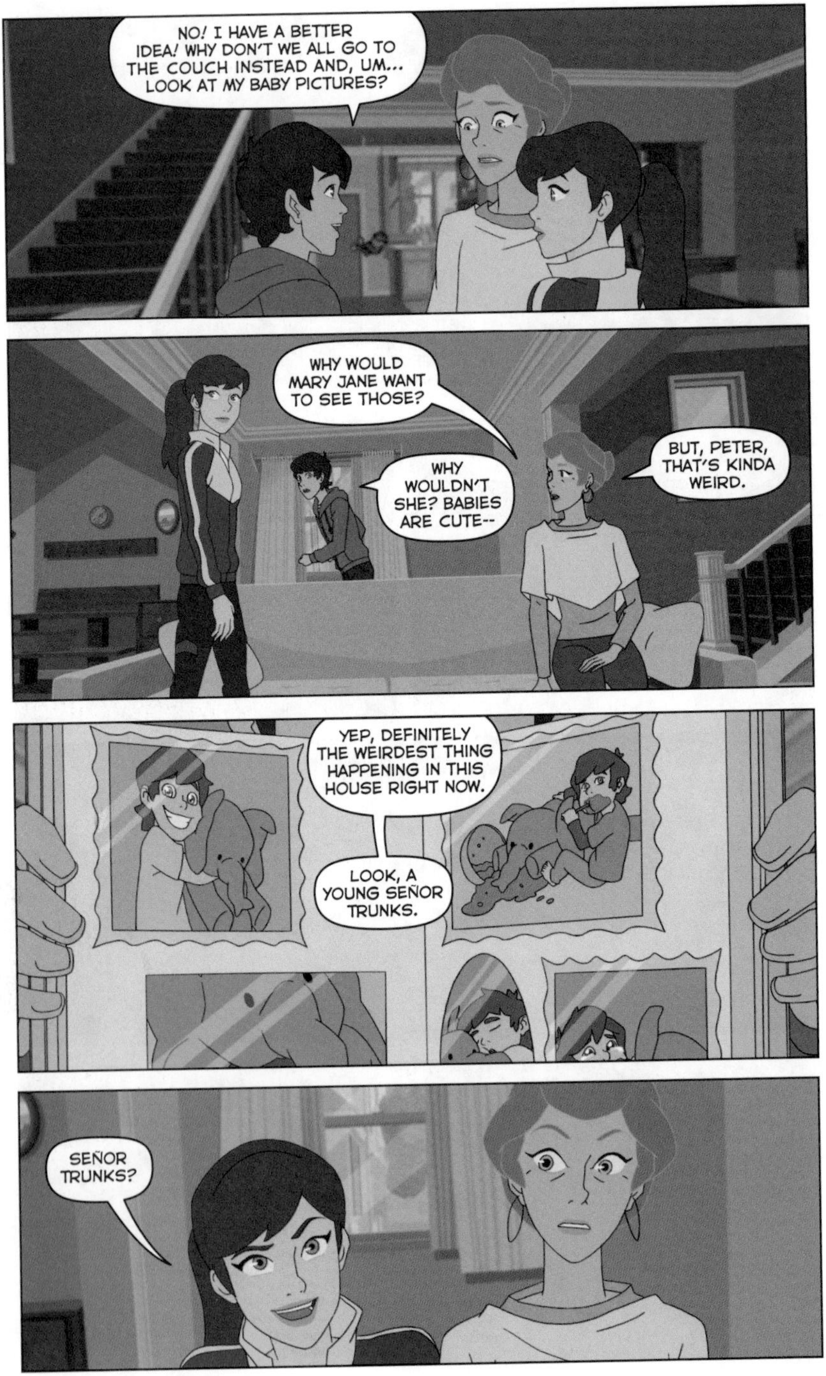
NO! I HAVE A BETTER IDEA! WHY DON'T WE ALL GO TO THE COUCH INSTEAD AND, UM... LOOK AT MY BABY PICTURES?
WHY WOULD MARY JANE WANT TO SEE THOSE?
BUT, PETER, THAT'S KINDA WEIRD.
WHY WOULDN'T SHE? BABIES ARE CUTE--
YEP, DEFINITELY THE WEIRDEST THING HAPPENING IN THIS HOUSE RIGHT NOW.
LOOK, A YOUNG SEÑOR TRUNKS.
SEÑOR TRUNKS?

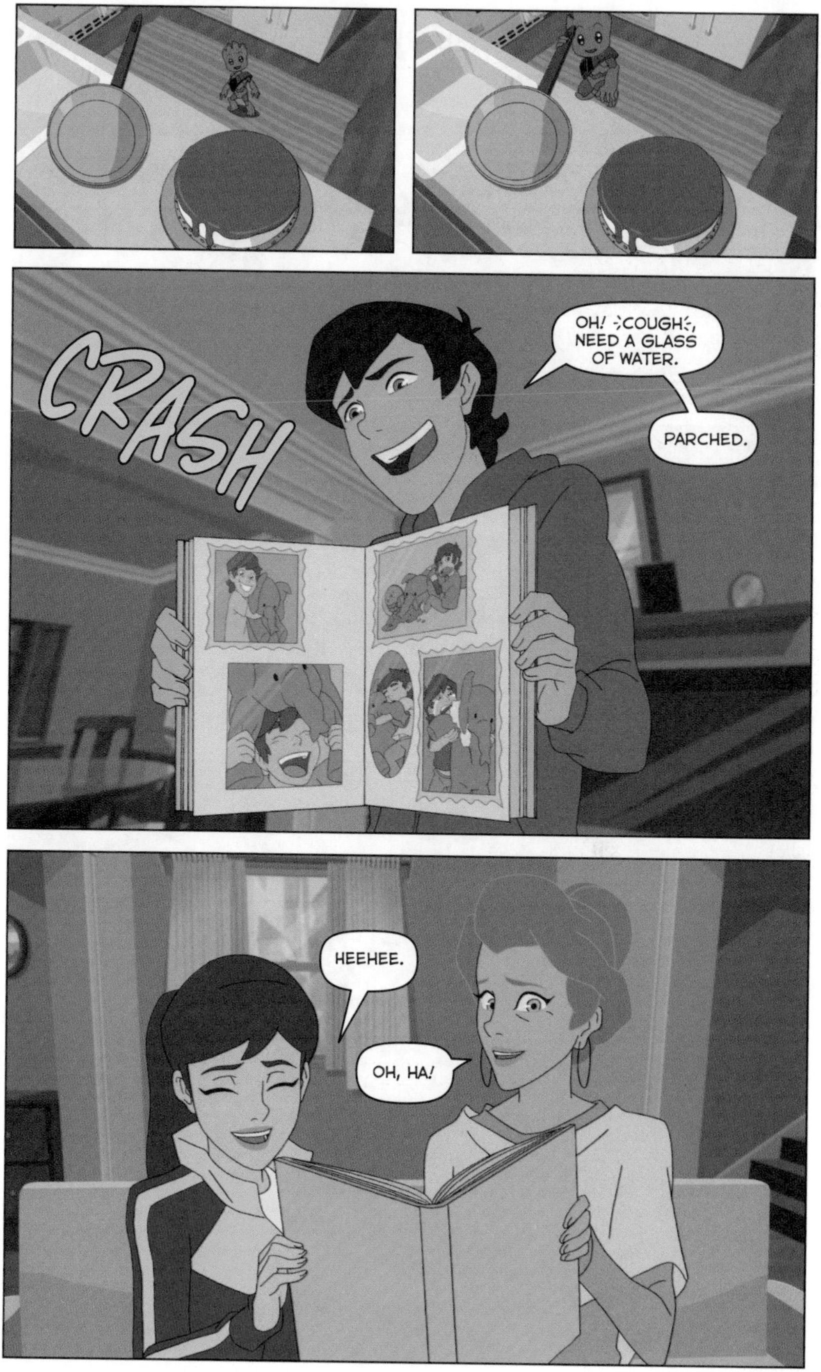
CRASH
OH! ⁖COUGH⁖, NEED A GLASS OF WATER.
PARCHED.
HEEHEE.
OH, HA!

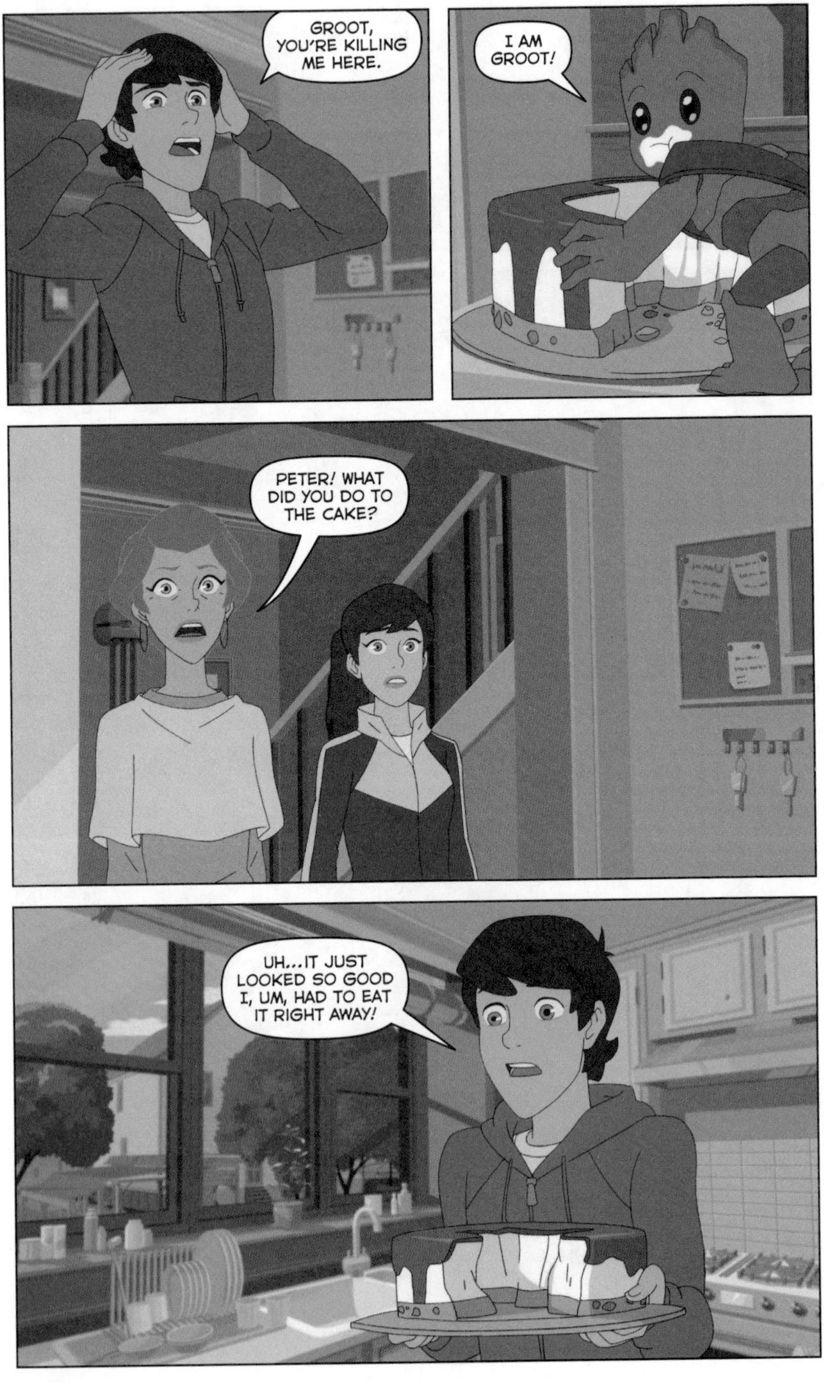
GROOT, YOU'RE KILLING ME HERE.
I AM GROOT!
PETER! WHAT DID YOU DO TO THE CAKE?
UH...IT JUST LOOKED SO GOOD I, UM, HAD TO EAT IT RIGHT AWAY!

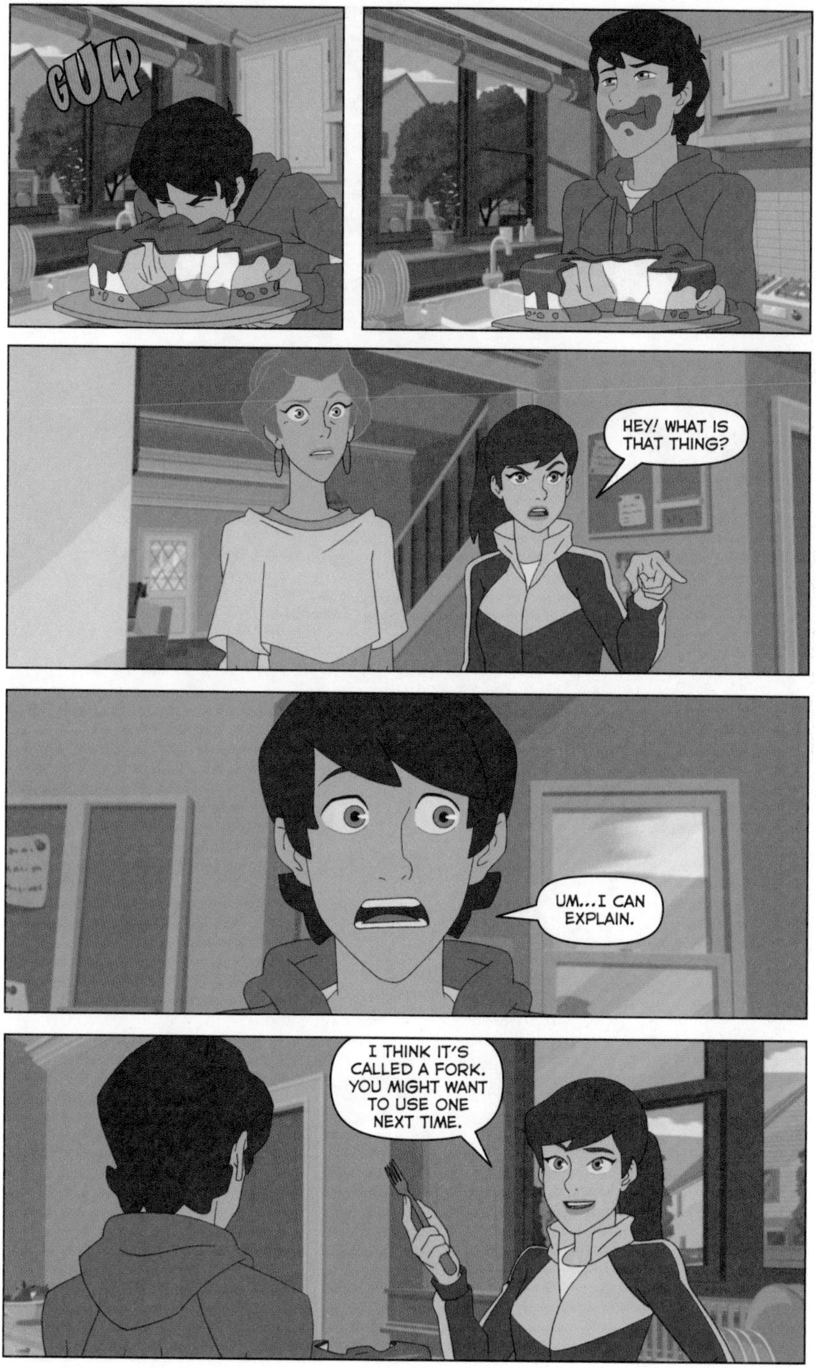
GULP
HEY! WHAT IS THAT THING?
UM...I CAN EXPLAIN.
I THINK IT'S CALLED A FORK. YOU MIGHT WANT TO USE ONE NEXT TIME.

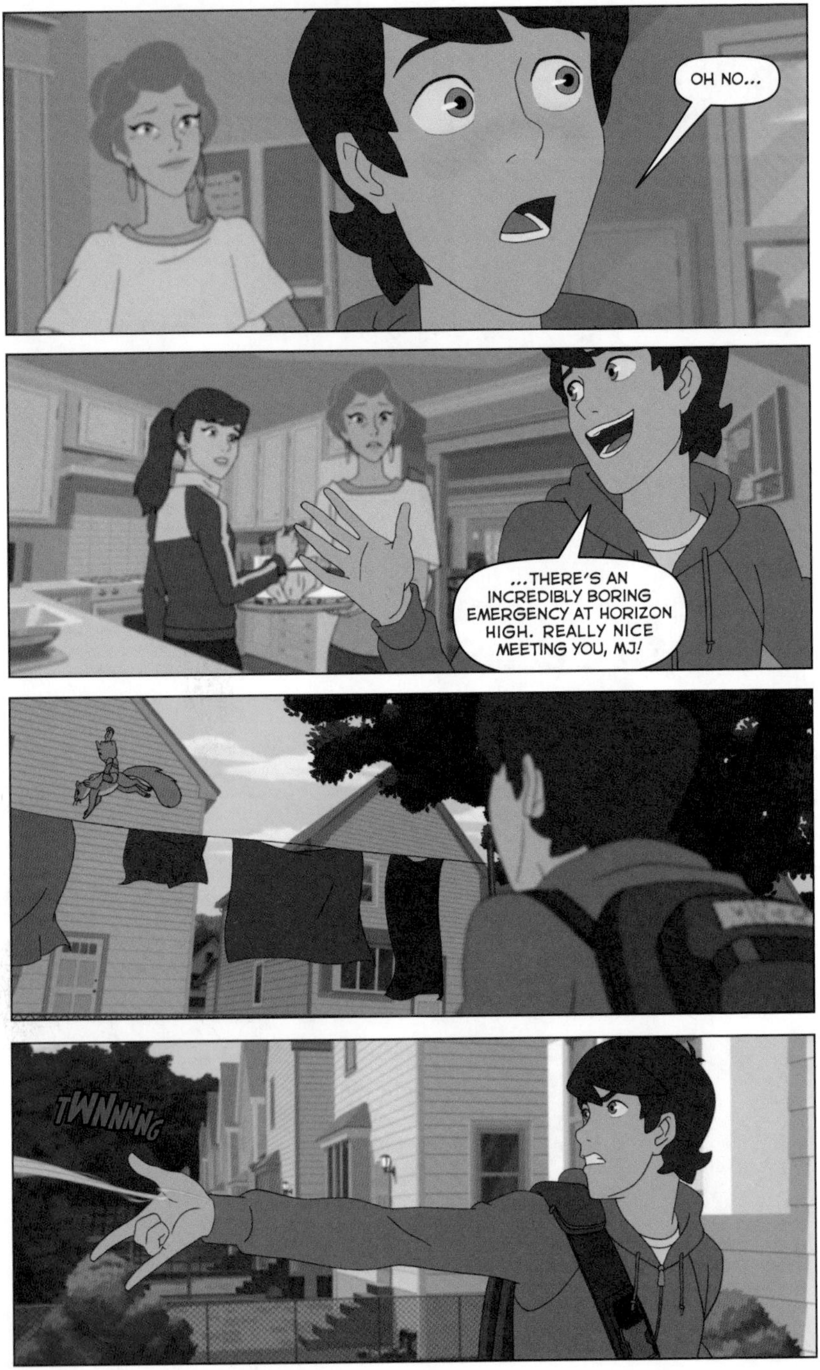
OH NO...
...THERE'S AN INCREDIBLY BORING EMERGENCY AT HORIZON HIGH. REALLY NICE MEETING YOU, MJ!
TWNNNNG

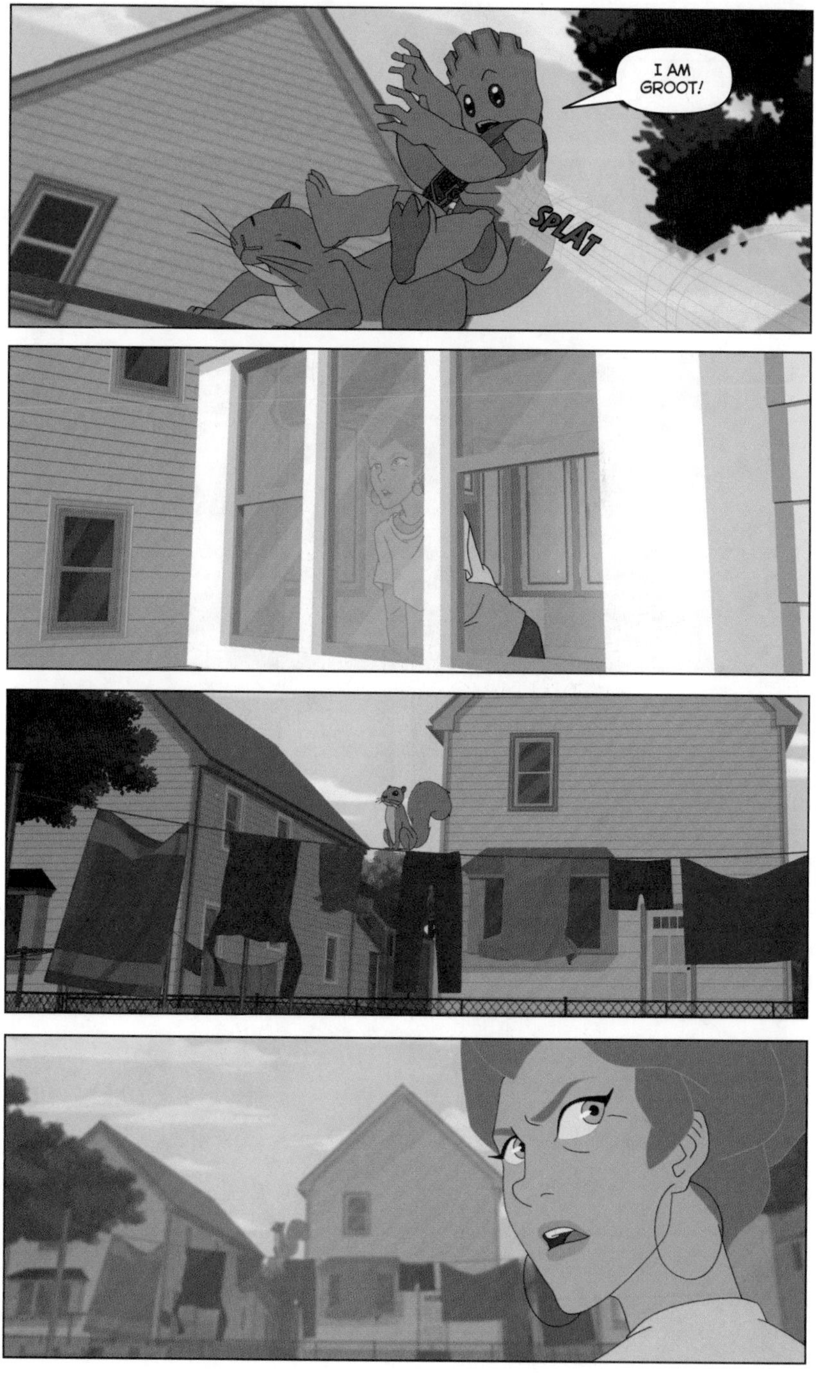
I AM GROOT!
SPLAT

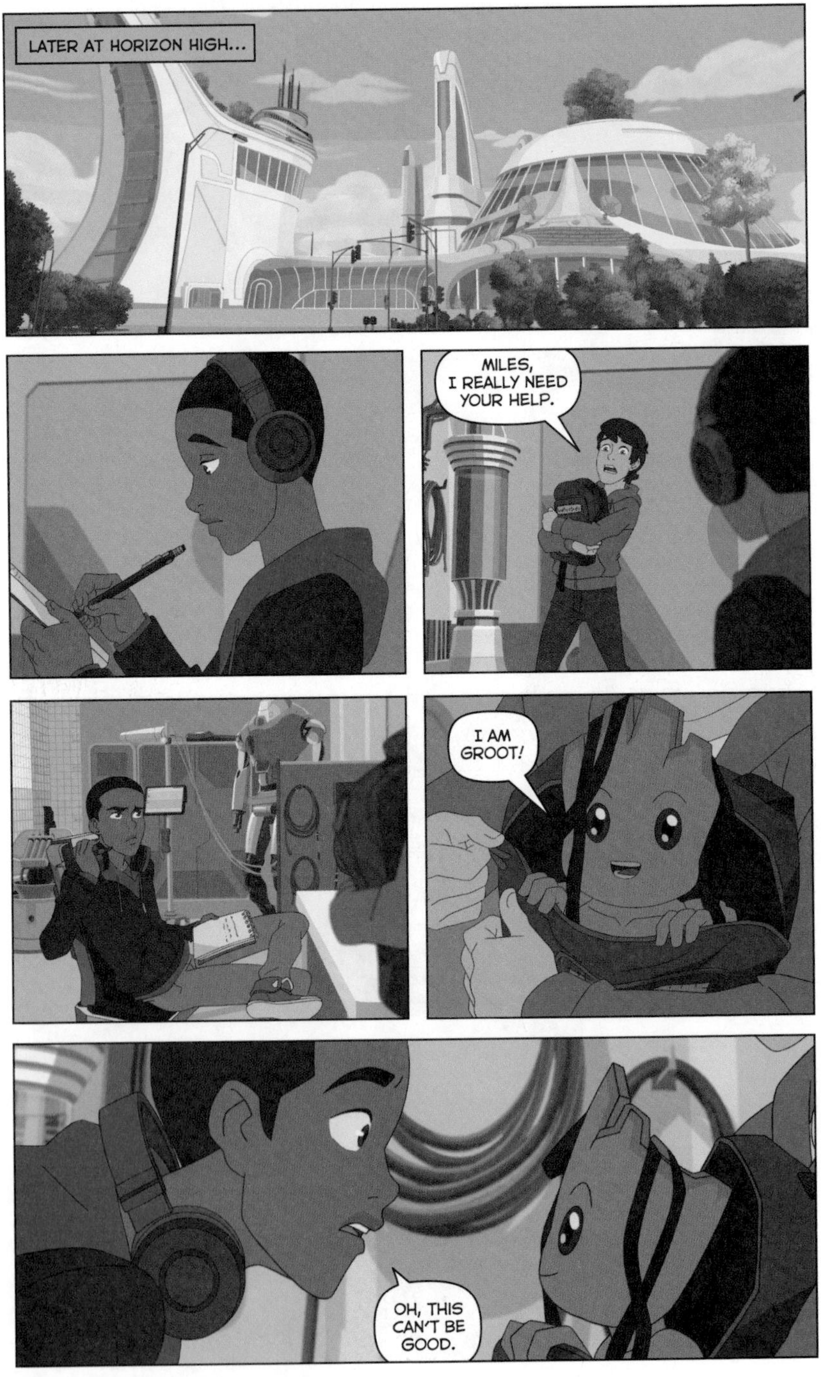
LATER AT HORIZON HIGH...
MILES, I REALLY NEED YOUR HELP.
I AM GROOT!
OH, THIS CAN'T BE GOOD.

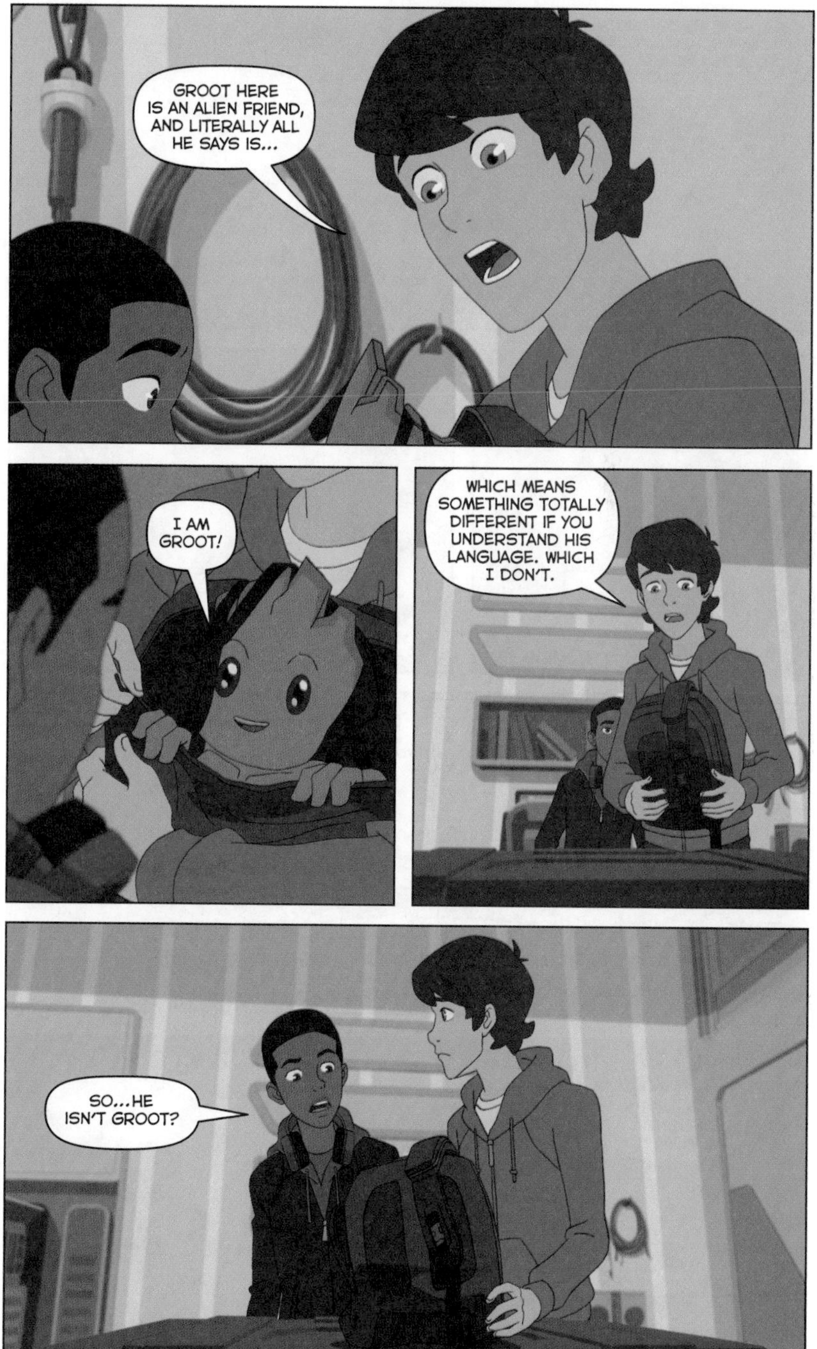
GROOT HERE IS AN ALIEN FRIEND, AND LITERALLY ALL HE SAYS IS...
I AM GROOT!
WHICH MEANS SOMETHING TOTALLY DIFFERENT IF YOU UNDERSTAND HIS LANGUAGE. WHICH I DON'T.
SO...HE ISN'T GROOT?

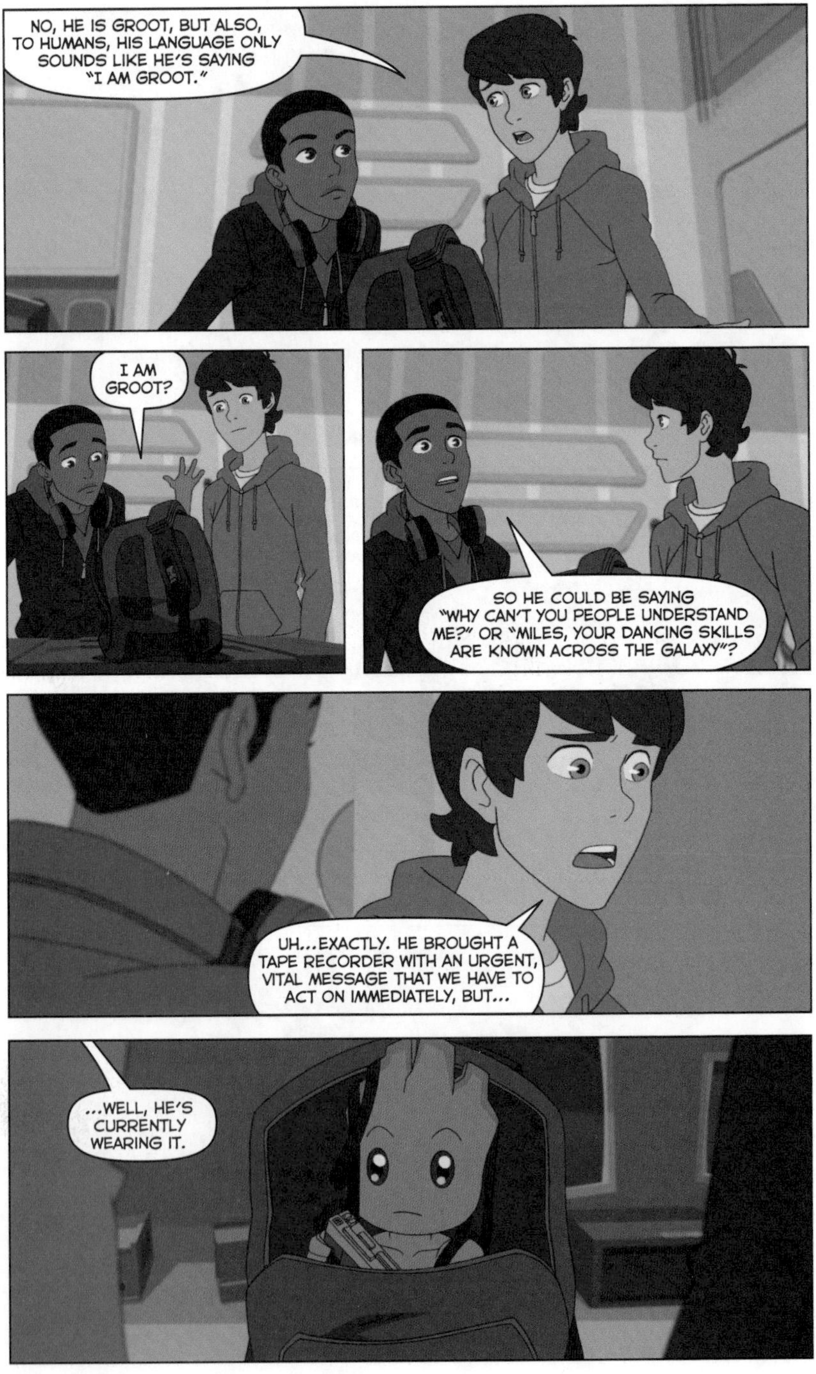
NO, HE IS GROOT, BUT ALSO, TO HUMANS, HIS LANGUAGE ONLY SOUNDS LIKE HE'S SAYING "I AM GROOT."
I AM GROOT?
SO HE COULD BE SAYING "WHY CAN'T YOU PEOPLE UNDERSTAND ME?" OR "MILES, YOUR DANCING SKILLS ARE KNOWN ACROSS THE GALAXY"?
UH...EXACTLY. HE BROUGHT A TAPE RECORDER WITH AN URGENT, VITAL MESSAGE THAT WE HAVE TO ACT ON IMMEDIATELY, BUT...
...WELL, HE'S CURRENTLY WEARING IT.

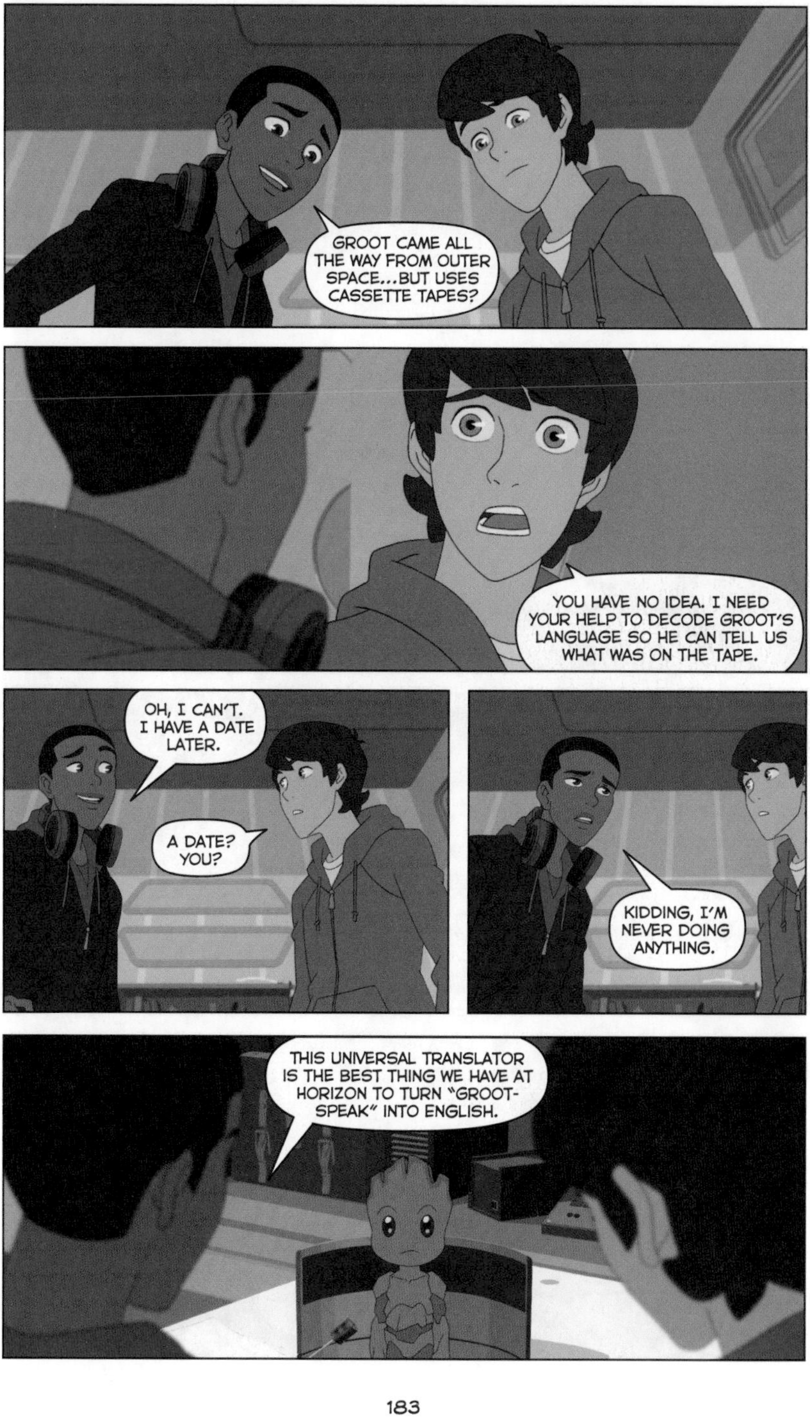
GROOT CAME ALL THE WAY FROM OUTER SPACE...BUT USES CASSETTE TAPES?
YOU HAVE NO IDEA. I NEED YOUR HELP TO DECODE GROOT'S LANGUAGE SO HE CAN TELL US WHAT WAS ON THE TAPE.
OH, I CAN'T. I HAVE A DATE LATER.
A DATE? YOU?
KIDDING, I'M NEVER DOING ANYTHING.
THIS UNIVERSAL TRANSLATOR IS THE BEST THING WE HAVE AT HORIZON TO TURN "GROOT-SPEAK" INTO ENGLISH.

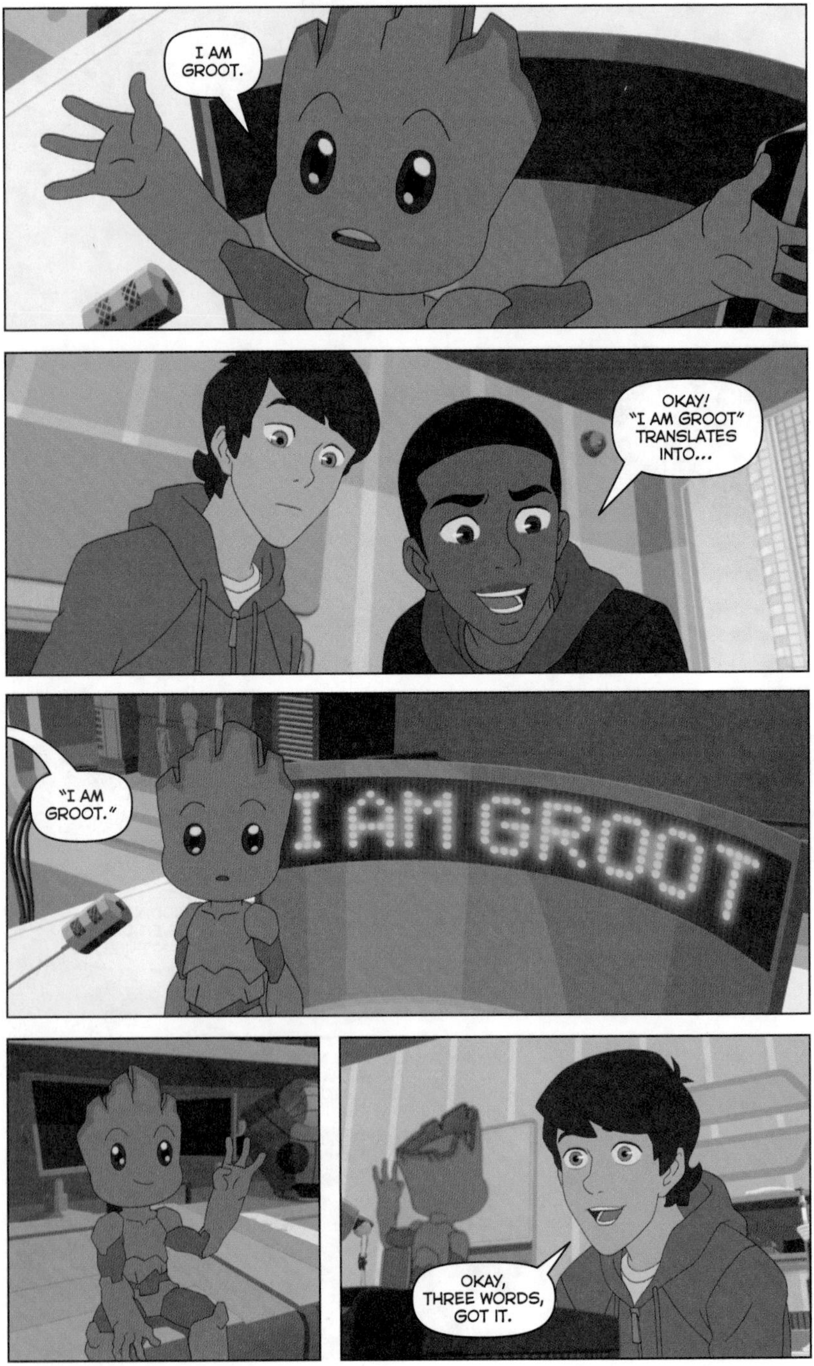
I AM GROOT.
OKAY! "I AM GROOT" TRANSLATES INTO...
"I AM GROOT."
I AM GROOT
OKAY, THREE WORDS, GOT IT.

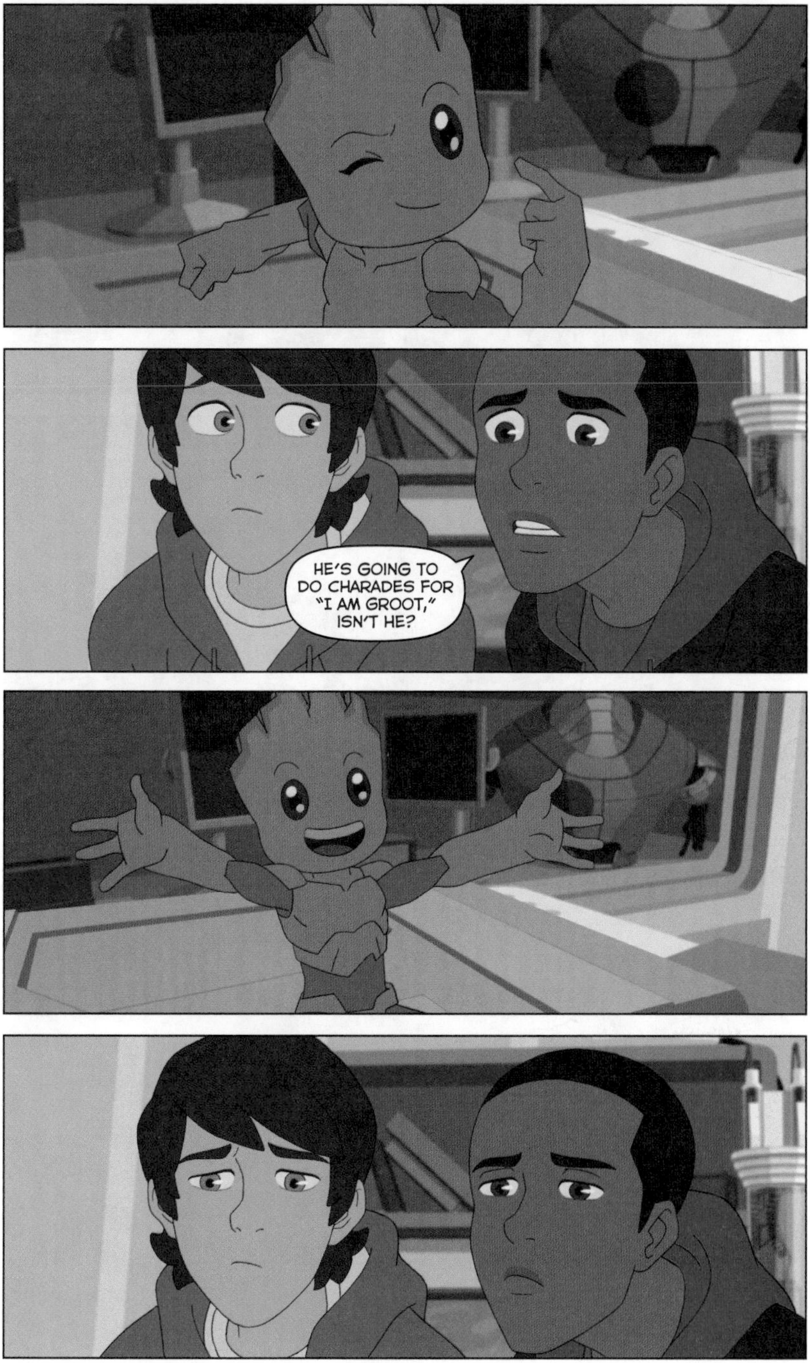
HE'S GOING TO DO CHARADES FOR "I AM GROOT," ISN'T HE?

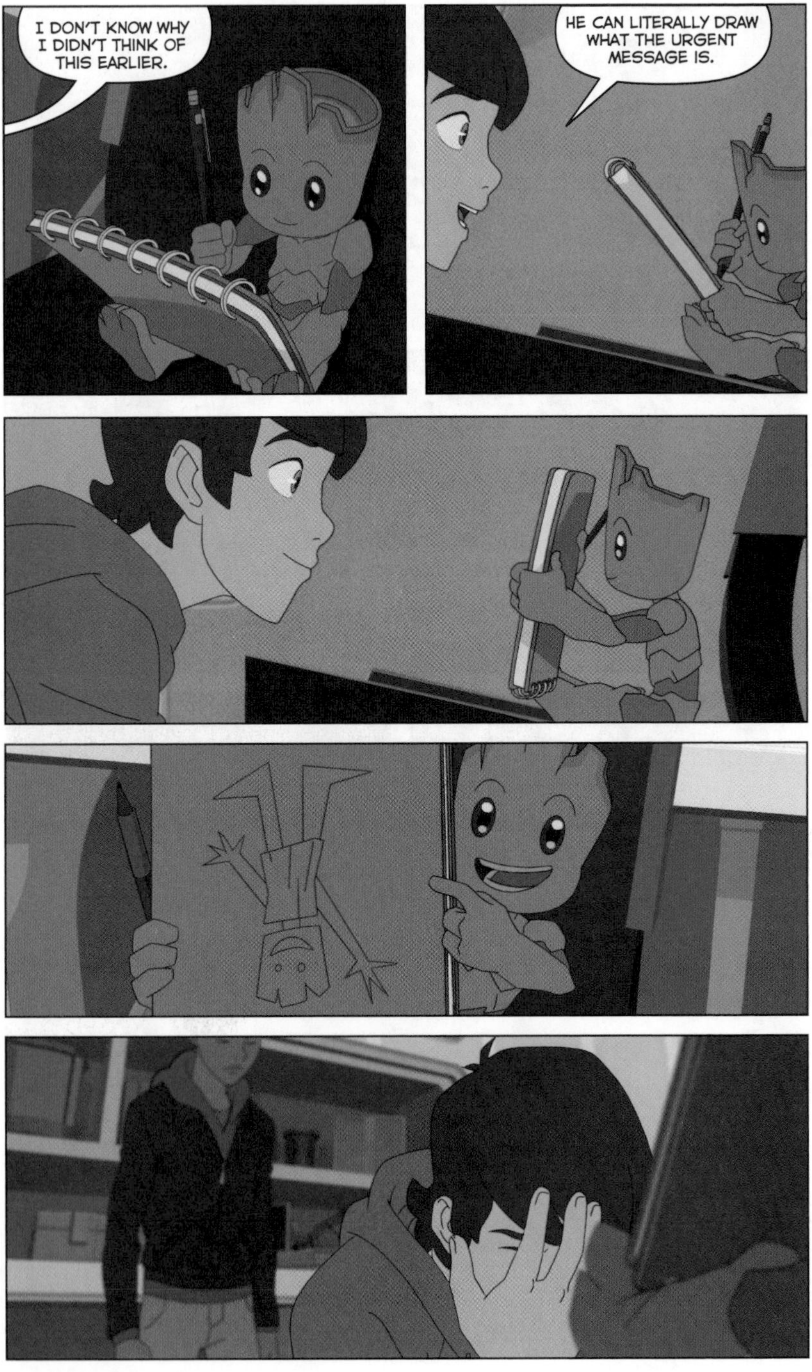
I DON'T KNOW WHY I DIDN'T THINK OF THIS EARLIER.
HE CAN LITERALLY DRAW WHAT THE URGENT MESSAGE IS.

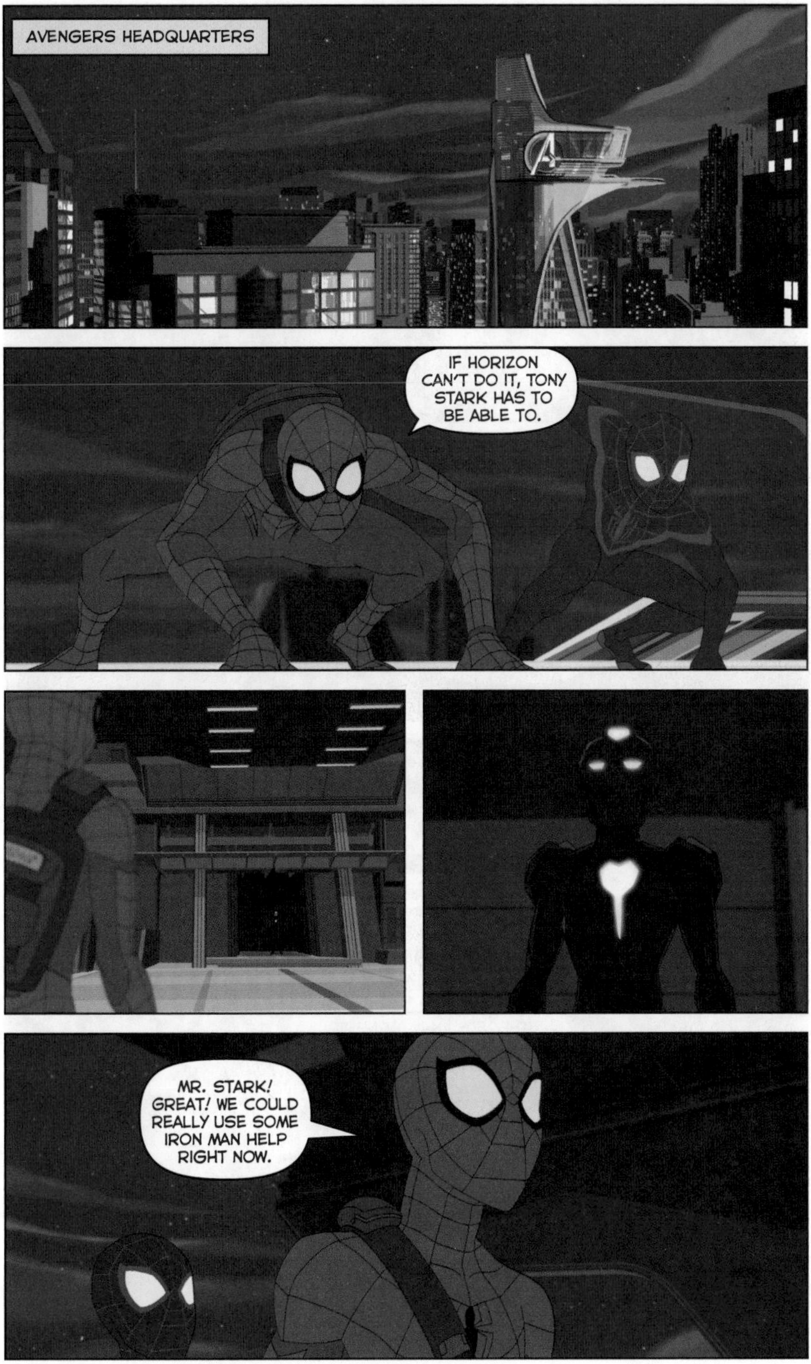
AVENGERS HEADQUARTERS
IF HORIZON CAN'T DO IT, TONY STARK HAS TO BE ABLE TO.
MR. STARK! GREAT! WE COULD REALLY USE SOME IRON MAN HELP RIGHT NOW.

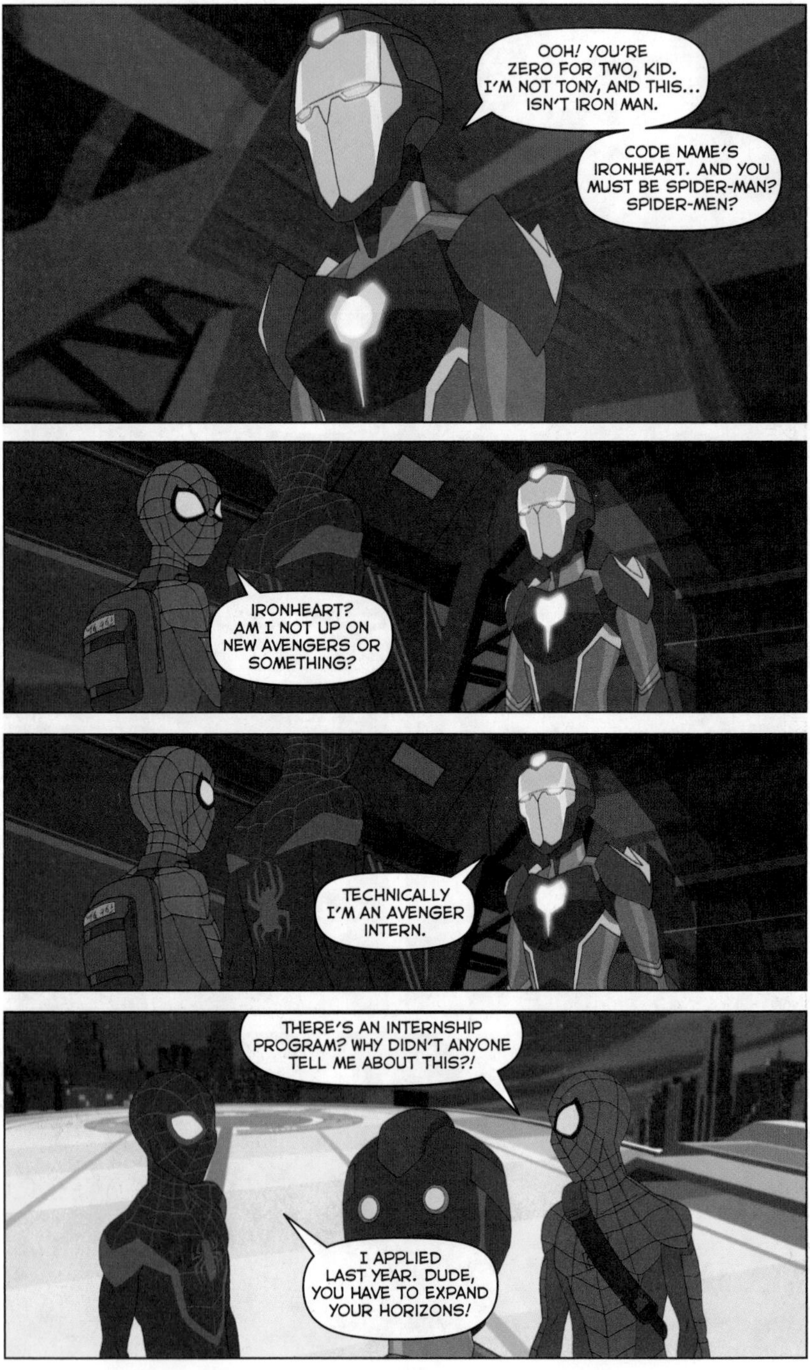
OOH! YOU'RE ZERO FOR TWO, KID. I'M NOT TONY, AND THIS... ISN'T IRON MAN.
CODE NAME'S IRONHEART. AND YOU MUST BE SPIDER-MAN? SPIDER-MEN?
IRONHEART? AM I NOT UP ON NEW AVENGERS OR SOMETHING?
TECHNICALLY I'M AN AVENGER INTERN.
THERE'S AN INTERNSHIP PROGRAM? WHY DIDN'T ANYONE TELL ME ABOUT THIS?!
I APPLIED LAST YEAR. DUDE, YOU HAVE TO EXPAND YOUR HORIZONS!

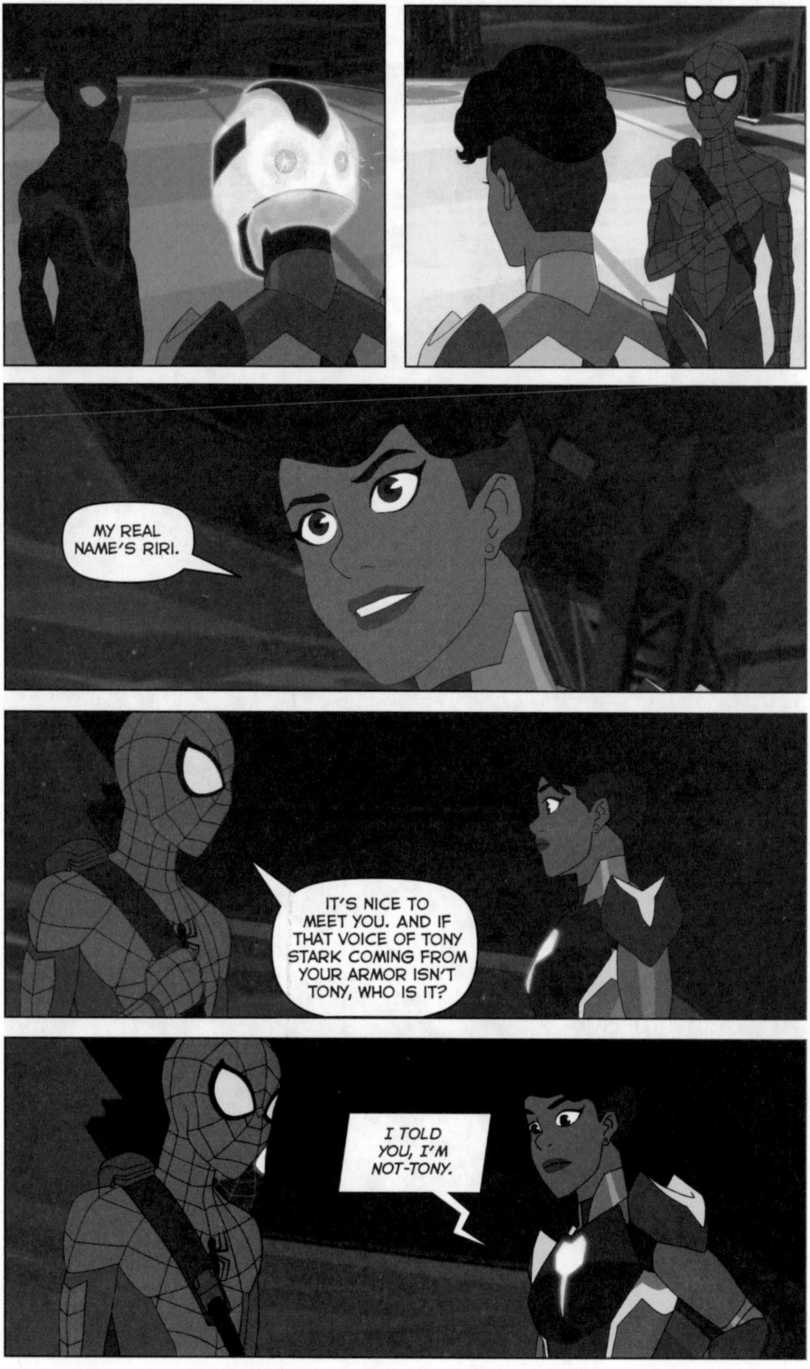
MY REAL NAME'S RIRI.
IT'S NICE TO MEET YOU. AND IF THAT VOICE OF TONY STARK COMING FROM YOUR ARMOR ISN'T TONY, WHO IS IT?
I TOLD YOU, I'M NOT-TONY.

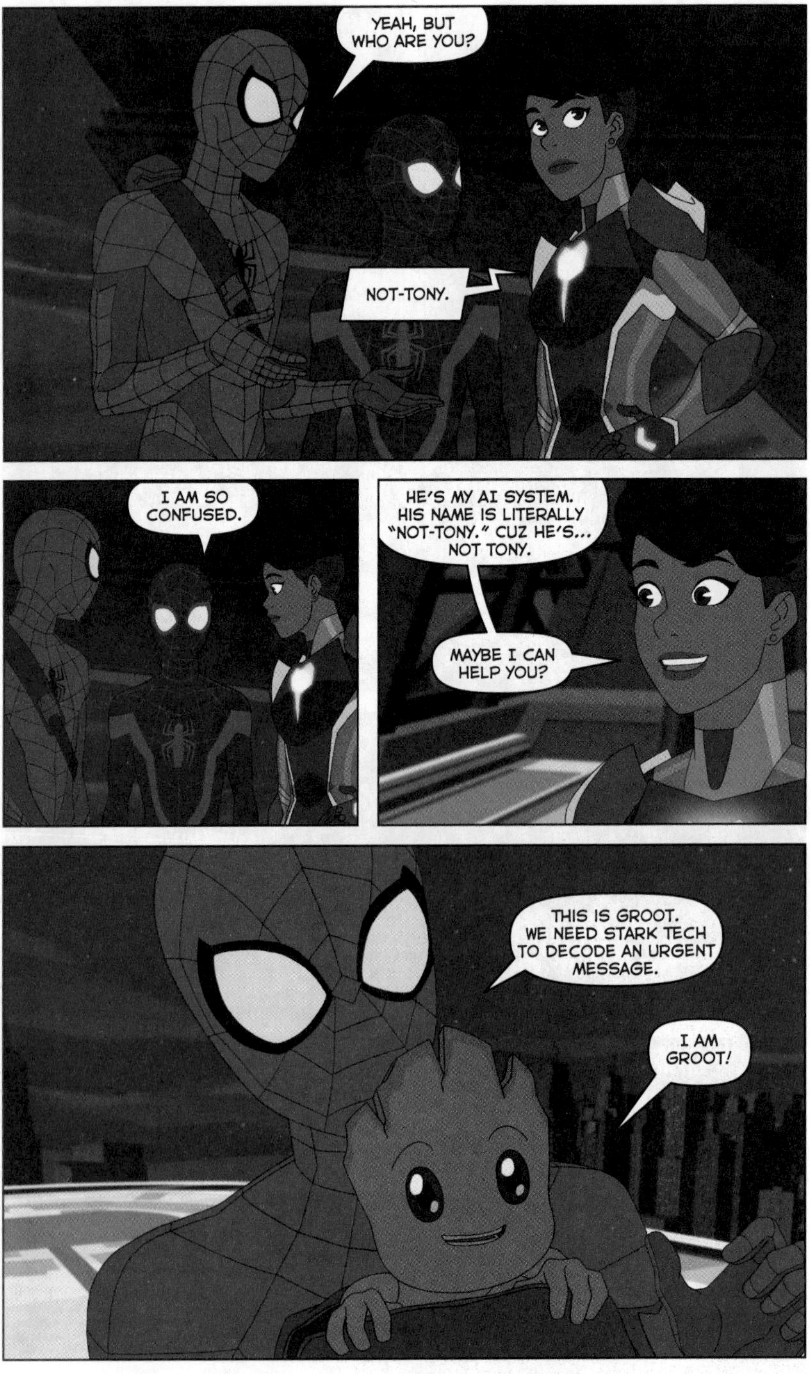
YEAH, BUT WHO ARE YOU?
NOT-TONY.
I AM SO CONFUSED.
HE'S MY AI SYSTEM. HIS NAME IS LITERALLY "NOT-TONY." CUZ HE'S... NOT TONY.
MAYBE I CAN HELP YOU?
THIS IS GROOT. WE NEED STARK TECH TO DECODE AN URGENT MESSAGE.
I AM GROOT!

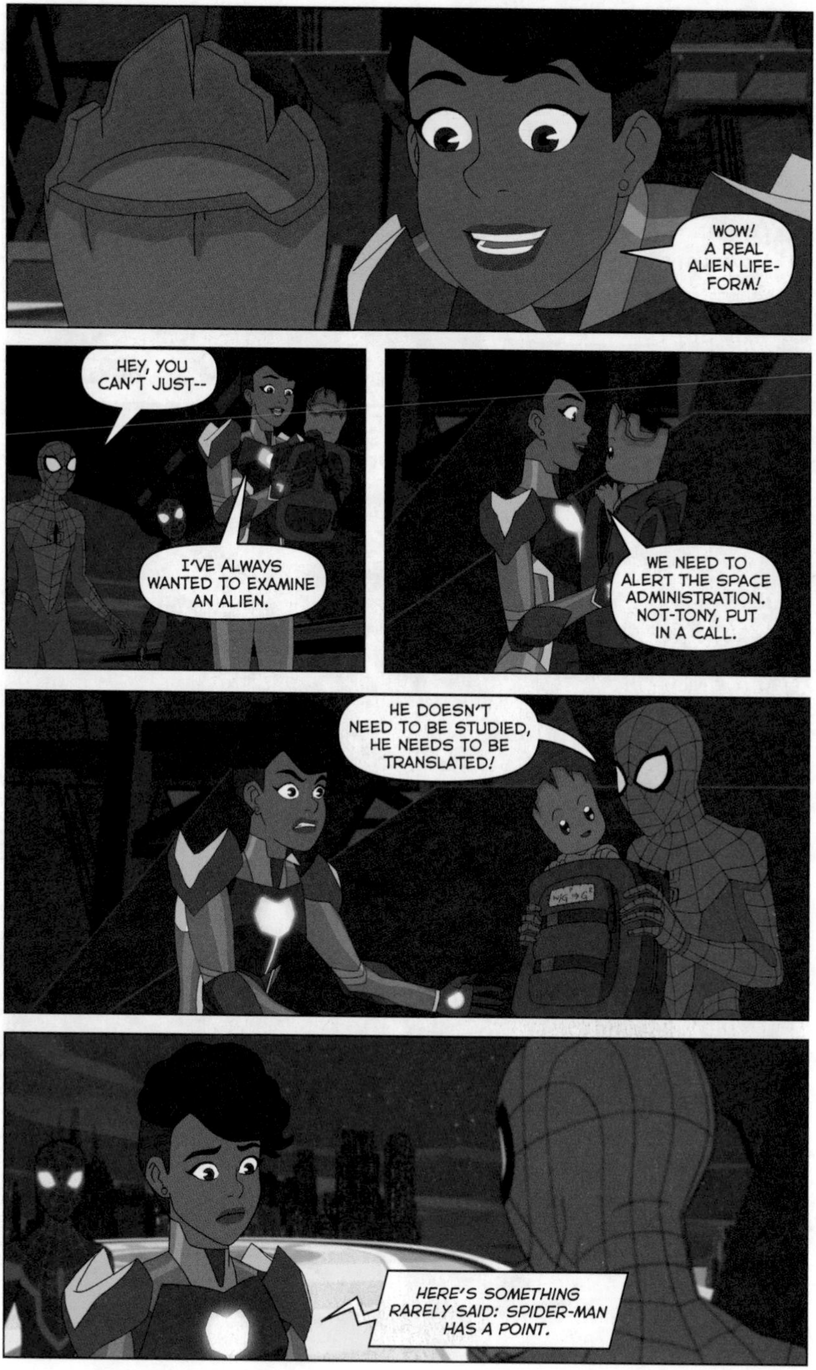

WOW! A REAL ALIEN LIFE-FORM!
HEY, YOU CAN'T JUST--
I'VE ALWAYS WANTED TO EXAMINE AN ALIEN.
WE NEED TO ALERT THE SPACE ADMINISTRATION. NOT-TONY, PUT IN A CALL.
HE DOESN'T NEED TO BE STUDIED, HE NEEDS TO BE TRANSLATED!
HERE'S SOMETHING RARELY SAID: SPIDER-MAN HAS A POINT.

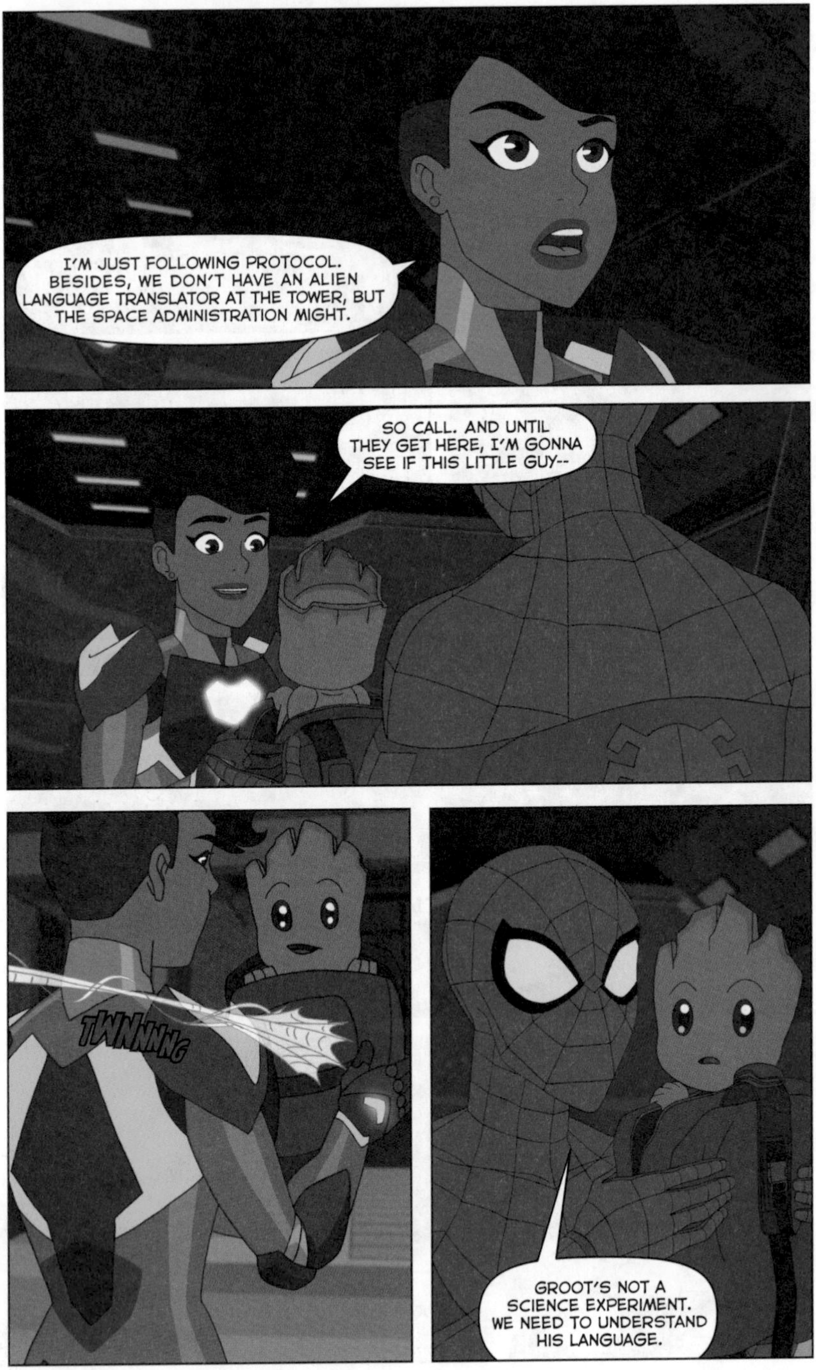
I'M JUST FOLLOWING PROTOCOL. BESIDES, WE DON'T HAVE AN ALIEN LANGUAGE TRANSLATOR AT THE TOWER, BUT THE SPACE ADMINISTRATION MIGHT.
SO CALL. AND UNTIL THEY GET HERE, I'M GONNA SEE IF THIS LITTLE GUY--
TWNNNNG
GROOT'S NOT A SCIENCE EXPERIMENT. WE NEED TO UNDERSTAND HIS LANGUAGE.

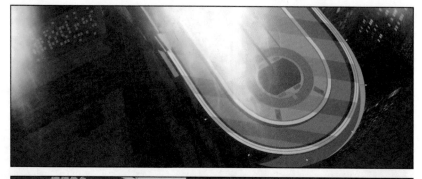

WHOA, THEY GOT HERE FAST.

WE'RE FROM THE SPACE ADMINISTRATION. WE RECEIVED A CALL FROM THIS LOCATION.

YES, SIRS, WE ENCOUNTERED THIS ALIEN--

AND WE NEED TO TRANSLATE HIS LANGUAGE.

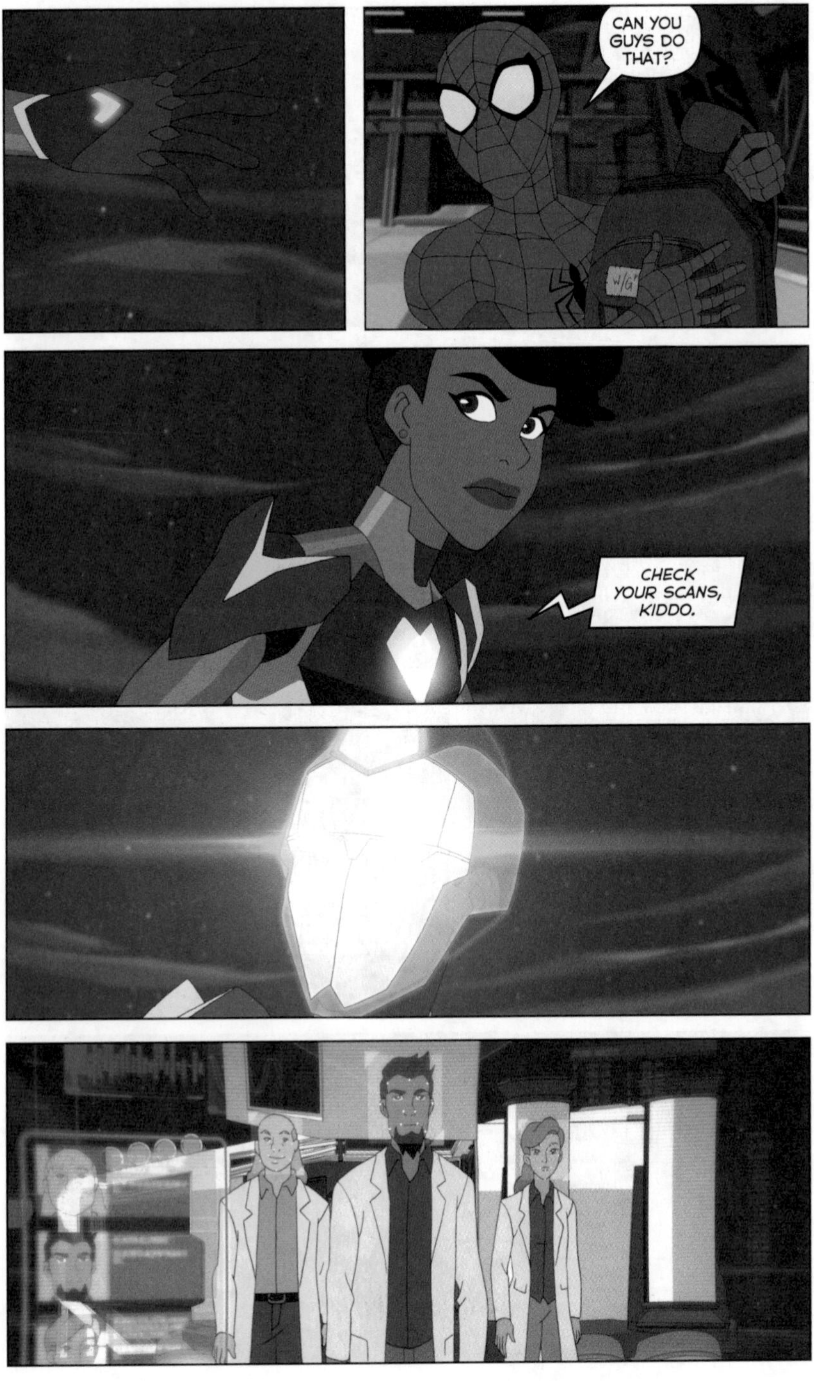
CAN YOU GUYS DO THAT?
W/G
CHECK YOUR SCANS, KIDDO.

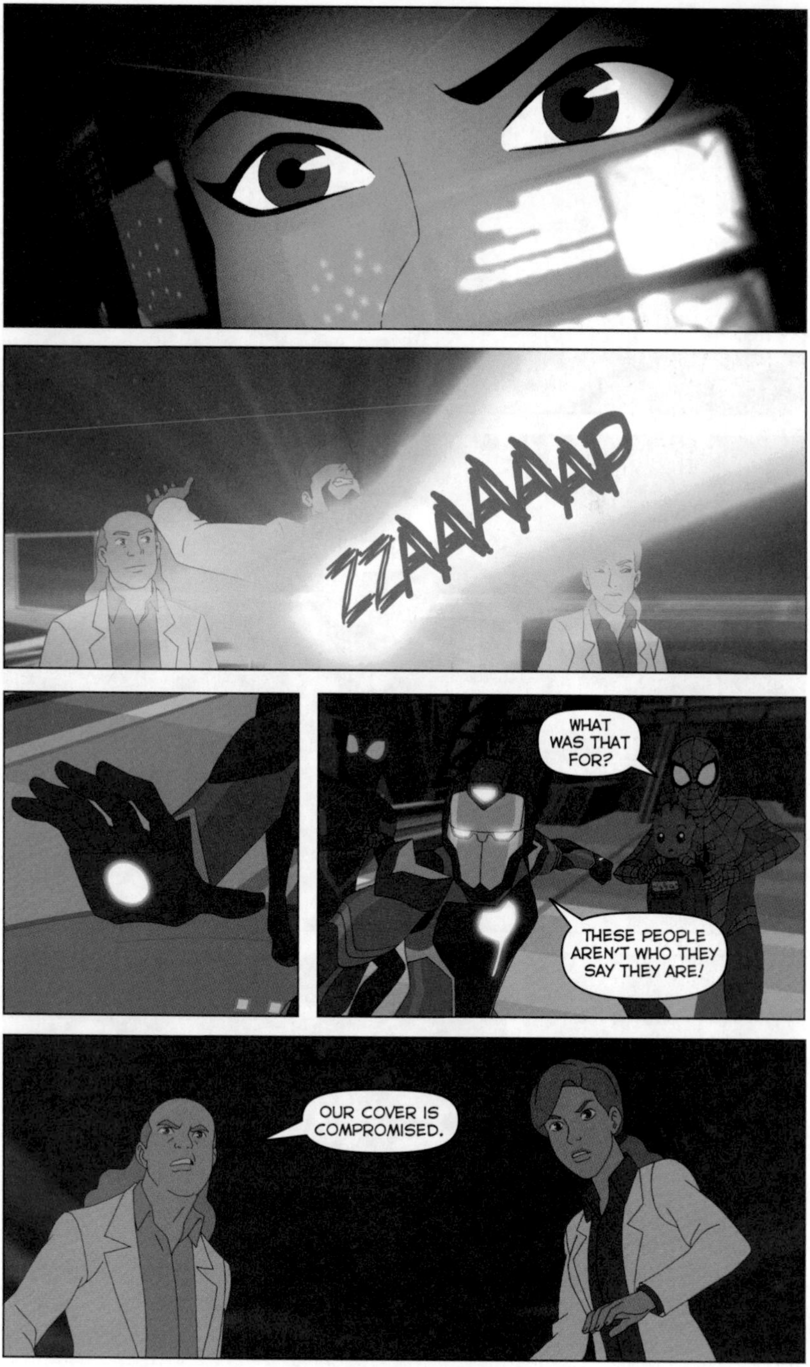
ZZAAAAAAP
WHAT WAS THAT FOR?
THESE PEOPLE AREN'T WHO THEY SAY THEY ARE!
OUR COVER IS COMPROMISED.

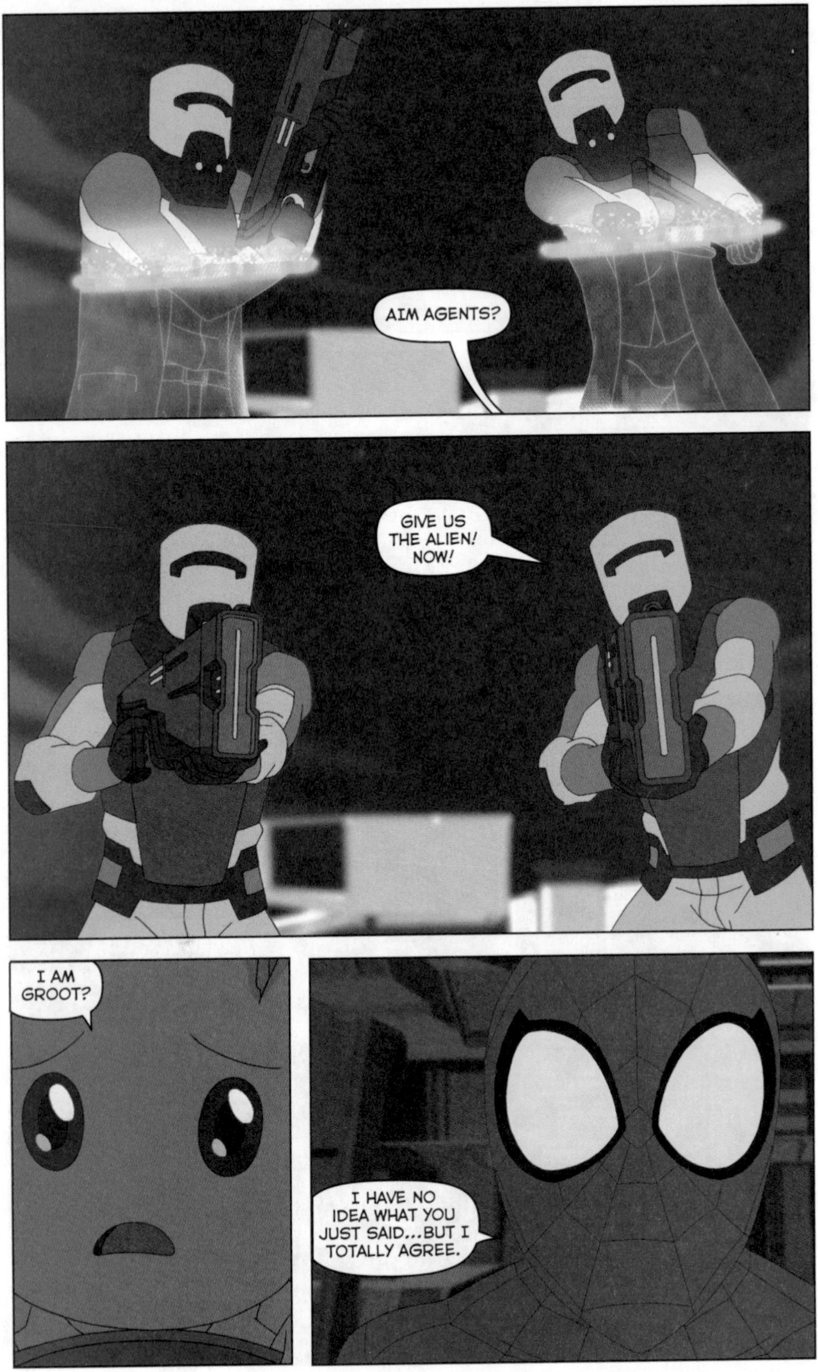
AIM AGENTS?
GIVE US THE ALIEN! NOW!
I AM GROOT?
I HAVE NO IDEA WHAT YOU JUST SAID...BUT I TOTALLY AGREE.

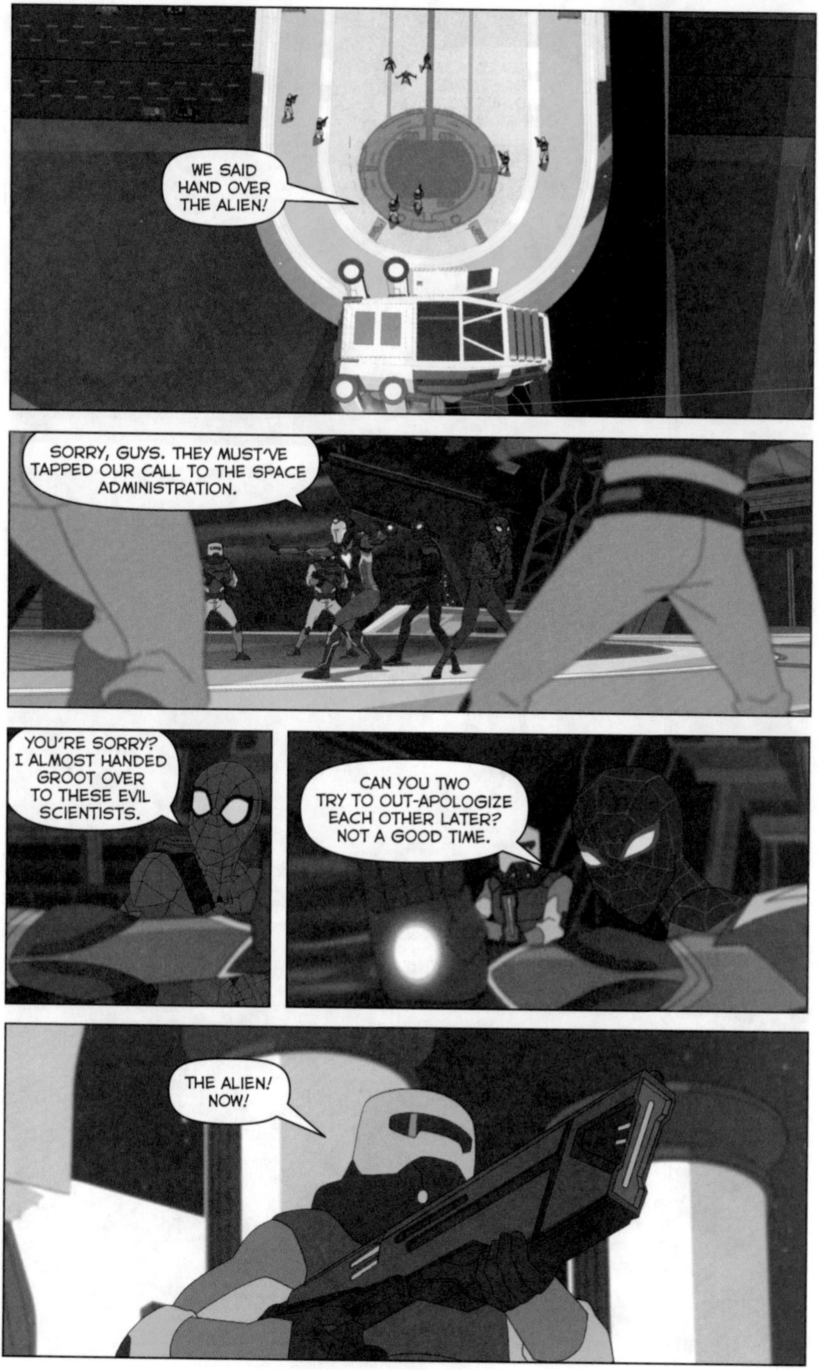
WE SAID HAND OVER THE ALIEN!
SORRY, GUYS. THEY MUST'VE TAPPED OUR CALL TO THE SPACE ADMINISTRATION.
YOU'RE SORRY? I ALMOST HANDED GROOT OVER TO THESE EVIL SCIENTISTS.
CAN YOU TWO TRY TO OUT-APOLOGIZE EACH OTHER LATER? NOT A GOOD TIME.
THE ALIEN! NOW!

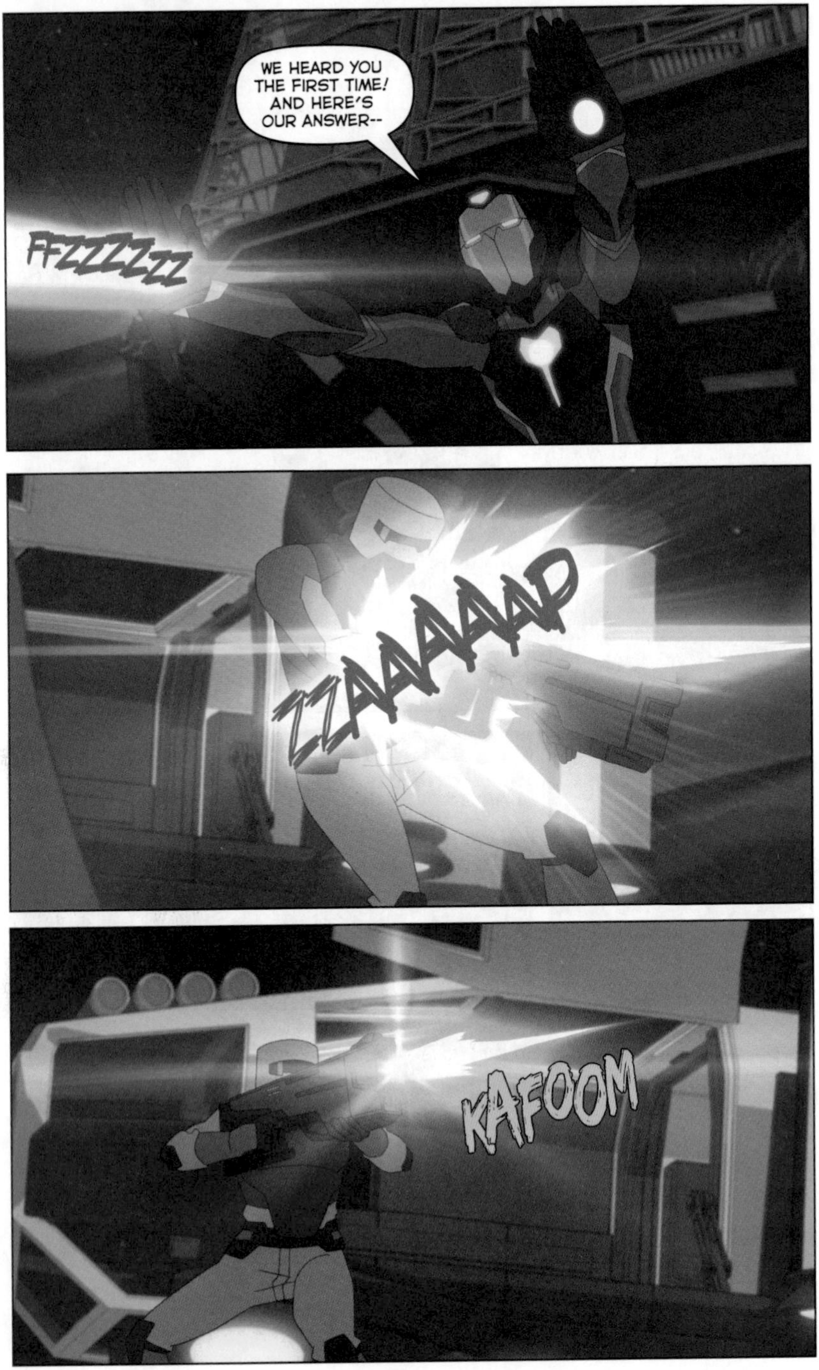
WE HEARD YOU THE FIRST TIME! AND HERE'S OUR ANSWER--
FFZZZZZZZ
ZZAAAAAAP
KAFOOM

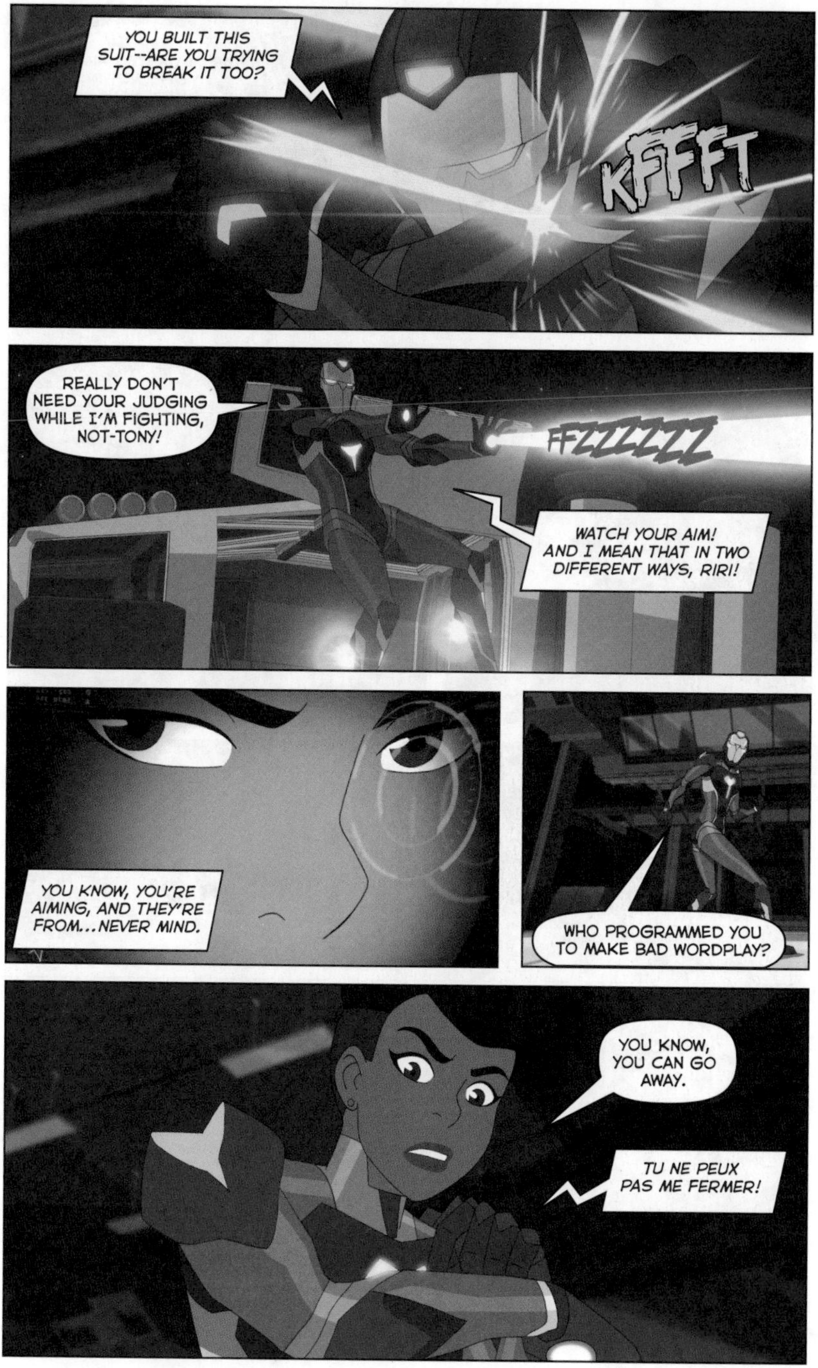
YOU BUILT THIS SUIT--ARE YOU TRYING TO BREAK IT TOO?
KFFFT
REALLY DON'T NEED YOUR JUDGING WHILE I'M FIGHTING, NOT-TONY!
FFZZZZZZ
WATCH YOUR AIM! AND I MEAN THAT IN TWO DIFFERENT WAYS, RIRI!
YOU KNOW, YOU'RE AIMING, AND THEY'RE FROM...NEVER MIND.
WHO PROGRAMMED YOU TO MAKE BAD WORDPLAY?
YOU KNOW, YOU CAN GO AWAY.
TU NE PEUX PAS ME FERMER!

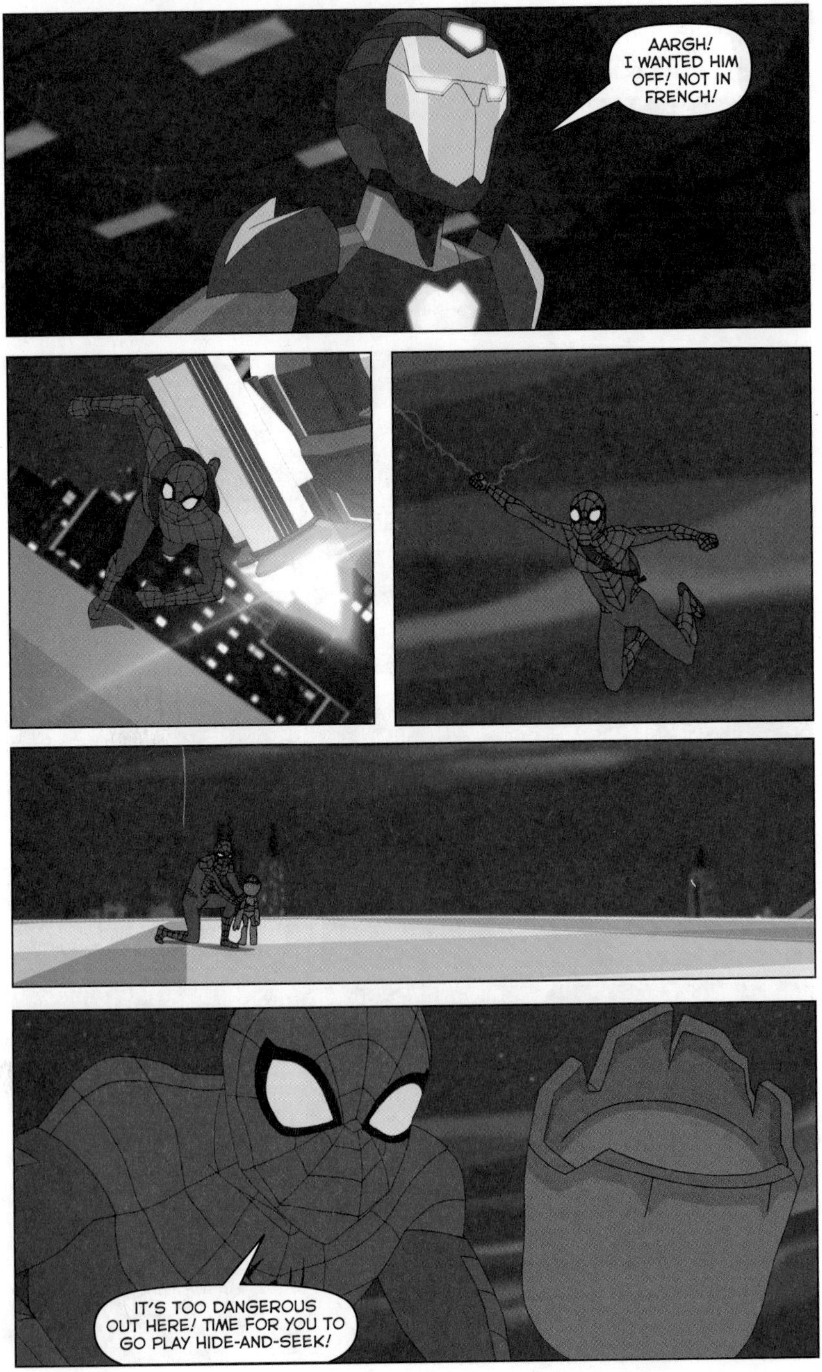
AARGH! I WANTED HIM OFF! NOT IN FRENCH!
IT'S TOO DANGEROUS OUT HERE! TIME FOR YOU TO GO PLAY HIDE-AND-SEEK!

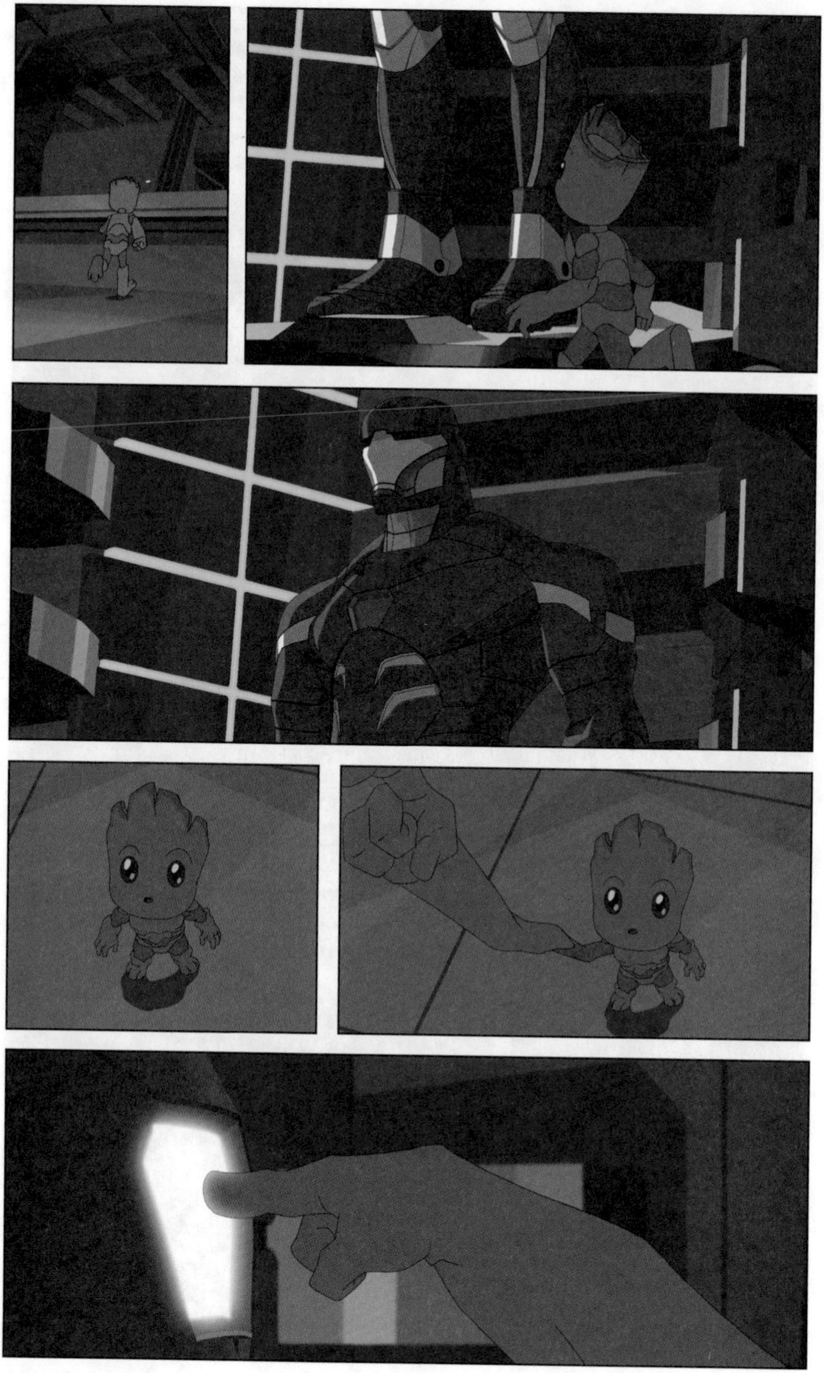

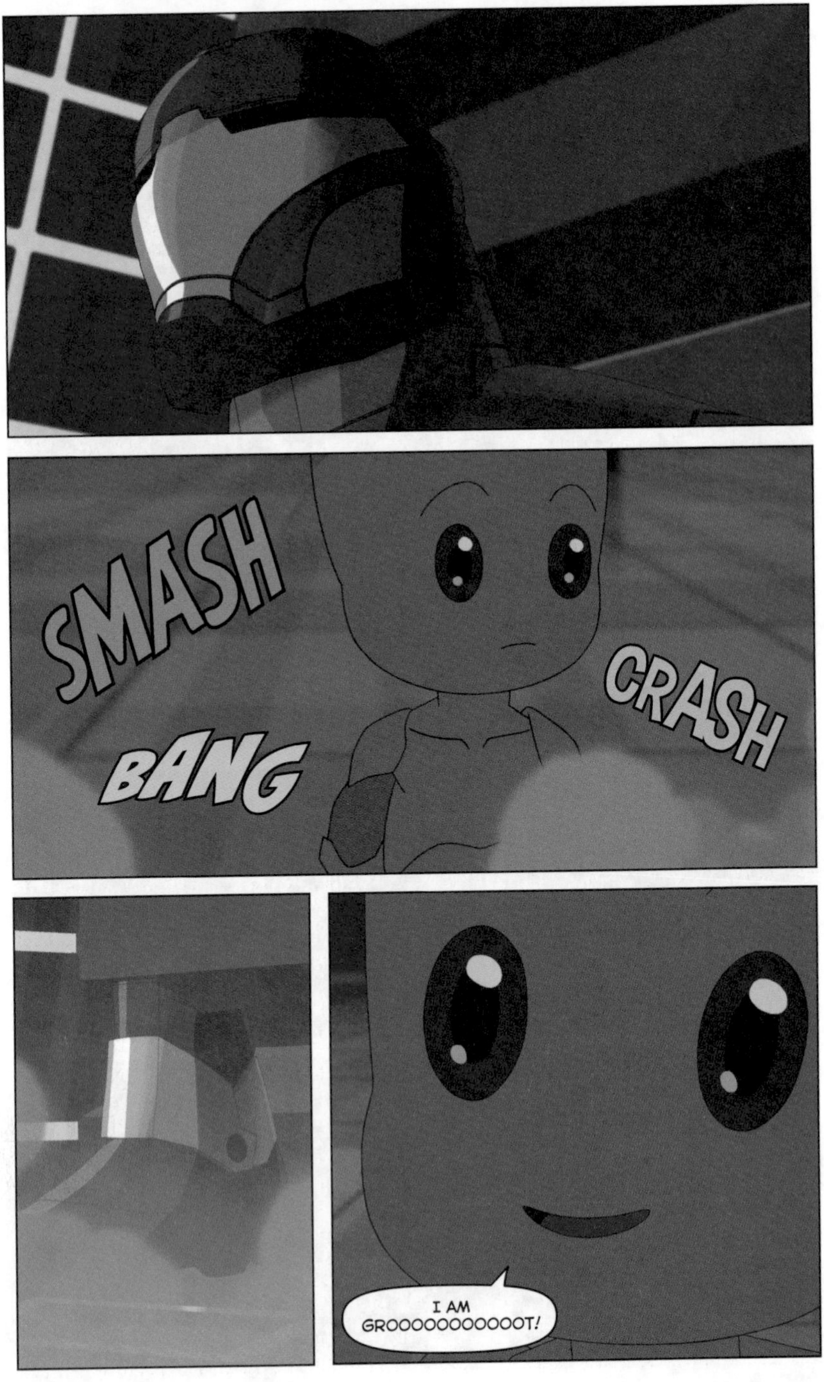
SMASH
CRASH
BANG
I AM GROOOOOOOOOOOT!

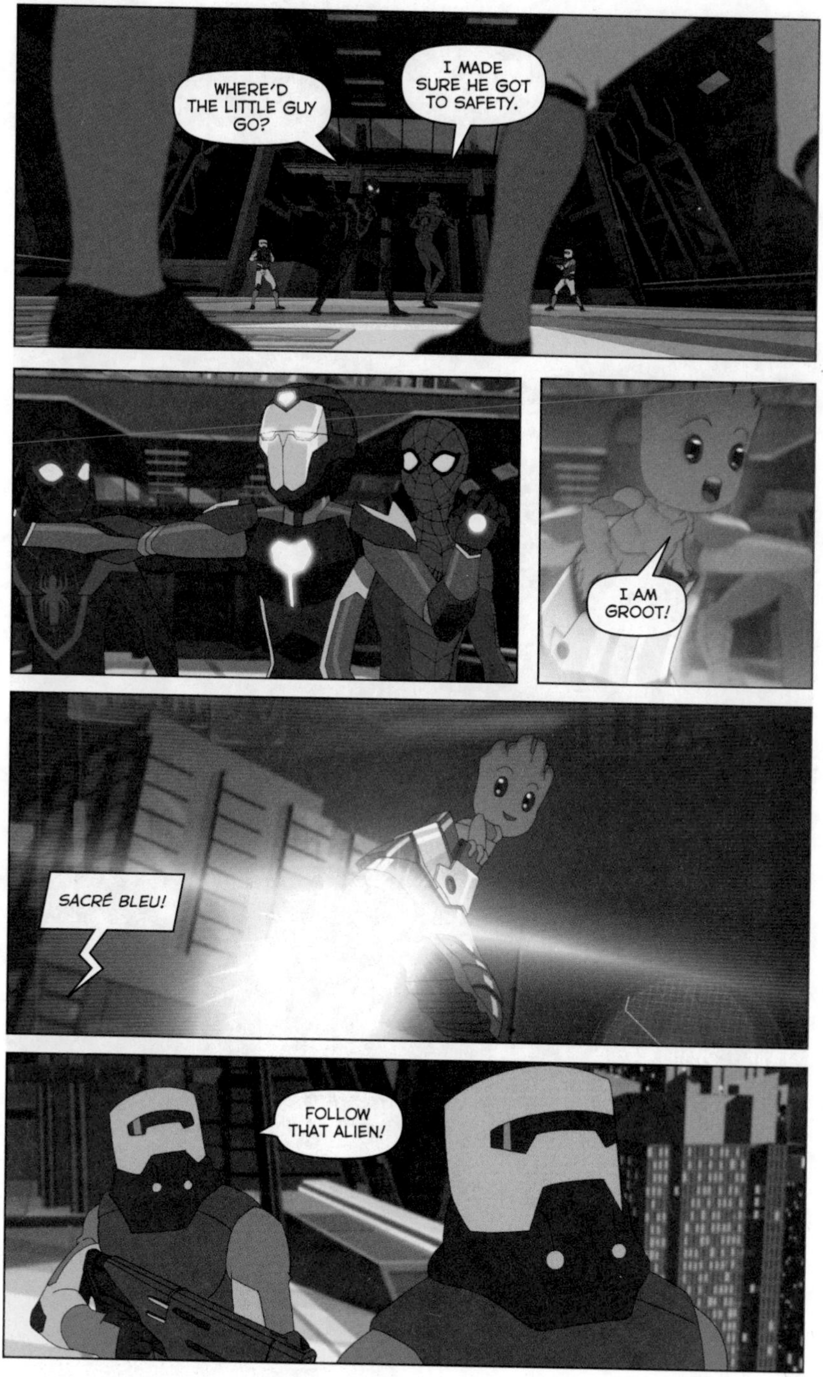
WHERE'D THE LITTLE GUY GO?
I MADE SURE HE GOT TO SAFETY.
I AM GROOT!
SACRÉ BLEU!
FOLLOW THAT ALIEN!

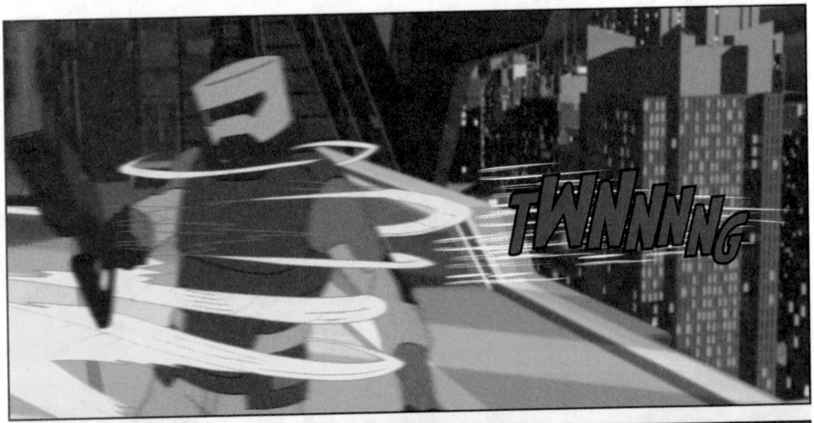
TWNNNNG

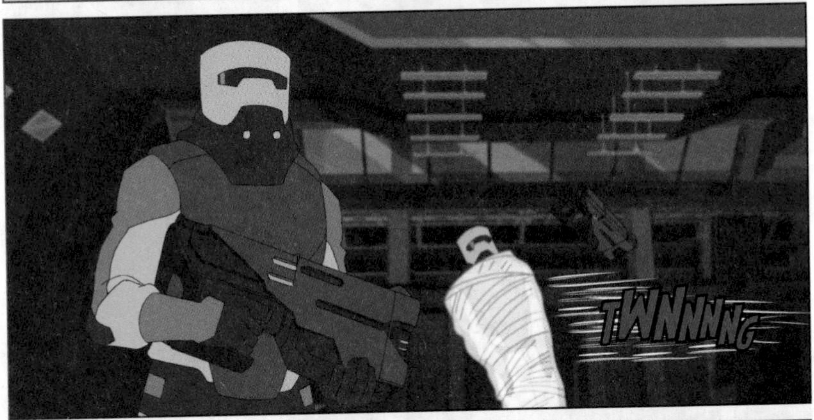
TWNNNNG

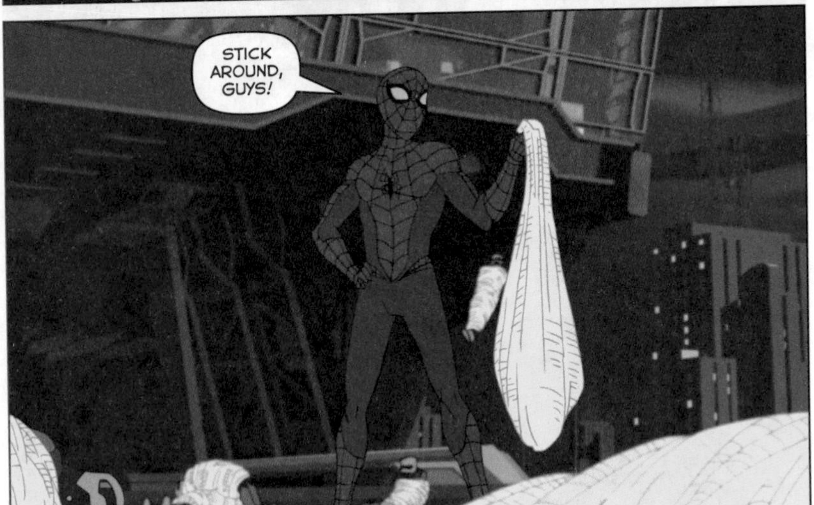
STICK AROUND, GUYS!

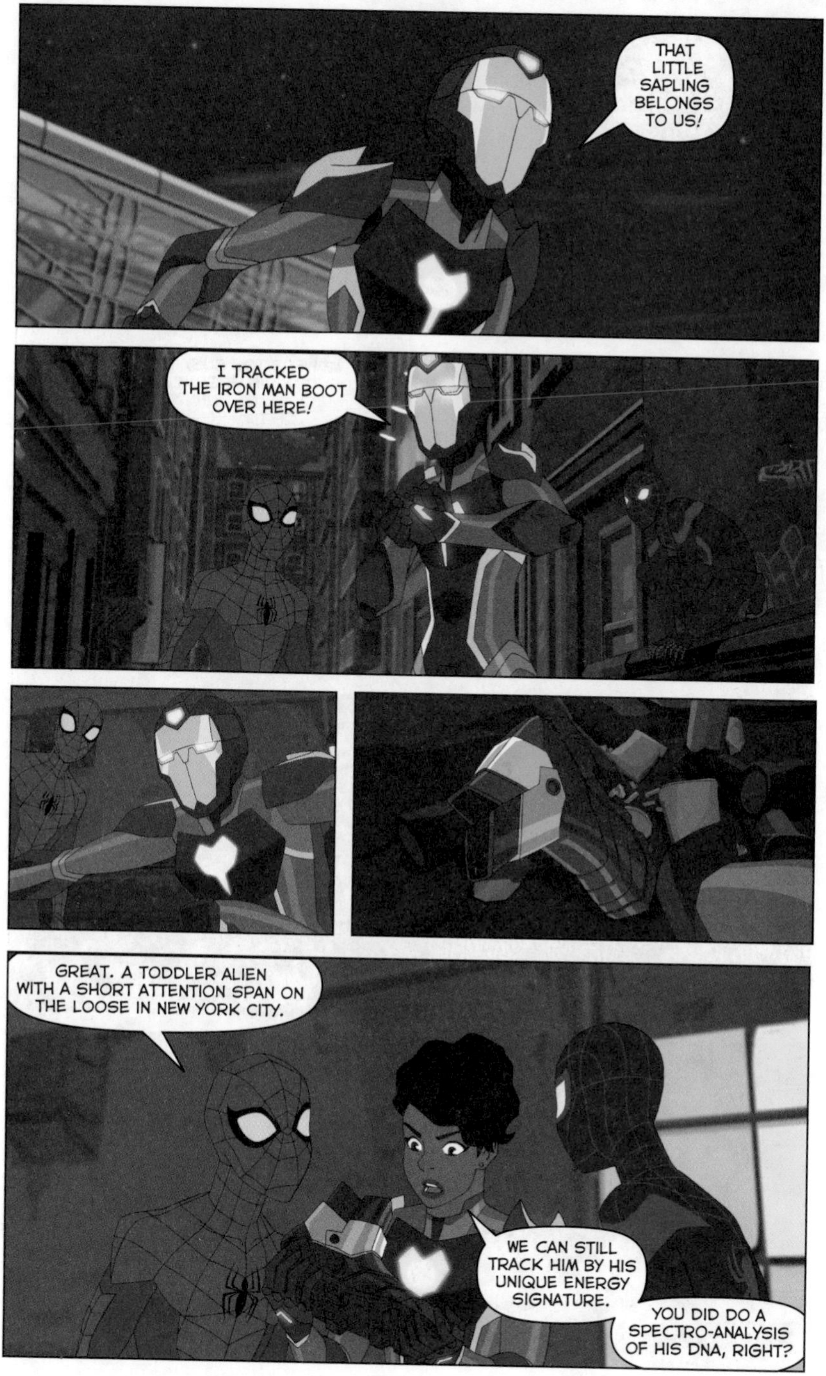
THAT LITTLE SAPLING BELONGS TO US!
I TRACKED THE IRON MAN BOOT OVER HERE!
GREAT. A TODDLER ALIEN WITH A SHORT ATTENTION SPAN ON THE LOOSE IN NEW YORK CITY.
WE CAN STILL TRACK HIM BY HIS UNIQUE ENERGY SIGNATURE.
YOU DID DO A SPECTRO-ANALYSIS OF HIS DNA, RIGHT?

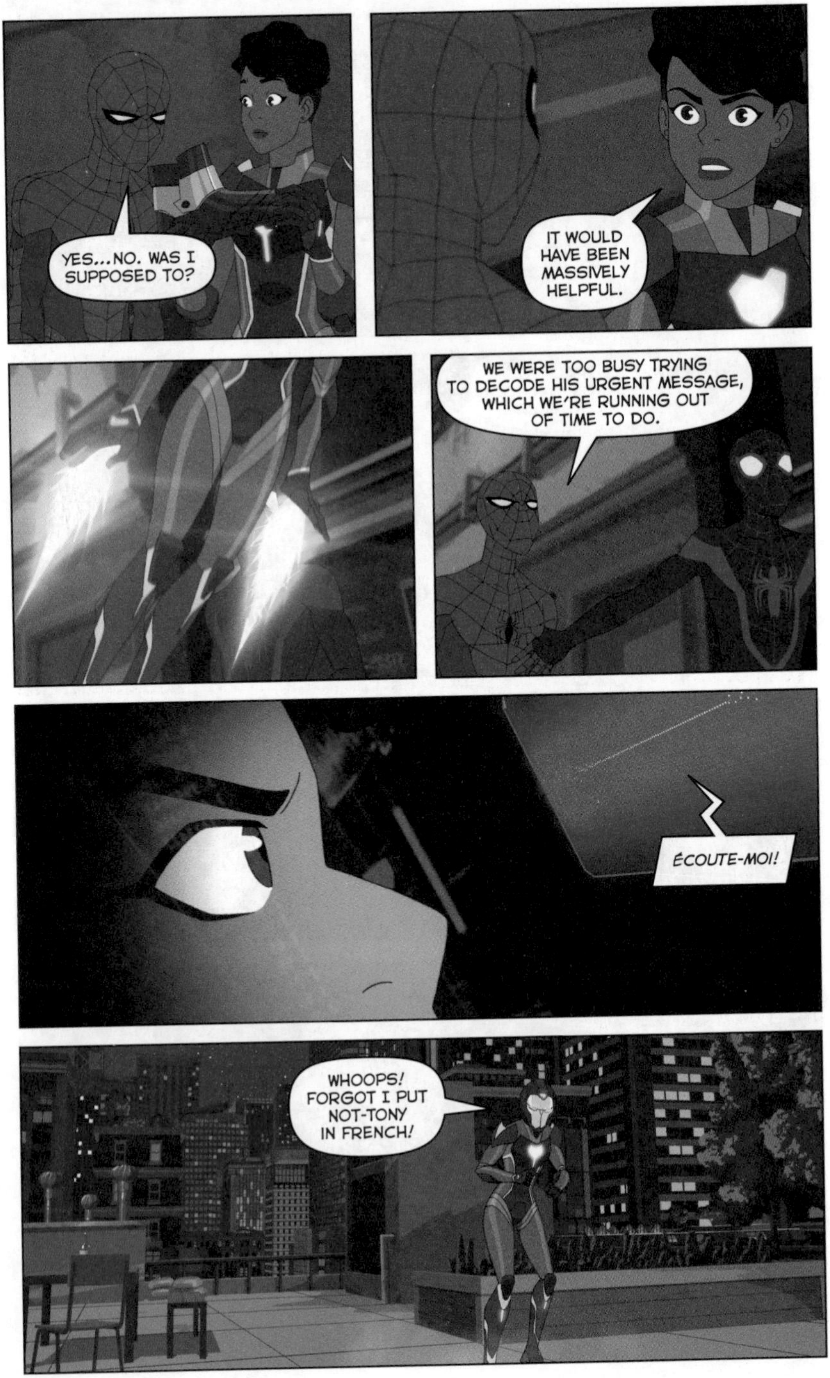

YES...NO. WAS I SUPPOSED TO?
IT WOULD HAVE BEEN MASSIVELY HELPFUL.
WE WERE TOO BUSY TRYING TO DECODE HIS URGENT MESSAGE, WHICH WE'RE RUNNING OUT OF TIME TO DO.
ÉCOUTE-MOI!
WHOOPS! FORGOT I PUT NOT-TONY IN FRENCH!

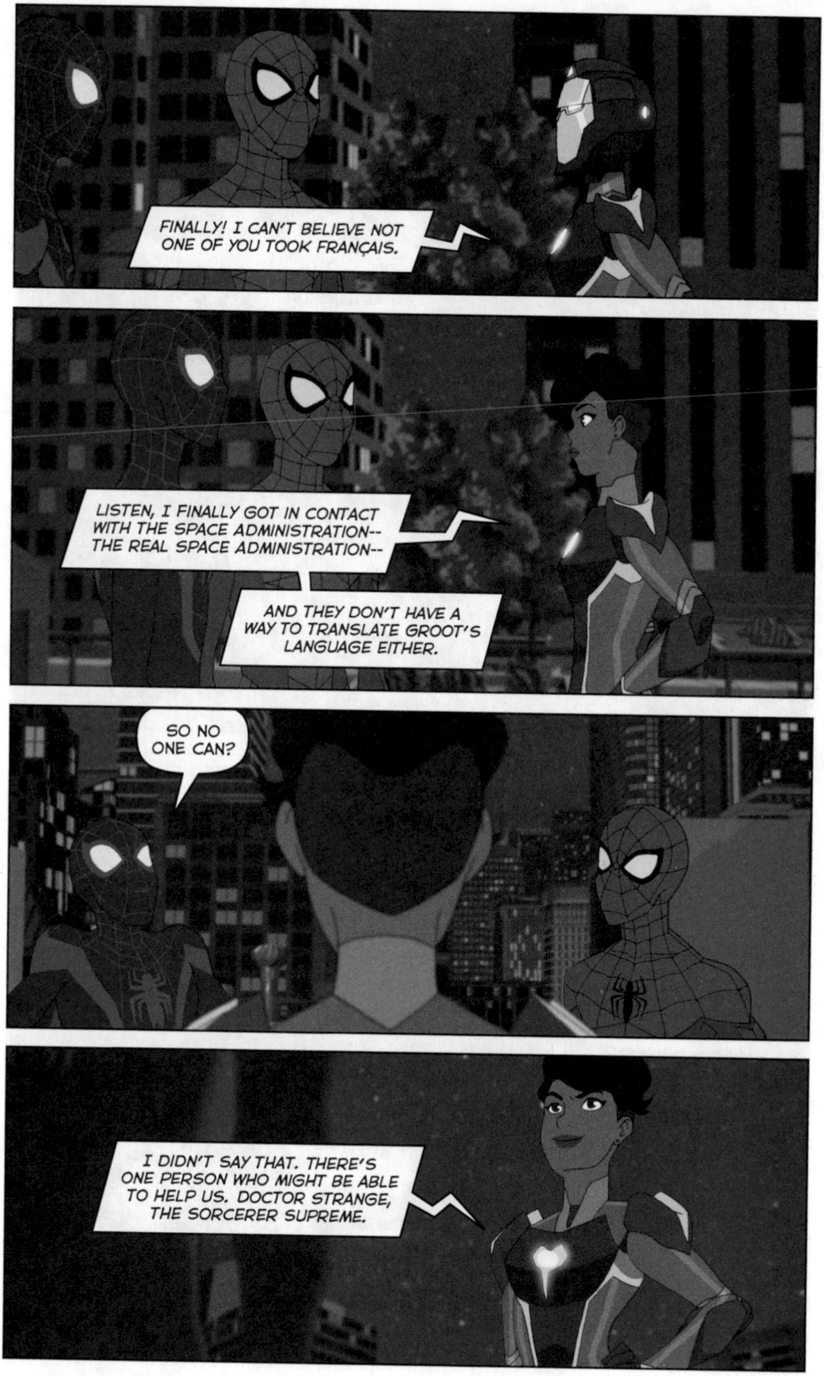
FINALLY! I CAN'T BELIEVE NOT ONE OF YOU TOOK FRANÇAIS.
LISTEN, I FINALLY GOT IN CONTACT WITH THE SPACE ADMINISTRATION-- THE REAL SPACE ADMINISTRATION--
AND THEY DON'T HAVE A WAY TO TRANSLATE GROOT'S LANGUAGE EITHER.
SO NO ONE CAN?
I DIDN'T SAY THAT. THERE'S ONE PERSON WHO MIGHT BE ABLE TO HELP US. DOCTOR STRANGE, THE SORCERER SUPREME.

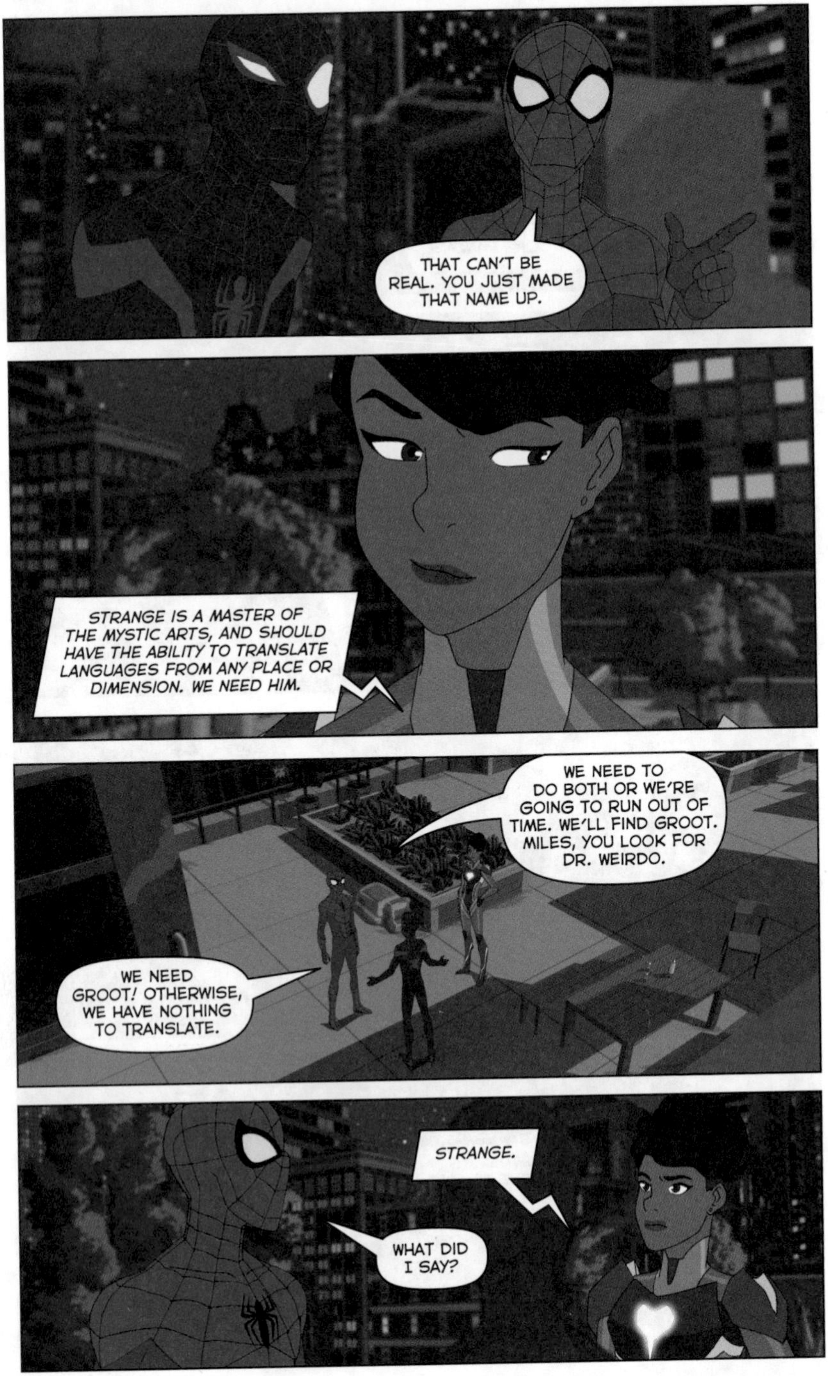
THAT CAN'T BE REAL. YOU JUST MADE THAT NAME UP.
STRANGE IS A MASTER OF THE MYSTIC ARTS, AND SHOULD HAVE THE ABILITY TO TRANSLATE LANGUAGES FROM ANY PLACE OR DIMENSION. WE NEED HIM.
WE NEED GROOT! OTHERWISE, WE HAVE NOTHING TO TRANSLATE.
WE NEED TO DO BOTH OR WE'RE GOING TO RUN OUT OF TIME. WE'LL FIND GROOT. MILES, YOU LOOK FOR DR. WEIRDO.
WHAT DID I SAY?
STRANGE.

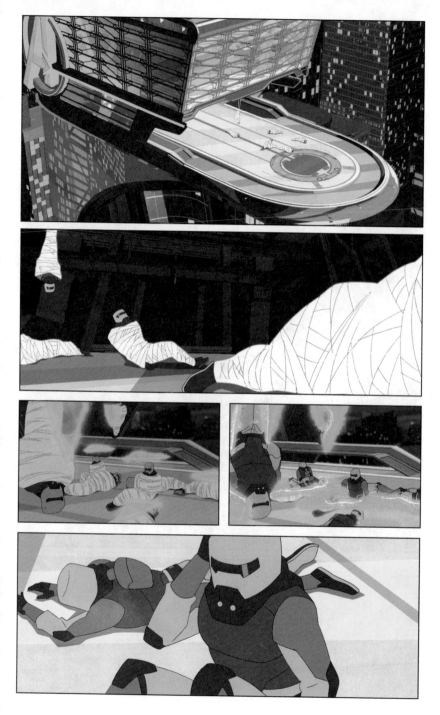

209

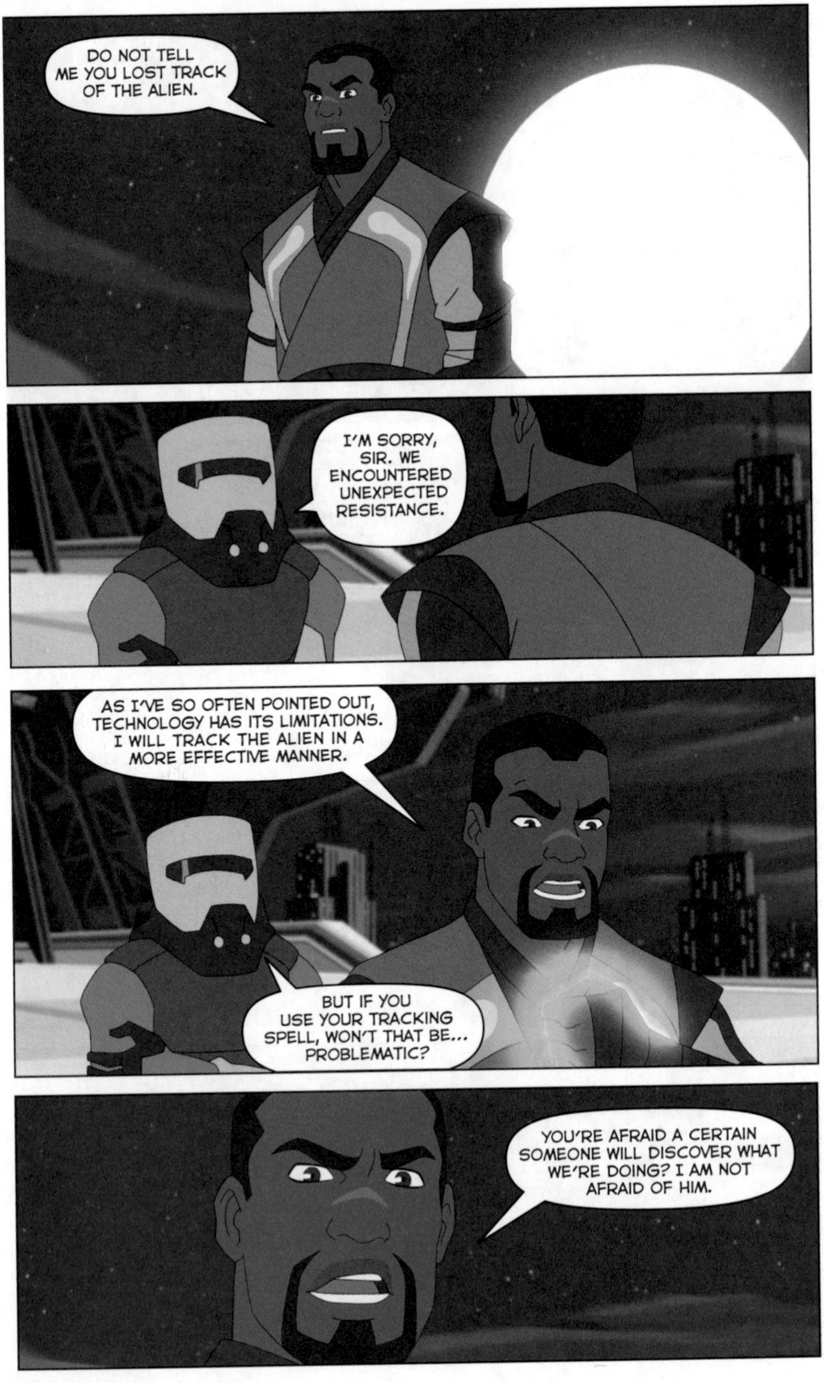
DO NOT TELL ME YOU LOST TRACK OF THE ALIEN.
I'M SORRY, SIR. WE ENCOUNTERED UNEXPECTED RESISTANCE.
AS I'VE SO OFTEN POINTED OUT, TECHNOLOGY HAS ITS LIMITATIONS. I WILL TRACK THE ALIEN IN A MORE EFFECTIVE MANNER.
BUT IF YOU USE YOUR TRACKING SPELL, WON'T THAT BE... PROBLEMATIC?
YOU'RE AFRAID A CERTAIN SOMEONE WILL DISCOVER WHAT WE'RE DOING? I AM NOT AFRAID OF HIM.

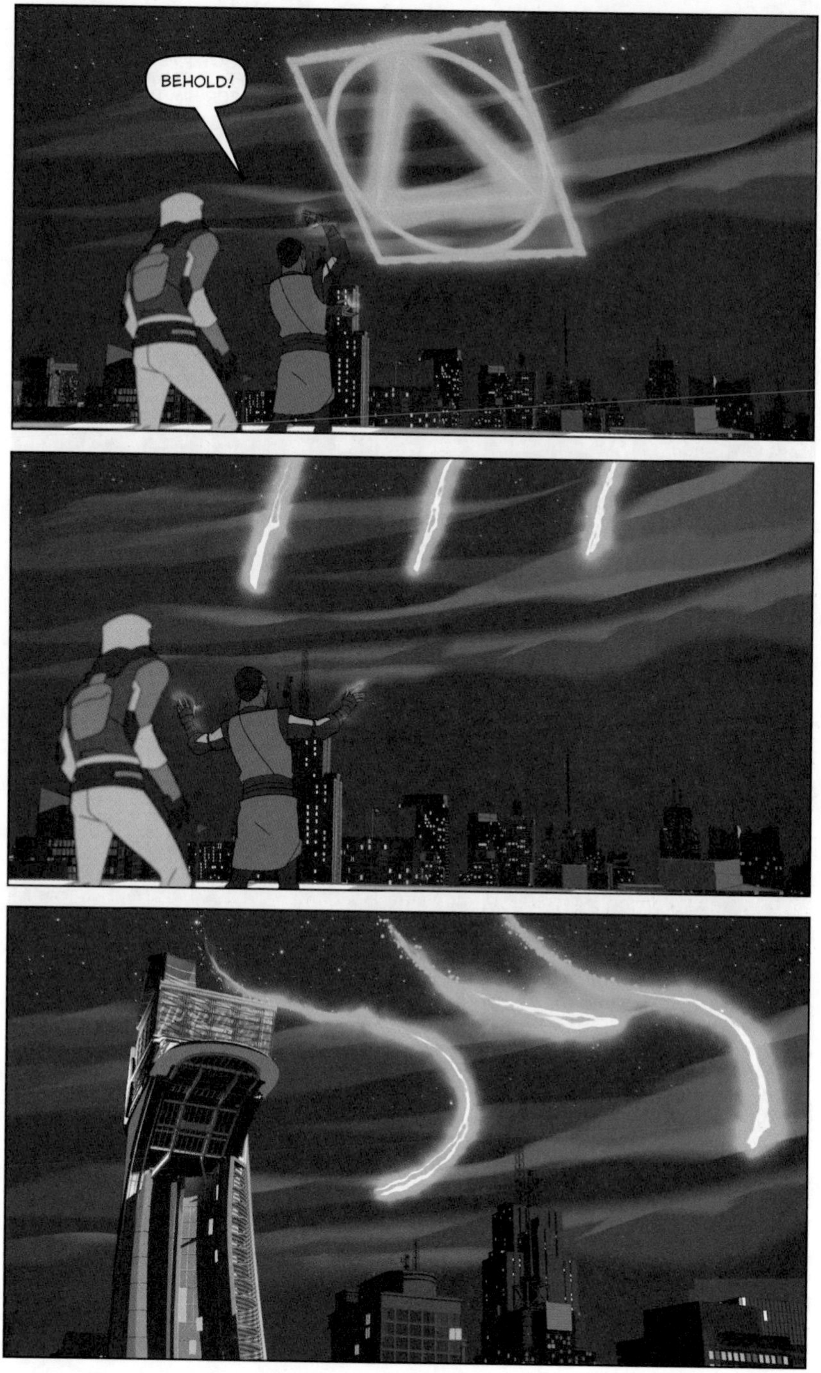
BEHOLD!

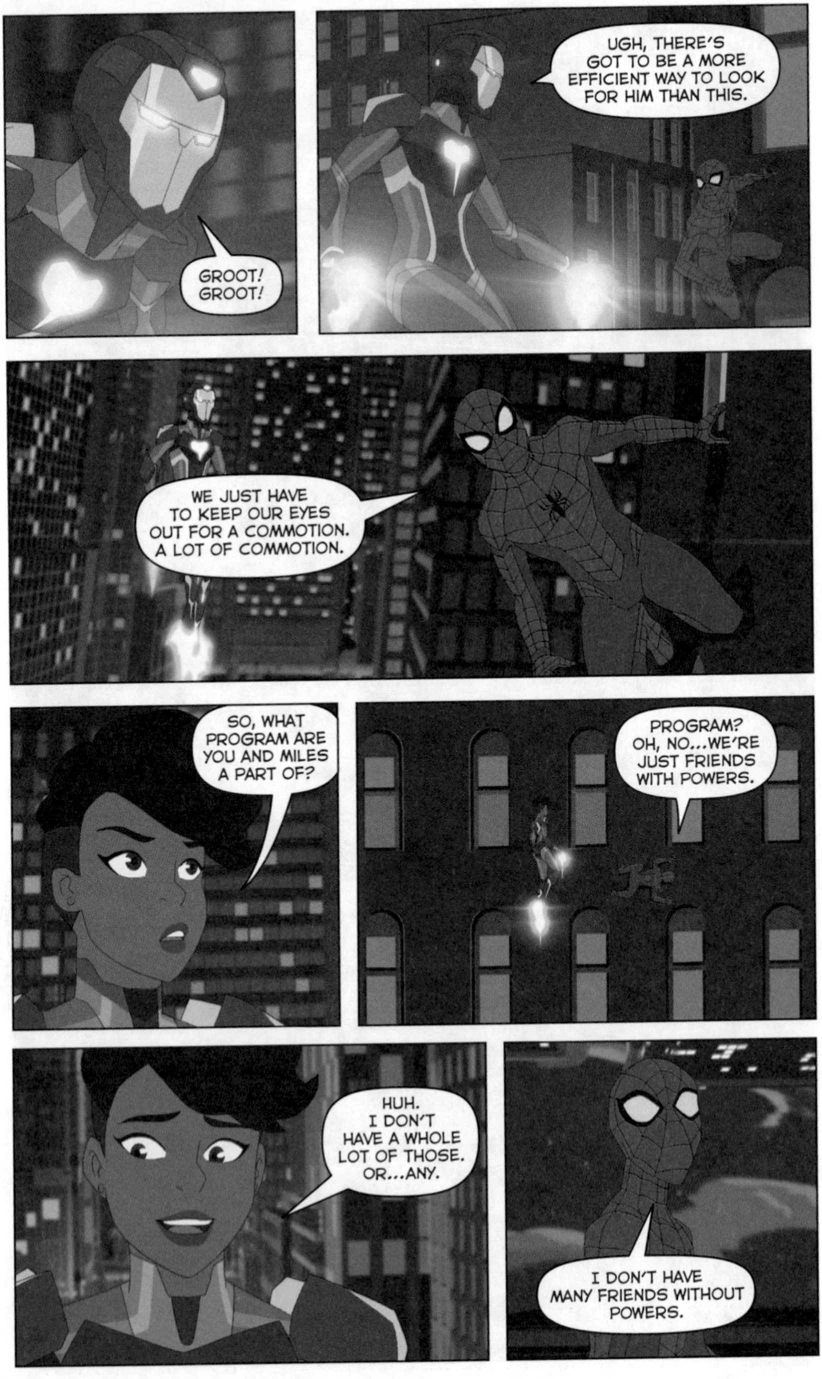
GROOT! GROOT!
UGH, THERE'S GOT TO BE A MORE EFFICIENT WAY TO LOOK FOR HIM THAN THIS.
WE JUST HAVE TO KEEP OUR EYES OUT FOR A COMMOTION. A LOT OF COMMOTION.
SO, WHAT PROGRAM ARE YOU AND MILES A PART OF?
PROGRAM? OH, NO...WE'RE JUST FRIENDS WITH POWERS.
HUH. I DON'T HAVE A WHOLE LOT OF THOSE. OR...ANY.
I DON'T HAVE MANY FRIENDS WITHOUT POWERS.

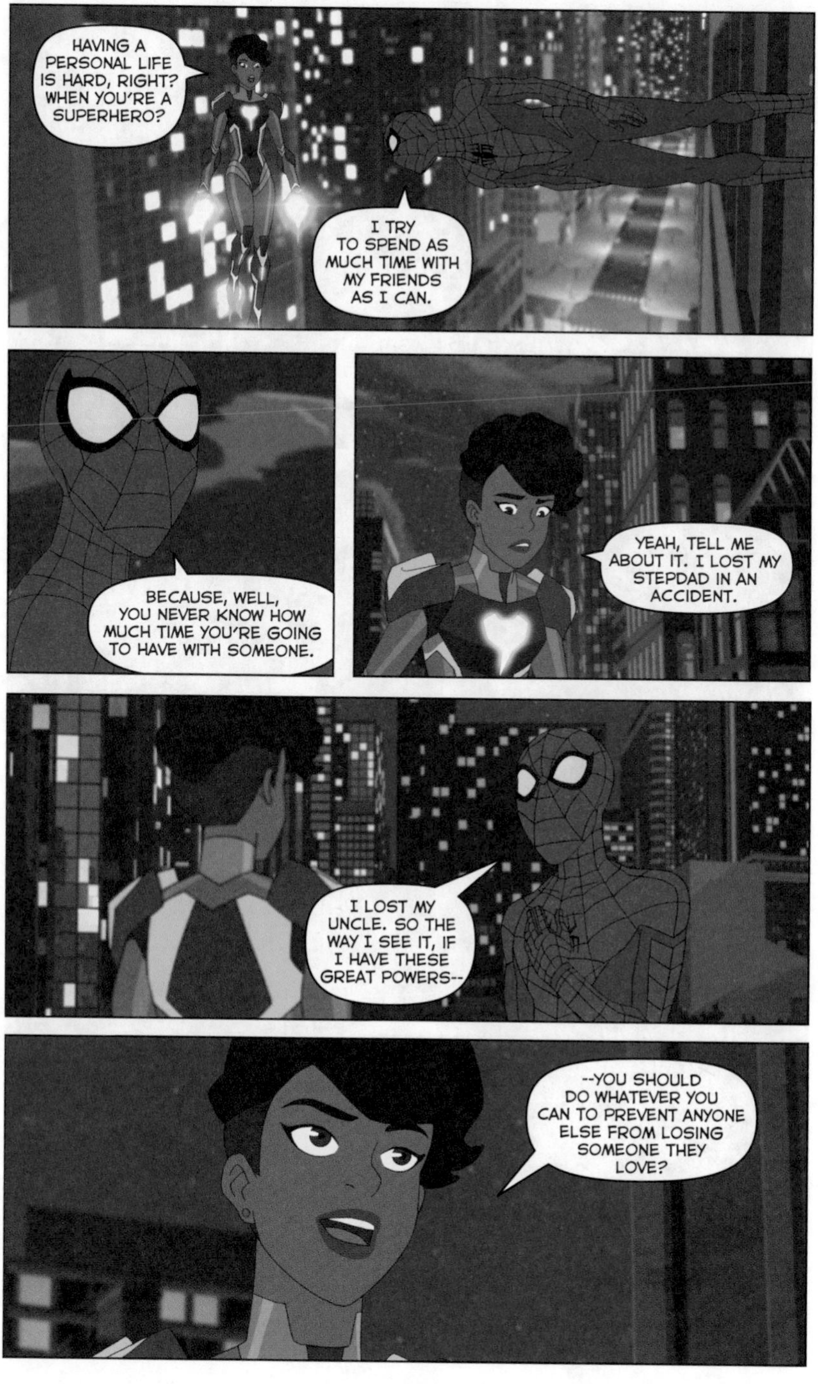
HAVING A PERSONAL LIFE IS HARD, RIGHT? WHEN YOU'RE A SUPERHERO?
I TRY TO SPEND AS MUCH TIME WITH MY FRIENDS AS I CAN.
BECAUSE, WELL, YOU NEVER KNOW HOW MUCH TIME YOU'RE GOING TO HAVE WITH SOMEONE.
YEAH, TELL ME ABOUT IT. I LOST MY STEPDAD IN AN ACCIDENT.
I LOST MY UNCLE. SO THE WAY I SEE IT, IF I HAVE THESE GREAT POWERS--
--YOU SHOULD DO WHATEVER YOU CAN TO PREVENT ANYONE ELSE FROM LOSING SOMEONE THEY LOVE?

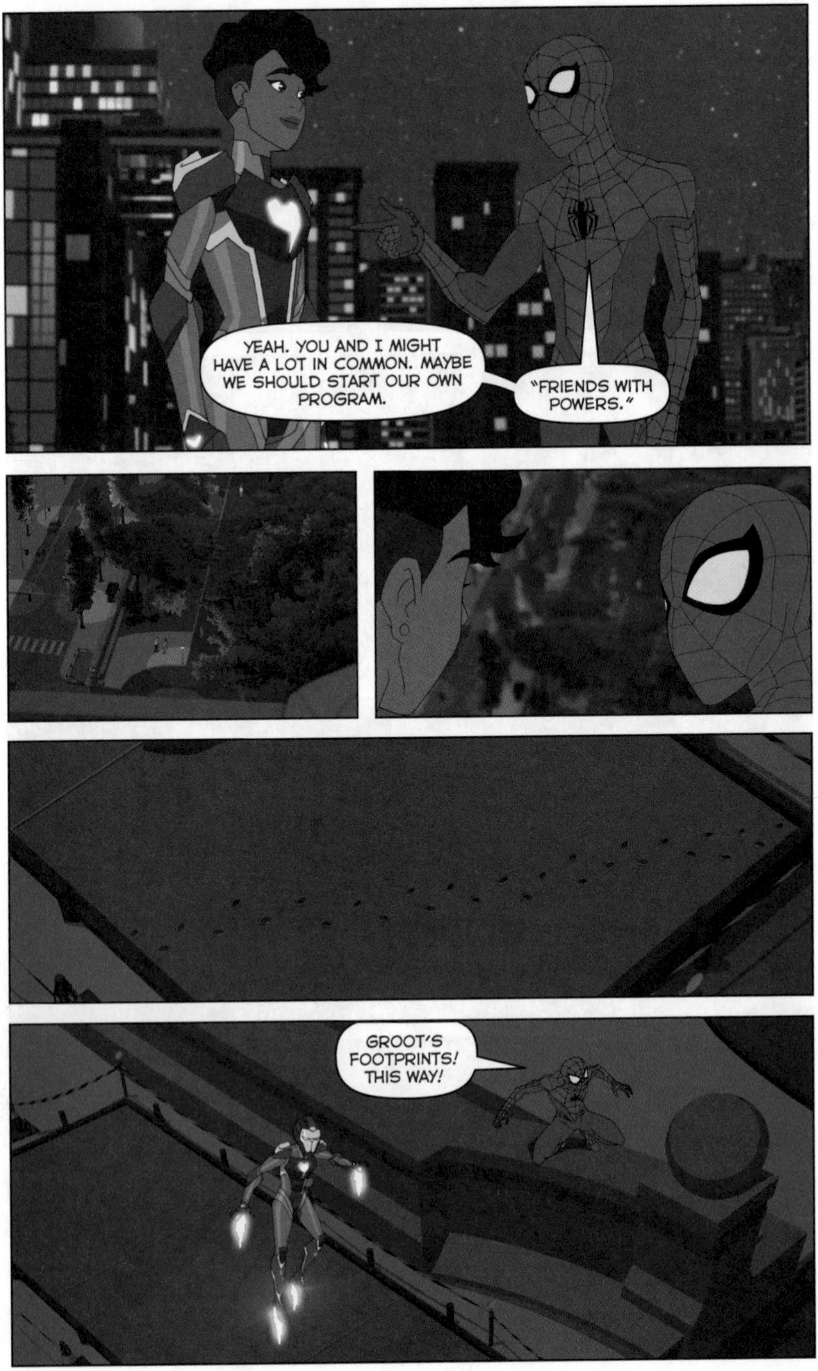
YEAH. YOU AND I MIGHT HAVE A LOT IN COMMON. MAYBE WE SHOULD START OUR OWN PROGRAM.
"FRIENDS WITH POWERS."
GROOT'S FOOTPRINTS! THIS WAY!

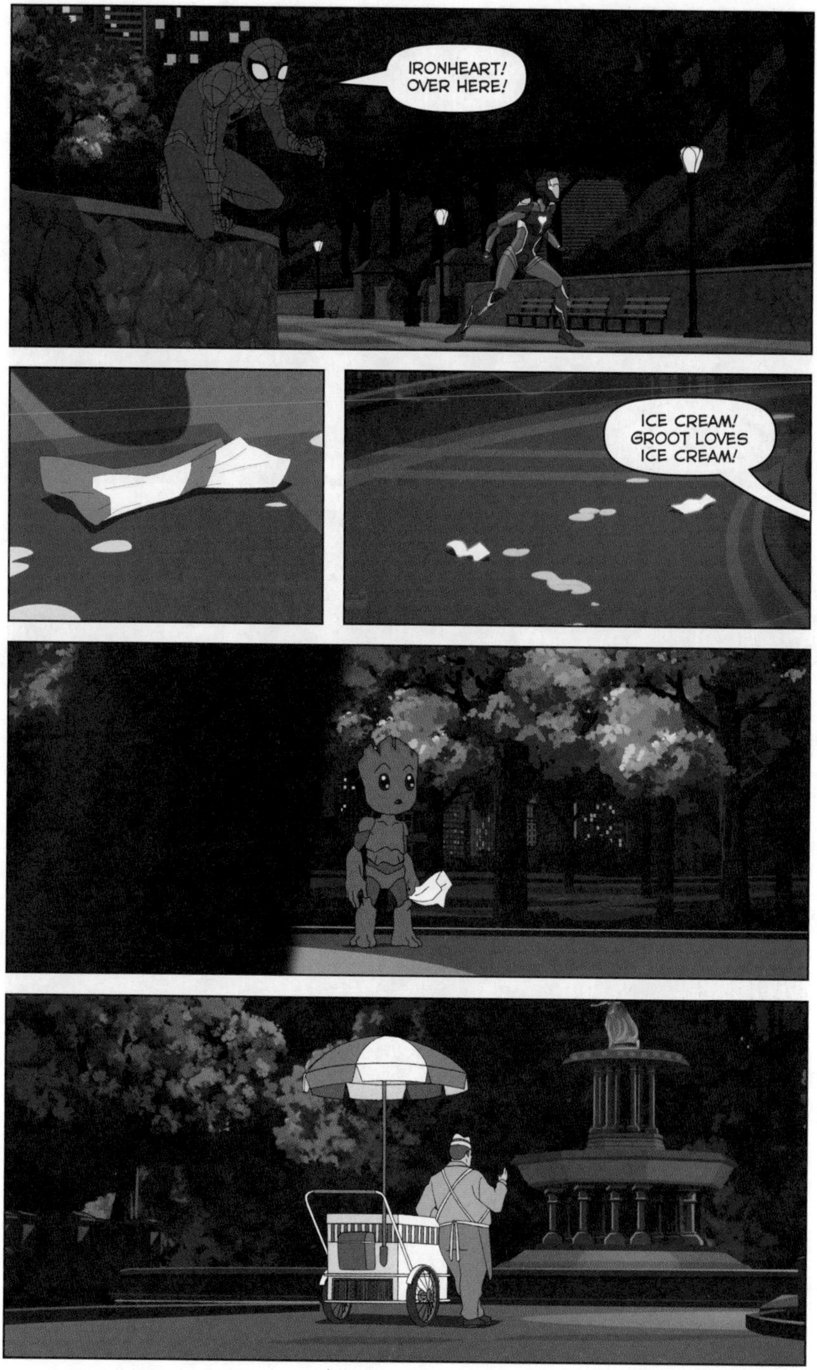
IRONHEART! OVER HERE!
ICE CREAM! GROOT LOVES ICE CREAM!

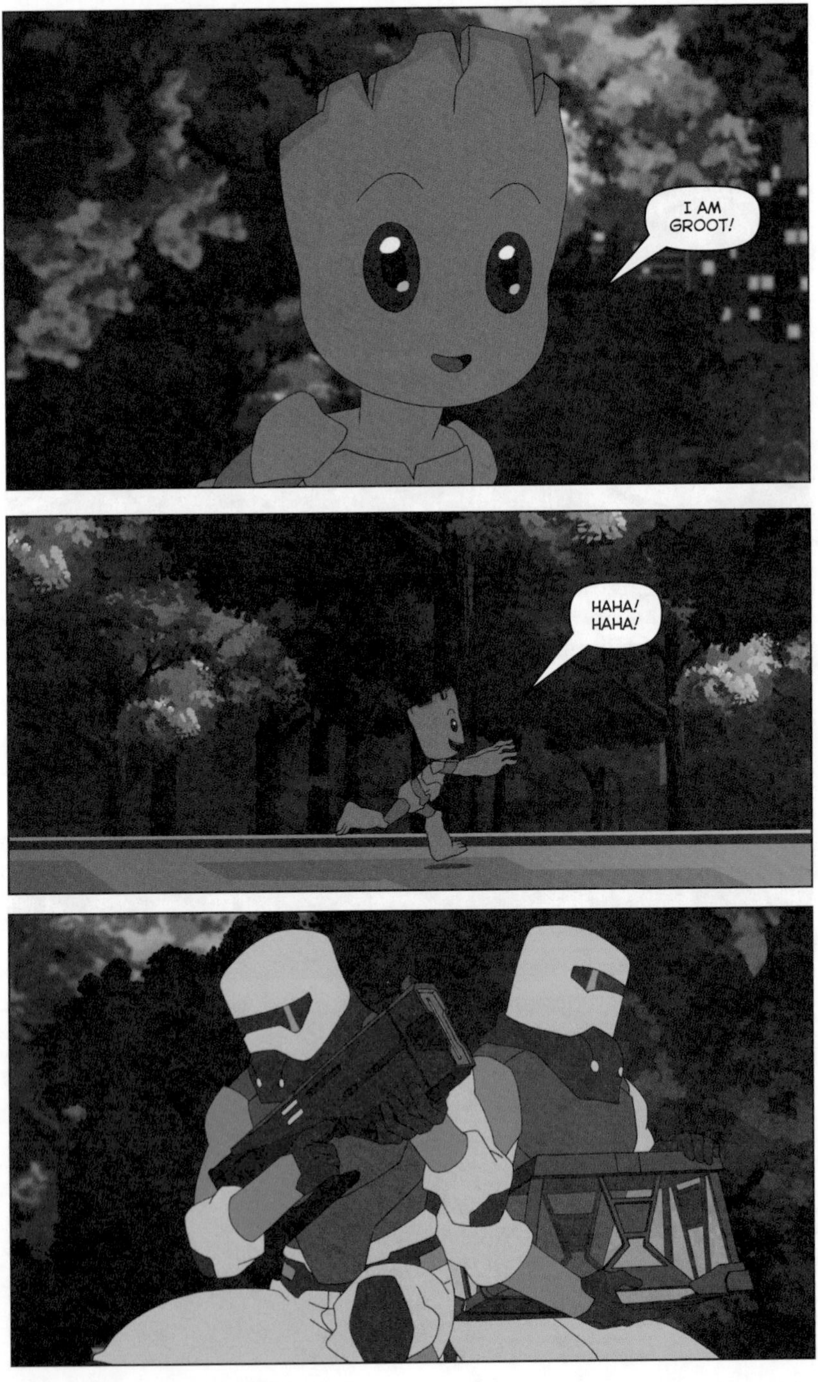
I AM GROOT!
HAHA! HAHA!

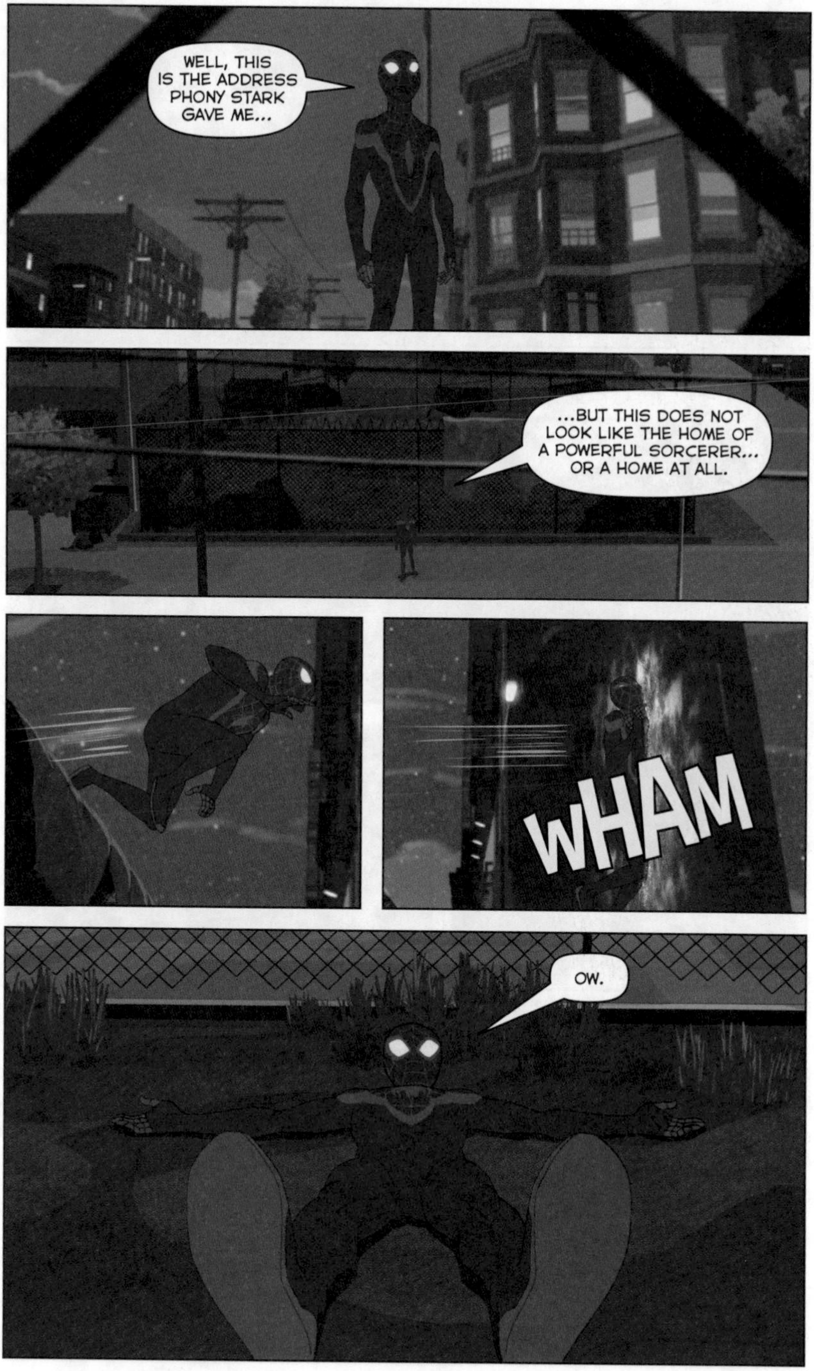
WELL, THIS IS THE ADDRESS PHONY STARK GAVE ME...
...BUT THIS DOES NOT LOOK LIKE THE HOME OF A POWERFUL SORCERER... OR A HOME AT ALL.
wHAM
OW.

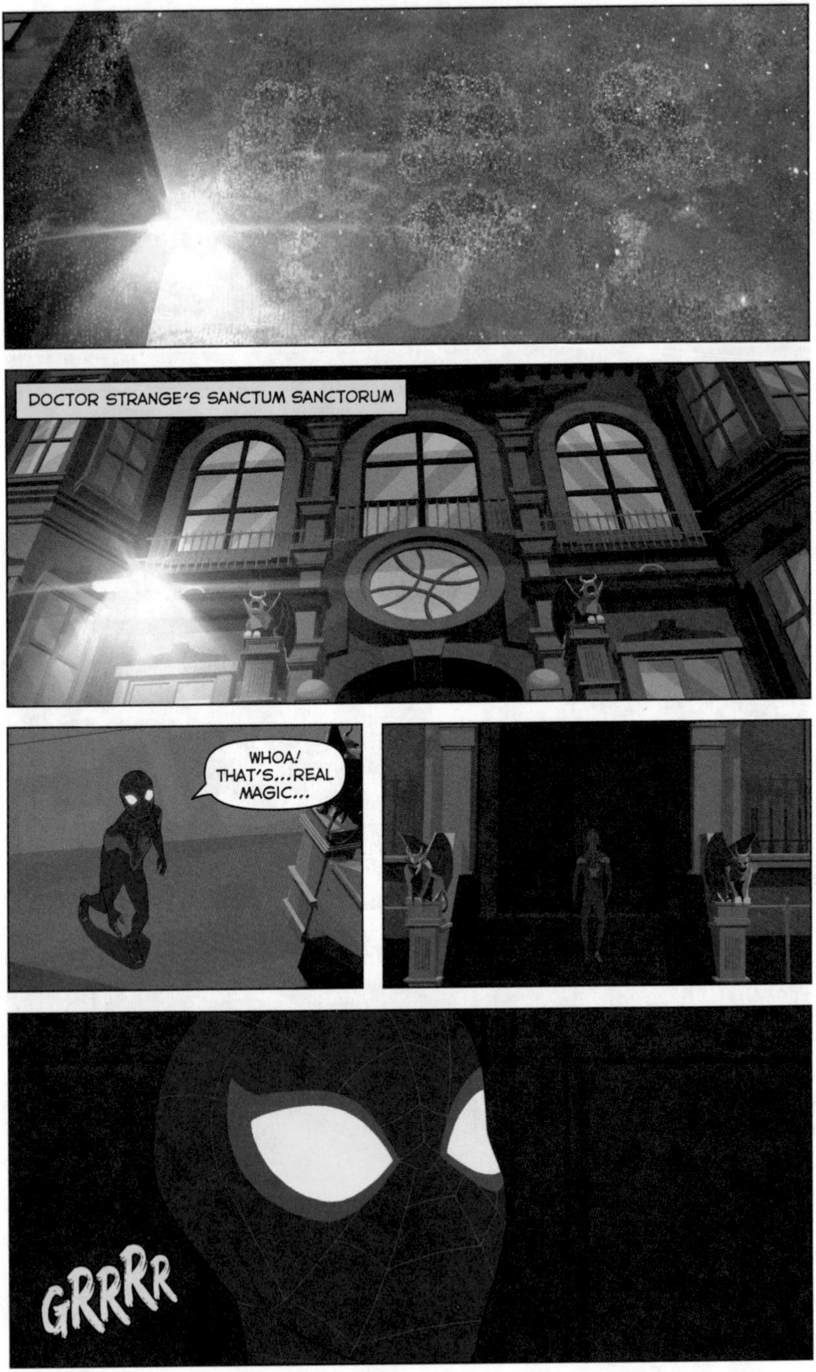
DOCTOR STRANGE'S SANCTUM SANCTORUM
WHOA! THAT'S...REAL MAGIC...
GRRRR

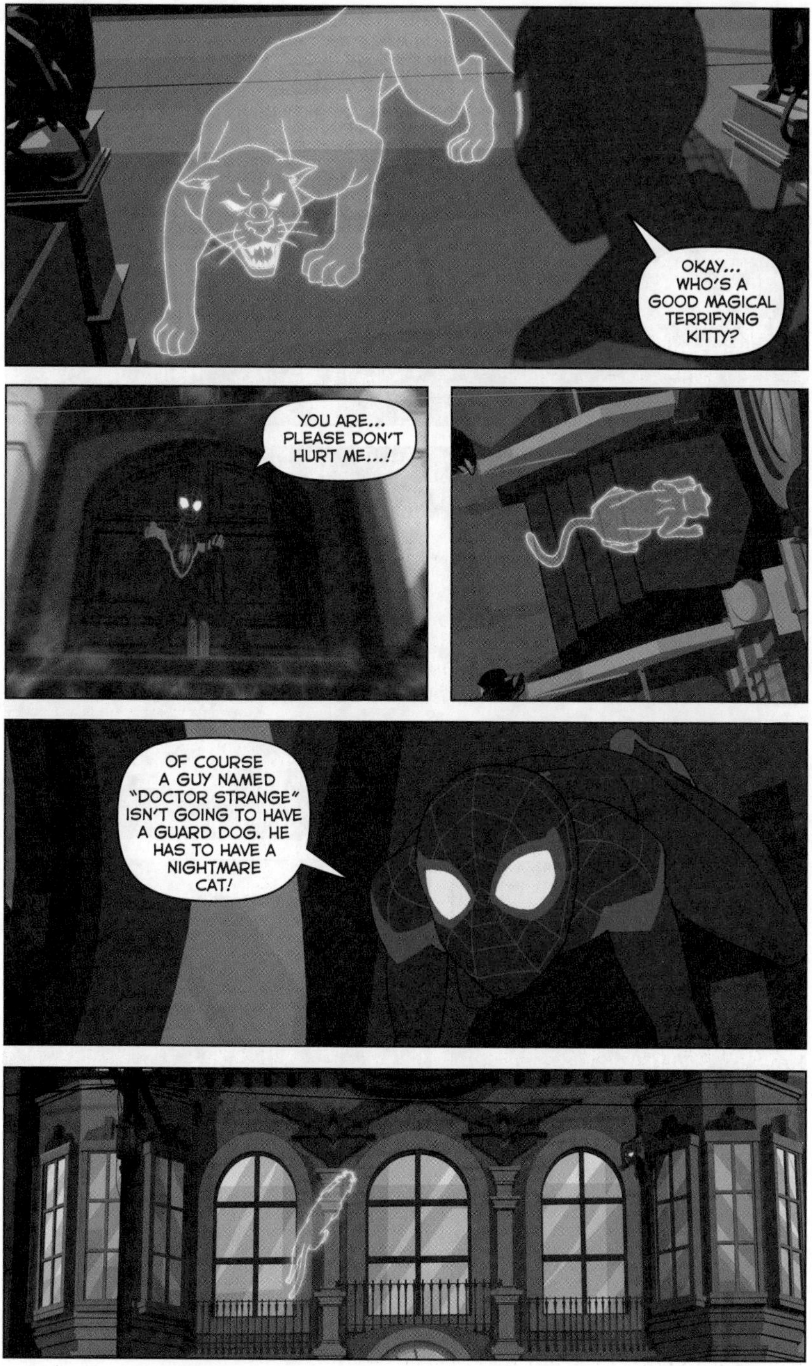
OKAY... WHO'S A GOOD MAGICAL TERRIFYING KITTY?
YOU ARE... PLEASE DON'T HURT ME...!
OF COURSE A GUY NAMED "DOCTOR STRANGE" ISN'T GOING TO HAVE A GUARD DOG. HE HAS TO HAVE A NIGHTMARE CAT!

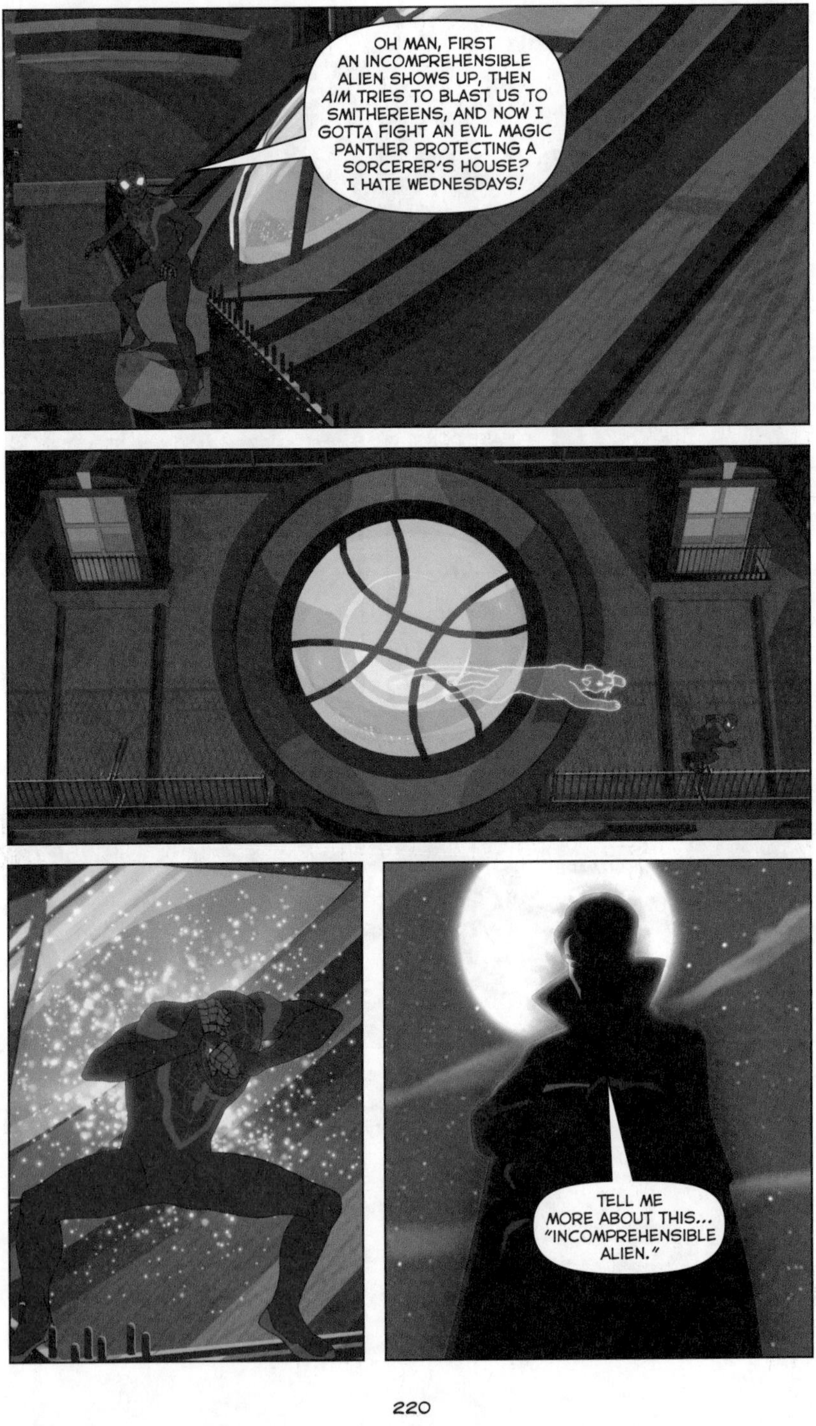
OH MAN, FIRST AN INCOMPREHENSIBLE ALIEN SHOWS UP, THEN AIM TRIES TO BLAST US TO SMITHEREENS, AND NOW I GOTTA FIGHT AN EVIL MAGIC PANTHER PROTECTING A SORCERER'S HOUSE? I HATE WEDNESDAYS!
TELL ME MORE ABOUT THIS... "INCOMPREHENSIBLE ALIEN."

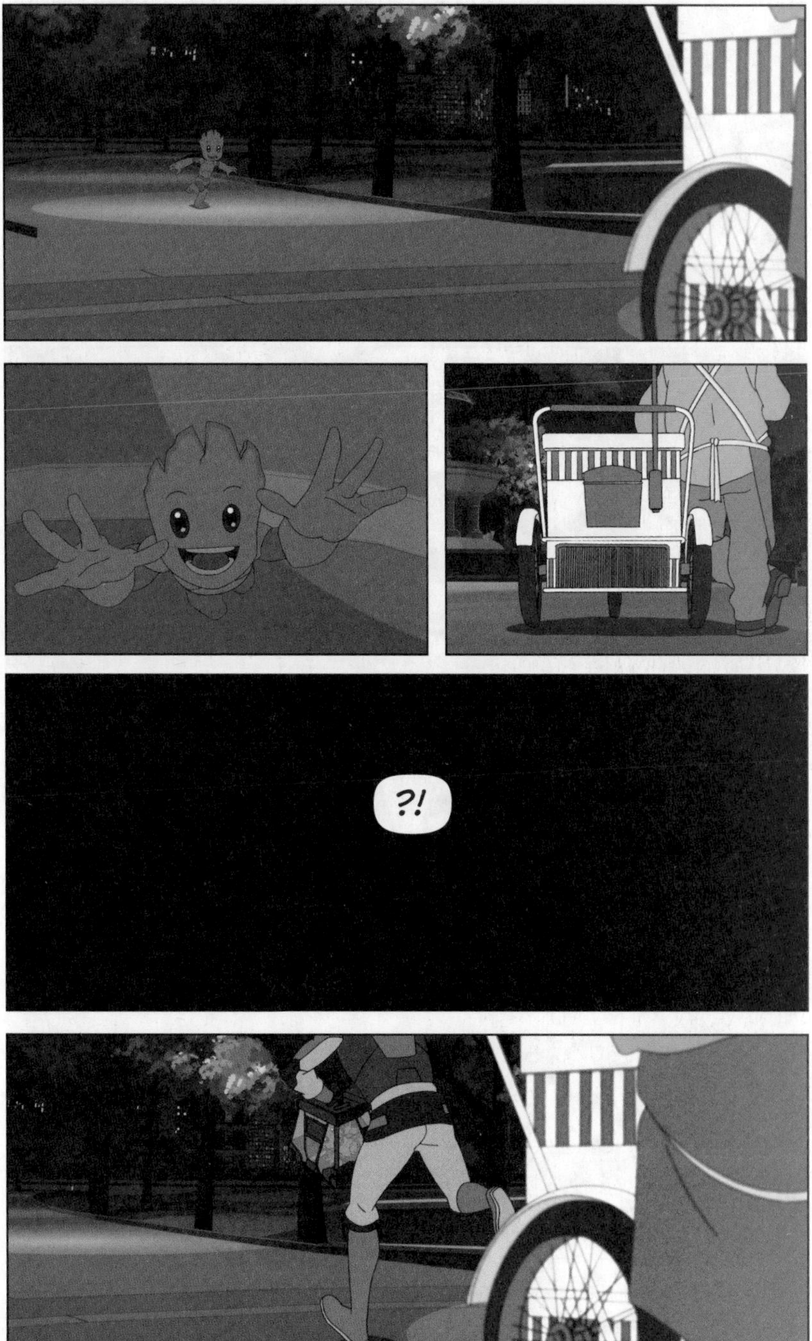
?!

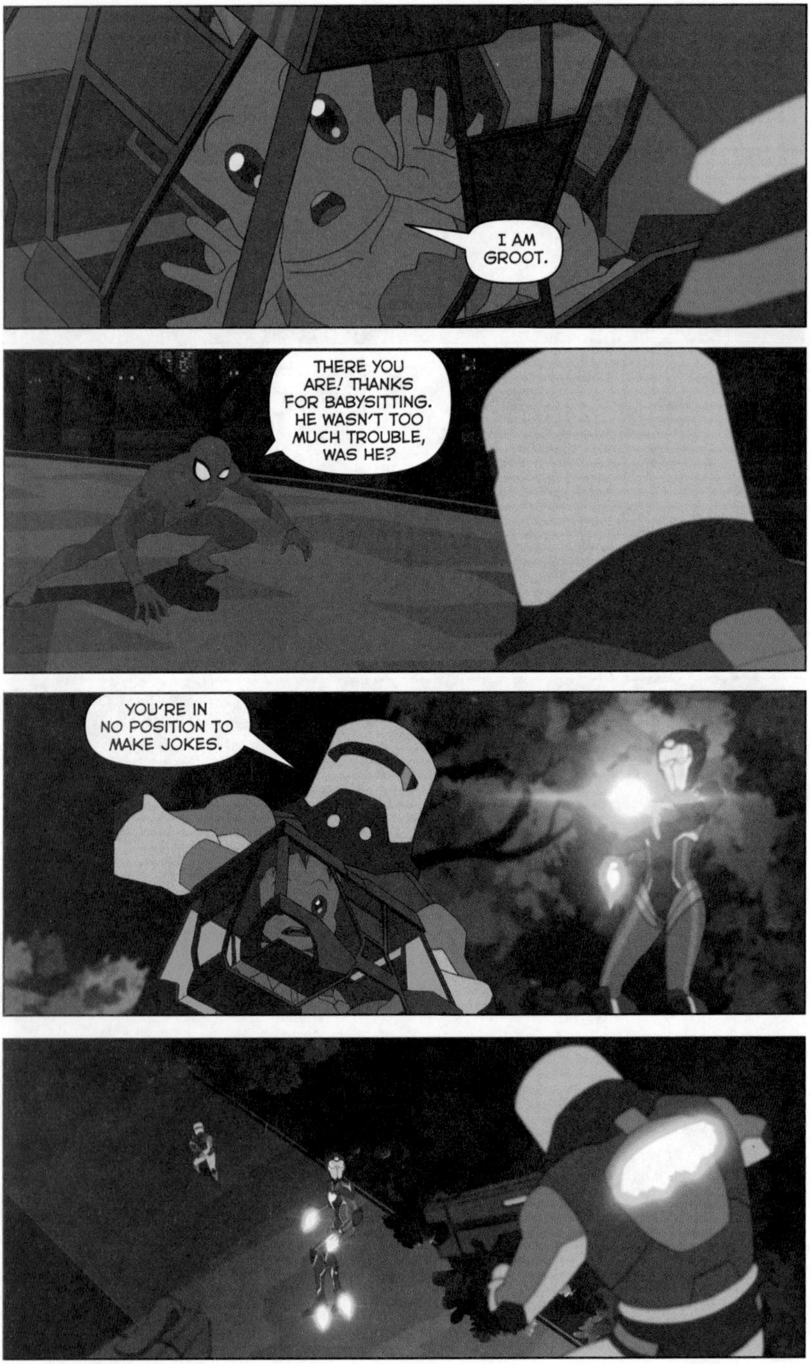
I AM GROOT.
THERE YOU ARE! THANKS FOR BABYSITTING. HE WASN'T TOO MUCH TROUBLE, WAS HE?
YOU'RE IN NO POSITION TO MAKE JOKES.

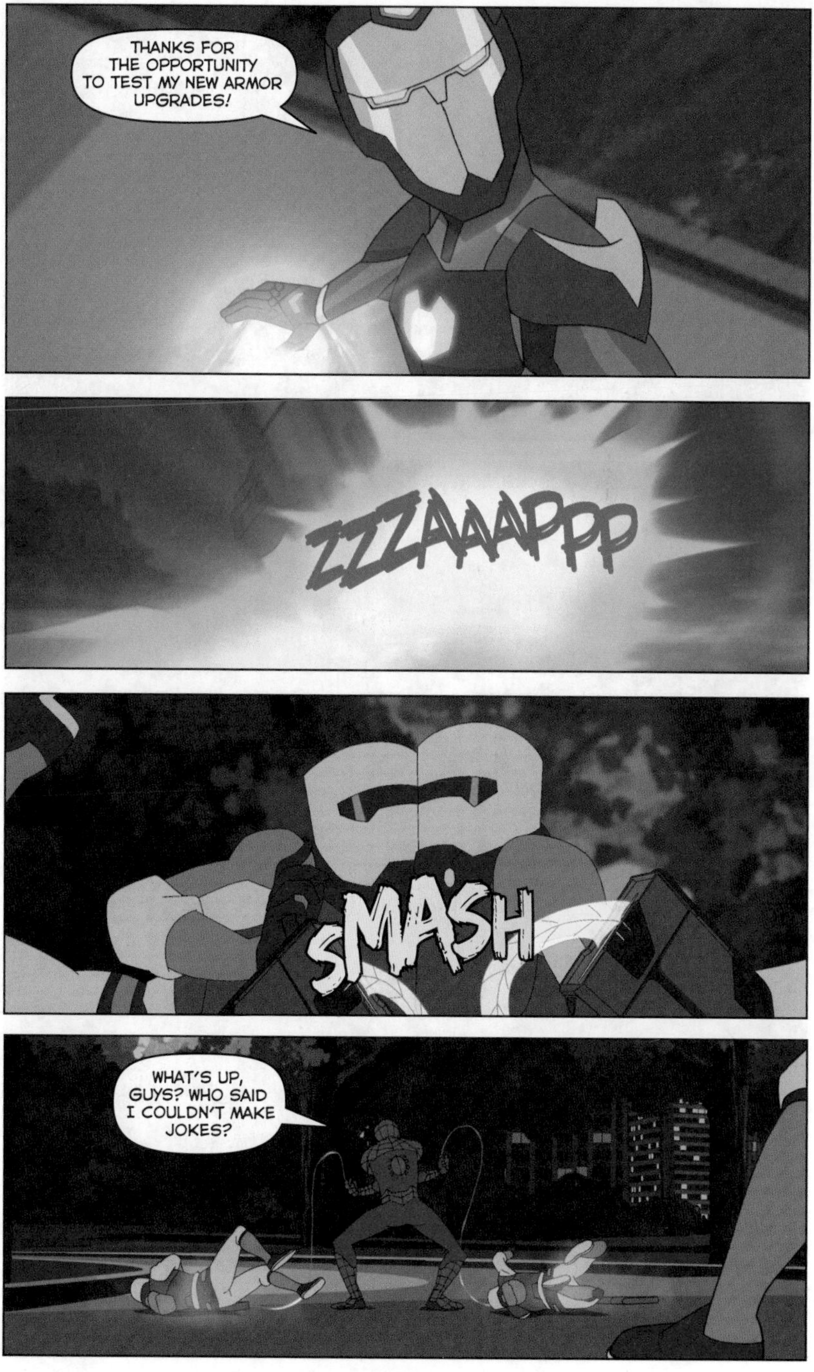
THANKS FOR THE OPPORTUNITY TO TEST MY NEW ARMOR UPGRADES!
ZZZAAAPPP
SMASH
WHAT'S UP, GUYS? WHO SAID I COULDN'T MAKE JOKES?

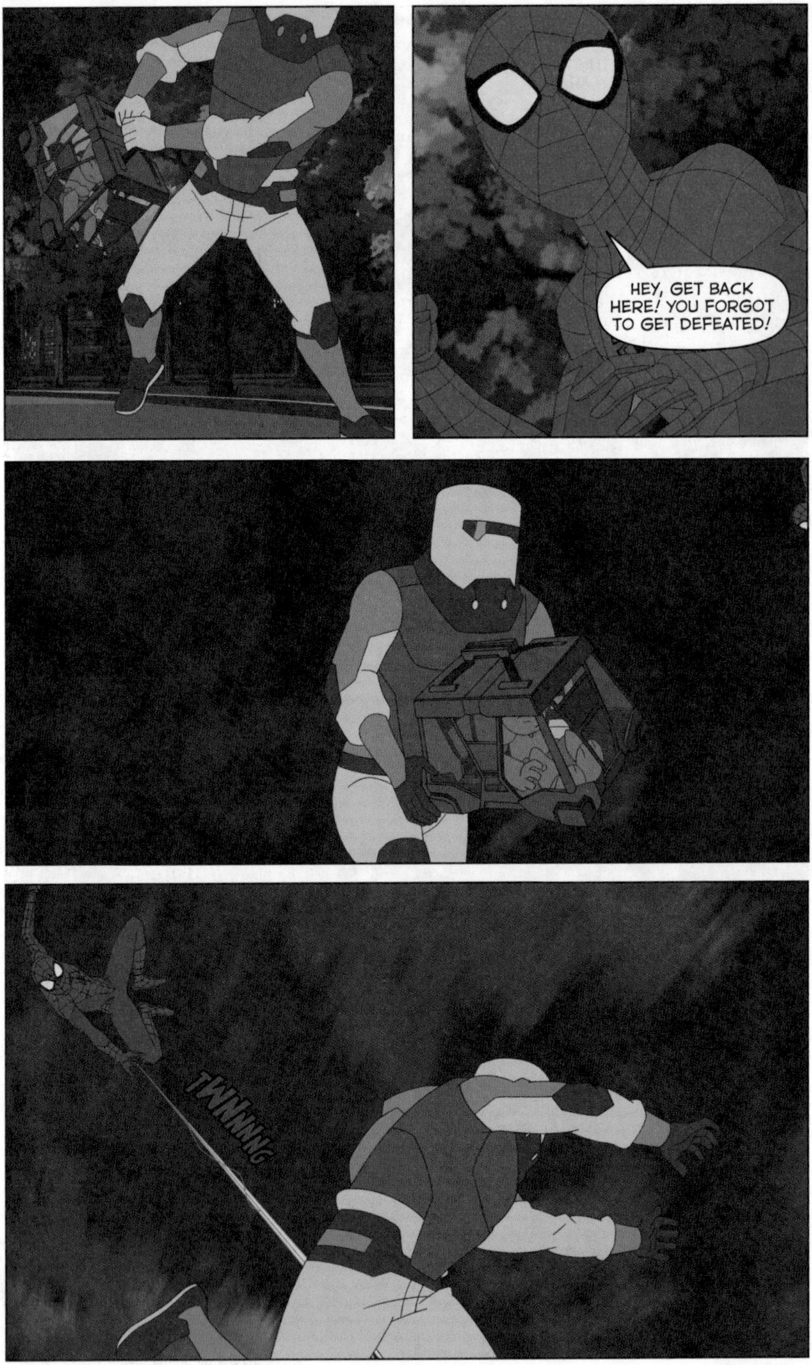
HEY, GET BACK
HERE! YOU FORGOT
TO GET DEFEATED!
TWNNNNG

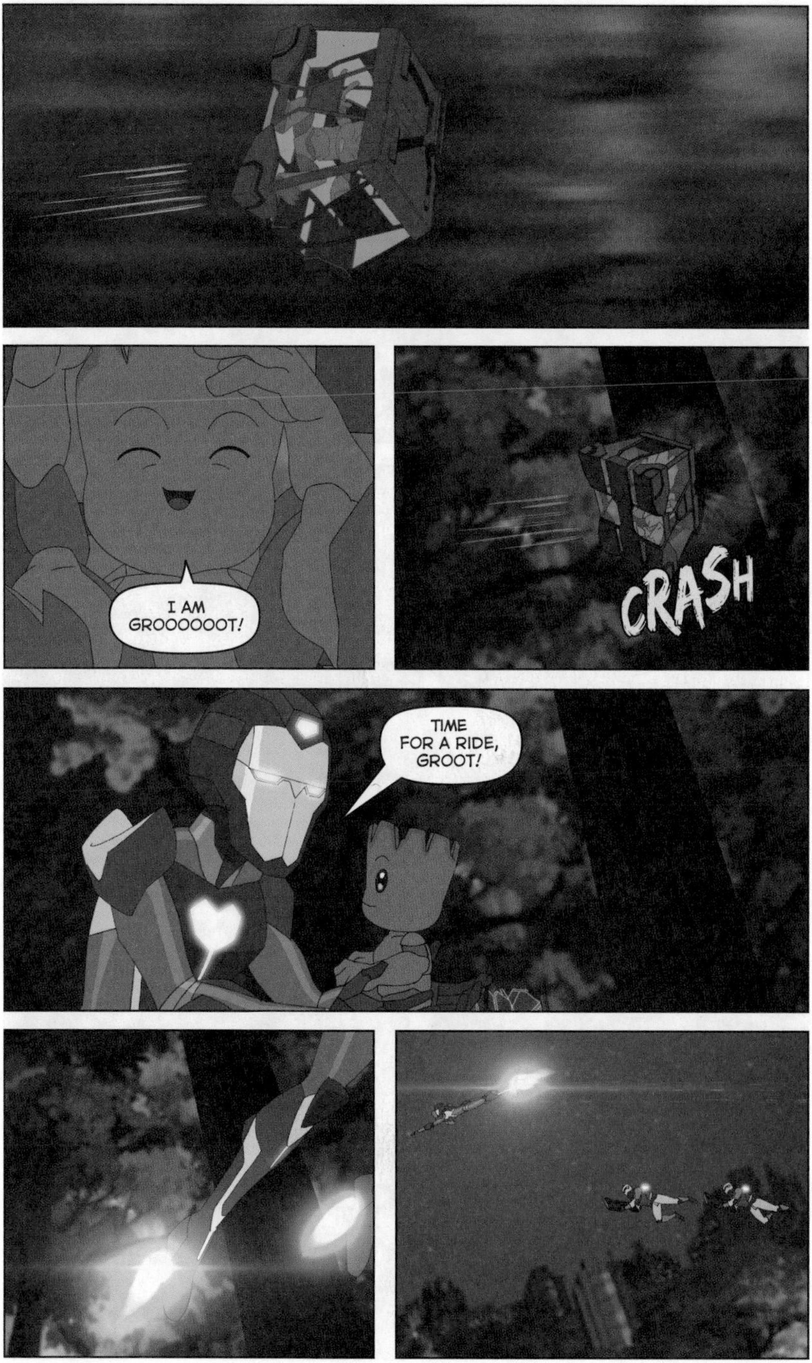
I AM GROOOOOOT!
CRASH
TIME FOR A RIDE, GROOT!

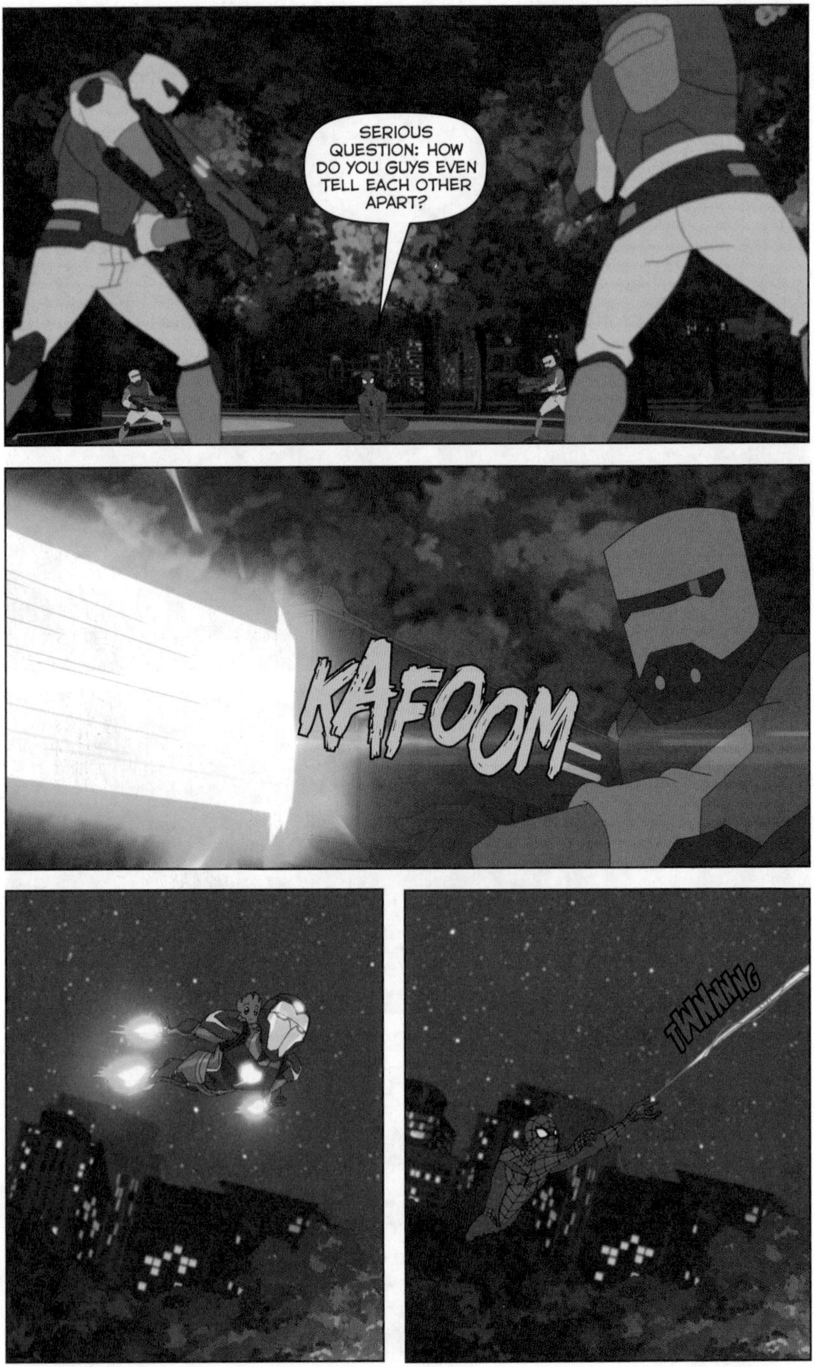
SERIOUS QUESTION: HOW DO YOU GUYS EVEN TELL EACH OTHER APART?
KAFOOM
TWNNNG

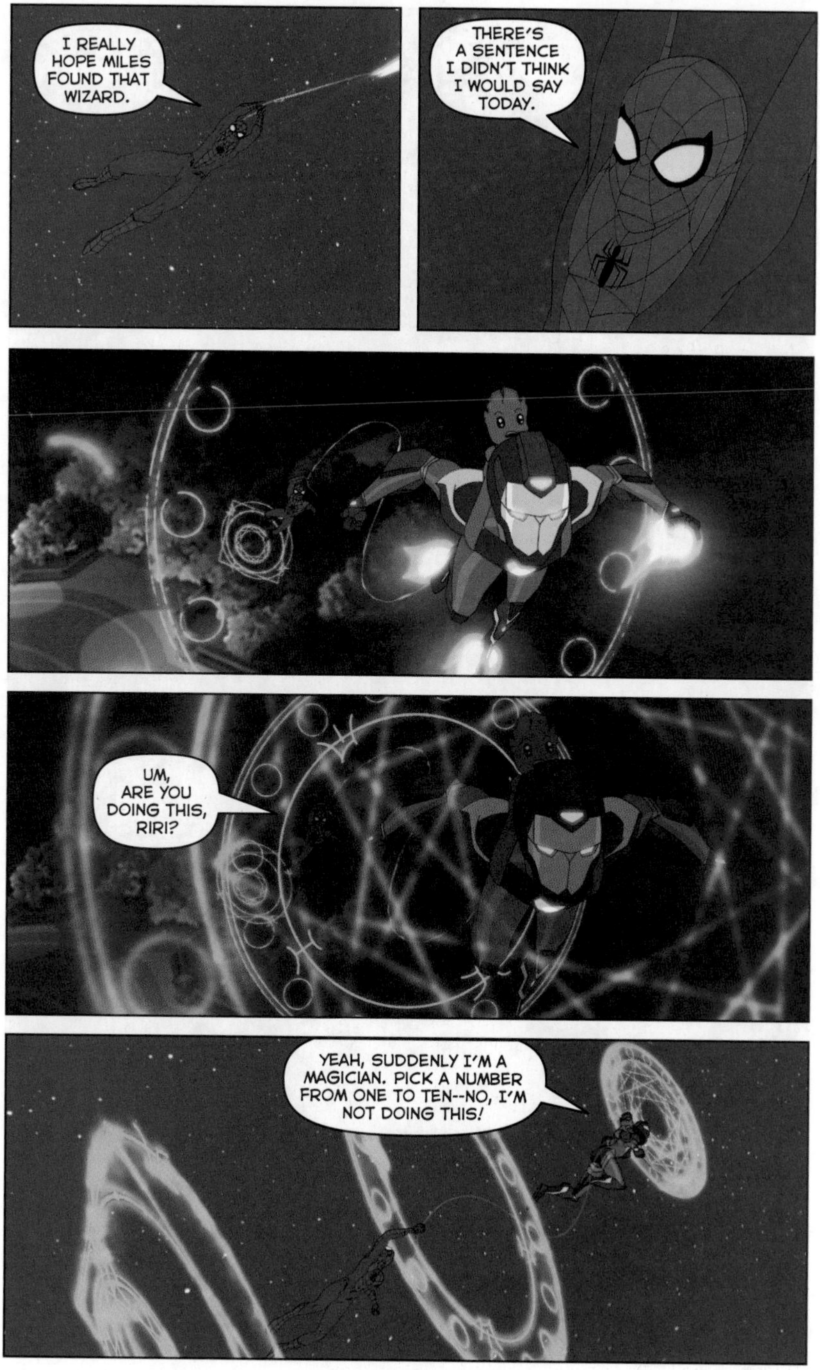
I REALLY HOPE MILES FOUND THAT WIZARD.
THERE'S A SENTENCE I DIDN'T THINK I WOULD SAY TODAY.
UM, ARE YOU DOING THIS, RIRI?
YEAH, SUDDENLY I'M A MAGICIAN. PICK A NUMBER FROM ONE TO TEN--NO, I'M NOT DOING THIS!

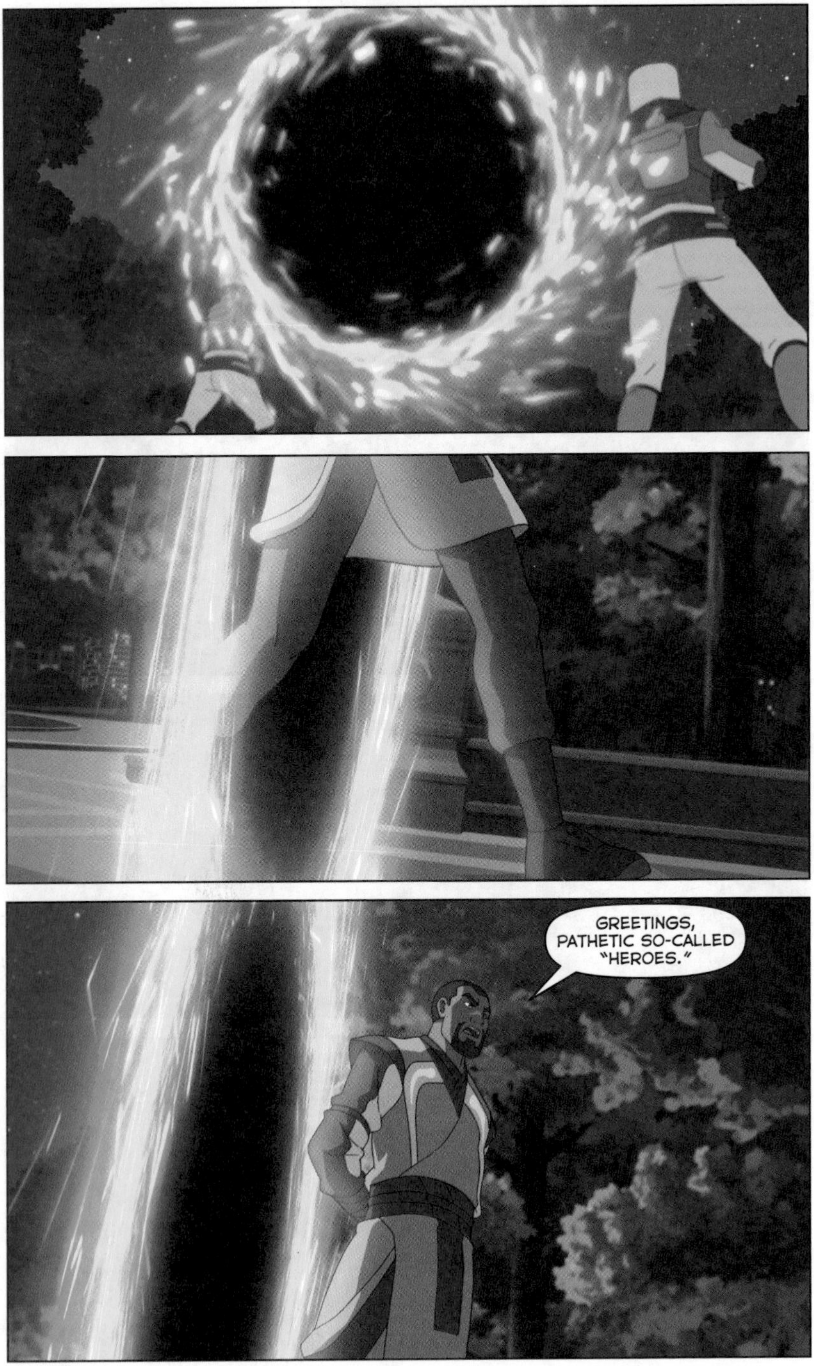
GREETINGS,
PATHETIC SO-CALLED
"HEROES."

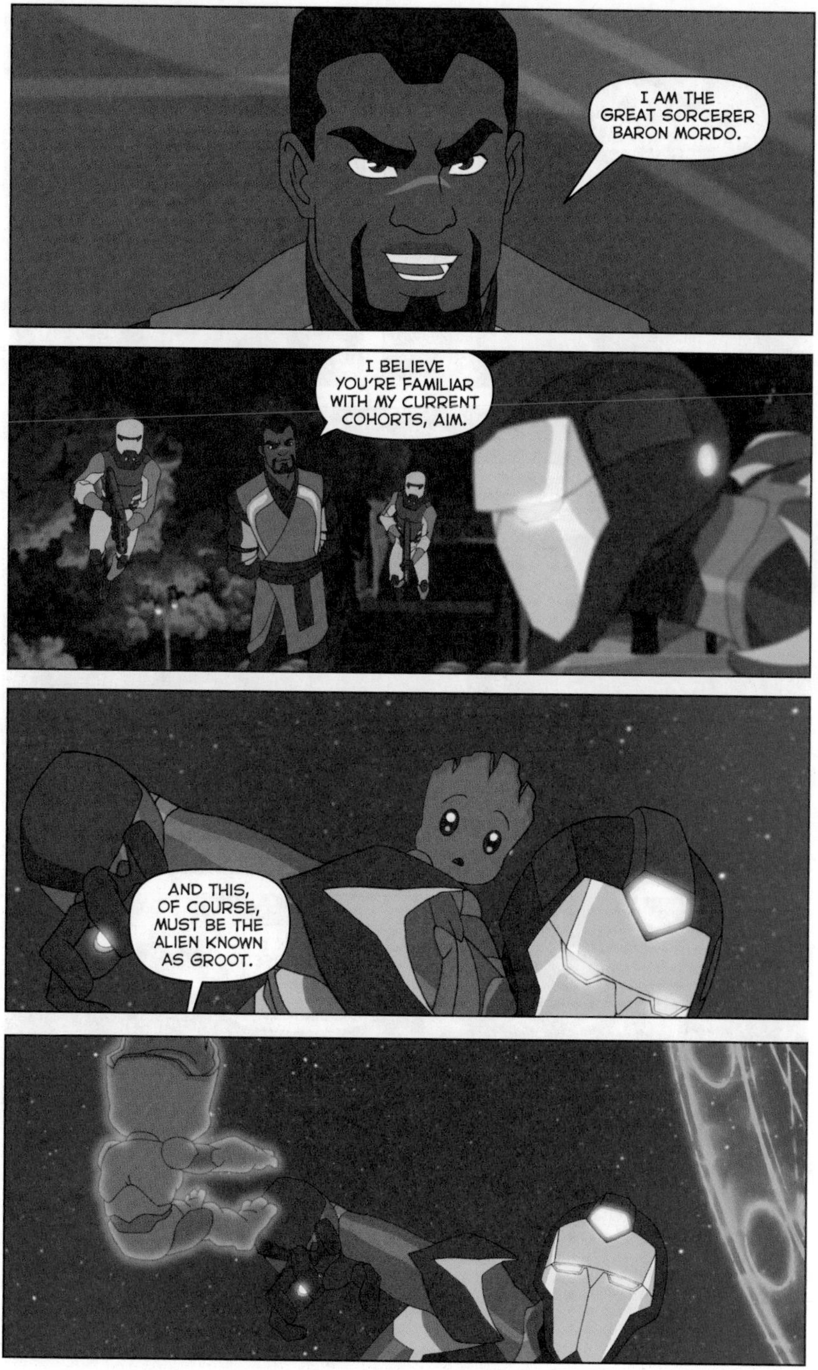
I AM THE GREAT SORCERER BARON MORDO.
I BELIEVE YOU'RE FAMILIAR WITH MY CURRENT COHORTS, AIM.
AND THIS, OF COURSE, MUST BE THE ALIEN KNOWN AS GROOT.

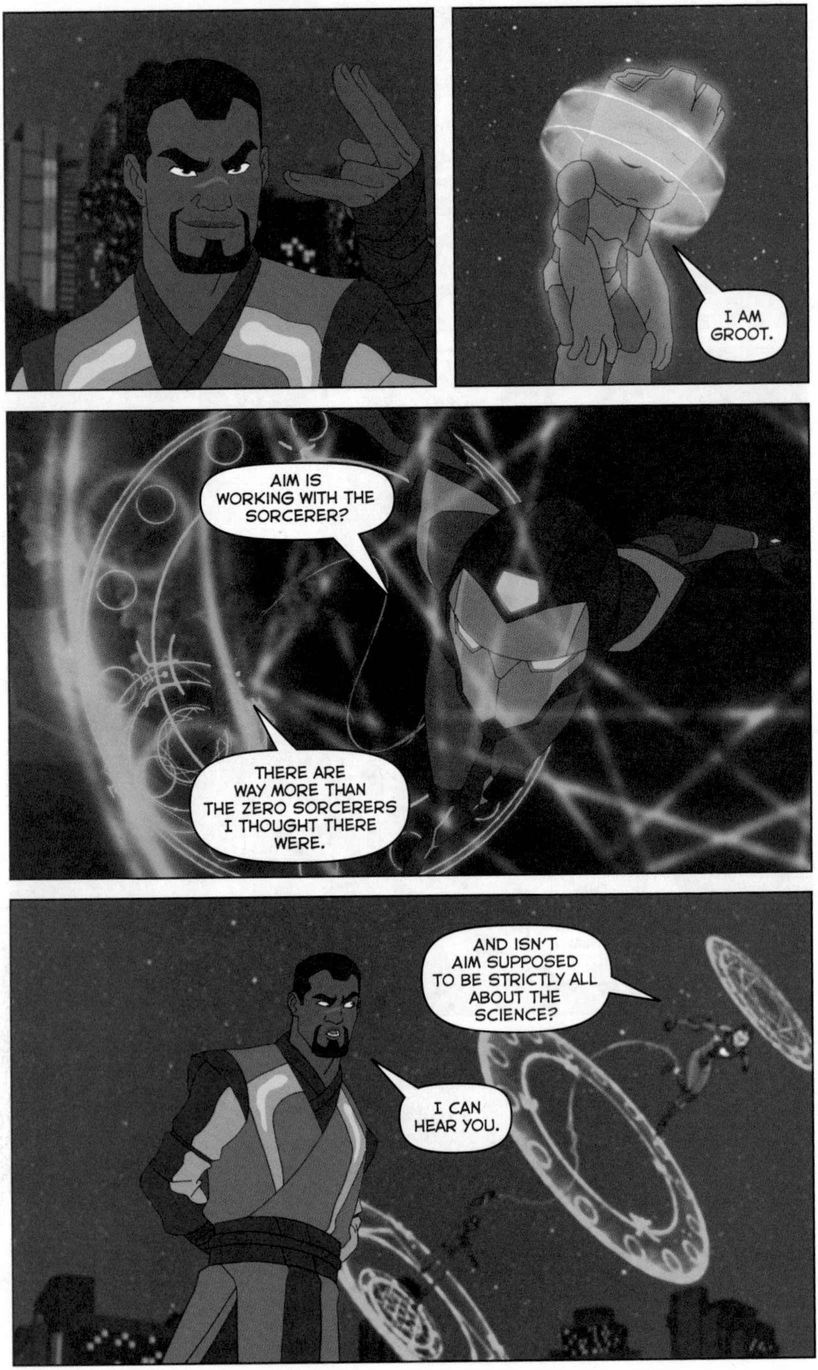
I AM GROOT.
AIM IS WORKING WITH THE SORCERER?
THERE ARE WAY MORE THAN THE ZERO SORCERERS I THOUGHT THERE WERE.
AND ISN'T AIM SUPPOSED TO BE STRICTLY ALL ABOUT THE SCIENCE?
I CAN HEAR YOU.

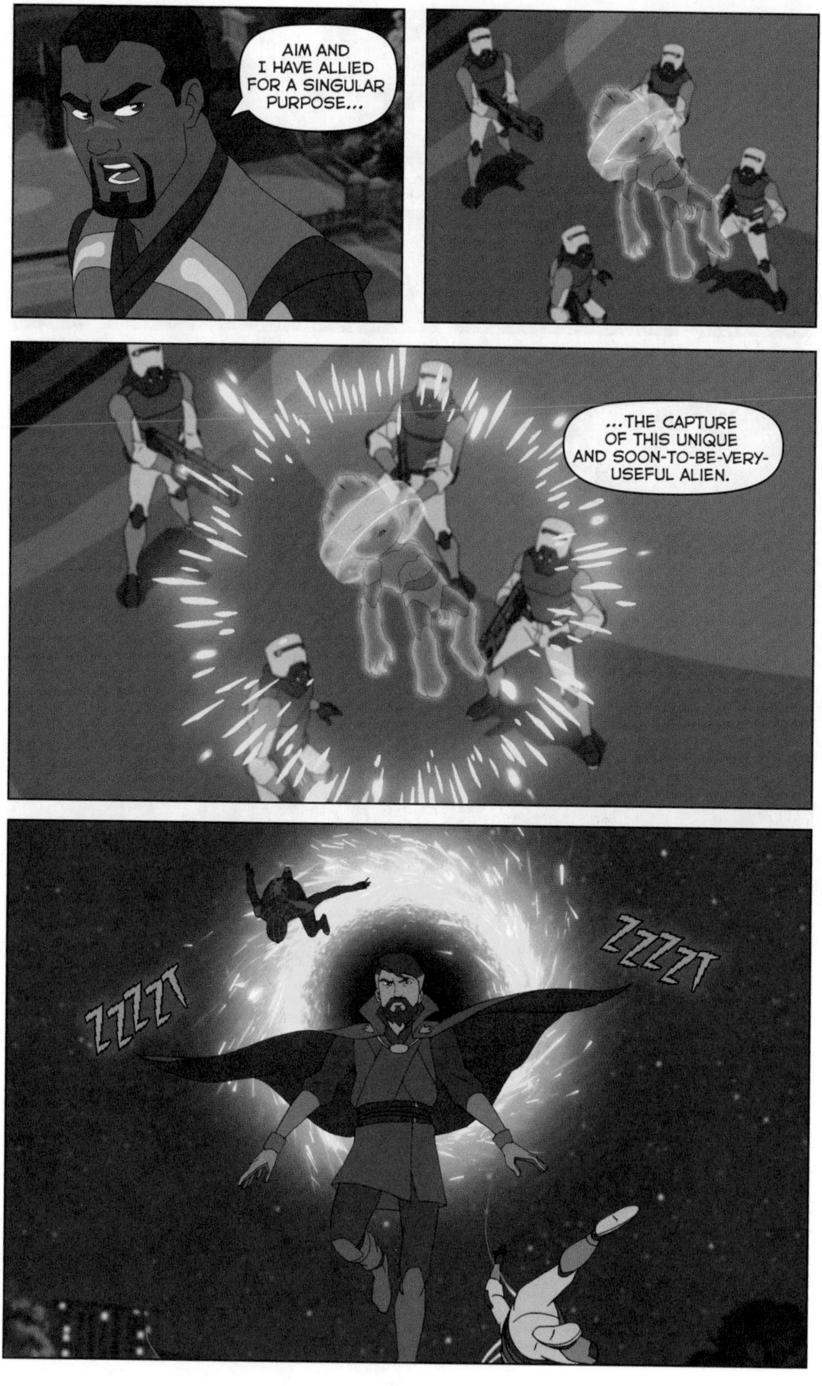
AIM AND I HAVE ALLIED FOR A SINGULAR PURPOSE...
...THE CAPTURE OF THIS UNIQUE AND SOON-TO-BE-VERY-USEFUL ALIEN.
ZZZZT
ZZZZT

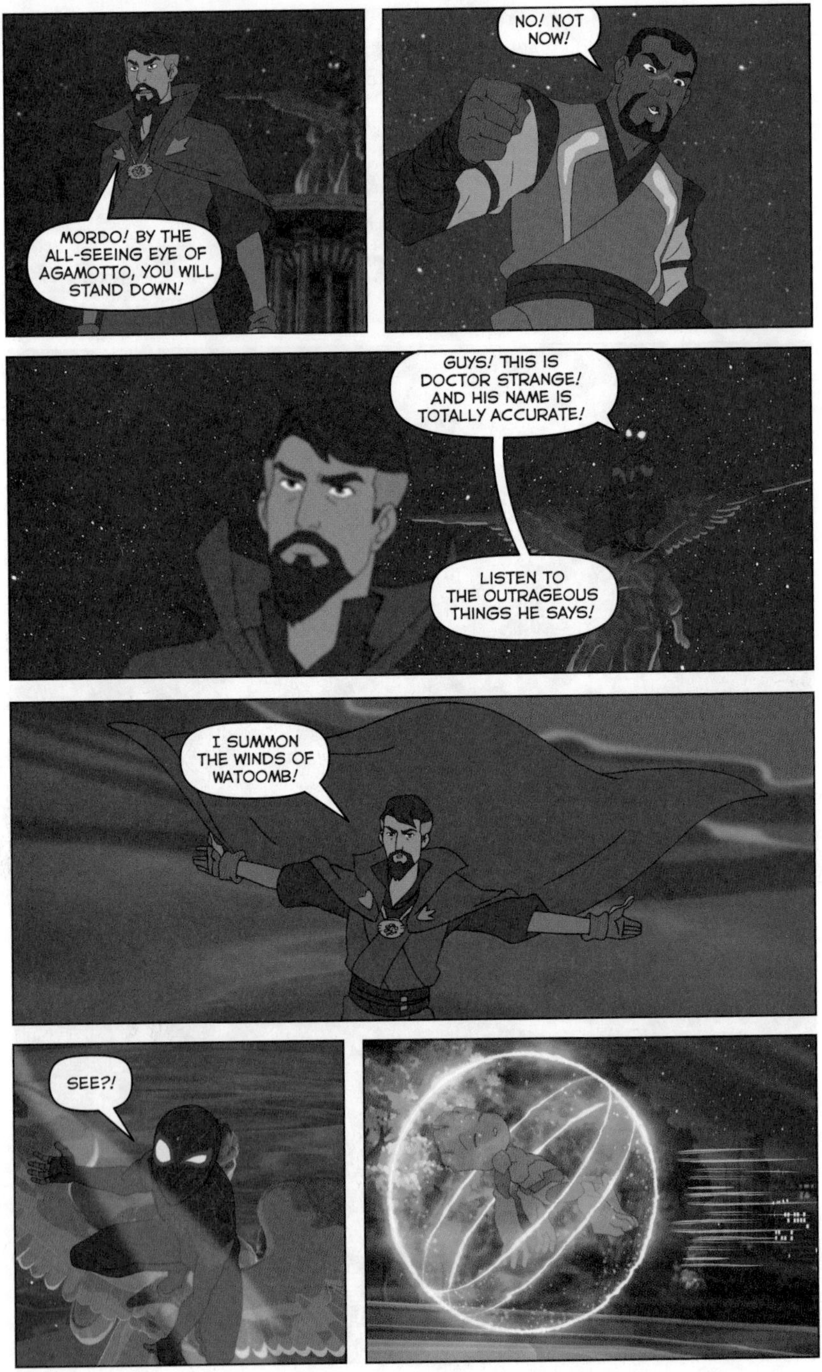
MORDO! BY THE ALL-SEEING EYE OF AGAMOTTO, YOU WILL STAND DOWN!
NO! NOT NOW!
GUYS! THIS IS DOCTOR STRANGE! AND HIS NAME IS TOTALLY ACCURATE!
LISTEN TO THE OUTRAGEOUS THINGS HE SAYS!
I SUMMON THE WINDS OF WATOOMB!
SEE?!

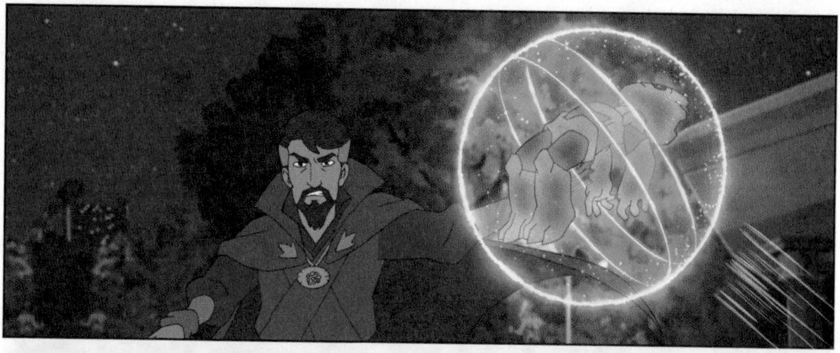

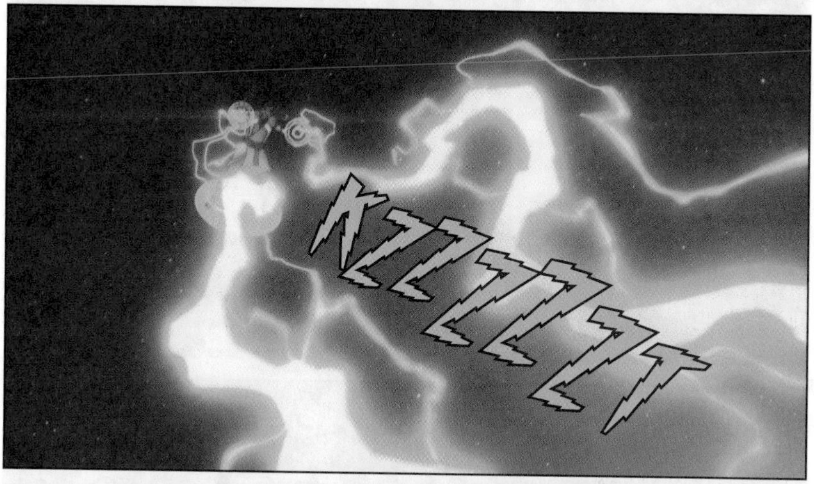
KZZZZZZT

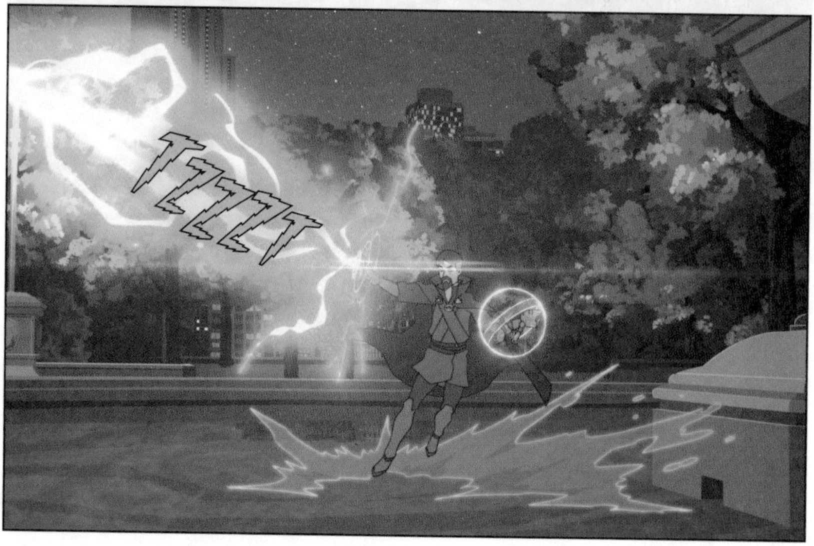
TZZZZT

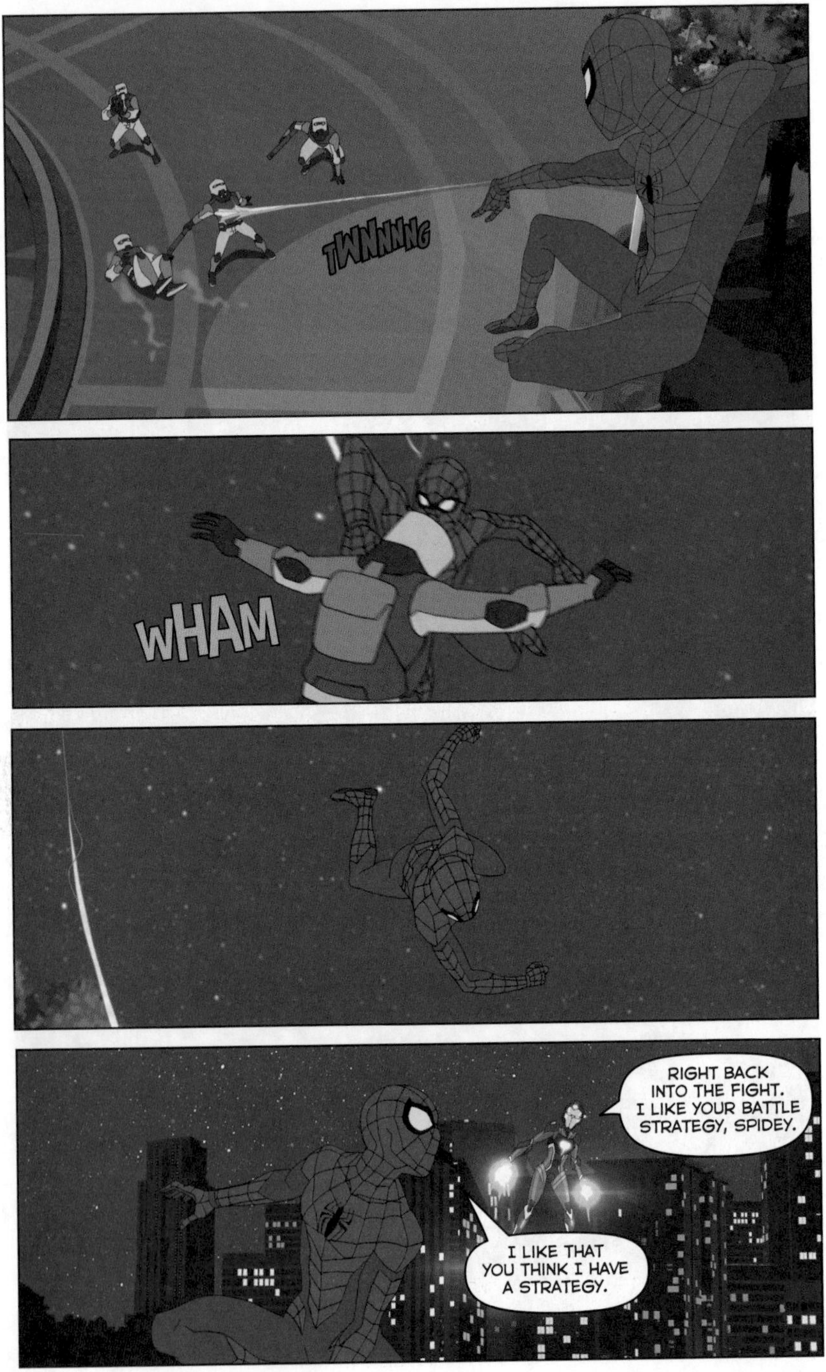
TWNNNNG
WHAM
RIGHT BACK INTO THE FIGHT. I LIKE YOUR BATTLE STRATEGY, SPIDEY.
I LIKE THAT YOU THINK I HAVE A STRATEGY.

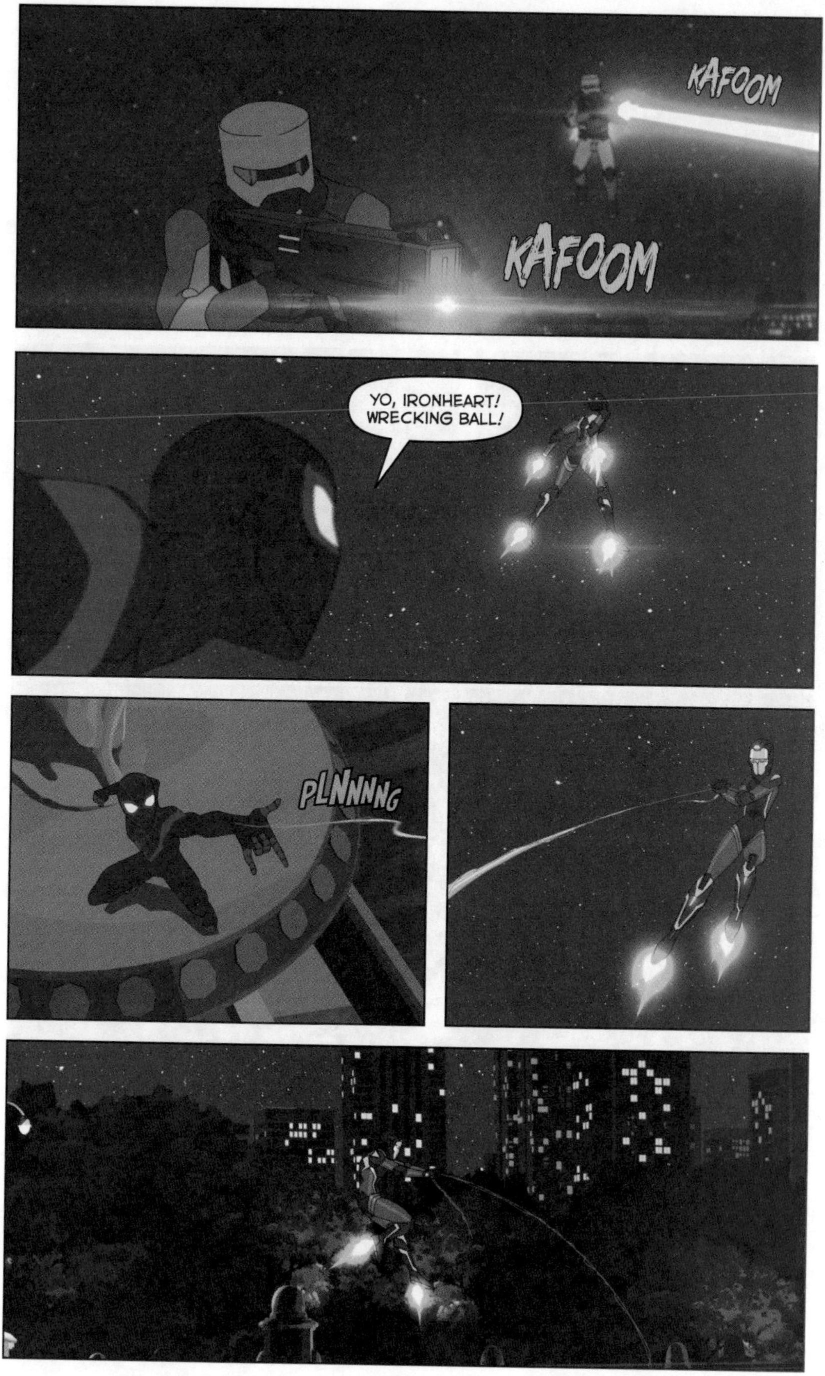
KAFOOM
KAFOOM
YO, IRONHEART! WRECKING BALL!
PLNNNNG

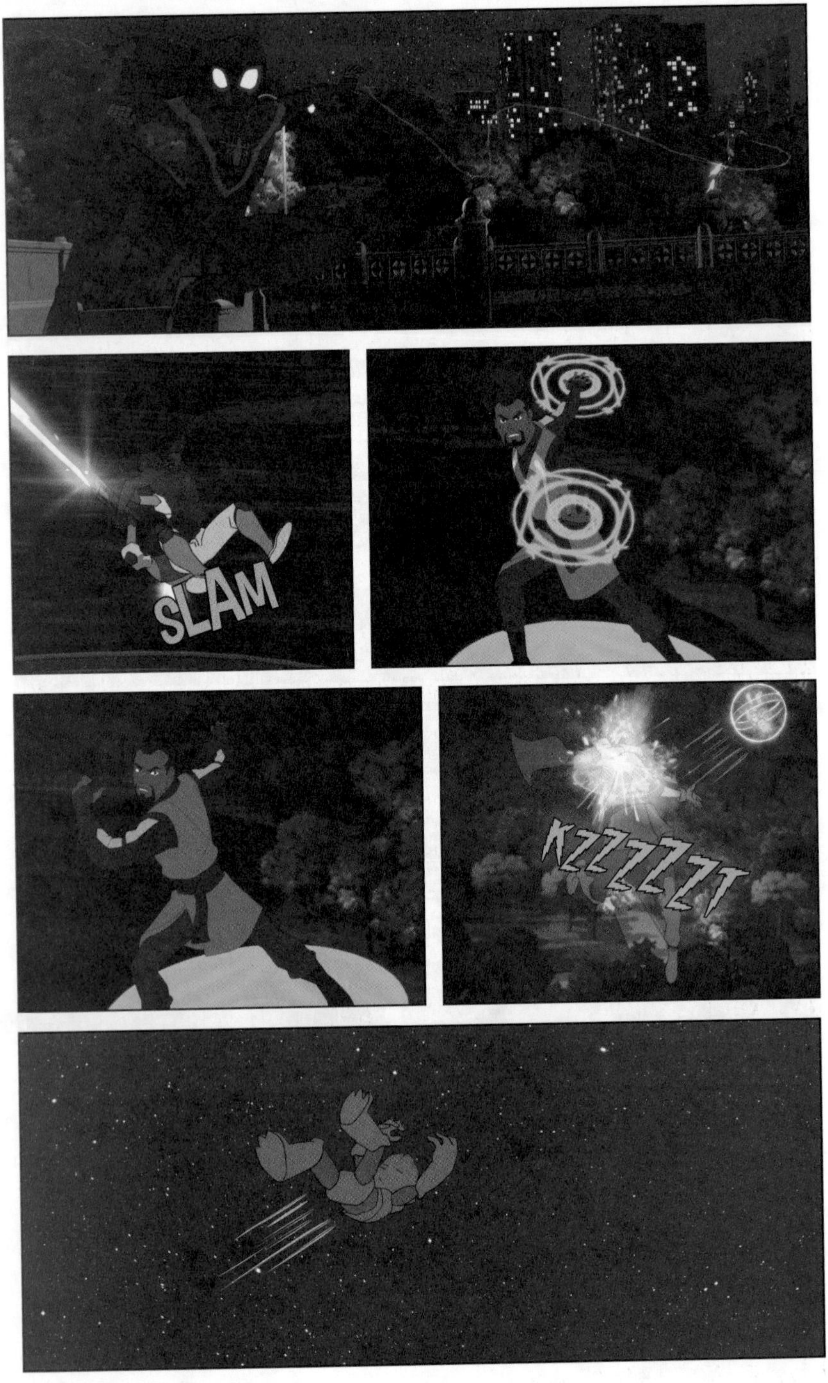
SLAM
KZZZZZZT

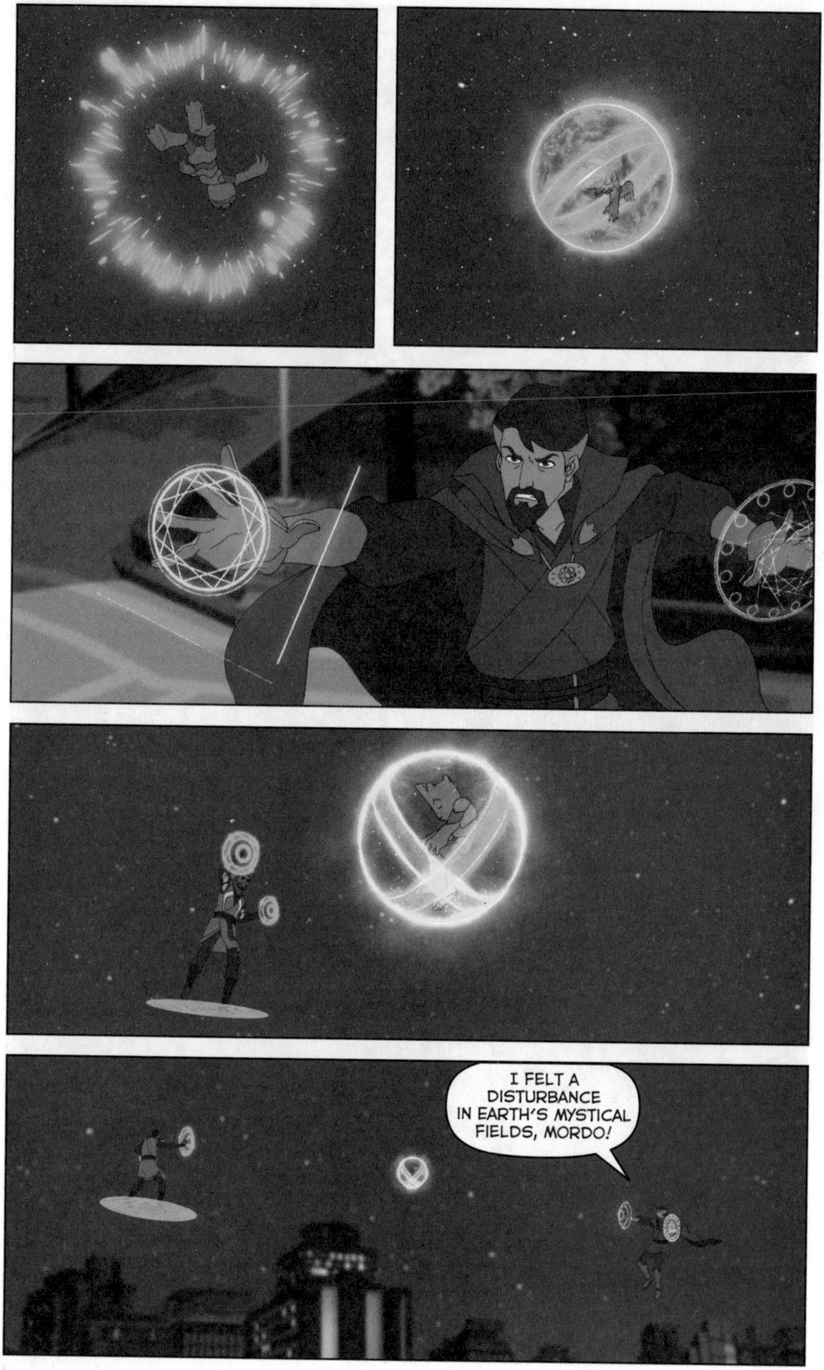
I FELT A DISTURBANCE IN EARTH'S MYSTICAL FIELDS, MORDO!

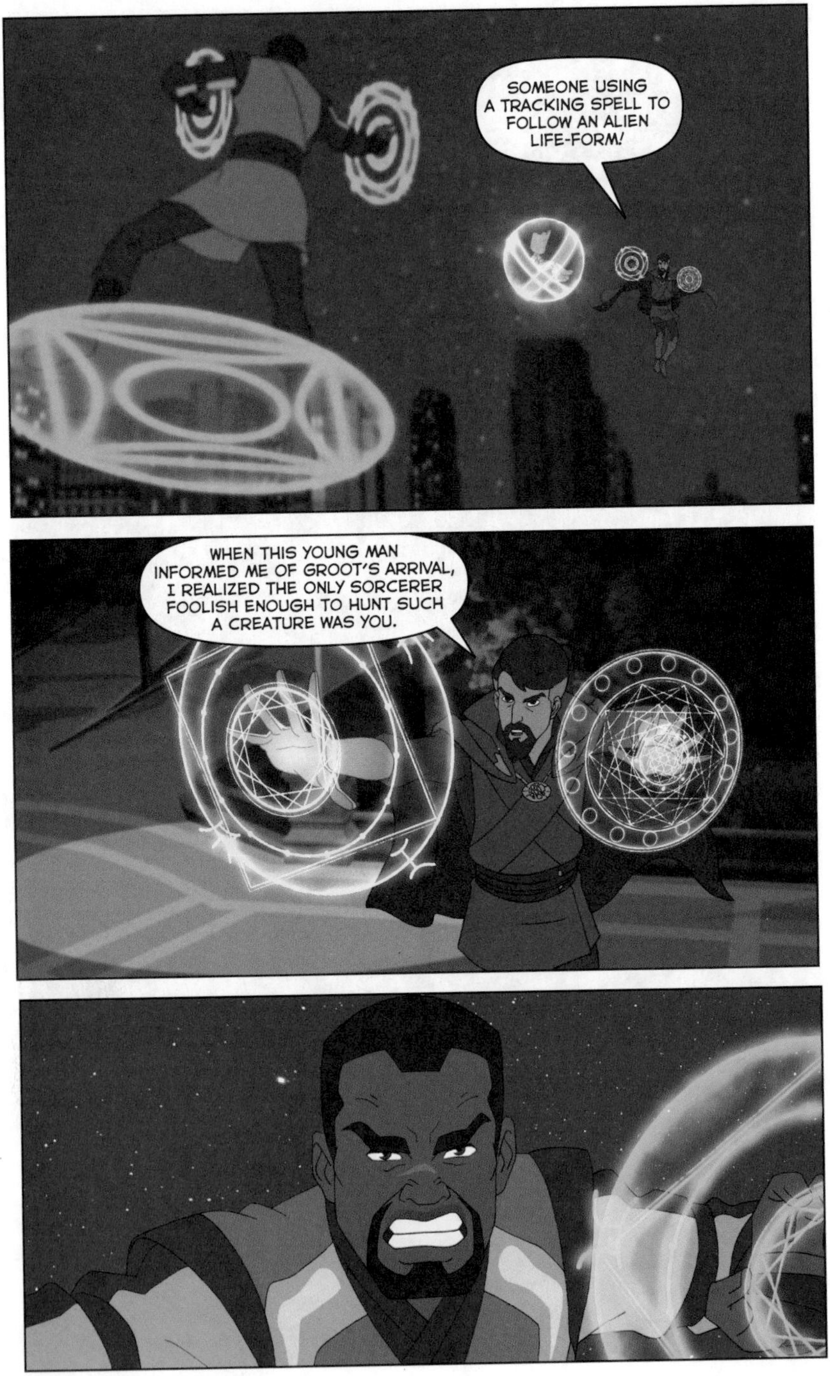
SOMEONE USING A TRACKING SPELL TO FOLLOW AN ALIEN LIFE-FORM!
WHEN THIS YOUNG MAN INFORMED ME OF GROOT'S ARRIVAL, I REALIZED THE ONLY SORCERER FOOLISH ENOUGH TO HUNT SUCH A CREATURE WAS YOU.

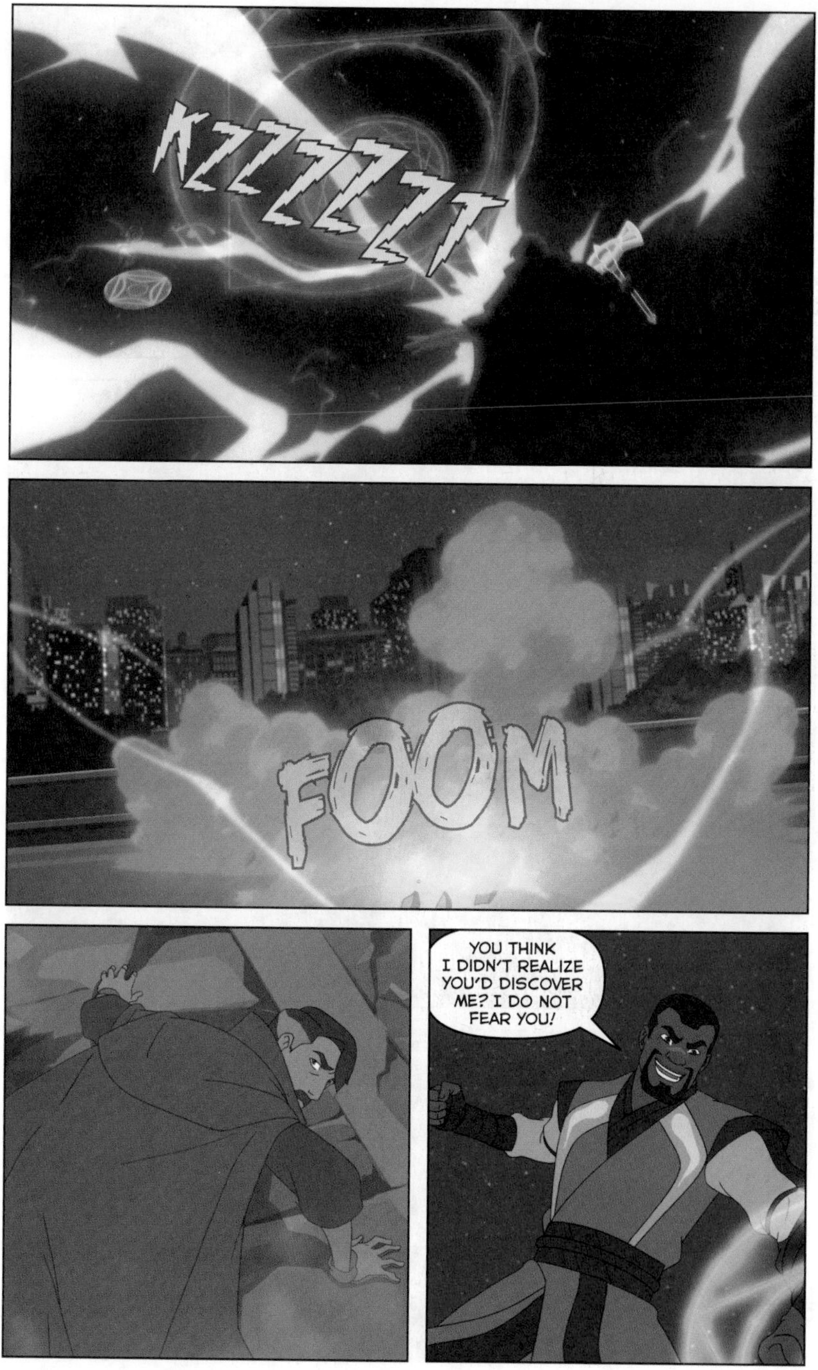
KZZZZZZT
FOOM
YOU THINK I DIDN'T REALIZE YOU'D DISCOVER ME? I DO NOT FEAR YOU!

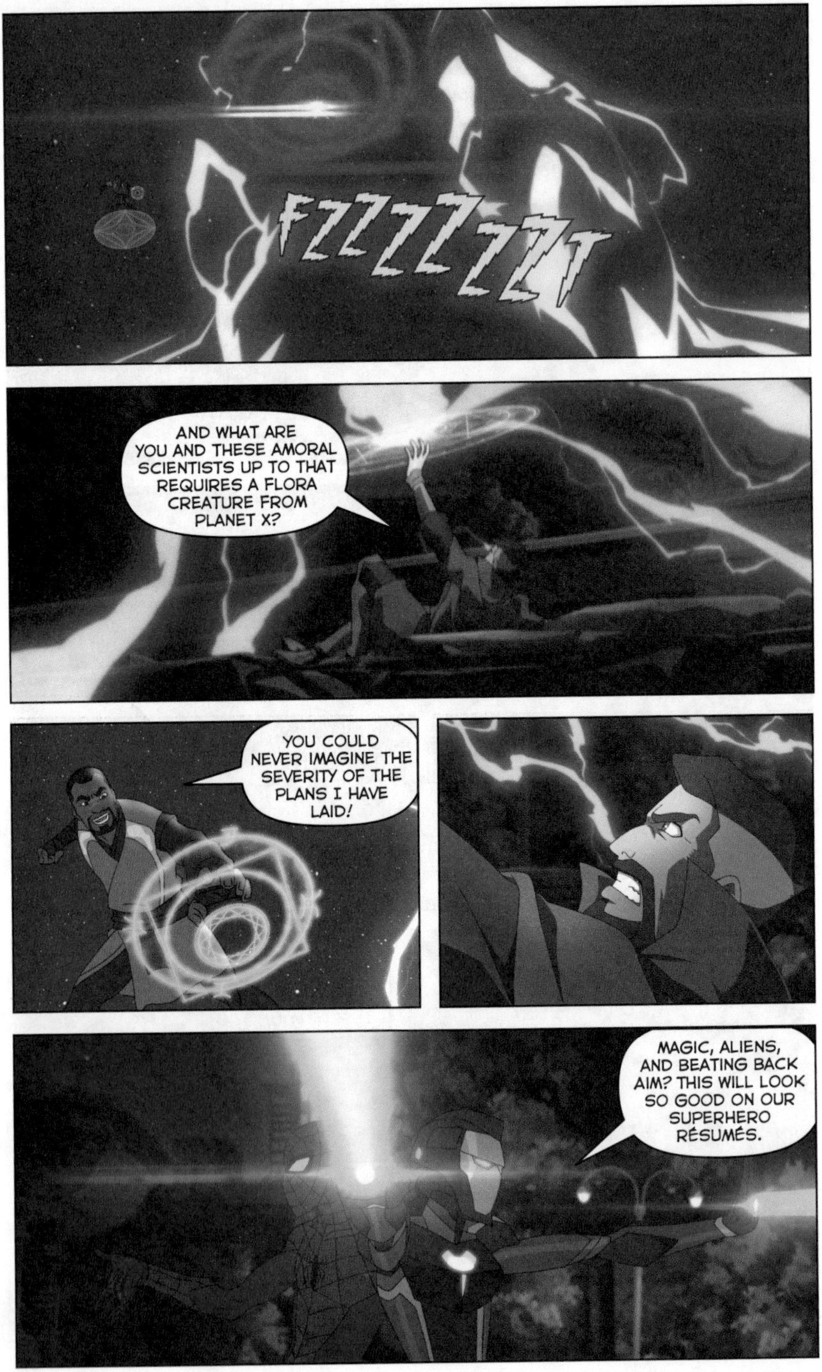
FZZZZZZT
AND WHAT ARE YOU AND THESE AMORAL SCIENTISTS UP TO THAT REQUIRES A FLORA CREATURE FROM PLANET X?
YOU COULD NEVER IMAGINE THE SEVERITY OF THE PLANS I HAVE LAID!
MAGIC, ALIENS, AND BEATING BACK AIM? THIS WILL LOOK SO GOOD ON OUR SUPERHERO RÉSUMÉS.

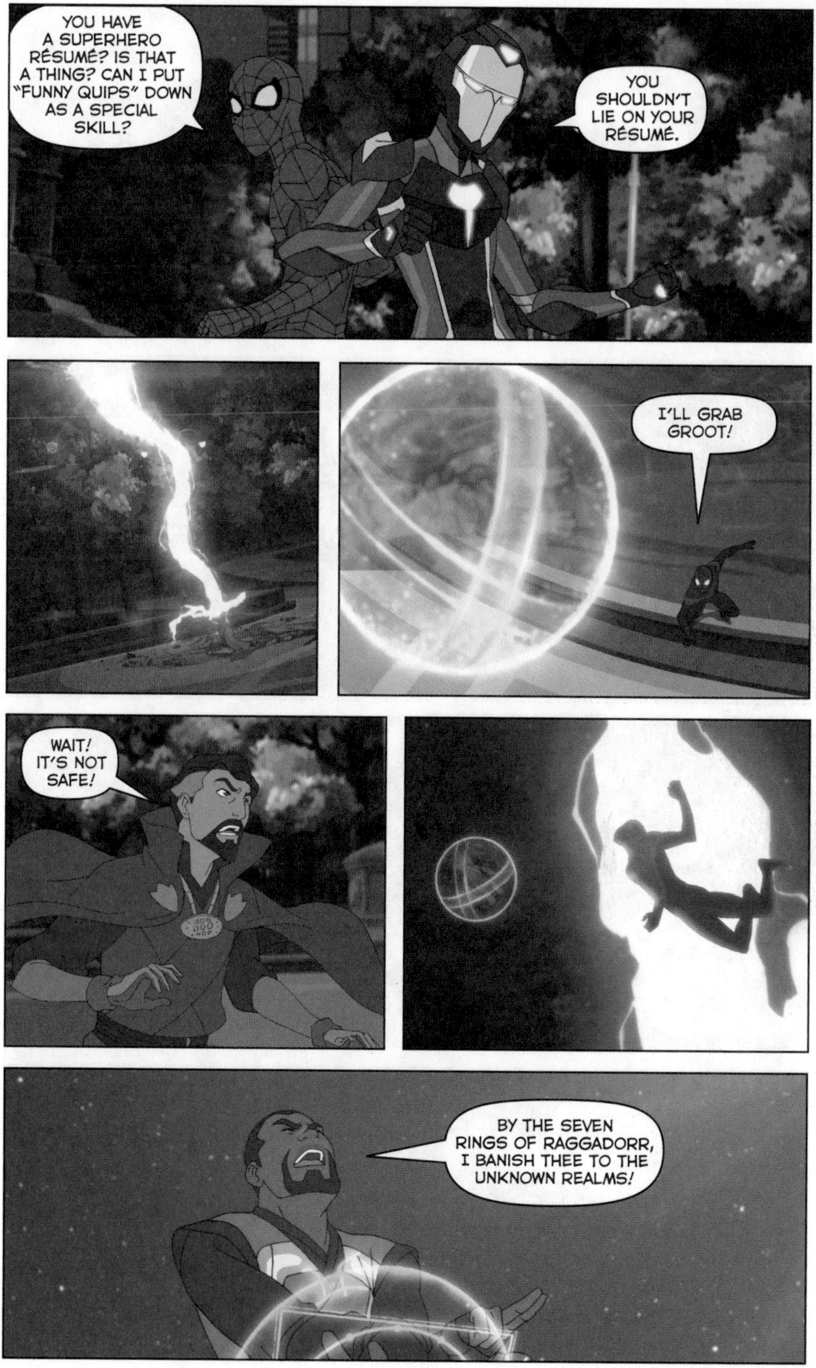
YOU HAVE A SUPERHERO RÉSUMÉ? IS THAT A THING? CAN I PUT "FUNNY QUIPS" DOWN AS A SPECIAL SKILL?
YOU SHOULDN'T LIE ON YOUR RÉSUMÉ.
I'LL GRAB GROOT!
WAIT! IT'S NOT SAFE!
BY THE SEVEN RINGS OF RAGGADORR, I BANISH THEE TO THE UNKNOWN REALMS!

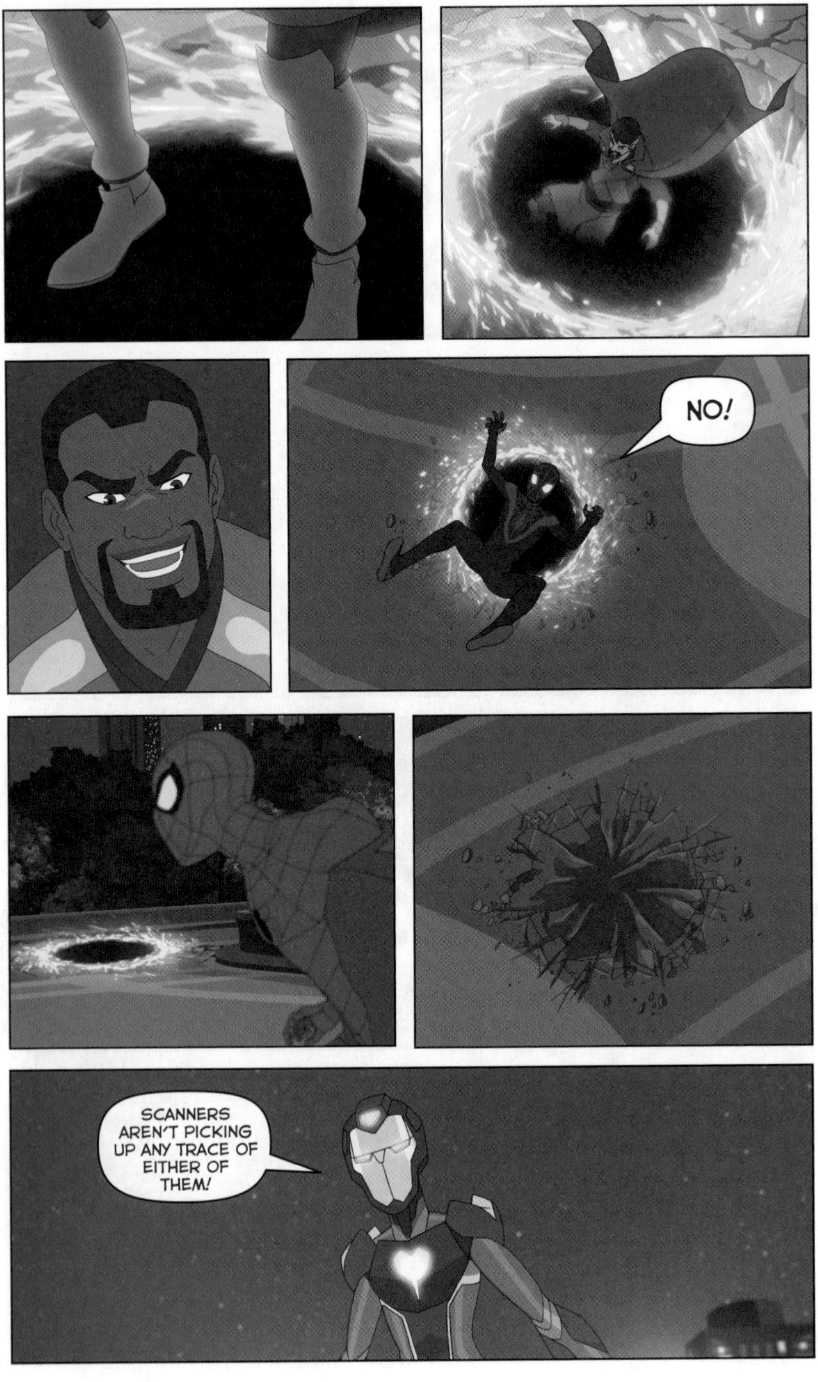
NO!
SCANNERS AREN'T PICKING UP ANY TRACE OF EITHER OF THEM!

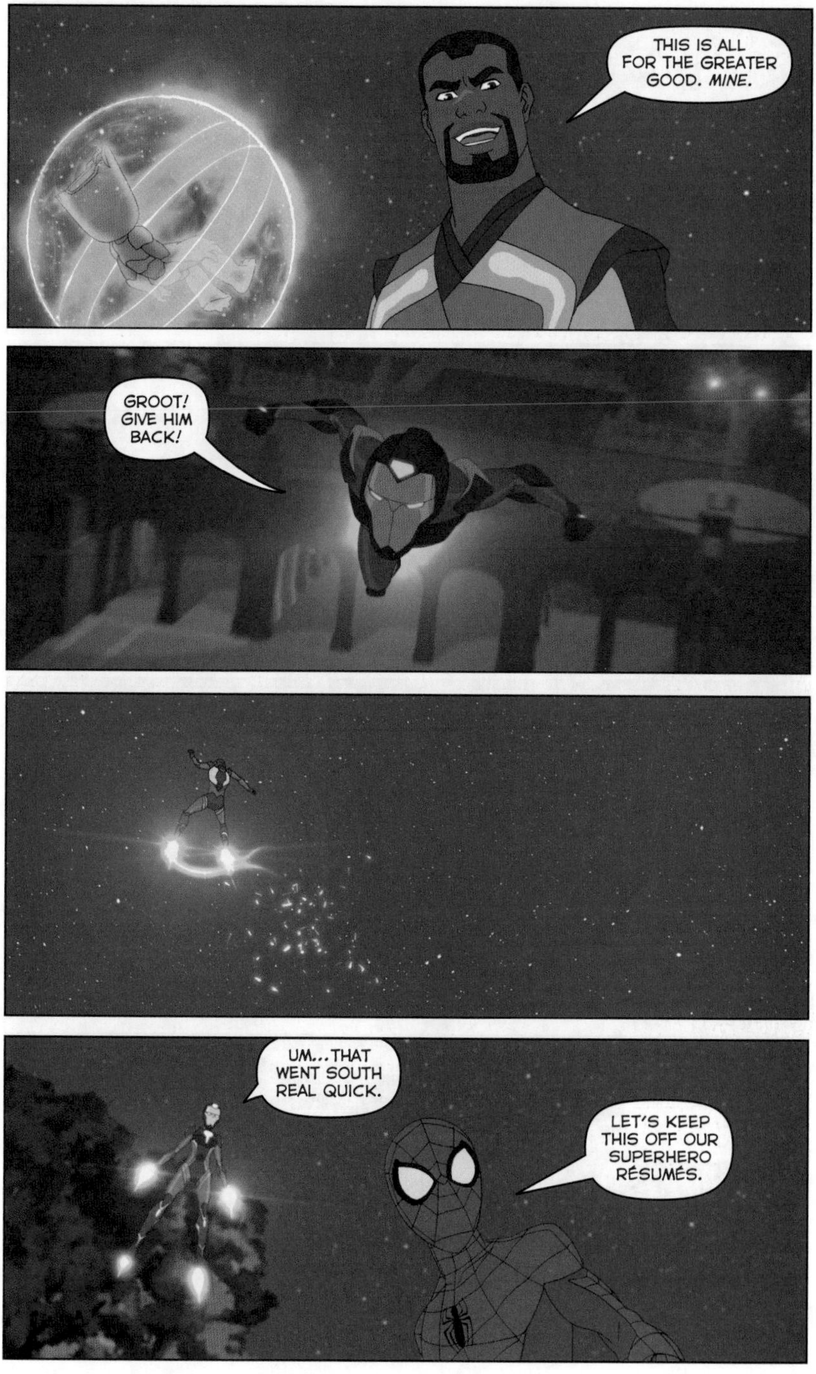
THIS IS ALL FOR THE GREATER GOOD. *MINE*.
GROOT! GIVE HIM BACK!
UM...THAT WENT SOUTH REAL QUICK.
LET'S KEEP THIS OFF OUR SUPERHERO RÉSUMÉS.

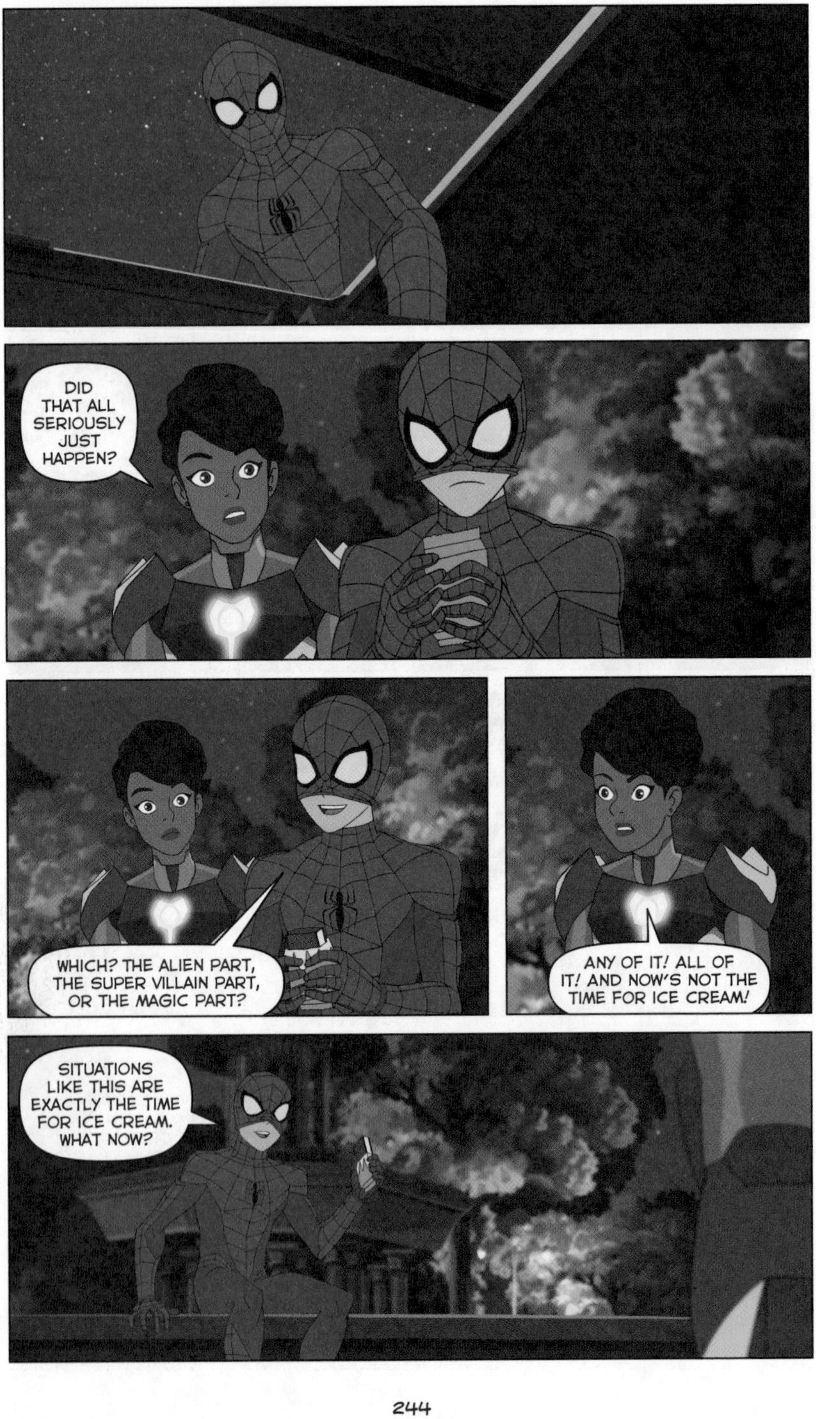
DID THAT ALL SERIOUSLY JUST HAPPEN?
WHICH? THE ALIEN PART, THE SUPER VILLAIN PART, OR THE MAGIC PART?
ANY OF IT! ALL OF IT! AND NOW'S NOT THE TIME FOR ICE CREAM!
SITUATIONS LIKE THIS ARE EXACTLY THE TIME FOR ICE CREAM. WHAT NOW?

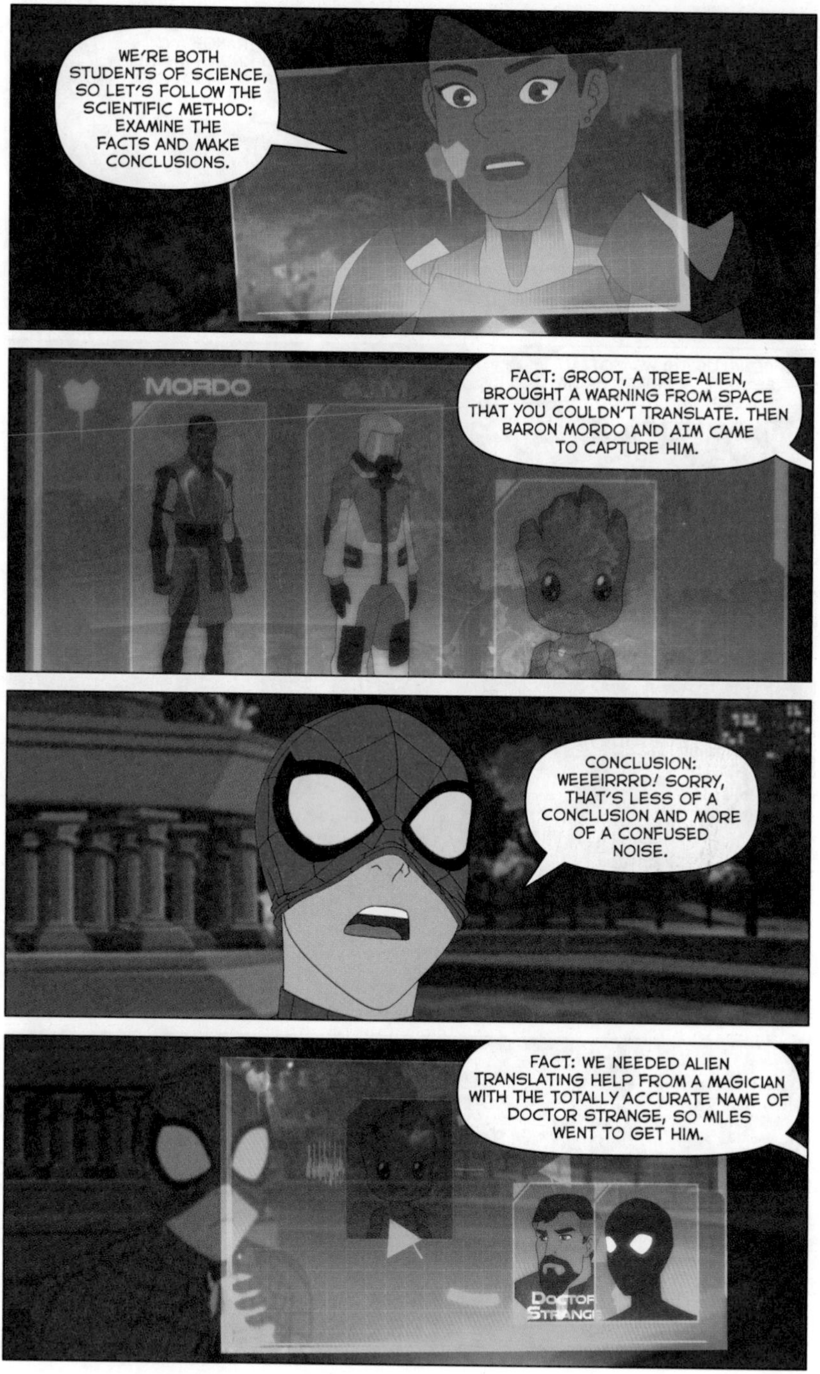
WE'RE BOTH STUDENTS OF SCIENCE, SO LET'S FOLLOW THE SCIENTIFIC METHOD: EXAMINE THE FACTS AND MAKE CONCLUSIONS.
MORDO
FACT: GROOT, A TREE-ALIEN, BROUGHT A WARNING FROM SPACE THAT YOU COULDN'T TRANSLATE. THEN BARON MORDO AND AIM CAME TO CAPTURE HIM.
CONCLUSION: WEEEIRRRD! SORRY, THAT'S LESS OF A CONCLUSION AND MORE OF A CONFUSED NOISE.
FACT: WE NEEDED ALIEN TRANSLATING HELP FROM A MAGICIAN WITH THE TOTALLY ACCURATE NAME OF DOCTOR STRANGE, SO MILES WENT TO GET HIM.

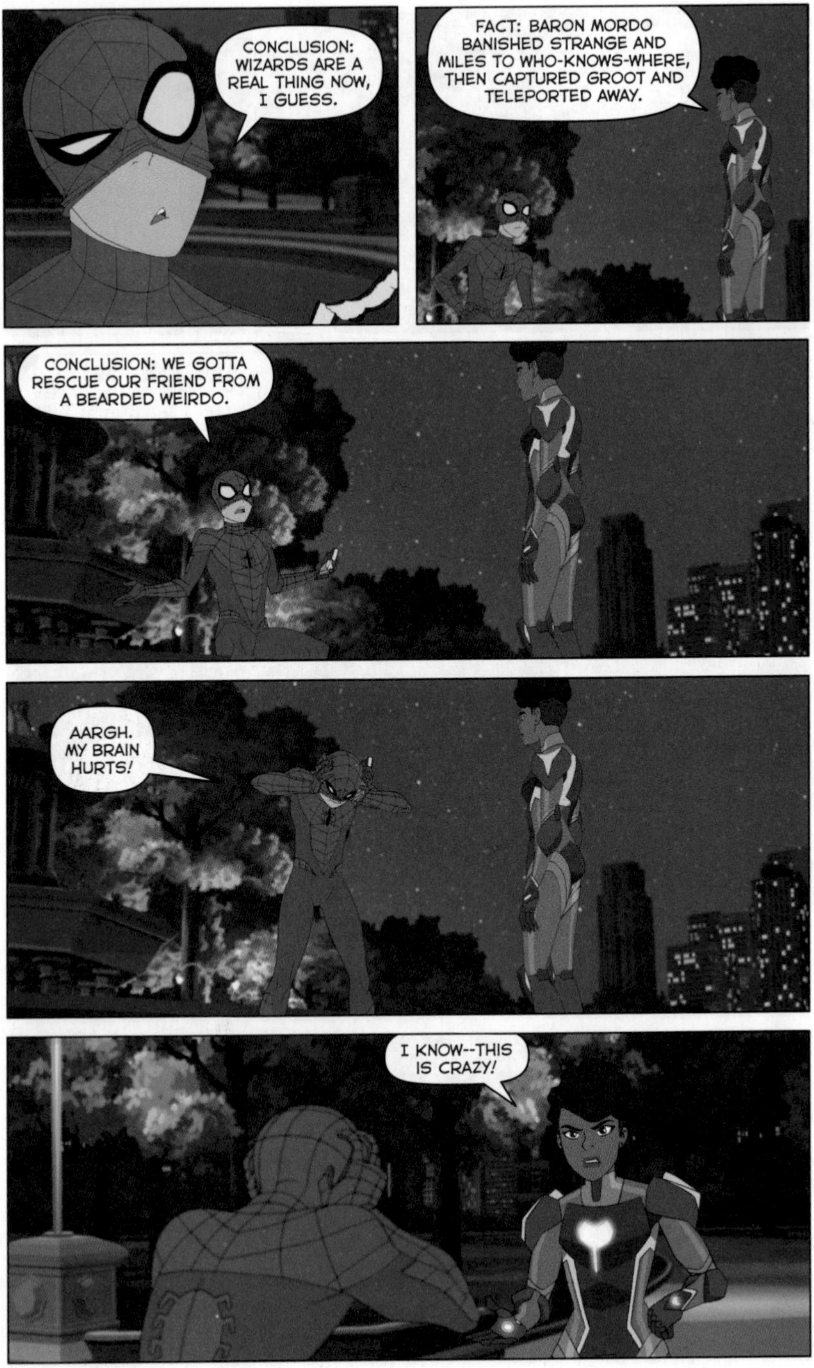
CONCLUSION: WIZARDS ARE A REAL THING NOW, I GUESS.
FACT: BARON MORDO BANISHED STRANGE AND MILES TO WHO-KNOWS-WHERE, THEN CAPTURED GROOT AND TELEPORTED AWAY.
CONCLUSION: WE GOTTA RESCUE OUR FRIEND FROM A BEARDED WEIRDO.
AARGH. MY BRAIN HURTS!
I KNOW--THIS IS CRAZY!

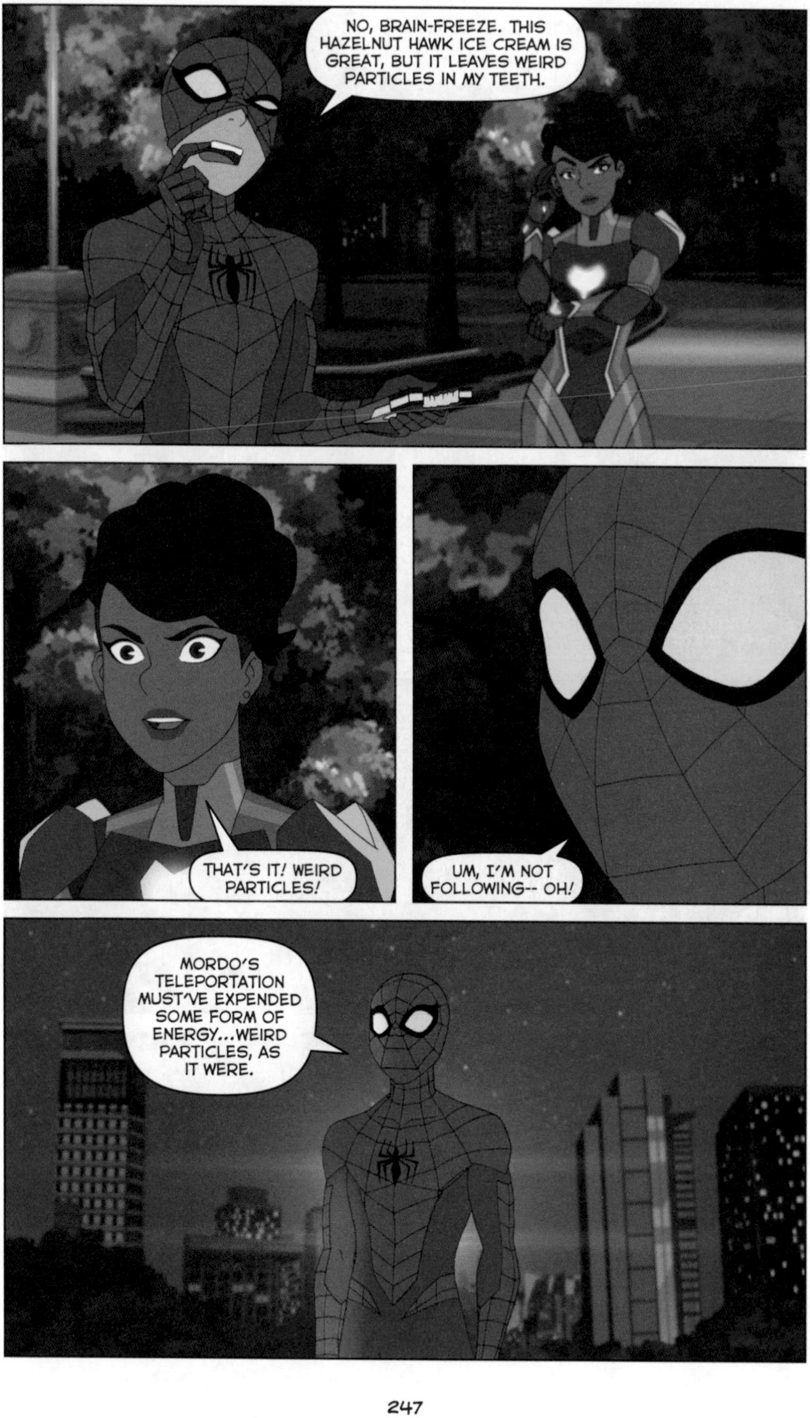
NO, BRAIN-FREEZE. THIS HAZELNUT HAWK ICE CREAM IS GREAT, BUT IT LEAVES WEIRD PARTICLES IN MY TEETH.
THAT'S IT! WEIRD PARTICLES!
UM, I'M NOT FOLLOWING-- OH!
MORDO'S TELEPORTATION MUST'VE EXPENDED SOME FORM OF ENERGY...WEIRD PARTICLES, AS IT WERE.

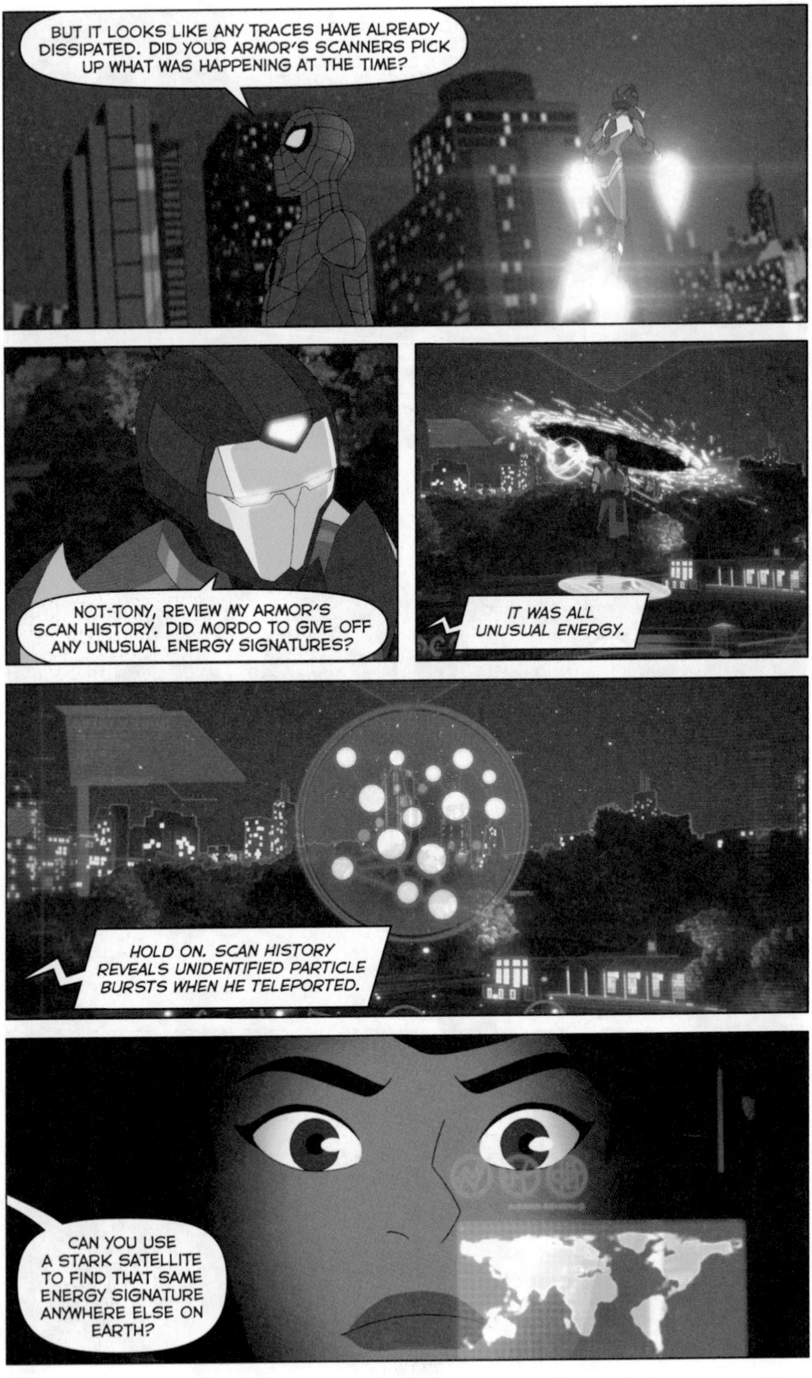
BUT IT LOOKS LIKE ANY TRACES HAVE ALREADY DISSIPATED. DID YOUR ARMOR'S SCANNERS PICK UP WHAT WAS HAPPENING AT THE TIME?
NOT-TONY, REVIEW MY ARMOR'S SCAN HISTORY. DID MORDO TO GIVE OFF ANY UNUSUAL ENERGY SIGNATURES?
IT WAS ALL UNUSUAL ENERGY.
HOLD ON. SCAN HISTORY REVEALS UNIDENTIFIED PARTICLE BURSTS WHEN HE TELEPORTED.
CAN YOU USE A STARK SATELLITE TO FIND THAT SAME ENERGY SIGNATURE ANYWHERE ELSE ON EARTH?

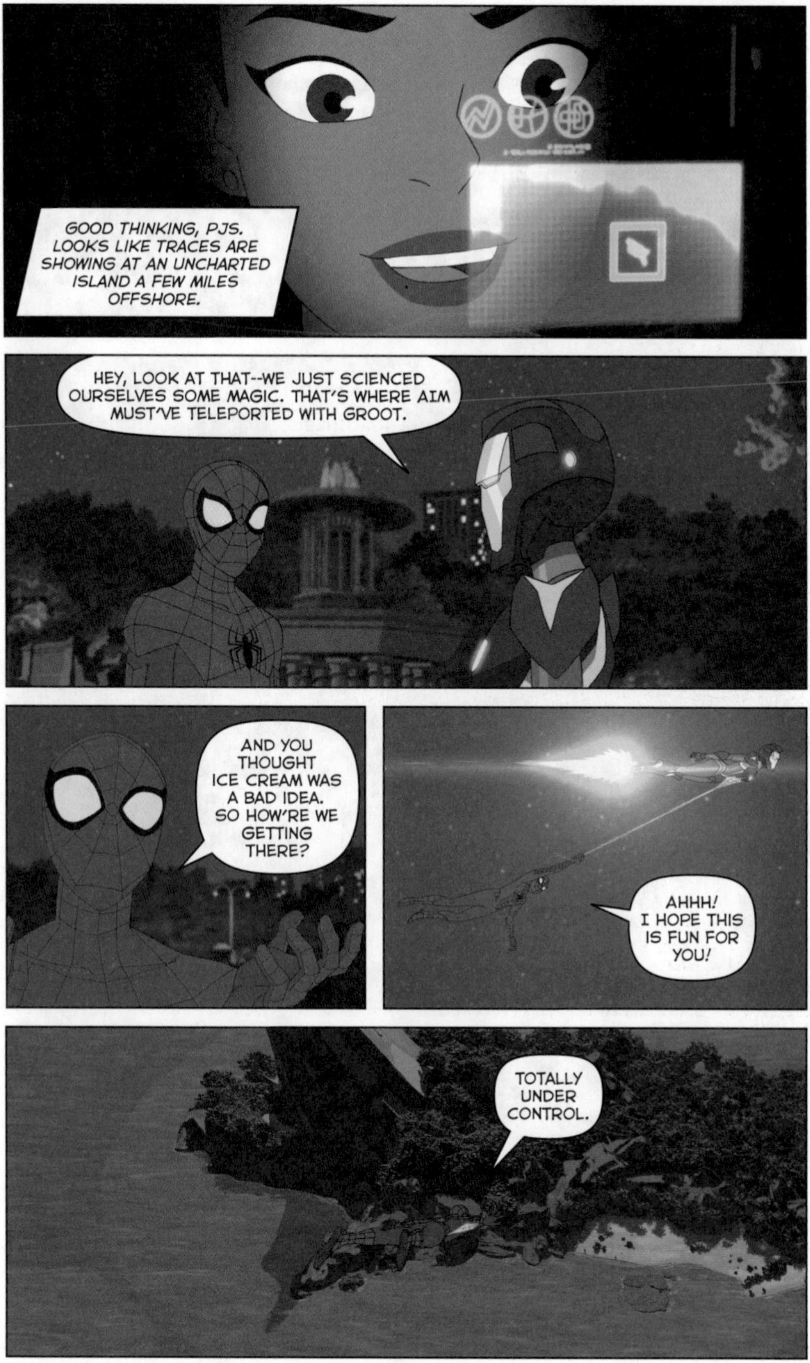
GOOD THINKING, PJS. LOOKS LIKE TRACES ARE SHOWING AT AN UNCHARTED ISLAND A FEW MILES OFFSHORE.
HEY, LOOK AT THAT--WE JUST SCIENCED OURSELVES SOME MAGIC. THAT'S WHERE AIM MUST'VE TELEPORTED WITH GROOT.
AND YOU THOUGHT ICE CREAM WAS A BAD IDEA. SO HOW'RE WE GETTING THERE?
AHHH! I HOPE THIS IS FUN FOR YOU!
TOTALLY UNDER CONTROL.

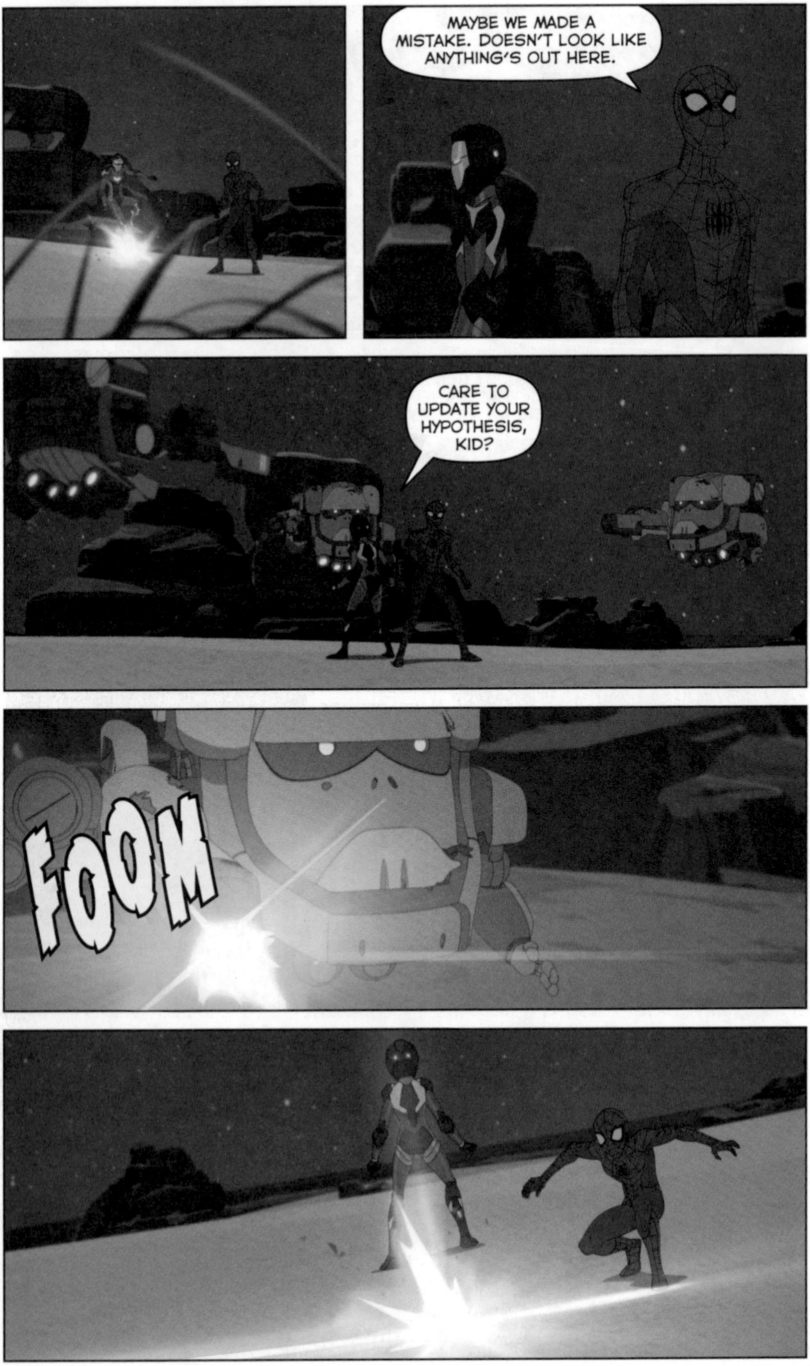
MAYBE WE MADE A MISTAKE. DOESN'T LOOK LIKE ANYTHING'S OUT HERE.
CARE TO UPDATE YOUR HYPOTHESIS, KID?
FOOM

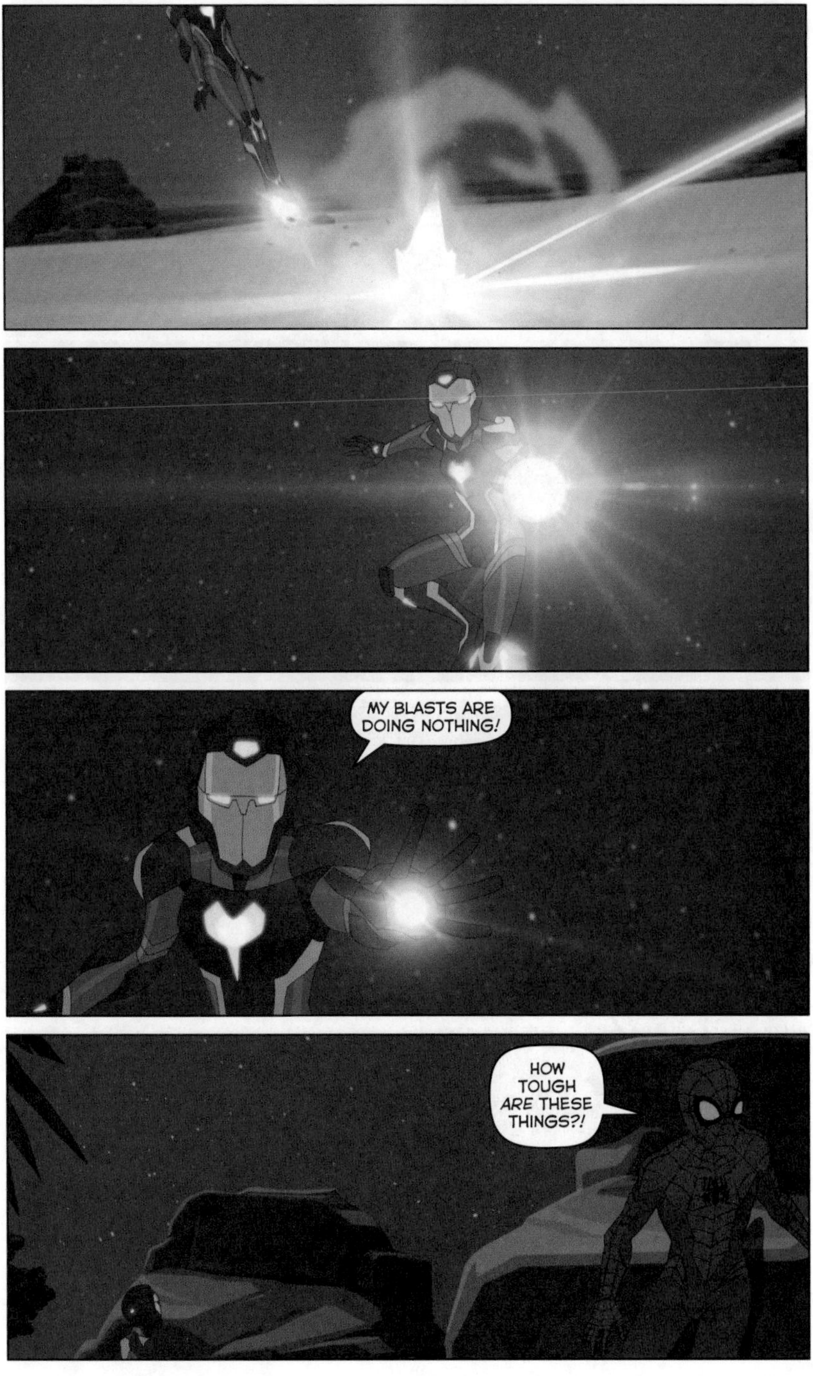
MY BLASTS ARE DOING NOTHING!
HOW TOUGH *ARE* THESE THINGS?!

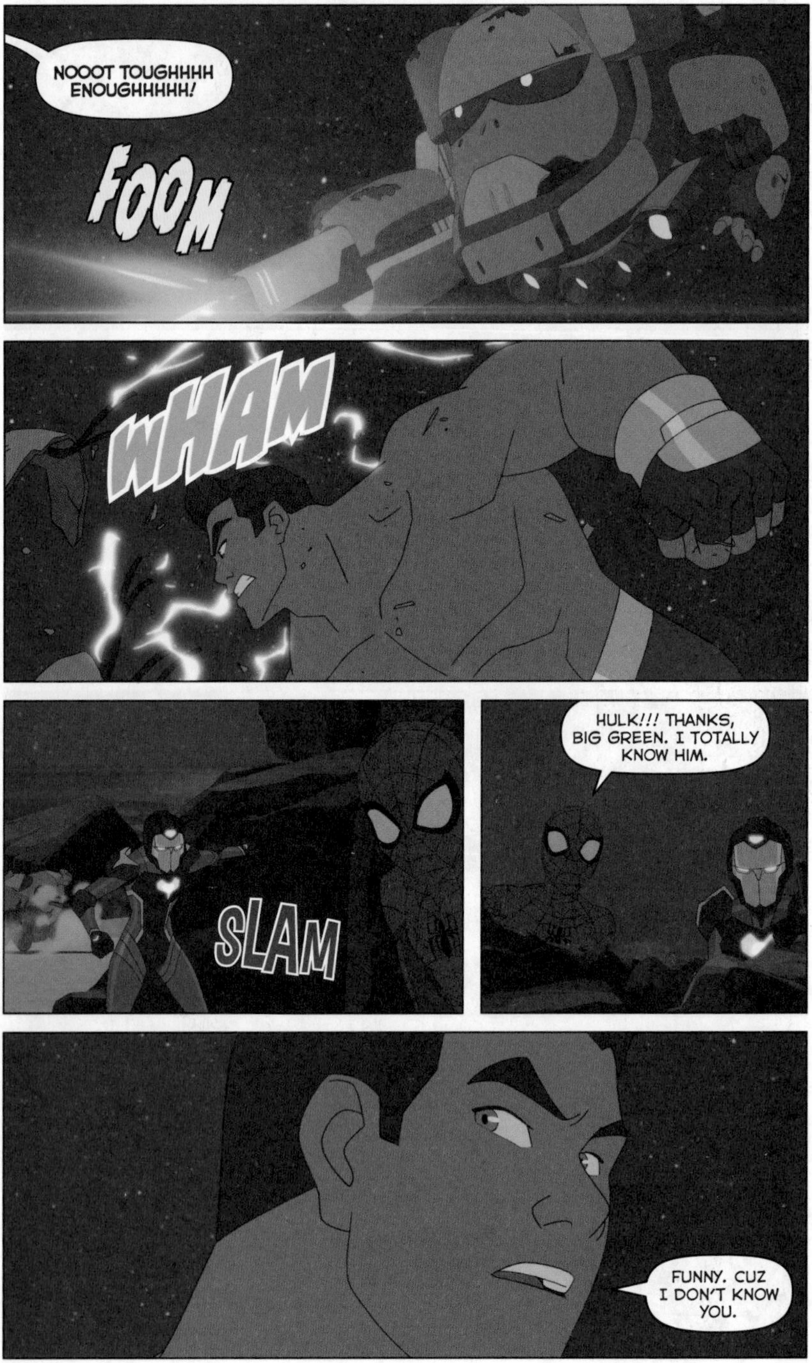
NOOOT TOUGHHHH ENOUGHHHHH!
FOOM
WHAM
SLAM
HULK!!! THANKS, BIG GREEN. I TOTALLY KNOW HIM.
FUNNY. CUZ I DON'T KNOW YOU.

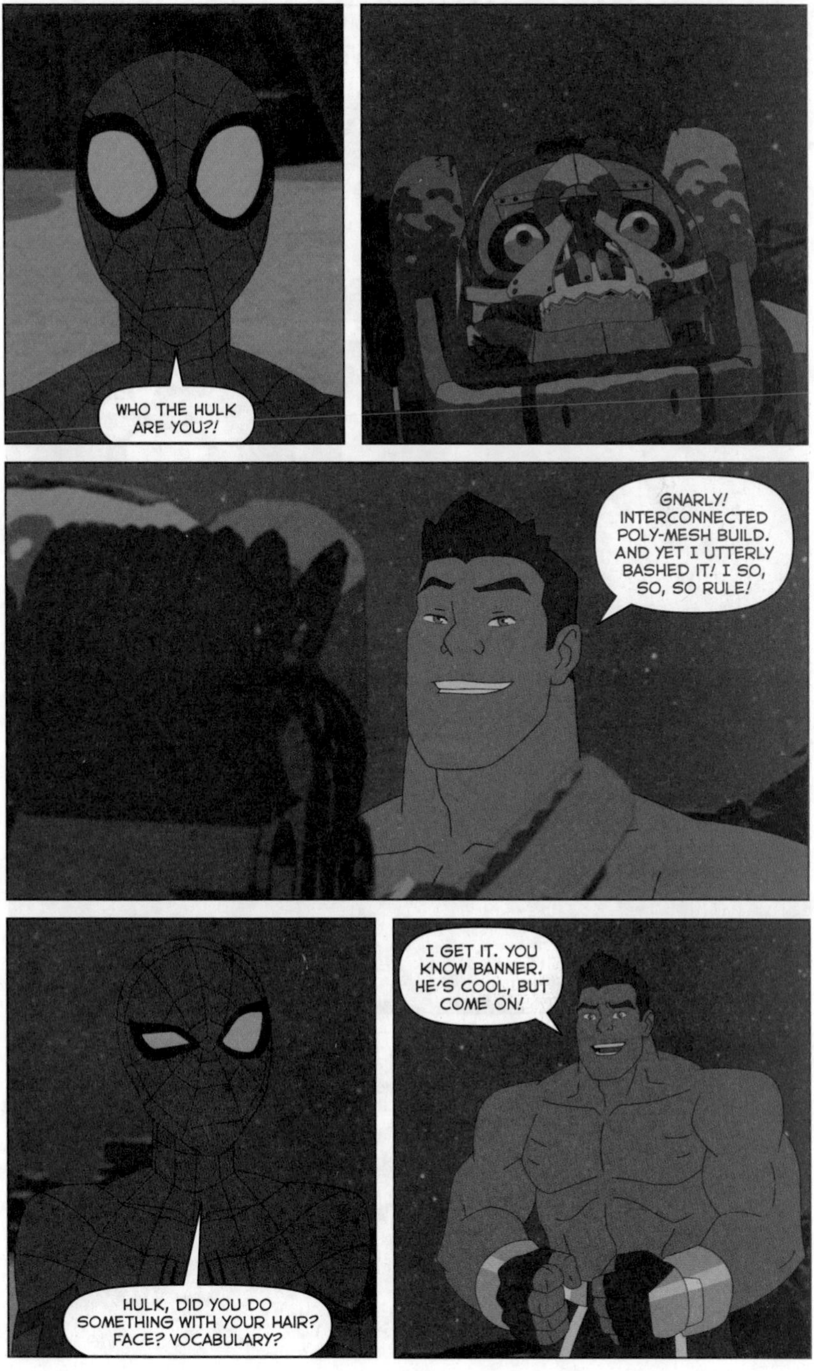
WHO THE HULK ARE YOU?!
GNARLY! INTERCONNECTED POLY-MESH BUILD. AND YET I UTTERLY BASHED IT! I SO, SO, SO RULE!
HULK, DID YOU DO SOMETHING WITH YOUR HAIR? FACE? VOCABULARY?
I GET IT. YOU KNOW BANNER. HE'S COOL, BUT COME ON!

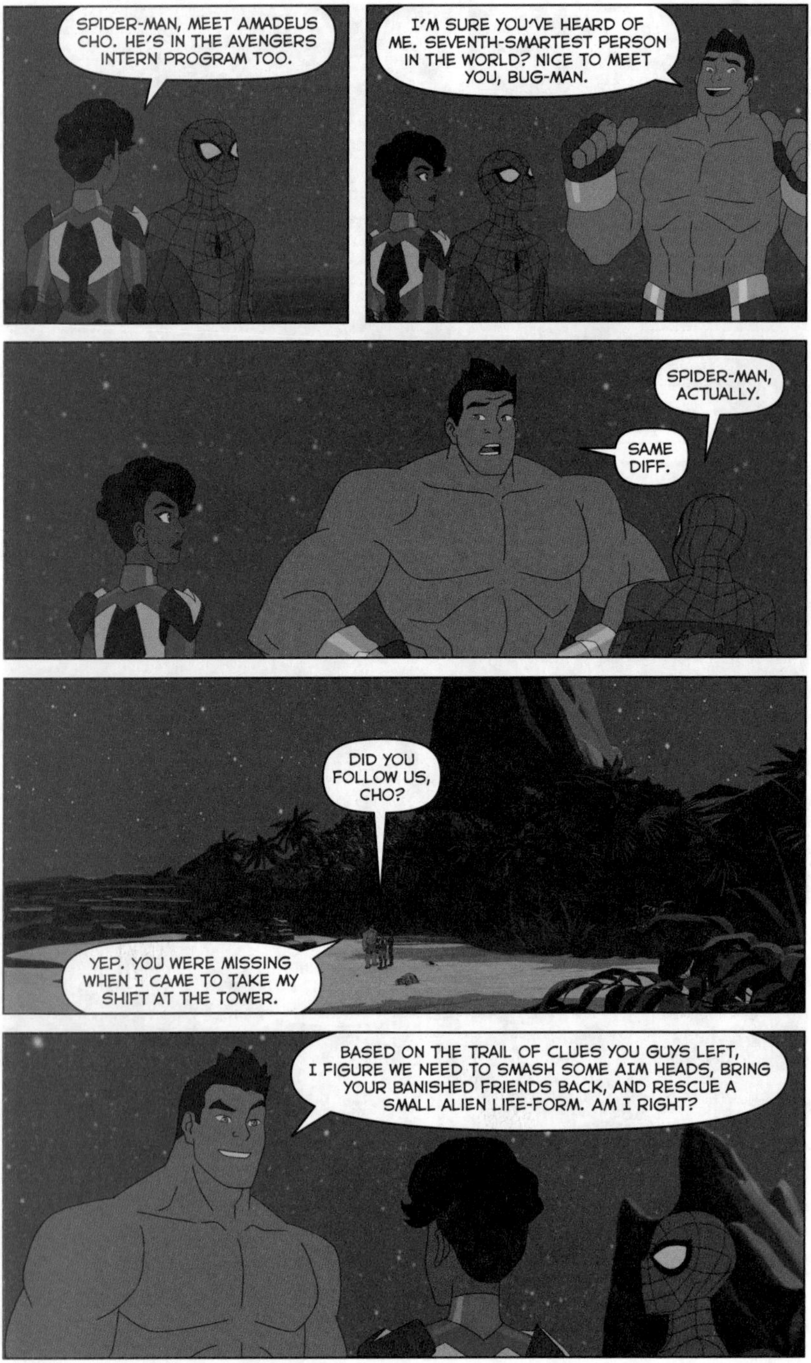
SPIDER-MAN, MEET AMADEUS CHO. HE'S IN THE AVENGERS INTERN PROGRAM TOO.
I'M SURE YOU'VE HEARD OF ME. SEVENTH-SMARTEST PERSON IN THE WORLD? NICE TO MEET YOU, BUG-MAN.
SPIDER-MAN, ACTUALLY.
SAME DIFF.
DID YOU FOLLOW US, CHO?
YEP. YOU WERE MISSING WHEN I CAME TO TAKE MY SHIFT AT THE TOWER.
BASED ON THE TRAIL OF CLUES YOU GUYS LEFT, I FIGURE WE NEED TO SMASH SOME AIM HEADS, BRING YOUR BANISHED FRIENDS BACK, AND RESCUE A SMALL ALIEN LIFE-FORM. AM I RIGHT?

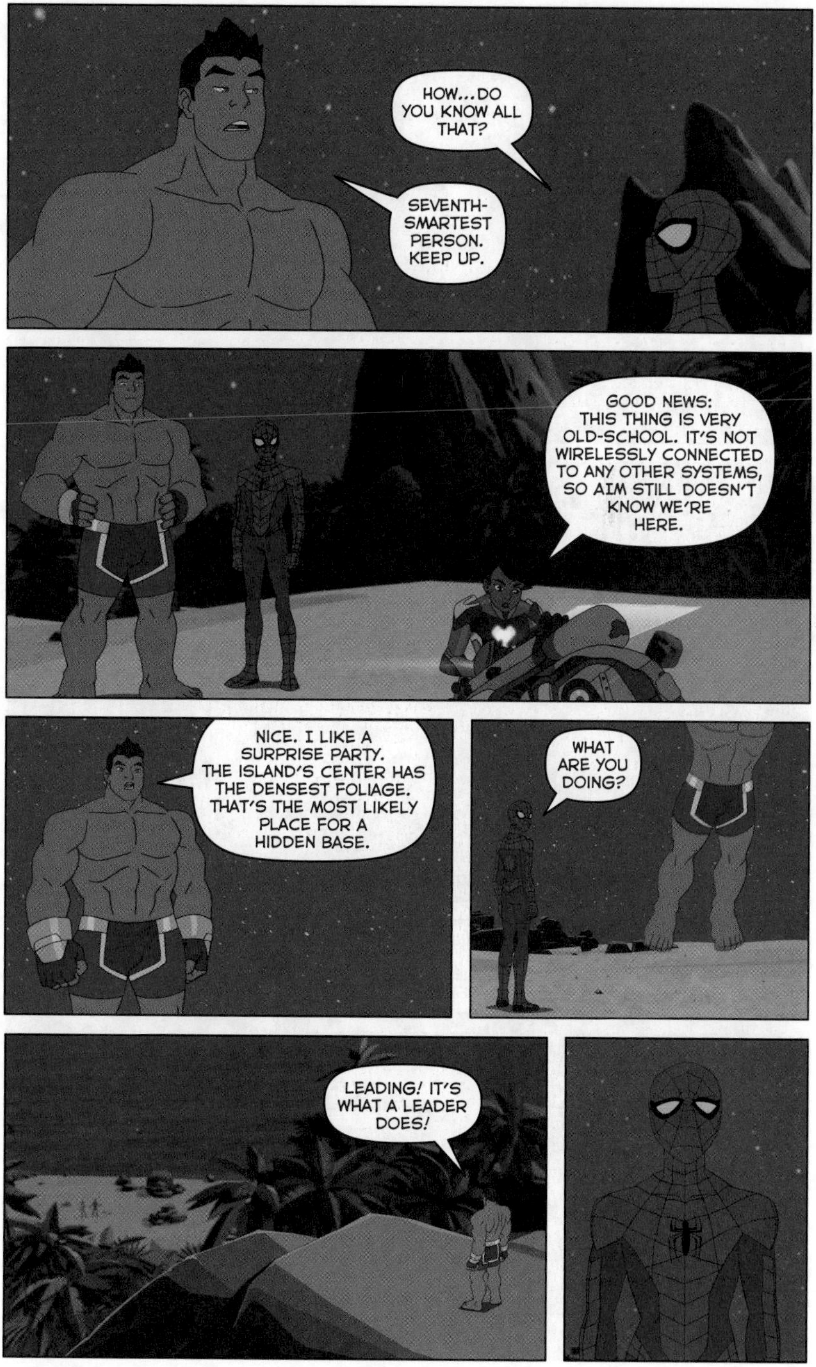
HOW...DO YOU KNOW ALL THAT?
SEVENTH-SMARTEST PERSON. KEEP UP.
GOOD NEWS: THIS THING IS VERY OLD-SCHOOL. IT'S NOT WIRELESSLY CONNECTED TO ANY OTHER SYSTEMS, SO AIM STILL DOESN'T KNOW WE'RE HERE.
NICE. I LIKE A SURPRISE PARTY. THE ISLAND'S CENTER HAS THE DENSEST FOLIAGE. THAT'S THE MOST LIKELY PLACE FOR A HIDDEN BASE.
WHAT ARE YOU DOING?
LEADING! IT'S WHAT A LEADER DOES!

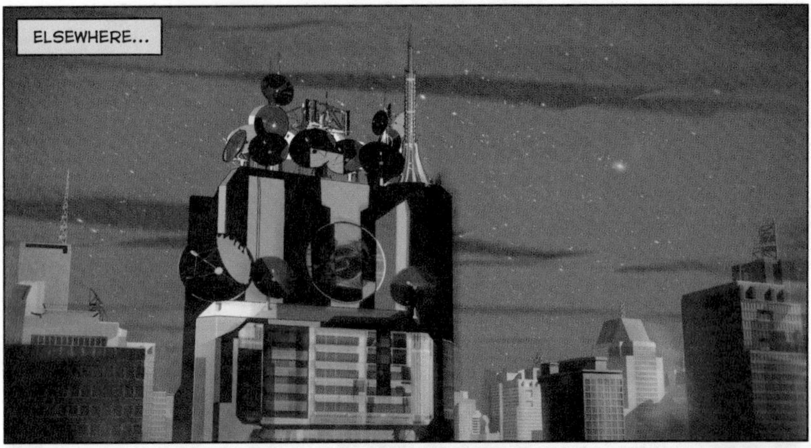
ELSEWHERE...

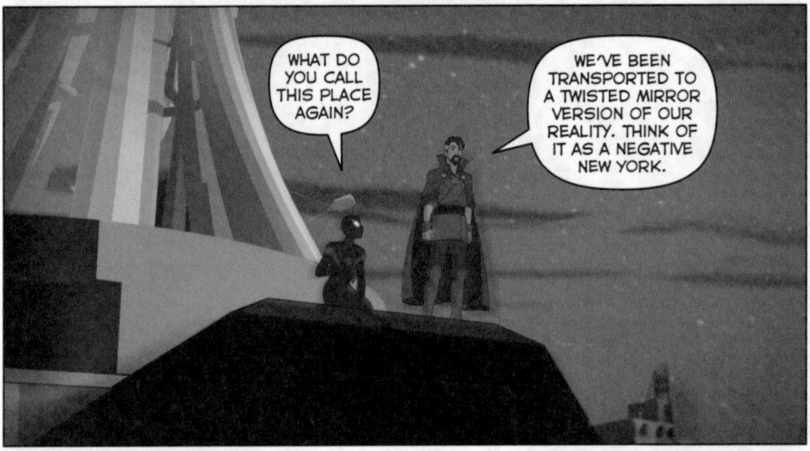
WHAT DO YOU CALL THIS PLACE AGAIN?
WE'VE BEEN TRANSPORTED TO A TWISTED MIRROR VERSION OF OUR REALITY. THINK OF IT AS A NEGATIVE NEW YORK.

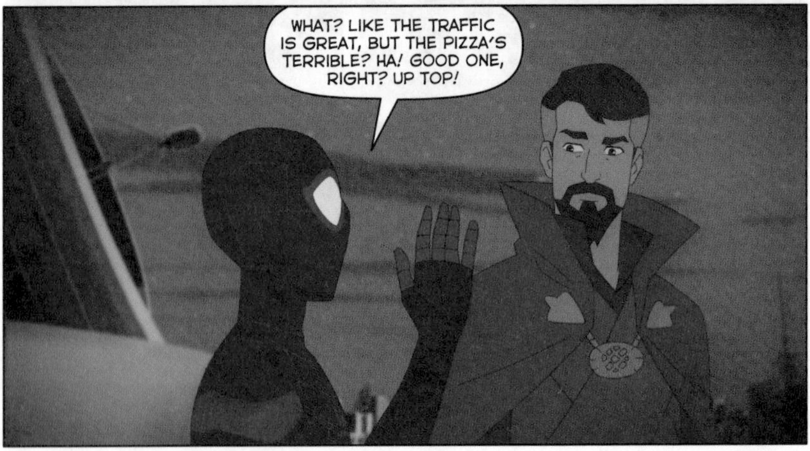
WHAT? LIKE THE TRAFFIC IS GREAT, BUT THE PIZZA'S TERRIBLE? HA! GOOD ONE, RIGHT? UP TOP!

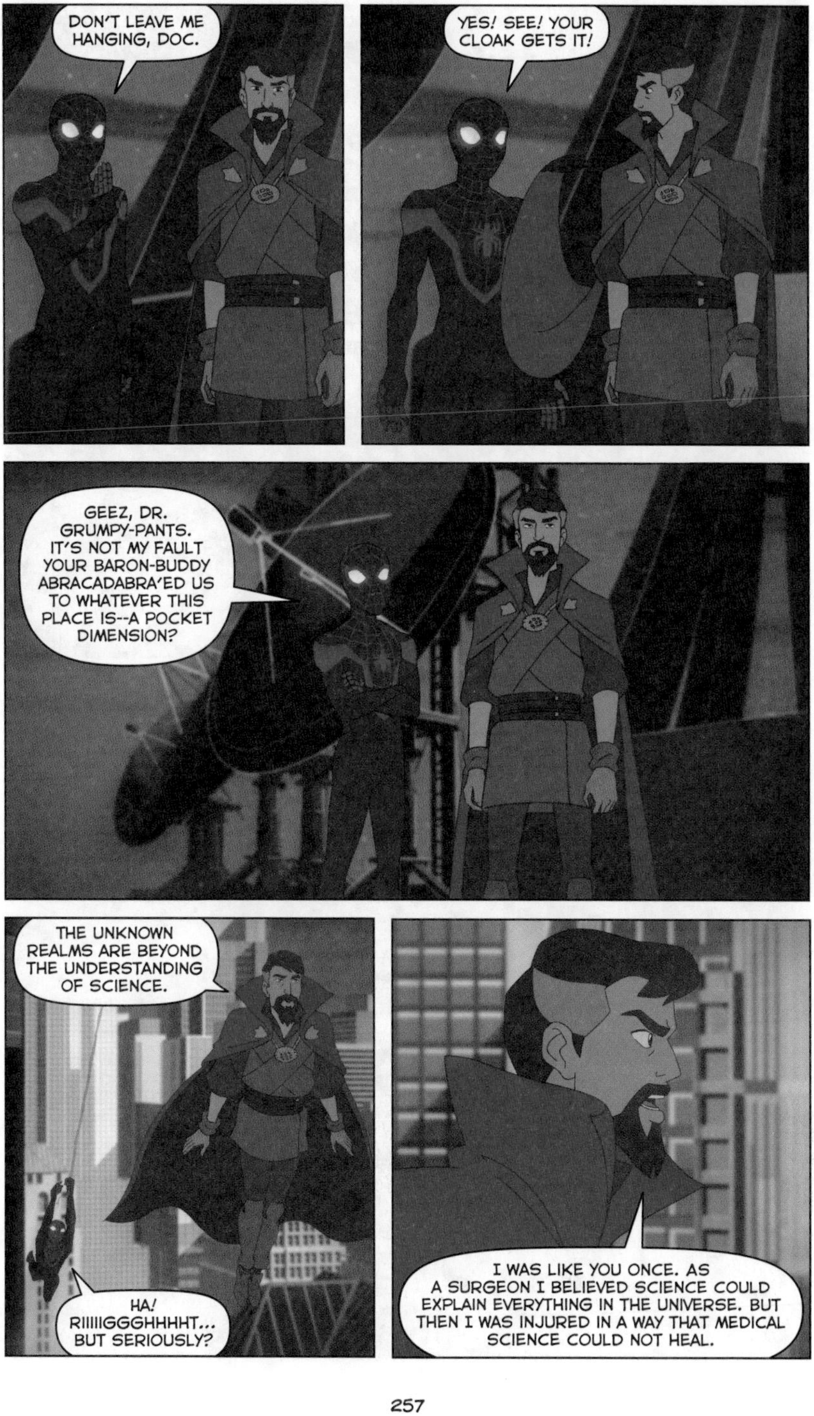
DON'T LEAVE ME HANGING, DOC.
YES! SEE! YOUR CLOAK GETS IT!
GEEZ, DR. GRUMPY-PANTS. IT'S NOT MY FAULT YOUR BARON-BUDDY ABRACADABRA'ED US TO WHATEVER THIS PLACE IS--A POCKET DIMENSION?
THE UNKNOWN REALMS ARE BEYOND THE UNDERSTANDING OF SCIENCE.
HA! RIIIIGGGHHHHT... BUT SERIOUSLY?
I WAS LIKE YOU ONCE. AS A SURGEON I BELIEVED SCIENCE COULD EXPLAIN EVERYTHING IN THE UNIVERSE. BUT THEN I WAS INJURED IN A WAY THAT MEDICAL SCIENCE COULD NOT HEAL.

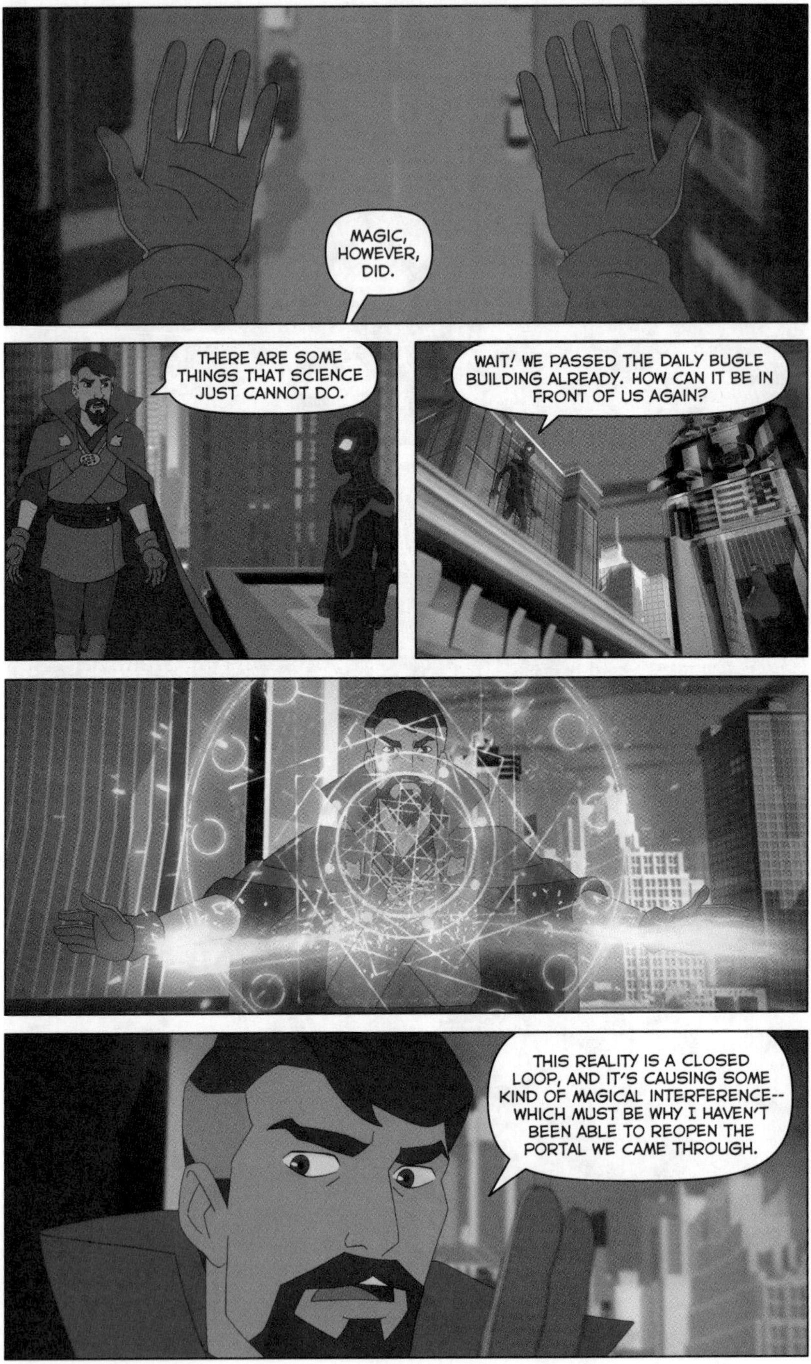
MAGIC, HOWEVER, DID.
THERE ARE SOME THINGS THAT SCIENCE JUST CANNOT DO.
WAIT! WE PASSED THE DAILY BUGLE BUILDING ALREADY. HOW CAN IT BE IN FRONT OF US AGAIN?
THIS REALITY IS A CLOSED LOOP, AND IT'S CAUSING SOME KIND OF MAGICAL INTERFERENCE-- WHICH MUST BE WHY I HAVEN'T BEEN ABLE TO REOPEN THE PORTAL WE CAME THROUGH.

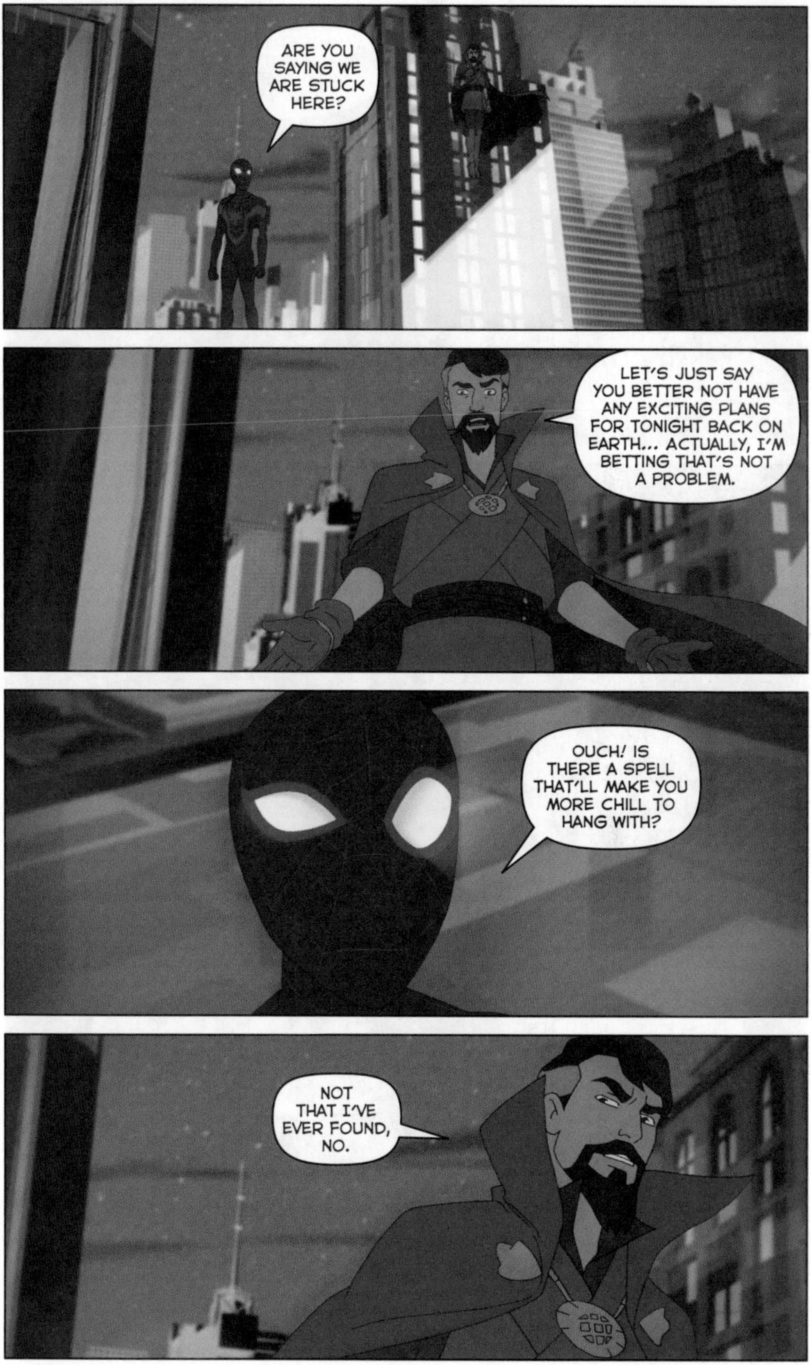
ARE YOU SAYING WE ARE STUCK HERE?
LET'S JUST SAY YOU BETTER NOT HAVE ANY EXCITING PLANS FOR TONIGHT BACK ON EARTH... ACTUALLY, I'M BETTING THAT'S NOT A PROBLEM.
OUCH! IS THERE A SPELL THAT'LL MAKE YOU MORE CHILL TO HANG WITH?
NOT THAT I'VE EVER FOUND, NO.

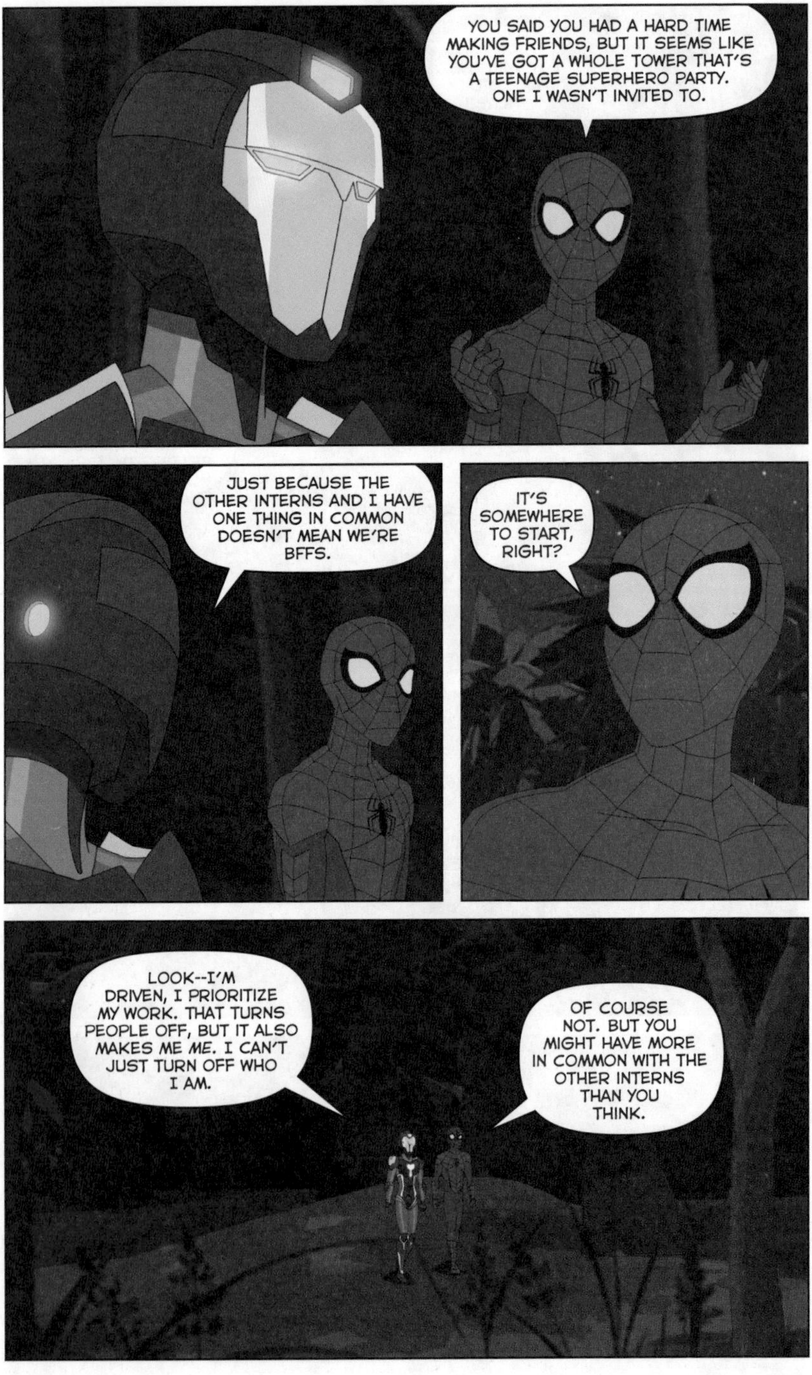
YOU SAID YOU HAD A HARD TIME MAKING FRIENDS, BUT IT SEEMS LIKE YOU'VE GOT A WHOLE TOWER THAT'S A TEENAGE SUPERHERO PARTY. ONE I WASN'T INVITED TO.
JUST BECAUSE THE OTHER INTERNS AND I HAVE ONE THING IN COMMON DOESN'T MEAN WE'RE BFFS.
IT'S SOMEWHERE TO START, RIGHT?
LOOK--I'M DRIVEN, I PRIORITIZE MY WORK. THAT TURNS PEOPLE OFF, BUT IT ALSO MAKES ME *ME*. I CAN'T JUST TURN OFF WHO I AM.
OF COURSE NOT. BUT YOU MIGHT HAVE MORE IN COMMON WITH THE OTHER INTERNS THAN YOU THINK.

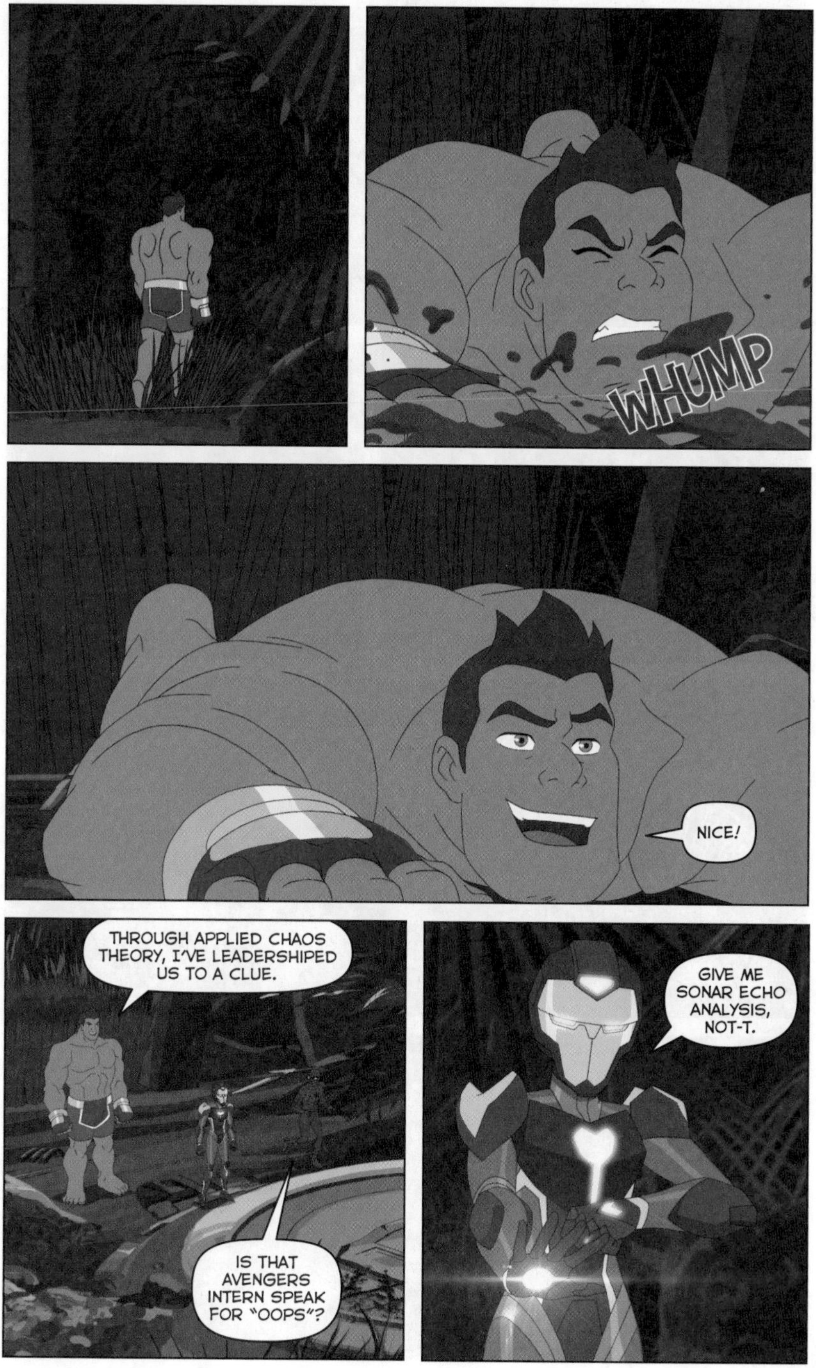
WHUMP
NICE!
THROUGH APPLIED CHAOS THEORY, I'VE LEADERSHIPED US TO A CLUE.
IS THAT AVENGERS INTERN SPEAK FOR "OOPS"?
GIVE ME SONAR ECHO ANALYSIS, NOT-T.

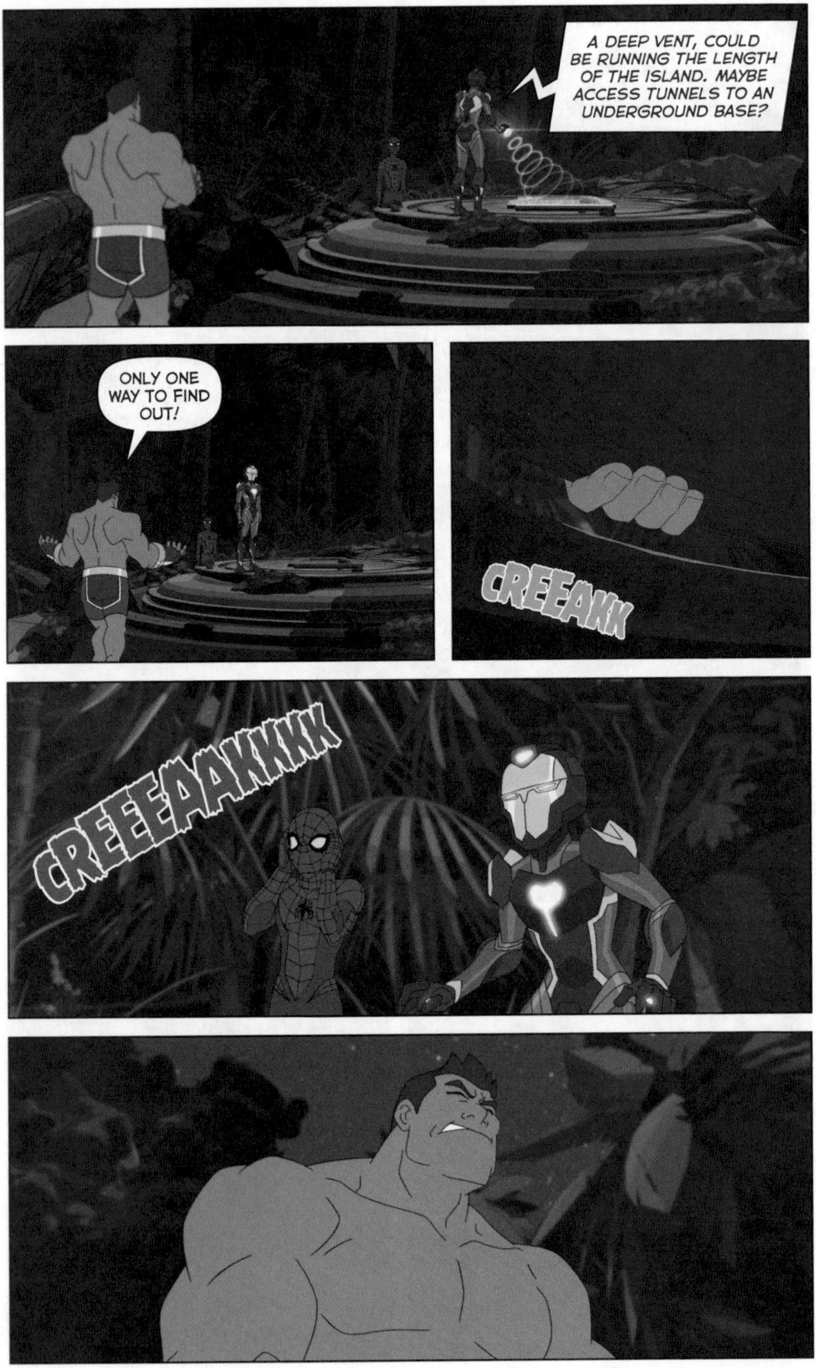
A DEEP VENT, COULD BE RUNNING THE LENGTH OF THE ISLAND. MAYBE ACCESS TUNNELS TO AN UNDERGROUND BASE?
ONLY ONE WAY TO FIND OUT!
CREEAKK
CREEEAAKKKK

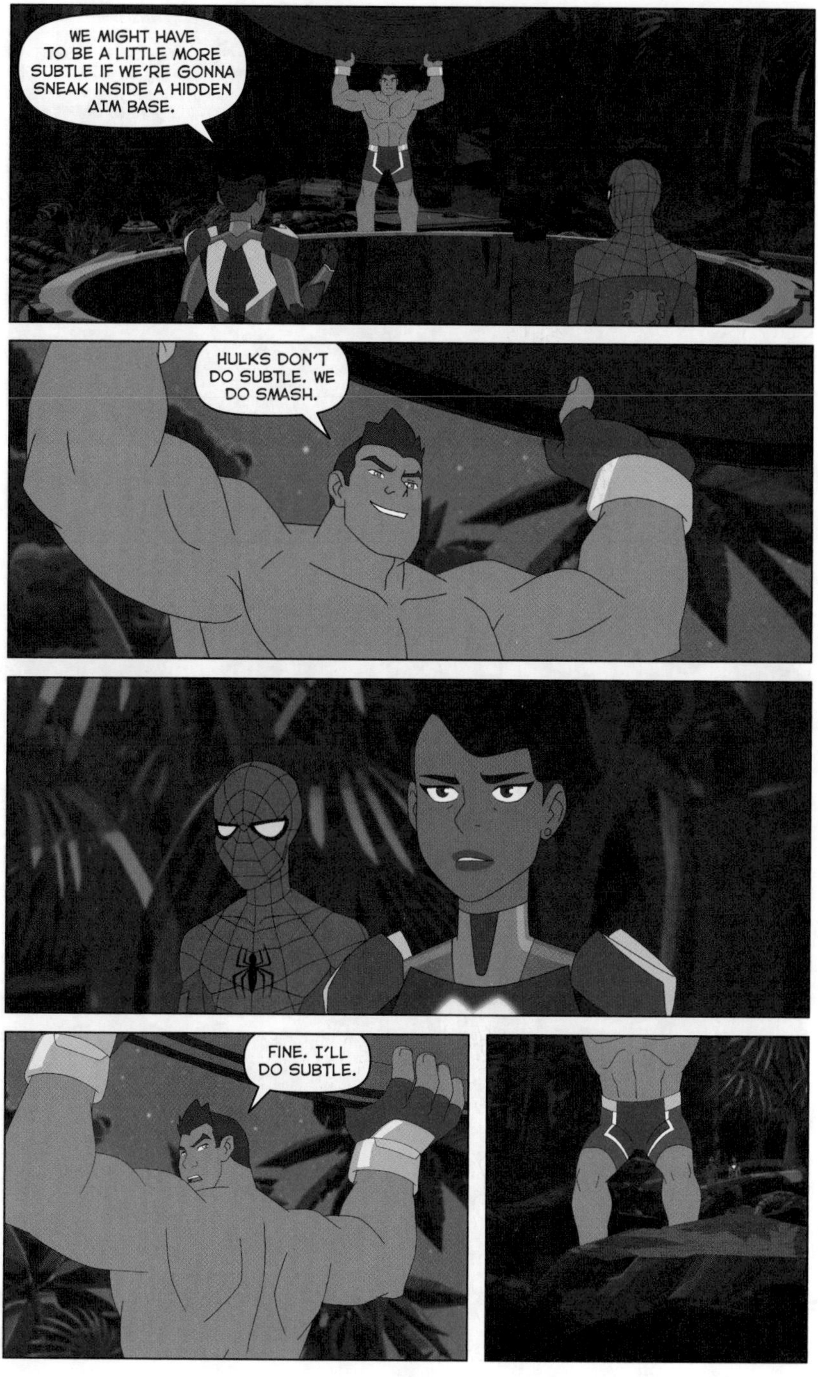
WE MIGHT HAVE TO BE A LITTLE MORE SUBTLE IF WE'RE GONNA SNEAK INSIDE A HIDDEN AIM BASE.
HULKS DON'T DO SUBTLE. WE DO SMASH.
FINE. I'LL DO SUBTLE.

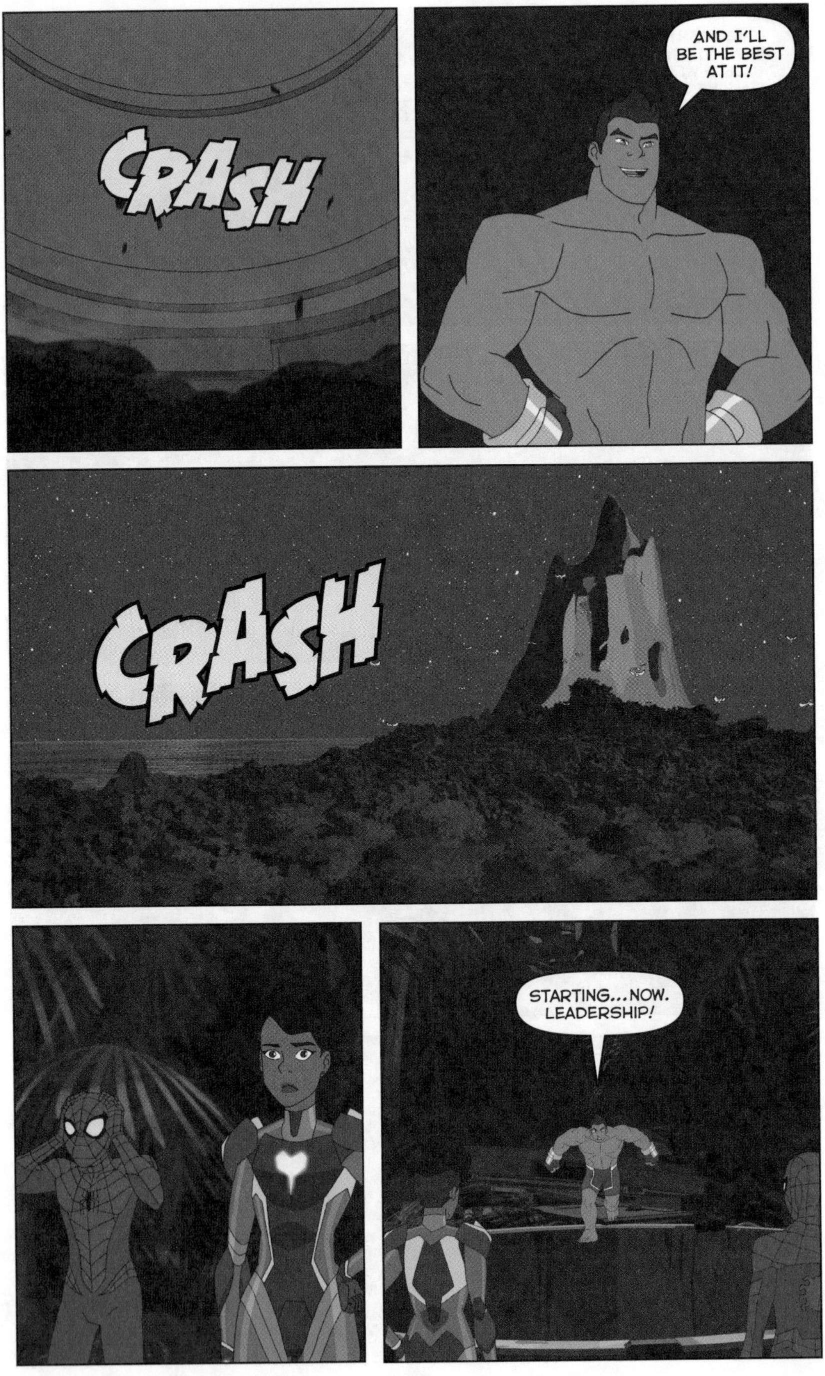
CRASH
AND I'LL BE THE BEST AT IT!
CRASH
STARTING...NOW. LEADERSHIP!

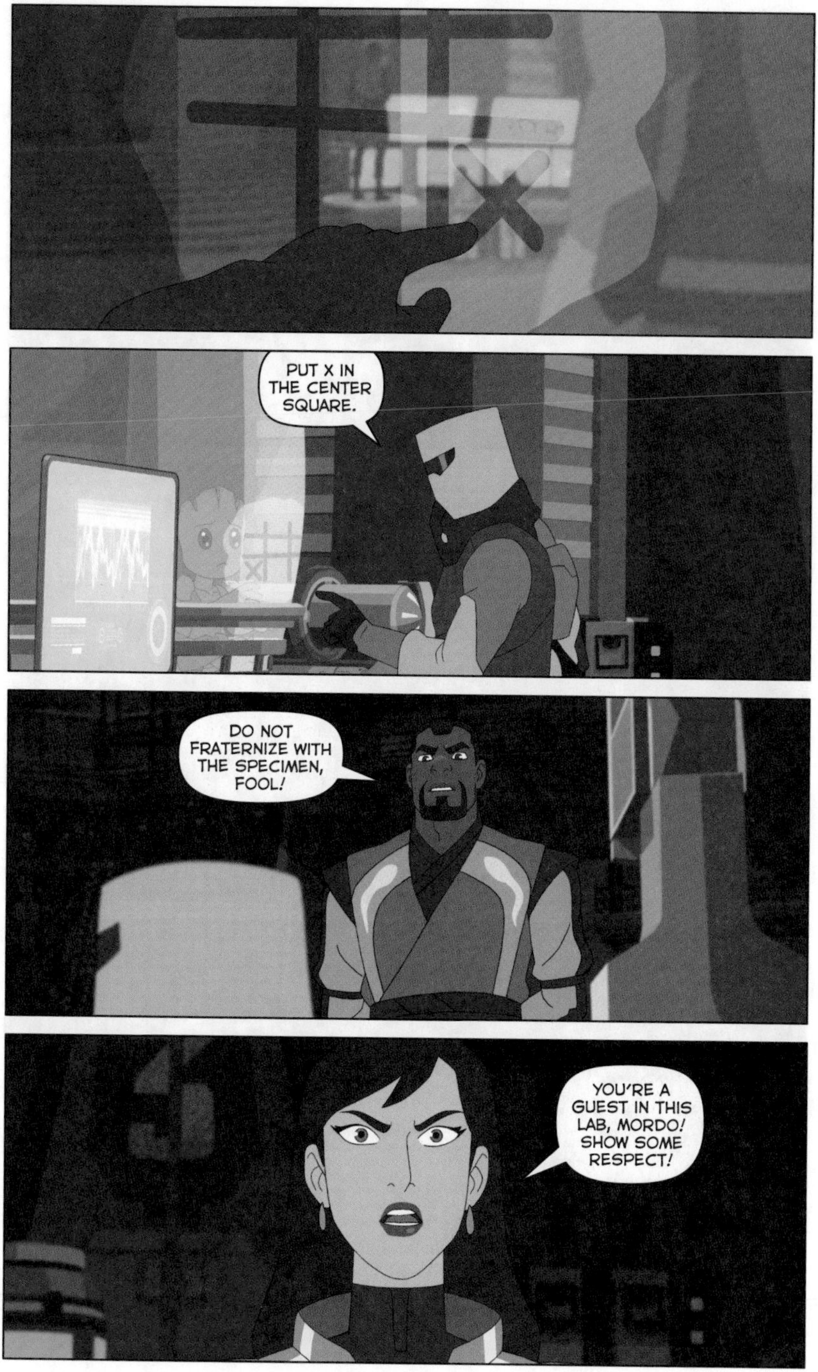
PUT X IN THE CENTER SQUARE.
DO NOT FRATERNIZE WITH THE SPECIMEN, FOOL!
YOU'RE A GUEST IN THIS LAB, MORDO! SHOW SOME RESPECT!

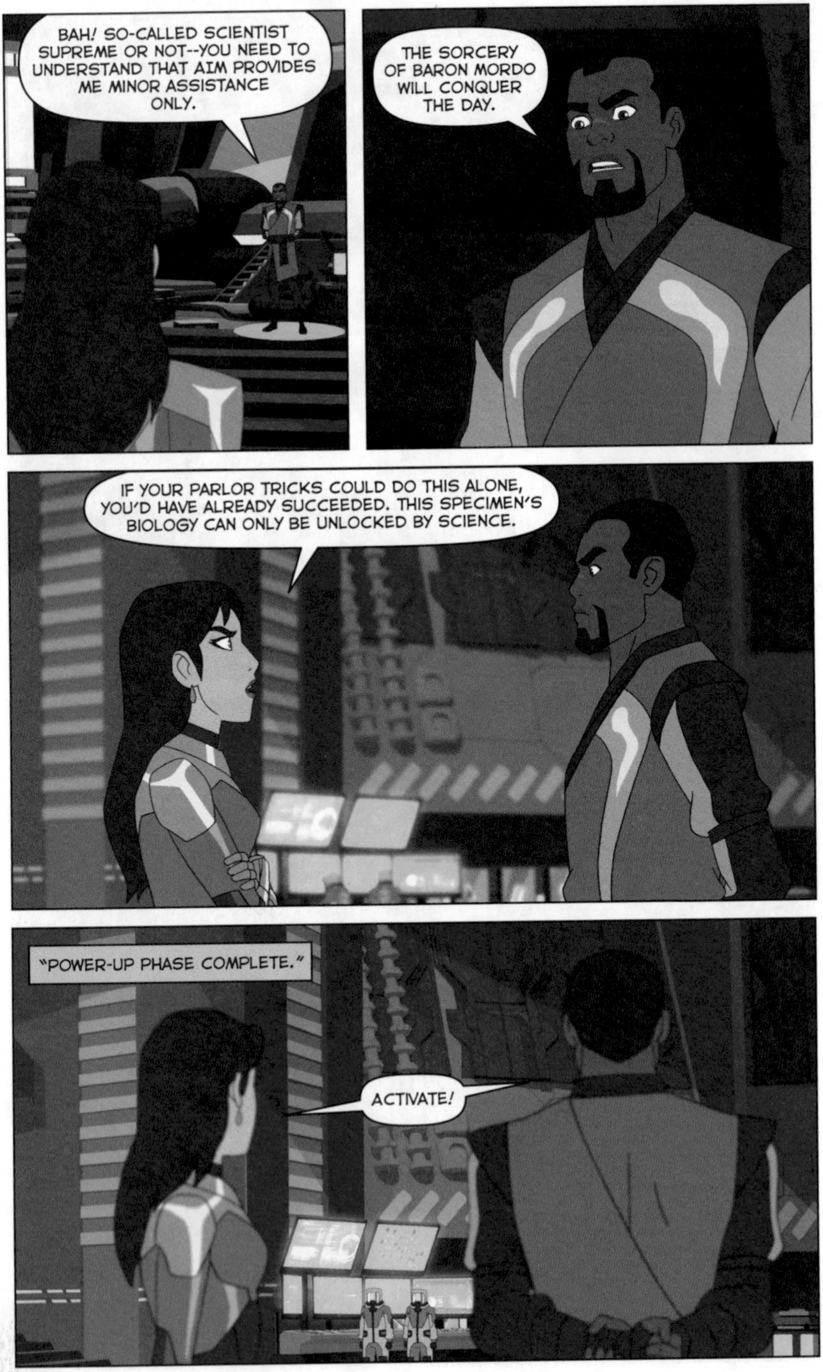
BAH! SO-CALLED SCIENTIST SUPREME OR NOT--YOU NEED TO UNDERSTAND THAT AIM PROVIDES ME MINOR ASSISTANCE ONLY.
THE SORCERY OF BARON MORDO WILL CONQUER THE DAY.
IF YOUR PARLOR TRICKS COULD DO THIS ALONE, YOU'D HAVE ALREADY SUCCEEDED. THIS SPECIMEN'S BIOLOGY CAN ONLY BE UNLOCKED BY SCIENCE.
"POWER-UP PHASE COMPLETE."
ACTIVATE!

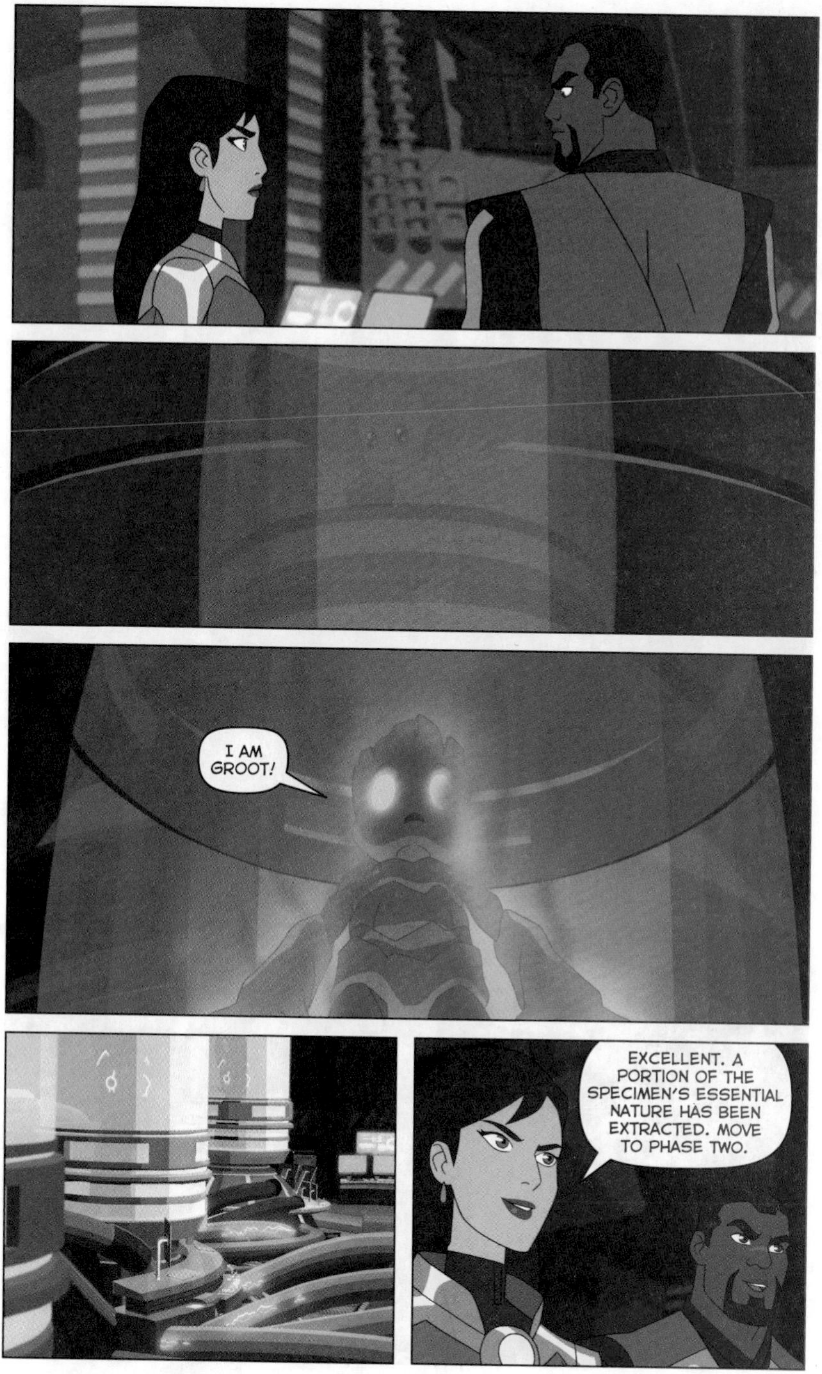
I AM GROOT!
EXCELLENT. A PORTION OF THE SPECIMEN'S ESSENTIAL NATURE HAS BEEN EXTRACTED. MOVE TO PHASE TWO.

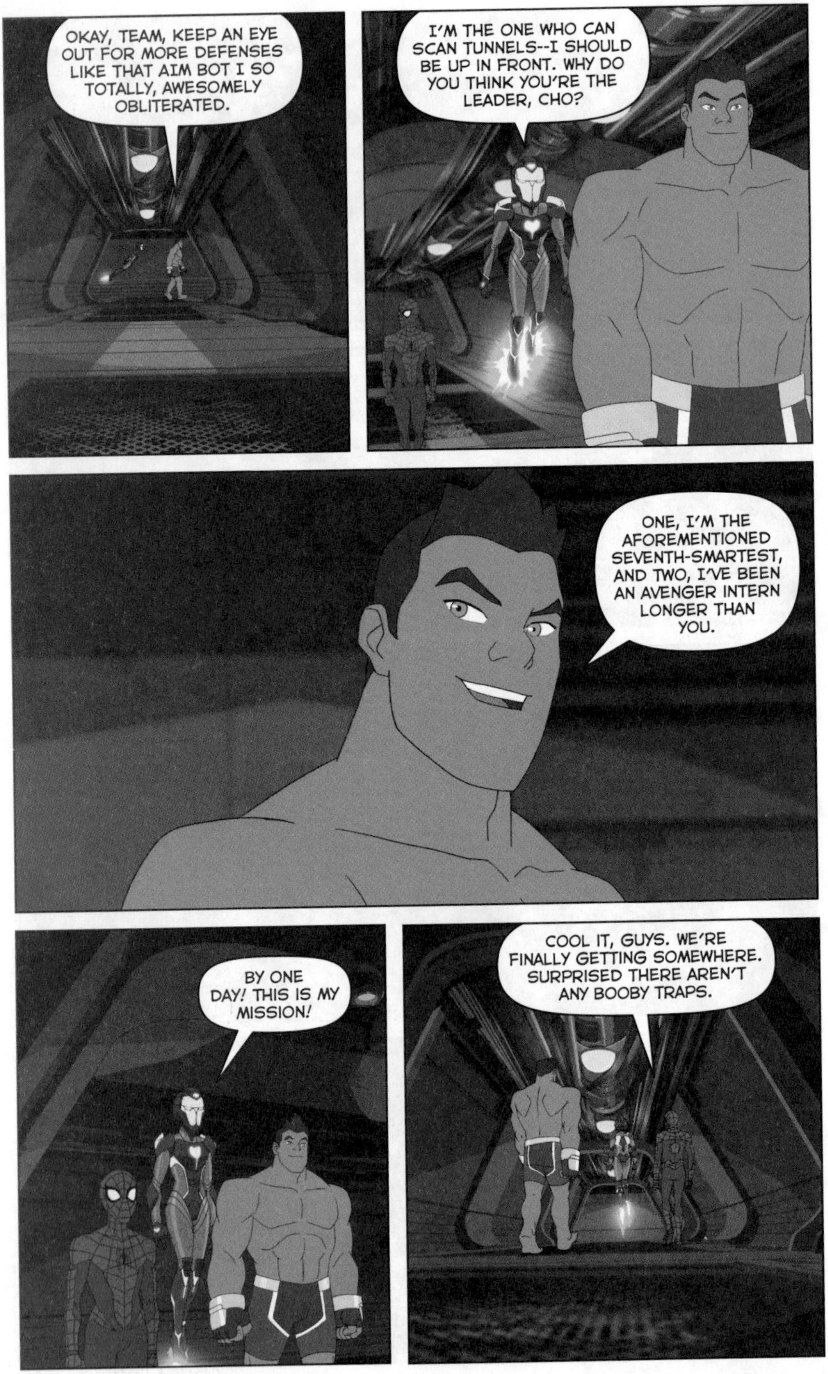
OKAY, TEAM, KEEP AN EYE OUT FOR MORE DEFENSES LIKE THAT AIM BOT I SO TOTALLY, AWESOMELY OBLITERATED.
I'M THE ONE WHO CAN SCAN TUNNELS--I SHOULD BE UP IN FRONT. WHY DO YOU THINK YOU'RE THE LEADER, CHO?
ONE, I'M THE AFOREMENTIONED SEVENTH-SMARTEST, AND TWO, I'VE BEEN AN AVENGER INTERN LONGER THAN YOU.
BY ONE DAY! THIS IS MY MISSION!
COOL IT, GUYS. WE'RE FINALLY GETTING SOMEWHERE. SURPRISED THERE AREN'T ANY BOOBY TRAPS.

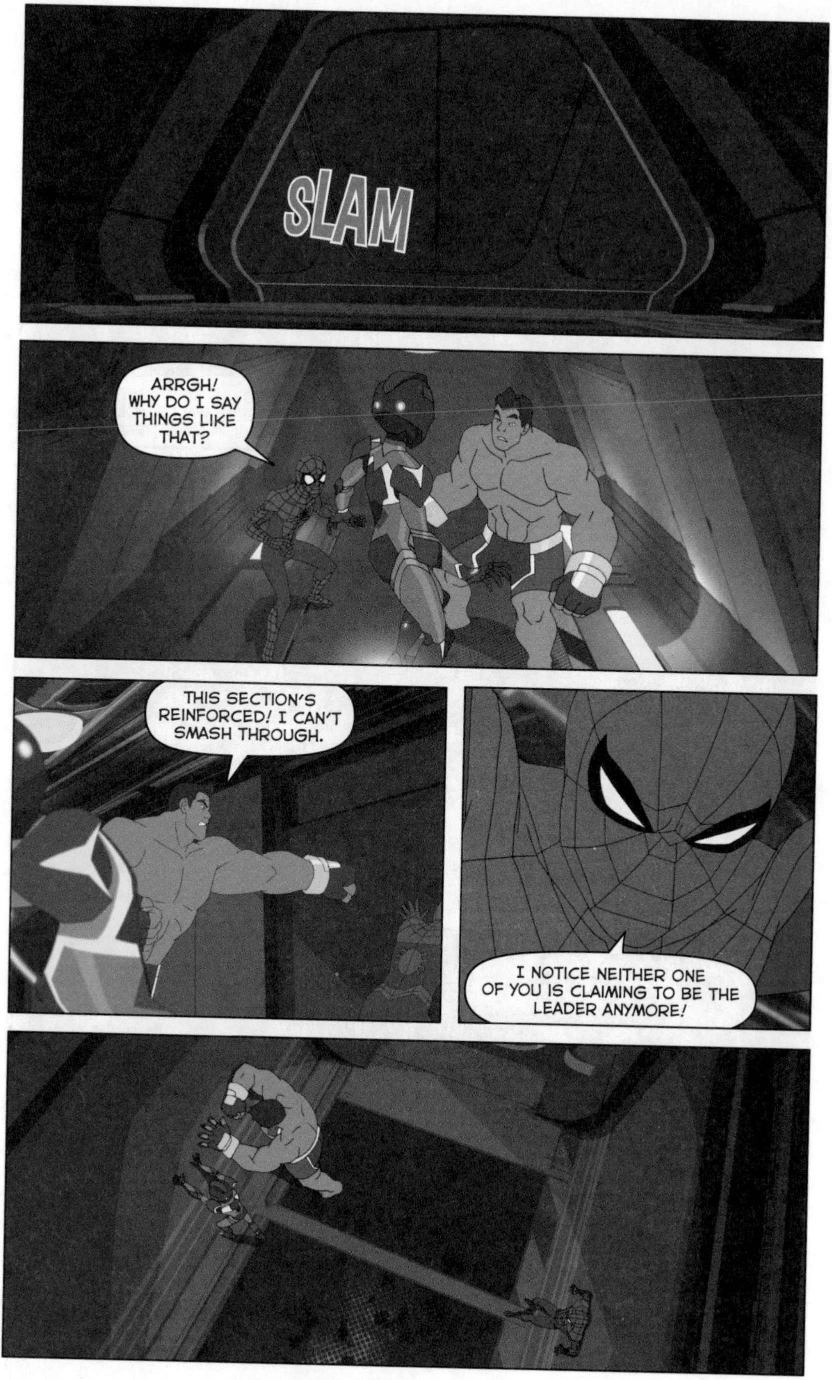
SLAM
ARRGH! WHY DO I SAY THINGS LIKE THAT?
THIS SECTION'S REINFORCED! I CAN'T SMASH THROUGH.
I NOTICE NEITHER ONE OF YOU IS CLAIMING TO BE THE LEADER ANYMORE!

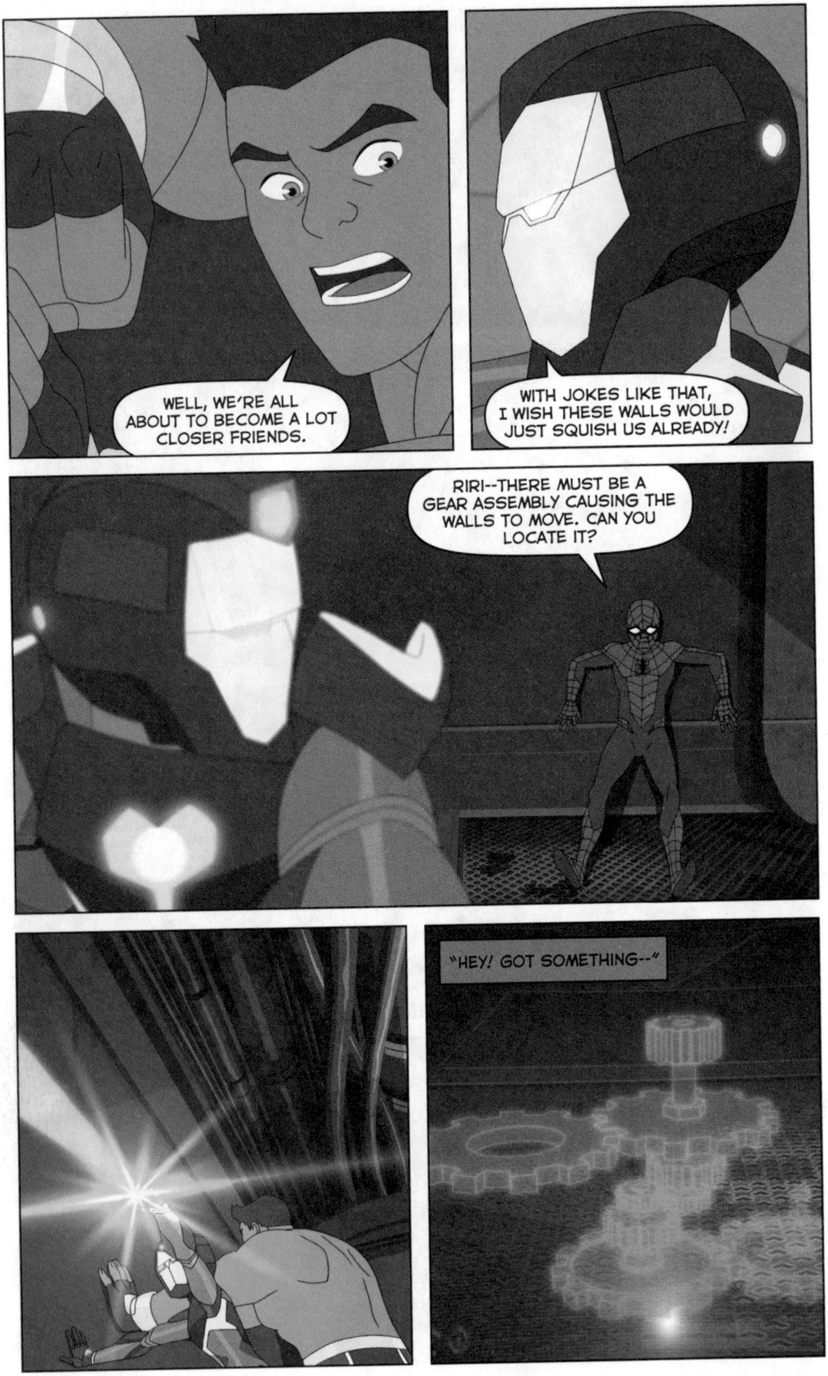
WELL, WE'RE ALL ABOUT TO BECOME A LOT CLOSER FRIENDS.
WITH JOKES LIKE THAT, I WISH THESE WALLS WOULD JUST SQUISH US ALREADY!
RIRI--THERE MUST BE A GEAR ASSEMBLY CAUSING THE WALLS TO MOVE. CAN YOU LOCATE IT?
"HEY! GOT SOMETHING--"

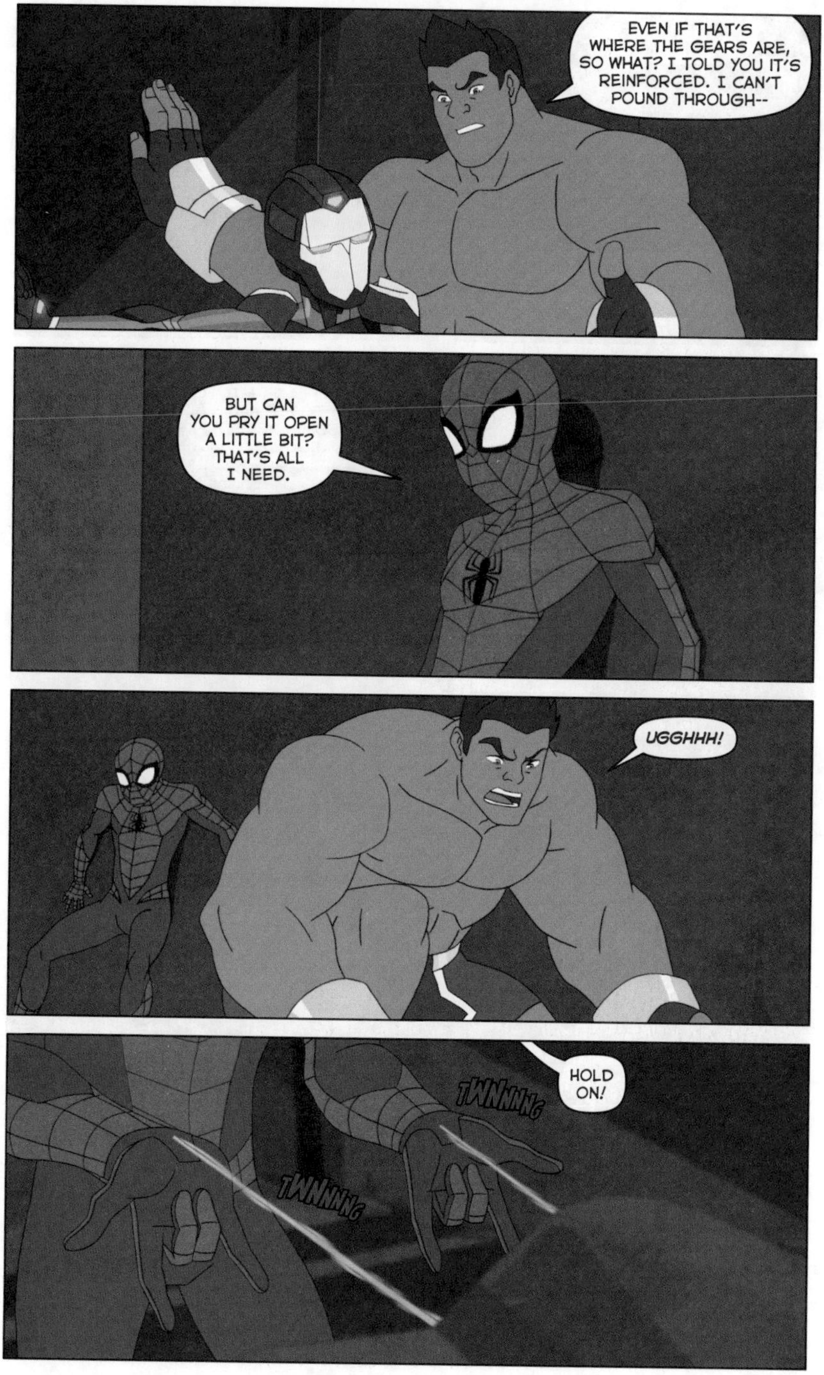
EVEN IF THAT'S WHERE THE GEARS ARE, SO WHAT? I TOLD YOU IT'S REINFORCED. I CAN'T POUND THROUGH--
BUT CAN YOU PRY IT OPEN A LITTLE BIT? THAT'S ALL I NEED.
UGGHHH!
HOLD ON!
TWNNNNG
TWNNNNG

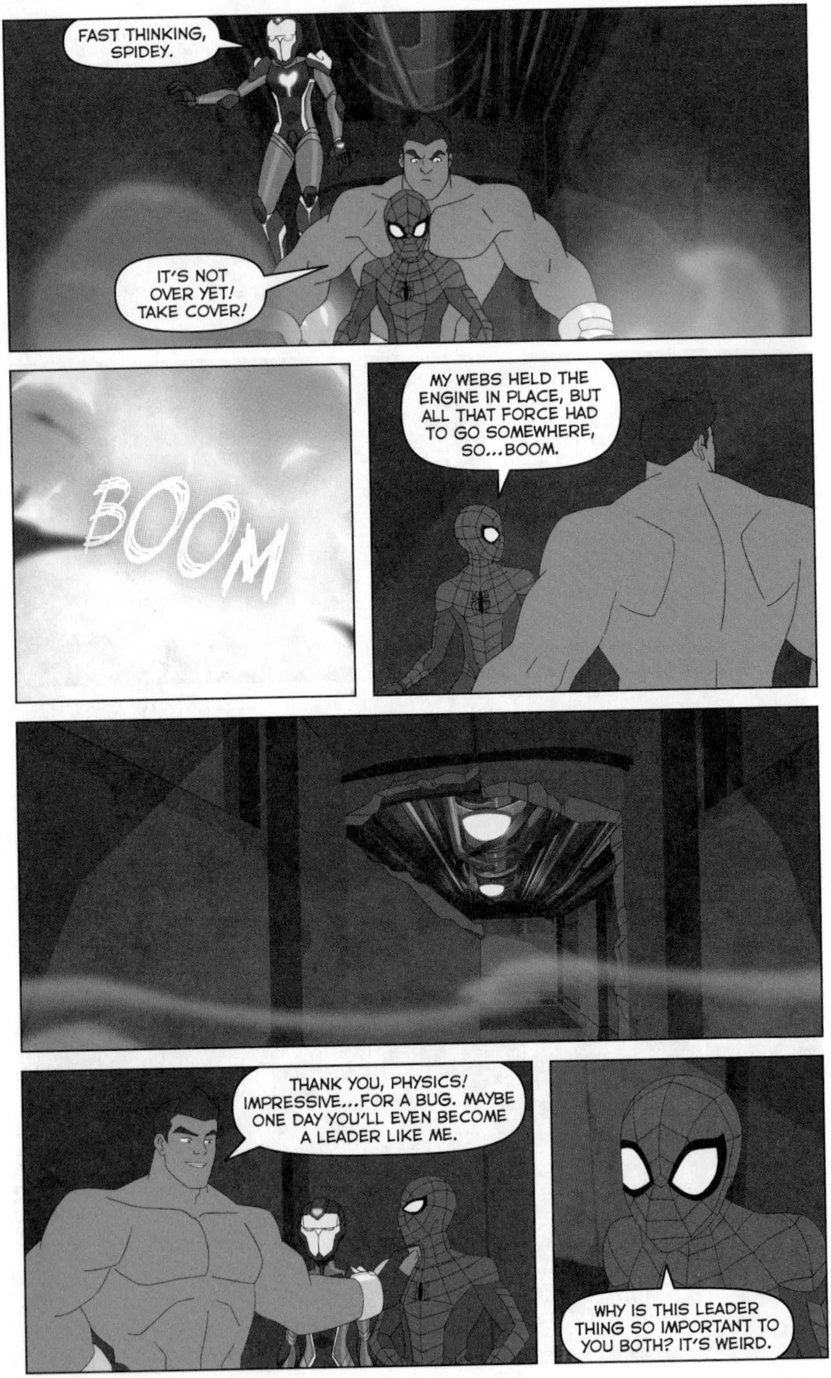
FAST THINKING, SPIDEY.
IT'S NOT OVER YET! TAKE COVER!
BOOM
MY WEBS HELD THE ENGINE IN PLACE, BUT ALL THAT FORCE HAD TO GO SOMEWHERE, SO...BOOM.
THANK YOU, PHYSICS! IMPRESSIVE...FOR A BUG. MAYBE ONE DAY YOU'LL EVEN BECOME A LEADER LIKE ME.
WHY IS THIS LEADER THING SO IMPORTANT TO YOU BOTH? IT'S WEIRD.

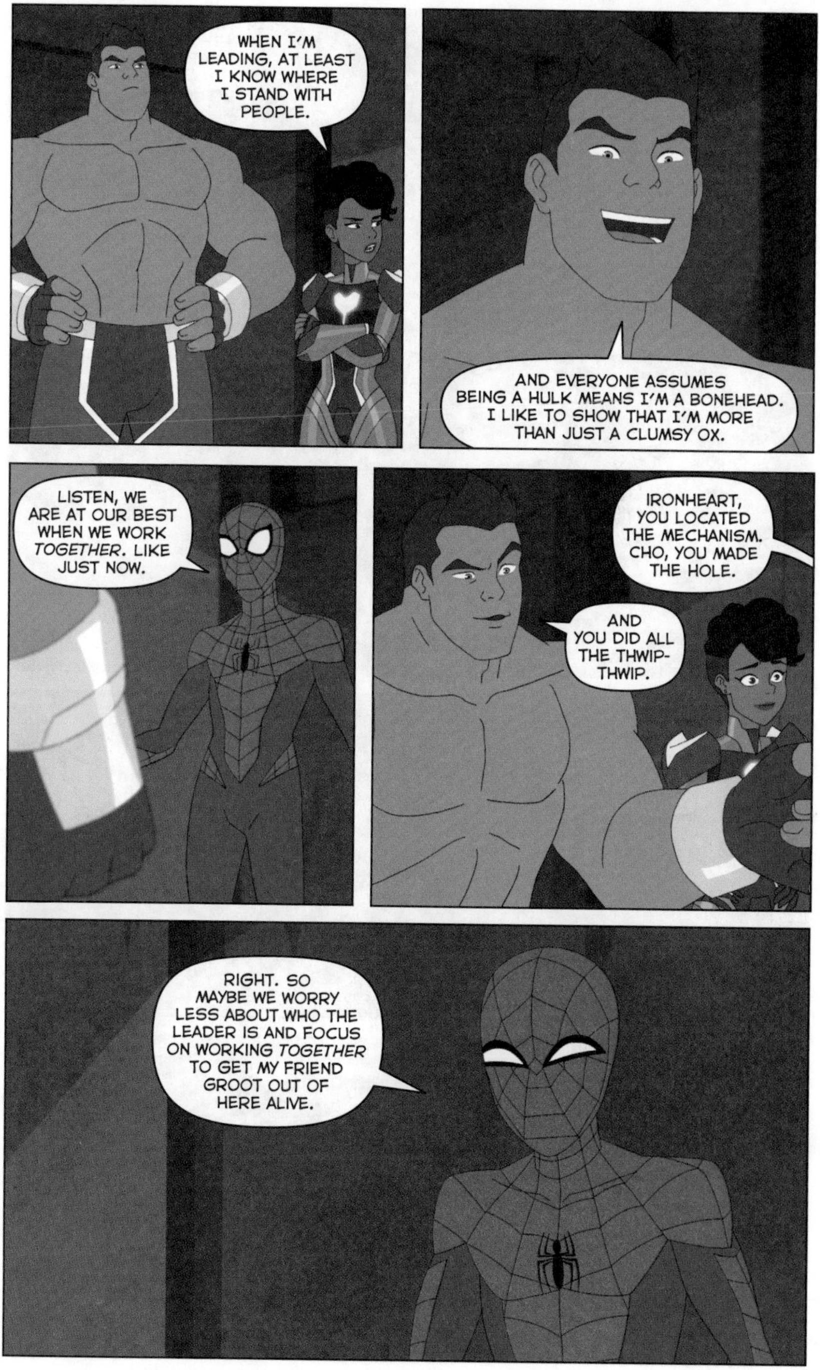
WHEN I'M LEADING, AT LEAST I KNOW WHERE I STAND WITH PEOPLE.
AND EVERYONE ASSUMES BEING A HULK MEANS I'M A BONEHEAD. I LIKE TO SHOW THAT I'M MORE THAN JUST A CLUMSY OX.
LISTEN, WE ARE AT OUR BEST WHEN WE WORK *TOGETHER*. LIKE JUST NOW.
IRONHEART, YOU LOCATED THE MECHANISM. CHO, YOU MADE THE HOLE.
AND YOU DID ALL THE THWIP-THWIP.
RIGHT. SO MAYBE WE WORRY LESS ABOUT WHO THE LEADER IS AND FOCUS ON WORKING *TOGETHER* TO GET MY FRIEND GROOT OUT OF HERE ALIVE.

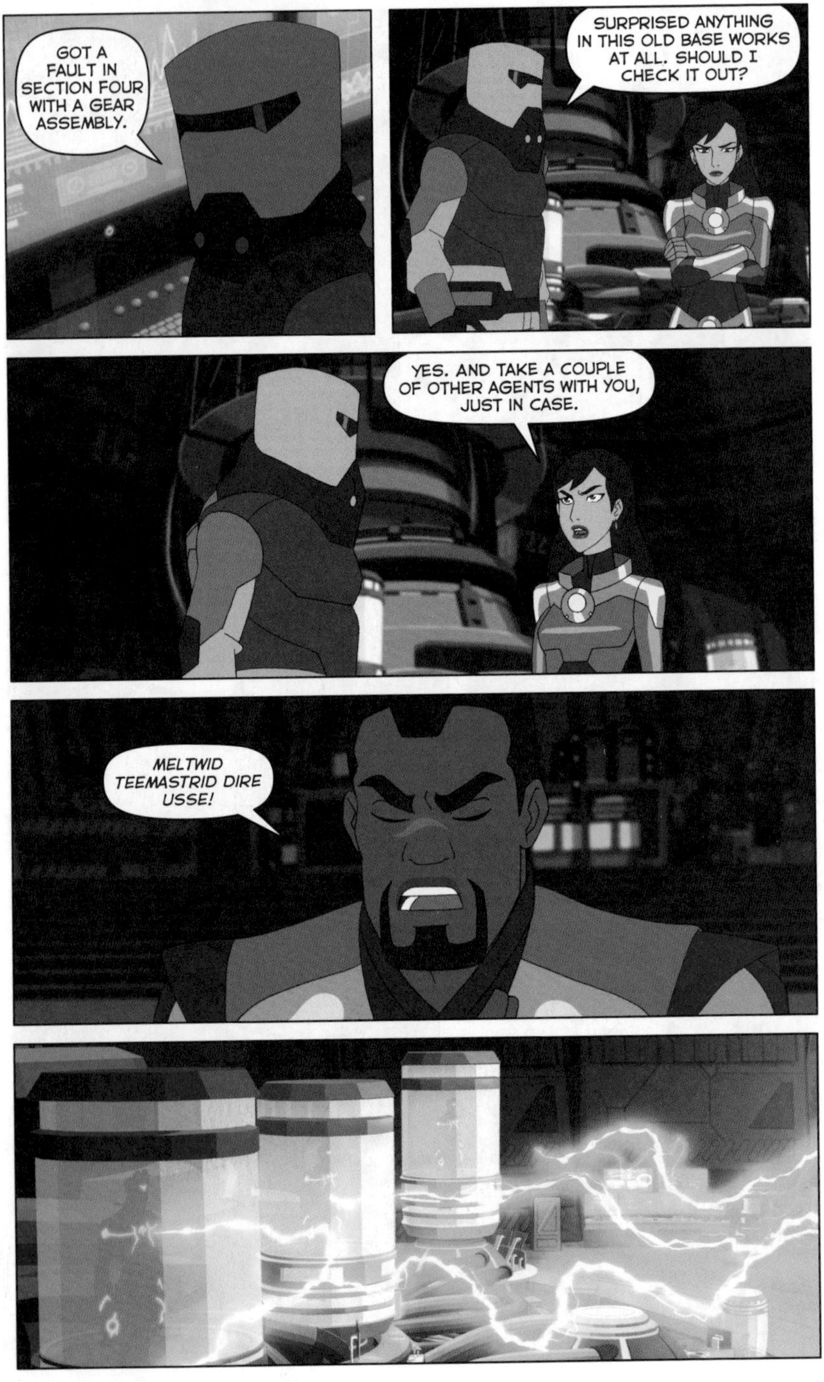
GOT A FAULT IN SECTION FOUR WITH A GEAR ASSEMBLY.
SURPRISED ANYTHING IN THIS OLD BASE WORKS AT ALL. SHOULD I CHECK IT OUT?
YES. AND TAKE A COUPLE OF OTHER AGENTS WITH YOU, JUST IN CASE.
MELTWID TEEMASTRID DIRE USSE!

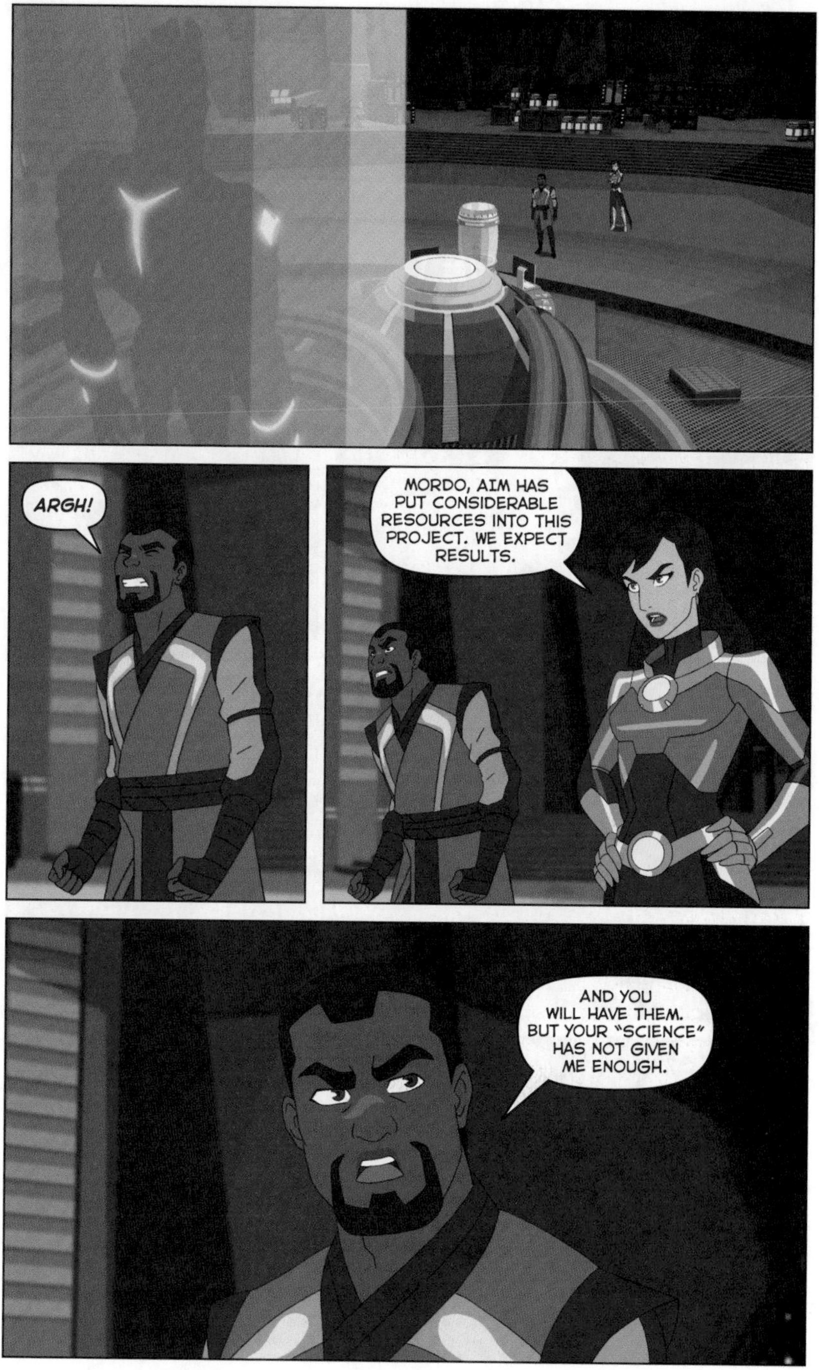
ARGH!
MORDO, AIM HAS PUT CONSIDERABLE RESOURCES INTO THIS PROJECT. WE EXPECT RESULTS.
AND YOU WILL HAVE THEM. BUT YOUR "SCIENCE" HAS NOT GIVEN ME ENOUGH.

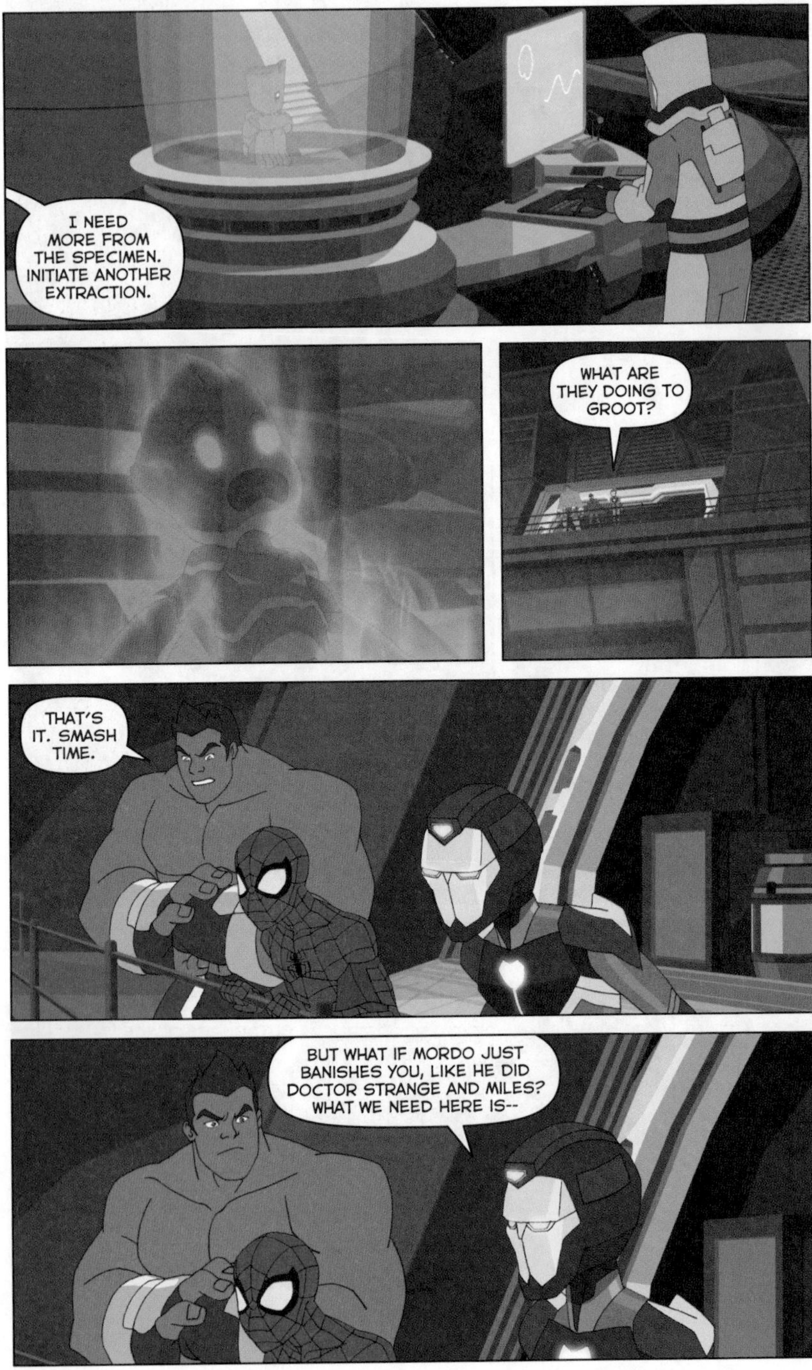

I NEED MORE FROM THE SPECIMEN. INITIATE ANOTHER EXTRACTION.
WHAT ARE THEY DOING TO GROOT?
THAT'S IT. SMASH TIME.
BUT WHAT IF MORDO JUST BANISHES YOU, LIKE HE DID DOCTOR STRANGE AND MILES? WHAT WE NEED HERE IS--

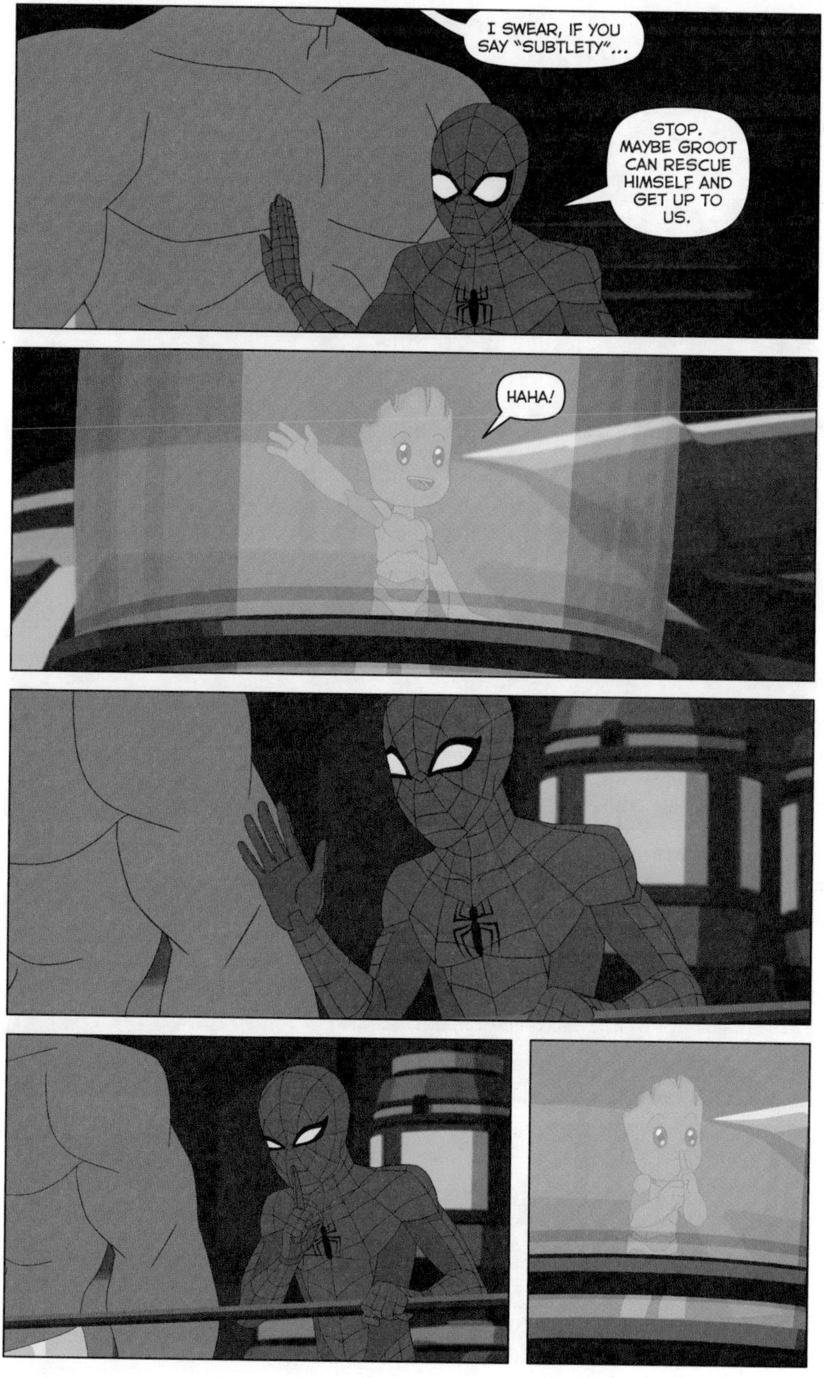
I SWEAR, IF YOU SAY "SUBTLETY"...
STOP. MAYBE GROOT CAN RESCUE HIMSELF AND GET UP TO US.
HAHA!

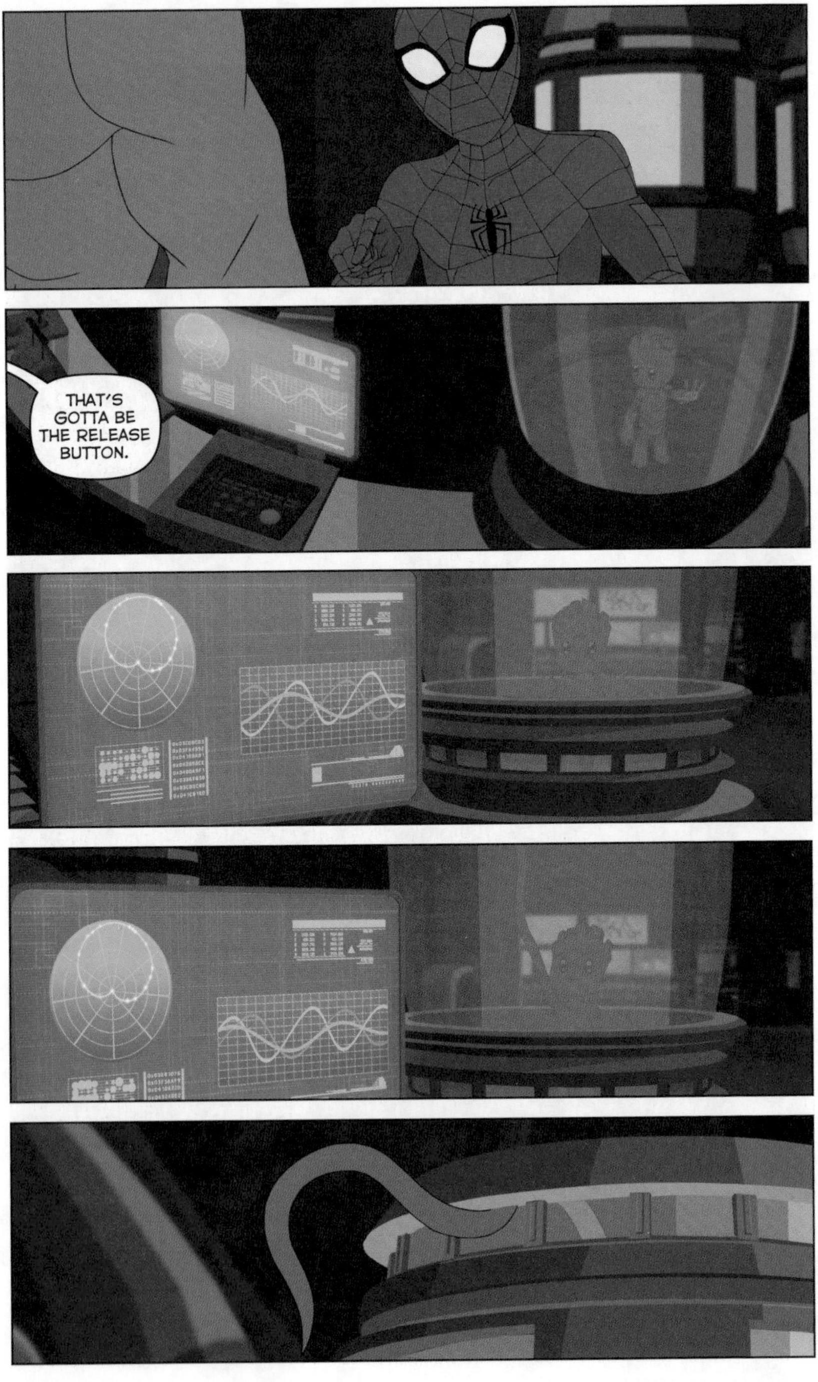
THAT'S GOTTA BE THE RELEASE BUTTON.

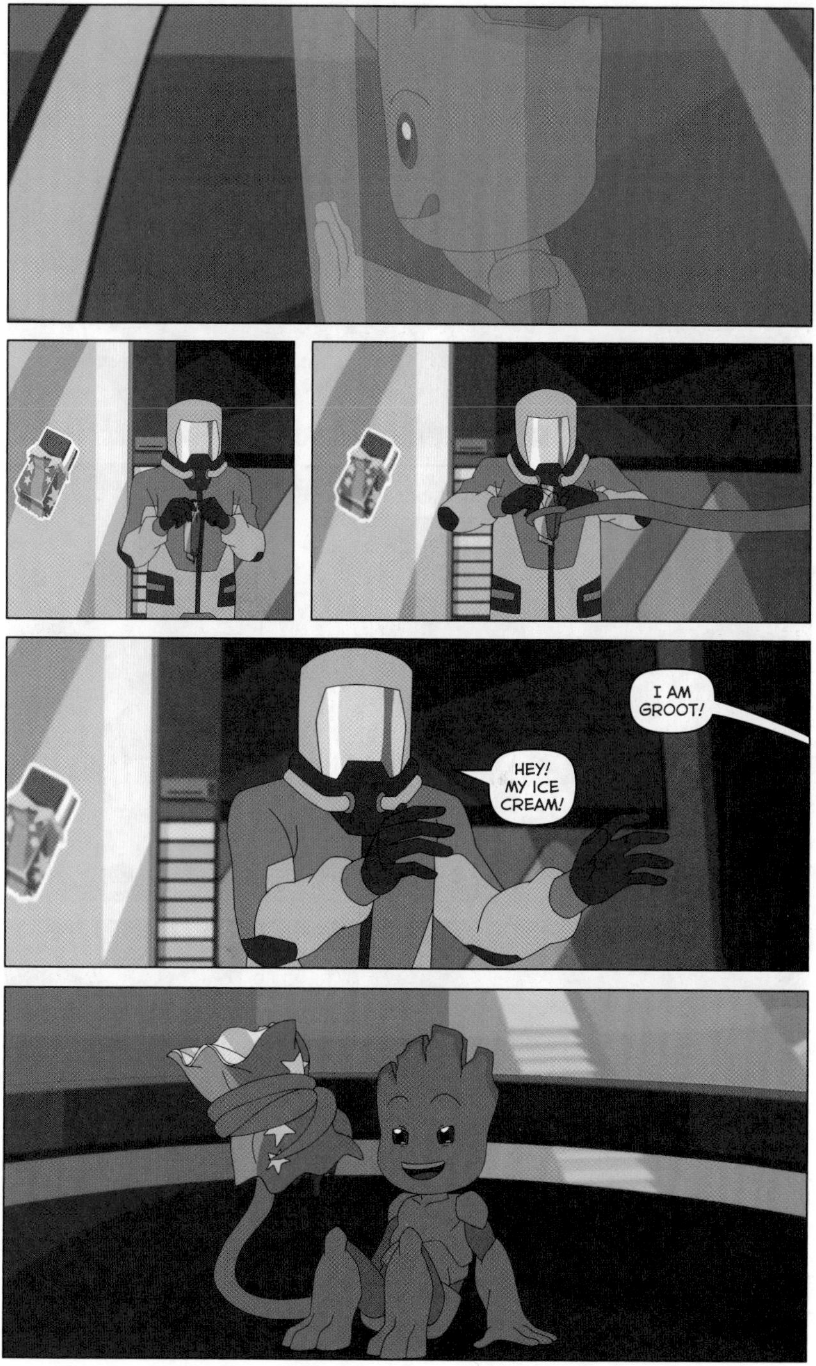
I AM GROOT!
HEY! MY ICE CREAM!

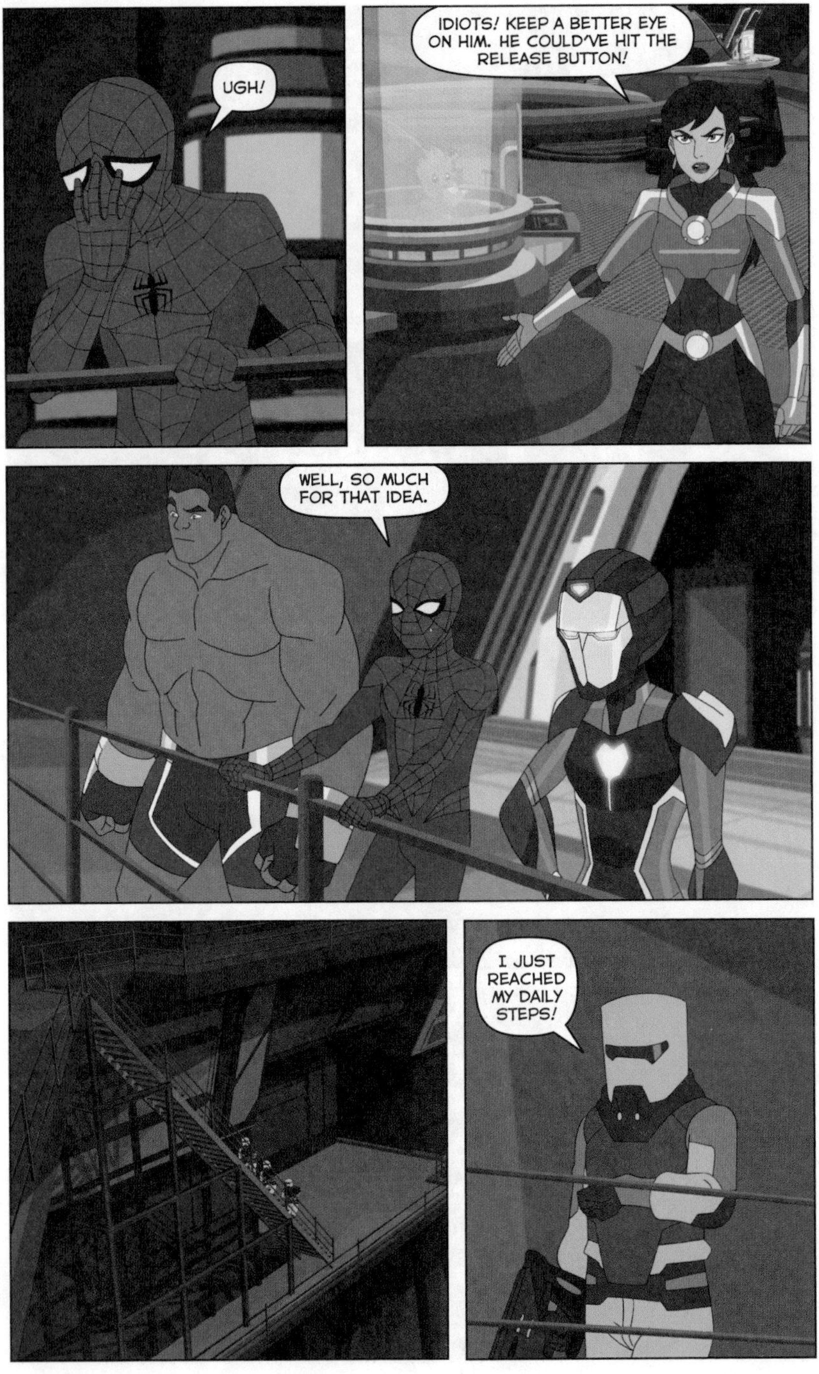
UGH!
IDIOTS! KEEP A BETTER EYE ON HIM. HE COULD'VE HIT THE RELEASE BUTTON!
WELL, SO MUCH FOR THAT IDEA.
I JUST REACHED MY DAILY STEPS!

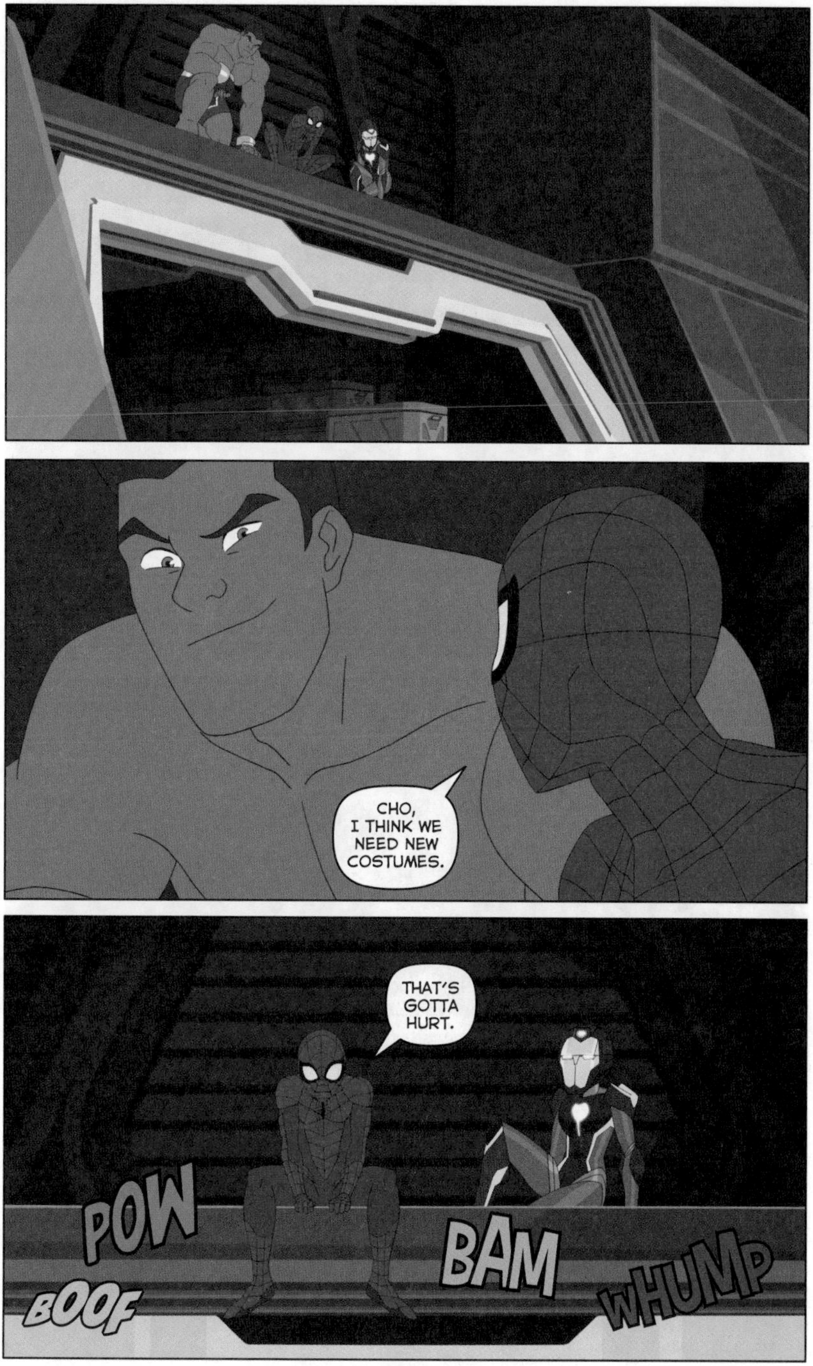
CHO, I THINK WE NEED NEW COSTUMES.
THAT'S GOTTA HURT.
POW
BOOF
BAM
WHUMP

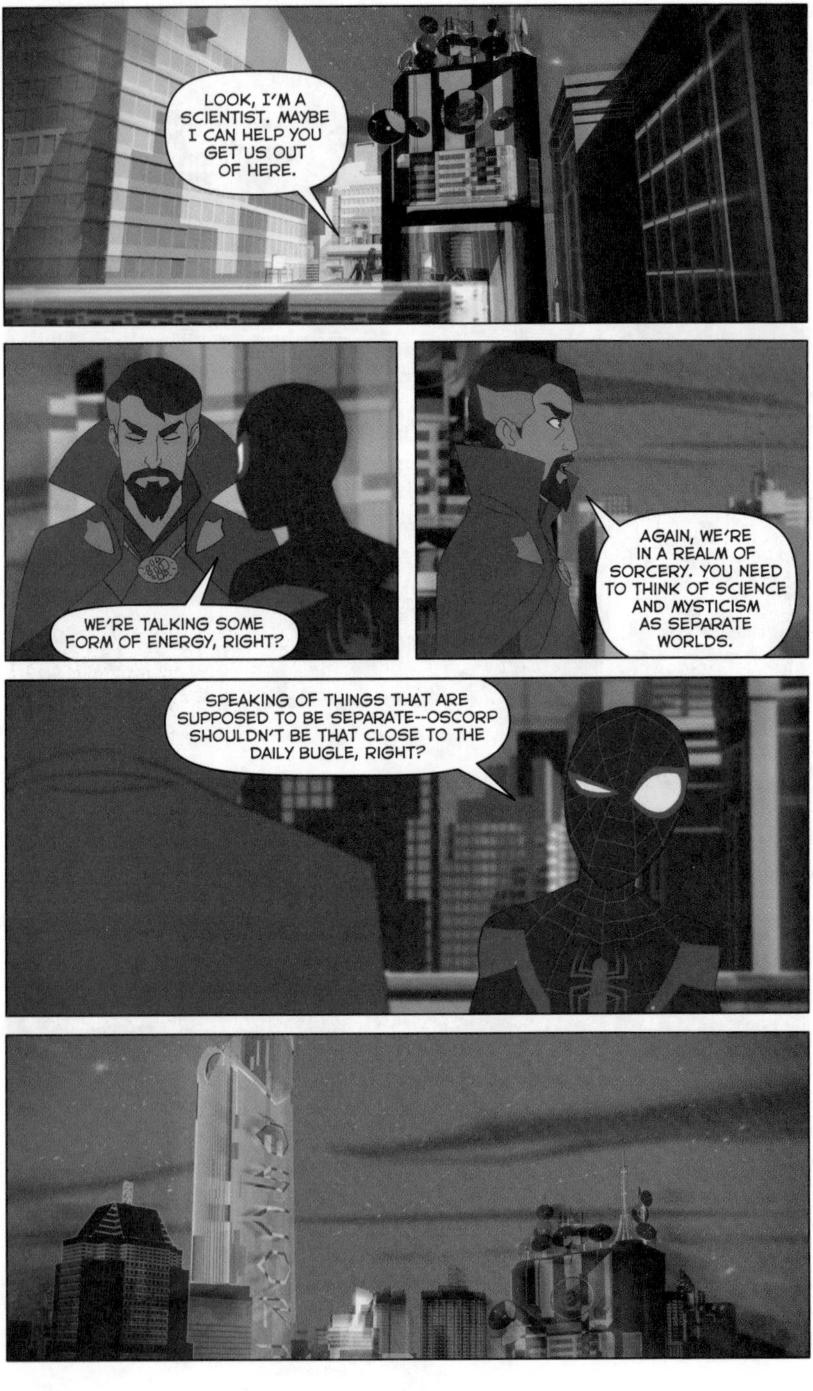
LOOK, I'M A SCIENTIST. MAYBE I CAN HELP YOU GET US OUT OF HERE.
WE'RE TALKING SOME FORM OF ENERGY, RIGHT?
AGAIN, WE'RE IN A REALM OF SORCERY. YOU NEED TO THINK OF SCIENCE AND MYSTICISM AS SEPARATE WORLDS.
SPEAKING OF THINGS THAT ARE SUPPOSED TO BE SEPARATE--OSCORP SHOULDN'T BE THAT CLOSE TO THE DAILY BUGLE, RIGHT?

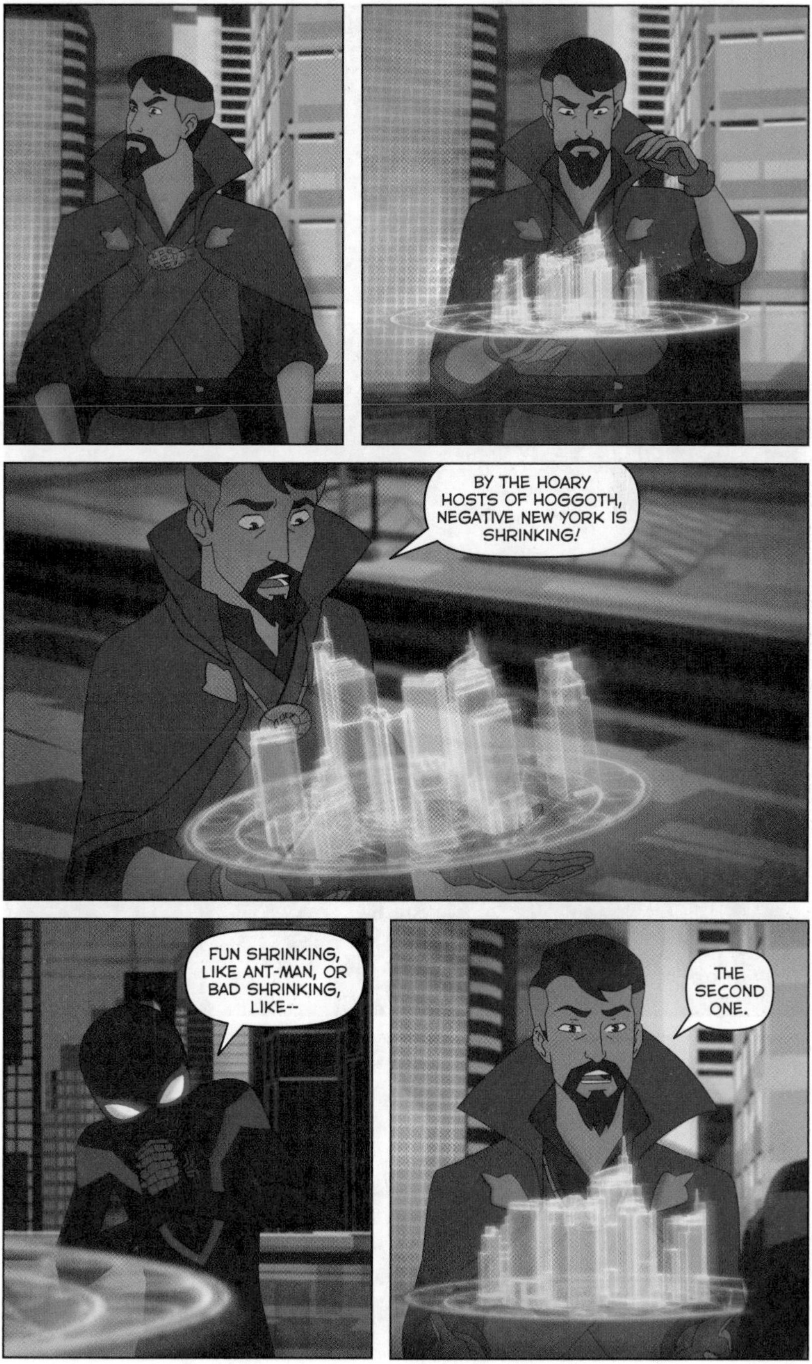
BY THE HOARY HOSTS OF HOGGOTH, NEGATIVE NEW YORK IS SHRINKING!
FUN SHRINKING, LIKE ANT-MAN, OR BAD SHRINKING, LIKE--
THE SECOND ONE.

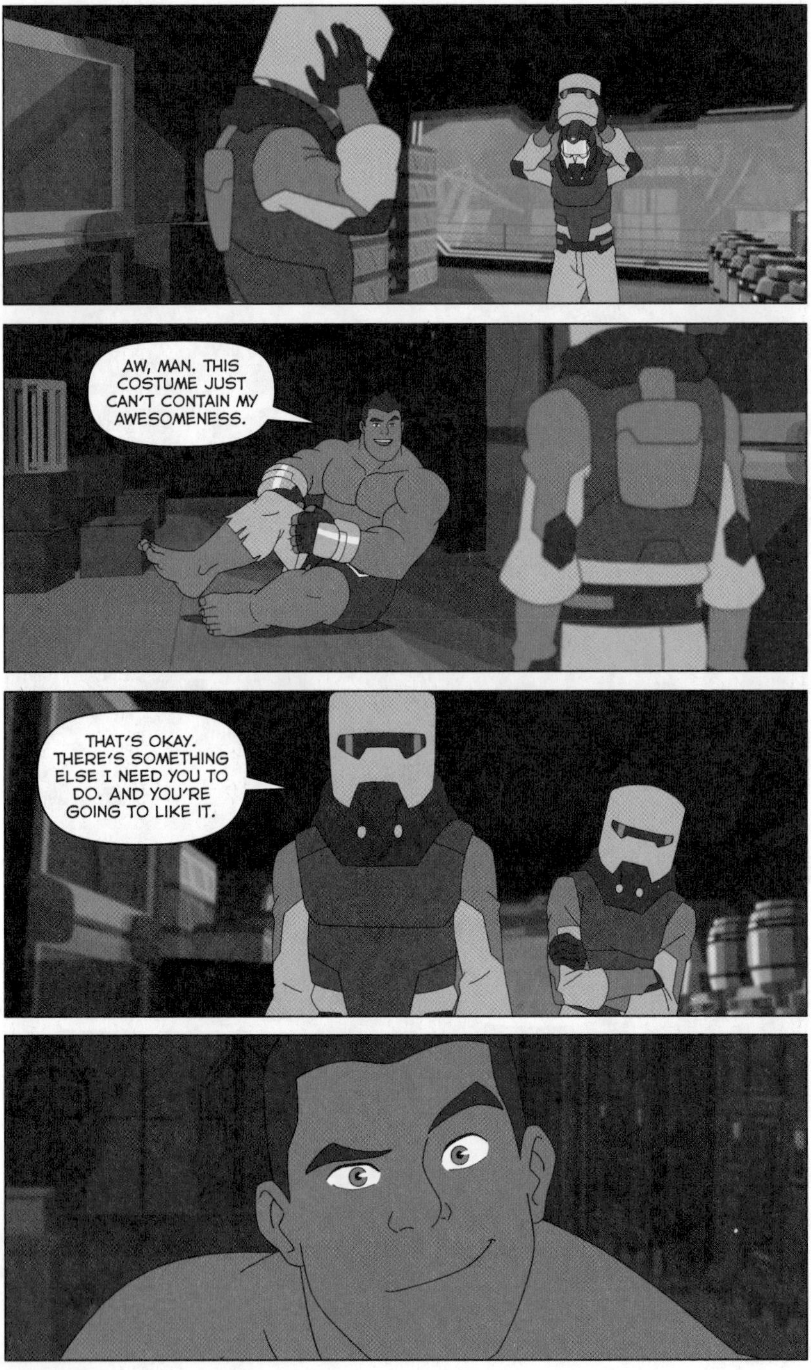
AW, MAN. THIS COSTUME JUST CAN'T CONTAIN MY AWESOMENESS.
THAT'S OKAY. THERE'S SOMETHING ELSE I NEED YOU TO DO. AND YOU'RE GOING TO LIKE IT.

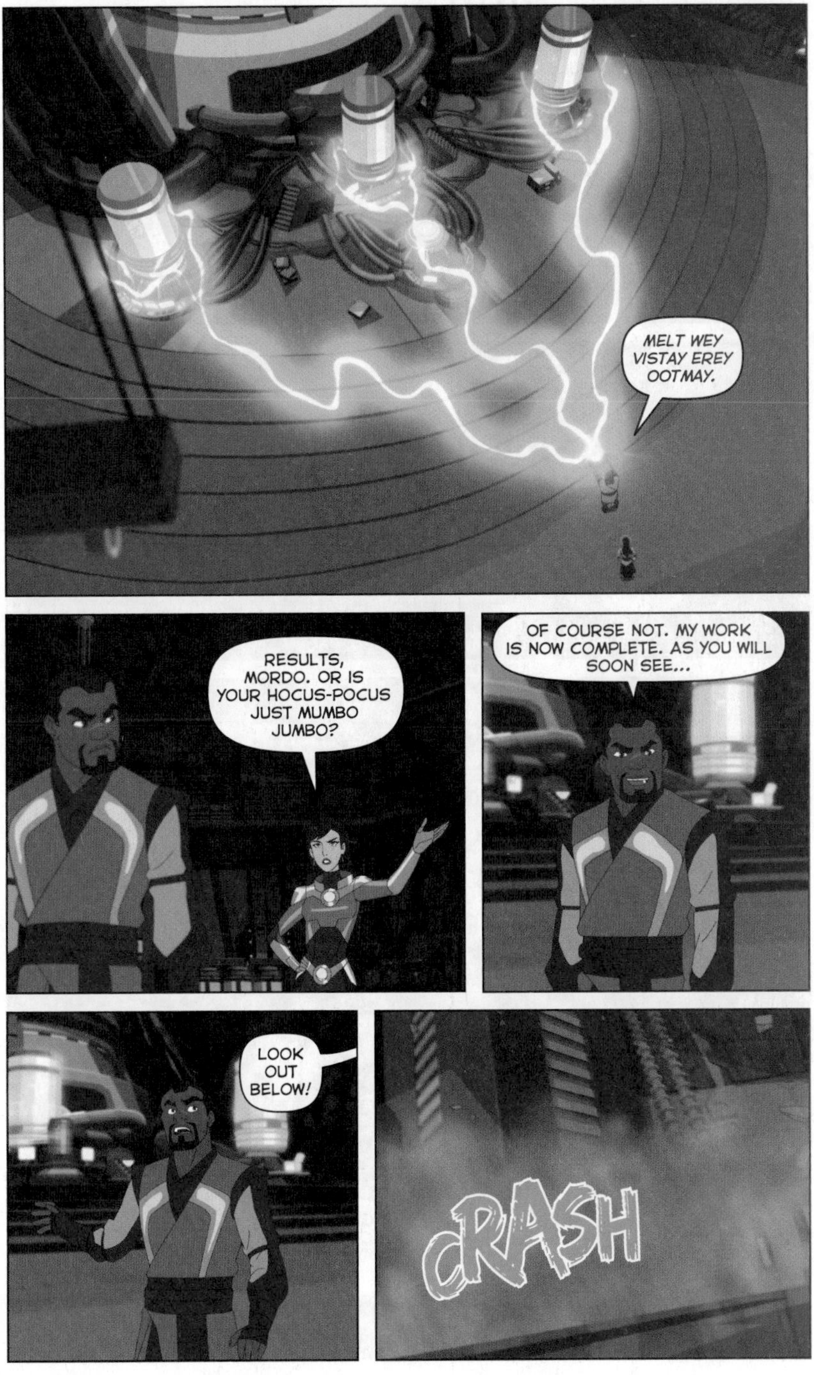
MELT WEY VISTAY EREY OOTMAY.
RESULTS, MORDO. OR IS YOUR HOCUS-POCUS JUST MUMBO JUMBO?
OF COURSE NOT. MY WORK IS NOW COMPLETE. AS YOU WILL SOON SEE...
LOOK OUT BELOW!
CRASH

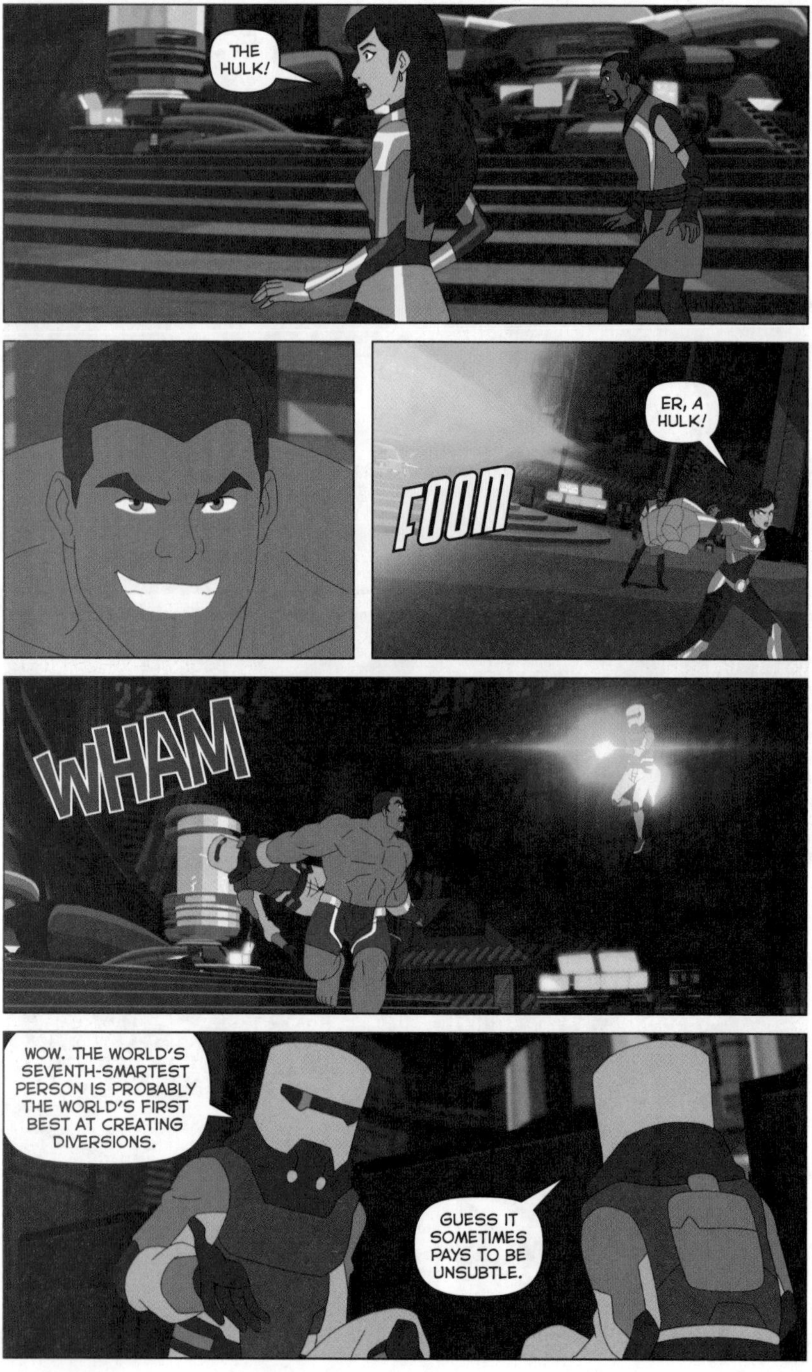
THE HULK!
ER, A HULK!
FOOM
WHAM
WOW. THE WORLD'S SEVENTH-SMARTEST PERSON IS PROBABLY THE WORLD'S FIRST BEST AT CREATING DIVERSIONS.
GUESS IT SOMETIMES PAYS TO BE UNSUBTLE.

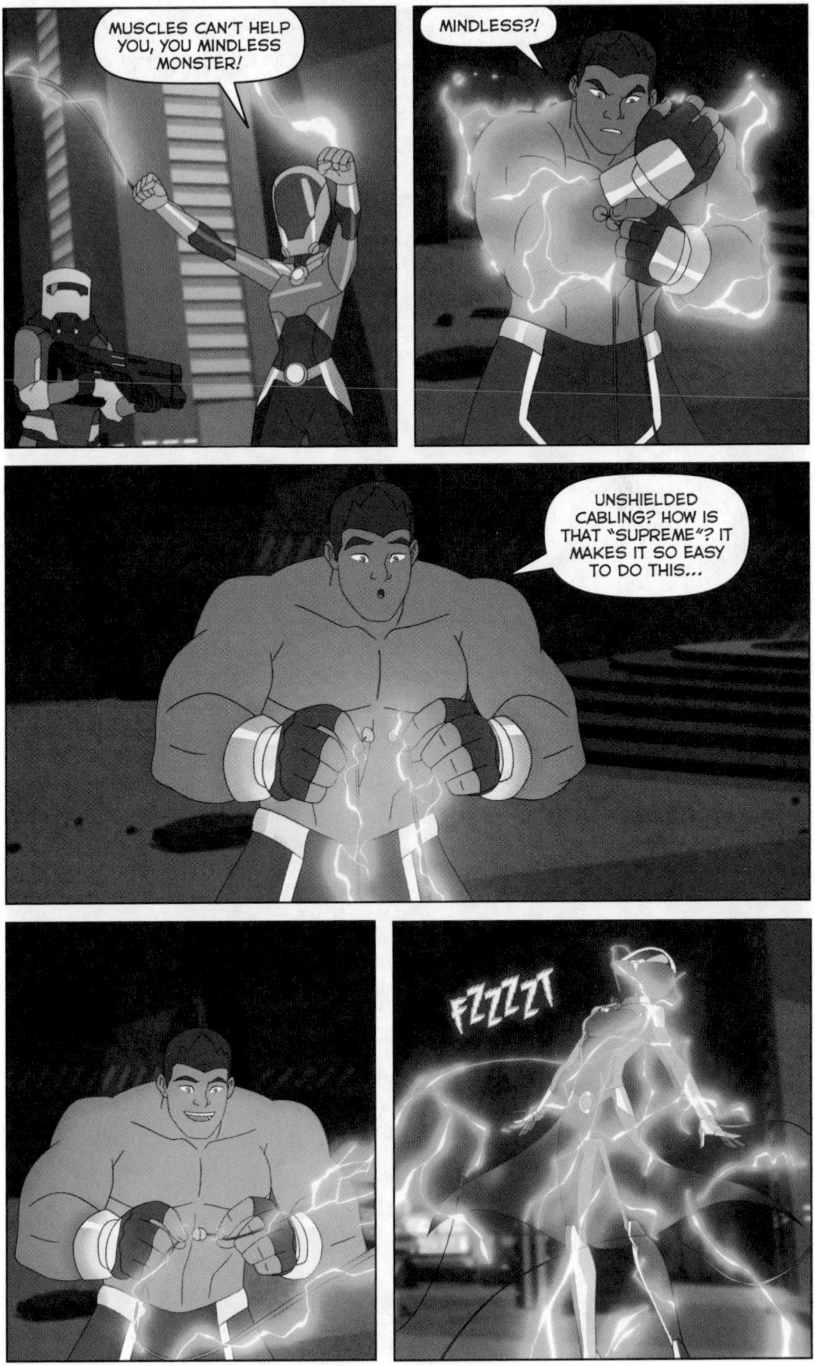
MUSCLES CAN'T HELP YOU, YOU MINDLESS MONSTER!
MINDLESS?!
UNSHIELDED CABLING? HOW IS THAT "SUPREME"? IT MAKES IT SO EASY TO DO THIS...
FZZZZT

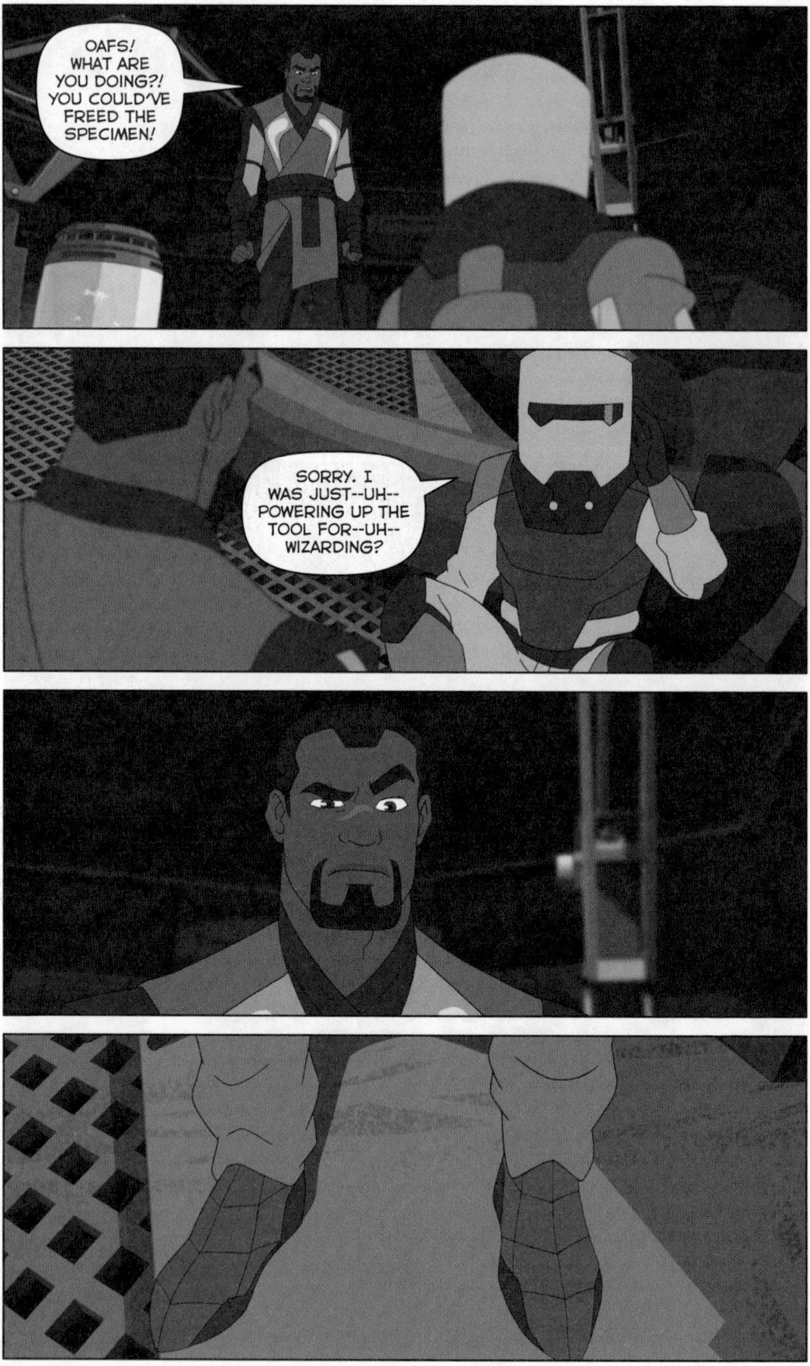
OAFS! WHAT ARE YOU DOING?! YOU COULD'VE FREED THE SPECIMEN!
SORRY. I WAS JUST--UH--POWERING UP THE TOOL FOR--UH--WIZARDING?

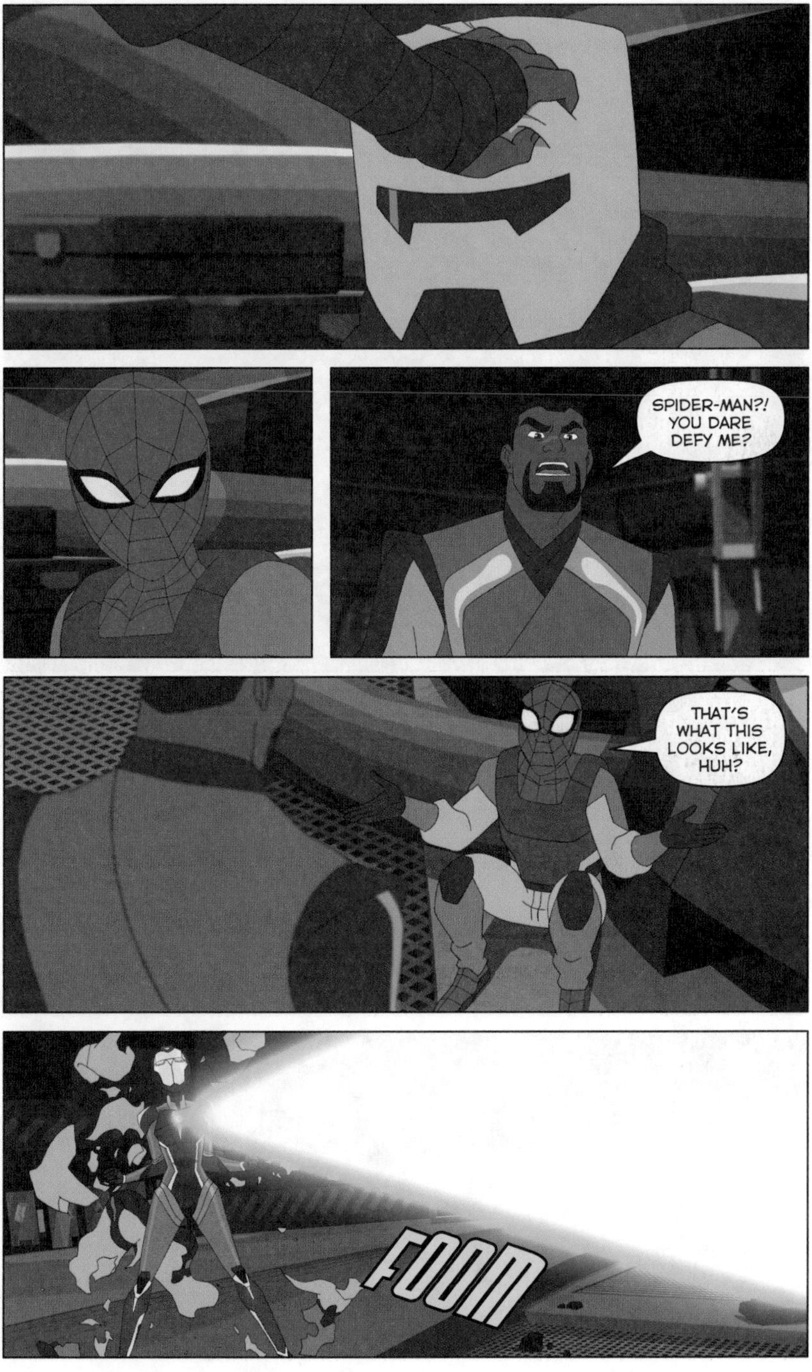
SPIDER-MAN?! YOU DARE DEFY ME?
THAT'S WHAT THIS LOOKS LIKE, HUH?
FOOM

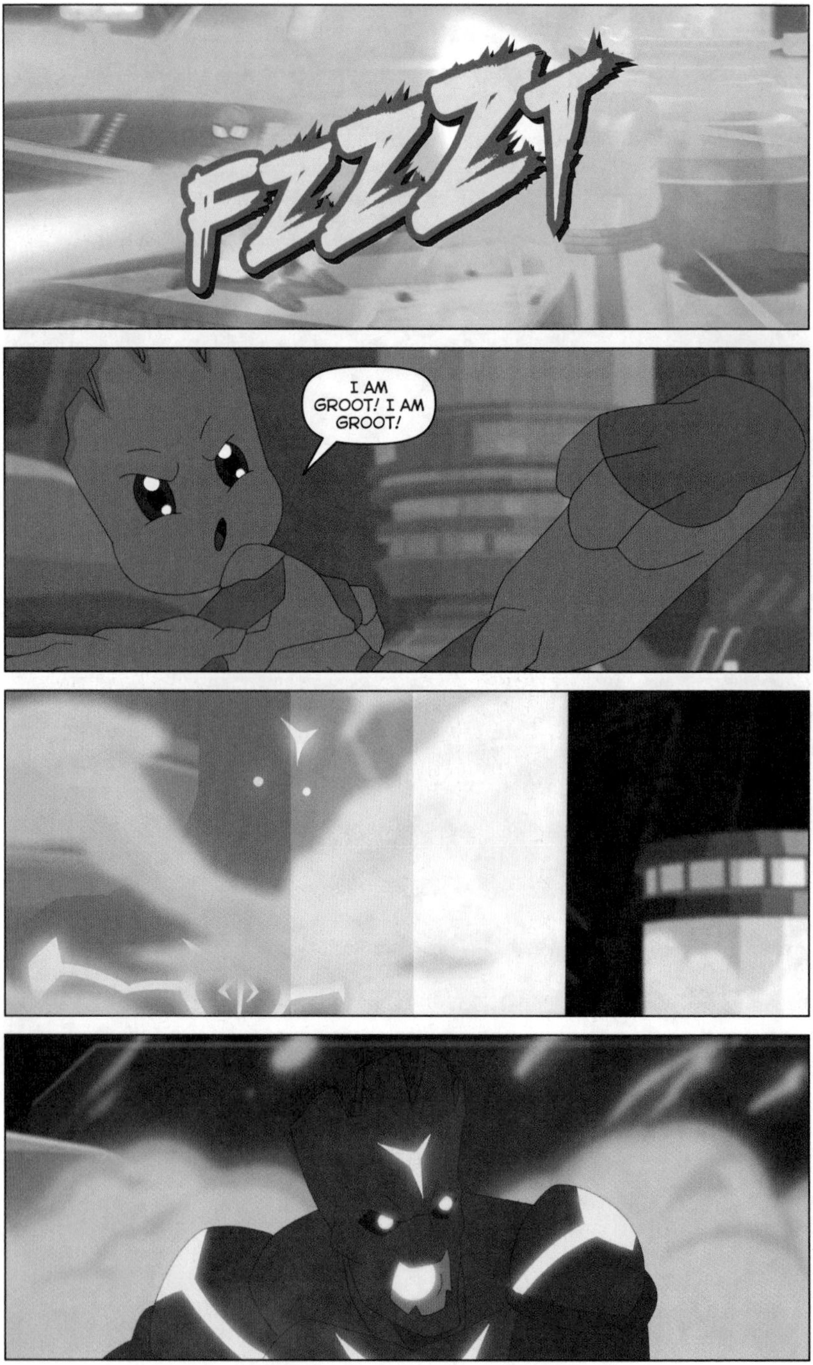
FZZZT
I AM GROOT! I AM GROOT!

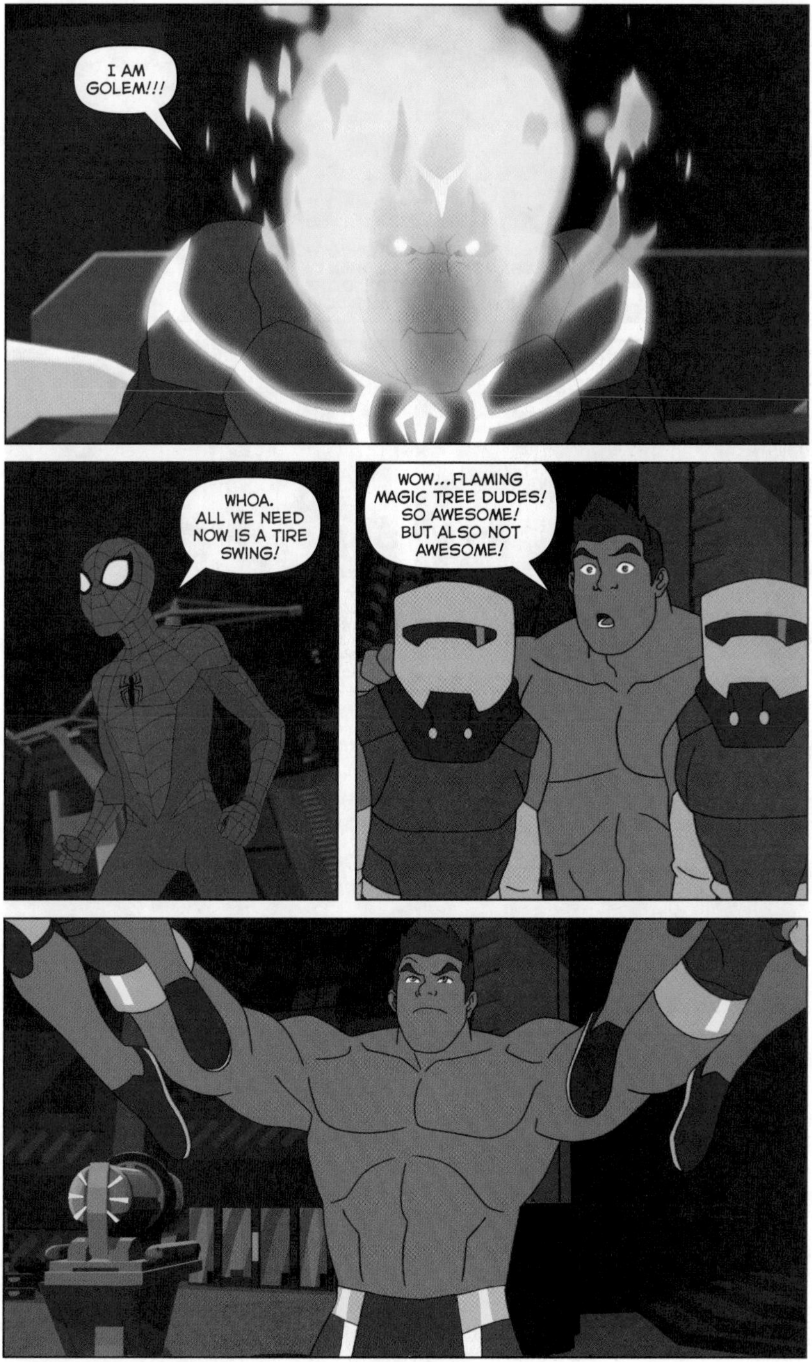
I AM GOLEM!!!
WHOA. ALL WE NEED NOW IS A TIRE SWING!
WOW...FLAMING MAGIC TREE DUDES! SO AWESOME! BUT ALSO NOT AWESOME!

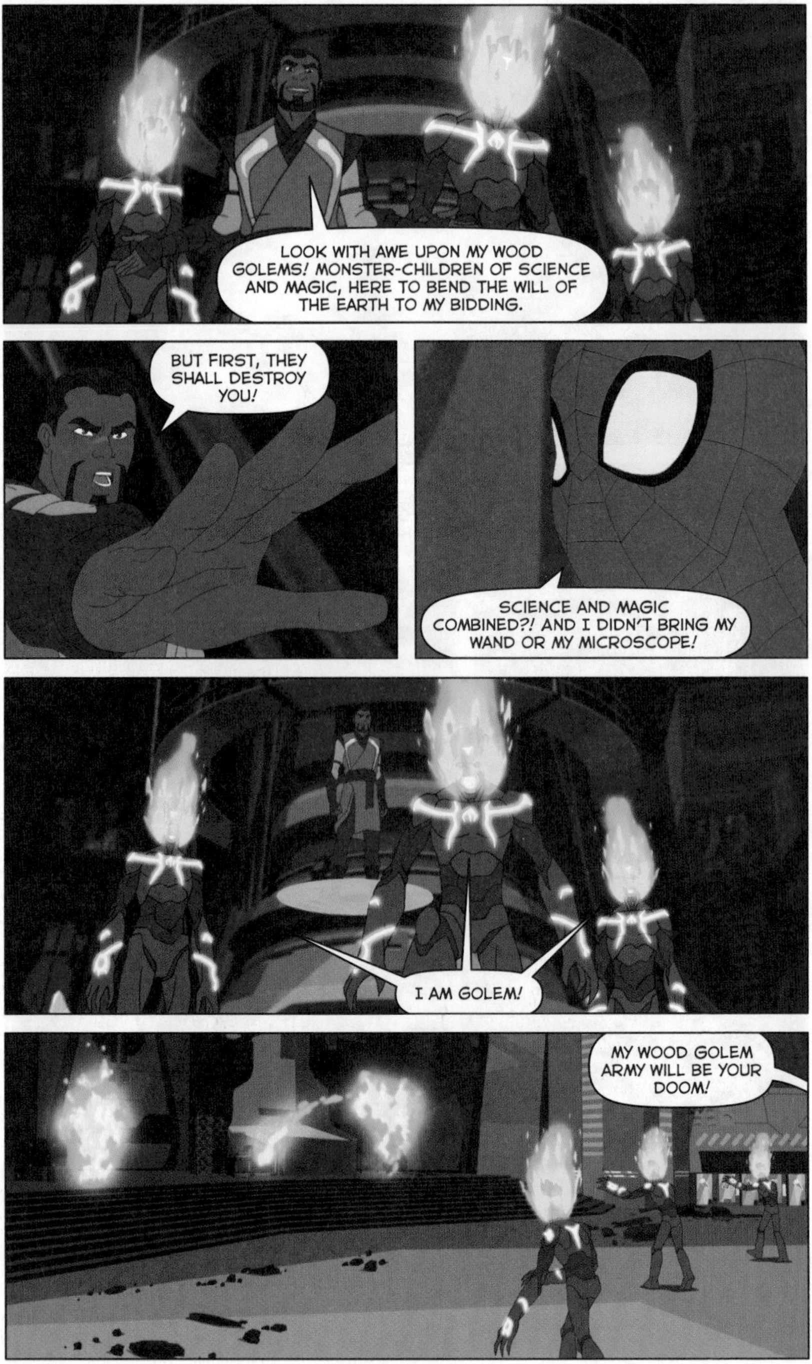
LOOK WITH AWE UPON MY WOOD GOLEMS! MONSTER-CHILDREN OF SCIENCE AND MAGIC, HERE TO BEND THE WILL OF THE EARTH TO MY BIDDING.
BUT FIRST, THEY SHALL DESTROY YOU!
SCIENCE AND MAGIC COMBINED?! AND I DIDN'T BRING MY WAND OR MY MICROSCOPE!
I AM GOLEM!
MY WOOD GOLEM ARMY WILL BE YOUR DOOM!

WHAT, THESE WALKING CAMPFIRES?

POW

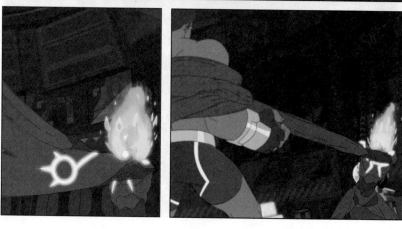

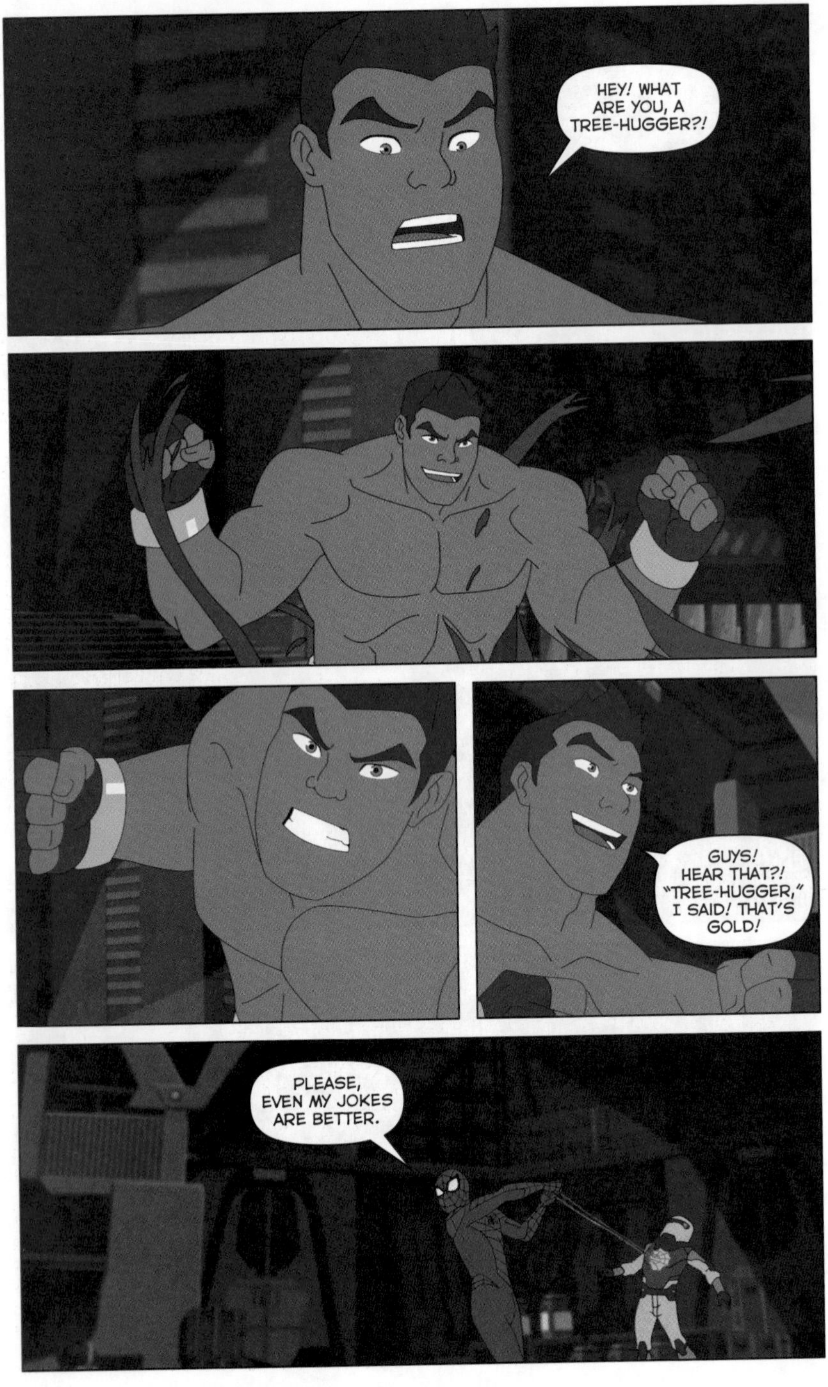
HEY! WHAT ARE YOU, A TREE-HUGGER?!
GUYS! HEAR THAT?! "TREE-HUGGER," I SAID! THAT'S GOLD!
PLEASE, EVEN MY JOKES ARE BETTER.

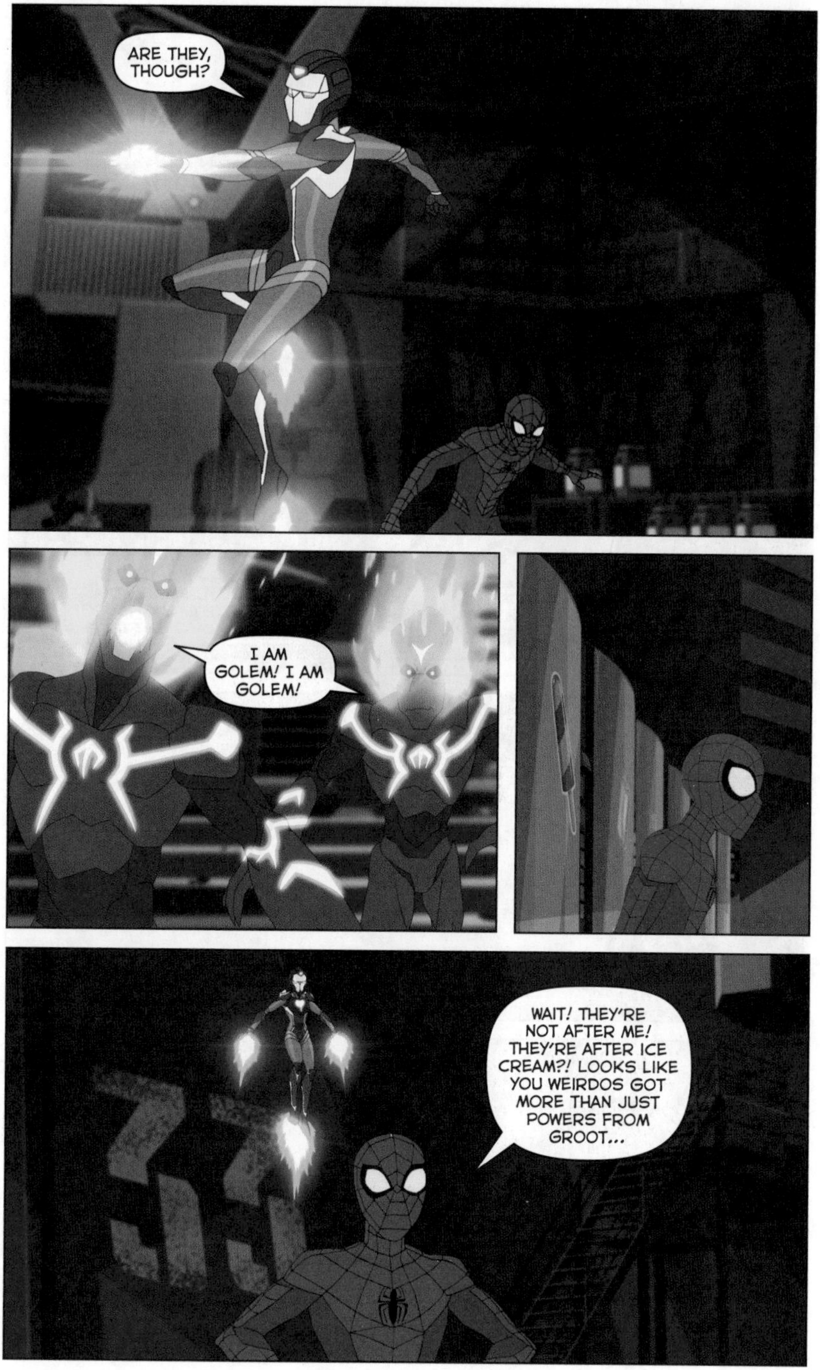
ARE THEY, THOUGH?
I AM GOLEM! I AM GOLEM!
WAIT! THEY'RE NOT AFTER ME! THEY'RE AFTER ICE CREAM?! LOOKS LIKE YOU WEIRDOS GOT MORE THAN JUST POWERS FROM GROOT...

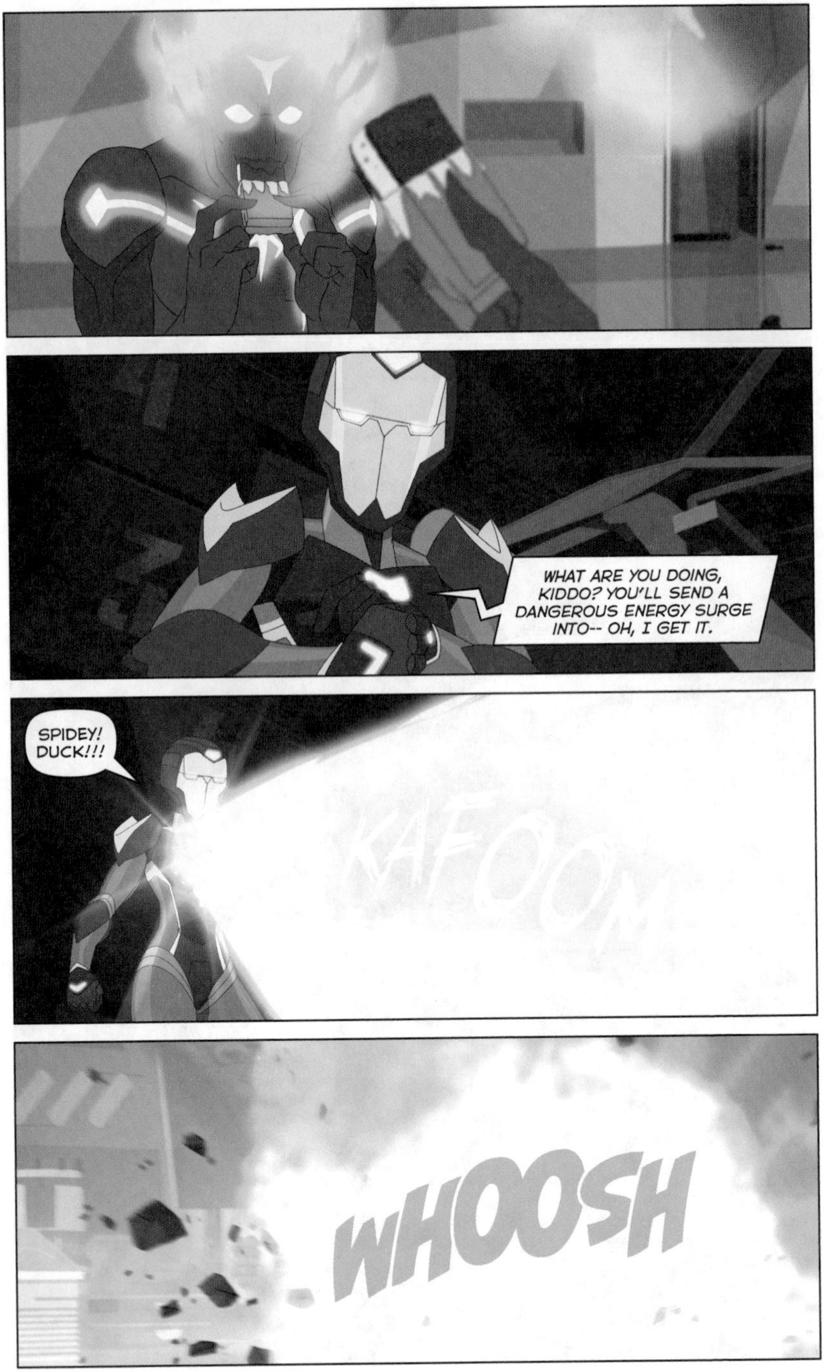
WHAT ARE YOU DOING, KIDDO? YOU'LL SEND A DANGEROUS ENERGY SURGE INTO-- OH, I GET IT.
SPIDEY! DUCK!!!
KAFOOOM
WHOOSH

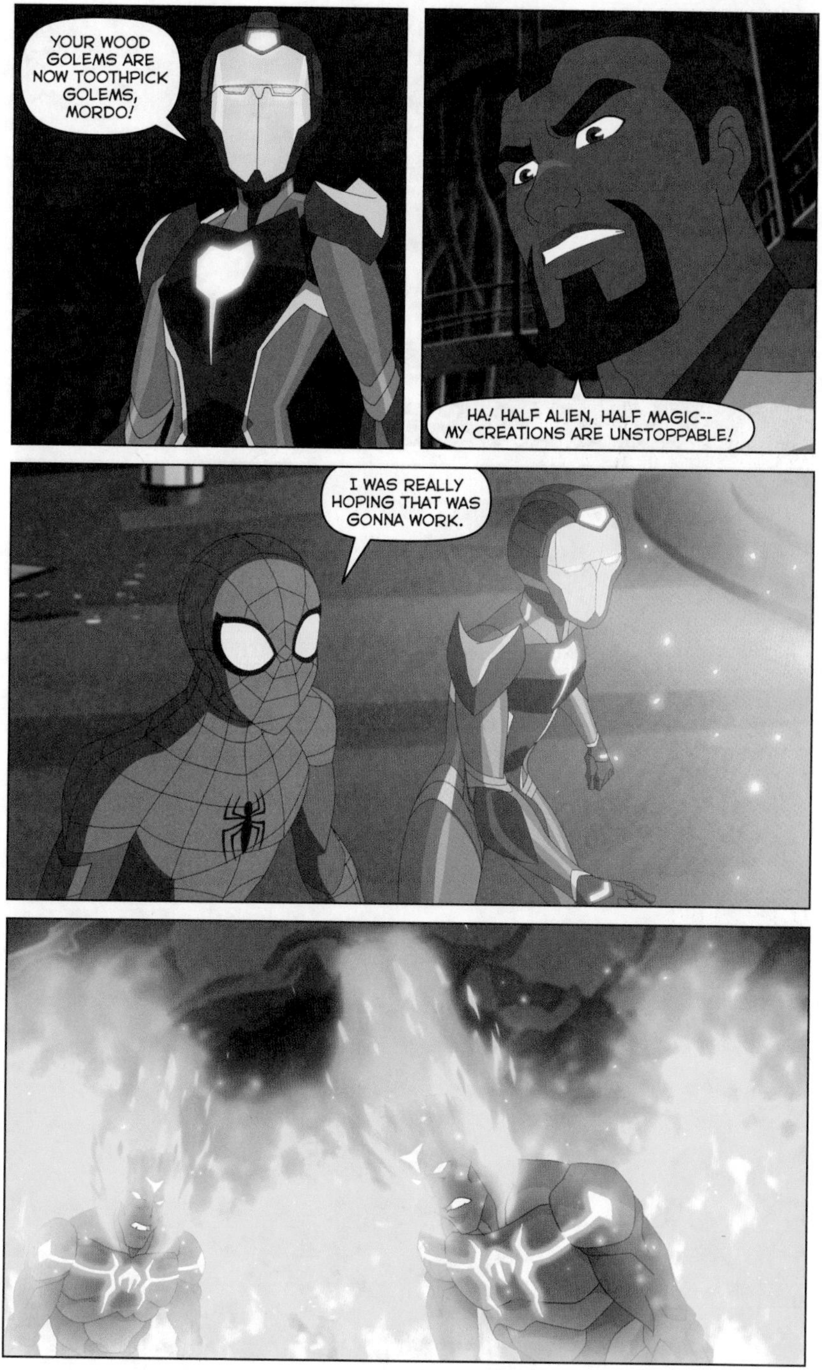
YOUR WOOD GOLEMS ARE NOW TOOTHPICK GOLEMS, MORDO!
HA! HALF ALIEN, HALF MAGIC-- MY CREATIONS ARE UNSTOPPABLE!
I WAS REALLY HOPING THAT WAS GONNA WORK.

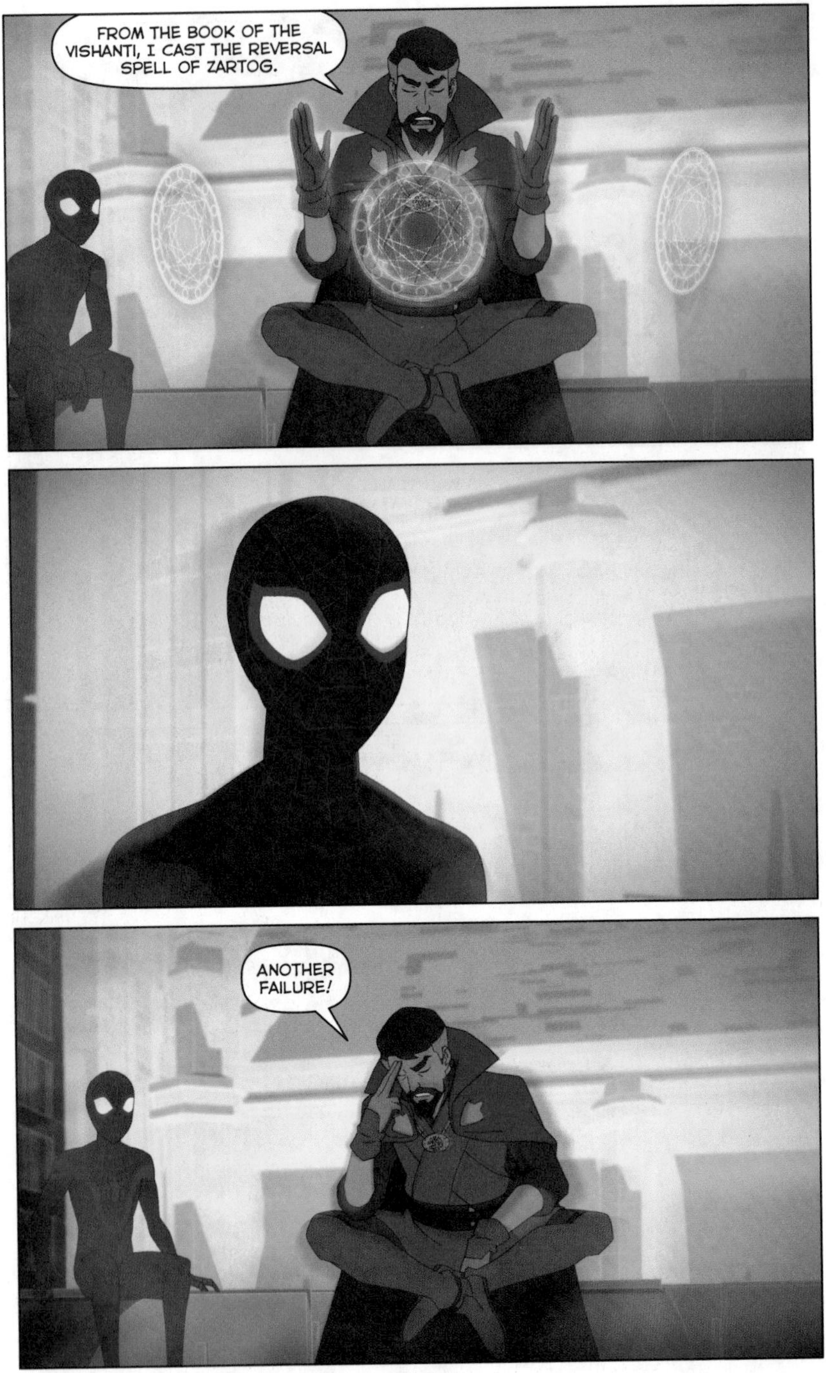
FROM THE BOOK OF THE VISHANTI, I CAST THE REVERSAL SPELL OF ZARTOG.
ANOTHER FAILURE!

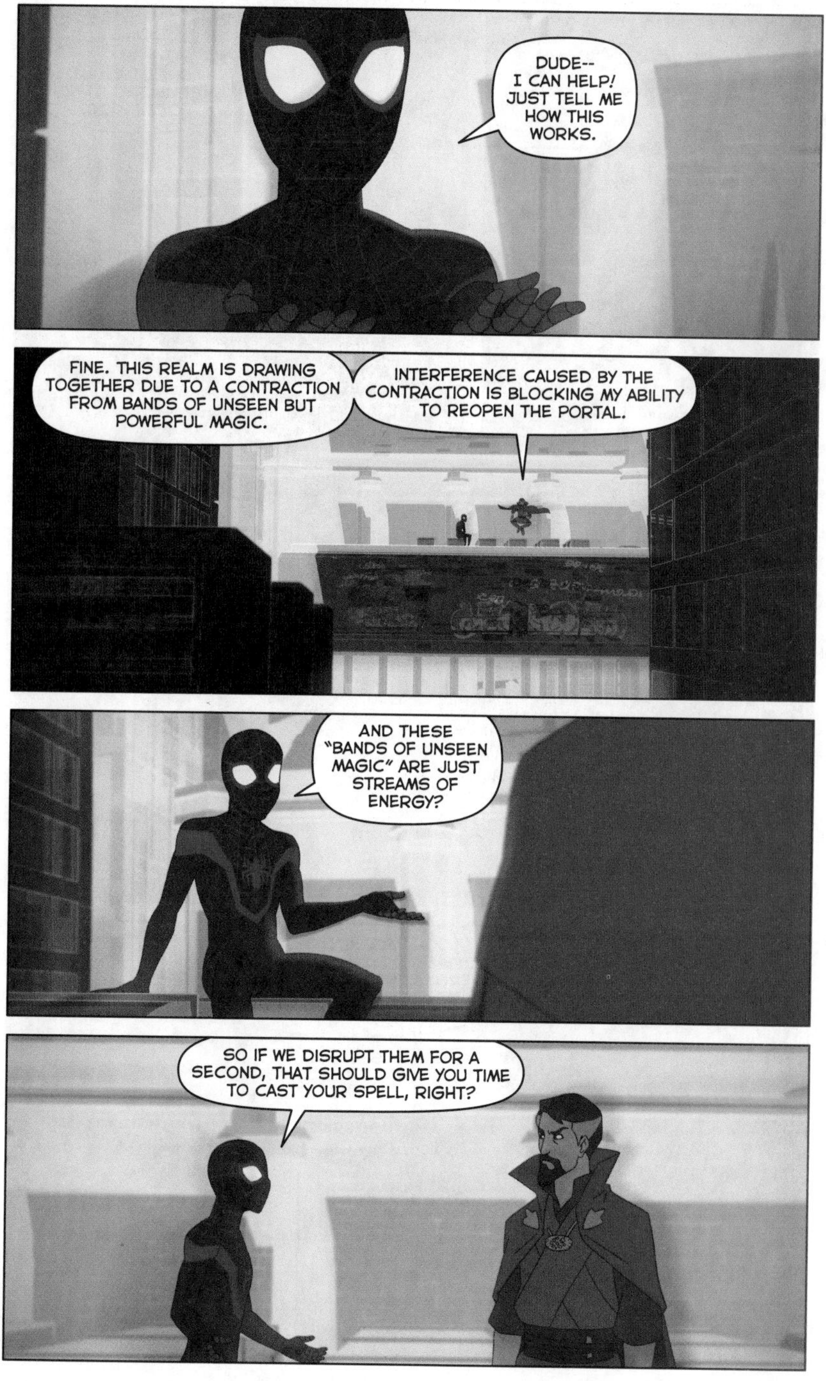
DUDE-- I CAN HELP! JUST TELL ME HOW THIS WORKS.
FINE. THIS REALM IS DRAWING TOGETHER DUE TO A CONTRACTION FROM BANDS OF UNSEEN BUT POWERFUL MAGIC.
INTERFERENCE CAUSED BY THE CONTRACTION IS BLOCKING MY ABILITY TO REOPEN THE PORTAL.
AND THESE "BANDS OF UNSEEN MAGIC" ARE JUST STREAMS OF ENERGY?
SO IF WE DISRUPT THEM FOR A SECOND, THAT SHOULD GIVE YOU TIME TO CAST YOUR SPELL, RIGHT?

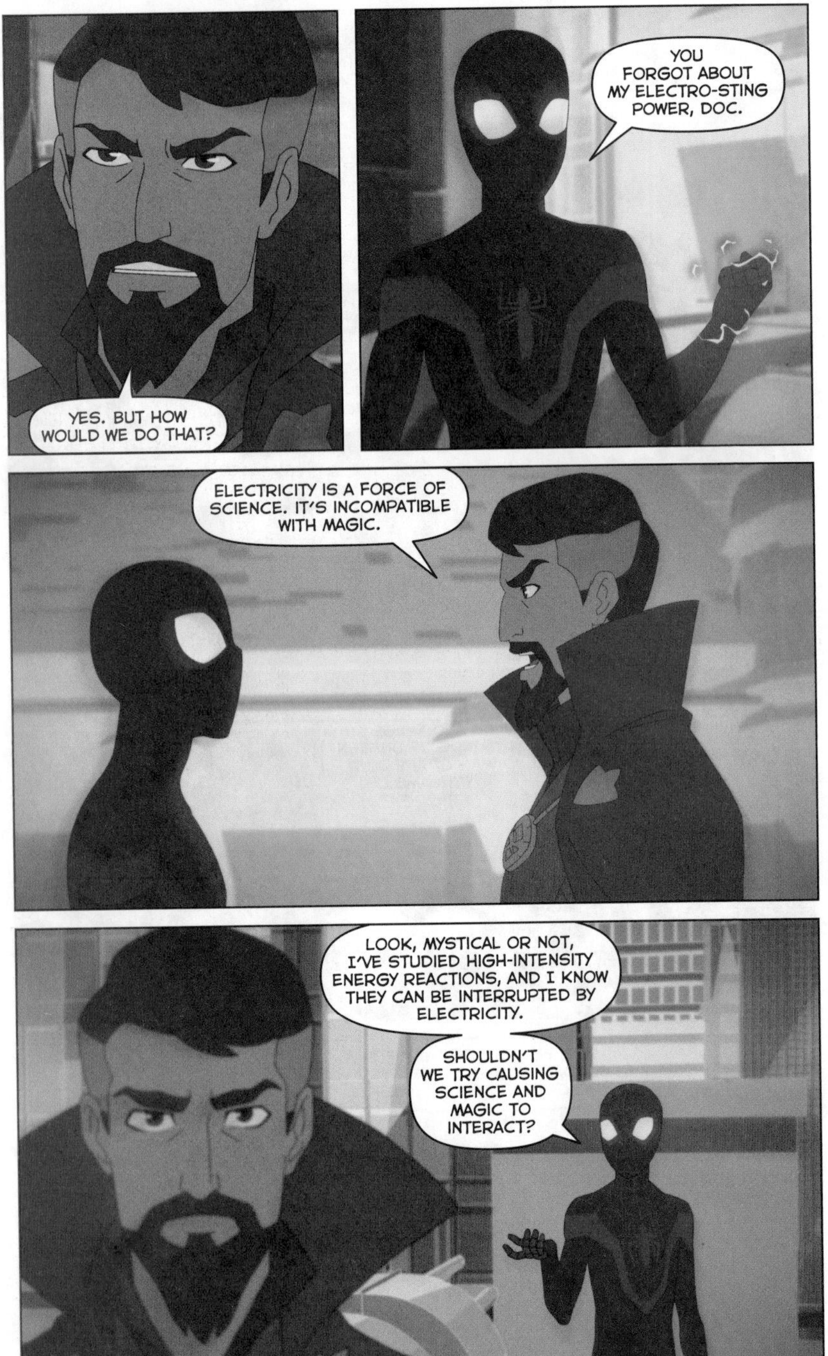
YES. BUT HOW WOULD WE DO THAT?
YOU FORGOT ABOUT MY ELECTRO-STING POWER, DOC.
ELECTRICITY IS A FORCE OF SCIENCE. IT'S INCOMPATIBLE WITH MAGIC.
LOOK, MYSTICAL OR NOT, I'VE STUDIED HIGH-INTENSITY ENERGY REACTIONS, AND I KNOW THEY CAN BE INTERRUPTED BY ELECTRICITY.
SHOULDN'T WE TRY CAUSING SCIENCE AND MAGIC TO INTERACT?

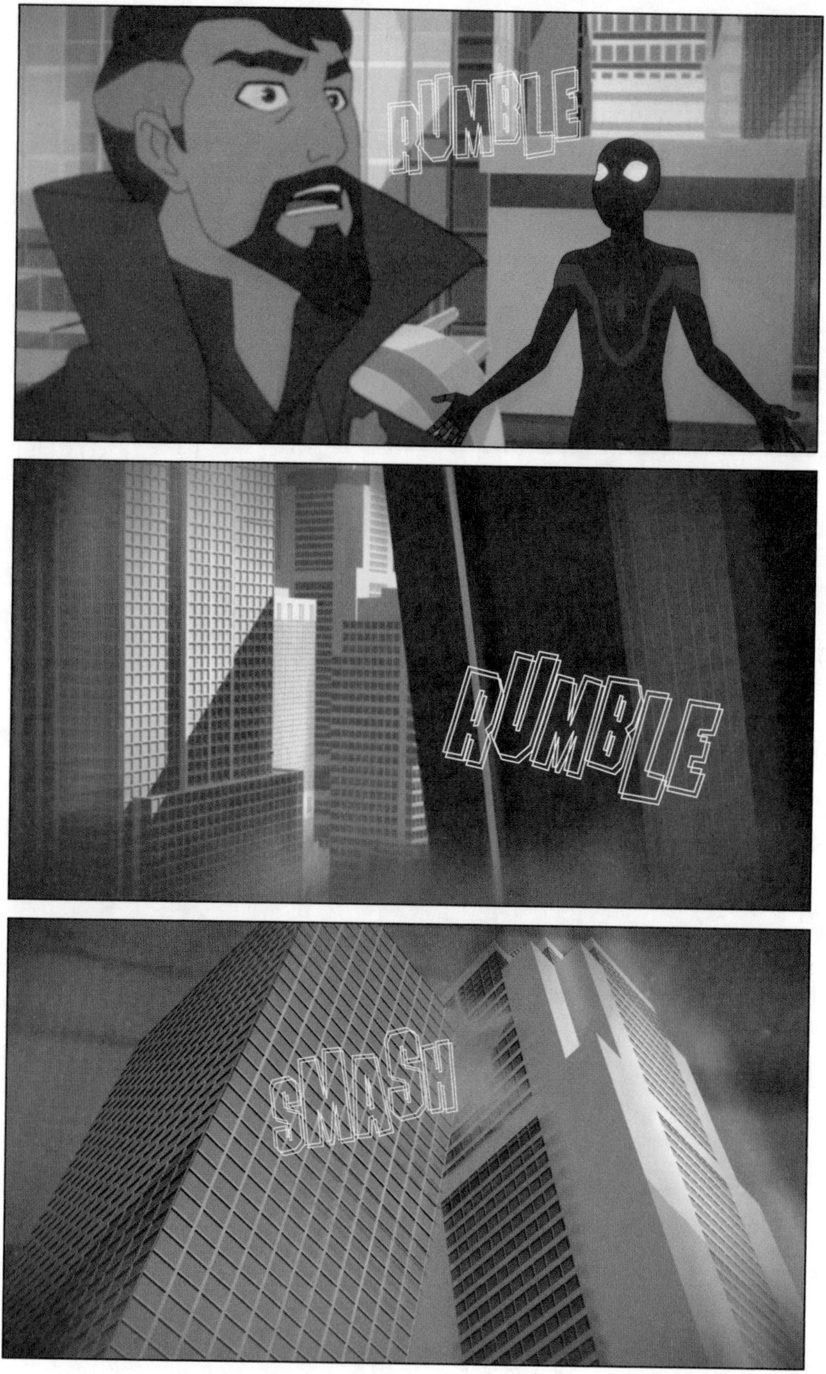
RUMBLE
RUMBLE
SMASH

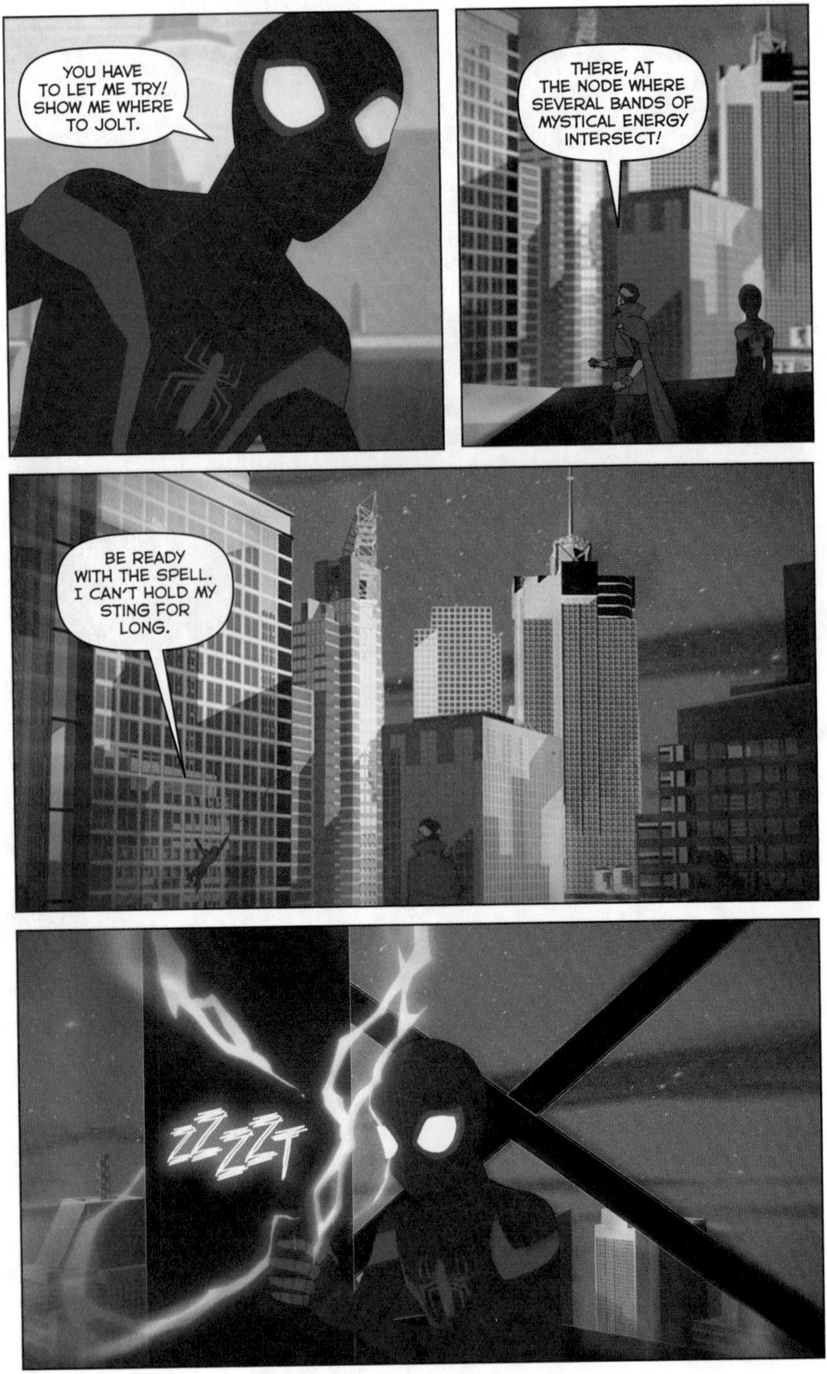
YOU HAVE TO LET ME TRY! SHOW ME WHERE TO JOLT.
THERE, AT THE NODE WHERE SEVERAL BANDS OF MYSTICAL ENERGY INTERSECT!
BE READY WITH THE SPELL. I CAN'T HOLD MY STING FOR LONG.
ZZZZT

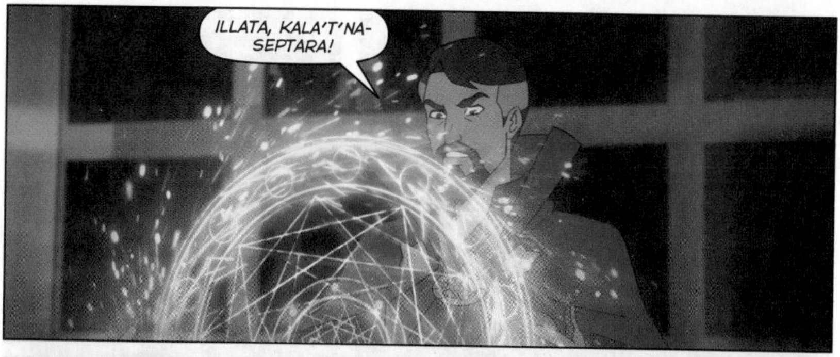
ILLATA, KALA'T'NA-SEPTARA!

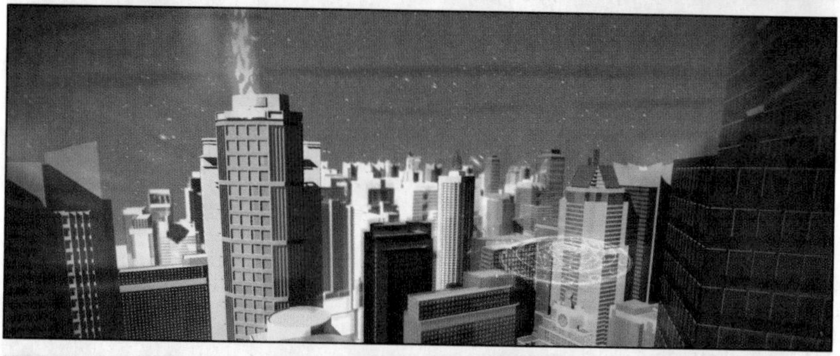

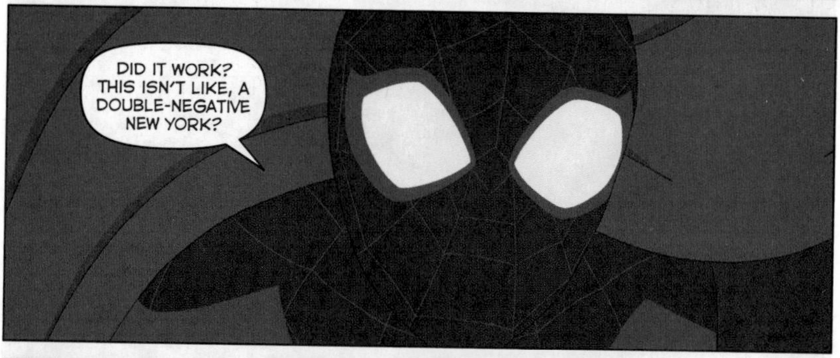
DID IT WORK? THIS ISN'T LIKE, A DOUBLE-NEGATIVE NEW YORK?

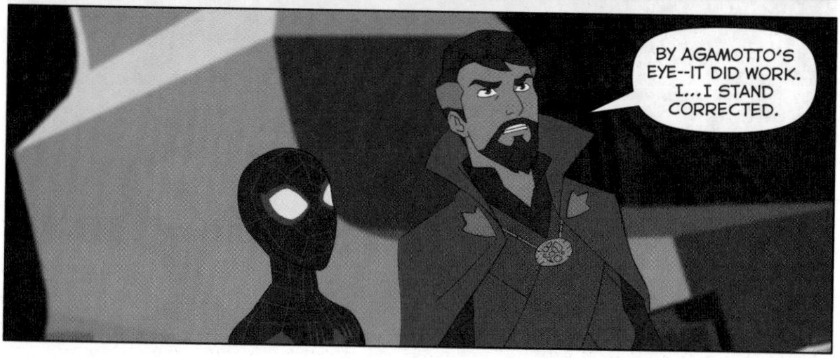
BY AGAMOTTO'S EYE--IT DID WORK. I...I STAND CORRECTED.

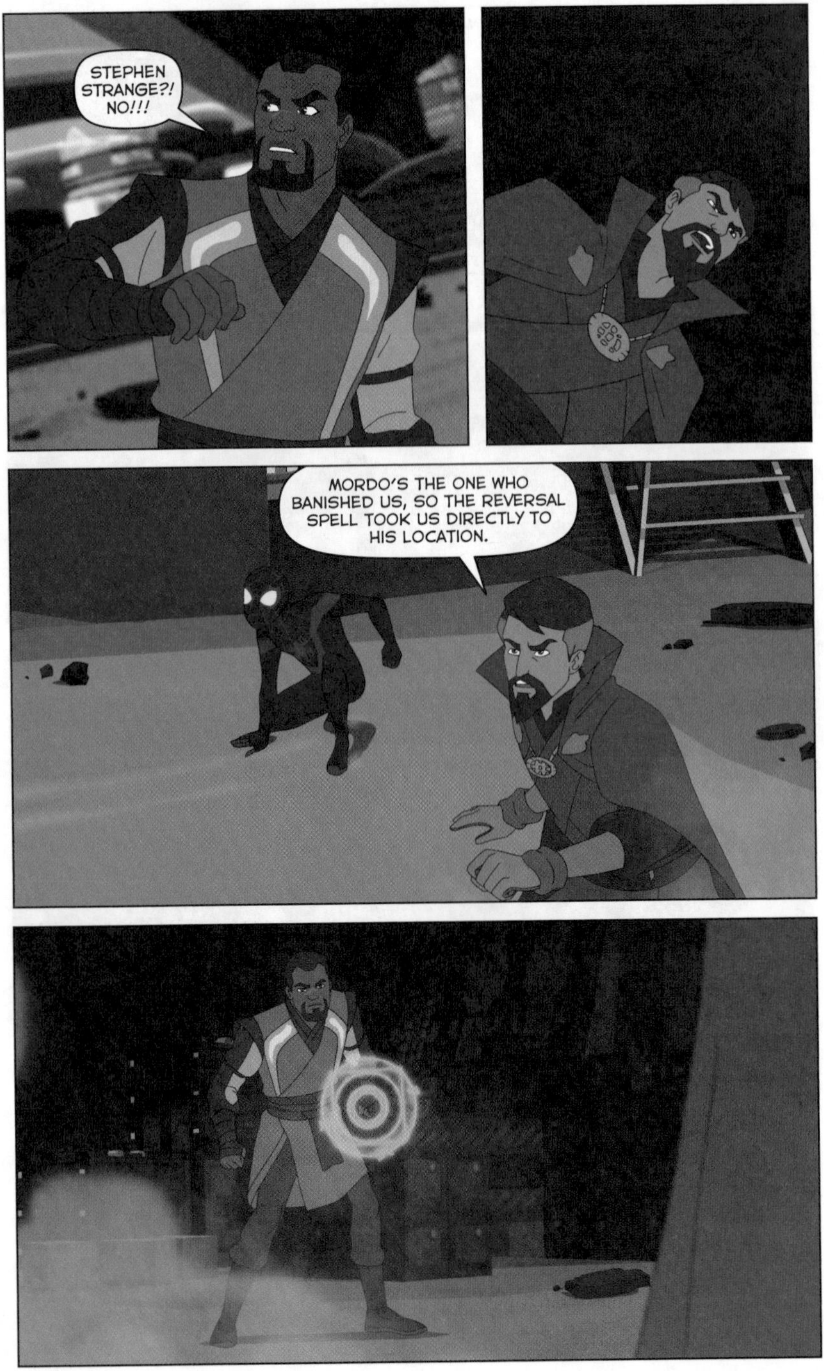
STEPHEN STRANGE?! NO!!!
MORDO'S THE ONE WHO BANISHED US, SO THE REVERSAL SPELL TOOK US DIRECTLY TO HIS LOCATION.

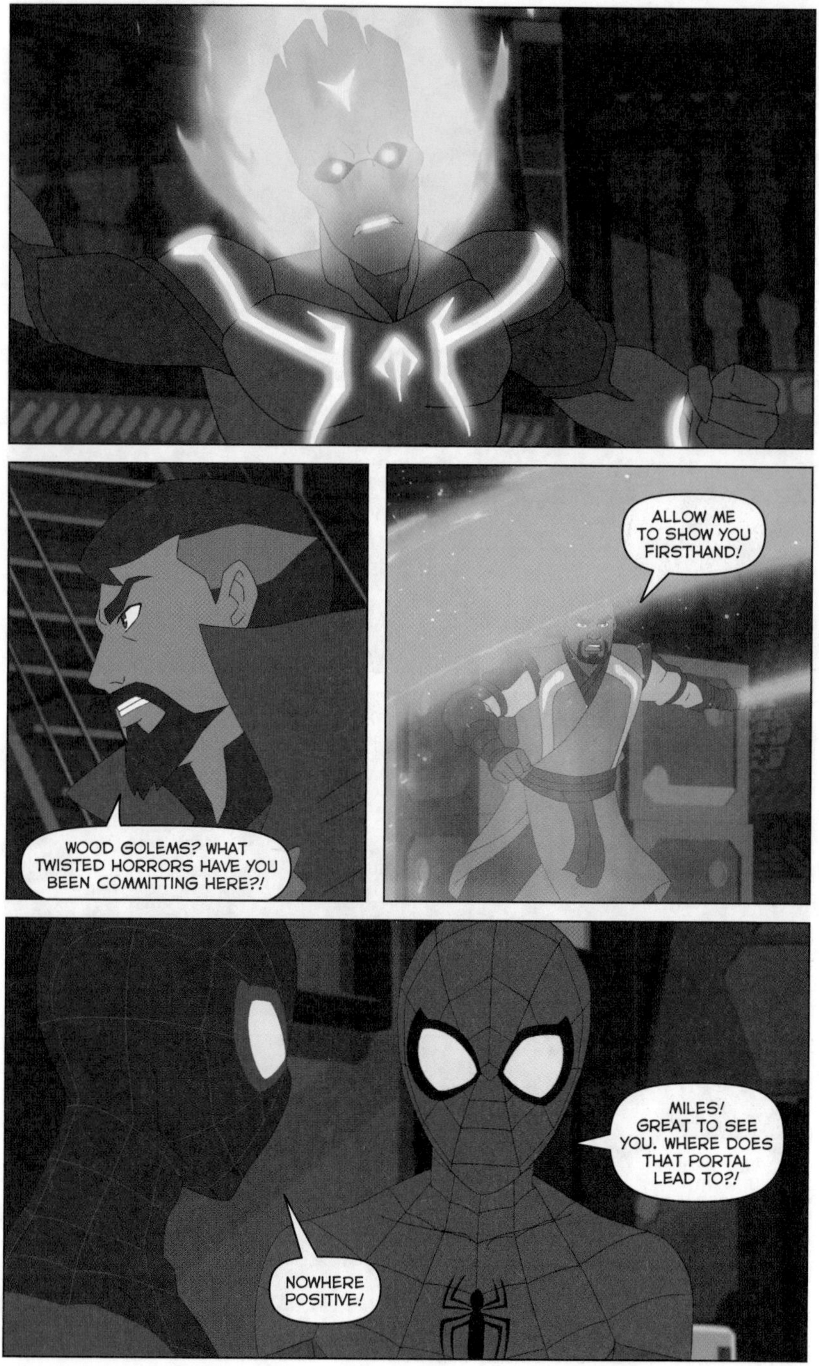
WOOD GOLEMS? WHAT TWISTED HORRORS HAVE YOU BEEN COMMITTING HERE?!
ALLOW ME TO SHOW YOU FIRSTHAND!
MILES! GREAT TO SEE YOU. WHERE DOES THAT PORTAL LEAD TO?!
NOWHERE POSITIVE!

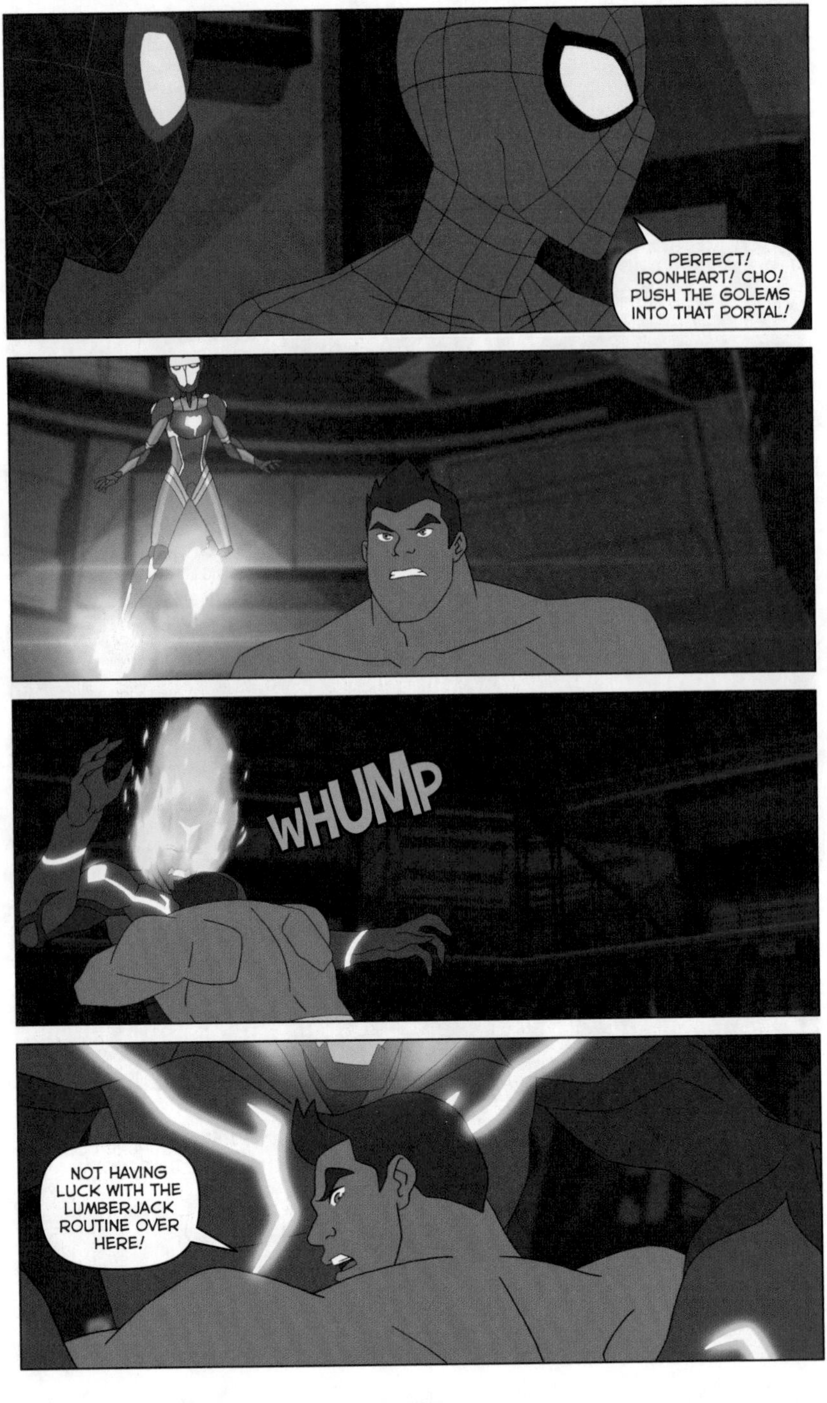
PERFECT! IRONHEART! CHO! PUSH THE GOLEMS INTO THAT PORTAL!
wHUMP
NOT HAVING LUCK WITH THE LUMBERJACK ROUTINE OVER HERE!

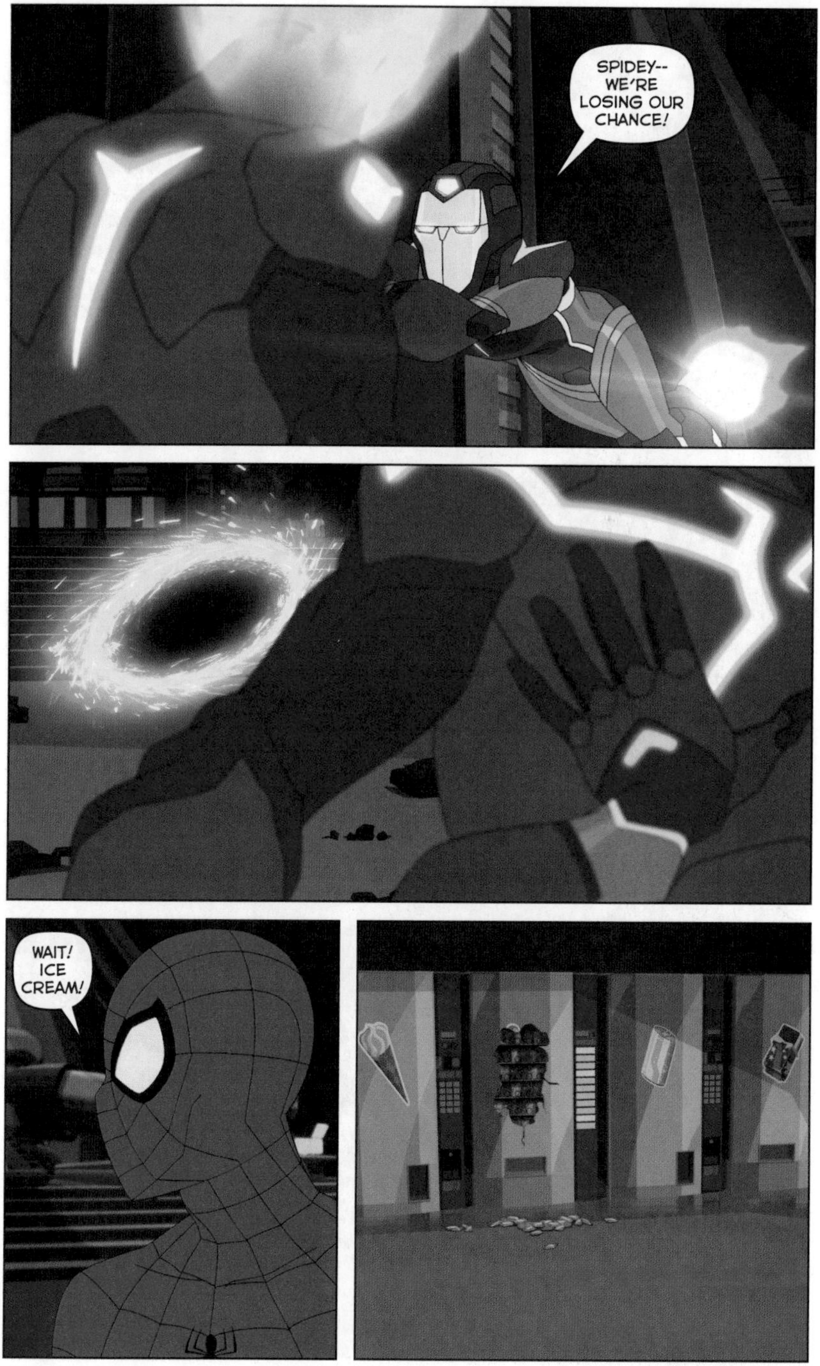
SPIDEY-- WE'RE LOSING OUR CHANCE!
WAIT! ICE CREAM!

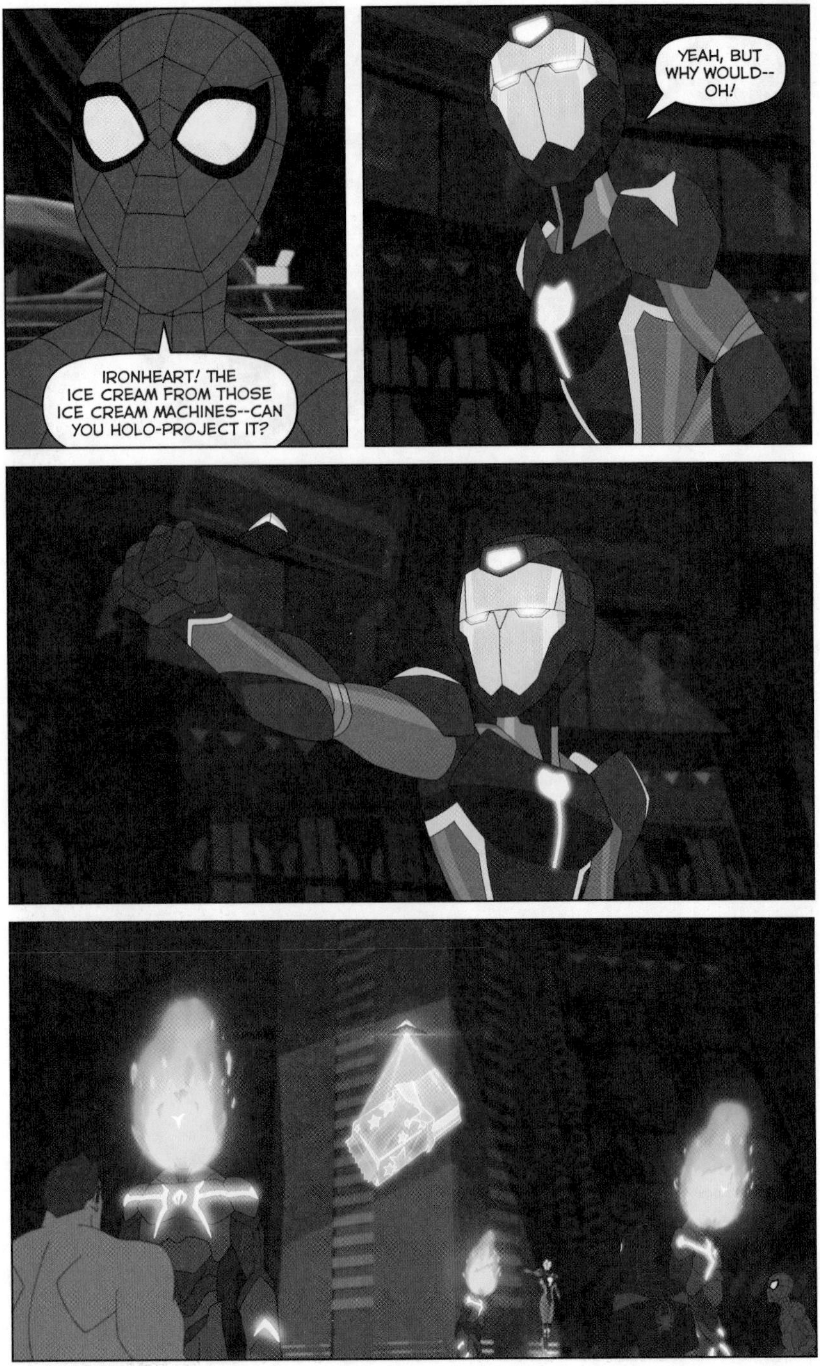
IRONHEART! THE ICE CREAM FROM THOSE ICE CREAM MACHINES--CAN YOU HOLO-PROJECT IT?
YEAH, BUT WHY WOULD-- OH!

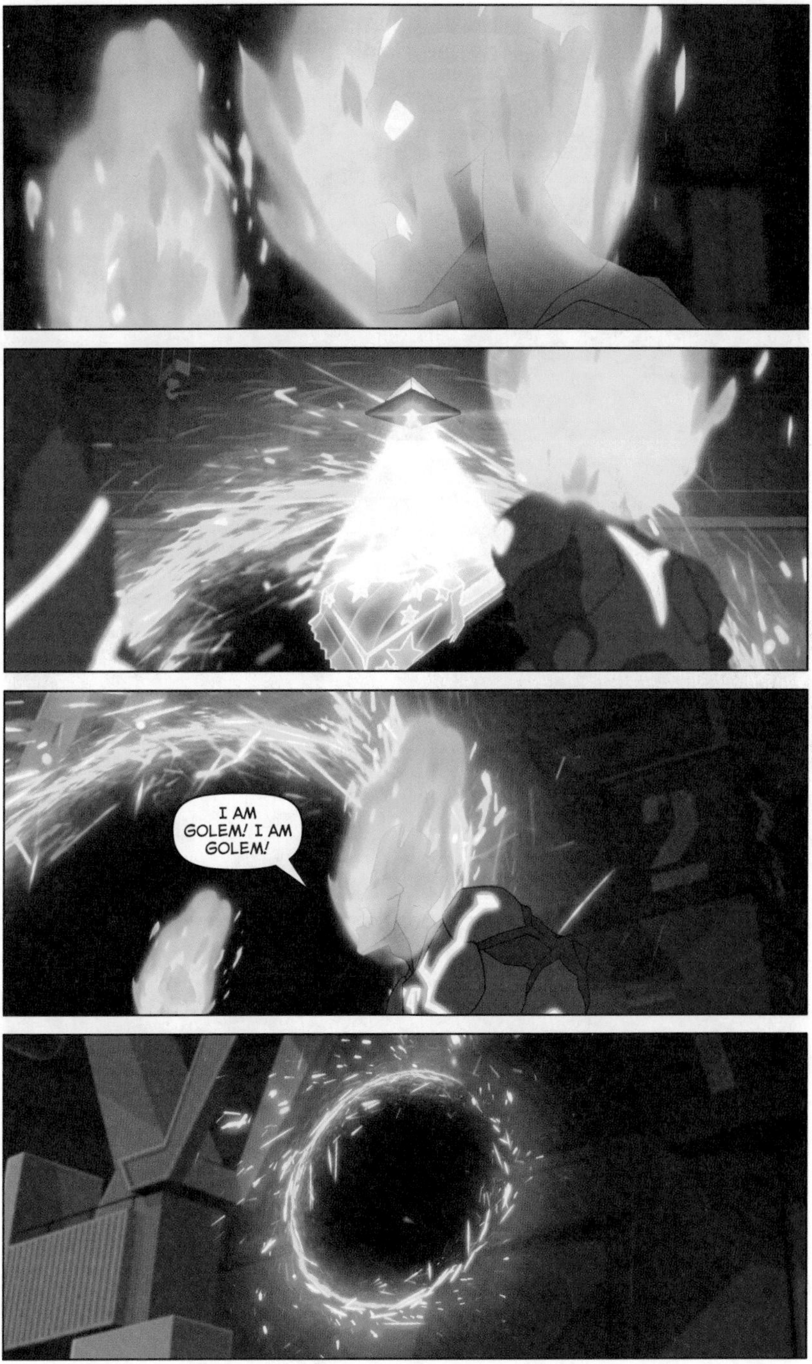
I AM GOLEM! I AM GOLEM!

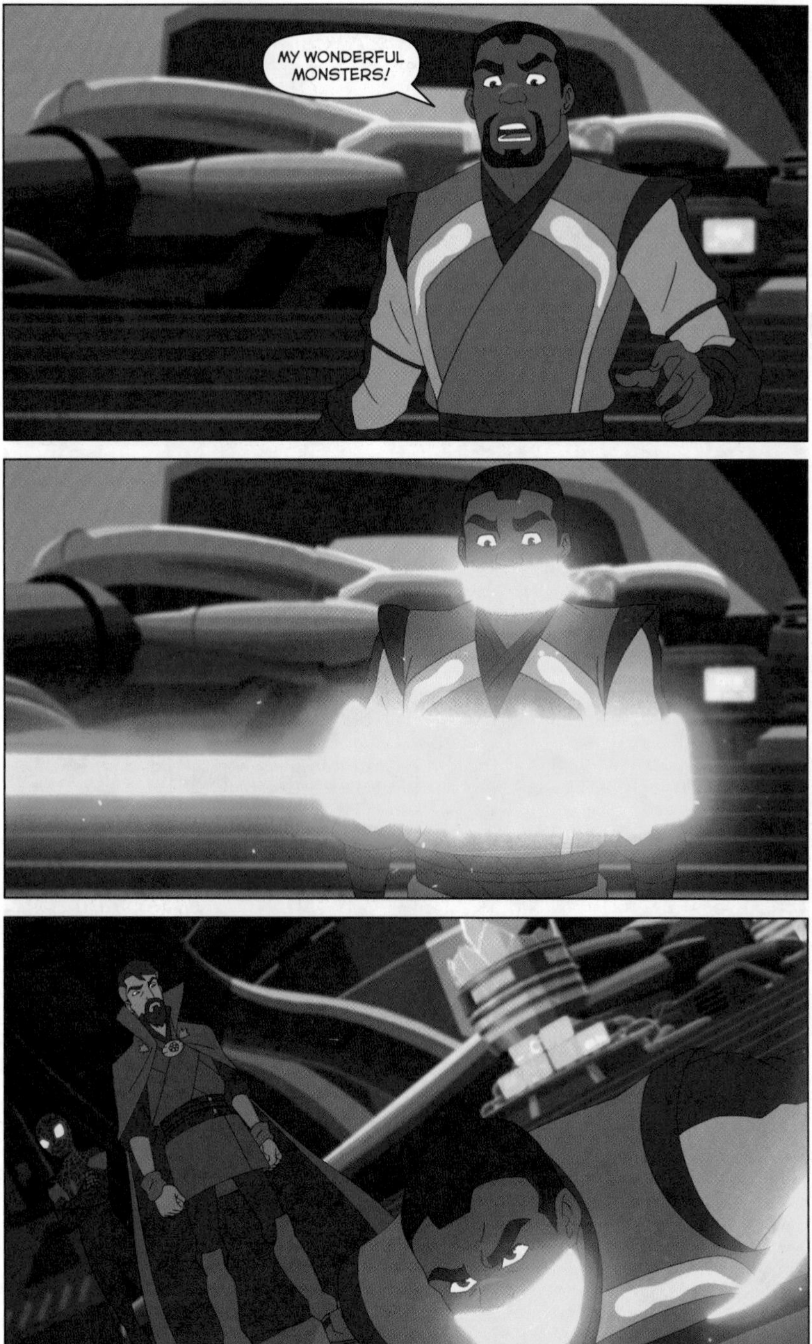
MY WONDERFUL MONSTERS!

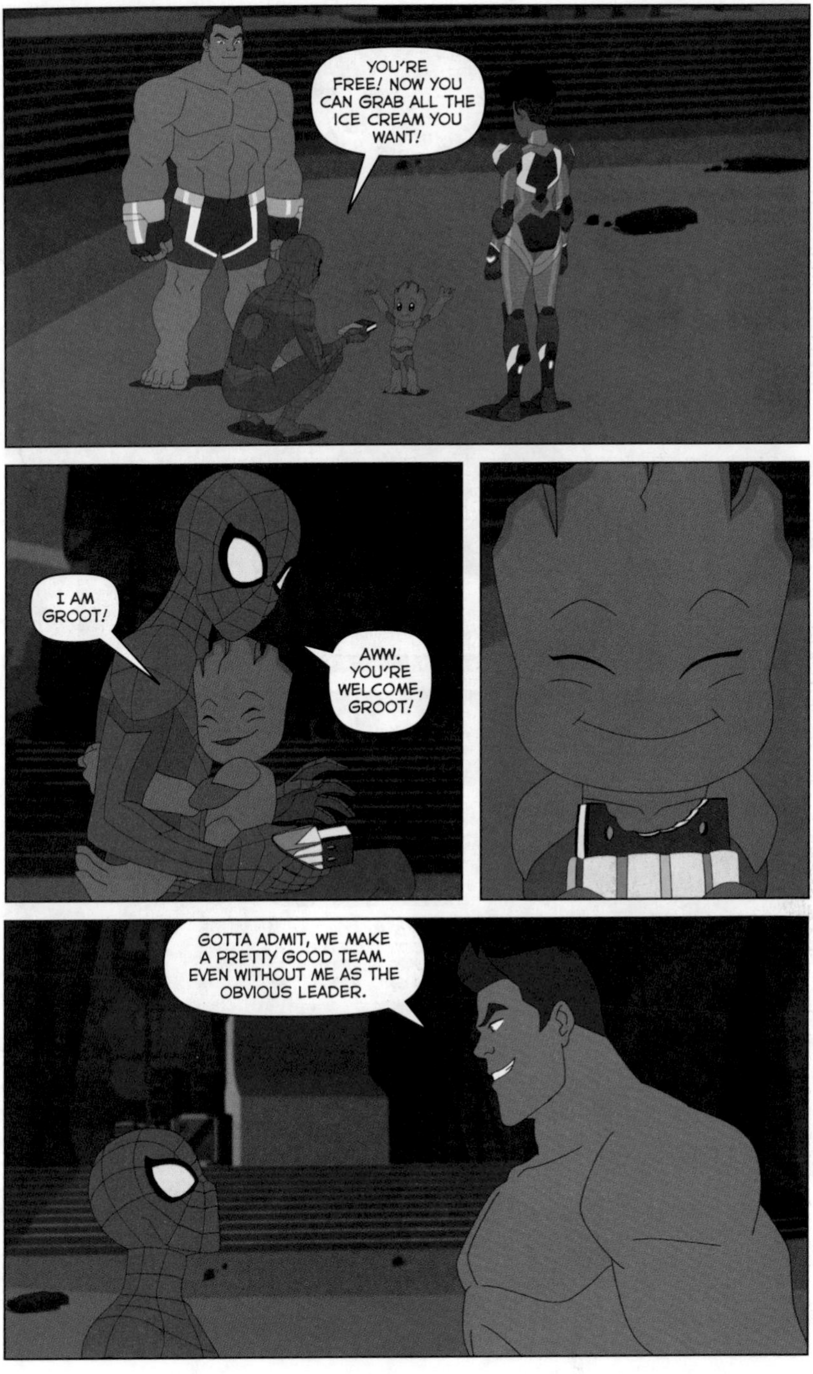
YOU'RE FREE! NOW YOU CAN GRAB ALL THE ICE CREAM YOU WANT!
I AM GROOT!
AWW. YOU'RE WELCOME, GROOT!
GOTTA ADMIT, WE MAKE A PRETTY GOOD TEAM. EVEN WITHOUT ME AS THE OBVIOUS LEADER.

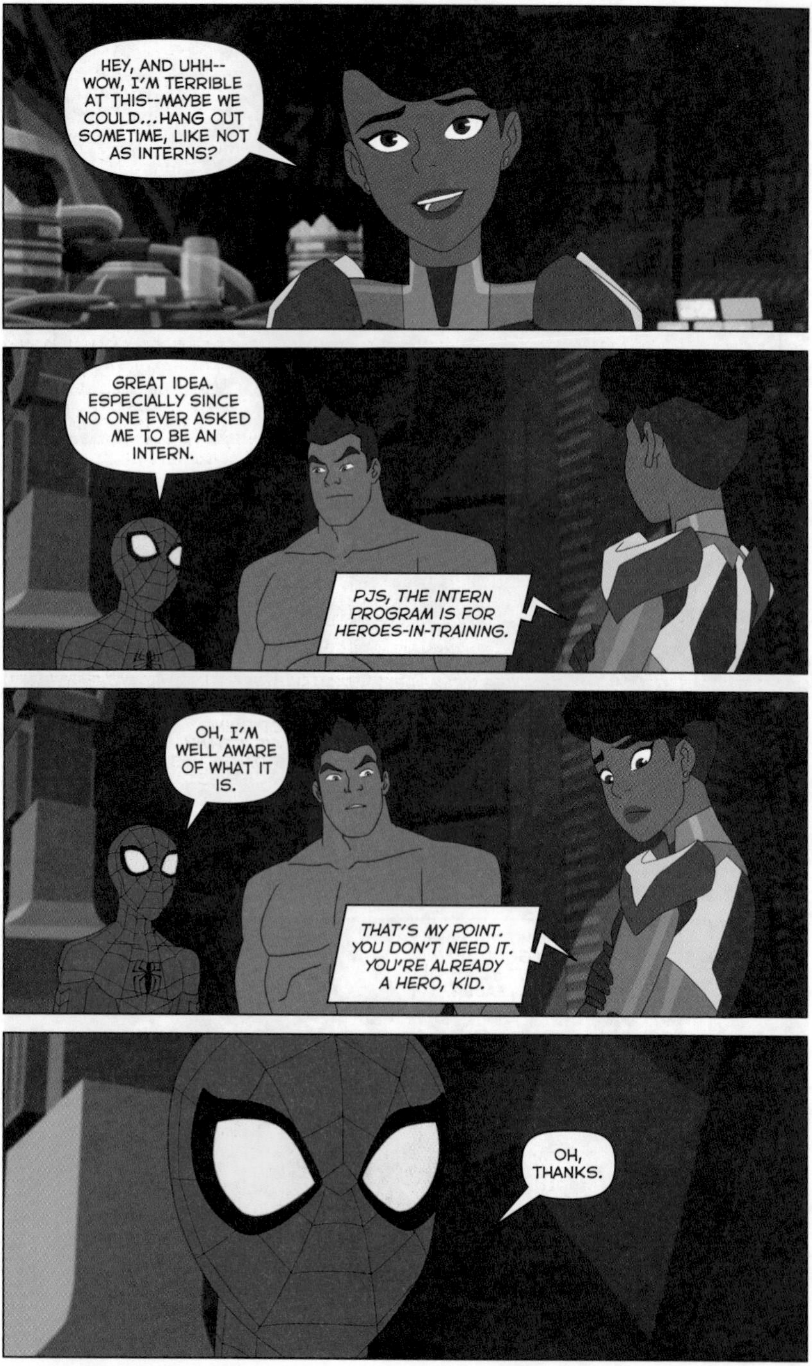
HEY, AND UHH-- WOW, I'M TERRIBLE AT THIS--MAYBE WE COULD...HANG OUT SOMETIME, LIKE NOT AS INTERNS?
GREAT IDEA. ESPECIALLY SINCE NO ONE EVER ASKED ME TO BE AN INTERN.
PJS, THE INTERN PROGRAM IS FOR HEROES-IN-TRAINING.
OH, I'M WELL AWARE OF WHAT IT IS.
THAT'S MY POINT. YOU DON'T NEED IT. YOU'RE ALREADY A HERO, KID.
OH, THANKS.

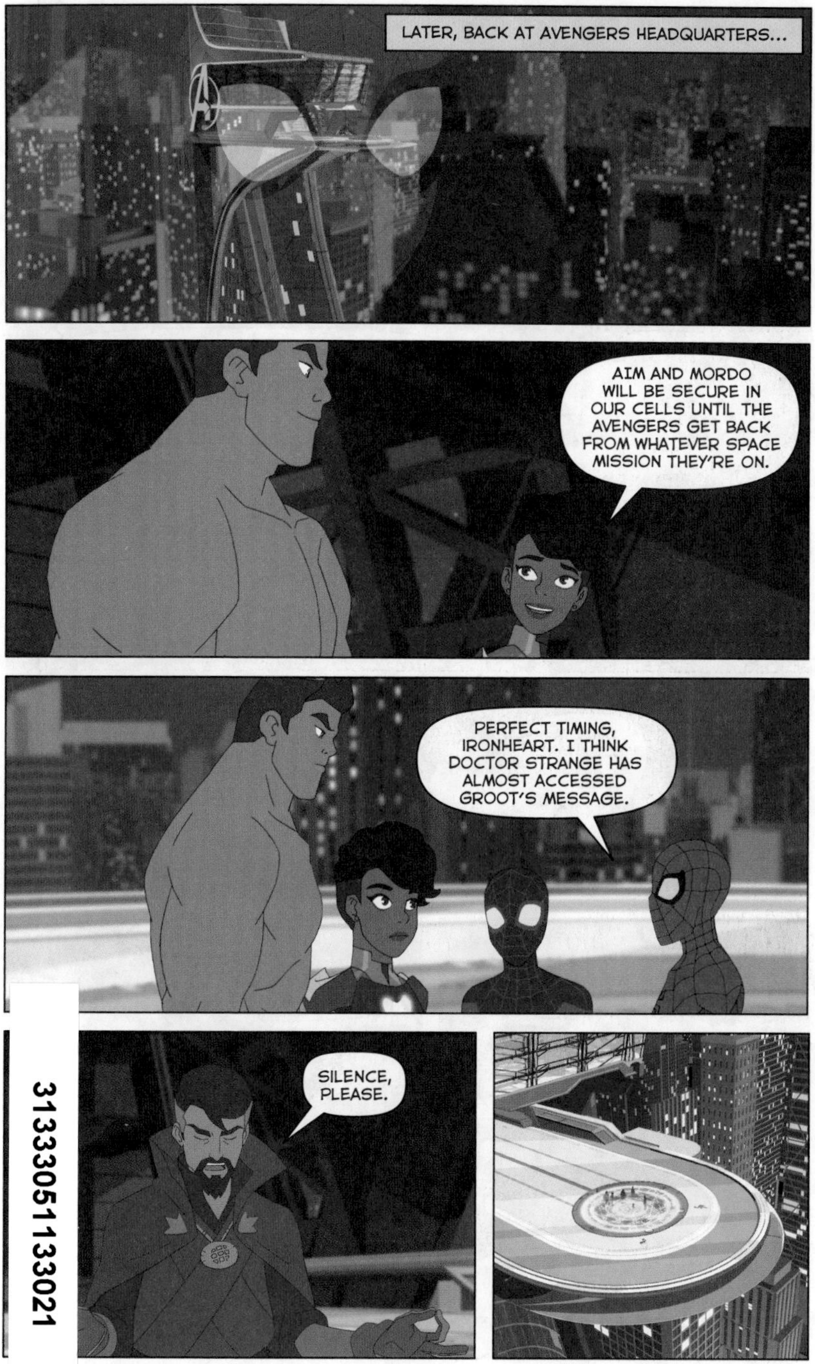
LATER, BACK AT AVENGERS HEADQUARTERS...
AIM AND MORDO WILL BE SECURE IN OUR CELLS UNTIL THE AVENGERS GET BACK FROM WHATEVER SPACE MISSION THEY'RE ON.
PERFECT TIMING, IRONHEART. I THINK DOCTOR STRANGE HAS ALMOST ACCESSED GROOT'S MESSAGE.
SILENCE, PLEASE.

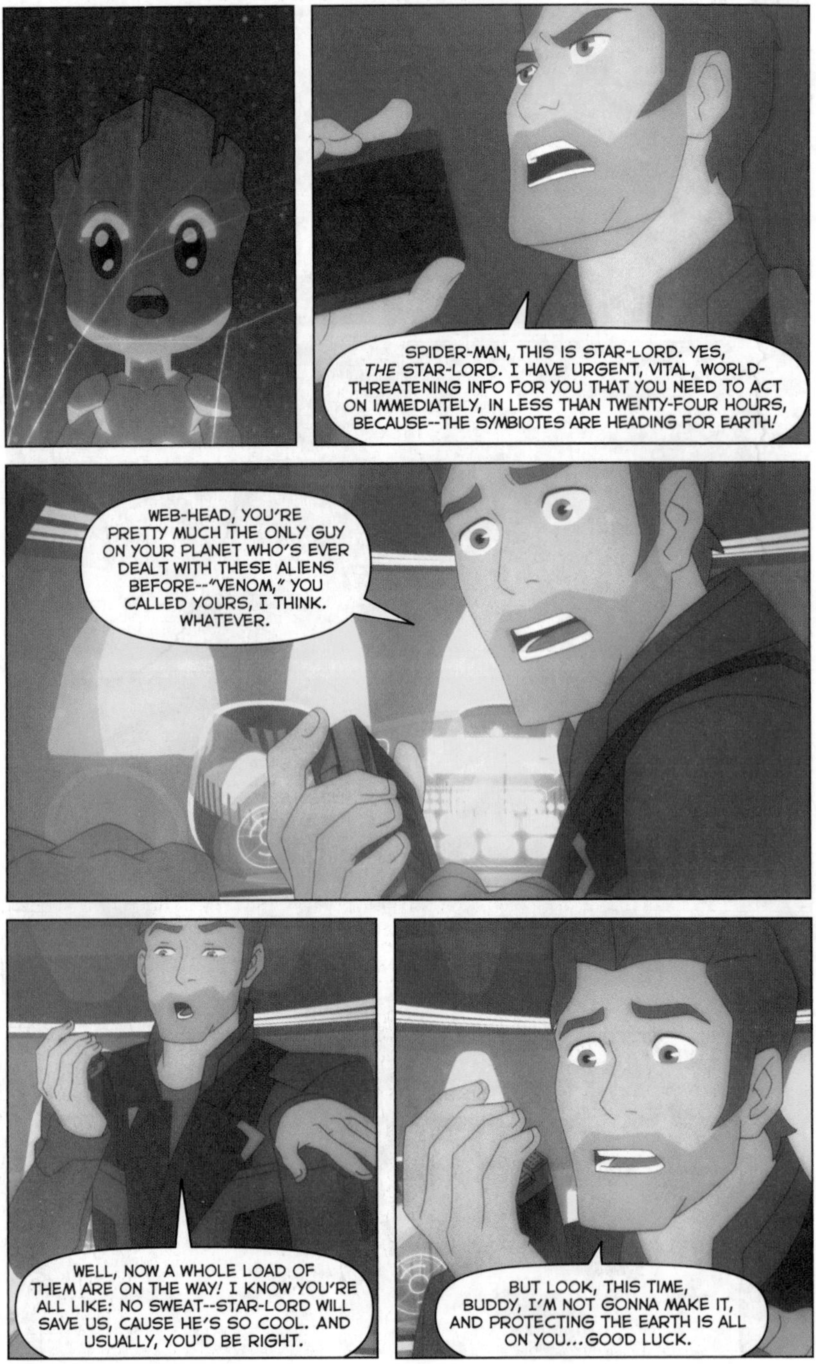
SPIDER-MAN, THIS IS STAR-LORD. YES, *THE* STAR-LORD. I HAVE URGENT, VITAL, WORLD-THREATENING INFO FOR YOU THAT YOU NEED TO ACT ON IMMEDIATELY, IN LESS THAN TWENTY-FOUR HOURS, BECAUSE--THE SYMBIOTES ARE HEADING FOR EARTH!
WEB-HEAD, YOU'RE PRETTY MUCH THE ONLY GUY ON YOUR PLANET WHO'S EVER DEALT WITH THESE ALIENS BEFORE--"VENOM," YOU CALLED YOURS, I THINK. WHATEVER.
WELL, NOW A WHOLE LOAD OF THEM ARE ON THE WAY! I KNOW YOU'RE ALL LIKE: NO SWEAT--STAR-LORD WILL SAVE US, CAUSE HE'S SO COOL. AND USUALLY, YOU'D BE RIGHT.
BUT LOOK, THIS TIME, BUDDY, I'M NOT GONNA MAKE IT, AND PROTECTING THE EARTH IS ALL ON YOU...GOOD LUCK.

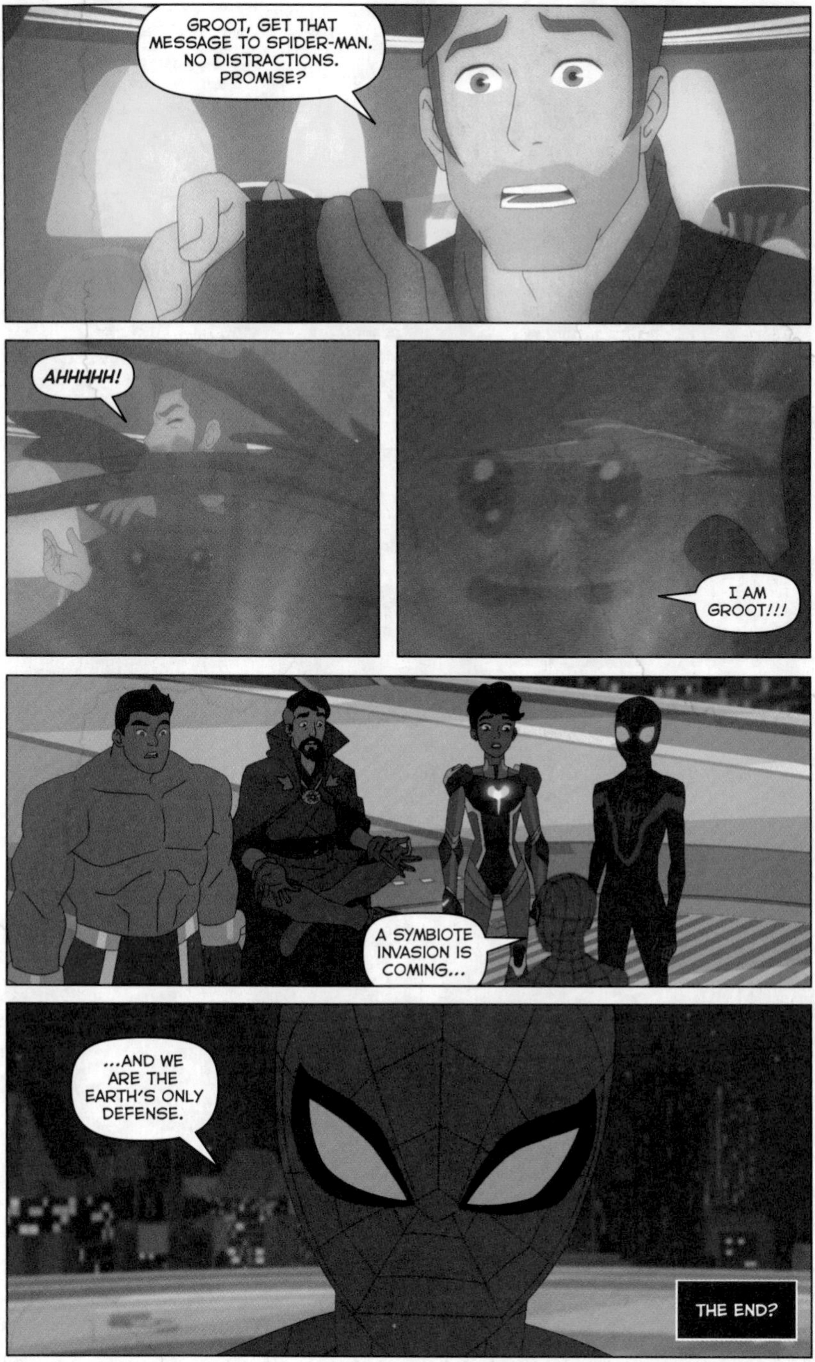
GROOT, GET THAT MESSAGE TO SPIDER-MAN. NO DISTRACTIONS. PROMISE?
AHHHHH!
I AM GROOT!!!
A SYMBIOTE INVASION IS COMING...
...AND WE ARE THE EARTH'S ONLY DEFENSE.
THE END?

CREDITS

WEB OF VENOM

EXECUTIVE PRODUCERS
Alan Fine
Joe Quesada
Dan Buckley
Cort Lane
Marsha Griffin

EXECUTIVE PRODUCER
Eric Radomski

SUPERVISING PRODUCER
Kari Rosenberg

SUPERVISING PRODUCERS
Kevin Burke & Chris "Doc" Wyatt

SUPERVISING CREATIVE DIRECTOR
Eric Radomski

SUPERVISING DIRECTOR
Dan Duncan

BASED ON THE MARVEL COMICS BY
Stan Lee & Steve Ditko

WRITTEN BY
Kevin Burke & Chris "Doc" Wyatt

DIRECTED BY
Tim Eldred & Sol Choi

AMAZING FRIENDS

EXECUTIVE PRODUCERS
Alan Fine
Joe Quesada
Dan Buckley
Cort Lane
Marsha Griffin

EXECUTIVE PRODUCER
Eric Radomski

SUPERVISING PRODUCER
Kari Rosenberg

SUPERVISING PRODUCERS
Kevin Burke & Chris "Doc" Wyatt

SUPERVISING CREATIVE DIRECTOR
Eric Radomski

SUPERVISING DIRECTOR
Dan Duncan

BASED ON THE MARVEL COMICS BY
Stan Lee & Steve Ditko

WRITTEN BY
Merrill Hagan & Denise Downer

DIRECTED BY
Tim Eldred & Sol Choi